To Virginia from Debbie Boswell 11/24/13

House of Mirrors

by
Debbie Boswell

authorHOUSE®

AuthorHouse™ LLC
1663 Liberty Drive
Bloomington, IN 47403
www.authorhouse.com
Phone: 1-800-839-8640

This book is a work of fiction. People, places, events, and situations are the product of the author's imagination. Any resemblance to actual persons, living or dead, or historical events, is purely coincidental.

Published by AuthorHouse   08/29/2013

ISBN: 978-1-4259-8181-5 (sc)
ISBN: 978-1-4685-5056-6 (e)

Library of Congress Control Number: 2006910489

Any people depicted in stock imagery provided by Thinkstock are models, and such images are being used for illustrative purposes only.
Certain stock imagery © Thinkstock.

This book is printed on acid-free paper.

Because of the dynamic nature of the Internet, any web addresses or links contained in this book may have changed since publication and may no longer be valid. The views expressed in this work are solely those of the author and do not necessarily reflect the views of the publisher, and the publisher hereby disclaims any responsibility for them.

To Martha, with gratitude

Author's Note

For the novel, I used a fictional Upper Hudson Valley village. I chose the name Gordonville. Recently, I discovered that the locale really existed. Named after the first settlers to come to the area, Gordonville became a part of the town of Rushford located in Allegany County.

"... you have sinned against the Lord;
And be sure your sin will find you out."
—Num. 32:23, NKJV

Prologue

Jenna Crandall was hiking up Thornbush Lane, a lonely stretch of road bordered by a forest on either side. Her red knapsack slung over her shoulder, she wiped away the sweat from her forehead. The spring morning was unseasonably warm.

She paused to check for oncoming vehicles, ready to dodge behind a tree if necessary. The last thing she needed was for a neighbor or worse a church member to see her on the quiet dirt path. They were sure to tell her mother. Jenna's eyes narrowed. The parishioners talked too much. Especially Norma Beery.

Jenna looked rueful. The sixteen-year-old high school junior didn't want anyone to see her, for this wasn't the way to Gordonville High School. Her mother was going to find out later anyway when the school reported her absent. She had no business playing hooky. Her grades were good, but the finals and the New York State Regents exams were coming up. She really should be in class.

Then again, Rosa would take care of it. She always took care of everything. Jenna wore a tiny smile. She didn't have to worry about a thing.

She continued looking down the road. No cars. No other hikers. No surprise there. It was unlikely she'd see another vehicle or pedestrian. Thornbush Lane was desolate and eerie with grotesquely shaped trees. They looked demonic causing the road to acquire an uncanny ambience even in the daytime. The trees closest to the road formed a natural canopy. Residents always wondered why the village's founders named the place Thornbush Lane. There wasn't even a thorn in sight. Maybe thorns used to be there, but the early settlers rid the place of them.

Jenna adjusted her knapsack. It never hurt to take precautions. Rosa taught her that. She resumed walking. She wiped some sweat off her brow. If she had known it was going to be this warm, she would've worn a lighter T-shirt and Bermuda shorts. Regardless of the hot weather, she just had to see Rosa. She had to get what she needed to say off her chest. Today. She had to make Rosa see reason.

Jenna reached the clearing where Rosa's house stood, a circa 1780's farmhouse. She was standing on the lower porch. Friends since the second grade, Jenna couldn't imagine life without her and yet she'd been considering just that . . . She walked toward the farmhouse as she fingered her amethyst choker.

"I was surprised you wanted to meet," Rosa said. The pretty, African-American teen was dressed in khaki shorts, a purple blouse and matching sneakers. She crossed her arms.

"Where're your parents?" Jenna asked ignoring her sarcastic tone. She hated when she folded her arms as if she were judging her.

"They left for work."

"Good," Jenna said. "We need to talk."

"You're at my house instead of school. Let me guess. You're still thinking of living without me?"

Jenna twirled a few stands of her thick coarse hair around her fingers. Rosa was a loyal friend, but she could be trying at times. "Let's go to the orchard."

The orchard was located in the back of the property. It was an apple orchard. Pink and white blossoms shined in the morning sun. The teens sat down on the ground underneath one of the apple trees.

Rosa watched Jenna take out her sketchbook, pencil and artist's crayons from her knapsack. Leave it to Jenna to be ready to draw no matter the situation. Soon, she was sketching one of the apple trees. She really was a good artist. She could be a pro.

Rosa sighed. The precocious high school junior knew what Jenna wanted and it was a stupid idea.

Jenna sensed Rosa's disapproval. It was an ongoing argument. She was almost seventeen. They both were. It was time to grow up. She wanted to stay out of trouble and live right. "I have to do this, Rosa."

"But you need me."

"I've made up my mind. I have to learn to fight my own battles."

"Can you?"

"I thought you were my friend?" Jenna's lips began trembling.

"I am. But do you really believe you can take on Bella by yourself?"

She was referring to Jenna's mother, her long time nemesis. Rosa didn't mean to hurt her feelings, but Jenna needed to hear the truth.

"Yes," Jenna replied. She had a plan. Rosa just hadn't given her the right opening to discuss it. That was the purpose of this meeting.

"So what's your grand plan for later on when you explain to your mother why you cut school *again*?"

"I didn't say I was going to go through with it today." Why was Rosa being so difficult? "Besides, you said your dad was moving your family to Hudson."

"He's letting me finish at Gordonville, Rosa said. "So if you thought you could get rid of me. You were wrong"

"I'm not trying to get rid of you."

"They'll eat you alive."

"I have to try, Rosa. "I don't want to be bad anymore."

"Is that why you're playing hooky?"

Jenna held up the drawing. "Consider me a work in progress."

Rosa winced.

"I want to start over again," Jenna continued. "No more mischief-making, no talking back. Maybe then I'll have what Lauren and Diane have." She turned the page over of her sketchbook and started drawing the old post and beam barn in the distance.

"How come you didn't mention Alan or Julian?" Rosa asked referring to Jenna's older brother and father, respectively. Alan was also Diane's twin. People often referred to them as The Twins.

Jenna concentrated on her art.

"Deep down you know Bella has no use for you or Alan. Not even Julian." Rosa stared at the amethyst choker around Jenna's neck. It was a gift from her mother. Last year, Bella took her to the jewelry store at the mall and let her pick out anything she wanted and for her birthday last month, she gave Jenna money for art supplies. Rosa sneered. *Just enough goodness to ease her conscience.* "You think by doing that Bella will suddenly love you as much as your sisters?" Rosa laughed without humor. She leaned over conspiratorially. "I'll get rid of Bella, Lauren and Diane. Just say the word."

Jenna stiffened. "I said no when you brought it up the first time."

"But it's the only way. Just think. You'll never feel pain again. And you'll be doing your brother and your dad a favor."

Jenna stared into space. She tried to imagine life without torment. She'd thought about it many times, but it didn't involve bloodshed.

"You know I'm right," Rosa said breaking into her thoughts.

"I just want to make peace with my mother and sisters."

"Good luck with that."

Jenna sketched the broad sign of the barn. "I've been thinking about college lately. The principal thinks I have a good chance of getting into some of the best art schools in the state. He's willing to put in a good word for me."

"Now this goody-two-shoes thing is starting to make sense," Rosa said. Ordinarily, she had no problem convincing Jenna about what was best for her.

"But I need to work on my attitude," Jenna said. "There's stuff on my record. Like that boxing match in gym class."

"I hope you're not blaming me for that. That was all you."

"I know." Jenna picked up a red crayon to color in the barn.

"That Maura chick deserved what she got." Rosa picked a blade of grass and held it between her fingers. "This is because of the fire isn't it?" Rosa threw her head back and laughed.

"It's not funny," Jenna said.

Last summer, they were in Jenna's bedroom dancing to her new hip-hop CD's, when Bella burst into the room and slapped Jenna for not washing the dishes. Enraged, Rosa waited for an opportunity, ran out to the backyard and set fire to the storage shed. Fortunately, Alan, who was home, discovered it in time. He put the fire out before it could spread.

"Your mother never touched you again though," Rosa sang.

Jenna didn't comment although she knew it was true.

"So you want to be an art major. I'm not surprised."

"With a minor in education," Jenna added. I'll support myself teaching art while I work in my studio."

"You mean here and in your mother's basement."

Playfully, Jenna swatted her.

"Anyway, I've seen your work. You've got the talent." Rosa yawned. "But Bella will never allow it."

The red crayon Jenna was holding slipped out of her hand and landed on the grass. "Why?"

"Because she's a dream stealer. So are Lauren and Diane."

"My sisters don't care about what I do."

"Mommy's little darlings will do anything to take you down. Remember the sweater?"

Jenna was seven years old, but she could still feel the sting from the smack she received from her mother for trying on Lauren's cashmere sweater. Needing to block the memory, Jenna searched the grass until she found the crayon. She resumed drawing.

"And don't forget what happened to Alan," Rosa went on. "Your brother had to wear long sleeves to school all because Lauren lied."

"Stop it," Jenna murmured between clenched teeth. She didn't need or appreciate the reminders.

"How about when Diane broke your mom's candy dish and said you did it," Rosa said, determined to make Jenna see reason. "Bella didn't think twice to go up side your head."

Jenna closed her eyes and put her hand to her temple. "You're trying to discourage me."

"I'm trying to protect you," Rosa said. "Alan would agree."

Jenna heaved a sigh. Rosa taught her to protect herself against anyone who disrespected her, namely, her mother and sisters. She even fought most of her battles. "Still, I have to try."

Rosa sneered. "Did you learn that in church?"

Jenna made a face.

Rosa cocked her head. "Your dad still doesn't know what they did to y'all."

"He doesn't even know about you," Jenna said.

Pain showed in Rosa's eyes. "After all this time. How come I have to be a secret? We're family. I think of you as family."

"So do I." Rosa was more of a sister than Lauren or Diane. "But that's the way Mom wants it."

"Haven't you ever wondered why?"

"Yeah." She couldn't begin to figure how to go about finding out why her mother was so secretive about Rosa. It's just always been that way. Plus mom threatened her, Lauren, Alan and Diane if they ever mentioned Rosa to anyone. No exceptions. Not even Lauren and Diane got a pass.

Yet, she couldn't begin to figure how to go about finding out why her mother was so hush-hush about Rosa's existence. "But it's always been that way." That and the fact that her mother threatened her, Lauren, Alan and Diane if they ever told anyone about Rosa. Not even Lauren and Diane got a pass.

The pain on Rosa's face took Jenna by surprise. Sentiment and Rosa didn't go together. When slighted, she simply laughed or remained eerily silent. Then, sometime later, days, months, perhaps weeks, when the person who offended her least expected it, she attacked.

"Someday I'm gonna go right up to Julian and introduce myself."

Jenna looked uncertain.

"Your father oughta know I exist."

Jenna knew that Rosa was right; yet, she wondered how that scenario would play out. Daddy would wonder why they hadn't introduced him to Rosa before. Mom didn't want him or anyone else to know about her existence, as if she were ashamed.

"Once they know I'm no longer around," Rosa began, breaking into Jenna's thoughts, "they'll work you over like they always do. You'll fold like a lawn chair."

Jenna continued drawing. Rosa was probably right, but she wasn't going to admit it.

"So it's like that, huh? Ignore me and maybe I'll go away?" As a goldfinch flew above them, Rosa smiled with cunning. "How about a compromise?"

Jenna wavered then asked, "What do you mean?"

"Let them think we're not friends. You feed them that line about wanting to be good and I won't come around anymore. Your mother and sisters won't miss me 'cause they can't stand me anyway. We'll just continue to meet in secret."

Jenna nodded. "I like that." She didn't really want to live without Rosa. She just didn't want to risk her future. "Can I tell Alan?"

"No," Rosa said. "Leave him out of it. Besides, I think I make him nervous." She looked puzzled. Alan was an okay guy. She'd never hurt him.

"But you're still gonna fight my battles," Jenna said.

"Only if you ask me to. Deal?"

"Deal."

They smiled and shook hands.

1

Sixteen years later

"Let's get them from this angle," a photographer from Essence Magazine said.

It was the event of the year. The marriage of Nelson Door, notable film producer and founder of Door Productions, whose slogan, "Enter the Gateway to Success," and one of Hollywood's sexiest men, to Lauren Crandall, renowned New York State assistant district attorney. The couple was posing in the rose garden, one of several formal grounds on his twelve-acre estate in the Westchester County town of Pound Ridge.

Jenna looked striking in a champagne-colored blackberry ball gown. The thirty-two-year-old stood by a maple tree. Smiling. Her sister and brother-in-law were the picture perfect couple. Lauren in her satin bridal gown, a diamond necklace adorning her slender neck and matching diamond drop earrings dangling from her earlobes, long auburn hair, which she had styled in an upswept hairdo, emerald-colored eyes; Nelson, good-looking and debonair as always in a black double-breasted tuxedo.

Her eyes swept over the 1920's Beaux Arts mansion. The stately trees stood like sentries against the blue sky. It was as if the elements had gotten together and agreed that the newlyweds should have perfect weather for their special day.

Jenna nodded and smiled at a guest who walked by. She wondered if her jaw would ever be the same after today. She'd been wearing that same plastic smile since yesterday, when she and the wedding party arrived at *The Palace,* her secret epithet for Lauren and Nelson's manor. They all had to be present for the wedding rehearsal followed by the rehearsal dinner.

That's when it hit her. She and Everett were really over. They'd been over for almost two years. It seemed ludicrous that it should occur to her then but it did. The wedding preparations, the ceremony and now this reception were an-in-your-face testimony to yet another failed relationship. Last night during the rehearsal dinner she took in, the fancy spread, the myriads of wait staff. She listened to the pointless prattle of the wedding party. She felt like an egg after someone cracked it open then emptied the yolk and the white into a mixing bowl.

She shuddered at the thought of what might've happened during the ceremony. Rosa was sitting among the guests. Sporting cornbraids and wearing a scarlet strapless tea-length dress, she winked at Jenna then smiled derisively as she watched Lauren and Nelson exchanging their vows. Heaven only knows how she made it past security. But that was Rosa. Her cunning and her ability to confuse was what Mom, Lauren and Diane despised the most.

Jenna began yelling at herself for giving Rosa the details about the wedding. But with whom else could she talk to about her feelings? They were like sisters and in spite of her twisted streak; it was sweet of Rosa to come down from Hudson to Pound Ridge to attend the wedding. Then again, she had to keep an eye on her during the ceremony. Rosa was probably out to pull some crazy stunt. The woman was unpredictable.

Clasping her hands together, she tried not to think about what would've happened if her mother or sisters had seen Rosa. If Alan saw her, he would've found a way for them to escort Rosa off the premises without anyone being the wiser, that is, after he got over his initial shock. He, like the others, wasn't supposed to know about their ongoing friendship. So far, no sign of her. Maybe Rosa just wanted the satisfaction of crashing the wedding. Since she got her wish, maybe she went home.

She tried not to think about Everett. The available bachelors walking about did little to lift her mood. She just had to remember to smile and she'd get through this afternoon.

Jenna took in the plethora of cameras capturing some of the world's cream of society: politicians, lawyers, models and Hollywood celebrities. The last two groups came courtesy of Nelson and Diane, who became an international supermodel. Maintaining her flawless smile, Jenna looked in her sister's direction. Also dressed in an identical champagne-colored blackberry ball gown, the amber-colored beauty stood beside her boyfriend, the Jamaican-born clothing designer, Lawrence Belmar, Larry to his friends. He too could pass for a model. His maternal East Indian features turned many heads. Larry was looking stylish in a Mandarin collar tuxedo.

The photographer pointed to Jenna. "Let's get one with the bride and her sisters in the rose garden."

"More posing?" Diane asked in a teasing tone. "This is my day off you know."

Lauren laughed.

Jenna turned toward the sound. Her sister the bride had her mouth opened just wide enough for the cameras to see her lovely bridgework. For a moment, Jenna forgot about the paparazzi as her tranquil smile soured. She put her hand to her temple. Lauren's laughter was so proper. So lady-like.

So fake.

Jenna curled her lips. Suddenly remembering her "role," Jenna put on her happy face and headed toward the rose garden.

The photographer posed Jenna sitting between Lauren and Diane who stood on either side of her. Jenna tried to ignore the twisting in her gut. Her sisters' size two figures and lighter skin gave notice to her darker pigment and size sixteen body. Growing up, they never failed to scorn her shape and color, especially Lauren, who, like their father Julian, took after their Irish paternal great-grandmother.

After Adrian was finished posing them, he snapped the picture. "Great. One more."

The camera flashed.

"Good."

"Glad that's over with," Lauren muttered.

Diane snickered. "Aren't you glad she got rid of that weight?"

"You're not kidding," Lauren said. "Imagine what my wedding pictures would've looked like."

"I wish she'd done something more with her hair," Diane said. It bothered her that Jenna kept her hair natural. Diane kept her honey brown locks in a perm. "At least she could've straightened it. Or put in a weave."

"Just be glad she's wearing something besides those tie-dye shirts."

Jenna pretended not to hear. Why should she expect her elder sisters to be civil? Why should today be different from any other day?

"Now let's get one with the bride and her brother then with the whole family," the photographer said.

Jenna looked down at her sandals. The whole family. At least she wouldn't have to suffer another moment with Lauren and Diane. She was going to have company. Jenna watched her sisters walking across the yard. A wicked smile crossed her face. It would've been funny to watch Rosa hand Lauren a wedding present.

*

Ironically, Jenna wasn't the one who ended up being in agony. It was Adrian the photographer. Jenna was trying hard not to laugh. After today, he's probably going to quit photography. It was taking an awfully long time to, *"get one with the whole family."* Nelson was a film producer, yet his relatives couldn't pose to save their lives. *Maybe* he and *Lauren could use mannequins in their wedding photos. Who would notice?*

A giggle escaped from Jenna's lips. She glanced around. Her mother wasn't looking. The mother of the bride, was looking elegant in a two-piece gray chiffon dress and matching pillbox hat. She stood proudly, a humorless expression on her coffee-colored face. Jenna smirked. Bella Crandall was not amused.

Alan made eye contact with Jenna then winked. Their new in-laws were amusing him too. He was also glad to see Jenna at ease. He'd been concerned about her lately . . .

"Perfect," Adrian said, unmistakable relief in his voice. He finally got these people to stand right. "Now hold that pose. Nobody sneeze. Nobody scratch." The photographer thought he was taking a risk in asking them to hold still. He didn't think he'd get a pose out of them until Labor Day.

Finally, the camera flashed.

"One more. I know you're all dying to get back to the buffet table."

While everyone chuckled, Jenna noticed a giant earthworm by Lauren's foot. Her lips twitched. Her sister had an intense fear of creatures that slithered.

"Say cheese," Adrian cried.

Suddenly, Lauren shrieked.

Jenna struggled to hold in the laughter as her sister began to do a wild dance while yelling, "Get it off me! Get it off me!"

Everyone turned around to see what happened. Security dashed to the scene, along with other nearby guests.

Nelson quickly assessed the situation. The earthworm wasn't actually on Lauren. Just seeing it had caused her to wig out.

Not wanting his bride to be embarrassed any further, Nelson told security that he had the situation under control then dismissed them. He turned to Lauren who was now in tears. "It's okay."

Nelson scooped her up in his arms and moved her away from the immediate area. He too was familiar with her fear of things that crawled. His younger brother kept reptiles as pets. It didn't bother him, although they weren't his first choice for household pets.

"It's gone now, sweetheart," Nelson said. He turned to the photographer. "We'll take pictures later when my wife's calmer." With that, Nelson took his bride out of the rose garden.

The photographer took down his equipment. He had given up on them long time ago.

Diane looked at Lauren clinging to her husband like a frightened child. Her sister was always the strong one. The brave one. Rarely did she see Lauren become unglued. Gingerly, Diane glanced at their mother. The handsome, imperious woman had a reflective look on her face yet her eyes carried just the slightest hint of strong disapproval. Diane started nibbling on her lower lip. Mom hated negative public displays of emotion except for happiness.

Soon, the crowd dispersed. Only Jenna and Alan remained. He watched her sniff a yellow rose but not before catching a gleam in her eye. No. He didn't want to believe that Jenna had anything to do with what happened in the garden just now. How could she have? Jenna wasn't even near Lauren. When did she find the time? He wasn't a fan of their eldest sister, but today they should all put aside their differences and just wish her well. He just assumed that Jenna was all right. Perhaps he was mistaken . . .

"Are you okay?" Alan asked.

Jenna sniffed a red rose. "Of course."

"I mean about this wedding."

Jenna looked into her brother's anxious face, sighed, then picked off a piece of lint from his tuxedo jacket. "Why wouldn't I be? The weather's great. I feel pretty. Now Mom may not be happy after Lauren's little performance back there. You know how Mom feels about image."

Alan nodded. Their mother was a stickler for appearance and Lauren did put on quite a show. Maybe Mom will cut her some slack since she was one of her favorites and it is her wedding day.

"Do you think we'll see Lauren's performance on YouTube?"

"It's not funny, Jenna." Finding humor in their sister's public humiliation wasn't a good sign.

Jenna rolled her eyes. "You're thinking about me and Everett? Well, forget it. It's over. How does it go? 'To everything there is a season . . . ' "

Her attempt at quoting from Ecclesiastes was a dead giveaway. Jenna was anything but religious. She was hurting. She had to be. Everett Long broke up with her almost two years ago. Shortly after the split, Lauren and Nelson announced their engagement. Alan didn't know the details leading up to the breakup, but he was always a little suspicious about it. Everett really liked Jenna. The timing of Lauren and Nelson's engagement was tacky. Talk about in your face. Jenna didn't go through the grieving process. Instead, she remained calm.

Too calm.

He'd had his share of heartaches and you don't get over it just like that. Jenna's heartache had to be going somewhere . . . *No. Jenna couldn't be hanging out with Rosa.* He was so glad for some peace in the family he just assumed all was well. Rosa Garrison had been out of Jenna's life and theirs for sixteen years. Jenna was easier to handle. Alan shivered. What was Rosa like now?

"Stop worrying." Jenna cut into his thoughts.

"I can't help it. I care about you."

Jenna smiled. That was true. He'd been looking out for her since childhood, often at his own risk.

"Telling secrets?"

They jumped at the sound of their mother's voice. Bella stood as if posing for a magazine, her countenance, was the epitome of congeniality. She glanced around then regarded them with an expression of foreboding.

Alan, who was six-foot and well built, took a step back from his five-foot two-inch mother. "We were just talking."

"About what?" Bella looked squarely at Jenna. "Invertebrates?"

Jenna wore an innocent look.

"She had nothing to do with what happened," Alan said with more bravery than he really felt. "She was standing there with the rest of us?"

"Quick to come to her defense aren't we?"

Surreptitiously, Jenna gave Alan a warning look. Unfortunately, he didn't look in her direction.

"Jenna would never intentionally humiliate Lauren on her wedding day," Alan said. Experience told him to stop talking. His mother was going to get scary mad, but he couldn't stop. He had this need to prove Jenna's innocence and more than ever to prove to himself that she's as happy as she says she is.

Jenna blew out a breath of frustration then turned to look at the rose garden. For a couple with very little personality, Lauren and Nelson had an aesthetic eye. She pointed to a bush filled with lavender roses beside a trellis. "Don't you think they would look beautiful in watercolor?"

"Yes," Alan said, relief coming over him. "It would." Jenna loved art. Drawing and painting was what she did often when they were growing up. Maybe art was her way of channeling her depression after the breakup. Maybe she wasn't hanging out with Rosa after all.

Alan watched his sister stare longingly at the rose garden no doubt was envisioning what it would look like on canvas. Their mother, however, was glaring at her with that familiar menacing stare from childhood. Alan swallowed. His solace disappeared. "What's wrong?"

Bella turned around slowly and deliberately and looked at him. "Nothing that concerns you."

Alan's heart sank. He was wrong. Jenna and Mom hadn't reached some kind of truce after all. He and Jenna had a horrendous history with their mother, Jenna in particular; but ever since Rosa's mysterious departure, they were on good terms. At least he thought they were. However, his mother's animosity and Jenna's withdrawal were all indications that life at home was anything but pleasant.

"Jenna." Bella spoke in a surly tone. Don't. Start." Bella refused to allow Jenna to indulge in her crazy antics especially today of all days.

Alan held his stomach. He looked from his mother to Jenna. The tension. The fear. It was as if he had stepped back in time.

How long has this been going on?

"Oh, Bella."

The fortuitous arrival of the church's coordinator for youth ministry broke the rigid atmosphere between mother and children.

With the skill of a veteran actor, Bella instantly became all charm. "So glad you could make it." She strolled over to her fellow congregant, quickly dismissing her son and daughter.

Alan wet his lips. What's so bad about painting? Mom knows Jenna likes that stuff. And why imply that Jenna was responsible for what happened to Lauren in the garden?

Deep down, he knew the answer. Rosa. He didn't want to believe it. Mom would've nipped it in the bud if it were true.

Wouldn't she?

"All right," Alan began, "what's going on?"

"I told you everything's fine."

"Then why did things feel creepy between you and Mom just now?"

Her brother was right, but she couldn't tell him. He'd want to investigate making things worse for her and him. "Forget it. This is a wedding. Time to partay!"

Alan watched Jenna half walk, half dance across the lawn to where the band was playing. He began to hold his stomach.

Jenna pushed down her dark mood and gyrated to the rhythms of hip-hop, rap, funk, R&B, calypso and reggae. Her dancing drew the attention of some of the male guests who came over and joined her. She wasn't forming connections. Just having a good time. It was safe. No danger of getting hurt.

Alan stood by the two-tier fountain watching Jenna and wishing that she would contain her enthusiasm. He wasn't buying this celebratory mood at all. It felt forced. Was she just putting her best foot forward or was Rosa Garrison behind this?

What's really going on, Jenna?

His wife, Elise, stood beside him sipping ginger ale. "I didn't know Jenna could move like that. We could barely get her to dance at our wedding."

That was true. Alan wore a nervous smile. Jenna was sweet but shy throughout their reception. Now here she was five years later tearing up the dance floor. No matter what Jenna told him, something wasn't right.

"It's good to see her loosening up," Elise continued as she watched her youngest sister-in-law twirling with a cute production assistant from Nelson's film set. "She's always been so reserved around others." Elise took another sip of ginger ale. "I thought it came from living with Bella."

"Don't go there." With the exception of Jenna and his father, Julian, Elise didn't get along with anyone on his immediate side of the family, especially his mother who was against their marriage. Regardless, he could always count on his wife for support. Elise was the voice of reason in the insane world of his family. She was his mental armament, his source of strength. Her patience and understanding made her loved by her students and one of Gordonville Elementary School's finest teachers.

"So far we're all having a good time," Alan added.

"I'm behaving myself. Didn't I do the reading for my dear sweet sister-in-law?"

Alan kissed Elise, ignoring her facetiousness. "I was very proud of you." Her reading from I John 4:7-19 was beautiful . . . *Let us love one another, for love is from God* . . .

"I've even been civil towards Diane." Elise made a face. "The giggler."

Alan shook his head. She just couldn't resist taking a swipe at his twin sister. He smiled at Elise. The mocha-colored beauty was turning heads in a cornflower A-line gown. He wasn't bothered. She had eyes only for him.

"Anyway," Elise continued, "Jenna's make up looks great. You know I asked Diane if her makeup artist had done Jenna's cosmetic work. And she looked at me as if I suddenly grew an extra head."

Alan adjusted his cummerbund. "Okay, so she did her own makeup."

"It's amazing," Elise said. "There's a talent I didn't know she had." She took another sip of ginger ale. "She's coming out of her shell, attracting guys. I can't believe she's the same person."

Alan took a deep breath. He wished Elise would drop the subject. He shuddered.

A waiter passed by with a tray of coconut shrimp. Elise took one. Alan declined. He helped himself to the rest of his wife's ginger ale instead.

Bella, Lauren and Diane stood by the guesthouse also watching Jenna.

"You weren't kidding, Mom," Diane said in a low voice. "Jenna and Rosa really are together again. Check out those moves."

"When she told the band, 'Come on, y'all, let's get this party started.' I wanted to crawl under a rock," Lauren said. Inwardly, she was nervous. Jenna was too celebratory. She wished that Jenna would go off somewhere. "I can't believe Jenna changed my music."

"Larry liked it," Diane said. "Especially the calypso and reggae if it's any consolation."

"She didn't ask me for a special request. This is *my* wedding."

"Lauren, relax," Bella said. The last thing she needed was another scene. She didn't care for Lauren's dance steps in the rose garden.

Bella pulled at the hem of her chiffon dress. Obviously, Jenna sweet-talked the bandleader into changing the music. Jenna could be a charmer. That's why men were following her on the dance floor like a pied piper. She knew exactly what she was doing when she altered the music. She knew that Lauren, the bride, wouldn't make a fuss or Diane, who was her maid of honor. Crandall's didn't air their dirty laundry out in public despite Lauren's histrionics notwithstanding.

Yes, Jenna had an excellent coach.

Rosa.

"I thought Jenna's partner in crime was gone for good," Diane said, breaking into her mother's thoughts.

"We all did," Bella said.

Lauren adjusted her veil. "I wish you'd told me." "When did you find out?"

"I caught them talking—"

Lauren gasped. "What were you doing at Thornbush Lane?"

"—In Jenna's room," Bella finished. "Don't interrupt me."

Lauren lowered her eyes. "Sorry." Her mother was the one person she couldn't defy.

"Another time Jenna was talking to Rosa on her cell phone," Bella said.

Lauren and Diane groaned.

"This was about a month ago," Bella went on. "So who knows how long their meeting of the minds has been going on?"

"I don't get it," Diane said. "What would make Jenna decide to contact Rosa after all these years?"

Bella sniffed. "Methinks Rosa never left." Why hadn't she come by the house? It was so unlike Jenna not to have her over. What did they have up their sleeve? "I haven't confronted Jenna with what I know. Let them play their little games. For now."

Anxiety came over Lauren. Mom had everything under control. She always did, but . . . *I thought that maniac was finally gone.* Rosa was a family burden. An embarrassment. Now she could be roaming around somewhere. On *my property*. Lauren began scowling.

Bella caught the look on her eldest daughter's face. "Stop that before you end up on camera. You gave them enough of a performance for one afternoon."

Lauren felt a lump in her throat. She didn't choose to embarrass herself, especially on her wedding day. But she couldn't tolerate creepy crawlies. *Mom knew that.* She blinked back tears. *I can't cry. I can't cry. Not these type of tears. For gladness yes, sadness no.* She'd been dreaming about this day her whole life and she refused to have it ruined by her mother's insensitivity or by her Jenna's antics. She took a deep breath and started thinking about the Costa Rican honeymoon awaiting her and Nelson. *Tomorrow this time, we'll be enjoying our first full day as husband and wife.* They'd take long walks along the beach, go dining and dancing. Plan their futures together.

Lauren began to smile.

Unaware of her sister's inner struggles, Diane admired the way Lauren could tolerate Mom's harsh words without falling apart. She wished she had her sister's strength.

Unconcerned by the effects of her words on her daughter, Bella said, "I don't like being made a fool of."

"Jenna played us all," Diane said.

"Mom," Lauren began when she found her voice again, "when were you going to tell me about Rosa?"

"Eventually. I didn't want you to worry, dear. You were planning the wedding, finishing court cases. You didn't need the added stress."

Her mother's term of endearment in addition to her not wanting to add strain to her wedding plans made up for her insensitivity a moment ago. "Thanks, Mom. But did Jenna have to come?"

"How would it look if you didn't invite your own sister to your wedding? Think of the notoriety. We can't take that chance. And did you really think that your father would've let that pass? Even I couldn't have justified that."

"Smile ladies," said a photographer for *The Journal News*. Bella, Lauren and Diane posed for the camera.

As soon as she left, Lauren said, "Jenna better not bring that weirdo to *my* wedding."

"She won't," Bella said.

"How do you know?"

Bella sniffed. "She wouldn't dare."

"Rosa wasn't at the rehearsal dinner," Diane said.

"That's true," Lauren said.

"So, we're not going to do anything now that Rosa's back?" Lauren asked.

"No."

"Alan's gonna have a field day," Diane said.

"Your brother doesn't know. And I expect it to stay that way. Is that clear?"

They nodded. The sternness in their mother's voice caused Lauren and Diane to look at Bella as if they were two little girls again.

"Lauren, you're a bride," Bella said. This is your day. Smile. Both of you."

And they did.

The band switched to a ballad. Jenna excused herself from her current dance partner, a marketing consultant in the governor's office, and left the dance floor. She headed to the stone fence then leaned against it. She spotted the bride and groom holding hands and smiling at each other. Jenna took a few deep breaths. *I'll be fine. I'll get through this.*

Her body tightened when her parents and Nelson's parents joined the newlyweds. Julian and Bella Crandall stood together, the picture of perfect contentment. Although not legally separated, they lived apart since Jenna and her siblings were children. And no one was the wiser. She scowled. Appearances. It was always about appearances.

Suddenly staged laughter filled the air. Diane, Larry and some of their modeling and celebrity friends joined the newlyweds and their in-laws.

Jenna watched her mother basking in her daughters' fame and fortune. Now, she had an influential son-in-law for the entire world to see.

She felt the dark clouds coming over her again. No. She didn't want to go there. She had to be happy. She had to get through this day. Perhaps this was a good time for a glass of Pinot Noir.

At that moment, Lauren, Nelson and the rest of the happy crowd left. Jenna was glad to see them go. With the exception of her father, Julian, she couldn't the sight of them. Yes, the setting was lovely and the ceremony was beautiful, hypocrisy and religiosity notwithstanding. Alan was right. She was unhappy. She didn't even want to be here, but she couldn't tell him. He'd start asking questions. He'd want to get involved.

Jenna closed her eyes. *Breathe.* Take deep cleansing breaths whenever she felt stress. Rosa taught her to do that. Jenna took another deep breath. So what if she looked weird. Who cares if the cameras caught her? Maybe the caption would read *Sister of the bride takes break.* Jenna continued her relaxation exercise, breathing in the aromas of earth and shrubbery. Blocking out all aggravations. No annoying older sisters, no hypocritical parents. No broken heart.

No dwelling on a certain best friend who refused to take orders . . .

When she opened her eyes again, she was startled. Standing a few feet away was a tall, dark-skinned black man in his early forties. He was tall, with short black tightly curled hair and brown friendly eyes. He was doing justice to his smoky gray, single-breasted tuxedo. The gold vest underneath added a sophisticated touch. He was holding a glass of wine and talking with another man who she recognized as the governor's nephew.

Jenna felt a stirring within. She remembered reading somewhere that when you met that special someone, the pain of the past didn't matter. All that mattered was you and that person. The now. She stopped believing that.

Until now.

2

Sensing that someone was watching him, Dr. Malachi Chase turned around and saw a pair of beautiful chocolate-brown eyes staring at him. Captivated, he too stared. He saw a lovely face. Smooth skin, full lips. High cheekbones. A single red rose adorned the side of her kinky afro. She reminded him of a noblewoman. *Nice work, Lord.*

Judging from her gown, she was one of the bridesmaids. Now he wished he had attended the ceremony instead of coming to the reception. Dr. Malachi Chase smiled at her. Jenna returned a shy smile.

When Brendan Cole asked Malachi a question and he didn't respond, he realized that his friend wasn't listening. He followed the direction of Malachi's gaze. The governor's nephew grinned, his slightly long blond hair blowing in the June breeze. "Are we having a good time?"

"I am now." Malachi took a sip of cabernet sauvignon. The lady impressed him one of the few who had. This reception was more like a gathering of Who's Who than a celebration of nuptials. He only agreed to come as a favor to Brendan whose wife, Audrey, had a family emergency and was unable to attend.

Brendan's blue eyes sparkled. It was good to see Malachi show some interest in the opposite sex. It had been a while since he was in a serious relationship. The last real relationship he had was in college. And that was a long time. All the other ones after that were unspeakable. He didn't want to jump to conclusions, but he was hoping that maybe something wonderful would happen between Malachi and Jenna. Married life suited him and Audrey. She brought sweetness and stability to his life. He wanted his friend to have that too. Brendan laughed to himself. After less than three years of marriage, he had become one of those individuals who tried to set up their friends, which he swore he'd never do.

Malachi took another sip of wine.

Brendan's face contorted. "How long are you going to nurse that drink?" He took the glass of wine from out of Malachi's hand and drank it.

Malachi looked around to see if anyone noticed Brendan's gauche behavior. "I can't take you anywhere."

"Lauren didn't invite me because I sip tea with one pinky in the air."

His uncle, the governor, had a friendly working relationship with the prosecutor. On the other hand, Brendan, a defense attorney with Gordonville's esteemed law firm Mirsky, Mirsky & Walden and her professional adversary, did not. Brendan was only here because he and the governor were a package deal.

"You've been holding that drink long enough, Mal. What're you waiting for? To see if a vine will grow out of the glass?"

"I'm savoring the bouquet."

Brendan rolled his eyes. Malachi drank only on occasion or if he was under stress. Otherwise, he could sip the same glass of alcohol until the cows came home. Nowadays, he cut back. A lot. He remembered when Malachi could drink under the table. Thankfully, Brendan could still relate to people even after becoming a Christian.

He didn't get weird or isolate himself. He could talk to Malachi about anything at all from the stock market to his favorite choices of peanut butter without Malachi "Bible-ing" him to death. Brendan yawned. "Just think, someday you'll be able to tell your grandkids about how you hobnobbed with the rich and famous."

Malachi snorted. He knew all about Lauren, Nelson, Diane and Larry's respective careers. Along with the rest of the world, he'd seen and heard enough about them on TV and magazines. He also saw through to their true characters: pompous asses.

Raucous laughter drew their attention. Mayor James Urbanowski was chatting with the newlyweds. In his late fifties, the slightly stocky politician also had a close working relationship with the bride. Together he and Lauren kept Gordonville's streets crime-free.

Brendan looked as if he bit into a lemon.

Malachi grinned. "You're not jealous that you and your uncle aren't the only political stars here are you?"

Brendan put down his empty wine glass on a nearby table. "The guy's a blowhard. I don't have to get up into Lauren's face. We've crossed swords in the courtroom often enough."

Malachi smiled knowingly. Lauren was a formidable opponent. At the end of a day dealing with her, Brendan was tense, jittery, not his usual relaxed devil-may-care self. Much to his wife's dismay, he would come home and polish off a bottle of scotch, even if he did win a case. Just dealing with Lauren Crandall had that effect on him.

Malachi gestured toward Jenna. "I'd much rather tell my grandkids about her." She was speaking with a guest by the hydrangeas. "Who's that woman? Is she from West Africa?"

"No. She's very much American. That's Jenna Crandall, sister of the bride."

"Sister?" Malachi frowned. He didn't see a resemblance to either Lauren or Diane. Perhaps Jenna took after one of her parents who he hadn't seen yet. Or maybe she resembled another relative. That happened in some cases. How often did people say he looked like his Uncle Harris on his father's side?

"What made you think she was West African?"

"Her features."

"I thinks she takes after her mother." Brendan muttered, "And Bella Crandall's a real character. Anyway, I met Jenna once. She's bright.

A little on the shy side. But once she got over it she was quite the conversationalist." Brendan lowered his voice. "It's amazing she and Alan come from the same gene pool."

"Alan?"

"Her brother. Try to keep up. He's the architect who designed the Olympia and Diane's twin. Poor guy."

Malachi whistled. The Olympia was the new mall in Gordonville, a village in the Upper Hudson valley where he recently relocated. The Olympia consisted of Victorian-style edifices in keeping with the town's architectural character.

"Alan's a nice guy," Brendan added. "So's their father. "You'd like Julian." He sighed. "About Diane . . . When you look into her eyes you can see the back of her head."

"So what is it about the mother exactly?"

Brendan whistled. "Bella Crandall. A real case study. The woman thinks that anyone who comes within inches of her should first check themselves for impurities."

Jenna finished talking to the guest then began to walk away. Malachi groaned.

Brendan chuckled. "I'll personally see to it that you get to meet her? Come on." He led Malachi to the open bar. He ordered a Chardonnay for himself and Malachi ordered an iced tea.

"I'm glad you came," Brendan said. "I needed the company."

Malachi looked around. "Where's your uncle? I haven't seen him in awhile."

Brendan wore a sheepish grin. "He left."

"What?"

"He just came long enough to show his face," Brendan said.

"Where is he?"

Brendan winced. "He went back home to watch the Yankee game. He adores Lauren, but he wasn't missing this game."

Malachi had that shocked look on his face, as if he'd just bit into an hors d'oeuvres laced with cayenne pepper. Brendan pretended to brush something off his lapel. When he dared to look at Malachi again, his friend was wearing a deranged smile.

"Give me one good reason why I shouldn't kill you now." He had planned to spend his afternoon the same way after a grueling week at Gordonville State University where he was working as a sociology professor.

"Because you're a Christian."

"God will forgive me."

"But I'm a fellow Christian." Brendan spoke with exaggerated innocence. "One who you've led to Christ."

"Don't try to sweet talk me." Malachi crossed his arms. "Did Audrey even have a family emergency?"

"I wouldn't lie about a thing like that, bro. I'm representing, my uncle, the governor." He hoped Malachi wouldn't be too angry with him. Audrey was supposed to be his buffer. Lauren had a certain aura about her that made him feel uncomfortable even though they matched wits in the courtroom from time to time; and since his wife couldn't be here and the governor wasn't staying, he needed Malachi. This was Lauren's crowd. Only his uncle, the governor, could work this crowd and enjoy it. Brendan sighed. "I'm sorry. I'll make it up to you."

"How?"

"I'll think of something. Now, somewhere on the grounds, there's a beautiful woman. Fate awaits you."

"First of all, don't call me bro. Second, you're not getting off that easily. I should be home right now watching the game in my sweats, feet up on the table with a big bowl of popcorn, potato chips, beer, loads of artificially flavored drinks . . . "

While Malachi continued lamenting about his ruined afternoon, Brendan saw Julian and Alan then waved them over. After he introduced Malachi to Lauren's father and younger brother, respectively, Brendan explained how Malachi came to be at the wedding. "Mal's also a new resident of Gordonville."

"Nice to meet you," Julian said. And welcome. Although it's strange welcoming you to Gordonville in the middle of Westchester County."

Laughing, Malachi said, "Thank you." Right away, he liked Jenna's father. He could tell that he was a good man and he was hoping that Jenna was like her father. Since he hadn't met her mother, he was looking for Jenna's features in Julian's face. He thought he saw a little resemblance in the eyes; however, Lauren, Alan and Diane definitely looked like their father. *I guess Jenna takes after her mother. In features, only I hope.*

"Malachi's a sociology professor at Gordonville State University," Brendan said.

Julian gave Malachi an approving look. "Excellent."

Embarrassed, Malachi simply smiled. Having the admiration of Jenna's father was important to him. *What's the matter with me? I haven't even met Jenna yet.*

"My daughter Jenna graduated from there."

"Really?" Malachi smiled.

He hoped he didn't look like an idiot. Something about walking the same halls, being in the same rooms, eating in the same cafeteria as Jenna made him feel fuzzy inside. I wonder what her favorite sandwich was.

"So you have a doctorate." Alan made a mock bow. "I got as far as a masters degree and vowed never to enter a classroom again."

"And did you stick to that vow?" Julian asked in a teasing voice.

"Continuing education classes don't carry the same pressure, Dad."

"I used to be a stockbroker," Malachi said. "The PhD was just a little something I decided to pursue.

"Don't be so modest." Julian looked speculative. "I admire a man who uses his mind."

Alan nudged his father with his elbow. "Somewhere in between he sold used cars."

Malachi patted his hair. Alan had no idea how close to the truth he came. "You might say I found my true calling."

"Well it's good to have more than one talent these days, Julian said.

"You're lookin' fly, Julian," Brendan said.

Malachi looked at his friend sideways. *What's with the urban slang?*

Julian struck a dramatic pose. "Think Diane can hook me up with a modeling agent?"

That brought on a round of laughter.

"I know the bridesmaids are dressed alike," Brendan began, "but Jenna looks especially striking."

"Watch it, Brendan," Alan kidded. "You're a married man.

Julian smiled proudly. "Well, I can't argue with that. And I'm not just saying that because she's my baby girl."

"Where is she by the way? I want to say hi." Brendan patted Malachi on the back. "I also want to introduce her to my friend."

Lord kill me now. Malachi shook make-believe dirt off the right foot of his black leather shoe. He was going to kick Brendan with it later. He wanted to meet Jenna. But did Brendan have to be so obvious?

"Jenna must've wandered off somewhere," Julian said. Alan flinched. *Please let her be alone.*

Julian looked around at the wedding guests. "The crowd must've gotten to her. He addressed Malachi. "Jenna doesn't socialize much. She's gone off to hide. That's easy enough. This place is like a park. She'll resurface."

Alan cringed. Malachi played as if he didn't notice Alan's uneasiness. What was the big deal in Jenna having some time alone?

Jenna walked by copses and a variety of formal gardens until she arrived at the topiary garden. The landscapers trimmed each plant into a shape of a character from Lewis Carroll's, *Alice's Adventures in Wonderland.* She went over and sat on a stone bench near a shrub in the shape of the Mad Hatter. A brook was there. She listened to the sound of the trickling water. A honeybee was pollinating among the marigolds.

The garden reminded her of all the good times she and Everett had in Lakewood Park back in Gordonville. They held hands while they took long walks along the lake. They cuddled while they watched the sunset. They went on picnics and talked about everything and anything. Jenna shook her head as if that could stop the flow of memories.

Soon, her thoughts returned to the man in the single-breasted tuxedo. She blinked back tears. She didn't dare entertain thoughts about a man. Thanks to her mother and Lauren, her last break up felt like surgery without anesthesia.

Like her secret ongoing friendship with Rosa, Alan didn't know that their mother had been sabotaging her relationships. He would've tried to help, like in the old days. It would've only made things worse for both of them. That encounter with Mom in the rose garden was a reminder . . .

Jenna recalled Rosa's words sixteen years ago. "*They're dream stealers.*"

She put her hands on her temples. So what if she ended up alone for the rest of her life? Maybe it wouldn't be the worst thing in the world. She took a deep cleansing breath and enjoyed the sweet fragrances of flowers and shrubs. Her thoughts returned to the man in the single-breasted suit. He was looking chic. Sophisticated. *I wonder what he's doing now. Is he with someone? Probably.* He was too handsome to be single.

Anxiety and loneliness taunted her. She closed her eyes and clenched her hands into fists. *I can get through this. The day's almost over. Then I can go home and forget all about* . . .

"This should've been your wedding day."

Jenna opened her eyes. *Rosa.* She took a deep breath. This was risky. A guest could pass by and ask about her friend or a photographer wanting to take pictures of the topiary gardens could decide they want to take photos of them. Still, it was sweet of her to drive all this way for her. She knew exactly what she was going through right now.

"Why are you still here?" Jenna asked. "And how did you get in anyway?"

Rosa smiled her familiar sly smile. "I got in."

Jenna let out a frustrated sigh. She should've known better than to ask. "Suppose Mom saw you?"

"With all these people?" Rosa sucked her teeth. "What did Lauren do? Invite all of Westchester and Los Angeles? I can't wait 'til tonight. With all those diamonds she's wearing, I wanna see if she glows in the dark."

"You won't be here to see that."

Rosa ignored Jenna and sat down beside her on the bench. "You're lookin' good."

"You too," Jenna said. "Now go home."

"Did you really think I was gonna let you go through this day by yourself."

"I'm fine," Jenna said.

"Uh huh. And those were tears of joy you were shedding during the ceremony."

"I shouldn't have told you where the wedding was going to be."

"Like they didn't talk about it to death on the news," Rosa said. "That ceremony was whack. Your mother reading from the Book of Isaiah in that phony religious voice. Lauren stage cryin' as Nelson put the ring on her finger."

"Actually, I think those tears were real." Her sister really was happy.

Rosa snorted. There was more bologna being tossed around that church than a deli counter."

"And what kind of a name is Door?" Rosa asked. "What're they gonna name their first-born? Exit? Maybe they'll have twins, Push and Pull."

Laughing, Jenna said, "Go home."

Again, Rosa ignored her. No matter what she said, she needed her. "The best thing about this day is that you met someone."

Jenna looked at her wide-eyed.

"Yeah. I saw you and that luscious guy checking each other out."

"Oh. Him."

"Curb your enthusiasm."

"You were you spying on me." Where was Rosa standing to see that? "Anyway, what's the point? Nothing's gonna come of it."

Rosa swore. "See what they've done to you?" You've given up before you've even tried." She clenched her teeth. "I should've taken them out when I had the chance."

Jenna shivered. This was precisely why she kept Rosa at bay. She still had it in for her mother and sisters even after all these years. "You know I hate that kind of talk. It's evil."

"You're kidding right? Look at your life, Jenna. You're a receptionist. I thought you wanted to be an artist. What happened? I'll tell you what happened. Bella torpedoed your ambitions. Just like I knew she would. And she's messing with your love life."

"I don't want to talk about this."

"Any guy who so much as looks at you twice she scares off.

"I said I don't want to talk about it."

"Remember Peter your first boyfriend? Bella made you feel guilty for being in love. Made you feel dirty. I coulda ripped her head off."

Jenna blew an anxious breath. Rosa would've done it too.

With just a word from her.

"And what happened to you and Peter?" Rosa asked.

"I broke up with him."

Rosa nodded. "For the sake of peace. And did you earn your mother's respect?"

Jenna shook her head.

"What about your other boyfriend Adam, the screenwriter? Bella insisted he was just using you to get to Nelson so he could show him his screenplays. 'Adam doesn't love you,' she said. Bella nagged and nagged until even you believed it."

Jenna held her hands to her temples.

"I told you she was lying. Adam was in love with you. And you lost him because of your mother and her head games. Now you can add Everett to the list. Bella's not trying to protect you from the deceitful man. She just hates to see you happy."

Jenna stared at the honeysuckles shaped like the Duchess and the red and white roses fashioned into the Queen of Hearts. Rosa's words penetrated her already fragile mood. Why did she have to go there? Jenna regretted letting Peter go and she hated herself for the mistake she made with Adam. She accused him wrongfully of using her. Why did she listen to her mother? Rosa told her the reason when she cried on her shoulders.

Because it was easier to believe a lie than to argue with her mother.

"Lauren." Rosa spat out the name as if it were a curse and at the same time snapping Jenna out of her reverie. "For Bella to get that she-wolf to do her dirty work was low. They badgered Everett until he couldn't take it anymore. Now you're making nice-nice at Lauren's wedding."

"Must we talk about this?"

"Yes. Because Lauren and Diane are living their lives while you're stuck in—I don't even know what to call it. Even Alan's living his dream of being an architect and he's only one step above the bottom of your mother's food chain. And he's married in spite of her." Her brother's love for Elise gave him the courage that he needed to stand up to their mother. Her loathing of her prospective daughter-in-law wasn't going to cheat Alan out of a chance at love. *I wish I had his guts.*

Jenna let out a frustrated sigh. She didn't need Rosa pointing that out to her or any other miserable part of her so-called life. Especially on a day like today.

Rosa shouldn't even be here. If anyone saw her, it could lead to trouble for both of them. "Roe, it was sweet of you to come. Now, you have to leave."

"Why are you helping Lauren? Why do you keep supporting this family?"

Rosa's tone altered. Jenna pursed her lips. She knew that tone. It was the harbinger of trouble. No matter how horrible she was feeling the last thing she needed was bloodshed at her sister's wedding. There would be no winners.

"It's all about their precious image isn't it?" Rosa asked. "They're still conning the world with that holier than thou show and you and Alan play along. Like you always do. Like two marionettes." She made puppet-like motions with her body. "And then there's your dad." She laughed dryly. "Completely clueless."

Jenna gave her a dirty look.

"I do adore the guy. But you know I'm right.

Jenna did know. She blew out a frustrated sigh.

"He's a good man," Rosa said. "I want to meet him." "You will."
Rosa brightened. "Really? When?"

"I don't know. Soon." Meeting Dad was a long-time time desire of
Rosa's besides annihilating her mother and sisters.

Rosa's smile suddenly turned cruel. "They'd go wild if they knew
I was here."

Jenna flinched. Nothing would please Rosa more apart from slaughter
than to disgrace her mother and sisters especially today of all days. How
remarkable that she behaved during the ceremony. "I can't rewrite yesterday.
Everett's gone and Lauren's married." She yawned. "I'm tired."

"Because you kept me up on the phone half the night stressing about
today," Rosa said.

"Don't you have a project to work on?" Jenna asked, referring to
Rosa's job as a freelance graphic artist.

"Today's Saturday," Rosa said. "It's my day off."

"Then you should be with Gary." Jenna was referring to Rosa's
boyfriend.

"We're going out tomorrow. And don't try to change the subject."

Jenna rolled her eyes. "You made your point. My plan failed.
Nothing I did pleased Mom. Chores, favors." Tearfully, Jenna added,
"Being good was a dumb idea. You win."

Rosa was glad she didn't listen to Jenna's order to stay away. Attending
Lauren's wedding can't be easy. To watch her sister get married after she
ruined her relationship with Everett had to be torture for her.

Jenna's voice was barely above a whisper. "I miss Everett."

"I know." Rosa opened her handbag, pulled out a tissue and began
dabbing Jenna's eyes. It really looked as if Everett was going to be
around for a long time. For once, Jenna would have a relationship that
worked. Unfortunately, their bond wasn't strong enough to take on the
Crandall's. Rosa frowned. If only Jenna would let her handle things.
She lost her edge since she made me stay in the background. "Don't mess
up your make-up. You wanna look good for Mr. Luscious, don't you?"

Jenna sniffled and smiled. She blew her nose then said, "You're
persistent."

"You know what has to be done."

Jenna quickly looked around. Then, in a low voice she asked, "What good would come from me committing murder?"

Rosa smiled. "Not you. Me."

Jenna's temple began to throb. She sniffled again. She stood up. Daintily, she picked up the sides of her ball gown and started heading back to the reception. She'd been away long enough. Mom might start wondering.

Rosa followed. "Go on to your afternoon of fancy food and phony pleasantries. You can lie to the world, but you can't lie to me."

Jenna didn't comment. She couldn't.

"I'll still be here for you," Rosa said.

"I know. Now go home."

"When you get back, find Mr. Luscious."

"Been there done that."

"I have a good feeling about him," Rosa said.

"Why? Is he Bella-proof?" Jenna asked

"I told you I could help with that."

Jenna stopped. She crossed her arms. "No more appearances, Roe. Go home. I mean it."

"Could I at least have a shrimp?"

3

Alan half walked, half jogged over to the wading pool where Bella was chatting with Reverend Brooks, the senior minister of the Gordonville Community Church, a non-denominational congregation. The ruddy middle-aged Alabama native who knew the bride and her family for years and was their spiritual advisor officiated over the ceremony. Alan greeted the Reverend then asked to speak with his mother in private.

When Reverend Brooks excused himself, Bella commanded, "Pull yourself together." She was annoyed at her son for approaching her with such undisguised anxiety in front of company. Hopefully, she wouldn't have to come up with an excuse for the Reverend as to why her Alan was so agitated. "Remember where you are." She adjusted her pillbox hat. "What do you want?"

Alan had to fight the urge not to run. Although his mother's face appeared beatific for appearances sake, the sound of her voice could freeze time.

"Have you seen Jenna?" He asked.

"Why?"

"Dad said she wandered off."

Bella tugged at the hem of her dress. Rosa Garrison was not on her daughter's property. If he knew that Rosa was here, he would interfere.

Alan always interfered. Naturally, the autocratic woman wasn't going to let Alan know that an uninvited guest may be among them. "So what if she wandered off?"

"I thought . . . maybe . . . Jenna's been acting overly festive. I thought." Alan shuddered. "That . . . *she* was here."

"You're talking about Rosa." Bella looked at Alan warily. Did he know she was back? He and Jenna have always been close. Could that be what he and Jenna were talking about in the rose garden earlier? "Did I *say* she was back?"

"No."

"Don't you think I would've been the first to know if she were?"

Alan stared. The answer was yes, but he didn't reply.

"And so what if Jenna takes a walk? What do you care?"

Bella regarded her son as if he were a fool then watched as an expression of doubt came over his face.

"I was just wondering," Alan said.

"Don't lie to me, boy."

Alan inhaled sharply. The word infuriated him. It was just another way of degrading him. Now that he was pushing forty, it was even more painful coming from his own mother.

"You came here to protect Jenna."

Alan began having flashbacks of his mother's beatings. His mouth went dry as if cotton were inside of it. He envisioned himself standing up to her and telling her just what he thought of her and what she did to him and Jenna during their childhood. He also fantasized about telling his father about other things . . .

Bella's eyes flashed. Alan was looking like a terrified child. The only thing left for him to do was to snivel. Disgusted, she stared him down.

Alan turned away and looked down at the grass. He couldn't look into his mother's piercing stare. He never could.

"You're the one who wanted to get married, go tend to your wife."

As Alan was turning to leave, Bella said, "The only reason you came rushing over was because you think Rosa's skulking around. Well, Jenna's not a little girl anymore for you to protect. She's fine."

"Is she?"

His mother wanted to go off on him. He could tell. She just couldn't. She wouldn't dare. Not in front of witnesses.

With a slight smile, Alan turned around and walked away. He may not have gotten the answer that he came for, but at least he found a bit of courage to say something.

Diane giggled as she rang a small hand bell.

Jenna returned just in time to see Nelson plant a kiss on Lauren's lips. She put on her happy face, applauded along with the other guests. She listened to the toasts, the laughter, couples stealing kisses. All of a sudden, Jenna began daydreaming about herself in an ivory wedding gown and Everett in a tuxedo kissing her. She didn't want to have this fantasy, but she couldn't stop it. It played mercilessly in her head. Then, it changed. Instead of Everett, it was the man in the single-breasted tuxedo kissing her.

She searched the crowd, hoping for a glimpse of the man in the single-breasted tuxedo regardless of her feelings. What would she do if she saw him? Walk over and start a conversation? Unlikely. What would she say?

I *can't go down that road again. Ever. I've got to forget about him.*

If Rosa were here, she'd probably suggest a shot of whiskey. Or vodka.

She decided to have a salad instead.

Malachi was also searching the crowd. *Where was . . . what was her name again? Oh, yeah. Jenna.* He winced. His stomach was rebelling. It wasn't due to the cuisine, which came from one of the finest restaurants in nearby New Canaan, Connecticut. It was because he had already eaten a handful of mini quiche, mini crab cakes, coconut shrimp and assorted canapés. A server came by with a tray of mini beef Wellington. Over his stomach's protestations, Malachi took one.

Brendan cringed. He was no stranger to Malachi's tendency to overeat when nervous. "Would you cut it out? You're gonna make yourself sick."

"I'll be fine," Malachi said, his mouth full of beef Wellington.

"Uh huh. Nothing spells romance like upchucking all over the girl of your dreams."

Malachi relaxed his tensed shoulders. *She did smile at me.* That was a good sign. He started imagining them making conversation perhaps even getting in a dance or two, but soon insecurity returned. "What if she thinks I'm a loser?"

Another server passed by with a tray of tomato and mozzarella appetizers. Malachi took two.

Brendan gritted his teeth. What happened to the cool, suave, sophisticated guy he befriended in college.

Malachi spotted Jenna at the salad bar. "Quick introduce me." He spoke with his mouth full of appetizers.

"Eww! You're disgusting."

Malachi started pulling Brendan towards Jenna. "Hurry before she disappears again."

"You mind not wrinkling my tux?"

"Sorry."

*

"Excuse, me," Brendan said after he and Malachi arrived at the salad bar and stood near to Jenna.

She turned around. Jenna smiled at Brendan, but when she saw the man in the single-breasted tuxedo standing beside him, she jumped. A slice of lettuce landed on Malachi's sleeve. "Oh, I'm so sorry."

Malachi smiled. "It's okay."

Right away Jenna realized that she was standing in the presence of someone who was authentic. If a piece of lettuce had gotten on Lauren or Diane's clothing, they would have had a fit. She wore a tiny smile. The scent of his spice-scented aftershave was teasing her senses.

Brendan cleared his throat. "You may not remember me. I'm—"

"Brendan Cole," Jenna finished taking her eyes off Malachi.

The attorney's eyebrows shot up.

"I've been told that I have a mind like a steel trap," Jenna said. She smiled brightly. "I met you and Audrey at Lauren's housewarming party when she was living in Bronxville."

"You're good." Brendan was impressed that Jenna remembered him, never mind his wife. He turned to Malachi. "Lauren and I were on a case where our clients decided to settle. That was the year my uncle was running for reelection. Hence, the invite to my opponent's get-together."

Malachi cleared his throat. This was all very interesting trivia, but he couldn't care less. He was only standing at the salad bar for one reason.

"Jenna," Brendan continued, "allow me to introduce you to my friend with the lettuce on his sleeve, Dr. Malachi Chase. Malachi, Jenna."

Malachi removed the lettuce, wondering to himself why he didn't remember to remove it and at the same time feeling silly but trying his best to disregard it and move on. He shook Jenna's hand.

From the moment his warm, firm hand touched hers, Jenna felt a wave of comfort and protection. This had to be a dream. She was shaking hands with *him* and now she knew his name Malachi Chase.

Malachi tried to control the muscles in his mouth. Jenna made him want to smile like a goofy teenager. He could've held Jenna's hand and gazed into her chocolate-brown eyes all afternoon. She smelled like strawberries and cream.

"Malachi just moved to Gordonville," Brendan said. "He's a sociology professor at Gordonville State University."

Jenna tried not to smile like a dope. *He lives in my hometown. Wait'll Rosa hears this.*

Putting aside her pessimism, Jenna thought about what it might be like to have him as a friend. A very special friend.

Malachi and Jenna didn't realize that they were still shaking each other's hands.

Finally, Brendan sang, "Hellooo. "I'm still here."

Wearing silly grins, they released each other's hands.

"So, you teach sociology," Jenna said.

"Uh, yeah. The behavior of individuals and groups of societies along with their social mores has long been a favorite topic of mine."

Brendan's mouth fell open. "I think I see my boss. Please excuse me." As he walked away, he murmured in Malachi's ear. "Good luck."

"I sounded like a geek didn't I?" Malachi asked as he watched his friend making a quick exit.

Jenna giggled.

He liked the sound of it. "I'll take that as a yes." Encouraged by her humor, Malachi asked, "Mind if I join you?"

"Yes, I mean no. I'd like that."

Malachi breathed a sigh of relief. So far so good despite the awkward start.

"I recommend the Asian salad," Jenna said.

"Then Asian it is." Already feeling stuffed from nervous eating; Malachi wondered where he was going to put the salad.

They found an empty table beside a bronze sculpture of Loki, the Norse god of tricks. Something about it gave him the creeps. One could say it was art for art's sake, but it didn't fit with Lauren's image. She prided herself on her Christian values. She even made a show of it in the media. Malachi shuddered. He hated creepy things, since he was a kid.

"Eerie isn't it?" Jenna asked. She was feeling excited and nervous. It had been awhile since she had a conversation with a man she felt attracted to and Lauren's icky statue made a great icebreaker.

Malachi didn't comment about the creepiness of the statue although he agreed with her inwardly. He put their salads and drinks on the table. He pulled Jenna's seat out for her before sitting down.

"How long have you known Brendan?" Jenna asked.

"Since college. He was pre-law and I double majored in finance and economics."

"You must be smart."

Sometimes for my own good. "I did all right."

"Dean's list?"

He chuckled. "All right you got me. I made the Dean's List. Four years in a row. I'm a certified egghead. The only thing missing is a pair of glasses." Malachi went on to talk about his friendship with Brendan, his family; he had a younger brother and sister and about his move to Gordonville.

Jenna ate a forkful of noodles as she listened eagerly. She liked the sound of his voice. He could probably make a boring subject sound interesting. She took a sip of Merlot and tried to picture what a date with Malachi might be like. It would be nice to go to the movies or for a walk and just try to connect. There was something calming and uplifting about him. Soon, however, the vision changed and she saw the ghosts of past relationships that failed. Her head was telling her that whatever happened with Peter and Adam was in the past. She should embrace this moment, but her heart was too busy remembering. And crying. Jenna took another sip of wine then asked, "Where are you from?" Conversation would drown out the memories.

"Brooklyn," Malachi answered.

"Wow. Gordonville must be a culture shock for you."

"Not really. I'm familiar with small town life. I went to college upstate."

"Tired of the city?"

Malachi twirled some noodles around his fork. "I just needed a change of scenery."

Jenna smiled enigmatically. "My intuition says it's a little more than that."

He laughed to hide his discomfort. "Once upon a time, I graduated from college with a Bachelor of Arts in economics and in finance, got a job as a stockbroker, excelled in my career at a company willing to pay for my MBA."

"And you took up sociology after dealing with bulls and bears."

"That's another story."

Malachi jabbed at a bell pepper then ate it. Clearly, further discussion of his earlier life was off limits.

So, he has a secret. Like Rosa and me. "Do you like your new place?"

"Very much." He told her about his house on Midland Avenue, a brick Federal home that only needed some cosmetics. Importantly, it was a bargain.

"You're close to us." She could hardly contain her excitement. He was good-looking, giving her the time of day and lived nearby. "We're over on Haven Road." Jenna looked wistful. "I love the city. I used any excuse to go to Manhattan. It's museum heaven."

"No, it's Museum Mile," Malachi teased, referring to the museums along a stretch of Fifth Avenue.

She smiled as she picked at a water chestnut. *What a dork. But at least he's handsome.* "I could spend all day in New York and never get bored." Jenna talked about the great times she had at the Metropolitan Museum of Art, the American Museum of Natural History, the Brooklyn Museum and her favorite mediums, Impressionism and post-Impressionism. "Sometimes I went there on school trips. Other times, Alan took me. Sometimes he did independent studies. Alan liked to examine New York City buildings. He's an architect."

"I heard," Malachi said.

With a shy expression, Jenna told him about her love of painting and drawing. "I experiment with other mediums too, but oil's my favorite."

He grinned. "Let me guess, you're an artist."

Jenna studied the wine in her glass. "I'm a receptionist. Not bad for a person with a B.A. in business."

"That's how you supplement your income as an artist." He posed the question as a statement.

She took another forkful of Asian salad. How appropriate would it be to tell a comparative stranger that her mother doused her dreams?

She could still hear her mother's words from when she was in her senior year of high school. They were having breakfast when Jenna told

Bella about her desire to go to art school. As she did with Rosa, she laid out her plans. Bella laughed as she poured a cup of Darjeeling. "*You want to be an artist? By the time they discover you, you'll be dead. Who will take care of you when I'm gone? Rosa?*

Jenna gripped her wine glass.

Malachi looked at Jenna with concern. "Jenna? You okay?"

She blinked then smiled with embarrassment when she realized that her mind wandered. "I'm fine."

"Careful with that glass."

Jenna looked at how tightly she was grasping it then immediately relaxed her hold on it. *I can't tell him the details about what Mom said. It's inappropriate. We just met.* "I work as a receptionist because it's my job. My mother thought I needed a more stable job."

"With all due respect to your mother," Malachi began, "what is stable? Especially nowadays. I could walk into my office on Monday and be told my services are no longer needed." Right away, that old guilty feeling returned. This conversation was running dangerously close to a past he'd rather forget.

Jenna shrugged. "I'm settled in my job. It doesn't matter anymore."

"It does to you. You shouldn't take a job just for the pay. I know we have to make a living, but one needs to have a passion in life. More so, if you have a gift, then you should use it. Otherwise, you'll spend the rest of your life feeling unfulfilled. In fact, you're obliged to use your gift.

"Jenna, I saw your enthusiasm when you were talking about art. I bet a day hasn't gone by that you don't wish you were sitting in front of a canvas or a studio instead of a desk."

Jenna played with a slice of Chinese cabbage. "I sketch in between phone calls at work."

"Ah ha!"

"Ah ha what?"

"You're restless," Malachi said. "You're at a job that doesn't allow you to use your God-given talent."

Jenna bristled. It didn't occur to her that her talent came from God. No one ever told her that before. Maybe she was asleep or her mind wandered in Bible class. Rosa had asked her once that if God had given her artistic talent, why didn't He see to it that she got the opportunity to carry out her dreams. She still didn't have an answer.

"You haven't even seen my work."

Malachi smiled. "True. But I have a feeling it's spectacular." There was an awkward pause. "I hope I get a chance to see them some time."

Jenna began twirling a strand of hair. Showing him her artwork meant seeing him again. Like on a date. Rosa would say go for it.

With his fork, Malachi played with an almond. Jenna wasn't comfortable with his suggestion. It was obvious. "Think of me as a potential client."

Jenna smiled timidly. If she accepted his roundabout offer for a date, her mother would be furious. Isn't this what Rosa was so upset about earlier? Her mother's previous interferences and her pathetic inclination to obey; only this time her mother wasn't involved. Yet.

Malachi could see as well as sense Jenna's indecisiveness. *Was she seeing someone?* Guilt could cause a person to act squirrely. *Then again, wouldn't she have brought her date to the wedding? I hope she doesn't have a boyfriend.* He made a fan out of his napkin. "If you're uncomfortable, I'll understand." Wearing a mischievous grin he added, "I know how temperamental you artists are about your work."

Jenna appreciated Malachi's graciousness. Still, she worried about the impression she was making. Her hesitance. Her silence. She must look seem like a teenager to him. "Okay. I'll show you my work." Already her stomach felt funny.

"All right then." It was all he could do not to jump out of the chair and holler. He couldn't wait to spend more time with Jenna in a more informal setting. "How about a week from today?"

"Great."

After they exchanged phone numbers, Jenna summoned a server to refresh her drink. There was going to be trouble. Still, Malachi was worth it. She laughed to herself. Imagine getting a date at her sister's wedding. *Rosa's going to love this.*

Lauren was passing by the gazebo when Diane stopped her.

"What?" She sounded snappish. "Nelson's waiting for me. He has a ton of relatives for me to meet."

"Who's that guy over there with Jenna?" Diane asked.

Lauren followed the direction of her sister's gaze. When she saw Malachi sitting with Jenna, she raised her eyebrows. "I have no idea." She sniffed. "I didn't invite him."

Alan was walking by with Elise. Lauren grabbed his arm. "Who's the guy with Jenna?"

"He's a friend of Brendan's," Alan replied.

"Oh?"

Alan told them about Malachi's background. A haughty look came over Lauren's face. Diane looked amused.

Alan turned to Elise. "You go ahead. I'll catch up."

Elise gripped his hand. She should've known that feeling of well-being between wouldn't last. Alan was going to have it out with his sisters. She sighed then muttered, "Try not to make a scene."

As soon as Elise walked away, Alan turned to Lauren. "You're not gonna do to Jenna and Malachi whatever it was you did to her and Everett." He looked at Diane. "The same thing goes for you."

"What makes you think we did anything?" Lauren asked.

"Your scent is all over this."

"If Everett was so in love with Jenna, there was nothing we could've done to stop him," Lauren said.

"That's a copout," Alan said.

Diane glanced around. They were attracting attention. Her twin brother's face could be friendlier and his tone a lot softer. They were in a garden full of family, friends, neighbors and colleagues. Diane smiled and between her teeth, "Alan, image."

Lauren and Alan plastered on award-winning smiles.

"I didn't like him," Lauren said.

"It wasn't about you," Alan countered. "Everett was Jenna's boyfriend."

Lauren shrugged. Her diamond earrings jiggled.

Alan looked at her suspiciously. Like their mother, Lauren and Diane had a history of acting callously toward him and Jenna. "I guess you think every time you donate to *a certain charity* it makes up for everything."

Diane cast a nervous glance from her twin brother to Lauren. Why did he have to go there?

Lauren held out her hands and admired her French manicure. "If we weren't in front of company, you'd be a very sorry person."

Alan looked at his sister's nails. He never told Elise the truth about how he got that nasty scratch across his forehead last year. If she knew, it would've started World War III. Only Jenna knew because she was there. He was defending her against Lauren, for the umpteenth time.

"Mom didn't want Jenna getting involved with anyone," Diane said.

"What do you mean by that?"

Lauren gave her sister a dirty look. The least their brother knew the better. Where was her common sense?

Diane cringed. She regretted her words the moment she opened her mouth. She was just trying to relieve the tension, not make their brother suspicious.

By their reactions, Alan knew the answer. He looked horrified.

Diane looked around again. "Image."

"Screw that," Alan muttered anger mixed with a twinge of anxiety in his voice. How could she be worrying about what others think at a time like this? A potentially disastrous situation was at hand. "Are you saying that Rosa's back?" He looked from his twin sister to Lauren, confusion registering on his face. Didn't Mom make him feel foolish for even asking about Rosa?

"It was just a precaution." Lauren sidestepped the question. She wasn't about to disobey her mother. "We don't want outsiders getting involved, remember?"

"Yeah." Alan's mouth went dry. Rosa Garrison was the family secret. "So she hasn't returned? This whole keep-Jenna-away-from-men scheme was all because Mom was suddenly afraid that she was gonna blow her cover." Annoyed and disgusted, he said, "That doesn't make sense."

Diane shrugged.

"Jenna associates with men and women every day at work," Alan said.

"She's not forming any serious relationships there," Lauren said.

"Still don't see the logic," Alan said. "Jenna's entitled to have a life. And if Mom's worried about her telling anyone about our so-called close-knit relationship, she need not worry. Jenna and I don't even discuss it among ourselves much less with people."

"Mom didn't do anything to you and Jenna," Lauren said defiantly.

"Is that why Mom's so afraid of the world finding out that we have *another* sister."

"Shut up," Lauren hissed.

"If Rosa were around," Alan continued, "I hope that Mom would say something. She isn't somebody you mess around with."

Diane giggled.

Lauren gave her a warning look. This was no time for her to get nervous.

Alan glowered. "Is Rosa here?"

"Did we say she was?" Lauren answered the question with a question.

"No. But why's she," he indicated Diane, "acting like a goofball? More than usual that is."

"Did Mom say Rosa was here?" Lauren asked. She had to steer Alan away from the truth.

"No."

Diane started giggling again.

"You think this is funny?" Alan asked.

"Aw, lighten up," Diane said.

"There's nothing funny about Rosa."

"Drop it," Lauren said. "I have to go."

"I can't believe how blasé you two are acting."

"I said give it a rest," Lauren said.

Diane struggled to keep from laughing. She couldn't help it.

"It's not funny." Alan forgot himself. Annoyed with his twin sister's childishness, his voice was a tad too loud once again bringing unwanted attention to their little group. Guests in the immediate area looked at them with a mixture of curiosity and apprehension.

Embarrassed, Diane started pouting.

"Nice going, Alan," Lauren said, wearing a calm expression so as not to reveal to the others that there was a problem. She turned toward her guests and smiled reassuringly.

Julian came over. "Is everything okay?"

"We're fine, Dad," Alan replied.

Julian stared at Diane who looked anything but fine.

"I hurt her feelings," Alan said.

Oh boy. It didn't take much to upset Diane. "I'm sure your brother's sorry about whatever he did."

Diane was still sulking.

"By the way, Lauren," Julian began as he was leaving them to return to relatives he was chatting with, "Nelson's looking for you."

"Tell him I'll be right there, Dad." She smiled reassuringly for the benefit of guests who were watching. "We're lucky, it was Dad who came over and not Mom."

Diane sniffled.

"Don't cry," Lauren said. "Just ignore him."

Diane sniffled again. "It's Lauren's wedding day, Alan. You could have some consideration."

He looked over at where Jenna and Malachi were sitting. They were talking, laughing, enjoying each other's company.

"This occasion isn't stopping either of you from looking for trouble." Alan looked back at his sisters. "I'm asking you. Leave. Them. Alone."

Reverend Brooks stood with Bella and some of the other members of his congregation by the mansion's summer porch. "You're holding up well, Bella," he said.

"Believe me, Reverend, I'm exhausted."The mother of the bride put her hand on her forehead for dramatic effect. "But for putting up with her and this wedding, Lauren bought me this new hat." The mother of the bride playfully struck a dramatic pose. "And a new teakettle. Both imported from England."

The Reverend and his congregants exchanged knowing smiles. They were familiar with Bella's love of tea. In addition, she was a well-known Anglophile.

"My Lauren was organized." Bella smiled proudly. "Now Diane is going to drive me crazy when she gets engaged."

"Then get ready," one of the choir members warned. "According to *inTouch Weekly,* Larry was seen shopping for engagement rings at Harry Winston. Not that I'm in the habit of reading the tabloids," she added quickly after Reverend Brooks wore a mischievous grin. "The magazine just happened to be lying on the table in my chiropractor's office."

Reverend Brooks shook his head and chuckled. He turned and noticed Jenna and Malachi. The couple was in deep conversation. "Looks as if Jenna's found herself an admirer."

Everyone looked in the direction in which Reverend Brooks was staring.

"It would be wonderful if Jenna could find some happiness too," Reverend Brooks said. There was something a little sad about Jenna, he thought. He frowned slightly as he recalled the few times he tried to minister to her, but was unsuccessful.

Bella wore an engaging smile. "Well, I should go over and get acquainted. Please excuse me."

As soon as she walked away, her smile disappeared.

"'A penny for your thoughts,'" Jenna said wearing a tiny smile.

Malachi, who'd been staring at a slice of cabbage, looked up at her and smiled. "I want to say something and I don't want you to misunderstand me."

"Go on."

"Okay." Malachi let out a deep sigh. "You're pretty."

Jenna smiled shyly.

"And you have a beautiful smile." He said it fast so that the words came out sounding all jumbled together. Malachi went back to looking down into his salad bowl.

"Thank you." Jenna decided to change the subject. She loved the compliments. Malachi seemed like a sweet guy, but he was feeling shy and uncomfortable. "I can't wait for this day to be over."

"I thought you'd enjoy all the grandeur and the romance."

She wished he hadn't used that word. Jenna emptied her glass of Merlot. A waiter refreshed her glass.

"And then there's getting dressed up," Malachi said.

"I'm more of a jeans and T-shirt kinda girl."

"Now I like you even more."

She fought back a giddy smile. She didn't want to appear goofy.

"I don't miss wearing a suit to work," Malachi said. "To tell you the truth, I can do without the tuxedo. That's a beautiful choker you're wearing, by the way."

"Thanks." Jenna told him about the gift from her mother.

"You two must be close."

Jenna smiled then took another sip of merlot.

"Did you know that the ancient Egyptians used the amethyst to guard against guilt, fear and self-deception?" "Really?"

At that moment, Malachi turned around. He didn't know the woman coming toward them, but her imperial stride and self-aggrandizing expression spelled trouble.

"Don't look now, but we're about to have company."

Carefully, Jenna looked up. She felt a slight pinprick of pressure. "My mother."

4

Bella's very presence filled the atmosphere. Malachi and Jenna stood. She moistened her lips then made the introductions. Malachi extended his hand, but Bella didn't take it. She simply stared.

His mouth twitched slightly. *Okaay.*

Jenna closed her eyes as if in pain. She just met Malachi and already her mother was trying to intimidate him. That penetrating glare kept her and Alan in line when they were kids. She wanted to say something to fill the nerve-racking silence, but she couldn't. Feeling helpless and embarrassed, she just stood there watching them stare at each other like a moviegoer watching a film in a theater.

Malachi's eye contact never wavered. Mrs. Crandall didn't surprise him at all. It wasn't Brendan's earlier warning to him about the mother of the bride. It was her body language. The way she approached them said it all: haughty. Now she's trying to show him who's boss. Malachi laughed to himself. *Lady, you do not know who you're dealing with.* This tactic was child's play. He would know. He'd done it before. And worse. Obviously, she didn't like him. Why? Nevertheless, he was fast becoming annoyed. He did not like this woman.

And she was Jenna's mother.

Great. Lord, You know I have a mouth. Please don't let me say or do anything I may regret.

Bella's eyes began to burn as Malachi continued to meet her stare. Hiding her bewilderment, she lifted her chin in defiance. Finally, she dropped the gaze then began smoothing the front of her dress.

Jenna blinked. This is historical. No one ever won a staring match with her mother. She looked on in wonderment.

Her awe vanished, however, when suddenly, the scent of green tea perfume filled the air. Lauren and Diane decided to join them. Of course.

"Good Afternoon," Lauren greeted their little group in a bubbly tone.

Jenna sat down. She clenched and unclenched her hands. Mom, Lauren and Diane had a way of absorbing the atmosphere around them like a hostile alien life force.

Why were they here? This was her moment with Malachi.

"Jenna was just introducing me to her friend, *Dr.* Malachi Chase," Bella said.

Malachi noted the sarcastic way in which she kept uttering his title.

Lauren smiled as if she was enjoying a private joke. "I hope you're having a good time."

"As a matter of fact I am." He took a glimpse at Jenna who was now sitting with her arms crossed.

"When did you join our church *Dr.* Chase?" Bella asked.

"I didn't," Malachi said. *And you knew that.* "And please, call me Malachi." Bella stared in stony silence. "Or not."

"Have we met before?" Lauren asked.

"No." *I would've remembered that.*

Malachi offered no further explanation. Lauren blinked. "My brother says you're a sociology professor."

"That's right."

Diane smirked. "So, where do you teach . . . *Malachi?*"

"At Gordonville State University." Alan must've mentioned it to her since she already knew his profession. And what's with the sarcasm? He had been sizing up Diane. He could see why she was a successful model. Diane was beautiful and shapely. Apart from that, the woman was vapid. "I'm lecturing on dysfunctional families."

Bella, Lauren and Diane exchanged glances. Lauren coughed and Diane smothered a smile. Bella gave her daughters warning glances. Right away, Lauren composed herself. Diane, however, was struggling to hold in the laughter. Again, her mother looked at her with a slight frown. Immediately, the super model managed to control herself.

Malachi was studying the women. Something was disturbing them, especially Ms. Crandall. He glanced at Diane. What was so funny? He looked over at Jenna. She wasn't amused. She just sat there looking silent and miserable. "Did I miss something?"

"You live in Gordonville?" Bella asked, ignoring the question.

"Yes. I moved there a month ago."

"How nice." He was going to be trouble.

"Is there something funny?" Malachi asked.

"No." Bella glanced at Diane with disapproval.

The supermodel started biting her lower lip. She didn't mean to tick off Mom.

He was about to make a point about the brokenness of adults who came out of families unable to function as a unit when he felt the message in his heart.

Not yet.

He recognized the Source. He listened to It and dropped the subject. Still, something was making them feel ill at ease. Malachi didn't think it was possible for the atmosphere to become anymore uneasy yet it did. Lauren's coolness wasn't fooling him.

Breaking the ice, Malachi turned to the bride. "Congratulations, Mrs. Door. I wish you and your husband many years of contentment."

Lauren glared at him, her big green eyes flashing. "That's Ms. *Crandall*-Door."

Malachi blinked. *She's a Venus flytrap in a wedding gown.*

He looked in Jenna's direction again. She was still sitting quietly only this time with her hands in her lap. What happened to the astute woman he was speaking to a while ago? *Lord, Jenna needs Your strength.*

Lauren was still looking at him with indignation when without warning, a camera flashed, capturing her sour expression.

Jenna tried not to laugh.

"My apologies, *Ms. Crandall-Door,*" Malachi said, smiling brightly. "I didn't mean to offend you. He was also glad to see Jenna with a half-smile on her face. "Brendan Cole didn't tell me how you wanted to be addressed."

"You know the governor's nephew?" Lauren asked skepticism in her voice.

Malachi's mouth twitched. Sometimes name-dropping was fun.

"They're college buddies," Jenna said, wearing a big grin.

Malachi coughed to cover up his laughter as Bella's face began contorting. *Score!*

Bella sniffed. First, Malachi defies her. Then, he causes Lauren to look bad on camera, which was the second time she let her guard down. And on top of everything else, Jenna was inviting this professor into her life.

And ours.

"Oh, there's the blushing bride."

Everyone turned to see Norma Beery, Gordonville Community Church's secretary and Bella's friend and neighbor. Clad in a hunter green jacket dress, her brown hair in a simple bun, she came over and joined their group. Bella smiled with genuine delight. Norma was a dear friend. She also felt relief. Her timing was perfect. Professor Chase was pecking on her nerve.

"It was a beautiful ceremony," Norma said.

Recovering from her battle of wits with Malachi, Lauren beamed and said. "Thank you, Mrs. Beery."

"And you look positively radiant," Norma said. "Oh and Nelson is so handsome. You both make a lovely couple. Anyone can see that you're very much in love."

Malachi looked down at the grass and realized how they got it to look so green.

"I've waited a long time to meet a man like Nelson."

"Like they say, 'Good things come to those who wait. I just wanted to thank you again, Bella, for contributing to Haley's day camp," Norma said. "She hasn't stopped talking about the great time she had on their field trip to Playland." She turned to Lauren and Diane. "Blessings have to fall on you girls," Norma added. "You're mother is a saint."

Bella, Lauren and Diane were all smiles.

Malachi prayed to keep his food down. *Hello? What about Jenna? Mrs. Whosiwhatsit's acting as if she's not there.*

"I can see where you girls get your generosity," Norma said.

Finally, Norma took notice of Malachi. She gave him a curious look.

Jenna was about to make the introductions when Bella said, "Oh, where are my manners? Norma, this is Dr. Malachi Chase, one of Gordonville's newest residents." She went on explain about his background as if she were the one who met him first.

"A professor," Norma said. "Impressive."

"But you can call him, Malachi," Lauren said.

Malachi didn't miss the subtle mockery.

He knew some hand gestures he'd like to use right about now, but he showed restraint. Making a good impression outweighed his need for vindictiveness. He didn't want to upset Julian or Alan. He really liked them. Importantly, he didn't want to embarrass himself, Brendan or the governor.

"Well, Malachi," Norma began, "the Crandalls are fine outstanding members of the Gordonville community."

"Really?"

Norma went into a sermon about all the donations that Bella, Lauren and Diane made in the past. Malachi struggled to look interested. He resisted picking up his salad fork and stabbing himself with it.

Jenna shifted. *Go away, Mrs. Beery. And while you're at why don't you, Mom and my sisters go—?*

Lauren suddenly switched the topic to wedding cakes and the tough decision she had in selecting one.

Malachi shoved his hands into his pockets. Couldn't they have this conversation elsewhere? *Do we really care about pineapple, white or* almond cake with butter cream frosting? These women were invading his and Jenna's space. He looked in Jenna's direction then did a double take. She was glaring at her mother, sisters, and Mrs. Beery. Then, in a flash, Jenna's expression changed back to discomfort before finally becoming unreadable. The others were too absorbed with cake and frosting to notice Jenna's foul demeanor. Again, his curiosity was aroused. Something was off about this family.

When Norma finally left, Bella, Lauren and Diane turned to Malachi and smiled. He recalled a documentary on the Discovery Channel about how sharks react when they smelled blood.

"Is something wrong, Dr. Chase?" Bella asked.

"There's nothing wrong with me," Malachi replied in a meaningful tone. He wasn't in the least bit fazed by their shocked and appalled stares. He had "turned the other cheek" long enough. Bella's little game was trite and out of line. In addition, Lauren was rude and Diane was a dimwit.

Jenna straightened up in her chair. She had a look of glee in her eyes.

Bella's eyes narrowed, but before she could retort, there came the sound of running footsteps. Everyone turned. Alan was racing toward them.

The architect's legs couldn't move fast enough. He was eating with Elise and some cousins when he saw his mother and sisters with Jenna and Malachi. Why didn't Lauren and Diane do what he said and leave Jenna and Malachi alone? Of course, they wouldn't. Not with Mom there. Her presence only encouraged them. They were probably putting Malachi through all kinds of misery.

Poor guy.

Alan was putting his own emotional well-being at jeopardy by going over there. His mother would resent his being there, especially after she just finished lecturing him about interfering in Jenna's life, but he liked Malachi. Importantly, Jenna seemed happy around him. She deserves a little happiness.

The moment Alan joined their group Bella started glowering. He placed his hand over his stomach while at the same time trying hard to remind himself that he was a grown man, not the little boy who ran half-naked through the house trying to escape from her beatings. He was no longer the awkward teenager struggling to define his masculinity while facing his mother's repugnance toward him. Winded from running, Alan nodded at Malachi before turning toward Jenna. "Everything okay?"

"Yes," Jenna replied, her smile giddy.

Alan frowned slightly. He turned to Malachi and jokingly asked, "These ladies treating you okay?"

"Yes." Malachi didn't feel badly about lying. This time. Why complicate matters by saying your mother and sisters are disgusting and ill mannered? Didn't Alan already know that? Why else did he come dashing over here?

Bella wore a sardonic smile. What would it take to get through to him that he should stop interfering in Jenna's life?

Alan stepped back. He was creeped out by her grin.

Malachi examined his cummerbund. It was understandable for a stranger to feel unnerved around Bella. *But her own son?*

"You didn't mention that Malachi was pals with Brendan," Lauren said.

Alan shrugged. He did tell her, but she was so obsessed with making Jenna miserable and so prejudiced towards others who in her eyes were beneath her, she wasn't listening or she didn't believe him.

"I was also best man at his wedding," Malachi added enjoying the scenario.

Lauren was turning beet red at the same time Nelson and Larry approached.

"There you are," Nelson said. He looked at Lauren quizzically. "What's wrong?"

"She's just overcome with emotion," Alan said. He introduced his brother-in-law and Larry to Malachi.

Malachi shook hands with Nelson and Larry. It was all he could do to hold in the laughter.

"Laur, they want to take pictures of you, Larry, Diane and me by the conservatory." Quickly, they said goodbye then left.

Malachi wore a slight frown. Nelson and Larry didn't even acknowledge her. *That's it.* Jenna shrunk after the women showed up. Again, it was as if Jenna was invisible. When he looked at Jenna, she was moving her salad bowl back and forth.

As Jenna toyed with her salad bowl, she began thinking about the meadow. She saw the wide-open space, the grass, the flowers. A tiny smile began to appear on her face.

Alan cringed. *She's in her own world. We must look like winners to this guy.* He had to snap her out of it. "They'll want us in other photos, Jen."

No response. Evidently, she's still in her happy place.

"Alan, where is your wife?" Bella asked. She'd seen enough. Jenna was acting weird and Alan was behaving like a nitwit in front of company.

"Elise is with Cousin Bertrand."

"Well, don't you think you should be with her?"

Alan looked at his mother as a trapped animal looks at its predator.

Bella gave Malachi a sideways look. Having him witness her son's edginess or Jenna's weirdness was not good. He may appear unfazed, but he wasn't missing a beat. She could tell. Jenna's old boyfriend, Everett, was very corporate and very smart. Malachi was smart too. A different kind of smart. He was sharp and bold. That made him dangerous.

He had to go.

Alan cleared his throat, snapping Jenna out of her reverie. She looked at Alan who seemed ill at ease. A meaningful glance passed between her and her brother.

"It's okay," Jenna said. "I'm fine."

Alan hesitated before finally going over to Jenna and kissing her on the cheek. He did a fist bump with Malachi then left.

"Jenna is a very busy girl," Bella said. "She has her priorities." She gave Jenna a stern look then left.

Malachi watched her walk regally across the park-like grounds. *Jenna definitely did not have a date for this wedding.*

Jenna sat with her hands clasped, staring ahead, trying not to cry.

"You know, it's natural for the family to be protective of the daughter," Malachi said. "Especially the mother."

Jenna looked up at him, gratitude showing in her eyes. This man who hardly knew her was saving her pride. Again.

Calypso music began playing.

"Did I tell you my parents come from Trinidad?" Malachi asked using the quaint dialect and speaking with a flawless accent. He took her hand and using the same accent said, "Let I show you how we do it in Port o' Spain."

To Jenna's delight, Malachi was already dancing as he led her to the dance floor.

Later that evening, Malachi stood on the back porch of his house. It felt good to be home, out of his tuxedo and into his New York Knicks T-shirt and light sweat pants. Except for his family and Brendan, he didn't tell anyone that he felt that the Lord had led him to the upper Hudson River village. That kind of talk usually turned people off or sent them running. Understandable. Liars, hypocrites and religious nutjobs talk that way too except he was not "out there."

He looked up at the stars and thought about Jenna. If anyone needed a friend, it was she. He wanted to be that friend. Malachi laughed to himself. He wanted to be more than that.

Warped doesn't begin to describe her mother and sisters. That was an awful lot of drama just for him and Jenna to have a salad. *Why don't they like me? They don't even know me or my past . . .* And what's this hold they have on Jenna? She lost her essence and retreated into herself. She was fearful and wherever there's fear, there's anger. He'd never forget the animosity he saw in her eyes when she looked at her mother, Lauren, Diane and Mrs. Beery. The eyes he admired held so much hatred. Even Alan became different around his mother. He showed grit then all of a sudden froze when his mother started bullying him. *He must be angry too.*

Malachi returned indoors. He headed for the kitchen, straight to the freezer and took out a quart of strawberry ice cream that he purchased on the drive home.

He developed a taste for strawberry at the wedding . . .

"I did it. I survived my sister's wedding." Jenna spoke aloud to herself as she lay on her back in her bed in her attic floor bedroom. It was her room since the age of fourteen. She asked her mother's permission to move up there. Jenna was surprised she said yes. The attic lacked the opulence of Lauren and Nelson's master bedroom or the luxury of Diane's Upper West Side condo, no Persian rugs or Renaissance pieces to brag about, but that didn't matter. The attic was her sanctuary.

Near the window was a chair, a desk and a laptop computer. On her dresser was a statuette, a unicorn that she won at the county fair for playing skee ball when she was eleven years old. Lauren thought it was "kitschy" which only made Jenna love it even more. In a corner was an upholstered chair. Jenna often curled up in it with a good book. Posters of her favorite Impressionist artist, Claude Monet and post-Impressionist artist Henri de Toulouse-Lautrec hung on the walls. Her bookshelf was an eclectic mix of art, gothic romance and crime novels. An antique fairytale book sat on the right-hand dormer window. Alan had given it to her for her sixth birthday and she cherished it ever since. It was a big book with thick colorful pages. It filled many lonely painful hours during her childhood. Even now, she still read from it.

Jenna turned on her side and faced the wall where her poster of Monet's *Garden of Givenchy* was hanging. She started thinking about Malachi. His handsome face, his warmth, the smell of his spicy cologne. She sat up then picked up her cell phone that was on the night table. She didn't have to wonder about whether Rosa was back home. The lateness didn't matter either.

Rosa answered on the first ring. "'Bout time. How'd it go?"

Jenna told her all about her chance meeting with Malachi including what Lauren, Diane and Bella tried to do to him.

"The brother stood up to 'em. I like him already."

Jenna was grinning. "Guess what? We have a date."

Rosa gasped. Jenna told her how it happened.

"You go, girl! I'm proud of you."

"You gave me the courage," Jenna said shyly.

After promising to call Rosa back tomorrow she hung up. Jenna switched off the lamp and smiled in the darkness.

5

A week later, Jenna stood before her bedroom mirror. She wore a sleeveless plum-colored top, her favorite pair of jeans and cloisonné earrings. She picked put her hair into a ponytail. The sun was shining through her window, illuminating her bedroom. She was glad the weatherman predicted a warm, sunny afternoon. Today was special. She wanted every moment with Malachi to be perfect. Like her birthday or Christmas, the day had to be just right. Her mother despised Malachi. He stood up to her. He's not in awe of Lauren and Diane's celebrity status.

She began twisting a strand of hair. Malachi would be arriving soon and her mother still didn't know that he was coming or that they were going out. She wanted to tell her about their date ever since they returned home from the wedding, but she knew that once she told her about her weekend plans with Malachi, her mother would be livid. She didn't relish the idea of dealing with her mother when she was in that mood, especially when she had no buffer. She even stayed up late last night reading from her fairy tale book. She found solace in The Brothers Grimm's *Cinderella* and *Hansel and Gretel*.

Jenna applied a touch of raspberry-colored lipstick. As she was placing it back into her makeup bag, she got an idea. If she thought of their date as an outing, it would be easier to tell her mother. Jenna checked her watch. Fifteen more minutes. *Why does this have to be a problem? I'm just showing him my artwork.*

She sighed. She knew why. A potential hurricane was coming. And its name was Bella. Rosa flew into her mind. One phone call would change everything. *"Just say the word."*

There'd be no more worries. No more tears. Only freedom. But if Rosa got involved, it wouldn't be like the way it was before.

This time there would be blood.

Jenna picked up her shoulder bag and walked over to the bed. On top of it lay her art portfolio, one of several that she brought up from the basement closet. The rest were either in her bedroom closet or at the farmhouse. She put them away ever since Bella put down her ambitions.

She was about to leave her bedroom when, at the last minute, she opened the drawer of her night table and took out a small sketchpad. She put it into her shoulder bag. Then, she took a deep breath and left the room.

When Jenna reached the second floor, she paused. She became tense. *Breathe.* Bella was in the hall. She was about to head downstairs. That's where Jenna expected to meet her; perhaps in the kitchen or the living room her mother's two favorite places in the house.

Her mother stared at the portfolio in Jenna's hand. Then, her eyes shifted to her daughter's ensemble. Bella's stare became ominous. Jenna was going out and it wasn't to the office.

There was no time to rehearse what she was going to say even if she wanted to. "I'm going out with Malachi. He's picking me up." Jenna tried to swallow, but she couldn't.

Bella gave her *the look*. Jenna's body went cold. "Why am I hearing about this now?"

Jenna explained about showing him her artwork. "It's just an outing."

Four eyes locked.

Jenna swallowed. Her confidence was quickly slipping away. By the look on her mother's face, an outing made no difference to her. Unable to withstand Bella's burning gaze, Jenna looked down at a knot in the oak flooring. Like Alan, she too couldn't win a staring contest with her mother. Jenna was aware of the precious moments passing. Malachi would be arriving. If only she was as gutsy as Malachi.

Or Rosa . . .

"Why are you showing your artwork to *him*?"

"He asked." Jenna never took her eyes off the floor. "How did he know you could draw?"

Jenna raised her head and looked up into her mother's face. Her eyes looked venomous. "We were talking."

"You just met this guy and you told him your life story?" This was not good. Not good at all. How much did she tell him? "You know I could just . . . " Bella made choking gestures with her hands.

Jenna did not take that lightly. She quickly stepped out of the way. Again, Rosa's words came back to her.

Just say the word.

Jenna quivered. "He only knows about my art." "You still don't get it do you? You can't take care of yourself."

Her mother continued downstairs leaving Jenna frozen to the spot.

Bella entered the English country-style living room and sat down in a Chippendale chair. She put on her reading glasses then picked up the latest copy of *Vanity Fair*. She needed to relax. And think. Jenna took her by surprise yet she should've expected it. A date. She didn't know that Jenna and Dr. Chase would've acted so fast.

Jenna, portfolio in hand, entered the room. "What do you mean I can't take of myself?"

Bella looked up from her magazine. She smiled at Jenna like a Cheshire cat. "You've been talking to Rosa."

The portfolio in Jenna's hand dropped, landing on the parquet floor. Mom knew about her and Rosa all this time. How long had she known?

Did Lauren and Diane know? Of course, they did. They were Mom's pets. What about Alan? Did he know that Rosa was still in her life?

Bella crossed her legs, dangling her mule-clad feet. Just seeing the look on Jenna's face made it worth her while keeping back the knowledge until now. "Did you tell Dr. Chase about Rosa?"

Jenna looked at her mother strangely. "Why would I do that?"

"For the same reason you pretended to the rest of us that you weren't with her. Just for kicks." Bella went back to reading her magazine.

It wasn't for kicks. But she didn't bother correcting her mother.

Bella didn't look up from her reading. "Go have your fun. Just be sure you're back before four o'clock."

"Right." Jenna picked up her portfolio then turned to leave.

"One more thing," Bella began, "I don't want him in my house."

Jenna had to make a call.

Malachi turned down Haven Road, a residential street within walking distance of town. Bordered by woods, the homes stood on three to five-acre lots. He parked his Toyota where Jenna instructed—three yards away. He didn't comment when she called him on his cell, trying to sound as nonchalant as possible, with the instructions. He simply agreed to do as she asked. However, he marveled to himself at her instructions. They were peculiar to say the least. He hadn't dated in awhile, but he didn't think the rules had changed that much. Usually, the man parked in front of his date's house, got out of the car and rang the bell. He didn't park down the road and make the woman come out to him. He sensed Bella's handiwork.

Malachi got out of the car. He admired the house, a charming yellow 1850's colonial with green shutters and a brass knocker on the front door. Tea roses, daisies and hollyhocks grew in the front yard. On the either side of the stoop two planters stood, each containing gardenias. Window boxes filled with multicolored impatiens adorned the windows on the first floor. He looked up at the attic floor . . .

Malachi cut through the property to the backyard. Tall hedges offered his six-foot-one frame some camouflage. He was grateful for that. Trespassing was wrong, especially when he wasn't welcome. What did Bella have against him? Obviously, she didn't want him in her house. Did she have something to hide?

Like a body? He wouldn't be surprised with her personality. Mrs. Crandall was one seriously scary woman.

The backyard had an English theme complete with Victorian garden furniture and an array of wildflowers. Birds sang and splashed in a ceramic birdbath.

Malachi scratched his head. The place looked like a page from one of those gardening magazines. Given the oppressive energy that Mrs. Crandall gave off, this storybook setting was paradoxical much like Lauren and Nelson's topiary garden. Jenna had given him a tour of the grounds at the wedding reception. The *Alice's Adventures in Wonderland* theme was beautifully but completely unexpected. Then again, the flowers shaped like the Queen of Hearts and the Duchess made sense. The Crandall women, with the exception of Jenna, did see themselves as sovereign. They were apt to cut off the head of anyone who crossed them.

Malachi sighed. This family was beginning to look like a jigsaw puzzle where not all the pieces fit.

Jenna was standing by his car waiting for him by the time he returned to the car. Malachi grinned sheepishly. He was supposed to get back before she did. "I was just admiring your grounds."

Jenna gripped her portfolio. She was admiring his grounds too. The sight of Malachi made her heart dance. He managed to make a plain crew neck shirt, a pair of jeans and vintage high-tops look so fantastic. So masculine. *Like a Greek god.*

She didn't mind him checking out the place. Mom was absorbed in her magazine. There was no chance of her stepping outside and catching

Malachi intruding. She was more concerned about what he thought of her last minute phone call. What kind of woman asks her date to park so many feet away from her house? She dreaded the thought of what could've happened if he had come before she even had the chance to call him.

Jenna also noticed the cross pendant hanging around his neck. She recalled his talk about God-given talents. Jenna pushed the thought out of her mind then smiled at him reassuringly.

Malachi gazed admiringly at Jenna. "You look great."

She looked down at the pebbles in the road, embarrassed by the way he was looking at her. It was exciting and scary at the same time. "Thank you." Her voice came out almost sounding like a child's squeaky toy. Now she wanted to hide herself.

Malachi smothered a smile. Jenna was cute when she was embarrassed. "Are you hungry?"

Definitely. She was hoping that her stomach wouldn't choose that moment to growl. She was so nervous this morning she couldn't eat. But was there time to have lunch, show him her artwork and return home by three, three-thirty?

"I could use a bite myself," Malachi said breaking into her thoughts.

She was hesitating again. Like at her sister's wedding.

"It would be my treat," he added.

Finally, Jenna said, "Okay."

As Malachi was opening the car door, Jenna ignored the nagging doubt. He took the portfolio and placed it on the floor of the backseat. *Who or what is she afraid of?*

They sat in a booth at Kalamona, a local Thai restaurant on Main Street. The aroma of coriander, ginger and other spices was making her feel even hungrier. She checked her watch. She had three hours to work with. The moment would've been perfect if she didn't have to worry about the time.

"So are you the one with the green thumb?" Malachi asked after the server took their orders and they handed her back their menus.

"No. The garden is mom's baby."

Malachi tried to picture Bella kneeling in the dirt wearing one of those big gardening hats. "How about your dad? No let me guess." He put his hand on his forehead as if he was a soothsayer. Speaking with a Romany accent, he said, "I see him in a garden. He's lying on a hammock. Next to him is . . . a radio. And I see . . . a can of beer."

Jenna giggled.

"Ah. I am losing picture."

Soon, though a sad smile came over her face. "Daddy moved out after I turned five. I don't know the details. She listened to the sound of xylophone music. Then added, "No one talked about it. I remembered him saying, 'It's better this way.'"

"I'm sorry."

She took a sip of water. "They're still married you know."

"Still it must've been awful for you, your brother and sisters."

"Lauren and Diane didn't seem to care and Alan was never the same."

Malachi studied his glass of water. This might shed some light about the relationship between Alan and Bella. "What happened to him?"

"He got nervous."

"About what?"

Jenna took another drink of water. "I don't know. He just developed a nervous stomach."

But what or whom made Alan nervous? To pump her for more information would be inappropriate. "Tell me more about you. I already know you love art."

"I like acting."

"Really?"

"I think I like it almost as much as art. My theatre professor thought I had a future in it."

"What else do you like to do?"

"Feeding the birds and the squirrels. Going for walks."

"Where?"

"Oh, lots of places. There's Lakewood Park. The meadow.

Malachi took a drink of water. "By yourself?"

"Uh huh." Jenna didn't blink. Rosa joined her on her walks sometimes, but he didn't need to know that. She still couldn't believe that Mom knew about their ongoing friendship all this time. She thought she was doing an ace job of keeping it a secret. As secret as her mother's habit of beating her and Alan when they were kids . . .

"Anybody ever join you on your walks?" Malachi asked breaking into her thoughts.

Jenna looked at him slyly then smiled. "I'm not seeing anyone, Malachi."

He laughed. "Was I that obvious?"

Before Jenna could reply, the server, a college-aged Thai-American, returned with their orders. She placed their meals on the table then left. Jenna was about to start eating when Malachi asked, "Aren't you going to say grace?"

Jenna took her time spreading her napkin on her lap while the soothing sounds of the xylophone, the buzz of conversation of patrons and wait staff, the clanking of plates filled the stillness that suddenly fell between them.

Finally, she said, "I'd rather not if you don't mind."

Respecting her wishes, Malachi nodded then said a brief silent prayer over his meal. Inwardly, he was shocked and puzzled. Jenna's reaction didn't make sense. She came from a Christ-centered home, rudeness notwithstanding. How much of His teaching did she receive?

Okay. Back it up, man. I'm no prize either.

Jenna looked around to see if anyone else was watching Malachi praying. A family at another table was praying over their meal. One or two patrons rolled their eyes, but most didn't care. They continued with their meals and conversations.

"You're religious," Jenna said when Malachi finished praying. She realized then that the cross he wore around his neck wasn't just a piece of jewelry.

"I have a *relationship* with God," Malachi said. "There's a difference." He took a bite of his spring roll. "Christianity isn't a religion. It's a lifestyle choice."

Jenna thought of something else that was a lifestyle choice, but she didn't say it. He might not appreciate it.

Malachi took another bite out of his spring roll. Jenna's attitude could have something to do with her family's dynamics. Her parent's marriage was a sham. What type of relationship did the siblings have with each other? Her reaction to prayer and her apparent lack of understanding about having a relationship with God was an indication of spiritual thirst. He had a problem. He was attracted to a woman with an unstable faith.

"I was raised Anglican," Malachi said. "And I wasn't into Jesus. I only went to church because my parents made me. When I got older, I went sporadically. After I started making it big on Wall Street, I thought Christianity was for pansies." A faraway look came into his eyes. "One day, I came to a point where I needed Him. Long story short I became a Born Again Christian."

Jenna stabbed a cucumber shrimp with her fork.

Malachi kept his eye on Jenna's fork. The prongs protruded through the appetizer as she raised it to her lips. "So, you don't say grace."

"I don't remember the last time I even prayed," Jenna said. "Mom does." In between bites she added, "Mom prays all the time. She even attends Wednesday night prayer meetings."

Malachi took a forkful of pineapple rice. *If you can't say something nice . . .*

"What made you suddenly decide you needed Jesus?" He was surprised that Jenna was continuing with the conversation. "I came to the end of myself." The perplexed look on her face was so comical that if the situation weren't serious, he would've burst out laughing. He was relieved that she didn't ask him for any more information. He was glad he was able to avoid it last week at the wedding.

"As you probably know, we grew up in the church," Jenna said. "Mom's an elder."

Malachi began choking on some rice. He coughed again. "That's nice," he managed to squeak out.

"I stopped going to church after I turned eighteen," Jenna said. "Mom didn't seem to care. It was one of the few things she didn't force me to do." Embarrassed, she put down her fork. Jenna picked up her napkin and dabbed at the corners of her mouth.

"Don't sweat it," Malachi said. "It's how you feel." He got a taste of Bella. She must've been a bit much growing up. "Like I said, my folks made me go to church. By the time I was a teenager, it became just a routine thing."

"When I was a little girl, our old Reverend said that God speaks to us. Does He speak to you?"

"Sure. Not audibly, of course, but in my heart. It's a feeling. His presence is a feeling like no other. You just know it. Sometimes He talks to me through people He sends into my life."

Malachi played with his stir-fry vegetables. She was asking questions about God. That was a good start. He didn't dare tell her that he felt guided by God to live in Gordonville and that he was beginning to think she was part of the reason. She'd go ballistic. He couldn't dismiss what she did to the cucumber shrimp with her fork. Plus, there were knives on the table.

"If God ever spoke to me," Jenna began, "I never heard Him." She frowned. "I believe in Him you know. It's just that every time Mom said His Name, it was right before she screamed, 'The wages of sin is death' then beat the mess out of me."

Malachi's fork clanked when it hit his plate. This explained a lot.

Jenna looked pained. "Forget what I said." She yelled at herself. Twice she said more than she should have.

"Don't worry," Malachi said. "I won't tell anyone." She's still afraid of her mother. *Just like Alan.* Mrs. Crandall must've mistreated him as well. No wonder he quivers when he's around her. "I'm sorry about what happened to you. But believe me your mother misrepresented God and the quote. May I give you the proper quote?"

Jenna shrugged.

Malachi quoted, *"For the wages of sin is death, but the gift of God is eternal life in Christ Jesus our Lord."* Jenna looked as if she were having abdominal pains. Clearly, she had her fill of Scripture. Even hearing the passage cited accurately didn't make her feel even a teeny bit better. Bella Crandall left an indelible mark on her daughter where Christianity was concerned. For a church elder, the woman was careless about scriptural accuracy and stingy with her kindness. Mrs. Crandall took Romans 6:23 and screwed with a child's mind—her own daughter's. Leaving out the other half of the quote changed the entire meaning for an impressionable little girl. What was she thinking? How many other passages did she twist to suit her purpose?

Where was Julian? What role did he play? Not living with his family didn't make him any less responsible. On impulse Malachi asked, "Do you want to learn about God?"

Jenna shrugged again. "I don't know. Maybe."

"I'm talking about forgetting everything your mother told you or did to you and get to know Him all over again."

Jenna looked down at her plate and stared at what was left of her Thai shrimp. She wasn't sure if she liked the direction this conversation was taking.

"Could I say one last thing about God? He gave you those beautiful brown eyes."

Jenna looked up at Malachi and grinned.

"And that gorgeous smile."

"What if I said I'll think about it?" Jenna asked.

"Fair enough."

For the remainder of the meal they talked about their jobs, the presidential election, growing up in Gordonville versus growing up in New York City.

Throughout their conversation, Malachi noticed that Jenna kept checking her watch.

"Why don't we go to Lakewood Park and take a look at your work?" He suggested.

Jenna sighed with relief. Just over an hour to go. She felt a heavy cloud hanging over her before she even left the house. She was having fun; unfortunately, her time wasn't her own.

"Let's go to the meadow," Jenna said.

It was closer to her house.

Malachi laughed as he carried Jenna's portfolio across the meadow. She was practically skipping. From the moment he parked the car and got out, she was acting like a happy child not unlike the ones he saw in the distance playing on the old-fashioned merry-go-round.

She stopped at a shady area of the meadow that offered views of white, yellow and pink daylilies. They sat down on the thick, green grass.

"Okay," Jenna said as Malachi set the portfolio down. "Ready for inspection."

"First, tell me why you love this place?"

"If I do, will you promise not to laugh?"

Malachi crossed his heart.

"We are a few feet away from the entrance to the Enchanted Forest."

His eyes twinkled. "I just didn't know it existed."

"I made it up when I was a little girl, silly. Actually, I got the idea from my fairy tale book." Jenna told him about Alan's birthday gift to her. "It was my favorite place. No one knew about it. Not even Alan." She pointed to a pine tree nine yards away. "The entrance was over there."

"A vivid imagination. No wonder you're an artist and future thespian. "Tell me more about your secret world."

Jenna liked the way Malachi paid attention to what she said. "There were pixies, talking trees, talking animals. Humans." She frowned slightly. "Some of them were bad."

"By any chance, did these humans happen to bear a slight resemblance to certain family members?"

Jenna responded with an enigmatic smile.

"Who else did you play make-believe with?"

She looked toward the Catskill Mountains. She barely mentioned her mother's beatings and that was only by accident.

"*Did you tell Dr. Chase about your friend?*"

She still couldn't believe her mother asked that. She'd forbidden them from talking about Rosa to Dad never mind outsiders. It had to be a trick.

Or she's trying to aggravate me.

And it was working. She should be enjoying herself with Malachi instead of watching the clock.

Jenna felt the grass with her hands. "I played with Rosa Garrison." *How's that, Mom?*

She felt a sense of triumph for her friend. Telling Malachi about Rosa may not be the same as telling her father, but at least she was giving her recognition.

"Who's Rosa?" Malachi asked.

"An old friend. We *used* to be friends. We split before our senior year in high school." She twirled a strand of hair. She hated lying to him, but she had to. It was enough that her mother knew that Rosa was still around. Now she and Rosa would have to change strategies. She didn't think it would mean trouble. As long as she continued keeping Rosa at bay.

"Did you ever have a perfect friend?"

"No one's perfect, Jenna."

"Rosa was. She was beautiful and smart. And confident. Everything I'm not." She winced.

Malachi looked at Jenna with tenderness. Like in the restaurant, she let something else slip. Whether she knew it or not, Jenna had a need to confide. Bella damaged her self-esteem. The question was how deeply? He recalled Norma Beery promoting Bella, Lauren and Diane.

Imagine having to listen to that all the time.

He wanted to tell Jenna that only God was perfect. Not her mother or her sisters or even Rosa, but he held his tongue. This wasn't the time for preaching. This was a time for listening.

"Before I met Rosa," Jenna continued, "I got picked on. But after we became friends, she had my back. She taught me to stand up for myself."

"Who picked on you?" He asked, already knowing the answer.

Jenna picked a blade of grass. "Mom. My sisters. Some classmates. Teachers who thought they were demigods."

Malachi wondered what happened to the confidence she once had. It was noticeably absent. When Mrs. Crandall, Lauren and Diane showed up Jenna transformed into a frightened little mouse. "You used past tense. What happened between you and Rosa?"

Jenna ignored her nagging conscience. "I didn't want to do bad things anymore and hanging out with her got me into trouble."

"*You?*" Here was yet more information to file.

"I told you. I stood up for myself. I wouldn't take garbage from anyone. Not even from my mother or my sisters."

Remembering how cowed she was at the wedding, he would've loved to have seen her standing up to Mrs. Crandall, Lauren and Diane. *What happened to her after Rosa left?*

"The principal, the teachers *and Mom* said I had no respect for authority," Jenna went on. Remembering Malachi was a Christian, she added, "You think I'm a terrible person now, right?"

"You were a kid. Besides, I don't know what you did." Jenna didn't offer any examples and he didn't ask. "Now, let's see your creations."

What if Malachi hated her work? Was her mother right to discourage her from becoming a professional artist? The thought of her mother being right nauseate her. Jenna toyed with a lock of her coiled hair.

"Relax," Malachi said. "Look, I know we just met, but I want you to think of me as a friend."

Friend.

She liked the sound of that. She liked the feeling that went through her too.

"Besides," he continued, "after telling me about the Enchanted Forest, you can't back down now."

Jenna reached into her shoulder bag and took out the small sketchpad. "Start with this one."

Over the next few minutes, Malachi examined the drawings. She watched his expression go from approval to amazement.

"These are incredible!" Malachi exclaimed.

"You really think so?"

"I wouldn't say it if I didn't believe it. Each one draws me right into the scene. Pardon the pun. Your attention to detail is extraordinary." Malachi turned to another page. "Hmm."

He studied a pastel drawing of an anaconda. A dainty hand was protruding from its mouth, the last of its meal going down. So far, Jenna's subjects consisted of ballerinas, farm animals, nature scenes and mythical creatures. This genre was macabre. It didn't fit with the other subjects. Yes, it was art and individuals sometimes deviated from the norm. How many of his ultra-conservative colleagues found release by watching adult cartoons?

The detail was amazing, although he wasn't fond of it. He hated anything ghoulish. When he was a little boy, his older cousin, Omar, used to get a kick out of torturing him with scary tales about demons, shape-shifters, devil dolls and haunted mirrors. To this day, he refused to sleep with the closet door open. Even now, his childhood fears were coming back as he stared at the drawing.

Jenna sucked in her breath. She forgot about that picture. She had to say something.

"It's nothing," Jenna said. "I was angry when I drew it."

"May I ask why?"

"I don't remember. It was a long time ago. She smiled to cover her unease. "It was during my rebellious teenage years."

"Remind me never to get on your bad side." Malachi returned the sketchpad to her then opened the portfolio. After examining a few sketches and watercolors, he said, "Your work should definitely be in a gallery. And I'm not just saying that. I mean it. You can't let this talent go to waste. Remember what I said, 'you'll spend the rest of your life feeling unfulfilled.' Would you at least consider art school?"

"I don't know."

"It's not late, Jenna."

"Well . . . " It was so long since she entertained the thought of becoming a professional artist.

"And one of the best parts," Malachi added, "is that you get to wear jeans and T-shirts. No more restrictive office attire." In a high-pitched feminine voice he said, "Those suits, those skirts. My feet are killing me in these pumps."

Jenna doubled over with laughter.

In the same girlish voice he said, "Look what the wind has done to my hair." Malachi patted his head. "It's such a mess."

Jenna gave him a playful punch on the shoulder. Malachi turned to the next picture, a watercolor painting of a farmhouse. It looked beautiful and familiar. "That's that old farmhouse on Thornbush Lane."

Jenna faked calmness. "You know it?"

"I drove down there once." He shivered. "Never again. I couldn't get off that road fast enough. Even the trees look satanic."

He learned about Gordonville's reputed haunted street by accident when he was looking for a quick route to town. It was as if his childhood nightmares had come to life. Malachi shuddered. "I thanked Brendan later on for not warning me about that place." He gave her an odd look. "You must've made a gazillion trips there to do this." He looked back at the painting. Even that day he drove down Thornbush, the house bothered him. Something about it was disturbing.

Malachi wore a slight frown. The farmhouse was dilapidated when he saw it. "You spruced it up."

"That's how it looked when Rosa and her family lived there."

"Oh." Well, all shabby houses looked beautiful once. He just didn't expect to hear that Jenna's friend once resided there.

"They moved to Hudson years ago," Jenna said. Unfortunately, the property got seedy after they left. The second owners didn't keep the place up and it went into foreclosure. No one's lived there since then."

Jenna stretched out her legs and stared at her white canvas sneakers. Malachi had actually driven down Thornbush Lane. No one ever drives or walks down there. She couldn't tell him that the farmhouse was she and Rosa's retreat. He might want to come along one day. As fond as she was of him, it was their domain.

Jenna gasped. Talking about Rosa suddenly reminded her of the time—and her mother. She checked her watch. The muscles in her stomach did a flip like an Olympic gymnast. Jenna leaped up. "Gotta go." She broke into a run.

"Wait. Let me take you home."

Jenna kept running. "No, thanks."

Malachi stood up and called, "But your artwork."

"I'll call you," Jenna said.

He watched her run as if her life depended on it. "What did they do to you?"

6

Jenna tore through the woods. She cried out when a tree branch scratched her arm. She kept on running. Sweat was pouring down her face, neck and back. She felt as if she was in one of those nightmares where as she's running towards the end of the tunnel the entrance pulls farther away the closer she draws near to it. She almost wished that she'd taken Malachi up on his offer to drive her home, but she couldn't take any chances. Her mother could be standing outside ready to say something or do something to drive Malachi away. She didn't want him to go away. Despite the differences in their worldviews, she liked him. Even if their relationship turned out to be nothing more than platonic, at least she'd have that, his friendship.

Jenna's heart leaped when she finally saw the road up ahead. She might still make it home in time to prepare her mother's afternoon tea. Four o'clock. Sharp. She started voluntarily preparing it for her mother when she was seventeen. It was part of her plan to be good. Over time, however, her mother turned a kind gesture to a favor to finally, an obligation. How could she tell Malachi that she had to rush home to make afternoon tea for her mother? She wanted whatever was developing between them to work. Frantic, Jenna didn't see the rotted tree branch.

Suddenly, she was airborne. She landed on the ground, injuring her knee. She gritted her teeth and writhed in pain. She didn't care about the dirt staining her clothes or about what she might be rolling into on the forest floor. All she felt was agony. Tears of frustration stung her eyes. Gone was the urgency to get home. When the pain settled to a throb, she got up gingerly and limped home the rest of the way.

Injured, dirty and exhausted, Jenna stood in the woods facing her house. Her mother wasn't standing at the front door waiting after all; nonetheless, her parting words to her earlier haunted her.

Be sure you're back before four o'clock.

Jenna took a deep breath then hobbled across the road.

*

She entered the house, gently closed the door, then leaned against it. She stared up at the torpedo glass ceiling light, gritting her teeth from the soreness in her knee. Jenna blew out a puff of air before finally scuffling down the center hall passed the oaken grandfather clock to the kitchen, a pristine, English country-style room, her mother's pride and joy.

She saw the new teakettle Lauren bought for her mother on the stove. Steam was rising up from it, sending an aroma of fresh mint into the air. The table was set with a gold-colored place mat and matching linen napkin, a Wedgwood china cup and saucer and a plate filled with watercress sandwiches, blueberry scones and shortbread cookies from Delsey's, the trendy café on Main Street known for its gourmet foods and international coffee and tea. In the center of the table was the crystal vase, her mother's favorite. It was a wedding gift Grandma and Grandpa Crandall. Jenna looked up at the wooden wall clock. 3:58 P.M. She was late. She could not make this right. She looked toward the pantry. "Mom?" She was remembering how much fun she and Rosa used to have hiding in there when they were kids.

Suddenly, the back door opened. Bella came into the kitchen carrying a bouquet of fresh-cut red, white and purple-colored wildflowers. She placed them in the crystal vase, humming as she adjusted each stem. Afterward, she stepped back and admired the centerpiece.

Jenna was standing in the kitchen like a ghost. Only the ache in her knee reminded her that she was very much alive. She could barely move, mortified by her mother's silent treatment. Of all the punishments Jenna received over the years, she hated this one the most. At least, when her mother was hitting her she was acknowledging her.

She stared at her mother, looking attractive in a paisley ankle-length dress and short, curly well-coiffed hair. Self-conscious, Jenna ran her hand through her own tresses, which now felt like straw from the heat and sweat. She was imagining how bad it looked after her mad dash through the forest.

The teakettle whistled just as the grandfather clock in the hall struck four. Bella poured mint tea into her Wedgwood cup. By the fourth chime, she was sitting down to high tea.

Her teacup clinked against the saucer when she put it down after taking her first sip. She picked up a

watercress sandwich and daintily took a bite.

At last, Jenna found the courage to speak. "I'm sorry."

She had to do it. She had to apologize even though a voice within asked, *Why? You didn't do anything wrong;* but the silence was too much. She would do anything for a crumb of her mother's recognition.

"I wasn't late on purpose." Jenna managed to find her voice again. "Time slipped." She winced at the unintended pun.

"I told you when to get back." Bella never looked at her. She stared at the centerpiece.

Jenna brightened. Her mother was speaking to her. Actually, it could've been worse. Mom would've gone ballistic by now if it weren't for teatime. "I was having a good time and I had to cut it short to rush back here."

Bella took another sip of tea.

Jenna felt a tiny spark of anger. She didn't care. Rosa's words came to mind. *"She just hates to see you smile."* Jenna started wishing that Rosa were here regardless of the consequences. It would be the two of them against her. Like the old days . . .

Jenna watched her mother chew on a blueberry scone.

Afterward, the Anglophile picked up her cup of mint tea and daintily took a sip. "You make your own tea during the week, Mom."

Bella flinched.

"I would've enjoyed myself more if I didn't have to worry about rushing home to you."

Bella gave Jenna a long hard stare. She was talking back a little bit too much. Who's responsible for this? Rosa? Or that professor?

"I ended up getting hurt." Jenna told her how it happened. Her face twisted from pain. She pulled out a chair and sat down.

"If you came home when I told you to, that wouldn't have happened."

The angry spark within Jenna kindled. "Rosa was right about you."

Bella laughed dryly. "What did she say pray tell?"

"That you don't respect me. You hate to see me happy. And she's right."

Bella's eyes blazed with fury. "I am a good mother. How dare you defend her? She's a creep and a dirty liar."

"Don't say that. Rosa's a good person. That's why I kept our friendship going."

"You mean that's why you lied about it."

Jenna let out a frustrated sigh. "I can't keep cutting my dates with Malachi short."

"This is my time now. You're disrupting it." Bella gave Jenna the up and down look before turning away.

Jenna felt as if her mother took up a carving knife and cut out her heart. She stood up then slowly, limped out of the kitchen. She paused then turned to look at her mother.

Bella didn't see the glare on her daughter's face.

After bandaging her knee, Jenna took some ibuprofen, showered then changed into a nightshirt with a mandala symbol. Next, she turned on the fan, stretched her tired aching body on the bed, then cried.

All she wanted was for her mother to love her and for her sisters to, if nothing else, to like her, but they didn't. They despised her. And she didn't fight back. She wasn't confrontational like Rosa. Even her brother fought Mom to keep his relationship with Elise. *What's wrong with me?* Jenna began punching her pillow. She was in a situation in which there was no escape. But there was. *"Just say the word."*

Jenna turned on her side and put the pillow over her head, trying to drown out the sound of Rosa's voice. Frightened and frustrated, tears fell down her cheeks. She didn't want to resort to violence. She just couldn't. It wasn't who she was. She put the pillow aside then sat up. She opened the night table, took out her sketchpad and a pencil, then started drawing a picture of a tree. When she was done, she called Rosa.

"What're you doing home already?" Rosa asked by way of a greeting. "Don't tell me Malachi turned out to be a dud."

"Why are *you* home on a Saturday afternoon?" Jenna asked. "Shouldn't you be out with Gary?"

"I asked you first."

"Malachi's really sweet." Jenna hesitated.

"But—"

"He's Christian."

Rosa groaned.

"A Born-Again Christian," Jenna added.

Rosa groaned again. "That's the worst kind. To them everything's a sin including breaking wind."

"But he's cool. In a dorky kinda way." Then, Jenna told Rosa about everything that happened.

Rosa cursed then said, "I told you. Nothing you do will ever matter to your mother. And why are you still serving her tea? Ain't she got two hands?"

"She did make her own tea," Jenna said.

"To shame you for being late."

Like the silent treatment. Jenna didn't dare mention that she apologized. Considering it didn't work. Rosa would've flipped out.

"I should've made her tea," Rosa said with a laugh." "My own special blend."

Jenna could just imagine what the extra-added ingredient would be. "Anyway, Malachi must think I'm a ding-a-ling. He's not going to call me again."

"He might surprise you," Rosa said. "Are you sure you don't want me to take care of your mother?"

Now was her chance. She could take the deal that she gave up long ago. For a moment, Jenna studied the sketch of the tree. She cocked her head then frowned. She began to draw Bella hanging from it. "No thanks, I'm good." She realized at that moment that the pills had taken effect. The pain in her knee was gone.

She and Rosa talked for a few more minutes then hung up. Jenna put away her sketchpad and pencil. Physically and emotionally drained, she laid back on the pillow and fell asleep.

Later that afternoon, Jenna's cell phone rang. She stretched out her hand and picked it up. "Hello?" She said in a sleepy voice.

"Jenna?" When she heard Malachi's voice on the other end, she opened her eyes and sat bolt upright.

"Were you sleeping?" He sounded regretful.

"It's okay," Jenna hastened to say. She stifled a yawn while at the same time struggling to get her thoughts together. What did he want? What should she say?

"I was worried about you," Malachi said.

Jenna told him about her accident. She braced herself for his criticism. *You should've let me drive you home. What was the hurry?* Neither of which she wanted to discuss.

"Have you seen a doctor?"

"No, I haven't." A rush of warmth came over her. No scorn. No prying. A contrast to her mother's nonchalance. "I'm already feeling better."

"I can take you to the ER."

Now Jenna felt warm inside. "I'll just put ice on my knee and stay off of it." She paused then added, "I didn't think you'd want to see me again," Jenna said.

"Why?"

"Because of the nutty way I acted."

"I was confused," Malachi said. "Not angry. Besides," he added humor in his voice, "I still have your artwork."

Jenna put her hand to her mouth. She almost forgot about that.

"So you see we have to get together again." Malachi hesitated. "I was wondering if you were free tomorrow. But with that bad knee—"

"I'm taking ibuprofen."

Malachi chuckled. Her enthusiasm was delightful "Okay. It's a date. But we're keeping you off that knee as much as possible."

"Agreed." Mom would be at church all day so that would cover the afternoon tea situation. She'd still expect service regardless of the injury.

"But tomorrow's Sunday," Jenna said. "Don't you have church?"

"I'll pick you up afterward and treat you to brunch."

He attended morning service at St. Luke's Anglican Church.

After they hung up, Jenna hugged her pillow. Suddenly, the injury to her knee felt a lot less painful.

7

"'The eyes of the Lord are everywhere, Keeping watch on the wicked and the good.'" Malachi read aloud from Proverbs 15:3 while sitting up in bed and listening to the sound of the rainfall. In the back of his mind, he was thinking about how Bella distorted the Book of Romans. Now doubt, to discipline Jenna.

Malachi closed his Bible and put it on the night table. The digital clock read 10:15 P.M. Thunder boomed.

A colleague offered him his two tickets to see a performance of Shakespeare's *A Midsummer Night's Dream* at the Center for Performing Arts in Rhinebeck because he and his wife were unable to attend. Jenna would've loved it.

With her inclination to be fanciful, she would've enjoyed the production, but he declined. He was glad too. To drive in this monsoon would only be tempting fate. Heaven may be a wonderful place, but he wasn't in a hurry to get there. Besides, Bella would've found a reason to sabotage the evening now that he and Jenna were officially dating.

He could count on his fingers how many dates they actually had in the past four and a half weeks. If Bella didn't need some errand done, only then was Jenna available. Even Lauren and Diane were requesting favors. And Jenna was granting them. What happened to Nelson and

Larry? Didn't Lauren and Diane earn enough money to hire a personal shopper?

The strangest detail of all was that he and Jenna never go out for a whole day. She always had to be home no later than three-thirty. That put the kibosh on romantic picnics. One way around that was for them to go out after four o'clock. This whole arrangement, including the strange parking rules, was completely unorthodox. He didn't want to embarrass her by pointing it out.

Norma Beery was right about the Crandall's influence in Gordonville. Residents who knew them only had compliments. Malachi wore a wry smile. The only thing left for them to do was to erect a statute.

Would Bella ever allow him to enter *The Inner Sanctum,* the name he secretly dubbed the Crandall residence? She certainly kept her distance, making it clear that he was persona non grata. During the Independence Day weekend, he ran into her at the farmer's market. In spite of her prior chilliness, he decided to go over and say hello. Bella's "Good Afternoon," sounded dry and laborious.

Another time, she stepped out to water the front yard just as he and Jenna were on their way out late one afternoon. He honked the horn and waved at her, as they were driving pass the house. Bella barely waved back.

Malachi looked speculative. Bella was determined to keep him away. Was it because she hated him or was it because she was hiding something? He started thinking about the Crandall's attic. Every time he picked up Jenna, he found himself drawn to the attic window. He was fascinated yet drawn to it at the same time. *If I ask Mrs. Crandall, what's in her attic and she tells me, will she have to kill me?*

Malachi yawned, picked up the remote, then turned on the television. Political pundits were flaunting their rhetoric. After two minutes, he rolled his eyes then turned his thoughts back to Jenna. Something was very odd about that family.

He began rubbing his eyes. Commonsense dictated that he should break up with her. More like run. It wasn't just about Jenna having dubious Christian values. Bella Crandall was trouble. Plus, why stay where he wasn't wanted? Why stay with a woman like Jenna who clearly was incapable of asserting herself? *Because she's a beautiful, intelligent, fun-loving, talented human being.* Her docility was a byproduct of an unhealthy family life. Her brother managed to move on. He got married. Has a successful career. *But Alan's still scared of his mother.*

Malachi began to nod off. Jenna needed someone in her corner, someone to protect her. Protect? His eyelids flew open. He liked the idea of playing that role. He fell asleep. A tiny smile was on his face.

Malachi parked in front of the Crandall's yellow colonial. Earlier, after he got dressed, he decided to go against procedures by going to Jenna's house and parking in front of the house. He was going to go up the front walk and ring the doorbell. Jenna wasn't going to like it. Neither was Mrs. Crandall. Nevertheless, he made up his mind. Something was wrong and he was gonna find out what it was. However, as he sat in his car staring at the picturesque dwelling, his earlier determination began fading. Next, he was questioning his sanity.

Then he saw her, a black woman around Jenna's age. She came from around the back of the house. She jogged up the steps with the confidence of one who had a right to be there. She stood at the front door, her back to the street. Malachi watched the stranger take a key from her handbag and unlock the door.

Is she a relative?

Quickly, Malachi got out of the car. "Hello?"

The woman pushed open the door, stepped inside, then slammed it shut.

Malachi raised his eyebrows. "So it's like that, huh?"

He opened the gate and walked quickly up the brick walkway, forgetting his trepidation about showing up unannounced. He rang the bell. Expecting a prompt answer, Malachi looked puzzled when no one answered. Surely, Bella the Imperious would've come to the door and asked him in very colorful language what he was doing on her front porch. He used the brass knocker. Still no answer. What happened to the woman? Importantly, where was Bella and where was Jenna? Today is Saturday maybe they were out on errands.

Malachi went back down the steps. He looked up at the upstairs windows, his fingers toying with the cross pendant around his neck. His gaze stopped at the attic window. The curtain moved. Was the woman holding Jenna and Bella hostage?

Malachi raced up the steps and taking the stance of a martial artist, he lifted his leg and kicked down the door. "Jenna!"

The visitor stood in the foyer wearing a Loki mask.

Malachi recoiled. He remembered the statue on Lauren and Nelson's property. His childhood phobias began taking over. It couldn't have come to life.

Get a grip, man.

"Where're Jenna and Mrs. Crandall?"

The woman stared at him through the mask for a moment then said, "Everything's under control."

Malachi backed up until he hit the wall. 'Loki' spoke in a malevolent tone. Not even Bella sounded like that.

"That's not what I asked." Malachi attempted to sound tough although it was probably a lost cause. Loki already saw him panic.

She was staring at his cross pendant. He could feel her eyes burning into his chest where the cross hanged.

She began snickering.

Is she laughing at the Cross?

Irritated, Malachi brushed past Loki.

*

The house was eerily silent.

Malachi looked up the stairs, expecting to see Bella staring down at him holding a hatchet.

The woman in the Loki mask came up behind him. Malachi sensed her presence. He realized at that moment that he didn't have a weapon. He didn't think he'd need one when he decided to come over. Would she attack him? Malachi turned, keeping her in full view.

"Jenna, Mrs. Crandall!" Should he call the police? No. He couldn't. He was the trespasser.

Then there came the sound of a woman crying.

Jenna.

Malachi looked around, not knowing which way to turn, all because Bella wouldn't invite him into her home. Running from room to room was a waste of precious time. Frustrated, he turned toward the stranger. "Where is she?"

From behind the mask came the sound of twisted laughter. Malachi was more frightened than when she spoke. The laughter was scary.

"She doesn't need you," the mask said.

"That's your opinion."

"And wait 'til Bella sees what you did to her door."

"I don't give a flying fig about the door. Now. Where. Is. Jenna?"

"Ooh. Tough talk, *Christian*."

The sobbing continued. Where was Bella? She should've come out from by now. Was this new arrival responsible for her disappearance?

"Who are you?" Malachi asked wearing a puzzled frown.

She continued laughing as she pointed down the hall.

As Malachi followed the weird woman's direction, the sobbing became louder. He stopped in front of a closed door leading to yet another room. He entered. Malachi found himself inside the dining room a formal area with wainscoting, French doors and a chandelier, which hung from a crown molding. The room was empty and the sobbing got even louder. It was coming from the next room.

Malachi rushed through the French doors, which led to the kitchen then drew back in horror. Three skeletons sat around the table. Spread before them was a pewter tea service; standing by, wearing sorrowful expressions were Alan, Julian . . . and Jenna.

Suddenly, the skeletons turned toward Malachi and cried, "Rosa!"

Jenna screamed.

*

Malachi jumped out of his sleep. He looked around him confusedly. He was in his bedroom. The clock read 10:30 P.M. The television was still playing. There was a health segment on the benefits of green tea.

The rain continued to fall.

The raindrops began to lull Jenna to sleep. Finally, she'd get some much-needed rest. Insomnia and anxiety were keeping her company. Her relationship with Malachi was on borrowed time. She just knew it. Her mother's antics over the past month and a half were going to make it a *fait accompli*. Also keeping her awake were Rosa's constant reminders about offering to help her solve her "mommy problems." For now, she was putting those thoughts behind her. Jenna let out a contented sigh as long awaited sleep finally came . . .

"Jenna?" Bella pushed open Jenna's bedroom door an turned on the ceiling light.

Jenna started to blink from the sudden brightness. "Oh good, you're awake. Guess who was on the phone just now?"

"Diane." Bella spoke her daughter's name with the excitement of a teenager with tickets to a rock concert. Jenna continued blinking.

"She's coming to town. She has big news and she wants the whole family to meet here tomorrow. We have to make an early start."

Now Jenna was blinking *and* smiling without humor. The house would have to be in tiptop shape. Lauren and Diane were coming. *Woo hoo.*

"I'll see you in the morning," Bella said. She turned off the light and closed the door.

Alone once more, Jenna listened to her mother's footsteps descending the stairs. In the darkness of her bedroom, she gritted her teeth. An entire afternoon with Lauren and Diane. She sat up then turned on the lamp. She picked up her cell phone and pressed speed dial.

Rosa answered on the third ring. "Make it fast. I'm watching *Psycho*."

She hated to bother her. Rosa was fond of Sir Alfred Hitchcock's productions. Unfortunately, this couldn't wait.

"Guess who's coming to Gordonville?"

8

The next morning, Jenna was yawning as she stood before her bedroom mirror. After going through copious outfits, she finally settled on the gray tank top, a skull with a flower, her favorite—and a gift from Rosa. A pair of faded Levi's completed her ensemble. The jeans were old faded and extremely comfortable. She knew what she was wearing would never measure up to her sisters' fashionable wardrobes, but she felt good in it. That's all that mattered. Besides, today was Saturday. Her day off. She had a right to some comfort.

Jenna yawned again. She was up before eight a.m. scrubbing and vacuuming every room upstairs and downstairs. Not a speck of dust or a cobweb could be seen anywhere. Who knew what room her prima donna sisters might enter? Perish the thought Lauren or Diane might see a stain or horror of horrors a dust bunny? Before noon, Jenna was finished cleaning the house. Earlier, her mother was out shopping. She had to buy and prepare something special for the feast . . .

Jenna put on an elastic headband. Fortunately, she had styled her hair in twists from early in the week. It saved time getting dressed. In the mirror, she saw the reflection of the piles of clothes lying on top of her bed. It took her over an hour to decide what to wear. Wearing a sardonic smile, she put them back in the dresser drawers and closet.

There was a time when what she wore in front of Lauren and Diane wouldn't have mattered. She sighed. She forfeited her confidence years ago. Or did she? Rosa's offer still stood . . .

"Stop it." Jenna silenced the thought. She wasn't going there. She checked her watch. "Show time."

Julian arrived first followed by Alan and Elise. They gathered in the living room where Jenna was sitting in an overstuffed armchair. She got up and greeted her father with a great big bear hug. The family patriarch had on his Gordonville Mechanics cap the establishment for which he was the owner/manager. To Jenna, the headgear was his trademark. He would have worn it with his tuxedo to the wedding if he could have.

Bella entered the living room. Clad in a floral short-sleeve dress, she took her seat in the Chippendale chair.

Julian held back his annoyance. His wife looked like a queen sitting on her throne. That's why he avoided coming over as much as possible. Occupying the same space with Bella wasn't easy. The woman could wipe out the colors from a rainbow. When the children were growing up, he preferred to have them spend time with him at his house, a three-bedroom home on Lilac Street. It was three miles away. Not far enough from Bella, but close enough to the children. It's a wonder they didn't get divorced long time ago.

Julian looked fondly at Jenna. She was some kind of magic glue. Perhaps she could act as a buffer zone between him and Bella.

"So, how's Malachi?" Elise asked Jenna. She had the chance to meet him at the wedding and again when she and Alan ran into Malachi and Jenna at a café in Rhinebeck during one of those rare occasions that he and Jenna was able to have some quality time together without having to shorten it.

She looked down at the parquet floor. "He's fine." For obvious reasons, her sister-in-law didn't know about her mother's disapproval of Malachi or about her attempts to discourage their relationship.

Bella glowered. She didn't want to hear anything about Dr. Chase. This was Diane's day.

Jenna glanced at her mother. When she saw the bitter look on her face, she could hardly breathe.

Alan noted it too. Lauren and Diane said Mom didn't want Jenna dating. Jenna told him that everything was fine. None of this suggested that things were fine.

At that moment, they all heard a car pull up. Through the lace curtains, Jenna saw a light blue Mercedes-Benz parking in front of her Honda.

Lauren had arrived.

Having a twisted desire to torture herself, Jenna got up and went over to the window. She swaggered up the front walk. Back from her Costa Rican honeymoon, Lauren's skin was almost bronze. She was dressed in black tank top, gray trousers and accessorized with a gold wave necklace and matching gold earrings. She flipped her hair, which cascaded down her shoulders like an actress' in a shampoo commercial.

Jenna turned away from the window. She walked back to her chair. She was plopping back into it just as Lauren rang the doorbell.

Bella ran excitedly to the door.

Lauren *stepped* into the living room, arms at her sides. She graced everyone with a smirk that, was supposed to pass for an endearing smile. After the family greeted her, Bella excused herself and went into the kitchen. Still looking smug, Lauren surveyed everyone in the room. She shook her head then let out a long-suffering sigh.

Julian, Alan and Elise exchanged glances. Were they underdressed? Only Jenna stared long and hard at her eldest sister, who dismissed them all and was now looking around the living room.

Jenna glowered. *Lauren's inspecting the room.* After all that housework she did this morning, she'd better not be looking for dirt.

Lauren flipped her auburn hair again. English country. Mom hasn't changed the décor in over twenty years. She walked over to the settee.

She smoothed her hand across its fine cotton fabric before finally sitting down.

Jenna gritted her teeth. What an honor for the settee that Lauren was planting her lower posterior into it.

"So, Jenna, how've you been?" Lauren asked. "We haven't spoken since the wedding."

"I'm fine." *If you wanted to speak to me, you know where I live.*

"How's work?" Lauren asked.

"The same." Jenna looked at her sister guardedly.

"Still a receptionist?"

Jenna grabbed the arms of the chair. She dug her fingernails into them. *And there it is.* Lauren knows she hadn't changed jobs since she began working at Wheat, Prentiss & Associates ten years ago. In a fake nice voice, Jenna replied, "Yes, I'm still working as a receptionist." "Have you considered another career?"

Jenna smiled without humor.

"What's wrong with the job she has now?" Julian asked feeling aggravated.

"Nothing, Dad."

"Then why would you ask a question like that?" Alan asked between clenched teeth. He saw the look on Jenna's face. He didn't feel too comfortable. Apparently, Lauren didn't notice that their baby sister's smile did not reach her eyes.

"There's nothing wrong with having high ambitions," Lauren said.

"Like yours?" Elise asked breaking her rule to stay out of her in-laws disagreements. They hadn't arrived at her in-law's one hour yet and already she was aggravated. Lauren's attitude towards Jenna was a bit much and she felt the need to come to the aid of her youngest sister-in-law. The elementary schoolteacher looked at Lauren with disgust then picked up one of Bella's country lifestyle magazines and began flipping through the pages. "I suppose you think teaching math and science to fourth and fifth graders is as exciting as watching grass grow."

Alan, who was sitting beside Elise in the loveseat, put his arm around her. He was proud of his wife. Usually, Elise left defense up to him. Nevertheless, he wanted her to stay cool. For once, he'd like to visit his mother without needing an overdose of antacid.

Lauren held out her hand, displaying her manicured fingernails, platinum engagement ring and wedding band. She sighed. "You people blow things way out of proportion." She looked over at Jenna. "I'm sorry if I offended you."

Her sister was never sorry about anything in her life. Jenna wanted to march right over and slap her so hard that her face would sail across the living room. Time to decompress.

Breathe.

Just then, Bella returned carrying a tray of refreshments. She placed it on the coffee table—by Lauren.

Jenna, Julian, Alan and Elise exchanged knowing glances.

"Where's Diane?" Julian asked. He was becoming impatient. Lauren, like her mother, was a bit much.

Lauren poured a glass of lemonade from the pitcher Bella had brought in. "You have to give her time, Dad. Traffic is horrendous. Especially on the weekends. I'm only here now because I got up with the birds." She took a long sip of lemonade.

Jenna got up and came over to the coffee table. She picked up a celery stick and scooped it into the crab dip. Eying Lauren, she tore off a piece of the celery with her teeth.

Alan tensed. He still suspected that Rosa was back and was behind Jenna's odd behavior at the wedding regardless of what his mother and sisters were claiming.

Oblivious to Jenna's mounting fury, Lauren put down her glass and looked briefly around the room again. "Mom, when are you gonna move? You've lived here long enough."

Bella patted her hair.

"There is life outside of a Gordonville."

"True," Bella said with a slight smile.

"Nelson and I will even buy you and Jenna a house."

Bella simpered. Lauren's offer was tempting, but she wasn't interested in moving. At least, not now. She was comfortable here. Adjusted. The Crandall name was important in this town.

"Unless, Jenna's thinking about living on her own." Lauren smiled, displaying her perfect white teeth. "Can you, Jenna?"

"Now what's that supposed to mean?" Julian asked. "Nothing." Bella's tone was as hard as steel. "Does everything have to have a meaning, Daddy?" Lauren asked even as she realized that perhaps she might have gone just a tad too far in questioning Jenna's living arrangements. When the attorney saw the glare in her mother's face, she stopped smiling immediately. She went too far.

Bella clenched her fists. *What possessed Lauren to ask that? And in front of her father and Elise?*

Why put that thought that in Jenna's head? Especially since Rosa Garrison was in and out of her life now. Jenna cannot get an apartment.

That would be asking for trouble . . .

A glint appeared in Jenna's eyes then quickly disappeared. This time, Lauren saw it. For a moment, she wondered what was going on in her sister's mind. Then, she dismissed it. She put an olive in her mouth.

Alan held his breath. Lauren needed to slow her roll. She was provoking Jenna; however, raised a point. Did Jenna have to be under the same roof as Mom? Since Rosa wasn't around as they claimed, wouldn't it be better for Jenna to get away from here?

"I don't want to be a receptionist anymore," Jenna said.

She looked at the stunned faces around her. She was just as surprised as they were perhaps even more. She never intend on bringing up her career change now. Today. At this very moment.

If ever.

Recovering quickly from her faux pas of a moment ago, Lauren was looking amused. Annoyed, Jenna drew strength from that. Her sister was beautiful, successful, invested well and was therefore able to afford a piece of the good life. She never failed to let her know it. Now Lauren married well. Jenna moistened her lips. It was her turn to pursue her dream. "I'm going to be a professional artist."

Bella's face took on a look of crazed anger.

Jenna tried to keep her breathing steady. "I'm going to attend art school. I'll teach art to support myself. Just like I planned." Jenna took a deep breath. Then she added, "Malachi thinks I should show my work. And I think so too."

"Well, good for you," Julian exclaimed. "I was surprised when you didn't take it up in the first place. I agree with Malachi. You do great work. You were always drawing or painting something when you were kid."

Bella nibbled on a table water cracker. Dr. Chase needed to mind his own business. She became angrier as she listened to Alan and Elise commending Jenna and joking with the millions she was going to make from her first commission. Jenna seemed more reenergized as she talked about art.

"I can't believe you're bringing up that up again," Bella said. "I thought I told you no."

The words were barely out of her mouth before Bella found herself wishing that she could take them back. She looked around the room at the stunned looks on the faces of her husband, son and daughter-in-law. It was bad enough that Jenna's artistic ambitions were resurfacing, but for her to let it slip out that she was the one who had dissuaded her in the first place was a huge mistake. Bella chastised herself for allowing her emotions to get in the way all because of Dr. Chase. Julian, Alan and Elise were unaware of Jenna's aspirations and her attempts to quash it. Until now.

Bella looked at her eldest daughter with a stare that could wilt a flower. Lauren blushed then ate another olive.

"What do you mean you told her no?" Julian asked. "You've discouraged her before? Why would you do that?"

"I know what's best for Jenna," Bella said.

"And she doesn't?"

Jenna drummed her fingers on the arms of the chair. How lovely having your parents talk about you as if you weren't in the room.

"If you knew about her friend you wouldn't ask," Lauren muttered. Unfortunately, she didn't speak low enough.

"What friend?" Julian asked.

Alan became fascinated with the mantel clock. Was Lauren drunk? She knew they weren't supposed to mention Rosa to anyone outside of their circle. Especially to Dad. He watched the minute hand moving and pondered what was going to happen next.

Lauren blushed even deeper. She looked down at her engagement and wedding rings. She couldn't look at her mother. She just opened a forbidden door.

It was all Bella could do not to walk over there and strangle Lauren. But she couldn't. Too many witnesses. Plus, there'd been enough mistakes already. Lauren was making too many of those. Diane may be childish at times but not Lauren. Her eldest was shrewd, manipulative; however, her conduct this afternoon was strange. Bella watched Lauren staring at her left hand. *Was married life turning her brain to yogurt? It's only been a month.*

"I asked a question," Julian said, baffled by the behavior in the room. Just who was this friend? He was about to say something when another car pulled up.

Again, Jenna looked through the window. Her Honda was now sandwiched between Lauren's Mercedes and a silver Jaguar. "Diane's here." This time she didn't get up.

Bella smoothed down the sides of her dress. Diane's timing couldn't have been better.

9

A moment later, dressed in a beige peasant top with beaded lace, Capri pants and carrying a Fendi tote bag, Diane entered the living room as if she were on the catwalk.

"You look darling," Bella gushed.

"What's Larry up to these days?" Lauren asked.

"Oh, he left for Milan on a business trip yesterday."

Diane smiled mysteriously then launched into a detailed account of her photo shoot in Monte Carlo and the sightseeing that she and some of the other models did while they were there. "You would just love the Prince's Palace and the Place du Casino. "And the shopping."

Diane regaled them with some of the latest fashion trends. "Lauren, next time Nelson goes to Cannes for the film festival, you have to go with him. Some of the best shopping is at the Avenue des Beaux Arts and the Avenue de Monte Carlo."

Julian sighed. "Does any of this have to do with why you called us all here?" This health and beauty yak fest was working his nerve. And he'd had enough of these hors d'oeuvres and chick food. He needed a beer. Badly.

"Yeah," Alan said, feeling equally as impatient and annoyed. "Out with it."

Bella glowered. "Give her a break. She just got here."

Diane gave her mother an appreciative look. "Thanks, Mom. I'm tired and thirsty. I feel like I've been on the road forever."

Julian was about to point out that she wasn't too tired to chitchat about fashion, but he kept his cool. She would've started whining, Bella would get upset, Lauren would probably put in her two cents and he didn't come here to argue.

Alan stood up, yawned then asked, "Don't you travel with water?"

"I drank it all."

Alan grinned. "No wonder you took so long. You must've hit every rest stop along the way."

Diane gave her brother a nasty look.

"Ignore him," Bella said. "I bought your favorite brand of cranberry juice."

"Thanks, Mom."

Bella hurried to the kitchen.

Diane flashed Jenna a cutesy smile then gave her the up-and-down look. "We gotta get you some clothes." That macabre-looking T-shirt was a fashion faux pas.

Jenna felt the cold sensation of shame. Her eyes stayed focused on Diane. She knew the others were looking on. She could feel it, but humiliation prevented her from looking in their direction.

"And you could do more with your looks." Diane looked critically at Jenna's hair. Those two-strand twists had to go. "Starting with your hair. You should go to a professional."

"Maybe you can get her an appointment with your stylist," Lauren said.

Diane's face lit up. "Angelo does wonders. He'll probably do it for nothing 'cause we're sisters."

A voice within Jenna commanded *Tell them off!* But she couldn't. She just sat there, immobilized, staring at her sister's derisive grin.

Alan scowled at his twin and Lauren.

Diane caught his expression as well as her father and sister-in-law's equally appalled looks. "What? We're just looking out for Jenna. She is the receptionist. The first person a client sees when they enter the office."

"Says the one with the over-processed hair," Julian said.

Diane's mouth fell. Since when did Daddy put her down?

"There's. Nothing. Wrong. With my daughter." Julian wasn't affected when Diane started pouting. She could have a hissy fit for all he cared. Diane was wrong to make personal remarks about Jenna.

Alan straightened. He never felt so proud of his Dad.

"Diane's your daughter too," Lauren said.

Alan's eyes bugged out. Lauren could be cryptic at times, but that was a peculiar remark even for her. Did she know about—?

"What do you mean by that?" Julian asked interrupting Alan's thoughts. A shadow crossed over Julian's face.

Lauren led Diane over to the settee.

"I asked you a question."

"I didn't mean anything. It was just a statement."

"Well, it stunk." Julian adjusted his cap. "I've always treated each one of you the same."

"Relax, Diane," Lauren said. She smiled cunningly. "Besides, Jenna was just telling us she's going to be an artist."

Diane brightened. "Really?"

You got over your hurt feelings. Alan muttered something unrepeatable. "Why don't we talk about your big news, *Diane?*"

"Oh, that can wait." His twin sister took a tissue from out of her handbag and daintily dabbed her eyes. "I want to hear all about Jenna."

"Malachi encouraged her to go to art school," Lauren said.

"Oh? And how is the dear boy?"

"Don't call him that," Alan said. "He's not a boy. He's a man." He resented her referring to Malachi that way. He didn't like when his mother did that to him.

Jenna gave Diane a hostile look.

Alan's heart picked up pace. Diane and Lauren were so eager to make Jenna uncomfortable; they couldn't see that she was getting irritated. "Leave her alone."

"She can speak for herself," Diane snapped. "Except when Rosa's around." She gasped, put a hand to her lips, then burst into nervous giggles.

Lauren closed her eyes and sighed. *Mom is going to kill you.*

Alan put his hand over his stomach. He hoped that he could keep down the hors d'oeuvres he'd just eaten.

Diane must be on something.

How could Diane mention *her*? And in front of Dad? Lauren said too much. This was even worse.

Elise felt Alan's body quivering. She began rubbing his back to ease the tension. They'd visited her in-law before and while there were squabbles or tension at best, it was never like this. Mystery. Anger. Stress. Why were Lauren and Diane picking on Jenna? And why would Bella try to steer Jenna away from art if that's what she wanted to do?

Alan began relaxing. Elise's massage began to ease his muscles. Maybe this revelation was a good thing. Opening the forbidden door was the push he needed even though this wasn't how he pictured it.

I could tell Dad about the abuse.

When Bella returned holding a tall glass of cranberry juice and a plate of canapés, she saw the indignant looks on Julian and Elise's faces, the silly grin on Diane's face, the discomfort on Lauren's, the tension on Alan's and the narrowing of Jenna's eyes. "What's going on?"

"I was just about to ask the same thing," Julian said. "Who's Rosa?"

Very calmly, Bella put down the glass and the plate on the coffee table. This delicate situation required a cool head. Something most unfortunate transpired during her brief absence. First, she had to take care of this snag. Then, she was going to find out who spoke out of turn . . .

Alan looked calm, but inside he was a wreck. This was Mom's worse nightmare. There was so much that Dad should know. Alan swallowed. Here was his chance. After all these years, fate was handing him a gift. All he had to do was speak, but instead he stayed silent. Dread sealed his mouth shut. If only he had the courage to seize the moment. Alan clenched his hands into fists.

"Well?"

Bella didn't respond. Instead, she stood up and smoothed down the front of her dress.

Alan looked down at the floor, hiding his smile. He was deriving pleasure from watching his mother try to figure her way out of this one. If nothing else, he was grateful for that.

Diane struggled to hold in the laughter.

"I fail to see the humor," Julian said.

"She's just nervous," Lauren said. She squeezed Diane's hand, willing her sister to control herself.

"There's nothing humorous about Jenna planning her future," Julian said. "She's doing the right thing. Jenna's a very gifted young woman and—"

Diane doubled over with laughter. Lauren struggled to keep a straight face.

Jenna watched her sisters having fun at her expense. Like in the old days. Shame and rage competed within her. Rage won.

Jenna stood up and at the top of her voice yelled, "Stop laughing at me."

Lauren and Diane fell silent. No one else moved or spoke.

Bella pursed her lips. Jenna was asserting herself. This is Rosa's influence. It mustn't escalate any further. The situation required delicate handling. Julian went from alarm to confusion. Usually, Jenna was so mild. He couldn't recall ever seeing her get angry, even when it was justifiable. On the other hand, it was good to see her defending herself. Bella was handling her like a puppeteer. Like the way she decided Jenna's career. What made Bella decide that Jenna shouldn't be an artist?

In a commanding voice Bella said, "Sit . . . down."

Her mother's tone had no effect on her, however. Jenna remained standing, staring balefully at her sisters.

Alan felt his stomach churning. This could get ugly. He stood up and said, "It's okay, Jenna. Lauren and Diane won't bother you anymore."

"I'll handle this," Bella snapped. How many times did she have to tell him to butt out? "*I* am in control."

Alan sat back down. He stared at the floor, willing it to open up and swallow him.

"Bella, that was uncalled for," Elise said. She looked at her mother-in-law with daggers.

Up to now, she remained silent; maintaining her rule of impartiality, but this time Bella had gone too far. Her son was *stressed enough as it is.* He hadn't looked this way in years.

Elise looked from her mother-in-law to her older sisters-in-laws. "And what is wrong with you? Leave Jenna alone."

Alan cringed. *Of all the times for Elise to challenge Mom.*

"I suggest you stay out of what you don't understand," Bella said. She wouldn't even look in Elise's direction. She wasn't trying to score points with her. She neither wanted nor needed her daughter-in-law's respect. They already had a strenuous relationship. Damage control was the only thing that mattered.

"Alan is my business," Elise retorted. She would not be intimidated. "Enlighten me."

Ordinarily, Bella would never tolerate defiance from Elise, but her daughter-in-law was the least of her problems right now. Ignoring Elise, Bella concentrated on Jenna. "I said sit."

Seconds passed. Finally, Jenna sat. She closed her eyes for a moment. When she opened them again, her anger was gone; yet, she felt like a vase that had just fallen off a table and shattered into tiny pieces.

Bella adjusted the sleeve of her dress. Who was foolish enough to mention Rosa? She looked over at Alan. Her son reminded her of a whipped black Labrador retriever. No. He wouldn't dare. Next, she looked at Lauren. Their eyes met briefly, before her eldest daughter turned away and began staring down at her black designer pumps. No. It wasn't Lauren either. Bella turned toward Diane, who immediately looked away. She took a sip of cranberry juice.

Bella pursed her lips. *So it was you.* The elder woman addressed her elder daughters. "Enough." The sound of her voice turned the living room into a virtual freezer.

"Will somebody tell me what the devil's going on?" Julian asked.

"It's nothing," Bella replied.

"Don't tell me it's nothing. My little girl's upset and they," Julian pointed to Lauren and Diane, "drove her to it." He talked about Diane's disparaging remarks and Lauren egging her on. "And Lauren was putting down Jenna's job from the moment she came in here. Evidently, she bothers you. Now Diane mentioned someone named Rosa. I want to know who she is."

Bella gave a quick look at her elder children. Lauren was staring at her fingernails, Alan was looking down at his lap and Diane was nibbling on her lower lip. The matriarch decided not to look at Lauren and Diane. Her angry stare might kill them. Anyway, damage control was more important. She had an idea. The elegant woman smiled to herself. It was so simple; she wondered why she didn't think of it before. Bella patted her head. "Rosa was a friend that Jenna *used* to have." That ought to shut him up.

"Does this Rosa have a last name?"

"Garrison," Bella said.

"The same friend Lauren was referring to earlier?"

"Yes?"

Julian turned to Jenna. "I never heard you talk about her before?"

"And since when are you so interested in Jenna's social life?" Bella asked.

Julian gave her a look. "I've always been interested in my daughter. Now what about this Rosa? I keep sensing this atmospheric shift every time her name came."

"She was no good," Bella said before Jenna could get the chance to respond. She might've used this as an opportunity to establish Rosa as a fairy god sister.

Jenna looked keenly at her mother. Bella held up her chin in defiance, daring Jenna to refute her.

"Elise," Alan began, his voice sounding strained, "do you have any peppermint?"

She opened her handbag and handed him a roll of antacid. Alan looked relieved. Ever since the wedding, his stomach started acting up. He hadn't had an upset stomach since he left home for college. That's where they met. They took quantitative reasoning in freshman year. Alan sat in the in the back, sometimes gazing out the window as if lost in thought, but remarkably would come up with the correct answer when called upon.

Elise looked fondly at her husband. Outside of class, Alan was so shy. It was all she could do to get him to come out of his shell. In time, they went from being classmates to being friends to becoming a little bit more. It was then that Alan became comfortable enough to share his childhood with her. From what he said about his relationship with his mother, Lauren and twin sister, she was amazed that a sensitive stomach was all he had. She fiddled with her house keys. After five years of marriage, she knew when something was off. Why was Alan so nervous lately?

Elise went over to Jenna then placed her arm on her shoulder. "I could use a cup of tea. How about you?"

Grateful for the gentle touch, Jenna looked at Elise. She wanted to say thanks, but she didn't dare open her mouth. Her voice might crack. Crying in front of her mother and sisters was the last thing she needed to do.

Alan felt warm inside as he watched his wife take his kid sister by the hand and help her out of the chair. Elise's kindness was one of the reasons why he fell in love with her.

"Don't you want to hear my good news?" Diane asked as Jenna and Elise were leaving the living room.

"We'll catch up," Elise said. She rolled her eyes.

In the hall, Elise lowered her voice. "You you're your sisters are morons, right? And no offense but that includes your mother." Elise was still feeling miffed at the way in which Bella treated her and her son.

Jenna wore a weak smile. She would've burst out laughing if she were in a laughing mood. The rancor existing between Elise and her in-laws was not a secret within their family.

"You can rise above them," Elise added.

Jenna nodded. *With Rosa's help.*

But this time, she allowed the thought to simmer for a while.

10

"Well, don't keep us in suspense," Lauren said to Diane. "What's the big news?"

Diane held out her left hand. On her finger was a four-carat diamond engagement ring that she had twisted around before entering the house.

Lauren squealed. She and Bella began hugging Diane.

"Did you set a date?" Lauren asked.

"February. I want a Valentine's Day theme. Pink and white color schemes and pops of red. Oh and I'm going to give out tiny bottles of wine and heart-shaped cookies as wedding favors. Won't that be cute?"

"It sounds girlie."

"Larry doesn't care what I do as long as I agree to be Mrs. Lawrence Belmar."

Alan rolled his eyes.

"It's the middle of July," Bella said. "You haven't even booked a hall."

"Larry's associate is loaning us his Palm Beach estate."

Lauren gasped. "That place is gorgeous."

Diane giggled. "The perfect place to sprinkle red rose petals down the living room aisle." She turned to Julian. She looked at him with puppy dog eyes. "Daddy, you are going to walk me down the aisle, right?"

He blew a frustrated breath. He was appalled at how quickly she, Lauren and Bella dismissed Jenna's feelings. Still, Diane was his daughter. "How can I turn down a Florida vacation?"

She threw her arms around him. "Oh, thank you, Daddy. Mom, do you think Reverend Brooks will want to go to Palm Beach?"

"Of course, he will. If I know the reverend, he wouldn't want to turn down the chance to officiate over the wedding." She chuckled. "Not to mention a Florida vacation. I'll talk to him. Oh, he's going to be thrilled."

Diane turned to her brother. "Our wedding won't be the same without you and Elise."

"I got your back." She was a pain, but she was his twin. "As for my wife, you'll have to ask her yourself." He pointed to Elise, who along with Jenna was reentering the living room, each holding a steaming cup of tea.

Diane showed them her ring.

"Congratulations!" Elise exclaimed with a fake smile. "Yeah," Jenna said. "Congratulations." She was glad she was sipping tea. Hearing about another wedding in the family so soon was making her ill.

"Of course, you're both in the wedding party," Diane said.

Elise maintained her fake smile all the while sickened by Diane's giddiness.

Jenna blinked. "Oh, sure." *Rosa's gonna love this.*

Bella was about to speak when the telephone rang. She went to the kitchen to answer it. When Bella returned to the living room, she was smiling like an executioner. "It's for you, Jenna. It's Dr. Chase."

Jenna felt the electricity in the atmosphere. She didn't know why she had given Malachi her home phone number. It was taboo for him to use it.

Without another word, Jenna left the room.

"Everything okay?" Malachi asked after Jenna picked up. "Did I call at a bad time?"

"No everything's fine." Jenna took a sip of tea. She stood in the kitchen imagining what the folks must be saying back there in the living room.

"Good." Bella gave the impression he was interrupting something. She sounded hostile over the phone. No surprise there. It was a wonder she didn't hang up on him. Moreover, he needed to hear Jenna's voice. He couldn't shake off the memory of last night's nightmare.

Jenna took another sip of tea while she listened to Malachi explain why he called her on the landline.

Her cell phone was off.

Jenna wanted to kick herself. She turned it off last night after talking to Rosa and with all the preparations she had to make this morning, she forgot to turn it back on.

"Are you free this afternoon?" Malachi asked.

It was at the tip of her tongue to say yes, but she couldn't get it out. Leaving in the middle of a family gathering was unacceptable; another one of her mother's ridiculous taboos. She wasn't having a good time anyway. So why stay?

"I'm available." *What made me say that?*

"Great. We're just gonna chill. And no, I'm not bringing you back home at three-thirty. I'm putting my foot down this time."

Malachi's words hit home. Why should she stay here and subject herself to more misery? Lauren and Diane were insulting her repeatedly. Mom didn't care. She only censured them because she didn't want them talking about Rosa in front of Dad and Elise.

Let your little darlings fetch your four o'clock tea. "Give me twenty minutes," Jenna said. And you know the drill." Although she was about to break protocol, she didn't want to get crazy.

After they hung up, Jenna marveled at what she just did. She broke a house rule.

Rosa's going to be so proud.

Her triumph fled, however, when she heard her mother's footsteps coming down the hall. Jenna began twisting her hair around her finger. *I can do this. I can do this.*

"Get off the . . . phone." Bella frowned in puzzlement. When she stormed into the kitchen, she was certain that Jenna would still be on the phone, way past the limit she'd set for that call. She would rip the phone out of Jenna's hands if it came to that. *How dare that professor call my phone?*

Jenna pretended to be surprised, but deep down she was amused. Thought you were going to catch me red handed. *Psyche.*

"So, what did he want?" Bella asked.

"To go out." Jenna's amiable response masked her fast diminishing amusement. Their discussion was none of her mother's business.

"You told him no, of course."

"I told him yes."

Bella looked around the kitchen. Surely, Jenna was talking to someone else. "Excuse me?"

Jenna was equally surprised. She didn't know where this newfound courage came from, but it was liberating. She almost felt like laughing. "I said we're going out."

"You're not going anywhere."

Jenna began rubbing her temples. That tone of voice was working her nerve. She looked at her mother and said, "Yes, I am."

Bella smoothed the front of her dress. Jenna's forceful tone was unmistakable. Rosa's influence over Jenna was growing. Bella sniffed. She was not going to allow Rosa to take over. She lost control after the fire. Rosa was behind that wheat muffin incident with Lauren. She hated herself for not doing something about it, but what else could she do. Punishing Jenna or worse, revealing Rosa Garrison for the sicko she really was would've disgraced the family.

And brought down Julian's wrath . . .

She could not let her family go through that. She had to let the incident go. Besides, in the end Lauren was fine. Distraught but fine. She could not afford that.

The family could not afford that. Therefore, she let the incident go. Besides, Lauren was fine. Distressed but fine.

A cocky smile appeared on Jenna's face. She didn't back down. Now Mom doesn't know how to handle this. Jenna started walking out the kitchen.

Bella took a deep breath. No. She was not going to lose control again. She grabbed Jenna's arm. "You're not going anywhere."

Jenna felt shock before the pain finally began shooting up her arm. She looked into her mother's hate-filled eyes. Her mother hadn't touched her in sixteen years. Rosa's words came back to haunt her. *"You think your mother would suddenly love you . . . ?"*

"Now, call Dr. Chase and cancel whatever plans you made with him."

Bella tightened her grasp.

Jenna winced in pain. She picked up the phone with her other hand and began dialing. She glanced at Bella. Her mother's face showed pure satisfaction. *Mom's happy because I'm unhappy.* With her other hand, she began to rub her temple again. Jenna's assertiveness was gradually returning. She put the phone back in its cradle.

Bella's pleasure turned to outrage. "I said cancel the date."

Feeling bolder, Jenna didn't make a move. She just stood there staring at Bella. Suddenly, she started laughing—a looming, menacing, laugh.

Bella dropped Jenna's arm and immediately drew back. "This isn't you." Bella tried to stop her voice from shaking. "Rosa's behind this."

"She has nothing to do with this. I have a mind of my own."

"Since when?"

Jenna sucked her teeth and walked out the kitchen without a backwards glance. She was now more determined than ever to prove that she could fight her own battles without Rosa's help.

Bella looked on in disbelief. *She did not just turn her back on me.* "I am in control." She followed Jenna out of the kitchen and caught up with her in the hall. "If you walk this house you will be sorry."

Bella's protestation sent the rest of the family running out into the hall.

Jenna halted briefly at the foot of the staircase. This was uncomfortable. She didn't need nor want an audience.

"Now what's wrong?" Julian asked.

Bella explained, careful not to say anything about Rosa's influence on Jenna's decision. She couldn't risk having her name come up again.

"That's it?" Julian asked. "Jenna wants to go out with Malachi? So what?" There was no real reason for Jenna to stay. He didn't want to stick around either. Listening to his wife and older daughters discuss wedding plans wasn't his idea of spending a Saturday afternoon.

Bella didn't appreciate Julian undermining her authority. "Jenna knows the rules."

"What rules?"

Bella told him that she didn't allow the children to leave during family get-togethers. "It's unacceptable."

"They're not kids anymore, Bella. And it's not like today is so important."

Diane started to sulk. She just announced her engagement. How could Daddy write off this special occasion?

"See what you've done, Jenna?" Bella asked. "You're selfishness is ruining your sister's day."

"Woman, drink some chamomile," Julian said. "Diane, grow up. Jenna, go have yourself a good time."

"Thank you, Daddy." Jenna continued up the stairs. Halfway up, she stopped. The spirit that had been motivating her to lash out at her sisters earlier and to challenge her mother had suddenly disappeared and in its place was anxiety. If she went out with Malachi, what would Mom do to her when she returned home?

Jenna turned to face her mother. Bella was wearing that familiar look of triumph. *She knows I'm afraid.* Her mind returned to that spring morning at the farmhouse with Rosa sixteen years ago. "*Still think you can live without me?*" *I can do this.* Jenna's face broke out into a twisted grin. Then she turned and went upstairs. Moments later they heard a door slam.

Bella crossed her arms to prevent herself from shaking. That grin was just as disturbing as her laughter in the kitchen. She cleared her throat. In a bright tone she said, "What're we standing around for? We've got a wedding to prepare." She had a good system going all these years. She would not allow it to spiral out of control. She brushed past everyone then reentered the living room. Lauren and Diane looked at each other, shrugged then she followed leaving Alan, Elise and Julian standing in the hall. Alan put his hand on his stomach. Jenna would never defy Mom like that. Now he was certain. Rosa was back.

Later, Jenna returned downstairs. She had changed into a cotton top and a pair of khakis. Julian was standing by the living room.

Jenna kissed him on the cheek. "Talk to you later, Daddy."

"Where're you going?"

"Malachi's outside."

"What kind of man doesn't come to the front door to pick up his girl friend? I thought Malachi was a gentleman. Don't tell me I was wrong."

Jenna's face fell. *Oh boy.* "That's the way we do it."

"That's nonsense."

Julian opened the front door and stepped outside. He looked right then left. He turned around and looked back at Jenna. "Where's his car?"

Jenna swallowed. Very rarely did her father get angry.

Bella, who overheard her husband's questions, flew out the living room. She looked sharply at Jenna. Naturally, she didn't want her revealing where Malachi had his car parked.

Lauren, Diane, Alan and Elise stepped out of the living room.

Jenna cleared her throat as she looked at her mother. *Are you going to tell him or shall I?*

Seeing the silent exchange between them, Julian slammed his hand against the wall. "I could plant corn and raise it before I get an answer in this house."

Thereupon, Jenna told Julian where Malachi parked his car. She could hear her mother swearing telekinetically. Julian flung open the door and stormed out the house. Where did Bella get off treating this man so unkindly?

Meekly, Jenna followed.

Malachi was sitting in his car preparing notes for Monday's lecture. This arrangement of having to park away from Jenna's house may have been off-putting, but at least he was getting some work done. Every now and then, he kept looking out for Jenna. Malachi couldn't get the nightmare out of his mind. It was so vivid. Was it the flounder he ate for dinner last night or was it a sign? It was a long time before he was able to fall asleep again.

Malachi was jotting down some more notes. He looked up again then did a double take. Jenna was approaching . . . with Julian? Quickly, Malachi put away his notes then stepped out of the car.

Seconds later, Julian and Jenna arrived. Malachi was baffled.

And a little scared.

What was going on? Julian was looking kind of annoyed. Malachi's breathing became shallow.

"Relax," Julian said. "I'm not gonna eat you. Think you and Jenna can spare a few minutes?"

Malachi's shoulders slumped from relief. "Yeah. Sure.

"Good. There's a parking space by the house." He smiled. "Come in for a few." With that, Julian walked back to the house.

Malachi's mouth fell open. For weeks, Bella wouldn't allow him to come to the front door never mind enter through it.

A very puzzled Malachi looked over at Jenna who was admiring him in his blue polo top and Dockers.

"You look great," she said.

11

Malachi experienced an acute sense of déjà vu as he followed Jenna up the brick walkway. He started glancing around, convinced that a woman in a Loki mask would appear.

Jenna gave him a peculiar look. "Are you okay?"

"Yeah. I'm just excited to be here." How could he tell her he dreamed about a crazy woman in a Loki mask in her house and skeletons in her dining room? "And don't worry. I won't talk about anything that you told me."

Jenna smiled gratefully.

They arrived at the front door. He was about to enter the Inner Sanctum. He wondered if this was a dream, but it couldn't be. He was holding Jenna's hand and it felt warm.

As soon as they entered the house, a chill went up his spine. Except for the floral wallpaper and the grandfather clock in the hall, the first floor had the same lay out as his nightmare. Malachi panicked. Again, he looked around. Would "Loki" appear?

"Are you sure you're okay?" Jenna asked.

Malachi laughed nervously. "The wallpaper. Looks just like one I saw in a movie." *And please don't ask me which one.*

Jenna brought Malachi into the living room where the family, except for Bella, was gathered. She told him that her mother was in the kitchen preparing lunch.

Malachi laughed to himself. Bella didn't want to see him. Evidently, he was only here because of Julian.

After everyone exchanged greetings, Julian pointed Malachi to a ladderback Windsor armchair. Jenna returned to the overstuffed armchair she had occupied earlier wishing she could sit near to him.

Julian said, "How's the job? Student's giving you a hard time?"

"Some, but most of them are good kids."

Diane handed Malachi the plate of canapés, proudly displaying her left hand.

"I see congratulations are in order," Malachi said as he took an hors d'oeuvres. Why didn't Jenna mention that earlier? He bit into the cheese-topped cracker and wondered if he would be able to see Diane's engagement ring from an airplane at 30,000 feet.

Diane beamed. "We're having a Valentine's Day theme." She told him about where she was holding the wedding.

"I know the place," Malachi said.

"Oh?" Lauren gave him a smug look as she slouched in the settee.

"I've seen it on the news," Malachi said.

It was apparent that Jenna hadn't mentioned his former career to Lauren. Or Diane. They must be still under the impression that wealth overwhelmed him. He finished chewing the last of the canapé. Let them assume whatever they wanted. He didn't have to prove his worth to anyone who was biodegradable.

Thereupon, Diane started talking about the wedding. More like rambling on.

Malachi smiled, nodded at the appropriate times and threw in an "Uh huh" and a "Really?" After awhile his brain began to grow numb from listening to intricate details about bridesmaids in strapless red gowns, junior bridesmaids in ivory gowns with red trim and spaghetti straps and something about a flower girl dressed in candy apple red. When she brought up her choice of possible wedding songs, he thought he was going to run out the house screaming. Malachi searched his conscience for what recent sin he could've possibly committed to deserve this.

Jenna clasped her hands. Why was Diane discussing the wedding with Malachi? She doesn't even like him.

Julian glared at Diane. He didn't invite Malachi inside so that he could suffer through her mindless chatter.

Their father was about to speak his mind when Lauren, sensing trouble ahead, said, "Di, Mom probably needs some help in the kitchen." With that, they excused themselves and left the living room.

Malachi adjusted his collar. *Thank God.*

His feeling of relief was only temporary. They're going to the kitchen. *Would there be skeletons in there?*

Julian leaned back in the sofa. "Now, tell me Malachi, why was your car parked halfway down the road?"

Malachi hesitated. "You don't know?"

"Would I be asking if I did?"

Malachi rubbed his hand over his low-cut hair. Julian's tone wasn't friendly. *Note to file: Do not mess with this guy.* Evidently, Jenna's parents didn't communicate, otherwise her father would've known that the unusual parking was his wife's idea.

Jenna winced. This was so embarrassing.

"You know why, Daddy. I told you remember?"

"'That's the way we do it' is not an answer," Julian said. "And while you're at it you can explain why Malachi's never been inside this house."

Jenna looked at her father wide-eyed.

"Well, it's fairly obvious," Julian said. "So what's the story?"

Jenna looked down at her lap.

Malachi helped himself to another canapé. This time he chose the one topped with roast beef. He looked at Julian. The man was staring at him, waiting for an answer. Malachi wondered at which time he felt more uncomfortable now or at the wedding when Bella, Lauren and Diane surrounded him and Jenna. When Julian invited him in, he thought it would be interesting if not enjoyable. First, Diane nearly killed him with boredom with her nuptial plans. Now he's in the middle of some kind of uber dispute between Jenna and her parents. On top of everything else, the inside of Jenna's house resembled his nightmare.

Malachi concentrated on the roast beef canapé as he searched his mind for a polite way to exit. There wasn't any. They had to answer. He didn't have to look at Alan and Elise. He could feel the discomfort oozing out of their pores. Malachi turned his attention back to Julian. *Does this man ever blink?*

Bells started going off in his head again. *Leave. Go while you still can.*

Malachi finished chewing his canapé. The roast beef didn't stimulate his mind. He didn't have a clever speech for Julian Crandall. *Maybe I should've had the smoked salmon canapé. Fish is brain food.* Jenna's lap still fascinated her. *Terrific.* She wasn't going to be much help. Straightforwardness was the only way to handle this. Julian Crandall could smell a lie for miles.

Bella slammed the pepper mill on the kitchen counter. How dare Julian invite Dr. Chase into *her* home? She picked up the pepper mill and began to season the tenderloin. "What were you two thinking, provoking Jenna?" She lowered her voice. "You know when she gets upset she calls Rosa. Suppose she showed up while your father and Elise were here?" Bella put down the pepper mill. "I thought it was bad when Lauren opened the door about Jenna having a friend. But for you, Diane, to even mention Rosa's name was unbelievably stupid."

Diane's eyes started welling up with tears. She goofed. Royally. She couldn't look at the ferocity in her mother eyes. Instead, she stared into the pot of water boiling on the stove.

Bella saw her daughter's grief and she didn't care. Diane was dear to her, but she knew the rules. *Foolish girl.*

Lauren couldn't comfort her younger sister or defend their actions. They did ask for it. With a remorseful expression, she picked up a knife and began to peel the potatoes for the salad. She forgot what Jenna was like when Rosa was around. It'd been so long since they had to deal with that whack job.

"And you of all people, Lauren, "Bella went on, "should know that 'the fish dies by its mouth.'"

Lauren stopped peeling and slowly lowered her hands. She first heard the Portuguese proverb from her pre-law professor. Fond of the adage, she repeated it to her mother. Now she was using it against her. She turned away to blink back tears.

"What happened this afternoon must never happen again. "Is that understood?"

"Yes, Mom," Lauren and Diane replied in unison.

Lauren went back to peeling potatoes. She swallowed then turned her thoughts to Nelson. That would help her to feel better.

"Jenna's no longer content to go off and sulk," Bella said. "Something else is going on. I can't put my finger on it." They heard footsteps approaching. "We'll discuss it later."

Alan entered the kitchen.

"So, did Jenna and Dr. Chase finally leave?" Bella asked.

"No, but they're about to." Alan shoved his hands into the pocket of his khakis. "It would be nice if you said something to them." He thought about what Lauren and Diane had said about their mother not wanting Jenna to date. Maybe she did drive Everett away.

Bella turned her back to her son and resumed seasoning the tenderloin.

"So, what are you going to do? Stay back here and hide yourself?"

Slowly, Bella turned around and stared fixedly at Alan.

Diane gasped. Lauren raised her eyebrows. Still smarting from her mother's attack on her dignity, she wondered what had gotten into her brother.

Ordinarily, Alan would've been intimidated but feeling encouraged by his father's demands for answers and buoyed by Jenna's boldness even if the source of it was questionable, he decided to try once again to stand up to his mother.

"We know you don't like Malachi," Alan said. "He wouldn't have said anything, but Dad wanted answers."

Bella couldn't wait to hear what else he had to say. Her son had suddenly developed a spine.

When he saw how calm his mother was, Alan went on. "You have some explaining to do."

"I don't have to explain a damn thing."

Alan ignored his mother's swearing. "Did you, Lauren and Diane do that kind of stuff to Everett that you've been doing to Malachi?"

Bella picked up a bottle of allspice. She started sprinkling its contents over the tenderloin. Lauren and Diane stood by silently.

"You're so guilty you can't even come up with an excuse."

Bella turned and stared at him with cold eyes. "Feeling gutsy aren't we?"

Alan felt his confidence slipping away. Did he make a mistake in coming in here to confront her?

"I'll be right back." She walked past Alan, who instinctively, stepped aside.

When he turned back to Lauren and Diane, they were staring at him in disbelief.

"You have a death wish," Lauren said.

"What did you guys think about Jenna's behavior?" Alan asked, ignoring the comment.

Lauren sniffed. "What about it?"

"You saw the signs." Alan lowered his voice. "Rosa's back."

Lauren sighed with exasperation. "Didn't we have this conversation?"

"Yes, and I don't care what you say. Rosa's back. I know it."

"Well you're wrong," Diane said. Picking up the hint from Lauren and going along with the deceit, she played along. It's what Mom would've wanted. "And so what if she was? We've dealt with her before."

"You're kidding right? Have you forgotten the stunts that Rosa used to pull?"

"It's been sixteen years," Lauren said.

"So imagine what she must be like now."

"If Rosa was here, don't you think Mom would've said something?" Lauren asked.

"No." Alan looked over his shoulder before continuing. "She thinks she can keep on hiding her existence, but she's making a huge mistake. Rosa is dangerous."

"Oh stop exaggerating," Lauren said.

"She set fire to the storage shed or have you forgotten? And if I were you I'd be worried."

"Okay I'll bite," Lauren said. "Why should we be worried?"

"Rosa's sanity is questionable."

They stared at him in dubious silence.

"Come on," Alan said. "It must've crossed your minds."

"What difference does it make?" Diane asked. "Rosa went away."

"Uh huh. I fell into that same trap too believing that from then on it would all work itself out. Well guess what? She's back. How do I know? Jenna's behavior. At the wedding, she was a live wire. Do you know Jenna to ever be that exuberant?"

Lauren smirked. "Must you read into everything?"

"This is no time for your courtroom tricks. Every grievance Jenna has she tells Rosa." Alan refused to allow their skepticism to discourage him. "Don't you think she's going to tell Rosa how you two and Mom treated her just now? Her lashing out just now didn't convince you that trouble's ahead and that we need to do something about it?"

The water came to a boil. Diane poured the egg noodles into the pot. Maybe Alan had a point. Was it possible that Rosa Garrison was crazy?

"You two knew that Jenna wanted to go to art school didn't you?" Of course. They're Mom's right hand.

Lauren finished peeling the potatoes and began washing them off. "And what if we did?"

"You could've told me what Mom was doing to her."

"And what would you have done?" Lauren asked. "You were rapt up with Elise and your architectural career."

Alan clenched his teeth. "I have always had Jenna's back which is more than I can say for you two."

Lauren smirked. "And so far you've done a bang-up job."

Alan was about to retort, but changed his mind. He had something more important to say and he only had but so much time to say it. Their mother would be back shortly.

"It's time we did what should've been done a long time ago," Alan said.

"What do you mean?" Lauren asked.

"I think you know."

Lauren thought for a moment. Then her eyes widened. "Now I know you're an ass. No one can know about Rosa.

Diane gasped. "Think of our reputation."

"Mom made the three of us a part of this," Alan said. "And Lauren, you of all people know that you can't go to court with dirty hands."

Lauren looked at him with the take-no-prisoners expression she reserved only for the courtroom. She would tolerate a lecture from Mom but not from Alan. "Leave it alone, bro."

They stared at each other like two wolves, each waiting for the other one to charge.

Diane stared nervously at the kitchen's entrance. "Forget about Alan. Mom'll be back any minute and—"

She froze. Lauren and Alan relaxed their stance as they heard their mother's footsteps coming down the hall.

"All right, Dr. Chase and your sister just left, Bella said entering the kitchen. She stared pointedly at Alan. "And I spoke to *him*. Happy?" Noticing Lauren and Alan's frigid poses and the jitteriness of Diane, Bella grew wary. "What is it now?"

"Alan thinks Rosa's back," Diane said.

Lauren crossed her arms. And that we should tell Dad."

Bella squared her shoulders. "I see." She walked up to Alan and got up into his face.

He smelled a mixture of Givenchy and seasonings.

"I thought I told you that Rosa isn't here. So even if you did tell all of Gordonville about her you would look pretty silly."

Alan backed away. She was too close. He didn't like her being so close.

"So that's why you came in here trying to be manly. Have you told your wife about Rosa?"

Alan opened his mouth, but nothing came out. It wasn't that simple. The answer was more than a simple yes or no.

"You couldn't tell her could you?"

No. But only because it wouldn't have been fair to tell Elise about another sister without telling Dad first.

"*I* will deal with Rosa," Bella said. "If and when I see her."

"You never dealt with her properly in the first place." Surprise registered on Alan's face as he realized that he still possessed some residual nerves. He pressed on. "You promised Dad you'd take care of the baby. I overheard the whole thing."

Bella stood like a statue. The kitchen grew deathly quiet except for the sound of boiling water. Lauren and Diane drew near to each other, each wondering what was about to happen next.

Bella was aware of the sound of bubbling water and of her children's eyes on her. *Alan knew all this time.*

"I didn't understand what Dad meant at the time," Alan went on, aware that he was skating on thin ice, but now that he had let the cat out of the bag, he had to see the argument all the way.

Bella came out of her stone-like pose. "Are you threatening me?"

"No. I just think . . . I just think we should do the right thing."

"You keep your damn mouth shut," Bella said.

Alan felt something cold go through him as his mother swore at him.

"Now get the hell out of my house."

He shouldn't have been surprised and yet he was. His own mother was throwing out him and his wife from her home. His childhood home. A lump formed in his throat. Alan choked back tears. "You're playing with fire. And someday you're gonna burn."

He walked out.

"Jenna has got to get out of that house before they make her crazy," Elise said as she and Alan were driving home. I was glad you decided to leave."

Alan concentrated on the road. He couldn't tell her that her mother-in-law threw him out which technically meant that she had to leave too.

He had enough on his mind without having to listen to Elise screech all afternoon.

"Let's stop at Delsey's for lunch," Elise suggested.

"Sure." Not that he was hungry. He was still hurting from his mother's callousness. Elise was probably starving. She didn't eat much of the hors d'oeuvres and they did leave before lunch.

"So what's the deal with this Rosa?" Elise asked.

Alan went cold. And it wasn't from the car's air conditioning. "She was bad news."

"Jenna was really friends with someone that bad even your mother doesn't want to talk about her? That doesn't sound like Jenna."

Alan concentrated on the road.

"You never mentioned her before," Elise said.

Alan turned on the car radio. The soothing sound of jazz music filled the car. He concentrated on the smooth sounds of the trumpet and put all thoughts of Rosa Garrison and his family behind him. Unfortunately, the peace only lasted for a few seconds. *They're lying.* Why allow a crazed woman to run around? That's who're they're dealing with. A grownup demented female. *How could they be so idiotic?* Alan pursed his lips. His mother's need to keep a dark secret was stronger than logic or moral fiber.

"So how did Bella manage to stop Jenna from hanging out with Rosa?" Elise asked, cutting into his thoughts.

Alan nearly choked the steering wheel.

Let it go already.

She was poking into things that he wasn't prepared to share with her right now. He was relieved that they were approaching Main Street. Hopefully, she'll be distracted when they reached town.

"Mom didn't do anything," Alan said. "Jenna and Rosa simply disassociated."

At least that part was true.

"Why?"

Alan sighed. "I don't know."

That part was true too.

12

Malachi threw Jenna a quick glance. He was driving for nearly five minutes and she still hadn't uttered a word since they left the house. She just sat, there staring. No doubt, Jenna was embarrassed about having to explain the parking situation to her father. It got even worse after they told Julian about the weird dating schedule. Malachi grinned. It was a treat watching Lauren and Diane squirm when their father gave them the evil eye. He was also glad that Julian said he wouldn't confront his wife about her bad conduct in the past. He'd gone through enough conflict and discomfort for one afternoon.

It was irritating to listen to Mrs. Crandall greet him with her phony hello and making fake conversation. She must've been in great pain to do that.

He was just glad to be out of that house. It was a beautiful, sunny afternoon and he was determined to spend every precious moment with Jenna. Malachi sighed. "Forget about what happened and let's just have a good time, okay?"

Jenna played with the zipper of her handbag. She forced herself to smile. "Okay." *I'll try.* She looked out the passenger window at the cornfield. Mom was sure to seek revenge. *I defied her—in front of others.* She started rubbing her temple. Rosa's offer was beginning to look good.

"I have to attend a conference in L.A. on Wednesday," Malachi said.

"How long will you be gone?"

"The rest of the week."

"I'll miss you."

Malachi smiled. "I'll call you every day. I'll be back before you know it." They drove in silence for a few seconds. Then he said, "So another wedding."

Jenna didn't know what to say to that. So she said nothing.

Malachi was persistent. "That's some rock Larry put on Diane's finger."

Jenna snorted. "With any luck she'll knock herself unconscious with it."

"Well at least you're talking." He had to do something about her mood. "I have an idea."

Minutes later, they were standing at a rest area on a mountaintop. Before them were verdant hills and valleys. Villages and hamlets dotted the landscape.

With his arms around her, Malachi said, "This is *my meadow.* I come here whenever students or colleagues work my nerve or when I just need to hear myself think."

"It's beautiful."

For a while, they stood side by side watching the view. Then, Malachi led Jenna over to some nearby benches and picnic tables. When they sat down, he put his arm around her. She put her head on his shoulder. Malachi smiled to himself. Today she smelled like vanilla. "Talk to me."

His warmth surrounded her. She felt protected. Valued.

Jenna breathed in the scent of his spicy cologne.

Presently, she found herself telling him everything that happened, from the ridicule of her receptionist job to her decision to attend art school to Lauren and Diane's mockery of Rosa to her mother's resentment over her leaving during a family affair.

"Why didn't you tell me?"

"I was embarrassed. And explaining my family is complicated. I can't explain them to myself. I'm surprised you still want to go out with me."

Malachi smiled. "It's amazing what I overlook when I care about someone."

Jenna's heart leaped at his tender words.

"But something doesn't make sense," Malachi began. "Why were your sisters laughing about Rosa?" From the little Jenna told him, Rosa didn't sound like a funny person.

"I don't know."

He didn't believe her, but he gave her the benefit of the doubt.

"Rosa always hated them." Jenna pretended to inspect her fingernails. Being around Malachi made her feel so relaxed, she was becoming loose-lipped. She had to be more careful. "You know, forget what I said."

Malachi stared at a knot in the woodwork on the picnic table. He couldn't forget. The skeletons did call out Rosa's name. "Why did Rosa hate your mother and sisters?" Jenna listened to the finches calling. "I was seven. Lauren got a raspberry-colored cashmere sweater from Daddy for her Sweet 16. I love purple. When I got a chance, I went to her room to try it on." Jenna smiled at the memory. "The sweater was too big for me and it was oh so soft." She became serious. "Then, Lauren caught me with it. She went ballistic. She even accused me of trying to steal it."

"That was a bit much," Malachi said.

"It was quintessential Lauren," Jenna said with resentment."

Malachi hated that her sister caused her to feel this way. Yet, he was glad that Jenna was feeling something, much better than retreating into herself.

"She screamed for Mom," Jenna went on, "who naturally, took her side." She tightened her grip on Malachi's hand. "Mom took off her slipper and began beating me with it."

Malachi clenched his jaw. Jenna did mention that her mother used to beat her.

"She said that God was going to strike with me with a bolt of lightning," Jenna said.

"That's terrible."

"She always said that," Jenna said bitterly. "That frightened me more than getting hit. On stormy days and nights, I thought I was a goner even if I didn't do anything wrong."

Malachi imagined how frightening it must've been for her. It infuriated him too. For Bella, a church elder, to portray God as a vengeful deity to an impressionable child was reprehensible.

And to her own child. Where was Julian during all this?

"Anyway, Alan heard the commotion and ran into Lauren's room," Jenna said. "He told Mom to stop, but before he could blink, Mom grabbed one of Lauren's belts then started beating him."

Malachi groaned. No wonder Alan's relationship with his mother appeared edgy. His annoyance intensified remembering how Bella paraded herself around the wedding reception while all along she was guilty of child abuse.

"Sometimes at night I can still hear the sounds of the belt tearing into his flesh," Jenna said.

Malachi could feel Jenna's body becoming taut like rope. "Shh. It's over now. It's all in the past."

Her arm began throbbing, as if reminding her that the abuse wasn't over. Not wanting Malachi to notice her discomfort, Jenna surreptitiously rubbed the spot where Bella grabbed her. Her mother hadn't touched her in years. She didn't want to tell him about what her mother had done to her in the kitchen. It was upsetting. And she definitely couldn't tell Rosa . . .

"You don't have to talk about this anymore," Malachi said.

"Lauren hardly wore that sweater," Jenna went on in a petulant tone, hungry for someone to listen to her. "She hated the color. I know 'cause I overheard her telling Diane. I loved anything Daddy bought me because it came from him."

Malachi looked pensive. "How old was Alan when this happened?"

"The twins were fourteen." Jenna winced. "Alan suffered putdowns and threats from Mom most of the time. I was the one who got the beatings. The only time he got smacked around was when he defended me."

"He's a good brother," Malachi said.

Jenna smiled. "He's the best." Her smile faltered. "If I did something that didn't make her happy, she'd pretend I wasn't there. I died inside every time. Rosa called it the S.T."

"S.T.?"

"Silent treatment," Jenna explained.

Malachi shook his head. The silent treatment was a demoralizing form of punishment, especially for a child. The goings-on behind the Crandall's charming home stunned him. "So, this is why Rosa hates your mother and sisters." The question was why. "Those times when your mother was abusing you and Alan, what were Lauren and Diane doing?"

"Laughing. It's what they always did. That and instigating."

Jenna sat up. "One good thing happened that day with the sweater. I met Rosa."

"Wasn't she questionable?"

"Not at first, silly. We were just little kids. It's when we got older she got a bit wild. She had her good points. She taught me that God wasn't going to strike me with lightening for wearing my sister's sweaters."

"Okay, now I'm curious. I know you said she got you into trouble. What exactly did Rosa do?"

Jenna made a face.

"That bad, huh? Well, gimme an example."

"Lauren was hanging out with her friends in the back yard. I came outside to play. Lauren says, 'How could you make yourself get so fat?' I was so embarrassed. All her friends were there."

"That was cruel," Malachi said. "How old were you?"

"Thirteen."

He made a face. Jenna was probably self-conscious about her looks.

"I told Rosa about it in school the next day," Jenna said. "She suggested we should go to my house after school and bake muffins. So, we did—with wheat."

Malachi looked confused.

"Lauren's allergic," Jenna explained. "She looked like she got attacked by a swarm of bees." Laughing, Jenna added, "Mom and Diane were so freaked out."

"That's sick."

"Well, she hurt my feelings." Now Jenna wished she hadn't told Malachi that story.

"So it's okay to poison your sister?"

"Told you Rosa was a bad influence."

"What did your parents say?"

"Mom didn't know what happened exactly. If she did, she didn't say. And no she didn't tell Daddy."

Malachi blinked a few times. "Why?"

Jenna shrugged. "Anyway, Lauren and Diane left me alone. That's the only thing that mattered to me. They got mean again. Then they stopped—after the fire."

"Fire?"

Oops. Jenna winced. That wasn't supposed to come up. "I was fifteen. Rosa was visiting. I guess I was so busy talking I forgot about my chores. Mom slapped me for not washing the dishes. I was so embarrassed. Imagine your mother slapping you in front of your friend? I was going to do the stupid dishes. Eventually." She paused then said, "While I was in the kitchen, Rosa went out to the backyard and . . . started a fire in the storage shed."

"What?"

"Rosa may be a little out there, but she's loyal."

"She doesn't sound like a healthy person." *Or a sane one.* No hard feelings, but I'm glad she's not around anymore. "Please tell me your mother told your father about the fire."

Jenna watched a ladybug land on the picnic table. It crawled along the top until it flew away again. "Daddy came over that day and when he saw the damage, Mom lied about how it started. She said it was, 'A mishap with the barbecue grill.'"

"She lied because . . . ?"

"Daddy doesn't know about Rosa." She sighed. "Mom likes to keep him on a need-to-know basis."

Jenna struggled to keep from laughing. Malachi had such a funny look on his face. Naturally, it must've sounded strange to him that her father knew nothing about her best friend. Shouldn't a parent know about his child's pals? She decided not to tell him that her father only found out about Rosa this afternoon. Malachi was shocked enough for one day.

This explains a lot. Why does Mrs. Crandall have so much say-so? "Why do I get the feeling that your father didn't know about the abuse?"

Her silence said it all.

"It's all in the past," Malachi said. "You can let it go."

Carefully, Jenna began rubbing her injured arm again.

Malachi let out a slow breath. Regardless of her parents' living arrangements, Julian should've known what was happening in his own family.

"Explain something to me," Malachi began. "Why didn't you and Alan tell your father what was going on?"

Jenna wrapped her arms around herself as if she were standing in the middle of Main Street in winter without a coat. "Mom's powerful."

Malachi stretched out his legs. "Confucius said, 'The superior man is distressed by his want of ability.' In other words some people make themselves seem larger than life to hide their lack of self-worth."

"I never thought my mother had a problem with her ego."

"And something's troubling her."

"What could possibly be troubling my mother? Nothing ever upsets her."

"You'd be surprised what hurts some of us. Did you hear anything that might shed some light as to why your father moved out? Think. You might know, but don't know that you know."

Jenna shrugged.

"How about moving in with your dad?" Malachi himself came from an extended family. Therefore, an adult child living at home was typical. He wondered if Jenna stayed home out of duress or apprehension.

"Mom would go postal."

Question answered. "You're here with me now," Malachi said. "If your mother had her way, you'd be home listening to Diane blathering on about her wedding." *A fate worse than death.* "And you told them that you were going to art school.

"You're in the wrong environment, Jenna. Malachi pointed to the landscape. "There's a whole big world out there. You have a lot of warmth, friendship and talent to offer. And you're pretty."

Jenna smiled shyly.

You should be with people who will appreciate you. Like me.

Jenna giggled.

Malachi was glad to hear her laugh after her startling revelation. Now that he had an even better understanding of her upbringing, he could see why anyone or anything that pertained to God would make her wary. Mrs. Crandall, Lauren and Diane, all supposedly pious, were hypocrites. Cruel. A string held her parents' marriage together.

He was hoping to decrease Jenna's caginess about Christianity by spending more time with her and having her meet other mature Christians. Again, warning bells sounded. Jenna had issues. The same nagging questions followed. Why stay where you're not wanted? Are you sure about this relationship?

I stay because Jenna wants me. It doesn't matter what her mother thinks or her sisters. And yes, I'm sure I want to stay. Jenna's not the problem.

Malachi shivered. Who was the woman in the dream? Rosa? *This is ridiculous. She's not around anymore. And it was just a dream.*

"Stop it," Malachi said.

"What?" Jenna asked.

For answer, he leaned forward and kissed her.

This was just how she imagined it except they weren't dressed up in a tuxedo and gown. She was getting another chance at a relationship. It took great effort to ignore the old pain still lingering in her heart and the alarm bells ringing in her head, threatening to drown out the beautiful music playing in her soul.

Malachi's pride soared. *She's kissing me back.* He didn't plan to kiss her although he wanted to for the longest time. Too many interruptions or the mood was all wrong.

When the kiss finally ended, Jenna smiled and said, "Now I know I can start over."

Malachi began nibbling on her neck, loving the aroma of her vanilla fragrance. "I'm an expert at that."

The feel of his warm breath against her neck made her shiver. "Something happened to you at your old job didn't it?"

"Don't ruin the moment."

She repositioned her body and gave him a long stare."

Malachi sighed. He owed her an explanation. She shared a difficult part of her life with him. That couldn't have been easy. "Like I said before, I was a stockbroker. I was determined to get to the top." He paused then said, "If I had to crush someone to get there, so be it."

"What did you do?" Jenna asked.

Malachi cleared his throat. "I'd pretend to be a colleague's friend, gain his trust, then use whatever information I got against him.

Jenna raised her eyebrows. Malachi a backstabber? This was unbelievable.

"I'm not that man anymore," he said hastily. Seeing the shock in her eyes made him feel even more uncomfortable.

"I know. I'm just . . . shocked. That's something Lauren or Diane would've done."

"There's no need to be insulting."

"You must've gotten a lot of people fired," Jenna said.

Malachi looked grim. "Yeah. I did. And demoted."

"Was it worth it?" She was finding it hard to believe that this handsome Bible thumper was once a jerk. On the other hand, it was a relief to know that he wasn't so perfect.

"At the time it was. I was one of the company's best. Earned the big paychecks, had the big bonuses, had all the perks. I partied, bought expensive toys." He used air quotes around the word toys. Malachi looked uncomfortable as he added, "Had lots of women. Then one day it was over. The company merged. They didn't need me anymore. Just like that.

"I had to sell some of my *toys* to cover my expenses. Still, my lifestyle caught up with me. I had to move back home. The bank foreclosed on my condo." Malachi stopped to watch a dragonfly hover above a bush then take flight. Thanks to my mom and dad I didn't have to go through the remainder of my retirement fund."

"Was it hard to face them? I mean . . . "

"How big a jerk was I to my family?" He wore a tiny smile. "I looked after them. That was my one redeeming quality."

"What happened to your homies?"

"You mean my fair-weather friends?" Malachi laughed dryly. "My only true friend was Brendan. Unfortunately, for me, he was here in Gordonville practicing law. He came down to the city when he could or when he had a case in Manhattan. That's where I lived after I moved out of my parents' house. Sometimes he and I would hang out on the weekends. Try to cheer me up." Malachi looked down at the ground. "He'd even slip me a few bucks."

"Now that's a friend," Jenna said. "Did Brendan know about the real you?"

"Yeah, he did." Malachi watched a chipmunk scurry across the way. He was grateful to Brendan for not abandoning him. He didn't know how he would've survived without his friendship.

Jenna kissed his nose. "So, because your bosses kicked your butt you ran crying to God."

"Not exactly in that order but yes, smarty pants."

"So what started you on this God thing?"

He was surprised she asked, considering she was leery about the Lord. "One morning I was on the subway and not in a good mood. I was on my way to this temp job as a stock boy. I hadn't worked for minimum wage since I was a teenager. My ego was pureed. I missed my old life. I had no privacy 'cause I was back home with my parents. I repeat: I was not in a good mood."

"This woman comes into the subway car preaching about Jesus. Listening to a sermon wasn't high on my list. And I was doubly ticked off because I forgot my walkman."

Jenna chuckled. "You had no choice but to listen."

"Oh I tuned her out. Anyway, somewhere in the middle of her sermon, she said something that grabbed my attention, 'Friends will leave you, jobs come and go, but God will never leave you.' It got me thinking. And the rest as they say is history."

"Didn't you already know that? You grew up in the church."

"Like I said, I was going to church, but I was just occupying space. I'll never forget the goofy smiles on my parents' faces when I started turning my life around. They'd been praying for me all along."

A shadow passed over Jenna's face.

Whoops. Go slow, Mal. "I decided to go back to school and study sociology. It was a pet subject of mine. I took electives in it when I was earning my bachelors." He grinned. "Turns out it's what I really wanted to do all along."

"But weren't you happy working as a stockbroker?"

"I thought I was."

"Your faith seems to be working for you," Jenna said. "Whatever it is maybe someday I'll have what you have."

He grinned. That's what he was praying for everyday.

"Malachi?"

"Yes?"

"Exactly how many women were you with?"

Malachi took her on a tour of Olana, the home of Frederic Edwin Church, an artist who played a major role in the Hudson River School of landscape painting. Later over a steak dinner, Jenna thought of the excitement of what she could accomplish as a studio artist, illustrator or a prop designer and the joy of having Malachi in her life. Emboldened by Malachi's talk not once did she think about her mother or her threats until they returned and saw the house.

It was completely dark.

13

Not even the porch light was on.

Malachi shivered. A quarter moon was casting shadows over the house creating an atmospheric gloom. He imagined a force coming down the brick walkway. He looked over at Jenna in the passenger seat. She wrapped her arms around herself. *She feels it too.*

"I have to go," Jenna said. The longer she stayed in the car, the longer she was prolonging the inevitable.

"I'll go with you."

"No, thanks. I'll be fine." She could only imagine what was waiting for her on the other side of the door. She didn't want him getting involved.

"I'm not afraid of your mother, Jenna." Malachi spoke in a slightly offended tone.

She adjusted her handbag. It wasn't her intention to offend him. She just had enough drama for one day.

"It's pitch black out there. You'd have to have eyes like a cat to see in the dark. At least let me see you to the front door." Malachi reached into the glove compartment and pulled out a flashlight. Shortly he was escorting her to her door, lighting the way.

For the second time that day, Malachi was standing at Jenna's front door. The flashlight took the place of the unlit porch light. He held Jenna tightly and thought about what she told him about her mother. Bella Crandall did some horrendous things right under her husband's nose and the community's. The abuse may have happened years ago, but he still didn't trust her. Even Alan was afraid of her. Would Jenna be all right while he was away in Los Angeles? "Promise me something, the first sign of trouble, call the police. And me."

Jenna looked a little surprised. "What do you think is going to happen?"

"Just promise me."

"Okay. It's because of what I told you isn't it?" The light from the flashlight he was holding showed his sheepish expression. Jenna smiled. "Don't worry."

"Sure you don't want me to come in?" Malachi asked.

"I'm sure." His being on the porch was risky enough.

Malachi kissed her. Then, reluctantly, he let her go. Jenna watched him walk down the steps and return to his car. She wanted to stay in his arms for a little while longer where she felt good and safe. She sighed and opened the door.

Malachi was still feeling uneasy even before he reached the corner of Jenna's street. *Father, please protect Jenna. And help me get her out of that nut house.*

Jenna stood inside the dimly lit hall. The only sound was the ticking of the grandfather clock. She leaned against the wall. Her legs felt like cooked spaghetti. She wished that Rosa were with her. Her mother could be in that hall waiting to grab her. Jenna was hoping that she was asleep upstairs. Then again, maybe it was better to face the inevitable. Snippets of her conversation with Malachi came back to her.

"*Maybe I can start over . . . You have a lot of warmth, friendship and talent . . . Be with people . . . who will appreciate it.*"

She heard a chair scraping across the floor. She leaped at the sound. It came from the kitchen.

Mom is awake.

Jenna turned up the dimmer switch. It's best to face the music. She headed down the hall.

When she arrived at the entrance to the kitchen, she gasped. In the shadowy room, Jenna saw what she thought was a giant praying mantis. She felt along the wall for the light switch. As soon as the lights came on, they revealed Bella sitting at the kitchen table, arms poised like the greenish-brown predatory insect; fury emblazoned upon her face. Jenna turned to run then stopped. She wanted to make a change. If she was going to do that, she had to take a stand.

Bella arose from the chair. "Get over here."

Jenna didn't want to move, yet her legs seemed to have a mind of their own. She wanted those guts she had earlier to return. She wanted to feel that forceful energy, but she couldn't evoke it.

Where did it go?

Rosa's prediction came back to haunt her. " . . . *You'll fold like a lawn chair.*"

"I knew you were going to be trouble," Bella said. "I knew it from the start."

Jenna could barely speak. "Don't say that."

"You were a wayward child. Now you've grown up to be a degenerate woman."

"That's not true."

"I know you, Jenna. I know you better than your father or your professor." Bella smiled with contempt. "I know you better than you know your own self. Rosa was behind your shameful behavior."

Jenna felt a modicum of nerve. "Nothing I did had anything to do with her."

Bella shook her head. "This is not you. Rosa put you up to this."

"Stop blaming her. It was all me."

Bella looked at Jenna warily. "Is Rosa in this house?"

"I said no."

"So, have you told Dr. Chase about her?"

"As a matter of fact, yes."

Bella gave Jenna a quizzical look. "What exactly did you tell him?"

"That she was a good friend."

"Was? So he doesn't know you two are still in touch?"

"No." Jenna fiddled with her hair again.

"So you're lying to him." Bella posed the question like a statement.

Jenna wanted to tell her mother that she was in no position to ridicule. Didn't she have secrets too? Like how badly Mom treated her and Alan all these years and that she's been keeping Rosa a secret from everyone. However, she kept quiet.

"So what else did you tell him?" Bella asked.

Jenna rubbed her temple. "She had a few quirks."

"Is that what you call them? Rosa should've been committed long time ago."

Jenna's face fell. She was twelve years old the first time her mother said that to her. It hurt as much now as it did back then. Rosa was her best friend and her mother had believed that she was a mental case. She held back tears.

Usually she told Rosa everything, yet she never told her what her mother said about her. She couldn't. Rosa had a thick skin except when it came to her mom and sisters. She would've reacted fast.

" . . . *They'll work you over and you'll fold like a lawn chair.*"

Tears began falling down Jenna's cheeks. Rosa was so right about them. Why didn't she listen?

Bella stared at her with loathing. "You think you can move me with your tears?"

Jenna sobbed.

"I don't care what Julian, Alan or Elise thinks. If Dr. Chase calls my phone again or sets foot on my property, I'll call the police."

Jenna looked at her mother in dismay. Rosa acted more like a sister to her than Lauren and Diane ever were. In a short time, Malachi became her rock. Jenna put a finger to her lips where Malachi had planted kisses.

"And if I catch Rosa in this house, I'll do the same," Bella said. She stormed out the kitchen.

Jenna shook her head. "No."

She recalled Rosa's words from long ago. *"They're dream stealers . . . You know your mother has no use for you . . . It should've been your wedding."*

She was about to lose another love. *No. Not again. Not this time.* Despair turned to rage.

Jenna ran out the kitchen and confronted her mother in the hall. "Go to hell!"

Bella grabbed a fistful of Jenna's hair then started banging her head against into the wall. Jenna slid to the floor like sludge. She stared at her mother in disbelief. She knew she shouldn't have been surprised. Hadn't her mother been hitting her lately?

But not like this.

"This is my house," Bella began interrupting her thoughts. "And you will respect me and this family. Make sure you tell that to Rosa the next time you see her." Bella stormed down the hall. She stomped up the stairs. From upstairs, a door slammed.

Ashamed, Jenna felt as if a million pairs of eyes were watching her. She lay across the hardwood floor, staring at the molding running alongside the staircase and the railings then the spindles as if they held some kind of meaning. Jenna closed her eyes and brought forth the pleasant memory of the time she spent with Malachi. His warmth. His encouragement. His kisses. From that, she found the strength to sit up. Miraculously, her head didn't hurt. Just her pride.

At that moment, her cell phone rang, breaking the sepulchral silence. Jenna reached into the pocket of her jeans and pulled out her phone. Malachi's number appeared on the display. She wanted to let it go to voicemail. Ordinarily, she never refused to take his calls, but she was in no shape to speak with him now. Then again, he might think the worst and come rushing over. He was already nervous about her being alone with her mother. The last time they were together, he acted as if something terrible was going to happen.

Something did. *But I can't tell him.* He knows too much already. *Suppose Mom knew what I really told him? I'd be dead now. Maybe that was better.* Then a picture of Malachi formed in her mind. She remembered the good time she had. No. Death wasn't better. She had plenty to live for.

I think. Yes. She had to believe it. Jenna put on a bright smile then answered her cell before the call went to voicemail. "Hey, Mal . . . Sure, everything's fine." She heard water running upstairs. "Mom's getting ready for bed."

Bella stepped out of the hall bath then looked around. Empty. Quickly, she returned to her bedroom then closed the door. She went to her dresser then opened an antique English jewelry box. She rifled through it until she found an old-fashioned key. Shortly, she returned to the door, pushed the key in, then turned the lock. She sighed. At night, she liked to relax in her bedroom with a cup of Earl Grey and a good book. Not tonight. The last time she laid hands on Jenna Rosa set fire to the storage shed.

Bella walked over to the bed then picked up her blue nightie. Jenna must be talking to Rosa. She could feel it. She was probably on her way now. The nightgown shook in Bella's trembling hands. She put it down and decided to remove her makeup first.

Something was off. Rosa was the sassy one. Not Jenna. *She mouthed off to me.* She wished she hadn't insisted on Jenna taking part in Lauren and Nelson's wedding. Then she wouldn't have met Dr. Malachi Chase.

Nervous, she looked over her shoulder at the door. "No," Bella said aloud to herself. "I won't be afraid in my own home."

Finished with removing her makeup, Bella walked back over to the bed and started changing into her nightgown. That's when she heard the footsteps coming up the stairs. Bella rushed over to the door and tested the lock. It was secure. The footsteps came closer. Bella's breathing grew labored. She glanced over at her antique 1930's desk phone on the night table. Should she call the police? She'd have to tell them that Rosa was in the house. She wasn't ready to reveal details about that other Crandall. Some secrets should stay buried.

The footsteps stopped. *Outside her door.* Bella stopped breathing. She stared at the doorknob, waiting for it to turn. Now the footsteps started again. *She's walking away!* She didn't breathe until the footsteps faded.

Jenna didn't remember climbing the stairs. She didn't remember getting into bed either, yet somehow, she ended up in her bedroom. Still dressed in her street clothes, she climbed into bed. She picked up her pillow and held it against her stomach. The events of the day had taken their toll on her: preparing the house for her sisters' arrival, enduring their insults, the showdown with her mother and now this assault.

In the safety of her sanctuary, Jenna cried. She cried until she had no more tears left to shed. Not even thinking about Malachi restored her joy. Then, she began rocking. Back and forth. Back and forth. Back and forth . . .

The next morning, Jenna woke up to a sun-filled room, chickadees singing outside her bedroom window and a slight headache. She sat up, stretched, then groaned from sleeping in a bad position. She had fallen asleep with her head slumped over. Jenna stood up. She teetered. She sat back down on the edge of her bed and waited for the vertigo to pass.

Later on, Jenna showered then changed into a clean tie-dye T-shirt, walking shorts and put her hair in a ponytail. Then, she went to the bedroom window and looked out. She saw her mother standing by the gate. She was dressed in a beige pantsuit with matching fedora. She was holding her purse and her Bible.

Jenna narrowed her eyes at the sight of the huge black leather-bound holy book.

Bella was waiting for the church van when a chill went up her spine. Slowly, she turned and looked up at the attic window. Jenna was staring down at her. Bella held the Bible to her as if it would protect her from Jenna's wrath beaming down at her from the attic window. No doubt, she was still angry about last night. She didn't come down for breakfast. She hardly slept a wink last night. She had to use eye makeup to hide the dark circles under eyes from lack of sleep. How would it appear if the congregants saw her looking poorly?

Even though she closed her bedroom door, she kept listening out for the sound of a low crackling fire or the sound of a certain visitor . . . Lauren and Diane told her after about Alan's certainty that Rosa was a dangerous potential psycho. His talk of impending danger must have gotten into her head last night, causing her to overreact.

Bella snorted. "Alan is so concerned about Jenna. Bella turned away as anguish filled her chest. Well, I feel hurt too—about a lot of things . . . "

She saw the church van approaching. She looked up at the attic window again. A baleful looking Jenna was still looking down at her. Bella turned away as a sudden rush of panic and grief overwhelmed her.

"You promised Dad you'd take care of the baby."

Bella choked back a sob. Alan's voice reminding her of the past played over in her head. "Damn you, Amelia."

By the time the church van pulled up to the front gate, Bella was all smiles. She took one last peek at the attic window. Jenna was gone. Bella greeted her fellow church members as she boarded the bus.

Jenna went to her night table and picked up her cell phone. "Rosa, I need your help."

14

"You know what woulda happened if I was here last night?" Rosa asked after Jenna filled her in on everything that happened yesterday. They gathered in Jenna's attic bedroom.

Jenna sniffled. Things would've been—messy. For years she avoided this moment, but after last night, she realized that if she didn't do something to save herself, she might die.

Rosa started pacing the room. "So, Bella's threatening to call the cops on me."

"And Malachi."

Rosa got off the bed from where she had been sitting and walked over to the dresser. She picked up a statuette of a unicorn and threw it across the room. It shattered after it hit the wall. "She hasn't hit you in years. Suddenly, she's grabbing your arm one day and using your head as a battering ram another. She's gettin' bold, Jenna. And you know why?"

"I didn't listen to you." Jenna sounded tired. Defeated.

Rosa walked over to the dormer window. She stared down at the tea roses, daisies and hollyhocks in the front yard garden. She could've ripped off Bella's head from the moment she walked through the door . . . "You know what has to be done now, right?"

"I think I'm gonna be sick." Jenna sank to the floor.

"Easy, girlfriend." Rosa joined her on the floor. "Take deep breaths."

Jenna followed her advice. After the nausea passed, she said, "Maybe God can fix it." Perhaps there was a small chance that blood didn't have to spill.

Rosa studied Jenna. "You're backing out." She stood up then kicked a pair of Jenna's loafers out of the way.

"I like those shoes."

"*I'm* the only one you can depend on. If God cared so much, why'd He stick you with them? Enough about religion."

Jenna wanted to tell her what Malachi said; that it wasn't about religion. It was about having a relationship with God, but she kept quiet. It wouldn't have gone over very well.

"I'm gonna do it in chronological order," Rosa began. "First Bella, then Lauren then Diane."

"Sounds like you already figured it out," Jenna said.

"Girl, I've been waitin' for you to come to your senses."

"How are you going to pull this off?" Jenna asked. Lauren lives in Pound Ridge and Diane is in Manhattan."

"Once I take mama bear out of the picture, they'll come. I just need to work out a few details. In the meantime, play it cool. Let Bella think she has the upper hand." Jenna smiled satisfactorily. "She'll relax and then I'll strike."

Jenna twirled her hair around her finger.

"What's wrong?" Rosa asked.

"Mom knows you're still around."

"*What?* How?"

"I don't know. I was careful. At least I thought I was." All this talk was disturbing. She hated her mother for making her have to put this horrible plan into action. "Do your brother and sisters know?"

"They haven't said anything to me."

Rosa sighed. "Too late now anyway. If my name comes up, neither verify nor confirm. And whatever you do say nothing about this conversation to anyone."

"What about Alan? He still looks out for me."

"But he doesn't have the nerve to deal with Bella. He could become a problem. And I think I make him nervous."

"Yeah?"

"He gets jittery whenever I'm around. Didn't you notice?"

"No."

"Anyway, don't breathe a word of this to Malachi."

Jenna winced then told her that he already knew about their friendship. "But he doesn't know that we're still hanging out. She sighed. "I hate lying to him."

"Well you have to."

"But he's in my corner." Jenna told Rosa about Malachi's support. "He hates what Mom, Lauren and Diane have been doing."

"That's good to know. But may I remind you that Malachi's a Christian? You really think you could tell him you're planning to eighty-six your mother and sisters?"

"Well, no, but—"

"He can't know about the plan."

Jenna threw her hands up in the air. "Even I don't know the plan."

"You're on a need-to-know basis. Like your dad." Rosa's face lit up like a Christmas tree. "I'll finally get to meet Julian. And Bella can't stop me." She looked at Jenna fondly. "It's good to be back." Jenna smiled. It was nice having company again.

"I'm hungry," Rosa said. "Let's eat."

Jenna looked at the broken figurine. "Sure. After, we clean up your mess."

A half hour later, they were having tea, whole-wheat toast and scrambled eggs. Teacup in hand, Rosa walked around the kitchen. It had been a long time since she'd been in this room, let alone this house. She began chortling, recalling the times that she got underneath Bella, Lauren and Diane's skin.

Rosa returned to her seat. She buttered a slice of bread. She looked over at the dish rack. She saw a small cast-iron pan then smiled.

"What?" Jenna asked.

Rosa looked at the door leading to the backyard. "I want to walk around the backyard."

"You have a plan."

"Need-to-know-basis, Jen."

The church van dropped off Bella. She smiled and waved at her friends and parishioners as they drove away. Then her smile vanished. Before going through the gate, Bella paused to look up at the attic. Jenna wasn't at the dormer window. Bella breathed a sigh of relief then opened the gate.

From the foyer, the aroma of fresh brewed coffee and cinnamon greeted her. Jenna had finally come out of her room. Bella was about to close the front door when she heard a voice. A familiar voice.

She's here. Bella swallowed. *No. I will not be afraid.* Bella closed the door. All conversation ceased.

She could hear chairs scraping back and footsteps clicking across the floor. Then, she heard the backdoor open and close. Regaining her courage, Bella smiled. They didn't expect her home yet. It's a good thing she declined having another cup of tea and a third slice of Norma Beery's German chocolate cake.

Scowling, Bella marched down the hall to the kitchen. Finally she would put a stop to this. This was her home.

*

Jenna was clearing the table when Bella arrived, which she noticed, was set for two. Rosa was nowhere in sight. She looked suspiciously at the backdoor. Odd. Why didn't she stay and bait her? That was her style.

"So you waited until I left the house to call that freak," Bella said.

Jenna nearly smashed the dirty dishes as she was putting them into the sink. She resented her mother calling her best friend by that name. It was at the tip of her tongue to say something especially now that Rosa officially had her back again, but she remembered her instructions to play it cool. With great difficulty she calmly let the insult slide as her mother stood there holding the Good Book.

"I don't know what your game is," Bella continued, "but you tell your little friend she's not welcome here."

"Rosa's not little anymore, Mom." She just had to stay it.

Bella flinched. She looked at Jenna with distaste. "I won't be around forever. Then, you'll see how helpful Rosa is." She flounced out the kitchen.

"That's what I'm counting on." Jenna smiled like a fox.

15

The following Saturday, Jenna was humming a tune while she polished the dining room floor and thought about Malachi. He returned from the conference late last night. Even though he called her every night from Los Angeles, she still missed him and she wanted to see him. But there was a problem. Now that she and Rosa planned to get rid of Jenna's problem, there was no need for her to live with her father. Jenna leaned on the handle of the floor cleaner. Malachi was going to ask her if she'd spoken to her father about living with him. She didn't have an excuse for Malachi if he were to ask. Knowing Malachi, he would ask.

She had to buy herself some much-needed time before she saw Malachi. She hadn't asked her father about moving in with him. Of course, he would've said yes, but now that she asked for Rosa's help, it was no longer necessary. She needed to stay home. It was strategic.

Jenna's cell phone vibrated. Rosa.

"Meet me at the farmhouse 12:30," she said after Jenna greeted her. "And bring your mother's small cast-iron pan."

"Okaay."

Rosa hung up.

Jenna frowned in puzzlement. What could she possibly want with that? She was putting the phone back in its clip just as Bella was passing by. "I'm done with the floor. Anything else you want me to do?"

Bella looked at her suspiciously. "Who were you talking to?"

Jenna leaned on the handle of the floor cleaner.

"Was it Rosa?"

"No."

Her mother was looking at her suspiciously, but she kept cool. *"Let Bella think she has the upper hand."* That's what Rosa wanted. "If you don't need me, I'm going out."

"With Dr. Chase or Rosa?"

Jenna counted to ten. Refusing to dignify her mother with an answer, she picked up the can of floor polish and walked out the dining room.

"Be back in time," Bella commanded.

"Yes, Mom." It was frustrating having to follow Rosa's guidance sometimes.

Jenna was in her room changing when there was a knock on her bedroom door. "Yes?"

Bella entered, her face was as animated as a child in a toy store was. "I just got off the phone with Diane. She's back in town. She's staying at The Lorelei House. She's in the Water Lily Suite." The French Normandy manor was Gordonville's premier bed and breakfast inn. It was located downtown on picturesque Green Street a boulevard of antique residential commercial properties.

Jenna continued getting dressed. Why did her mother think she cared about the details of her sister's accommodations?

"She made an appointment with a realtor," Bella said.

"Oh?"

"Larry wants to be close by to some of his clients."

Jenna began rubbing her arms and hands with baby oil. By the nauseatingly happy look on her mother's face and giddiness in her voice, she was waiting for her to skip around her bedroom.

"Diane wants you, me and Julian to come along," Bella said. Be ready to leave in an hour. Wear sensible shoes." Bella turned to leave.

Jenna frowned in disbelief. Did you tell her that I had plans?"

"What for?"

"So she blows into town, makes a request and I'm supposed to drop my plans?" Jenna checked her watch. 11:15 AM. "Diane must've gotten here last night and she calls us now? Perish the thought we had something to do today. She has a fiancé."

"Larry is in Italy," Bella said in a cool tone. She lifted her chin. "We're family. We support each other."

"Alan and Elise are family too, but did Diane ask them to come along? No." To heck with not making waves. This was just another opportunity to ruin her plans and shop for real estate at the same time.

"I don't like your tone," Bella said.

"You and Daddy go with her. Better yet, let Lauren go. I bet she knew that Diane was here before you did."

From the thunderous look on Bella's face, Jenna knew that she had struck a nerve.

"You sound a lot like Rosa," Bella said.

"Would you leave her out of this?" A warning from deep within was telling her to be still, but she couldn't stop herself. "Why do I have to forfeit my afternoon? "Who's Diane anyway?"

Bella lifted her hand. Jenna put her arms up to defend herself against a blow. To her surprise, her mother didn't strike her. Instead, she lowered her hand. Jenna did the same only for her mother to use that moment to quickly raise her hand and slap her across the face.

She put her hand on her stinging cheek. How could she have forgotten about the element of surprise? Her mother used the tactic often during her early childhood. Bella looked at her with contempt. "Be ready in forty-five minutes." She left the room, slamming the door.

Jenna listened to the sounds of Bella's retreating footsteps. Afterward, she cried out then grabbed a jar of Vaseline and threw it across the room. It hit the wall then dropped to the floor, landing in a corner where it cracked open, petroleum jelly escaping from it.

Bella almost reached the second floor when she heard BANG. She quickened her steps. As soon as Bella reached her bedroom, she locked the door.

"Diane's back in town," Jenna said to Rosa.

"Like Santa Claus?"

She might've laughed off Rosa's facetiousness, but she was in no laughing mood. After her fit of temper, Jenna jumped on her cell to call her friend. She was still hyperventilating. "This means we can't meet."

"*Whyyy?*"

Slowly, Bella opened her bedroom door. She stepped out into the empty hall and listened by the attic steps.

Jenna told Rosa what happened. She added, "It's my fault. I blew it."

Bella heard angry murmurs, but she couldn't make out the words. Jenna must've been talking to Rosa. It's what Jenna always did. She complained.

To *her*.

Rosa cursed. "She hit you again?"

"I was supposed to play it cool," Jenna said.

"She's skatin' on thin ice."

*

Bella reentered her bedroom then closed the door. She turned the key in the lock.

"On the bright side," Rosa continued, "Diane's here. Find out how long Miss Prissy's in town for then we'll meet later. "And from here on do as I tell you." Bella wouldn't have had a reason to hit her if she had played it cool like she said to.

Jenna agreed then hung up. She checked her watch. Malachi should be up by now. She started to call him then changed her mind. He would definitely want to meet and she still hadn't come up with a plausible explanation for why she hadn't spoken to her father about moving in with him. She turned off her cell. Until she could think of something to say, she had to avoid him. On the bright side, her problems would be over very soon.

Julian started grumbling after they pulled away from the third property, a classic Greek revival on six and a half acres, a property situated. "Nine more houses to go. What in blazes was your sister thinking?"

Jenna wiped the sweat off her brow and smiled at her father's unintended pun. The temperature was brutal. They were riding together in his Ford Explorer. Bella and Diane rode with the realtor, Rena Lansing, who was all agog about having Diane Crandall and her fiancé, Lawrence Belmar, as clients.

"I can't believe she didn't like this house," Julian said. He imitated Diane. "'The kitchen depresses me.'" Julian snorted. "Like she cooks. All she has to do is change the darn room."

Jenna reached over and turned on the air conditioner. She stared out the window at the grand estates, evidence of the financial success of the residents of Coral Heights, an affluent section of Gordonville. Everett lived in Coral Heights. "I had to cancel my plans for this. I—I was going out with a friend this afternoon."

From the mischievous smile on her father's face, she could tell right away he assumed that Malachi was the friend. She left it that way.

"You didn't have to come," Julian said.

Jenna continued staring out the window at the posh scenery.

Julian stole a quick glance at Jenna. He took notice of her hobo bag. "Do you have plans with Malachi later?"

Now would've been a good time to bring up living arrangements. Jenna clutched the straps of the tote bag. "No."

"Going shopping later?"

The tote bag. She didn't want him asking about it. He mustn't find out about the cast iron pot. "Maybe I'll go by the mall, but I'm not sure. Depends on when we finish here." Jenna clasped her hands.

"You can talk to me you know," Julian said. Jenna seemed to be tense. "Just because I didn't live with you kids didn't mean I wasn't available."

Jenna turned to him and smiled. "I know."

Julian drove in silence for a minute. Then he asked, "Is there something you wanted to talk about?"

"No."

"You're going to love this property, Mrs. Crandall," Ms. Lansing said after they pulled up in front of a French Second Empire.

"You've been saying that about every house," Jenna murmured as she dragged her sneaker clad feet across the lawn, while at the same time admiring the dwelling. Its mansard roof, dormer windows and cornices reminded her of the estates in the gothic novels she enjoyed reading so much; the type of home she envisioned she and her intended living in someday.

" . . . And you don't have to do any work," Ms. Lansing said, praising the homes attributes. "Just move right in." She chuckled. "Unless you want to change the wallpaper or repaint."

Diane dazzled the realtor with one of her magazine-cover smiles. "Since we'll be working together, call me Diane."

Ms. Lansing gushed and insisted that Diane call her Rena. The realtor went on to say how she felt "privileged to be on a first-name basis with such a beautiful, charitable individual."

Julian rolled his eyes.

Jenna made a gagging gesture then watched her mother and Diane walking hand in hand towards the house. Her stare practically burned a hole through their clothes.

Bella felt a chill. The same sensation she felt when Jenna was staring down at her from the attic. Slowly, she turned and caught Jenna staring intently at her and Diane. Bella turned away. Still feeling shaken by whatever was going on upstairs in Jenna's room; she smoothed the front of her slacks. She couldn't get the sound of that *BANG* out of her mind. What was that?

She didn't say anything to Diane, who picked her and Jenna up earlier, about her sudden distrust of Jenna. She couldn't. Not with Jenna sitting with them in the car. If she had been thinking, she would've had Julian pick up Jenna at the house and she would've ridden with Diane. She thought about calling Lauren last night and this morning. She would have to admit that Jenna's relationship with Rosa was making her uncomfortable. What would Lauren think? Her mother has always been in charge. She would have to reveal that Jenna was becoming as belligerent as Rosa was and that she thought that Rosa was in the house last night, but it turned out that she wasn't. She only heard Jenna on the phone.

And she sounded vicious . . .

She'd have to tell Lauren about her and Jenna's . . . disagreement. Not that that was a problem. She would just rather not relive it.

Jenna walked ahead of Julian on the pretense of admiring a patch of flowers, which were close to Bella and Diane.

Bella noticed Jenna's proximity. She shivered.

"How'd you like to host a tea party here, Mom?" Diane asked.

Bella laughed a tad too loudly.

Diane gave her mother an odd look. "Mom?"

Bella cleared her throat. She had to get Jenna and Rosa off her mind. She had to maintain control. "When is Larry returning to the States?"

"Tonight. He's coming up to Gordonville tomorrow." "That's wonderful." Bella relaxed. The news was already taking her mind off her unease.

"I got him a room at The Lorelei House too," Diane said.

So, Diane's going to be in town a while. Jenna stopped by a patch of zinnias and smiled.

Malachi growled. His call went to voicemail. Again. He hung up, refusing to leave another message. He already left four. Where was Jenna?

He sat on the edge of the bed and stared through his bedroom window at the Hudson River view. Bella had a violent history.

Should I call the landline?

He groaned. Did something happen to Jenna while he was away? The last time he called the phone line Bella was caustic. But so what? He just wanted to know if Jenna was all right.

*

"Twelve houses?" Rosa couldn't believe how Diane made Jenna spend her day. "That girl's buggin.'"

It was after five in the evening. They were sitting in the kitchen of the old farmhouse. Jenna asked Julian to drop her off at Delsey's on the pretext that she wanted takeout. From there, she hiked over to the meadow.

"Actually, it was seven," Jenna said. "Or nine depending on your interpretation. She skipped three houses and stopped halfway through two because they didn't meet her needs."

Rosa rolled her eyes.

"At least I didn't have to make tea," Jenna said. "So, what's the plan?"

"You have a spare key to your house on you?" Rosa asked.

"No." Jenna sounded annoyed. Rosa didn't answer her question.

"Before you leave for work Monday, leave it where I can find it." Rosa smiled like a crocodile. "I'm paying your mother a visit."

Jenna nodded. *Monday. So that's when it's going to happen.* "I'll put the key under the left planter out front."

"What time are you coming?" Jenna asked.

"Need-to-know-basis. That way, if anyone asks, you can honestly say, 'I don't know.'"

Jenna had to admit that that was a good idea.

"So did you bring it?" Rosa asked.

Jenna reached into her tote bag and pulled out the small cast-iron pan that Rosa had requested. While Bella was changing in her bedroom, Jenna had sneaked down to the kitchen and placed it in her tote bag before Diane arrived. It was a relief to hand it over to Rosa. It was awkward carrying it around. At one point, her father had asked if she wanted to leave the bag in the car. Jenna thanked him but declined. She wouldn't take the risk of him lifting it then questioning her as to its contents. "I guess there's no point in me asking what you're going to do with it."

Rosa smiled. "You learn fast. Now what about Diane? How soon is she going back to the city?"

Now it was Jenna's turn to smile. She told her about Larry coming to Gordonville. "He and Diane are meeting with the realtor on Monday. Ms. Lansing's beside herself." Jenna cleared her throat and proceeded to imitate her. "'I'm actually going to meet Lawrence Belmar the famous fashion designer.'"

"There'll have to be a slight change of plans," Rosa said in between laughter. She always enjoyed Jenna's talent for doing impersonations. "After Bella, I'll pay a visit to Diane instead and leave Lauren for last."

"You mean you'd switch the order? I'm shocked."

"You gotta seize opportunity when you can," Rosa said, ignoring Jenna's wit. Then, she crossed her arms. "Any chance of anyone getting in my way?"

Jenna shook her head. "Mom'll be alone. She's attending a church meeting Monday evening."

Rosa sneered. "Good luck with that." She pulled out a pair of gloves and a piece of cloth from her handbag. Rosa slipped the gloves on.

Jenna watched Rosa take the cloth and wipe it across the panhandle. *She's wiping off my fingerprints.*

16

Malachi was sitting on the back porch of Brendan's colonial having drinks and trying his best to listen to the defense attorney talk about an intense trial that just wrapped up yesterday. He couldn't keep his mind off Jenna. He stopped by her house on his way to Brendan's. Regardless of the consequences, he walked right up to the door and rang the bell, just as he did in the nightmare and just like in the nightmare, no one answered. Not even a woman in a Loki mask.

If something did happen to Jenna, wouldn't I have seen some sign? Skeletons at the window maybe?

" . . . So, I did everything to convince the jury of my client's innocence except pull a rabbit out of a hat," Brendan said. "I thought I was about to lose the case. "Next thing I know, the forewoman finds my client not guilty."

. . . She could at least call. Where could she be?

"It was all I could do not to pass out from relief," Brendan said. "I think I convinced the jury of my client's innocence because—"

Brendan stopped talking. He studied Malachi's contemplative look. If he were to wave his hand in front of his face, would he come back to earth? His friend did seem a little distant before, but at least he was responding with the occasional yeah or grunt. Now Malachi just sat there with that glazed donut look on his face. That might explain why he was drinking beer instead of soda. Something's up. Brendan took a drink of beer. "So, I played the ukulele while dancing the hula in a coconut bra and grass skirt."

There has to be some explanation as to—Malachi stopped pondering. Startled. He looked at Brendan. "Wait a minute. What?"

"Finally got your attention. What's the big idea making me talk to myself?"

"Sorry, man. What were you saying?"

"Forget it," Brendan said. "What's on your mind? Everything okay with you and Jenna?"

"Yeah." Malachi took a drink of beer. "At least we were before I left for Los Angeles. Jenna knew when I'd be back. I was sure she'd want us to get together today. Instead, she's been scarce." He told Brendan about getting her voice mail. "I even stopped by her house." Jenna sounded okay when he called her back the night Bella turned all the lights off in the house. She sounded okay when he spoke to her over the phone while he was in California. Still, he never got that night out of his mind. Or that nightmare.

Malachi never told Brendan about it or about his fears stemming from it. That would've led to a conversation about Rosa, which might have led to her childhood abuse. Jenna wanted it to remain a secret. He couldn't betray her trust.

"Maybe she's busy," Brendan said breaking into Malachi's thoughts.

"Too busy to see me?"

"It's Saturday, Mal. She probably had errands to run. Or, she's probably under a lot of pressure and needs to decompress."

Malachi looked at Brendan quizzically. Keen observation considering . . . "What makes you say that?"

"Growing up with sisters like Lauren and Diane?" Brendan held up his beer bottle. "I'm surprised Jenna doesn't drink. I know attorneys who've crossed swords with Lauren and by day's end they're either at the bar or holed up in their office sucking their thumbs." Brendan grinned with pride. "I've stood up to Lauren—and survived.

I'm like a god around the office."

Malachi chuckled. "That's worthy of a raise."

"Damn straight." Brendan took a swig of beer. "You met the mother right?"

Malachi shuddered.

"Then you can imagine what kind of stress Jenna must've been under."

Malachi didn't comment.

"What I'm trying to say," Brendan went on, "is that Lauren and Diane are famous. And Alan does pretty well for himself even if he's not in the limelight. That's got to weigh on Jenna. I mean, how can she measure up?"

"She doesn't have to," Malachi said, sounding a little annoyed. "God made her unique. With her own special talents."

"What talents?"

"You don't know?"

"Do I look like I know?"

Malachi shrugged. Jenna spoke so animatedly about art when they first met. He just assumed that she mentioned it to Brendan too. Since her artwork wasn't a secret, Malachi told Brendan about it.

"They're amazing," Malachi said.

"I knew she was holding back," Brendan said. "But what I don't get is why wouldn't Bella talk about Jenna's talent? She loves to brag. The woman talks about Lauren and Diane every chance she gets."

Malachi turned away and winced. If only he could talk about the child abuse that Alan and Jenna had endured. He hated keeping things from Brendan. He was more than a best friend. He was like a brother. He stretched his legs out then said, "Why does she act like Alan doesn't exist? The guy's a genius at design."

Malachi watched the evening breeze stirring the leaves in the maple trees. Brendan can't know that Bella was trying to sabotage Jenna's career, not without bringing up her and Alan's difficult childhood.

Brendan saw the worried look on Malachi's face. "Is there something else?"

Malachi opened his mouth, but nothing came out. He cursed himself for not being unprepared.

"Don't you know you're supposed to tell your attorney everything?"

Malachi rolled his eyes then wore a tiny smile.

"Okay. I know that look. When you're ready to talk, you know where to find me. Meanwhile, why don't you go back over to Jenna's? You're lousy company anyway."

Malachi took the service road. Visions of teacups, skeletons and a Loki mask danced around in his head. To block them out, he put on an R&B CD.

He was almost at the intersection of Springfield Road and Thornbush Lane, when he saw a familiar figure. *Jenna?* He breathed a sigh of relief. He honked the horn and pulled over to the side.

Jenna looked up. She grasped her tote bag.

Malachi? What was he doing here?

She pasted on a smile. She was so busy making plans with Rosa she forgot to ask her for a good excuse she could give him for why she wouldn't be moving out of her mother's house after all. Rosa would've had a great one. Now she was in a pickle.

Forgetting about his fear of Thornbush Lane Malachi got out of the car. He ran towards Jenna and scooped her up in his arms. "Thank God you're okay."

"What do you mean?" Jenna asked taken aback by Malachi's display of emotion was unexpected.

"I didn't know where you were. He told her about his repeated phone calls going to voicemail. "It was making me crazy."

Jenna swore to herself. *If only I had checked my voicemail. I could've spared him the anxiety.* "Sorry. I got roped into house-hunting." She told him about Diane's return to Gordonville and the twelve houses they had to see. "I didn't call you because I figured you were still asleep." Jenna began twisting her ponytail. "When I got back, I felt like going for a walk. To clear my head."

"I'm a little insulted that you'd rather blow off steam going down this creepy street than use me as a sounding board," Malachi said, pretending to be offended, "but if my sister made me look at twelve houses, I'd probably have a nervous tic by now. Homeward bound?"

"Uh huh."

Malachi bowed with a flourish then said, "Your carriage awaits."

Malachi calmed down now that he knew that she was safe. Still, something was off. It was more than seeing Jenna coming down Thornbush Lane. She went there often enough. Her artwork proved that. "Usually, I like to give a person space," Malachi said. "But, in this case, I'll make an exception." He negotiated a right turn. "Remember when I said I wanted you to think of me as a friend? Well, obviously, I think of you as more than that, but you get my drift."

Jenna could scarcely breathe. *He's leaving me.* Malachi could no longer tolerate her family. She felt a lump in her throat. She couldn't lose him.

"I can't help you if you won't let me in," Malachi said. "Something's going on and I want to know what it is."

Jenna could hardly keep from smiling. *He's not kicking me to the curb after all.*

If it weren't for the seat belt, she'd have fallen face forward from sheer happiness. Then, almost immediately, her sense of calm diminished. Malachi wants to know what's going on.

I have to tell him about Mom's threats.

Jenna took a deep breath. "Mom said she was going to call the cops if you came back to the house."

The car screeched as Malachi almost swerved off the road then pulled over to the side. Jenna looked at him in shock. It took a few moments for her heart rate to get back to normal. It really was true that your life flashes before your eyes.

Malachi turned toward her with wild-looking eyes. He said something in Trinidadian Creole. It didn't sound like I'm taking you to lunch today. "I was at your house today."

Jenna widened her eyes. "What?"

He told her how worried he was. "I thought the worse that would happen is your mother would curse me out. Not have me hauled off to jail. Malachi envisioned officers leading him away in handcuffs. He saw himself in central booking. Wouldn't Brendan have loved to get that phone call? *Or the look on my priest's face when he heard about my arrest?* "She hates me that much."

Jenna too was horrified at what could've happened. At the same time, she realized just how much he cared. "You really thought something happened to me. My past really scared you didn't it?"

His silence said it all.

She was glad that she didn't tell him about what really happened last night.

"No offense, Jenna, but your mother's nuts."

Jenna's eyebrows shot up.

Right away, Malachi regretted his words. He should be respectful. After all, Bella was her mother. "I'm sorry. That was out of line."

Jenna started giggling before doubling over with laughter.

Malachi drew in his breath. Usually, he loved the sound of her laughter. But not now. It was disturbing. He chalked it up to stress. Yes. That was it. It had been a demanding day for her. He could just imagine what it must've been like having to spend an entire afternoon going in and out of numerous houses with two drama queens and a fawning realtor.

Jenna caught her breath. "Sorry. It's just that Mom thought that Rosa was crazy."

"She did?"

"It's great to hear someone else accuse her of being the same."

A mask fell over Malachi's face. Switching the subject, he asked, "Did you talk to your father about moving in with him?"

Jenna stopped smiling. The fun was over. Here was the question she was dreading. "No, Mal, I didn't. But I will." Another lie. But she had to say something.

Malachi started the car. They drove the rest of the way in silence, he concentrating on the road, Jenna looking out the window at the passing residences, farm stands and cornfields. The tote bag, now empty, sat on top of her lap. She gripped its handles as she held back her tears.

When they reached Haven Road, Malachi parked in the usual spot. He decided not to take a chance by parking in front of the house. He didn't have a police record and he wasn't in a hurry to get one now.

Taking Jenna's hand in his, Malachi said, "You have to get out of that house before something terrible happens."

"Oh. I thought you were mad at me."

"No, I'm disappointed that you didn't speak to your father."

Jenna didn't know how to face him. Something terrible was going to happen.

"Jenna?" Malachi asked. "You okay?"

Jenna nodded.

He leaned over and kissed her tenderly on the lips. Now that he knew that she was all right, he didn't want to let her go.

He hugged her. "Talk to your father."

"I will."

17

"I don't understand," Bella said. "It's just disappeared into thin air."

Jenna spread some mayonnaise on a slice of oat honey bread while her mother was tearing apart her pristine kitchen. She was packing her lunch a roast beef sandwich. There was no rain today. A perfect day to eat in the park. Jenna's hand shook as she put three thin slices of roast beef on the bread. Was her mother going to question her about the pan?

Jenna glanced up from her luncheon preparations. Pots and pans, the blender, food processor, a muffin pan and the waffle maker were scattered. "What're you looking for?"

"My cast-iron pan," Bella replied in a snippy tone.

Ignoring her mother's snippy tone, Jenna finished making her sandwich and put it into an insulated bag.

Forcing herself to sound sweet-tempered she said, "Use a different one."

"I want that pan. I'm making fried eggs and it fries them just right."

"So make scrambled."

Bella looked at Jenna suspiciously. "Do you know something about my missing pan?"

"No, I don't."

Bella sucked her teeth. Jenna shrugged, then placed her lunch bag by the front door with the rest of her things.

Later, Jenna was reading the latest issue of *ARTnews* while she and Bella were at the kitchen table having breakfast. Bella spread jam on her whole wheat bread. She was still miffed about her pan and was loathed to take Jenna's suggestion to have scrambled eggs even if it was a good suggestion. She glanced at Jenna from time to time, resisting the urge to take the art magazine she was reading and fling it across the room even though that may have gotten a rise out of her. The return of relative normalcy to the house encouraged Bella to regain her bravery and return to her usual unpleasantness.

Bella took a bite of whole wheat bread. Jenna had been polite and easy going all week. She wasn't making any secret phone calls nor did a certain unwelcome visitor show up. Nevertheless, something was strange. Bella took another bite of bread. "You're quiet this morning."

Jenna smiled, shrugged, then turned the page. She was still tense about Rosa coming. The not knowing when was unnerving.

"Did you tell Dr. Chase what I said and he decided to leave you?" She took a sip of green tea then said, "It's all for the best."

Breathe. Jenna didn't bother contradicting her mother. She remembered to play it cool by allowing Bella to make her own conclusions.

"What's the church meeting about?" Jenna asked.

"Since when do you care about church affairs?"

"I'm just making conversation."

Bella gave Jenna a cynical look as she ate another bite of whole wheat bread.

"Can we have a conversation without arguing? Am I so bad?"

Bella took another sip of green tea.

"Why do you look at me like that, Mom?"

Bella clenched her teeth. "I'm not doing anything except trying to enjoy my breakfast without fried eggs." She was still suspicious of

Rosa and the whereabouts of her cast iron pan. Jenna had to know something.

"You give me nasty looks. You act like I disgust you."

"It's your shame that's making you think that," Bella said.

Jenna blew out a frustrated breath. *Rosa's coming.* She didn't know when since Rosa refused to tell her. Jenna wiped some stray crumbs from the corner of her mouth with a napkin.

"What do I have to be ashamed about?"

"Why don't you ask yourself that question?"

"Because I didn't tell you about Rosa?"

"You lied to me," Bella said.

"What's the big deal? You all hate her anyway." Jenna looked down at the slice of half-eaten bread on her plate. "Why do you treat me the way you do?"

"It's all in your head."

Jenna looked up. "Every time I try to reach out to you, you crush me. You let Lauren and Diane pick on me."

"That is a lie."

"And you're mean to Alan. Why?"

"Liar!" Bella flung down her napkin and stood up. "I've always taken care of you."

Jenna looked at her mother in amazement. Where was this coming from? Up to now, she had been playing it cool, but it didn't matter anymore.

"Aren't mother's supposed to take care of their children?" Jenna asked.

Bella smoothed the front of her print silhouette dress. "*I* did not start this war."

"What war?"

"Never mind," Bella said. "I'm protecting you." "From what?"

"Bad relationships, Jenna. And if that makes me a bad mother, then that's too bad."

"I think I'm old enough to take care of myself."

"Oh?"

Jenna picked up her teacup. She took a sip of tea even as anger was firing up in her belly. "There you go again, being malicious."

"I'm malicious." Bella chuckled without mirth. "Rosa tried to burn down my house and you call me malicious?"

"It was the storage shed and it was payback."

Bella's nostrils flared. "Payback? I gave you an order. I told you to wash the dishes and you disobeyed me."

Jenna could feel her anger rising. *Play it cool.* "Why are we talking about this? It was seventeen years ago." Jenna picked at the crust on her bread. "You think I can't take care of myself. I'm helpless without you. I can see Lauren and Diane feeling that way but why you?"

"Because it's true."

Jenna stared at Bella, stunned. *She really thinks I'm incompetent.* It wasn't enough that she treated her like dirt. Rosa was right. Her mother didn't think much of her at all.

"Your professor's gone so deal with it." Bella sat back down. And let this be the last time you bring anyone else around here. I'm getting tired of this."

"And so am I." Jenna got up and cleared away her breakfast dishes.

Bella pounded her fist on the table, upsetting the remaining dishes on the table and startling Jenna. "I made sacrifices for you."

Jenna turned around. "What sacrifice?"

Bella stared into her teacup. "Never mind." She looked up at Jenna. "Since you love Rosa so much, why don't you go and live with her?"

"Maybe I will. She's more like family to me than either you, Lauren or Diane ever was." How ironic that her mother would suggest that she should leave to go live with Rosa when Malachi wanted her to leave home to live with her father.

Jenna was about to leave the kitchen when she turned and faced Bella. Her mother was openly glaring at her. Instead of feeling anger, however, she felt sadness. Her longing for her mother to love her had returned. Heavy-hearted, Jenna left the room, knowing that it would be the last time she would see her mother alive again. If only things could've been different.

In the hall, she overheard Bella say, "Freak."

Regret changed to resentment.

On the front stoop, Jenna reached into the pocket of her sienna-colored suit jacket, took out a spare key, and slipped it underneath the left planter where Rosa would find it later. Afterward, she headed for her Honda.

In her car, Jenna opened her handbag and pulled out her cell phone. She pressed Rosa's number.

"All set," Jenna said as soon as Rosa picked up.

"Good."

"She said I was a freak." Jenna burst into tears.

"Hey," Rosa began, "it's gonna be all right."

"She kept talking crazy about not starting a war and making sacrifices for me."

"How do you think she brainwashed you into staying home?" Rosa asked. "Mind games, Jenna. Don't listen to her."

Jenna went on to tell her about the many times that Bella used to say that she and Rosa should be committed. "I never told you," Jenna said tearfully, "because I was afraid of what you would do. I'm sorry. I should've told you." Hysteria was creeping into Jenna's voice.

Rosa, who didn't know the meaning of the word apprehension, was starting to worry. The last thing she needed was for Jenna to lose control. If she slipped up and made an error, they would both get into major trouble. Importantly, she couldn't concentrate on Phase 1 if she had to worry about Jenna's emotional stability. She had to get her to calm down. "Just relax. What Bella says doesn't matter. After today, she won't be a problem. I promise."

"She hurt me."

"I know, but you gotta relax and let me handle this. Now breathe."

Jenna did what Rosa told her to do.

"Feeling better?"

"A little."

"I need you to be strong."

"I can be strong." Jenna nodded. I can do this. She was determined to override the self-doubt and misery that Bella's poor evaluation had left within her.

"Good. Now listen up. 'Cause this is extremely important. Do not go back to your house until I tell you to. Understand?"

Jenna sniffled. "Yes."

"Good. Now I want you to go to work and act like it's any other day. Next time I call, you'll be a free woman."

"But what about Lauren and Diane? They're still around." Jenna hiccupped. "They're going to be so angry when they find out that Mom's dead."

"Trust me," Rosa said. "They won't be a problem." *They'll be too busy grieving.* "Now what are you *not going to do?*"

"Not go home until you tell me," Jenna replied with a smile.

"Good girl." Jenna was starting to relax. Good sign.

Bella stood by the living room window watching Jenna. "You can sit in that car and talk all day for all I care." She lifted her chin in defiance. If Rosa really were a threat, she would've done something already. Bella remained at the window even after Jenna finally pulled away from the curb and drove away.

The telephone rang. It was Norma Beery. Bella smiled then chuckled with relief.

10:35 A.M.

Jenna kept looking at the clock on her computer between typing file labels, answering phones and signing for deliveries. The telephone rang again. Her heart skipped a beat. Was it Rosa? She answered the phone.

Another client. She directed him to the senior account executive, and then began putting away stacks of files that, Bree, a college intern, had placed on her desk earlier.

10:40 A.M.

The phone rang again. Line 2. "Wheat, Prentiss & Associates." Jenna's professional voice belied her edginess. "How may I direct your call?"

"How's the firm's most attractive receptionist this morning?"

"I'm fine." *For now.*

"I hope you don't mind me calling you on the office phone instead of your cell?" Malachi asked.

"Not a prob."

"Free for lunch?"

"No." She needed to be alone for when Rosa called. "I am free for dinner." She should hear from Rosa before then. Maybe we can take in a movie." A mischievous grin spread across Jenna's face. "You can even drop me at the front door."

"Dinner," Malachi said.

"Yeah. Dinner." She suppressed a giggle. She could just see him gagging through the phone. After her mother's threat, why would he want to darken her doorstep? Jenna cleared her throat. "Mom has a church meeting this evening." Which was true. So what if she would be . . . indisposed later?

"All right," Malachi said. "Dinner sounds great." He agreed to pick her up at seven then hung up. Jenna played with her hair. It should be fine.

11:29 A.M.

Rosa still hasn't called.

Maybe she wasn't carrying out the plan this morning. Was it this evening? Just before Mom left for the church meeting?

Was I hasty in making dinner plans with Malachi?

She returned to her desk. Everything was going to be okay. It had to be. Rosa was in charge. She sighed, got up and picked up some more files.

12:55 P.M.

Again, she glanced at the clock on the computer. Just then, Bree walked over. It was the college student's turn to manage the phone while Jenna went to lunch. Jenna's stomach started growling as she was greeting the petite, stocky brunette. She laughed at herself and said, "I guess that's my signal to eat lunch now."

Usually she left for lunch at exactly one o'clock. What was five minutes? Jenna picked up her bags and headed for the elevator bank. Some time in the park might do her some good.

18

Rosa peered through her binoculars in her leather-gloved hands while she was standing in the woods facing Jenna's house. Bella wasn't at any of the upstairs or downstairs windows. She put away the binoculars into her tote bag. She looked around. No neighbors about. So far so good. Next, she removed her shoes, a pair of magenta-colored slip-ons that were a Christmas gift from Jenna and placed them into a shoe bag, which she then placed into her tote bag. She adjusted her silk headscarf, picked up her tote bag, slung it around her shoulder, then emerged from the woods.

Rosa was about to cross the road when she heard a car coming. She hid behind an evergreen. Jenna said there wouldn't be any visitors. Still, they say to *expect the unexpected.* She couldn't tell Jenna that if anyone showed up she'd have to take care of him or her . . . One Jenna couldn't handle that. Two, the least she knew the better. For both of them. There was always the chance of something going wrong.

Presently, the vehicle drove by. Rosa watched the car disappear down the road before finally stepping from behind the tree. Again, she looked around. Satisfied that the coast was clear, she crossed the road.

Quietly, Rosa opened the gate. Like a cheetah, she stalked across the brick pathway and up the front stoop where she lifted the left planter. Rosa slipped her hand underneath it. She smiled. The keys were exactly where Jenna said they would be. Next, she walked around to the backyard. She scampered over to the crepe myrtle and peeked around it. She took out her binoculars again and trained them on the upstairs windows. No one was standing by them.

Nice.

Bella was trying on her new silk hat in front of her bedroom mirror. She was going to wear it to the church luncheon on Sunday. She was in better spirits. Norma's phone call helped. She put this morning's clash between her and Jenna behind her. It brought up memories she would sooner keep buried . . . Still, it was worth going through all that pain and aggravation to find out that Dr. Chase was out of their lives. And a relief. The man was trouble. She could tell a snooper when she saw one. Still, there was the little matter of Rosa. It was puzzling that she had been in the house yet she didn't stick around to confront her. Rosa usually loved to challenge authority.

The telephone rang. Bella picked up her antique desk phone. "Good Afternoon, Reverend Brooks . . . Sure, I'll be there this evening . . . Diane and Larry are fine, thank you for asking . . . Yes, she narrowed her decision to four homes." Bella laughed. "Yes, *only* four. I think Larry had something to do with that." Bella laughed again. "Yes, he's in town for the day. He's viewing them with her later this morning."

Rosa stepped from behind the crepe myrtle.

Bella frowned. *Was that movement?*

She moved over to the window. The grass and the shrubs shined under the July sun.

Must've been a beaver. Norma was talking about the amount of beavers in the area lately.

Bella removed the hat and put it into the hatbox. " . . . Of course, I'll be at Sunday's luncheon too . . . She chuckled. "Yes, Reverend Brooks, I will make my baked macaroni and cheese. I'll even make an extra dish just for you."

Then, she heard a thud. Bella looked toward her bedroom door, which was open. She could see through to the hall.

Reverend Brooks continued talking.

Distracted, Bella held the receiver away from her ear. *What was that sound?*

She heard a key turning in a lock. A door opened then closed. The sounds appeared to be coming from the back. *Someone's in the kitchen.*

" . . . And tonight I also want you and Norma to cover . . . "

While Reverend Brooks was discussing the agenda for tonight's meeting, Bella began speculating. Lauren and Diane had keys to the house, but Lauren was litigating a case in Westchester County Court and Diane and Larry were house—hunting with the realtor. Anyway, if any of them were dropping by, they would've called first.

There was Julian. He had a key. No. He would've called. He'd never just drop by. She heard movement in the kitchen. Whoever was downstairs wasn't interested in keeping their presence a secret. That left Jenna. Bella pursed her lips.

Reverend Brooks went on. " . . . So, the choir director thought—"

"I'm sorry, Reverend," Bella interrupted, "but I'll have to call you back. Someone's at the door." It was difficult trying to keep up the conversation while trying to listen to what was going on downstairs in the kitchen. After promising Reverend Brooks she'd call him back, she hung up.

She walked over to the bedroom door, hips swaying. Jenna was on the phone before she left for work. No doubt, she was talking to Rosa. "She'd better not have made herself late for work and gotten fired."

Halfway down the stairs, Bella called out, "I know it's you, Jenna." Why did she put up with her? "You brought lunch today. So why are you back here?"

Bella reached the first floor landing. She walked down the hall to the kitchen. When she arrived at the threshold, she stopped and stared at the woman standing in the middle of the room. That cocky stance. That sneer. It had been sixteen years, but she'd know her anywhere.

"Hello, Bella."

19

Rosa.

It took Bella a few minutes to get over the initial shock of seeing her old nemesis. She stared at Rosa's black leather gloves, silk scarf and stocking feet. Strange accessories for a ninety-degree day. Where were her shoes? Bella crossed her arms, not wanting Rosa to know that her presence was distressing her. Up to this moment, she was confident about the idea of confronting Rosa, never truly expecting to see her, not after all these years; even when she learned that Jenna was still associating with her. Even so, Rosa spent days keeping away even after she knew she came to the house. Why? And why was she here without Jenna?

Bella stared into Rosa's eyes. They didn't look quite right . . .

In a voice belying her insecurity Bella asked, "What are you doing here?"

"Is that how you greet me after all these years?"

Rosa grinned.

Bella caught her breath. The grin on her face was hideous. "Where is Jenna?"

Rosa looked at her strangely. "At work where she usually is this time of day."

Bella smoothed her dress. "Leave or I'll call the police." Maybe that would scare her away. She wanted her out of here. Something was different about her. This was not the same Rosa and it was more than her being sixteen years older than the last time they spoke.

Rosa walked up to her. "I'm not going anywhere, you miserable old wolf."

Immediately, Bella forgot about her distress. Infuriated, she raised her hand to slap Rosa, but the younger woman was quicker. She grabbed Bella's mother by the wrist, wrenching it. Rosa held her grip even as Bella's face twisted in agony.

"You think you can smack me around like Jenna?" Mercifully, Rosa released Bella's wrist.

"What do you want?" Trepidation and pain was evident in Bella's voice.

Rosa began laughing.

Bella shivered. She looked into Rosa's eyes again.

Rosa's *crazed* eyes.

She gripped the sides of her dress. She often joked about Rosa's mental state. She didn't think that there was any real credence to it. She realized now that that hadn't been wise.

Alan kept insisting that Jenna and Rosa's relationship was twisted. Bella didn't initiate their friendship, but neither did she do anything to stop it. She just fanned the flames. She encouraged Lauren and Diane to follow her example. The woman was dangerous. She knew that now. She had to remain calm and focused. There was no time for fear and regret. She had to reach Jenna. She was the only one who could reason with Rosa except for maybe Alan and even he feared Rosa. Because he knew. She tried not to think about the things she said to her only son or about what took place the last time they were together in this very kitchen.

Alan's warning came back to haunt her. *"You're playing with fire . . ."*

No. I have to focus. Somehow, she had to get Rosa out of the house. That's not going to happen. She had to get word to Lauren. She would know what to do. It was vital that didn't involve police.

She never intended on calling the police on Rosa. She only said it to keep Jenna in line. She wouldn't call the police. She couldn't. This was a private matter. *I could run.* Rosa wasn't wearing shoes. She couldn't run if she wasn't wearing shoes.

Bella rubbed her aching, swelling wrist. Rosa grew amazingly strong over the years. She paused. The hairs on the back of her neck began to rise. Suppose Rosa was carrying a gun? She has been holding on to that tote bag . . . "Would you like to give Jenna a call? I'm sure she'd like to know where you are."

"Who do you think sent me?"

Bella edged to a chair. She didn't know when it happened, but the game changed. In the old days, Rosa did the dirty work while Jenna stood by and watched. They changed strategies.

Rosa smiled like a cat staring at a cornered mouse. Bella's fear was delicious. Keeping her eyes on her old rival, Rosa slowly reached into her tote bag . . .

Bella gulped.

Rosa pulled out . . . her cell phone.

Bella's shoulders sagged with relief.

Rosa guffawed then pushed the camera button. "Smile." She snapped a picture of a horrified Bella. "Know why I'm here?"

"No. I don't." Bella crossed her arms, resorting to bravado where she felt safe.

Rosa's eyes held a dangerous vibrancy. "Justice. You've been very mean to Jenna. That's not *Christian* is it, Bella?

She didn't answer. She couldn't. She held her wrist. It hurt terribly and she was too terrified to move.

Who gave you the right to hit her?" Rosa's voice developed an even more malevolent pitch.

Rosa got up into Bella's face. "Hit me. Go ahead. I dare you."

Bella looked into eyes filled with hatred. A bead of sweat was running down the side of her face.

"Can't do it can you? I wanted to take you people out long time ago. But Jenna stopped me from killing y'all."

Bella plopped into the chair. *I'm not going to die; I'm not going to die. Please, Lord don't let her kill me.*

Rosa walked about the kitchen. "I dreamed about it all the time. She looked at Bella and smiled. "Jenna didn't want me to harm you."

Bella cringed. Yes, they were mean to Jenna and in the process, they offended Amelia's child. Now Rosa wanted revenge. She had to stop dwelling on the past and concentrating on survival. She needed a distraction, someone to call the house or suddenly stop by. Her mind flew to Alan. She didn't know why. The odds of him calling were nil. She wiped the sweat off her hands onto her dress.

Then, Julian crossed her mind. The chances of him telephoning or dropping by were the same as Alan's. Slim. If it hadn't been for him writing her checks or giving her money, Julian wouldn't even have a key to the house. That meant that her only hope was for a neighbor to stop by, perhaps Norma Beery. She could quietly signal Norma to call the cops. But if Rosa did have a gun, she would shoot anyone who got in her way. She knew that with every fiber in her being.

"Jenna was protecting you from me this whole time," Rosa sang. "Bet you didn't know that?"

Bella could hardly breathe.

"Jenna was always pining for your attention," Rosa continued. "Always hoping, always believing that you and your divas would love her. I kept telling her she was wasting her time." Rosa's face became a mask of rage. "Well, guess what? Jenna's finally sick of you." She walked around Bella, staring at her as if she were observing a fascinating specimen. "You're ashamed of me."

"No." Bella's voice was barely above a whisper.

Rosa stopped circling. "Then, why won't you tell anyone about me?"

Bella didn't expect this question never mind this visit. "It—it's not good for people to know our business."

Rosa leaned over her. "Not even Julian? I know he doesn't know about me. Why is that *Bella?*" Rosa chuckled. "Methinks you don't want your husband to know what you've been up to. Well he's gonna know."

Bella stared at her open-mouthed. Rosa's knowledge came from whatever Jenna told her. Obviously, Jenna understood more than she realized.

Bella struggled to find her voice. "Let's talk."

"About what? How you all celebrated Lauren's marriage while Jenna was still hurting over Everett?"

Bella looked bewildered. It never occurred to her that Jenna was still thinking about him. And was she with Dr. Chase now?

"Did the food and the drinks slide down your throat with ease knowing that you screwed her at every chance she had to be happy?" Rosa grinned. "I was there." She whispered menacingly, "Hiding in the shadows."

Bella wasn't too surprised. Something was making her overconfident and giving off pheromones, but she couldn't tell Lauren what she suspected. She had to reassure her that all was well. Lauren had been upset more than once that day.

"Shadows, Bella. Your daughters hide their actions in the dark as much as you do. It's amazing what they said in front of Jenna because they thought she was ignorant. Diane passing herself off as if she's America's sweetheart." Rosa shook her head and laughed." She hasn't been *innocent* since the Reagan administration. The stuff your darlings were into would make a prostitute blush."

Bella looked disappointed.

"Wouldn't the church have loved to know about that," Rosa said. "Lauren was an amateur compared to perky Diane." Rosa cocked her head to the side. "You know I'm going to kill you."

It was the way she said it that filled Bella with intense fear. So calm. Unflappable. She might as well have said she was going down to the farmer's market to buy a few ears of corn.

"Then," Rosa went on, "I'm gonna take care of Diane. Jenna told me that laughing hyena is staying at The Lorelei House. I'm saving the best for last—Lauren. I'll be waitin' for her when she comes home. It's a long drive to Pound Ridge, but it's worth it. And you know the beauty of it? You won't be able to do a damn thing 'cause you'll be dead."

Bella fought back tears. "You can't just walk into The Lorelei House."

"I got into your daughter's wedding didn't I?"

"Larry won't let you get near Diane."

"You think that designer doofus is a threat to me?"

"No good can come from harming anyone." Bella threw her pride to the wind. Reasoning with Rosa was like going against the grain, but at least it was buying her some time. She had to protect Lauren and Diane. She had to protect the family's reputation. The idea of Reverend Brooks, Norma Beery and the rest of the congregation and all of Gordonville knowing about this other child was horrifying.

No. The public mustn't find out.

Rosa Garrison was out of the box. No. She was always out of the box. Just moderately contained. Jenna claimed she told Malachi about her. Bella rubbed her chafing wrist. She doubted that. Even Jenna didn't know the whole story.

"You all treated Jenna and Alan like crap. Even your own husband you pushed around."

"That's not true."

"He was just a joke to you, Bella."

"No."

Rosa laughed dryly. "Then why did he leave you and the kids?"

"He did not leave. Julian saw the children all the time. I never denied him access to this house or his kids." Just what information had Jenna been feeding Rosa?

"How *is* Julian these days? Have you finished emasculating him yet?" Rosa laughed at her own remark. "Speaking of male . . . ineffectiveness, I was floored when Alan got married. I didn't think he had it in him. Guess your son finally found his manhood in the jar you keep it in underneath your bed . . . along with your husbands." Rosa chuckled. "I'll be doing those men a favor killing you.'

"Please, don't do anything foolish."

Rosa gasped. "Is the great Bella Crandall, begging for mercy?" She laughed raucously. "I don't believe it. Are you really asking me, a crazy person, for compassion?"

Bella widened her eyes. *She knows what I've been saying about her.* How she regretted every time she carelessly tossed around the word committed or freak.

She shook her head vehemently. She had to deny it. She didn't dare admit that she made fun of her state of mind.

"You're not crazy."

"You do think I'm a loon. And you think Jenna is too. She told me. Like when you called her a freak this morning. That upset her." Rosa looked pensive. "Jenna always comes crying to me. She had Alan. But she talked girl talk with me. Especially about all the relationships you interfered with, *Bella.*"

Birds were singing in the backyard. Bella derived no comfort from their song. Jenna's friend, Rosa, was terrorizing her.

Their fifth child.

The world wouldn't understand her reason in keeping her existence a secret, but it was better to risk its anger and dismay as well as Julian's than to suffer reproach. The world and her husband would fault her for many things. Besides, no one needed to know about this imbalanced relation.

Again, Bella considered making a run for it but changed her mind. She could end up wrestling her. She looked down at her injured risk.

Rosa's strong. Stronger than I remember.

Rosa walked over to a drawer. "Do you still keep your good knives in here?"

Bella wanted to dash from the chair, but her legs refused to move. Bella stared at Rosa's tote bag. She still couldn't dismiss the possibility that the vindictive woman was carrying a carrying a gun. She couldn't outrun a bullet. *I could cry for help, but who would hear me?*

Bella held her breath as she watched Rosa open the utility drawer and pull out . . . a teaspoon. She stared, flabbergasted. She wasn't going to die from a stab wound or a gun shot. She was going to die from heart failure.

Rosa began to laugh. Bella's horror was so delicious. "Make me a cup of tea."

"Problem?" Rosa looked up at the clock. 1:18 P.M. "Oops! My bad. It's not four o'clock yet. I know you still have to have your afternoon tea." Her smile faltered. "And you still have Jenna fetching it for you."

"It's okay," Bella said. "I can drink tea anytime." She added, "Jenna doesn't have to make tea anymore."

"Oh, she won't."

Bella got up, then put the kettle on the stove. She had to use both hands because of her injured right wrist. She opened the cupboard. No tea. Bella cursed to herself. She had to go into the pantry. She shuddered. Would Rosa follow her? She hasn't done anything. Yet. It was like playing a cat and mouse game. "I have to get more tea. It's in the pantry."

Rosa shrugged.

As soon as Bella stepped into the pantry, Rosa took the small cast-iron pan from out of her tote bag. She put the bag on the floor then leaned sideways against the wall, hiding the pan.

When Bella came out of the pantry carrying a box of assorted teas, she stopped short. Rosa was now leaning against the wall, hands behind her back and smiling like the joker in a deck of cards. Bella smiled nervously as she put the box on the table. Next, she went to the cabinet and put her hand on the first set of dinnerware, a floral porcelain cup and saucer. Her hands shook as she set placed them on the kitchen table. She began to pray silently that anyone, anyone would call. Suddenly, she remembered that Diane was going to call her after she and Larry got through with the realtor. Her spirits soared. At any minute, the phone could ring. *I could give Diane a cryptic message.*

As her strength grew, her mouth began twitching. She envisioned the Gordonville Police Department bursting through the door. She and her daughters would be safe. Bella glanced at Rosa. She dare not smile. Rosa would wonder what was going on and she couldn't make her suspicious.

Bella opened the box of tea. She looked at the selections. She studied each individually wrapped packet. Each bag categorized by type and flavor. What type would Rosa want? It wasn't important was it? Decaffeinated. Yes. She could definitely use it. *I'll give her lemon and white decaffeinated tea.* Soon Bella was taking the tea bag from out of its packet. She placed it into the porcelain cup then stared into it. She had to put aside her long-standing resolve to keep Rosa Garrison a secret. As much as she wanted to keep them out of this, she needed them. There was no way around it. Not anymore.

"Don't you have something to go with tea?"

Startled, Bella went to the bread drawer. Inside was a box of buttery lemon squares she had bought fresh from Delsey's earlier that morning. Bella picked up the fancy white pastry box by its elegant red ribbon then brought it over to the table. Now resentment mixed with fear. She was planning to have the lemon squares during afternoon tea.

"Put them on a plate."

Presently, Bella took out a plate and a linen napkin. Afterward, she placing the lemon squares on the plate. She paused. "How many?" *Did it matter?*

Rosa rolled her eyes. "I don't care."

Bella nodded then began placing the pastries on the plate. She looked at the first one sitting all alone in the center.

Rosa moved closer to the table.

Bella contemplated the lonely lemon treat then decided to add another one before turning to stare at the kettle. The gift that Lauren bought for her, her precious gift she was now using to pour tea for her family's enemy.

Rosa moved a little bit closer.

Bella continued to stare at the teakettle. She no longer loved her English import and for the first time, she felt no pleasure in preparing tea.

Soon, the teakettle whistled.

Rosa smiled. "Tea time."

Her wrist still paining, Bella winced as she gingerly picked up the teakettle. Lost in thought, she began pouring the hot water into the cup.

Rosa raised the small cast-iron pan over Bella's head.

Bella didn't know what hit her.

Rosa put the cup, saucer, plate, teaspoon and napkin into her tote bag. Next, she put the bloodstained cast-iron pan into the sink. She walked over to the back door and was about to leave when she looked back at the lemon squares on the table. She turned back and picked up one. Then, she walked out the back door.

Bella lay on the kitchen floor, her head bleeding profusely.

The telephone rang.

20

Diane frowned as she closed her cell phone.

"What's wrong?" Larry asked. His Jamaican accent was almost hard to detect. He made a left turn on Old Mill Road. They were returning from their appointment with Ms. Lansing, the realtor.

"Mom's not picking up."

"Maybe she's out."

"She didn't say she was going out," Diane said. "Except church and that's not until tonight."

Larry grinned. "Maybe she doesn't want to be disturbed during her afternoon tea."

"It's not funny. And it's not four o'clock yet." Diane started wringing her hands. Mom was a creature of habit. If she said she was going to be home, then she was going to be home.

Larry wiped the grin off his face. He didn't realize she was that upset. He felt a twinge of guilt. He hated to see Diane upset. "Look, your mom's probably in the backyard picking flowers or chatting with Norma Beery and can't hear the phone. We'll swing by. If she's not home, we'll use your key and wait for her. She'll be pleasantly surprised." He put his hand on her lap. She looked adorable in a light blue tunic and white Bermuda shorts.

Diane turned to him. "You're just hoping that Mom'll have those white chocolate Macadamia nut cookies you love."

"That too. And we can tell her we settled for the English Tudor. She'll like that."

Diane twisted her engagement ring. It wasn't like Mom not to answer or not be home especially when she knew they would be in touch with her.

2:45 P.M.

Jenna finished typing a memo. She glanced at the computer clock. All afternoon, she had to keep up a pleasant appearance for the executives and their clients when it was all she could do to think about whatever was going on back home between her mother and Rosa.

Jenna started typing another memo.

2:47 P.M.

For a moment, Jenna stared at the clock on her computer. She began rubbing her left temple. She should've heard from Rosa by now. Something must've gone wrong. But it couldn't have.

Jenna closed her eyes. *Why hasn't she called?*

Then, her cell phone vibrated. *Finally.* She didn't have to wonder who it was. She nearly dropped the phone while she was pulling it out of its case. She cleared her throat. "Yeah, Roe?"

"It's done."

"Mom!" Diane called after she and Larry pulled up in front of the house and got out. Perhaps she was within hearing distance of the front yard.

No answer.

They headed for the backyard. Seeing no sign of Bella, Diane said, "I don't like this."

"I said she was *probably* in the garden," Larry said. "We'll wait for her inside. Come on." He led Diane to the back door. "Hand me your key." When they reached the entrance to the kitchen, Larry, who was walking ahead of Diane, saw Bella through the door's glass panel and gasped. Bella was lying across the floor through the glass panels. The amount of blood oozing from Bella's head was frightening.

"What's the matter?" Diane asked. Dread was evident in her voice. "What's going on?"

Larry didn't answer her, preferring to concentrate on opening the door and getting over to Bella, whom he prayed, was still alive. He shifted his body to block Diane's view of the grisly sight. That proved to be an impossible task, however. Realizing that something was indeed amiss, Diane was trying to get pass him.

Larry grabbed her by the shoulders. "Stay. Here."

"No, I'm going in with you."

"Diane—"

"What is it, Larry? What's wrong?"

He sucked his teeth then opened the door. He had no time to argue. Bella's life depended on swift action, assuming she was still alive. Larry found out quickly that he didn't need Diane's house key. The door opened with ease from the moment he put his hand on the knob. Diane screamed when she saw her mother's prostrated form. For a moment, Larry just stood there, stunned. He heard about these situations on the news, but they always happened to someone else in some other place. Never in a million years did he imagine that it would happen to someone he cared about in their own backyard.

There was so much blood. Its scent was pungent. Larry fought back the urge to hurl. He covered his nose, ran over to Bella, then checked her pulse. He found one. It was faint. Relieved, he called to Diane who remained riveted to the same spot, almost catatonic.

Mommy can't be dead.

"Call 9-1-1."

Diane remained transfixed. Mom was so still. So much blood. *Rosa didn't do this. I know she didn't.*

"Move, nuh!" In his anxiety, Larry's almost nonexistent accent came out heavier. He didn't mean to be abrupt either, but at least he had the right effect. Diane snapped out of her reverie, grabbed her BlackBerry and began calling an ambulance. His fiancée just suffered a shock and he felt for her. He didn't even want to imagine finding one of his parents like this but now wasn't the time for sentiment. Saving Bella's life depended on speed. Only God knew how long she'd been lying there.

Larry noted her injured wrist. There was also spilled water all over the floor mixed with Bella's blood. He stood up, careful not to step into it. He saw the bloody pan in the sink. He nearly gagged. He looked at the table. Part of the tablecloth was soaked with water. He moved closer to the table. Eleven pastries were in the box.

One was missing.

"They're on their way." Diane was hoarse. *Mom. I can't lose my mom.* "What happened?"

Larry shook his head. "Don't touch anything. I think there's been a robbery."

Or a discussion that turned into a fight.

Jenna couldn't wait for the elevator. She fled from her ninth floor office and down the stairwell. Larry's phone call relaying the graphic detail of what he saw brought home the reality of what she had permitted Rosa to do.

Sixth floor.

What did she expect? Rosa was gonna be trouble. Isn't this why she hesitated to call her in the first place? Now the authorities were involved. She collaborated with Rosa to kill her mother, which in this case, turned out to be attempted murder since Mom was still alive.

Fourth floor.

Her coworkers were stunned when she relayed the news. Their heartfelt responses were considerate, but they weren't important right now. She couldn't believe that Mom wasn't dead.

Third floor.

Jenna stopped to catch her breath on the landing. *What if Mom regains consciousness?* She had to talk to Rosa. Jenna continued down the stairs.

Inside her Honda, Jenna started shaking. She waited for her nerves to go steady, before taking out her cell phone and pressing Rosa's number. "Come on. Pick up. Pick up." She began rubbing her temples. Would she be able to get through the afternoon?

"Yes, Jenna?" Roe sounded tired.

"Mom's still alive." Getting to the point was more important than polite pleasantries.

"Oh." Then Rosa added, "Apparently, Bella's too pigheaded to die."

"This is no time for jokes. What're we going to do?"

"*We* aren't going to do anything. *You* are going to go home and play the shocked and dismayed daughter."

"I'm already shocked and dismayed."

"Good. Then, you're ready for your presentation." Rosa yawned. "You interrupted my nap." She giggled. "I had a busy afternoon you know. Gary and I are going out for Chinese later."

"I'm glad for you," Jenna said. "Don't you realize the seriousness of the situation? Suppose Mom regains consciousness?"

"Let me worry about that." Rosa sounded snappish. "Just do what I told you." She hung up.

Jenna sat staring at her cell phone. *I guess I should be grateful.* Based on how the way Larry found her mother, she'd be out of commission for a while. Perhaps permanently . . .

The clock on the dashboard read 3:15 P.M. Then she looked up and stared through the windshield. The spires of Gordonville State University stood before her like a beacon.

"Another aspect of the dysfunctional family," Malachi said addressing a group of sophomores in the lecture hall, "is unhealthy control." He wrote the terminology on the blackboard. "That's when a parent dominates every aspect of a child's life. It could leave the child feeling unlovable. Isolated. In some cases even angry."

His cell phone vibrated. He pulled it out of his jacket pocket. Jenna's number appeared on the caller ID. It said urgent. His adrenaline kicked in.

Malachi spoke to the class. "Excuse me, I have to take this. Uh, start reading chapter three."

He stepped out into the hall. As soon as he returned Jenna's call and she told him all that Larry and Diane found at the house, Malachi sank down into a nearby chair.

"Just stay where you are," he said. "I'll come get you." After he hung up, Malachi muttered, "My nightmare."

Malachi parked his car as close to the house as possible. Jenna caught her breath.

My house.

The police cordoned it off with yellow tape. The ambulance was also on the scene likewise, reporters and their camera crew. A crowd began forming as the news of Bella's attack began to spread.

Jenna surveyed the scene. *I hope Rosa knows what she's doing.* Too late now.

Despite the tragic situation, Malachi was glad he chose his designer blazer. He reached into the glove compartment for his comb and quickly ran it through his hair. Then, he and Jenna got out of the car and began walking toward the property.

Jenna saw an Asian-American man in his early forties. She studied him as he immediately began to heard toward them. His stride, his cool demeanor. The dark suit. Ornamental oxfords. Everything about him screamed cop.

Stay calm. She had to remember what Rosa taught her. Especially now.

"Detective Sergeant Richard Chang." He looked from Jenna to Malachi. "Is either or both of you related to the victim?"

"I am," Jenna said, noting the detective's handsomeness. She introduced herself and Malachi. "My mother is Bella Crandall. I—I live with her. Lawrence Belmar called me. He's my sister's fiancé." She hoped that Detective Chang didn't hear her heartbeat throbbing like conga drums. "My mother, she's . . . "

"Holding on. The paramedics are with her now." Chang looked grim. The sight appalled the detective who had seen a lot during his stint as a New York City detective. A victim sprawled out on the floor close to death. Evidence of the perpetrator having had a meal. In a city or a relatively big town, this might have been just another crime story, but in the village of Gordonville, this was horrifying. Yes, the village did have the occasional vandalism, truancy, breaking and entering. *But attempted murder?* Murder itself hadn't occurred here in over fifty years. Granted, Bella Crandall wasn't dead—yet. Hopefully, she wouldn't die. On top of that, this was a high-profile crime. He hated those. They added pressure on the department.

He sighed. *Mayor Urbanowski.* He was political bedfellows with the victim's eldest daughter, who happened to be New York's A.D.A. Hizzoner was gonna be on top of this. He could get a call from the governor. They were pals too. *I thought I escaped all this.*

The detective was at a place in his life when he needed a change of scenery. When he relocated from the Midtown South Precinct in New York City to Gordonville to take the job as detective sergeant, he thought it was the perfect opportunity. He didn't even mind the fact that he had limited manpower and had to handle more than one task, given that the department was small. Some of his team had multiple duties as well.

Jenna breathed a sigh of relief that would've made Rosa proud. She had to keep up the semblance of the worried daughter, which wasn't entirely an act. *Mom could wake up at any moment.* She looked over by the crepe myrtle. Diane and Larry were sitting on the ground, wrapped in each other's arms.

Detective Chang followed her gaze. Larry was cooperative when he was questioning him earlier. He'd seen the clothing designer on television and he was prepared to dislike him. The man was shallow but to his surprise, the man acted responsibly even if he did show a little resentment. He didn't see the need for the detective to question either him or his fiancée since they were the ones who might've saved Bella's life. Diane, on the other hand, was a trip. Interrogating her showed "a lack of sensitivity on his part." Detective Chang pursed his lips. The fashion model was laying on the grief a bit too thick. *Nervous perhaps?*

"Your mother managing to survive is a miracle in itself," Detective Chang said. "Considering how long she lay there before your sister and Mr. Belmar arrived."

Jenna groaned. Continuing with her act, she started heading toward the house, but Chang blocked her just as Malachi put his arm out to stop her.

"You can't go in there. It's a crime scene." Chang looked around at the spectators then frowned. It didn't take long for word to get around that the mother of the Crandall sisters was the victim of a brutal crime.

Detective Chang signaled to Jenna to follow him over to where Larry and Diane were sitting. Malachi followed, thanking God silently that Diane and Larry came to the house in time.

"Larry said there was bruising around her wrist," Jenna said when they arrived at the spot where Diane and Larry were sitting. She was stunned. She hadn't counted on her mother and Rosa getting into a fight.

Diane couldn't bear to hear the details. She *saw* the details. She had fond childhood memories of herself, Lauren and Mom preparing meals in the kitchen. Now the room was tainted. She'd never be able to get the picture of her mother lying half-dead out of her mind. Diane started whimpering.

"The suspect didn't leave any fingerprints on the teakettle or the dishes?" Malachi asked. Immediately, he adjusted his collar after Chang began sizing him up. He knew better than to interrupt police procedures.

Detective Chang's mouth slowly curved into a smile. "You from the city?"

Malachi relaxed. "Yeah. Brooklyn."

"Whereabouts?"

"Crown Heights."

"Flatbush," Chang said.

Diane got up and moved towards another part of the property. She couldn't care less about this Brooklyn love fest. Larry followed.

"Don't leave the area," Detective Chang instructed.

"We won't," Larry said.

"And don't touch anything."

He turned his attention back to Jenna. "Did your mother expect any visitors?"

"No."

"Someone was there. He or she had tea and dessert while your mother lay bleeding."

Malachi groaned.

Jenna gasped. Larry didn't say anything about that.

Detective Chang observed their reactions. "Yeah, I was disgusted too. You gotta really hate someone to be able to do that."

Malachi started kicking a small stone. Understandably, Jenna and Alan had serious issues with their mother. She was an abuser. A little known fact. Was either of them going to reveal that now? Probably not. They've kept quiet about it all these years. They couldn't have pulled off such a heinous crime. They didn't fit the profile. Alan didn't have a vindictive bone in his body. And Jenna didn't have the courage to leave home much less attack anyone.

Malachi looked toward the backyard garden. A chickadee pitched onto the rim of the birdbath. As he watched the bird take a drink, something Jenna said came back to him.

"Rosa always hated them."

Malachi put on his poker face to hide his growing agitation. Jenna's former childhood friend couldn't have had anything to do with this. She wasn't even around.

"What about DNA?" Malachi's need to stop his current line of thinking outweighed the good sense to keep quiet during an interrogation.

"Larry said the weapon was left in the sink," Jenna said. He told her about finding the bloody cast-iron pan in the sink. She felt queasy. Now she knew what Rosa wanted to do with it.

"It appears to be what the assailant used." Detective Chang looked at Malachi. Ordinarily he didn't answer questions. "We didn't find any used dishes."

"According to your sister your mother loves tea."

"Very much," Jenna said.

"Your mom's visitor must've surprised her," Detective Chang said.

Malachi shivered. In his mind's eye, he saw the three skeletons sitting around the Crandall's kitchen table.

Now there were two.

"Diane and Larry both said your mother has tea at four o'clock every day and yet the table was set for one and it was nowhere near four o'clock."

Malachi looked at Jenna with surprise, forgetting himself. She was looking at him, shamefaced.

Chang looked from one to the other. "Either of you care to share?"

"It's nothing," Malachi said.

"I'll be the judge of that."

"I prepare four o'clock tea for Mom when I'm home." Jenna glanced quickly at Malachi. *Now you know.* She twirled a strand of hair. Detective Chang's eyes seemed to pierce right through her, as if he were trying to read her mind.

"When you're home." Chang regarded her for a few unsettling seconds then added, "That would be weekends and holidays."

"Yes."

His silence begged the question, *why?*

"She's my mother." Jenna was relieved when Detective Chang finally stopped staring at her and began writing in his notepad.

Malachi stared steadfastly at Jenna. *So this is why you always ended our dates so early.* Why didn't she tell me? I would've understood.

"Did she make you do anything else?" Detective Chang asked.

Jenna continued twirling her hair. "She didn't *make* me do anything." *I must stay calm.* "It's just being a good daughter."

"I see. Suppose you wanted to go out on a Saturday afternoon? Then what?"

Jenna could feel Malachi staring at her. *Why didn't I tell him the truth?* He already knew about her and her brother's history with their mother. Malachi was supportive. He still stayed around even though her mother and her sisters had been rude beyond the pale. He would've understood about the tea.

Malachi must've noticed by now that I haven't said anything about the abuse. Diane hasn't said anything either. Detective Chang would've definitely said something. Of course, she wouldn't. Not in front of Larry.

Detective Chang waited for Jenna's reply. The silence was almost tangible. He was starting to lose his patience. He was about to voice his displeasure when the front door to the house opened. The paramedics came out carrying Bella on a stretcher. Diane ran toward them, as did Jenna, who was glad for the disruption.

Jenna gasped and Diane sobbed. The sight of the thick blood-soaked bandages around their mother's head was horrifying.

"Is she going to be all right?" Jenna asked. She felt troubled, confused. The woman who caused her so much misery lay lifeless before her. Maybe she was dying. She never wanted things to come to this, but her mother insisted on being adversarial. On the other hand, she would have peace from now on. She would wake up to a stress free life.

Unless, Mom wakes up . . .

"She's stabilized," one of the paramedics replied.

Malachi, who came up behind them, was equally aghast. Based on the extent of Bella's condition, the culprit's hatred was palpable. True, Jenna's mother disliked him from day one, but he couldn't find it within himself to rejoice about this. Regardless of Bella's faults, she didn't deserve this. Chang's remark about hating a person came back to him. Suppose the authorities found out about the hostility Bella held toward him. Malachi grew uncomfortable. They'd think he finally got tired and decided to clobber her if they knew about that. Bella wanted him out of her daughter's life, but trying to kill her wasn't worth it. Besides, it went against his principles. Would Detective Chang believe that? Then again, people killed for less.

Detective Chang joined them. He turned to Jenna and said, "I'm sorry, Ms. Crandall, but I need to ask you some more questions."

"I understand."

Diane gave her a dirty look. "What do you mean, 'you understand?'" She raised her voice an octave. "He's treating us like suspects. Can't you see that?"

Immediately, the cameras were on them. Various newscasters simultaneously began giving an account of Diane's outburst.

Diane stared angrily at Jenna. The initial shock of finding her mother almost dead was wearing off. Did Jenna's friend really do this? Was Alan right? Tension was making her reckless. Lauren couldn't get here soon enough. She wanted her big sister badly.

Jenna looked around at the cameras and the spectators. In a low voice Jenna asked, "What's wrong with you? People are watching." What was Diane thinking? Just because Mom was incapacitated didn't change the rules. Or did it?

Diane crossed her arms. Jenna had a lot of nerve reminding her about decorum.

Malachi shoved his hands into his pockets. You'd think Diane would be more sophisticated. Didn't she understand the detective was only doing his job? *She must be dumber than I thought.*

Chang scowled. Diane was going to be a problem. He didn't want to give the press fodder. And there was gonna be fodder. Already he sensed that something was off. Why was Jenna making tea for her mother? Her explanation didn't ring true. It was no secret that the Crandall matriarch was active in the church. Bella was a healthy woman. Her acts of charity were public.

If she drank tea at four o'clock everyday, why was she having it so early today? And what's with the attitude that Diane gave her sister a while ago? That wasn't very affectionate. He tapped his pen against his notepad. The Crandall's were supposed to have this close-knit Christian family thing going. Diane even made this big thing about it in on one of those tabloid shows.

"It's standard procedure," Detective Chang said. Diane held up her chin. "You tried to make us," she pointed to Larry, "feel guilty about having a key to my own mother's house. We were the ones who reported the crime to you people in the first place."

Her voice rose even louder. Detective Chang's face grew flushed. If he could find a reason to lock her up, he would go for it.

Larry could see that Chang was getting ready to blow a gasket. He could just see Diane's arrest on the evening news. Worried, he pulled her aside. "I don't like this anymore than you do, Diane, but we have to cooperate, okay?" He looked over at Bella. In a louder voice, Larry said, "Let's ride in the ambulance. That is, if it's okay with you, Detective."

Chang waved his hand in dismissal. "Go ahead." He'd had enough of Diane. If he needed to question her, he'd call her.

"No," Diane said. "I want to wait for Lauren."

"Are you sure?" Larry asked.

"Yes. She's on her way."

Although it was comforting to have Larry by her side, she couldn't face her mother's possible demise without her big sister by her side.

Soon, the paramedics drove away with Bella.

Jenna looked at the gawking crowd, the authorities walking through the garden, the reporters drinking up as much news and celebrity gossip as they could find. Thanks to her sister, they got a tidbit. Rosa said to "play the shocked and dismayed daughter", but this was too much. She just wanted to walk away. And keep on walking.

Jenna started rubbing her throbbing temples. She wanted to be alone—at home.

"Headache?" Malachi asked.

"Just tension."

"Come with me," Detective Chang said.

Detective Chang, Jenna and Malachi, took seats on the backyard patio. Malachi was grateful that the officer allowed him to be with Jenna as he took a seat in a Victorian garden chair with trelliswork.

"Can I get you anything, Ms. Crandall?" Chang asked.

"Call me Jenna. And water's fine. Thanks."

Chang gestured to George Davidson, a police officer in his early thirties. He removed his hat and wiped the sweat off his brow as he strode over to Detective Chang. His dirty blonde hair blew in the warm July breeze.

"You and Officer Tedesco bring us some water, please," Detective Chang said.

"Sure, Sarge."

"When you get back, I want you to stick around."

"Gotcha," Davidson said. He was grinning as he walked away. The boss wanted him to listen in on the interrogation. Later on, they would compare notes. It's what they did.

Chang turned his attention back to Jenna. The kettle was still warm even when he arrived at the scene. That put the time of the crime prior to two o'clock. "Where were you today?"

"Work."

"Where's that?"

"Wheat, Prentiss & Associates. It's a public relations firm downtown. I'm the receptionist." *Did he know that?*

"Tell me about your whereabouts between noon and two o'clock."

"I was at lunch."

"Where'd you eat?"

"I brown-bagged it."

"So, you ate in the cafeteria."

"No. In the park across the street from the office."

"Can anyone vouch for you?"

"I ate alone."

Chang was writing the information down in his notepad just as Officer Davidson returned with William "Bill" Tedesco. The rookie officer helped distribute the bottled water.

"Tedesco, make sure none of those curiosity-seekers get too close," Chang said.

"Right." He walked away.

Davidson was eying the dainty English garden furniture. He cringed before sitting down on a Victorian chair, which reminded the officer of a vanilla cupcake. *If the press takes a picture of me, I swear I'll sue.*

"What time did you return to the office?" Detective Chang asked.

"2:05." Jenna opened her bottle of water and took a long drink. "Bree was a little annoyed."

"Who's she?"

"One of the college interns who works at the firm."

"Why was she annoyed?"

"I cut into her lunchtime." Jenna smiled nervously.

"What were you doing before?" Detective Chang asked.

Jenna took another sip of water. "The weather was so beautiful I lost track of time." Jenna opened her handbag and took out a paperback. "I got engrossed in this." She showed

Chang studied the cover; an attractive 20th century woman fleeing from an eerie manor, her flowing gown billowing in what the reader could only imagine was a windy night by the moor. "I'm a spy novel man myself."

Jenna put the paperback away.

"Was your mother expecting anyone?"

Jenna smiled. "You already asked me that." Again, his eyes were boring into her. Jenna was cringing inwardly. "She was supposed to attend a church meeting later this evening. Mom's an elder."

Chang nodded. Diane already mentioned it.

Jenna looked down at her hands and for some reason, found herself wishing that she had the patience to sit down for a manicure like Lauren and Diane. "If Mom was going to do anything else today, it might've been with Diane and Larry." She told him about their meeting with the realtor.

Chang knew about that too. Diane and Larry mentioned it during their interrogation. "Are your sister and her fiancé staying with you and your mother while they're in town?"

He thought he saw a shadow pass over her face. "No. They're staying at The Lorelei House."

Chang turned a page over in his notepad. *Close-knit family my Aunt Minnie.* "I'm gonna ask you the same question I asked them. Did your mother have an argument with anyone?"

Jenna took another drink of water. "No."

Malachi started swinging his leg.

Chang twiddled his pen. *Was that apprehension in her eyes?* "Your cooperation is vital to this case."

"You think she's hiding something?" Malachi asked before he could stop himself. Unease got the better of him. Rosa as well as Jenna and Alan's brutal relationship with Bella was in the back of his mind.

"Since you live at home, Chang said, ignoring Malachi, "you would know more about your mother's habits. "You could know something and not realize it."

Malachi sang to himself as he played with the rock. *Told you so.*

"Now, what about your father?"

"Daddy doesn't live with us." Her tone was defensive, but she couldn't help it. The detective wanted to make her father a person of interest. On top of that a secret was about to come out. After a frustrated sigh, Jenna explained about her parents' de facto separation. "My father's not a violent man," Jenna said.

Chang and Officer Davidson exchanged glances. The Crandall's did a fantastic job of hiding things. The detective wondered again, about Diane's emoting when he was interrogating her and Larry earlier. She certainly neglected to volunteer that. His instincts began acting up. Was she hiding something? If so, what?

Detective Chang made another note then said, "Nothing was stolen. "From what I can see this crime was all about pure unadulterated hate. Does your mother have any enemies?"

Malachi looked down at his oxfords.

"Everybody loved Mom. She's very popular around here."

"Bashing someone in the head then enjoying a pastry while the victim lay bleeding on the floor is a clear indication," Chang said. He looked Jenna straight in the eye. "That person's still out there."

Jenna fought very hard not to turn away. *Stay calm. Breathe. That's what Rosa would say.*

"So, if you can remember something, anything at all," Detective Chang continued, "it would be helpful."

Jenna nodded.

"We noticed your artwork. It's pretty impressive."

"Thank you."

"Told you," Malachi muttered, relieved for the switch in topics.

"Forensics also found a broken jar of Vaseline in your bedroom," Chang said.

Jenna squeezed the now empty water bottle a bit too tightly, crushing it in the process. "Is that important?"

"Why would you leave that there?" Chang asked, answering a question with a question, at the same time making mental note of her reaction.

"I forgot." Her voice held a slight edge.

Malachi removed his blazer then loosened his collar. He could tell that Jenna was trying to keep it together. Why was she unnerved about the broken jar?

Detective Chang waited for Jenna to elaborate.

She sighed. "I was a little annoyed, all right?"

"About?"

Jenna told him about having to change plans last Saturday to go house hunting with Diane. He doesn't need to know that her mother slapped her or that she had arranged to meet Rosa.

Malachi corroborated Jenna's story. He was about to mention running into her at Thornbush Lane when Something kept his mouth shut. It was as if he was being told now wasn't the time to speak. He shouldn't have been speaking now.

Jenna too noticed that Malachi omitted her trek to Thornbush Lane. She thanked him silently. He really was trustworthy. She felt even sillier for not telling him about the tea.

Chang started clicking his pen. "Do you usually do as you're told?" Jenna sounded like a servant more than a daughter. He was unable to get the tea off his mind. "I don't understand the question."

"Well, clearly, you didn't want to look at houses, yet you went along."

"I was just having a bad day," Jenna said.

"I see. Chang wasn't buying it. He'd seen enough to know that all wasn't bliss in the Crandall family. The hostility Diane showed towards Jenna was blatant. The broken jar of Vaseline was a sign of irritation. Jenna was peeved that day.

Jenna put the water bottle down by the bench. Then, she folded her hands on her lap. *Breathe.* "Diane is family."

"That brings me back to my earlier question. Having to prepare four o'clock tea for your mother must've cramped your style."

"It didn't."

"You're contradicting yourself."

"How so?"

"You said you had plans Saturday. Your sister comes to town and your mother," he consulted his notes, "coaxed you into just abandoning your plans."

Jenna removed her suit jacket and rolled up the sleeves of her red cotton blouse.

"Mom felt that we should've all been there to support Diane."

Detective Chang gave her a piercing stare. "If you were angry about having to go out with your sister, you must've been seething about making tea for your mother."

"I don't let things bother me," Jenna said.

Malachi recalled her grisly picture. *No, you only draw a snake eating someone alive.*

Suddenly, a woman screamed.

Detective Chang and Officer Davidson ran toward the direction. Jenna and Malachi followed.

Lauren had arrived.

21

"Let go of me!" Lauren cried.

She was fighting and thrashing in the arms of Officer Tedesco and two other officers Nanci Vega and Jay Levi, who was trying to restrain her from running into the house. The crowd was gawking. Some were taking pictures with their camera phones. Newscasters reported on the drama unfolding. At the same time, Julian, Alan and Elise arrived and like the neighbors, they too were gaping at the scene.

More theatrics. Chang was livid. He could understand Jenna wanting to enter the premises. But Lauren? She's a lawyer. She knows the house is a crime scene. Chang frowned at the drama and wondered just how much of this show was for the cameras. Diane already gave them a production. Now Lauren was giving the tabloids more material.

"Lauren." Diane waved, relieved to see her big sister.

Lauren calmed down. When the officers thought she was composed, they released her. Lauren gave them dirty looks before adjusting her pinstriped summer suit.

After getting clearance, Julian, Alan and Elise joined Jenna and Malachi. Julian hugged Jenna.

Alan patted her on the shoulder. "You okay?"

"I'm fine," Jenna replied.

Malachi thought he detected something meaningful in Alan's question. Or did he imagine it?

Indignant, Lauren said, "She's not the victim. Mom is."

"What is wrong with you?" Julian asked, appalled by his eldest daughter's behavior.

Chang watched the exchange with interest and revulsion. Apparently, Lauren wasn't too fond of Jenna.

"I don't understand," Lauren said, not fazed by her father's disapproval or by what anyone else thought. "What happened? "Where's Mom?"

Diane's eyes began filling with fresh tears. "They took her to the hospital. The ambulance just left."

Lauren put a smooth, manicured hand on top of her upswept hair. In a grief-filled voice she asked, "Who would do this?"

"That's what I intend to find out. Detective Sergeant Richard Chang."

Lauren turned toward him with a haughty look.

Malachi raised his eyebrows. *You did not just dis a cop.*

Chang was familiar with Lauren's style in and out of the courtroom and he wasn't about to let her intimidate him. He dismissed her with a cutting look then proceeded to introduce himself to Julian, Alan and Elise.

Lauren's mouth fell open.

Malachi suppressed a chuckle. *Take that, Counselor.*

Diane dabbed her eyes. "He's questioning us."

"We went over this already," Larry muttered. He didn't want her egging Lauren on into having a fit over a routine police procedure. He looked around. He didn't like the attention Lauren was drawing.

"We're suspects?" Lauren's voice was shrill.

Larry sighed. *Too late.* He gave Diane a disapproving look.

Lauren stared defiantly at Detective Chang. "Do you know who I am?"

"As a matter of fact, Counselor, I do."

His tone clearly implied just how much he cared. Again, Malachi smothered a smile.

"And like the rest of your family," Chang continued, "you'll have to answer some questions."

"I'm in the middle of litigation when I get this horrendous message about my mother and this is how my family and I are treated?"

Chang crossed his arms. "And just how are you and your family being treated, Counselor?"

"For one, we could be missing our final moments with our mother." She looked at Julian. "My father should be with his wife. Instead, we're standing here. Instead of questioning us, *Detective*, you should be looking for the real culprit."

"Lauren's right," Diane said, feeling empowered now that her elder sister was here. She ignored the nagging feeling in the back of her mind. Rosa had been getting worse before she left. *But why did she come back?* She nibbled on her lower lip. Rosa couldn't possibly have done this. Could she? Lauren didn't think so. She was pointing the authorities to an outsider. And even if Rosa were guilty, they couldn't say anything. *No one was supposed to know about her.*

Larry started pinching the bridge of his nose. The detective offered them the opportunity to leave with the ambulance, but Diane wouldn't take it. She insisted on waiting for Lauren. Larry stiffened when he saw the ogre-like expression on Chang's face. He pulled Diane aside. "Enough."

Diane whispered. "But Lauren—"

"Your sister can do whatever the hell she wants," Larry interrupted. "I care about you. Stop asking for trouble."

Julian coughed. "Can the questions wait, Detective Chang? At least until after we get an update on my wife's condition?" He wanted to get Lauren and Diane out of there before they got themselves arrested.

Chang maintained his cool. Already he was tired of the Crandall's and the investigation hadn't even begun. "All right. He put his notepad away. He ran his fingers through his smooth black hair. "Whoever wasn't questioned I expect at headquarters later." He looked directly at Lauren. "No exceptions. The sooner I can wrap up the preliminaries the quicker this investigation can get under way. Jenna, do you have someplace you can stay?"

"Well . . . I . . . " She hadn't thought of that. *They* hadn't thought of that. After all the careful planning that Rosa did, Jenna was going to have to live elsewhere.

Elise spoke up. "She can stay with us." She and Alan lived in a large Cape Cod on Donnelly Drive in the Lakewood section of Gordonville.

Detective Chang nodded. "Fine."

Alan stood deep in thought. At least he could keep an eye on Jenna. Jenna smiled as she stuffed her annoyance down to the pit of her stomach. Who knew how long it would take the police to complete their investigation? She loved her brother and sister-in-law dearly, but not to live cheek by jowl.

On top of that, her dinner plans with Malachi was ruined. It was inevitable but no less annoying. Until now, she hadn't realized just how much she was looking forward to going out to dinner with him. She was planning to have a glass of wine in Rosa's honor. Then again, how would it look if she were to turn to him now and say, "I'm really in the mood for a T-Bone steak and some Cabernet Sauvignon? How about you?" She could just see his Born-Again eyes bugging out.

Jenna cleared her throat. "Thanks, Elise. My car's still in town." She explained about Malachi driving her over. "I was a wreck."

"That's understandable, dear," Julian said.

Alan adjusted his collar. "We'll swing by later and get it."

Chang lowered his voice. "We'll be posting an officer outside of your mother's room as a precaution."

Stillness settled over the Crandall's, Malachi and Larry. The assailant could strike again once he or she realizes that the job wasn't finished.

Jenna looked down at the ground. A guard wasn't necessary. Rosa wasn't going to do anything. Not yet anyway. But they didn't know that.

She felt eyes upon her. She looked up. Alan was staring at her.

A sudden wave of panic ran through her. *Does he know? He couldn't know. He hasn't even said if he knows about Rosa's return. He would've said. No. He's just worried about me.*

Jenna gave him a reassuring smile then looked away.

Unknown to them, Detective Chang was watching Alan and Jenna with keen interest.

"Sarge."

Officer Tedesco came over with a woman in handcuffs. The detective did not disguise his shock and anger.

"Mrs. Beery?" Julian wondered what other surprises this day held.

"You know this woman?" Detective Chang asked.

"She's our neighbor," Julian said.

Malachi knew it wasn't right, but he got a twisted pleasure seeing her in handcuffs. He remembered her from the wedding. She was a bore.

"We've known her since we were kids," Lauren said. She addressed Officer Tedesco and in an indignant tone said, "Uncuff her now."

"This is my domain, Counselor," Detective Chang said.

"And I'm representing her should she need counsel," Lauren retorted.

"She insisted on seeing who was in charge," Officer Tedesco said. "When we told her no she tried to break through. Claims she has information."

Jenna looked keenly at Norma. What could she possibly have to say? She couldn't have seen Rosa. Did she?

"All right, take the cuffs off," Detective Chang said. Once the officer uncuffed her, Chang took out his notepad. "Name?"

"Mrs. Norma Beery. I've been the Crandall's neighbor for over thirty years." She nodded at Lauren. "I was even at her wedding. Known her since she was nine years old."

"And what is that you had to say?"

Norma patted her hair. "I spoke with Bella this morning. We talked about the church meeting this evening."

"What time?"

"8:15. I know because I was making breakfast for my daughter Haley. Bella was good to her. She's good to everybody."

Jenna looked keenly at Mrs. Beery. She resisted the urge not to roll her eyes.

"The Crandall's are solid citizens in this community," Mrs. Beery went on. "And I can't imagine why anyone would want to—"

"Did she say anything out of the ordinary?" Detective Chang asked interrupting her. He wanted to move this impromptu interview along quickly. Mrs. Beery was what Mrs. Goldberg, his old neighbor back in Flatbush, would've referred to as a noodge.

"No. But she was glad I called. She said she needed to hear a friendly voice."

"Why's that?"

"She didn't say," Norma replied.

Jenna looked puzzled. Mom needed cheering? Was it possible she felt a little bad about what she said about me this morning?

"Sometimes a person just needs some cheer," Mrs. Beery continued. "Bella does so much for the community."

As the Crandall's, Larry and Malachi were leaving for the hospital, reporters called out to them to make statements.

Lauren addressed the reporters. "We will not rest until the guilty party has been brought to justice."

"I hope she did it," Detective Chang said to Officer Davidson in a low voice. "I want an excuse to lock her up."

Davidson laughed.

By 11:00 P.M., Detective Chang was back in his office. He rubbed his tired eyes. There was a knock on the door. "Yeah?"

Officer Davidson entered, holding a paper bag with the Delsey's logo on it. "Thought you could use this."

Chang pushed aside some files as the officer put the bag down on the desk and began taking out two Styrofoam cups of coffee, some crullers for himself and some black and white cookies for the detective. "What no donuts?"

"Too cliché." Davidson grabbed a chair by the azaleas and pulled it over to Chang's desk.

Chang took a bite of the black and white cookie as he stared at the plant. It was a gift from his mother. At first, he thought it was too frilly for the office. Why couldn't she have brought him a cactus or bamboo? *"The place needs color."* At least the azaleas were orange. She could've chosen pink, her favorite color. The guys would never let him live it down.

Chang took a sip of coffee. He closed his eyes and savored the taste. Delsey's knew how to make a cup of coffee. Regular. Just the way he liked it. No cappuccino. No lattes or café macchiato although they offered those too. He took another bite of his black and white cookie. Their pastries were good too.

He took another sip of coffee. Mom's recent visit to Gordonville was—uncomfortable. *"Why have you stopped going to Mass?"* How did he manage to let his mother get that information out of him so easily, he was a cop for heaven's sake? He was supposed to be close-mouthed. His mouth curved into a tiny smile. This was Mom. He had to explain. It started when he was at the Midtown South. He didn't have time for church. Any free time he needed for sleep. After awhile it just became easier to believe that somewhere between birth and death if he led a good life, he'd someday go to Heaven. Mom's interpretation: He was relying on his own strength instead of God's. He rather face ten hardened criminals than to see the disappointment on her face. All those years of CCD classes down the drain.

Gratefully, she moved on to a more comfortable subject. *"Maybe if you met a nice girl and settled down, she'd encourage you to go to church more often."* A vision of Nanci Vega with her brown curly hair and big beautiful brown eyes popped into his head. She loved the azaleas . . .

"Uh, Sarge?"

Chang snapped to attention. "What was that?"

"The latest on the Crandall case."

"Bella's in a coma," Detective Chang said. "So far, the family's alibis check out. Including Professor Chase's." He frowned.

"What?" Davidson asked.

"Jenna's boyfriend."

'What about him?"

"I think the professor knows more than he's saying. I can't prove it. Just a feeling."

Davidson took a sip of coffee. The department was familiar with the detective's instincts and often teased him about it. Nevertheless, he had to admit that his boss' gut feelings seldom ever failed.

Detective Chang told Officer Davidson what transpired between Alan and Jenna. He couldn't stop thinking about that look Alan gave to Jenna. What did he know? During questioning, he couldn't shake Alan. And Jenna seemed reluctant to talk about her little tantrum with the Vaseline jar. *Something tells me she wasn't very pleased with Mommy.*

"What do you think it means?" Officer Davidson asked interrupting his thoughts.

"Don't know. Anyway, Nelson Door arrives tomorrow from Hollywood for questioning." He took another sip of coffee. "Lauren's rabid. So's Mr. Door. He has to, and I quote, 'Postpone an important film project.'"

"Finding his mother-in-law's attacker isn't important?" Davidson asked. "By the way, one of us could've flown to Los Angeles to question him," Officer Davidson said.

"Looking for a taxpayer-funded California vacation, George? Anyway, I don't think he liked the idea of cops on his set."

Officer Davidson held up his cup. "To the devoted son-in-law." Detective Chang raised his cup and together they toasted Nelson Door. Then, Davidson said, "Something doesn't make sense."

"A lot of things about this case don't make sense," Detective Chang said.

"An attempt is suddenly made on this woman's life," Officer Davidson began, "and no one knows of an enemy?" He dunked his cruller into his coffee. "Nothing just happens. Somebody wanted her dead."

"Ya think?"

"The whole thing reminds me of a pressure cooker that exploded."

"Exactly!" Chang exclaimed and slammed his hand on the desk, nearly spilling their coffees. He talked about the coolness he witnessed between Jenna and her elder sisters, Julian and Bella's faux marriage and Lauren and Diane's unprofessional behavior. In addition, Diane and Larry's behavior when Malachi and Jenna arrived was cool. Both couples kept their distance. It continued even after Julian and the rest of the family arrived. The term special units came to mind. "And it seems like Bella was treating Jenna like a housekeeper."

"What's the deal with her having to make four o'clock tea?" Davidson asked.

"Hold that thought," Detective Chang said. "I found out from the daughter-in-law that she and Bella weren't exactly on friendly terms."

Davidson raised his eyebrows. The close-knit image was falling apart fast.

"Elise said they wouldn't destroy each other if you left them alone together," Chang said. "They were civilized but frigid. She also said that her mother-in-law initiated a lot of the let's say aggression in the family. Along with Lauren and Diane."

Davidson made a face. "Those people are one big bag of candy corn."

"She's the only one who bothered to mention that little detail."

"I never did buy into that lovey-dovey stuff the Crandall's were always putting out to the media," Officer Davidson said. "It's a load of crap? Like they have this need for the world to see how loving they are. Who the hell cares?"

Detective Chang broke off another piece of cookie. Davidson has a point. Why the need to display all that love and care to the world especially if it was fake? "Anyway, Elise was out grocery shopping with a neighbor around 1:30."

"Something's definitely weird between Jenna and Bella," Davidson said.

Chang leaned forward. "Go on."

"Bella wasn't bedridden. Why did Jenna have to serve her tea? And why did she have to look at houses? I don't think Diane would've cared whether she was there or not."

"She would if she wanted to annoy her sister. She was certainly instigating this afternoon."

"I love my mother too," Officer Davidson said. "But if I was still living at home and she was making those demands on my days off, I'd have left long time ago."

Chang held up his hand. "Demands? That's an interesting word?"

Davidson shrugged.

"Seemed fitting didn't it?" Detective Chang asked.

"Yeah. Guess it did." Officer Davidson paused to think. "Jenna has a steady job. What's keeping her home? She could afford to get her own apartment."

"So you conclude she's unhappy."

"Isn't she?" Davidson dunked his cruller into his cup of coffee. Between bites he said, "I don't care what Jenna says about courtesy and family. A tragedy occurs and everybody's on teams. No group hugs. No consolatory words for each other."

Chang nodded. "Regardless of her largesse, someone's unhappy with Bella Crandall."

Davidson looked thoughtful. "You mentioned that look between Jenna and her brother. Let's say he suspected her. That would mean she lost it. Why let it get this far?"

"You're assuming the family knows Jenna is unhappy."

"How could they not see?" Davidson asked.

"People see what they want to see." Chang picked up a pen and started tapping it on the desktop. Did Jenna keep her temper in check around her mother only to go ballistic when she was alone? Who could blame her? Bella Crandall didn't sound like an easy person to live with. *Jenna kept serving her mother. She went house-hunting last week Saturday with the family for Diane's benefit.* "I still can't get that broken Vaseline jar off my mind."

"Again, why doesn't Jenna just leave?" Officer Davidson asked.

Chang put down the pen. "Fear."

"Of her mother?"

Chang smiled enigmatically.

Now Davidson leaned forward. "Are you suggesting that Jenna had something to do with this? She's milquetoast."

"Don't be fooled, George. Jenna flung a jar. And she crushed that water bottle."

"It was plastic."

"But it demonstrates attitude—and latent strain."

"Sarge, come on, she doesn't have the strength to clobber her mother."

"Maybe not." Detective Chang took up the pen again and began twiddling it. "She's holding back something. So's her brother and her boyfriend."

"What do you think that is?" Officer Davidson asked.

"Don't know."

"Okay. If there were a *maternal* problem," Davidson began, "wouldn't the family have done something about it?"

"George, we're talking about people who seem to have a habit of hiding things. Like Bella and Julian's so-called marriage."

The younger officer chuckled. "That's not gonna stay secret for long."

"So who or what made Bella Crandall suddenly need cheering up?" Davidson asked.

"The person who entered the premises without leaving any fingerprints or footprints and attacked her," Detective Chang replied.

"And who likes lemon squares." Davidson chewed on another cruller.

"So far, the family believes it's an outsider," Chang said. "I'll assume the same. For now. However, I want you to check out Jenna's lunchtime alibi."

Malachi sat at the kitchen table listening to the crickets chirping outside his window. He popped open a can of root beer. He couldn't sleep, still reeling from the day's events and from his narrow escape with Detective Chang. When he accompanied Jenna and her family to the precinct for support, he thought he was in the clear. He wouldn't have to answer any questions. After all, Detective Chang acted indifferently towards him. *Wrong.* He dreaded the type of questions Chang would ask him; like for example, his relationship with Jenna's mother. The woman had no room for friendship; at least not with him. And her character was wanting. Plus, Detective Chang might have put him on the list of suspects.

He prayed for wisdom before he heard the first question. He couldn't lie, yet he didn't want to betray Jenna either. Didn't he promise her he wouldn't tell anyone about her stormy past? *But did that have to include lying to a cop?* Fortunately, Detective Chang was only interested in his whereabouts before two o'clock. He didn't have to reveal anything about Mrs. Crandall's hidden temperament or their unfriendly relationship. He was never so glad to have once been a snake in the grass. It trained him well. He was impassive throughout the interrogation.

He took a sip of ginger ale. If Mrs. Crandall knew she had an enemy, would she have stood around in plain sight? She certainly paraded herself at the wedding. She was active in church and community affairs up to the time of the attack. That woman was not in fear of anyone. *Assuming she was capable of feeling fear.* Slowly, Malachi put down the soda can. *She was serving tea.* In the nightmare, a tea service was on the table. The skeletons cried out Rosa's name.

Malachi groaned, stood up, then started pacing the kitchen. It's not possible. Rosa's ancient history. But she did hate Mrs. Crandall. The *real* Mrs. Crandall. *The one I didn't tell Detective Chang about.* The one that no one told the police about. Jenna did a fantastic job keeping quiet about it as did Alan. And naturally, Lauren and Diane wouldn't say anything not when they had a hand in Bella, Alan and Jenna's dark past.

He walked over to the window. A full moon was shining over the Hudson River. In his mind's eye, he saw two images of the Crandall house, one with scenic gardens and pretty window boxes and another one at night; dark, ominous, unwelcoming.

Alan lay in bed staring up at the bedroom ceiling. Soft lamplight illuminated the bedroom. He answered all of Detective Chang's questions with the poise and skill he acquired over the years from being a Crandall. He worked for R.B. Consulting, P.C. Between the hours of twelve and two, he attended a business lunch with a client and another colleague.

When asked if his mother had any disputes with anyone, he looked the detective straight in the eye and said, *"No, Mom's a very popular person. I can't imagine why anyone would do this."* He really laid it on thick. Alan sat up then started punching the pillows. Rosa finally got out of control. After she set that fire, it was only a matter of time before something terrible happened. The sight of Mom lying in intensive care was terrifying. He could only imagine how Diane must've felt. She and Larry clued him in on what their mother looked like, lying in a pool of blood. Mom made his childhood a living hell, even threw him and his wife out of her house just the other day; nevertheless, he'd never wish a thing like this on her.

Alan stared at the phone. The neurologist could call at any moment. *I regret to inform you that your mother passed away at . . .* He breathed a heavy sigh, turned on his side and faced the window. He wanted his mother's love. Maybe now he'll never have it. Rosa left. But she came back. The past sixteen years were a lie. There was never any peace. Dad should know about her. If he told him the truth at the family gathering when he had the chance, none of this would've happened. He sighed. Now he couldn't tell Dad or Detective Chang. Not without speaking to Lauren and Diane first.

I have to talk to them. Now they have to listen. Lauren's act was nothing but a show. She and Diane had to know that Rosa was responsible. He would've pulled them aside while they were at the hospital, but there was too much chaos. And Dad. And Elise. She would've been especially curious.

As if on cue, Elise entered the bedroom. Although his back was to her, she knew Alan was grieving. Gently, she closed the door. She climbed into bed and wrapped her arms around him. She could feel the tension in his body.

She began massaging his shoulder. "I checked on Jenna." Did he just stiffen? "She's okay," Elise added. "Relatively speaking. I put her in the larger guest room. She'll be happy there."

Alan sat up. "Did she say anything?"

"She's grateful for our support. She's distant though. Like her mind is elsewhere. But that's understandable."

Alan took her hand. "What did Detective Chang ask you?"

"Where I was around one o'clock." She told him that she talked about her and Bella's less-than-stellar relationship.

"Why'd you tell him that?"

"Somehow it came up."

"He's a detective, Elise. He has ways of getting things out of people." He was more worried about Jenna and the part that Rosa played in this crime. It hadn't occurred to him to tell Elise not to say anything about her relationship with his mother.

"What's the big deal?" Elise asked. "I told him we were civil. Just not affectionate."

"He didn't need to know. I didn't tell him about my past with Mom. I doubt Jenna did either."

Elise looked puzzled. "What about your past with Bella?"

Alan played with the cover. He'd never told her just how bad it really was. As far as his wife knew, his mother was just oppressive, difficult. She didn't know just how complicated things were. "I just don't want to talk about it."

"I doubt anything's gonna come of it. Besides, the authorities would be more suspicious of me not you." With a half-smile, she added. "I'm the one who admitted she didn't get along with her mother-in-law."

"Don't even kid about that."

"Al, there's absolutely no connection between you, Jenna and your mother. You were kids back then." Elise looked into her husband's anxious eyes. "I'm not going to pretend that this isn't difficult. But please try to relax. You have to be strong for Jenna." Elise kissed him. "*We* have to be strong." She began to massage his shoulders. "I still can't believe this happened."

"What if a person got so fed up that he snaps?" Alan asked.

"It happens." Elise stopped massaging his shoulders. "Do you suspect someone?"

"Keep your voice down," Alan snapped.

Elise's mouth fell open. He nearly bit off her head.

"And no, I don't suspect anyone. It was just a rhetorical question." He got out of bed then stormed into the master bath, slamming the door.

Elise looked mystified. What had gotten into him? They had arguments before but not where he copped an attitude. She saw him lash out at Lauren and Diane whenever they pushed his buttons but not her. Her eyes started welling with tears. She stared at the closed door, growing angry and more confused. *What did I say?* Finally, Elise flung the covers aside then stormed out the room.

Alan looked at himself in the bathroom mirror. Reflected back was a scared adolescent boy in the body of a thirty-nine-year-old man. He turned on the faucet then splashed cold water on his face. After, he looked at himself in the mirror again. The water was dripping down his face and down the front of his black crewneck shirt as he whispered, "Rosa."

Down the hall in the guest room, Jenna lay wide-awake in the dark. After a few minutes, she turned on the lamp and looked around the spacious bedroom. It was contemporary traditional, with two night tables, a telephone, a Tiffany lamp and a table clock. A small boom box sat on the floor in the corner. Floral curtains matched the bed skirt. Elise did a nice job decorating the room, but she longed for her sanctuary.

Jenna sat up and picked up her cell phone. For what she had to say, it was best if she didn't use the landline.

22

"The brutal attack on Bella Crandall has rocked the sleepy Hudson River town of Gordonville."

As she was getting dressed the next morning, Jenna listened to the television newscaster in a detached manner. She marveled that she was able to sleep at all last night. By the time she got finished talking to Rosa, however, she was much more relaxed. As usual, her friend put her at ease. *"So what if you have to spend a few nights with Alan and Elise? When everything blows over, you'll be back home in your own bed."*

Jenna picked out a floral T-shirt, a pair of jeans and a baseball cap. Elise said she was welcome to any clothes she found in the closet since Jenna's were back at the house. She was putting on a black leather belt when she heard the newscaster say something about "speculations about revenge." She paused. Apparently, they were launching an investigation into past criminal indictments by Lauren Crandall-Door. Jenna straightened out her shirt. Her mouth curved into a slight smile. They were right but for the wrong reasons.

Jenna turned off the television then finished getting dressed. Next, she phoned the office. She closed her eyes, inhaled and willed herself to feel shock and misery. Soon she was speaking with Mr. Prentiss who with great compassion told her to take as much time as she needed.

She also spoke to some of her fellow coworkers, who offered her their support. Before long, Jenna hung up. A complacent smile was on her face. *I don't have to go to work.*

She took a pair of sunglasses she found in a drawer then went over to the boom box. She turned the dial until she found a hip-hop station. She set the volume on low. Soon she began to bop then dance to the music.

Later, Jenna went downstairs to the kitchen. The room smelled of fresh brewed coffee from the automatic coffeemaker. Jenna grinned at her Christmas gift to Alan and Elise. They loved coffee almost as much as Mom loved tea. Jenna poured herself a glass of orange juice. She was glad that neither her brother nor sister-in-law was up yet. She wasn't in the mood for conversation. Jenna took a sip of orange juice and admired her sister-in-law's choice of petite rose floral design wall covering.

I'm definitely redoing the kitchen when I go back home.

She finished her juice, put the glass in the sink, then stepped through the sliding glass doors to the backyard. She breathed in the fresh morning air. She went over to the hammock chair. She needed to think. How should she spend her first day of freedom?

Elise entered the kitchen. She watched Jenna through the sliding glass doors. She was still watching her when she heard Alan's footsteps coming down the stairs. She hadn't spoken a word to him since last night. She was still hurt but mostly confused. What was wrong with Alan? Why did he lash out? She knew he was upset about what happened to his mother, but that was no reason for him to take it out on her.

Unknown to Elise, Alan was standing at the threshold to the kitchen, staring at Elise. When he came out of the bathroom last night and saw that the bed was empty, he knew then that he blew it. He behaved like a jerk. Dealing with a family secret gone awry and now running amok was bad enough, but alienating his wife was wrong. He needed Elise now more than ever. Troubling days were ahead. He just lost it when she asked him if he suspected anyone.

Alan took a deep breath then entered the kitchen. He came up behind Elise and put his arm around her. He gave her a peck on the cheek. "I'm sorry."

Elise said, "We were all stressed last night."

Alan flinched. Her graciousness pricked his conscience.

"How about some cinnamon French toast?" Elise asked.

Alan beamed. That was his favorite breakfast. She did forgive him. He gave her a tight squeeze, spun her around and kissed her.

Elise returned his kisses although she should've been fuming. Alan's behavior last night was rude and obnoxious, but she loved him and he needed her. She knew that.

Alan tightened his hold on her and groaned with pleasure. Elise opened one eye. She was enjoying herself and she hated to ruin the moment but . . . "Alan, Jenna's outside." Her sister-in-law was facing the opposite direction. If she were to turn around, she would've gotten a good view of a very private moment.

Alan noticed Jenna for the first time. Her clothing blends with the background. *Like a chameleon.* He chuckled. "So what? She's over eighteen."

Elise made a face and pulled away from him.

"We're more popular now than ever before," Alan said with irony.

She went over to the refrigerator and took out some eggs and a carton of milk. "Somehow, I don't think Bella would've wanted this type of publicity."

Alan winced as he poured himself a cup of coffee. Elise had no idea how accurate that was.

"We should give Jenna a key to the house," Elise said. "We don't know how long she'll be here."

"Yeah." He didn't really want Jenna to have a key. They could end up in Rosa's hands.

Just then, Jenna reentered the kitchen.

"Morning," Alan greeted. "How're you holding up?"

"Okay."

"We're leaving for the hospital at 11:00," Alan said.

Jenna hid her disappointment by watching Elise crack eggs, add vanilla, nutmeg, then cream. She didn't want to return to the hospital. She just wanted to be alone with her thoughts, but she had to maintain the grieving image. On the other hand, she wanted to enjoy her first full day of freedom. That was more comforting than the memory of her mother lying in the ICU. A feeling of regret came over her. *Why? Mom treated Alan and me horribly.*

Elise noticed Jenna staring. "Hungry?"

"Not really."

"You should eat something," Elise said. "You barely ate last night."

"I had some orange juice."

"You need more than that," Elise said. "How about a cup of tea and some fresh strawberries? I picked them up at the market yesterday." She cringed. While she was shopping with their neighbor, Bella had a not-so-friendly visitor.

"I'll take a rain check," Jenna said.

She took a roll from the breadbox and put it inside of a sandwich bag. Then she stuffed the whole thing into her handbag.

"I'll be back by the time you're ready to leave."

"Where are you going?" Alan asked.

"For a walk."

"But where?" Alan asked.

Jenna scowled. "Around."

Elise stopped whisking the batter. "Your brother's just concerned about your safety. We don't know who this creep is that's running around."

Alan took a sip of coffee.

Jenna forced herself to smile. *Play it cool.* "I appreciate your concern, Alan. I just need some air."

"Just be careful," Elise said.

"I will." Jenna headed for the backdoor.

Alan said, "One more thing. What did you and Mom talk about yesterday morning?"

"Not much. You know how things are with us."

Alan looked uncomfortable. That was precisely the problem.

"What?" Jenna asked.

Elise looked from Alan to Jenna. She had not forgotten Alan's enigmatic behavior last night.

Alan took another sip of coffee. "I thought Mom may have said something that would shed some light on what happened." *What set Rosa off?*

"She was her usual self." Jenna put on the sunglasses and went out the backdoor.

Elise stared into the French toast batter. Alan was probing. She had to admit it. Was it because he knew something? Or did he think Jenna knew something? She was about to ask him when she changed her mind. Last night was still fresh in her mind. She resumed whisking.

Jenna strolled down Donnelly Drive. A robin red breast was foraging through a front yard. A man was jogging up the road. A woman sped by on her bicycle. Periodically, one of Alan and Elise's neighbors stopped to offer their commiserations and declare their desires for justice. She thanked them and as she looked into their eyes, she saw their terror. Their bewilderment. Their sense of security was gone.

Jenna played with the ends of her hair and kept walking.

She reached Forest Avenue, where she could see the tops of the maple trees of Lakewood Park, one of her and Everett's special places. There, they held hands as they walked, kissed or talked for hours about anything and everything. She was feeling the pain from the memories, then resentment of how she lost Everett and why. Then, she started thinking about her mother lying in the ICU. She started twirling a few strands of hair. No. She wasn't supposed to care. She put on her blue tooth headset. Soon, she had Rosa on the line.

"Are you at work?" Jenna asked.

Rosa yawned. "No. Tomorrow. What's up? My day hasn't officially started yet."

"Sorry," Jenna said. "Can we meet?"

"Now?"

"We need to talk."

"Again?"

"It won't be long," Jenna said. "I have to leave for the hospital with Alan and Elise. We're visiting Mom."

"You don't *have* to do anything anymore remember?"

"So are we going to meet?"

Rosa yawned again. "All right."

"You're the best. Come to Lakewood Park. I'll be by the lake."

Jenna was sitting on a bench watching the ducks and geese on the lake. A middle-aged man sat nearby reading the *Wall Street Journal*. He gave her a cursory glance before turning the page of his newspaper. She felt split in two. She wasn't sure if she wanted her mother to die after all. Too late now. She was in it too deep. If Mom recovered, she would rat her and Rosa out for sure. The town was a wreck. What was supposed to be a simple solution to an old problem was now a police investigation. If Rosa didn't do this plan right, what kind of job would she do on Lauren and Diane? Stressed, Jenna put a hand to her temple. *What's wrong with me? She knows what she's doing.*

"Boo!"

Jenna leaped off the bench. Rosa was laughing. The middle-aged man, also startled, looked up from his newspaper. Recovering from her fright, Jenna saw his dumbfounded expression. She couldn't blame him. Such strange behavior coming from someone Rosa's age must've seemed strange. But that was Rosa wild, spontaneous. Unconcerned by what others thought. Jenna signaled for them to move to another area. Rosa created enough of a show for one morning.

The man continued to stare in open-mouthed silence.

"I didn't expect things to turn out like this," Jenna said after they sat on a bench in a secluded spot by some dogwoods. She went on to tell Rosa about seeing her mother in the hospital and about seeing the dread on neighbors' faces. "I'm supposed to feel great. But I don't. I feel terrible. Maybe this wasn't such a good idea."

"Oh, you had better be joking," Rosa said. "You feel sorry for Bella? Maybe you should have your head examined. You're obviously having a delayed reaction to that smack in the wall she gave you. Don't you remember the things she did to you and Alan? Remember what you told me when you spilled grape juice all over your party dress?"

Jenna nodded. "Mom locked me in the closet."

"For a whole hour," Rosa added. "Who heard your cries? Or Alan's when she was beating him? And no, I don't care what the town's people think. You were scared way before them."

Jenna watched a flock of birds fly down and peck in the grass. She reached into her handbag and took out the sandwich bag with the roll. She started breaking the bread into small pieces then tossed them to the birds.

"I was listening to the news," Rosa said. She held out her hand to Jenna for a few pieces to give to the birds. "I wanted to gag when they kept going on and on about 'how such a terrible thing could've happened to a wonderful woman like Bella Crandall. And what a family the Crandall's are.'" She sucked her teeth. "And of course, Reverend Tub-o'-Lard Austin moaning in front of the cameras." She deepened her voice. "'Poor Bella.'" Rosa wore a foxy grin. "I got a picture of her."

"Bleeding all over the kitchen floor?" Jenna shuddered. "I don't think so."

"No, fool. Bella was scared stiff."

"She was?"

"Check it out." Rosa pulled out her cell phone from her handbag and showed Jenna the photo of a terrified-looking Bella.

Jenna couldn't believe her eyes. Throughout her childhood, her mother instilled her with fear and shame. To see her scared felt weird. And strangely wonderful. Her mouth started twitching.

"Come on, let it out," Rosa said. "You know you wanna laugh."

Jenna didn't laugh, but she did smile. The picture of her mother petrified was wonderful. Alan would love this. But she couldn't show him the picture. She grew sober. She would have to explain. Alan was already unusually nosy. "What we did was wicked."

"*We* didn't *do* anything," Rosa said.

"I'm still an accessory. God said, 'Thou shalt not kill.'"

"What's with you and God lately? You knew what the deal was. I don't want to hear anymore of this religious-talk. I didn't *kill* anyone. Yet."

"Because you didn't whack Mom hard enough.

"Aren't we ungrateful?"

"Sorry," Jenna said. "I'm just nervous."

"Well, don't be. It's gonna be okay."

"How do you know?"

Rosa smirked. "Have a little faith."

Jenna made a face. "Anyway, Malachi says it's not about religion. It's about having a relationship with God."

Rosa groaned. It was great that Jenna had a new man in her life; especially one with the guts to stand up to Bella, Lauren and Diane, but right now his Christian faith was getting in the way. "Isn't God the one who let your family crap all over you?"

"Alan's weirding out on me," Jenna said. She told Rosa about him questioning her. "You don't think he suspects do you?"

"I doubt it. He oughta be doing somersaults instead of nagging. Even your dad should be dancin'."

"That would look great in the papers," Jenna said. "Daddy bustin' a move while his wife's in intensive care."

"He should. He may never have to write another check to her again," Rosa said. "You can get that money."

Jenna sat up straight. She could always use extra cash.

"That house has always been Bella's castle." Rosa's eyes lit up. "When things cool down, it'll be all yours."

"You really think this'll happen?" Jenna asked.

"Definitely."

"But Mom's not dead."

Rosa tossed the last of the breadcrumbs to the birds. "She will be."

Jenna didn't argue. Rosa spoke with such certainty that she was afraid to ask her what she knew, not that she would tell her.

"You can have Malachi over anytime you want," Rosa added.

Quietly, Jenna said, "They're posting a guard outside of Mom's hospital room."

Rosa snickered. "That's a waste of time."

Jenna looked out at the lake. The ducks and the geese swam contentedly. She wished she felt as cheerful as they did. "You won't do anything to Mom yet? Right?"

Rosa studied her friend for a moment. Sometimes Jenna was an enigma. After everything Bella had put her through, she was still worried about her. "No, I won't do anything to her." *For now.* Rosa brushed her hands on her pants. "Let's go out tonight. We'll celebrate your emancipation."

"Mom's in the hospital. What'll people say?"

"I think you're missing the point about emancipation."

"I guess I don't know how to be free," Jenna said.

"I'll teach you. We'll have a party."

"I don't know anybody. You and Malachi are my only real friends.

"Leave that to me."

Jenna stared at the dogwood trees. Filling the house with acquaintances even if they weren't friends of hers was tempting.

"Let's get some beer," Rosa said.

"It's not even noon."

"Your point?"

Jenna hesitated.

"See that's your problem," Rosa began. "You lack spontaneity. Consider this your first lesson in freedom." Rosa stood up.

Just then, Jenna's cell phone rang. Malachi. Dissatisfaction and uncertainty fled. All smiles, she told him she was feeling fine and that they were going to visit her mother later that morning.

"I happen to be free this morning," Malachi said. "I can meet you there."

"That'd be great." Jenna breathed a sigh of relief. Going to the hospital was less daunting knowing that Malachi would be by her side. Even now, she felt guilty having Rosa beside her when he believed that she was just a distant memory. "Thanks again for yesterday. I don't know how I would've gotten through it by myself."

"I was glad to do it."

After Jenna told him when they were leaving for the hospital, they hung up.

Rosa said, "Now, about that beer."

"No, Counselor, I don't have any new developments," Detective Chang said. "Uh huh . . . Uh huh . . . Yeah." He started pinching the bridge of his nose. "We're doing everything we can, but . . . " He raised his eyebrows. "What did you say to me? . . . Well, Good Day to you too, Counselor." Detective Chang hung up the phone then cursed.

Who does she think she is?

For someone who boasted about her faith, Lauren Crandall-Door had a mouth like the contents of a sewage treatment plant.

There was a knock on the doorjamb.

"Yeah?" He answered grumpily without looking up.

Officers Davidson and Vega entered. They took in their boss' disgruntled expression.

"What's wrong?" Davidson asked.

Detective Chang sat up, conscious of aware of the female officer's presence. *Did she hear me?* He straightened his tan suit jacket and bronze tie. He almost forgot that he was expecting George and Nanci back from interrogating Bella's neighbors and conducting more investigations on the Crandall property.

"Lauren Crandall-Door is what's wrong." Detective Chang sighed. "She's looking for updates."

"Already?" Officer Vega asked.

"She demands it."

"In less than twenty-four hours?" Davidson made a rude noise. "She's full of it. What does she expect?"

"Don't get me started." Detective Chang was feeling frustrated enough without Lauren pressuring him. The perp was clever. No fingerprints. No footprints. The only ones they found so far were Bella's, Diane's and Larry's. "And if she doesn't get it, she'll go over my head."

Chang was about to make a colorful reply when he glanced at Officer Vega. Naturally, she'd heard profanity before. Nanci transferred to his unit from the town of Hudson. Still, he wanted to make a good impression. It was important to him ever since the day she walked into his squad room. He tried not to lose himself by staring into her big brown eyes and brown silky hair.

He cleared his throat, stood up and picked up the watering can. Detective Chang began to feed the azaleas. He was too glad to have something to do away from looking at Nanci Vega. "I have to attend a press conference and I want to be in a proper frame of mind. "Besides, Mayor Urbanowski will be there front and center." He let out a long-suffering sigh.

"No wonder Ms. Crandall-Door's showing off," Officer Vega said. "Lauren's got her backer."

Detective Chang harrumphed. Urbanowski was even more difficult than Lauren was if that were possible. He was demanding round the clock investigation. He was going to stay on top of things. He'd turn the heat up on the police department if he'd have to. Chang blew an exasperated sigh. No doubt, the mayor was using his close relationship with her and this high profile case as a stepping-stone to advance his career.

Detective Chang put down the watering can then sat back down at his desk. "So what did you two find out? And don't tell me about how exceptional the Crandall's are. I heard enough about the family's virtues. One more time and I'm gonna lose my lunch."

"Okay we won't," Officer Vega said laughing as she and Officer Davidson pulled up chairs.

To the detective sergeant her laughter sounded like musical chimes.

Officer Vega tucked a stray hair behind her ear. "For starters, Jenna's polite, keeps to herself, quiet."

Chang recalled her suppressed temper and wondered about how quiet she really was. "Friends?"

"None that we're aware of," Davidson replied, "except for Chase, but technically he's her boyfriend."

"Is there a difference?"

"I place friends in a different category. A significant other . . . "

"Shouldn't a significant other be a friend first?" Officer Vega asked. Officer Vega smiled. "Dr. Chase is fine."

Chang smiled thinly.

Davidson tried to keep a straight face. In addition to knowing about his boss' instinct, Davidson knew about his feelings for Nanci. His partner's compliment, albeit good-natured, was painful.

"Can we get back to the subject?" Chang asked. He was taking Nanci's view seriously and was trying not to let visions of becoming friends with her distract him—until her opinion of Prof. Chase's looks spoiled the image.

"Bella is as sociable as Jenna is quiet," Officer Vega continued. "She's either friends or acquainted with neighbors or congregants. Everybody knows Bella for her generosity."

"It's a wonder the mayor hasn't erected a statue in her honor," Detective Chang commented dryly. He rubbed the back of his neck. He didn't believe that Jenna Crandall was that quiet. She has a boyfriend for crying out loud. "You may be interested to know that Jenna stopped attending church," Officer Davidson said.

Chang raised his eyebrows. "Really? How did Bella feel about that?"

"We got that little tidbit from Mrs. Beery," Davidson said.

"Oh, her." Her intrusion during his investigation still aggravated him.

"She kept going on and on about Bella, Lauren and Diane, Officer Vega said. "'They're wonderful. They're fantastic.'" She rolled her eyes.

"Did Beery mention anything at all about Alan, Julian or Elise?"

"No," Officer Davidson replied.

Officer Vega added, "I know she and Julian are estranged, but Bella's groupie talked as if he didn't exist. It was weird." She gestured to Davidson. "George and I got the feeling that Mrs. Beery didn't like Jenna."

Detective Chang leaned forward. "Really?"

Nanci nodded. "When she told us about Jenna not going to church, she made it sound so shocking."

Chang bristled. Not being a regular churchgoer himself, he felt a little on the defensive. He considered himself a model citizen and he defied Norma Beery or anyone else to refute that. "Did Jenna associate with anyone at church while she was still a parishioner?"

"Not really," Davidson answered. "But no one had anything bad to say about her."

Chang smiled derisively. "In other words Jenna was the invisible girl." No wonder she left. "Anything turn up on her laptop?"

Just some E-mails from Alan and Elise," Davidson replied. "Nothing significant."

E-mails from her brother and sister-in-law. Detective Chang frowned. Maybe Jenna really has no friends. "What were on those E-mails?"

Officer Davidson answered. "Alan asking her how she's doing, Elise sending her cutesy e-greetings, invites to spend the weekend."

"Jenna was using her computer mostly for surfing the Net or downloading music."

"What kind of music?" That revealed a lot about a person.

"Hip Hop, rap," Officer Vega answered. "And classical."

"The classical I could see," Officer Davidson said. He had a hard time accepting the fact that Jenna listened to hip-hop music and rap. "She doesn't come across as the type who'd like that style. She's, you know, bookish."

"Oh you'd be surprised what people like," Officer Vega said.

Detective Chang agreed. He was convinced that Jenna had another side to her. He caught a glimpse of it.

"I had this American history professor who was really conservative," Officer Vega began. "He always wore suits, voted Republican. But I heard that on the weekends he was kinky. I used to think it was just gossip. Until they arrested him. You should've seen the stuff campus police took out of university housing along with the people caught with him." She nodded knowingly.

Detective Chang grinned. "What type of stuff was she looking up?"

"Art, art history, art schools," Officer Vega replied.

"You think she likes art?" Davidson quipped.

"Okay, so we have a reticent woman with a talent for art, a love of fantasy and adoration for urban music. What else?"

"She bookmarked several bookstores and the Gordonville Library," Nanci said. "Recently she had them hold some gothic and fantasy novels. She also likes murder mysteries. Oh and she surfs department stores."

"Not unusual," Detective Chang said.

"Pretty clothing and accessories," Officer Vega said.

"Pretty as in pretty pricey," Officer Davidson added. "A tiny shoulder bag for two thousand bucks? I can think of a lotta things to do with two thousand dollars. Buying a dainty handbag isn't one of 'em."

"She didn't actually buy them?"

"None of those items appeared on her credit card," Vega said.

"And she's never been seen wearing anything relatively expensive," Davidson added.

Chang started drumming his fingers on the desk. "That's the kind of stuff Diane and Lauren would wear. She may be harboring jealousy." *Anger she allegedly doesn't have.* Her sisters had all the publicity, adored by their mother and the world, had successful men in their lives. Chang smiled scathingly. "Outside of teaching Sunday school, Bella's a homemaker," Officer Davidson said.

"How does she support herself?"

"The check is in the mail," the officers sang in unison.

"And she was seen at Delsey's two days ago buying a dozen lemon squares," Officer Vega said. "And yes she was happy," before Detective Chang could ask about Bella's mood.

"Are you going to question Jenna again?" Davidson asked.

Chang leaned back in his chair. Two opposites living in the same household. "Yeah, I'm gonna question her. But first, I'm going to pay a visit to the Gordonville Community Church. Methinks Bella Crandall has another side to her." Detective Chang stood up. "She may be 'known for her generosity,' but someone out there does not like her."

"You take such good care of that plant, Sarge," Officer Vega said, as she and Davidson were getting ready to leave. "I love the flowers. They're so beautiful. *!Qué linda!* And they make the office look nice."

Chang smiled. "Thank you, Nanci."

Davidson smothered a smile.

23

Feeling more relaxed, Jenna returned to Alan and Elise's house. Rosa's parting words played repeatedly in her head. *"Stop feeling guilty."*

As soon as she entered the foyer, she heard, "Where have you been?"

Alan.

He was standing right at the front door.

What is he was timing me now?

"Have you any idea what time it is?"

"No."

"It's twelve-thirty." He let out a worried sigh. "I've been trying to reach you for the past hour. What's the point of having a cell if you're not going to turn it on?"

Jenna leaned against the doorjamb. "Sorry."

It was Rosa's idea to turn off the phone so they "could chill" while she taught Jenna a little something about emancipation.

"Where did you go?"

Jenna glared. "Lakewood Park." Alan was really starting to get on her nerve. Plus, she really needed to sit down.

Alan looked at her for a moment. "We'll take my car."

"I need the bathroom." Jenna teetered as she headed for the stairs.

Alan frowned. "Have you been drinking?"

Jenna stiffened. "What's the big deal?" She started up the stairs. Alan, who had always been her ally, had suddenly become an interrogator. She loved him, but she didn't ask Rosa for help only to end up playing the good girl to please Alan. Did he know about Rosa? She decided to worry about it later. She just wanted to get away from him for a few seconds.

"You're not supposed to drink on an empty stomach that's the big deal." Alan raised his voice higher as Jenna kept on going, ignoring him.

Jenna stopped on the middle stair. Rosa's words came back to her. *"Stop feeling guilty."* In a voice like steel Jenna said, "I'm not a child, Alan. And I don't have to answer to you."

Alan stepped back. Jenna never used that snippy tone with him before. Now he knew for sure that Rosa attacked their mother. No. Tried to kill her. *With Jenna's consent.* He was letting his nerves get the better of him again. He shouldn't do that. That wasn't wise. He smelled Rosa Garrison's influence over his little sister. Literally and figuratively. He had to tread lightly.

Elise appeared at the top of the stairs. "What's going on?"

"Suppose someone saw you drinking?" Alan asked in a calmer voice. He didn't mean to ignore his wife, but right now, his priority was Jenna. "You know how the media is. They'd just make a thing out of it. They're already getting a thrill from Diane and Lauren's little performance yesterday."

"They are?"

Alan ran his hand over his head. "One of those tabloid TV shows. It spread like wildfire. It's only a matter of time before they find out about Mom and Dad's . . . quasi separation."

Her sisters and mother were finally gonna get some *real* publicity. Jenna started grinning.

With an admonishing tone Alan said, "It's not funny."

Jenna rolled her eyes then stomped up the stairs, brushing past Elise.

Alan stared into Elise's confused face. Before she could ask him any questions, he said, "I'll wait for both of you in the car."

Crowds of reporters were camped outside of Gordonville General Hospital. When they recognized Alan, Elise and Jenna, the reporters ran over and began bombarding them with questions.

"How do you feel?"

"Can you give us a statement?"

"Is there any truth to the rumor that Lauren Crandall-Door is calling in a special investigator?"

"No comment," Alan replied repeatedly as he, Elise and Jenna walked briskly towards the hospital's entrance. His face hid his surprise about the special investigator. *What was Lauren thinking?*

"Jenna Crandall," a male reporter for the *Gordonville Gazette, began, "*any truth to the rumors you were seen drunk this morning?"

Jenna stopped, causing Alan, Elise and herself to bump into each other.

"You were seen buying beer at a convenience store," the reporter continued.

Jenna blinked. Where was that reporter hiding? Now Alan was never going to let her hear the end of it. "I neither confirm nor deny." She'd heard Lauren make that statement many times.

"Let's go," Alan said, visibly uncomfortable. He ushered Jenna and Elise to the hospital's entrance. "And I suggest we stop at the cafeteria and get you a cup of coffee."

Alan sighed. This was only the beginning.

They rode the elevator in silence. Just like the car ride to the hospital. Elise absorbed their tension like a sponge. Alan stared intently at the floor number display. Jenna was fascinated with the elevator's control panel. Elise inhaled the fresh brewed hazelnut coffee coming from the Styrofoam cup in Jenna's hand. She wished she had purchased a cup too. This scenario was unnatural. Alan and Jenna were always so close. Now they were standing as if a wall were between them.

Alan finally told her in the elevator car why he and Jenna were arguing. Elise shook her head. Years of living under Bella's regime must've made him image-conscious. So what if Jenna was drinking? She's an adult. And she needs to grieve. Maybe beer was her way of finding release. Elise glanced at Alan. Jenna rejected her cinnamon French toast for a six-pack and she wasn't upset over it.

As soon as they arrived on their floor and stepped off the elevator, Elise pulled Alan and Jenna aside. Fed up she said, "Both of you knock it off. This is neither the time nor the place for your petty little differences. Your mother needs you. And you need each other."

Alan and Jenna allowed Elise's words to sink in. Alan held out his hand to Jenna.

She looked down at her brother's outstretched hand. Outside of Rosa and Malachi, Alan was her only defender. Jenna wore a tiny smile as she took her brother's hand and shook it. Then, the three of them walked down the hall to the intensive care unit.

"Visiting hours started already," Diane said by way of a greeting when Alan, Elise and Jenna arrived outside of the intensive care unit. Lauren and Larry were also present. "Where've you been? Thought you would've been the first one."

"Had some business to take care of first," Alan replied and hoped that that would be enough of an explanation. He wasn't about to clue them in on Jenna's drinking binge. He looked from Lauren to Nelson. "I didn't expect to see you guys here already."

Jenna bristled at the sight of her sisters, brother-in-law and Larry. They looked as if they stepped out of a page of a fashion magazine. They're here to visit a sick relative. She mentally calculated how many paychecks she'd have to save up just to afford the tunic blouse Diane was wearing.

"I was in no shape to return to Pound Ridge," Lauren said. She flipped her hair over shoulders. "I booked The Lilac Room last night."

Jenna smiled demurely then took a sip of coffee. Lauren's staying in town. *Rosa's going to love this.*

"Nelson took the red eye from Hollywood," Lauren added, her pretentious voice rising loud enough to cause some hospital staff, patients and visitors in the immediate area to look in her direction.

Jenna counted to ten. Did the whole world have to know from where Nelson was arriving?

Lauren frowned. "When did you start drinking coffee?"

Jenna looked into her sister's cold emerald eyes. Should she tell her she was drinking? What she drinks wasn't any of her sister's business. Who died and left Lauren in charge?

If Mom dies, will Lauren be in charge?

"Why are you drinking coffee?" Diane asked. "You love tea almost as much as Mom."

"How's Mom?" Alan asked. The last thing he needed was for Lauren and Diane to fixate on Jenna's sudden taste for coffee. He'd discuss it with them later.

Lauren's eyes lingered on Jenna before finally turning to her brother. "They managed to stop the bleeding."

"That's a relief," Elise said.

"Otherwise there's no change," Lauren added.

Alan frowned. "Where's Dad?"

"He was here then he stepped out." Lauren sighed.

"Said he'd be back."

"This ordeal must be hard on him," Elise said.

Lauren shrugged.

"Just because they're not together doesn't mean he doesn't love her," Elise said.

"I have to stop by Detective Chang's office for questioning," Nelson said, changing the subject. "I wasn't even in town when the crime occurred."

Larry clapped him on the shoulder. "They questioned me too. Don't you watch detective shows? You could be the unhappy husband. I could be the unhappy fiancé. Perhaps your mother-in-law and *my* future mother-in-law was a nuisance to both of us . . . "

Diane made a face and Lauren put her hands akimbo. Larry's immaturity was unbelievable.

Nelson scowled. "I had reporters calling me during production. It was annoying and embarrassing. I've got better things to do than clubbing my mother-in-law."

Jenna took another sip of coffee. "They questioned Malachi."

Lauren, Diane, Nelson and Larry looked dumbfounded, as if they suddenly remembered she was present. Then, they exchanged glances with each other and shrugged.

Jenna's face fell. What made her think that she could take part in their discussion?

Again, Alan jumped in. This was no time for their haughtiness. He recalled the argument he and Jenna got into earlier and how the way she reacted to him. Considering what he knew, making her angry might not be such a good idea. He pointed out that he had left work to bring Jenna to the crime scene as well as stick around to support her considering their mother didn't even respect the man.

He looked from Lauren to Diane with a censorious stare. "Malachi played one heck of a role yesterday." He turned to Jenna. "Bet he didn't expect to get sucked into this, huh?" Alan asked, filling in the silence that followed.

"No," Jenna's tone matched her beaten spirit. She took another sip of coffee. She wanted to say that he was coming to the hospital, but she couldn't. She lost the ability to speak.

"Will you be seeing Malachi today, Jenna?" Alan asked.

Somehow, she managed to respond. "Yeah."

Malachi's kindness meant nothing. Dismayed, she walked over to the waiting area and sat down.

Lauren looked baffled. "What's the matter with her?"

"You're way too old to be playing cute," Alan said.

"Whoa!" Larry exclaimed. He and Nelson stepped back.

Lauren gave her brother a look that could curdle milk. Diane drew closer to her sister in a show of solidarity.

"You were all insensitive," Alan said in a low voice. "To Jenna *and* to Malachi."

Nelson put up his hands. "I don't even know the guy."

"He's Jenna's boyfriend," Alan said.

"And I should know this because . . . "

"We introduced you at your wedding."

"Alan, do you know how many people I was introduced to?" Nelson asked.

"And he wasn't her boyfriend then," Lauren said.

Elise rolled her eyes. She looked at Jenna who was leaning over and dabbing her eyes with the hem of the T-shirt. Elise considered going over to comfort her but didn't. Jenna needed her space.

"I got a room at The Lorelei House too," Larry said changing the subject. "I was lucky to get a room. Considering its summertime

It's not luck, you dumb twit. It's because you're Lawrence Belmar. Jenna stared at the floor as she quietly listened in on their conversation. The Lorelei House would've stuffed a guest into a broom closet to accommodate the famous designer, who just happened to be engaged to Gordonville's Diane Crandall, international supermodel who was also the sister of Gordonville's own Lauren Crandall-Door, New York State assistant district attorney." She wiped her tears with the back of her hand. Soon, a smile touched her lips. Larry booked a room. That means Diane was going to be staying in town for a while . . .

"I'm in The Tulip Room," Larry said. He made a face. "There goes my manhood."

"Assuming you had one," Nelson said.

Larry fake-punched him. "Are those reporters still out there?"

"Yeah." Alan looked disgusted. Neither Larry nor the rest of them understood that their behavior towards Jenna was thoughtless. "So, what's all this about a special investigator?"

Unnoticed, Jenna returned to the group.

Lauren put her hair into a ponytail holder. "Detective Sergeant Richard Chang isn't moving fast enough. I threatened to have someone else appointed to handle the case."

Alan rubbed his jaw. *She really thinks someone other than Rosa is guilty.* "Lauren, can I talk to you and Diane a minute?"

"No."

Diane checked her watch. "Alan, don't you think you should be spending your time with Mom?"

Alan sighed. His twin was right. Nevertheless, he still needed to speak with them as soon as possible.

"Can I go in first?" Jenna asked.

Larry, who now happened to be standing close to her sniffed then said, "So it is true what they're saying about you." He turned to the others. "I heard on the radio she was so stressed about her mother that she tied one on today."

Diane gasped. "Why didn't you tell me?"

Lauren looked at Jenna with contempt. "You have got to be kidding?" She looked accusingly at Alan. "So that's why you have little sis drinking coffee. You knew."

Alan took a deep breath.

Nelson groaned. "That's just great."

"Do I look drunk to you?" Jenna asked. She was calm, but her tone of voice had a trace of annoyance.

"They said you were acting strangely," Larry said.

"That's to be expected when you're drunk," Nelson said, his tone testy.

"Can we let it go now, please," Alan said.

"I'm standing right here," Jenna said, enraged he would disregard Malachi's support, but jump to criticize her about having a drink.

Nelson raised his eyebrows. Jenna hardly speaks. What got into her?

Alan looked at Lauren. Her face was unreadable. Next, he looked at Diane who refused to meet his gaze.

"Okay," Larry said. "We'll go with tipsy."

"How about we drop it?" Jenna said.

Lauren regarded Jenna with disdain. "Chill out, all right."

"You chill," Jenna retorted. She was livid and buzzed from drinking one beer too many.

Lauren raised her eyebrows. "Watch your tone."

"Don't tell me what to do."

The desk nurse, a tall curly-haired male, looked in their direction.

"Like I said, let it go," Alan said. The last thing they needed was to have Jenna flipping out.

Nelson looked at Jenna with disapproval. "Jenna should've been mindful of her behavior. She knows her family is in the public eye."

Jenna's eyes flashed. "I'm going to see Mom now." She swaggered down the hall without a backward glance.

Alan watched her retreating figure. "Lauren," he spoke so that Larry and Nelson couldn't hear. "Can we talk?"

"No." Lauren moved away.

Her anger now dissipated, Jenna nodded at the guard in front of her mother's room, a big broad-shouldered man. She took a deep breath then opened the door. For the second time in less than twenty-four hours, she entered the ICU. Bella lay powerless, hooked up to monitors. Unable to lay a hand on her. Unable to utter another hurtful word. Jenna pulled up a chair and sat down. She'd already seen her mother in this condition last night. She hadn't come to herself about it yet.

In a voice just above a whisper she said, "I'm sorry, Mom. I never wanted this to happen. I wanted us to have a relationship." She began crying softly. "But you wouldn't give me a chance. I couldn't take it anymore."

She jumped when she felt a hand on her shoulder. She turned around. Malachi was standing beside her.

"Sorry. Didn't mean to scare you. They told me you were here."

"How long were you standing there?" Jenna asked.

"I didn't hear what you were saying if that's what you're worried about."

Relief flooded through her. Having Malachi overhear her would be the worst thing to happen next to having her mother wake up and reveal her attacker.

Malachi pulled up another chair and sat down beside her. "You're doing the right thing. Talking to your mother. I understand that people in comas can hear you even though they can't respond."

He looked at Bella, recalling the first time he met her. She was so proud. So haughty. Now she was lying comatose in a hospital, a very dark secret locked up inside her. It seemed so unreal.

Was it possible this was Rosa's doing? That would mean she was still around and Jenna would've been lying to him. She didn't have to. She was the one who told him about Rosa in the first place. Then again, she did omit the fact that she had been making tea for Bella at four o'clock all this time.

He pushed aside the idea. Why would Jenna's friend go through such an extreme measure to make Bella pay for past offenses?

Attempted murder?

No. Whoever attacked her was someone with a grievance. Despite her popularity, Bella could get under a person's skin easily if he or she didn't measure up to her standards. Whatever those are. And evidently, she ticked off the wrong person.

Malachi stared at the blue summer blanket on his unmade bed. What if Jenna and Alan had something to do with this? No.

Don't go there. Not now.

He brushed aside the thought of Jenna, Alan or Rosa seeking revenge and instead focused on Bella. "Mrs. Crandall, it's me, Malachi. I know you and I didn't hit it off, but I heard about what happened and I came to visit. Hope you don't mind. Now I know that you're a strong woman. You have to get better."

Jenna smiled tightly.

"And after you get better," Malachi continued, "You can go tell me off. In the meantime, I'll pray every day for your recovery." *And for you to get a new personality.* He put his arm around Jenna and kissed her. "Oh. So it is true."

"What?" Jenna asked.

"Your liquid breakfast."

Jenna groaned. "Don't tell me my family's out there discussing my business in the hall."

"That and the mixture of beer and coffee. Maybe your family is concerned."

"Yeah. They care."

"Maybe they really do."

"Don't defend them," Jenna snapped.

Malachi's mouth fell open. Where was this hostility coming from?

"Sorry." Just because Mom's out of the picture didn't mean she should get careless and start mouthing off. *Stupid move.*

Malachi waved his hand in dismissal. "Remember those parties I talked about? I used to get plastered. It's not a good place to be. Trust me."

"Don't worry. I'm not going to turn into an alcoholic I promise." Jenna looked at her mother's unconscious figure. "Why do people do bad things?"

Thinking about his checkered past, Malachi said, "God gives us free will. Some of us choose to do evil. We feel insecure. Or misguided."

Jenna gestured towards her mother. "You'd never do something like this."

"Well, no, but if it weren't for the Holy Spirit I would've been sued, incarcerated or maybe someone would've punched my lights out. Just last week I was this close to pouring sugar into a colleague's engine."

Jenna giggled. "Are you serious?"

"Dr. Edward Brightmore. He always has something to say about my teaching methods."

"With a name like that you don't have to ask if he's a geek."

"He's British."

"What's that supposed to mean?"

"Just sayin.' And he's got that snooty accent."

"It's not snooty," Jenna said. "It's classy."

"He's a pain in the butt." Malachi's face got that faraway look. "Just know that when you do wrong there are consequences."

Jenna studied him. "You're thinking about your past again."

Malachi looked at a copy of a still life painting by Van Gogh that was hanging on the wall. *I can't tell her about that other part. Not now.*

He felt himself getting emotional. He couldn't talk. All he could do was nod.

"When I was a little girl, Mom always said I was bad," Jenna said. "She said I was the devil's baby."

Malachi looked aghast. Was there no end to Bella Crandall's cruelty? In a low voice he said, "With all due respect, I think your mother was either ignorant, or deeply disturbed."

"About what?"

"I don't know," Malachi said. "Something."

"Mom is mistress of her own kingdom."

"Not everything is what it seems, Jenna. You're talking to a master at deception."

They sat quietly watching Bella and listening to the hum of the monitors. Suddenly, the door flew open. Lauren stepped into the room, her wedge sandals clapping across the floor. Her cold stare froze Jenna and Malachi to the spot. He wondered how someone as beautiful as she could emit such negative energy.

"You're only allowed a certain number of minutes," Lauren said her tone as frigid as her stare. Her bangles jangled when she put her hand on her hip. "There are other's you know."

Malachi restrained himself before he said something he would regret. "We were talking. Time got away from us."

Lauren gave him a withering look.

Okaay. Malachi looked at Jenna. She had that same vacant expression on her face that she had at the wedding. He reached over, took her hand, and willed his strength to pass through to her. Then, he rose from the chair, urging Jenna to rise with him.

She was aware of standing up. Her legs felt like lead, slowing her gait. Malachi had to help her to the door.

Impatient, Lauren sucked her teeth and moved toward the bed. Nelson entered just as Malachi and Jenna were exiting the room. He walked past them without a word and sat beside Lauren.

As soon as Jenna and Malachi stepped outside of the ICU, she knew right away that the guard heard everything. She could see it in his eyes. The embarrassment.

The pity.

Jenna's insides felt cold. Mortified, she wanted to disappear.

Disrespected—again.

Jenna turned away from the guard's uncomfortable stare. Diane, who was sitting a few feet away chatting with Larry, turned. She glanced from Jenna to Malachi. A sly smile formed on her pretty face. Then, went and turned back to Larry.

Jenna felt a sudden jolt. Her sister was mocking her.

Alan and Elise were coming from the cafeteria when they saw the pained and awkward looks on Jenna, Malachi and the guard's faces, respectively. Immediately, panic set in.

"What happened?" Alan asked.

Malachi was about to reply when Diane said flippantly, "Lauren had to set them straight."

"What's that supposed to mean?" Alan asked.

He turned to Jenna then blinked, as did Malachi. Jenna had that same look he saw on her face at her sister's wedding. Rage. Elise, Diane, Larry and the guard saw her expression too. They exchanged startled glances. Forgetting her manicure began to chew her nails.

Just then, Lauren and Nelson came out of the intensive care unit. They looked indignant.

"What's all the yelling?" Lauren asked.

Alan took a deep breath. "Jenna, just relax."

"He's right," Malachi said. "It's not worth the fuss. It's okay."

"It is not okay," Jenna exclaimed in a loud voice startling Malachi, Elise, Larry and the guard. Patients and hospital staff in the immediate area stopped to look at the group. She was aware of the attention, but she didn't care. "Nothing they do is ever okay."

Diane drew closer to Larry. Jenna looked scary mad.

"Don't you think you've drawn enough attention to yourself for one day?" Lauren asked.

"Good question," Nelson said.

"You two shut it." Alan muttered the command between clenched teeth. Couldn't these two geniuses see that Jenna was irate?

"Excuse me," the desk nurse began, his voice stern, "but you're going to have to keep your voices down. There are patients."

"We're sorry," Alan said.

Rosa would've wanted me to stay calm. I blew it. This is all Lauren's fault.

She stomped down the hall. Malachi rushed after her. A camera flashed. A reporter had sneaked on to the floor and was capturing the scene. Nelson swore.

Alan pulled Diane aside. She wrenched her hand away.

"We need to talk," Alan said.

Another flash went off. Larry yelled at another reporter. While hospital security was taking care of the reporters, Lauren and Nelson returned to Bella's room. Alan pulled Diane aside again.

"What do you want?" She asked. "Leave me alone."

"You and Lauren better lay off Jenna." Alan spoke in a low voice. Who knew if another reporter was listening in?

"Rosa is back. She's the one who attacked Mom. I know it.

Diane groaned. "This again?"

Alan would have conniptions if he knew that Rosa was back and that she, Lauren *and* Mom lied about it. He was already convinced she was dangerous. Diane rubbed her shoulders nervously. Rosa could be influencing her. Jenna's behavior was a little off. She didn't want to believe that Rosa attacked their mother. It had to be the work of some psycho. Rosa wouldn't brutalize anyone.

"You, Lauren and I have to come forward with what we know."

"Are you crazy?" Diane looked towards the closed door where behind it Lauren and Nelson were visiting with Mom. "Rosa's just a rebellious kid. She's not a kid anymore, Diane. Now, what did Lauren do?"

Malachi caught up with Jenna on the main floor of the hospital. He had to catch his breath. She was so angry she was walking as if she were jet-propelled.

Jenna shed angry tears. "They're doing it again. Even now."

Malachi glanced around. Some staff was looking at Jenna. He could tell by the faces of others that they recognized her. "You want to go somewhere and talk?"

Jenna shook her head. "Mom's life is in limbo and that still doesn't change them." She sniffed. "Lauren disrespected me. And you. That's why the others went away."

"Others? Who're you talking about?"

"No man wanted to stay with me."

Oh. Malachi rubbed the back of his neck. He had to be reasonable. Not jealous. Jenna had a life before she met him just as he had a life before he met her.

"I'm not going anywhere," Malachi said.

"Where have I heard that before?"

Malachi flinched. Her cynicism was coming from pain and betrayal. Nevertheless, it stung.

"Eventually, you'll get tired of the insults," Jenna continued. "I don't have a backbone."

"Huh?"

"That's what Everett said. My ex-boyfriend. He got tired of the family politics. He hated that I wouldn't stand up to them."

Malachi didn't have to ask who she meant by them. Jenna started trembling. Malachi took Jenna into his arms. If any reporters were around, they could take all the pictures they wanted. He stroked her quaking body and tried not to be too gleeful that he was the one comforting her instead of Everett.

"I'd lie awake in the dark wondering if I'd ever meet anyone," Jenna said. "Have a life partner to talk to, laugh with. Everyday I'd wake up knowing that I had to face another day. Alone."

Malachi's heart was aching for her. She really believed that he was leaving. "Jenna, how can I convince you that—"

"What? God is with me?"

Malachi looked around again. A crowd was gathering. Great.

Jenna laughed bitterly. "Next you're going to tell me that I'm not *really* alone? I went to Sunday school remember? 'God is with you.' Isn't that what all you religious folk say? When I'm hurting, Malachi, I need someone with a heartbeat and real arms."

Malachi was at a loss. Now rage and pain was in Jenna's voice. Fury blinded her.

Jenna pushed herself away from him. "I hate Lauren!"

Malachi drew her back into his arms and began whispering soothing words to her. That outburst was only going to lead to more gossip. And speculation. Significantly, Jenna wasn't just sad. She was incensed.

He kissed the top of her head. He didn't take her outburst toward religious folk personally. She had been injured and let down repeatedly. Unfortunately, a segment of the church was responsible for this starting with her mother and sisters. And who knew what went on among the congregants at The Gordonville Community Church. His stomach turned at the thought of Norma Beery. More than anything, he wanted to ease her pain and at the same time, convince her that he wasn't going to leave her. No matter what anybody else may have done to her, he was different.

Suddenly, the elevator doors opened and Alan came rushing toward them. He stopped short, surprised yet glad to Jenna and Malachi. He was certain that they would've driven off by now. Alan glanced around at the curious onlookers staring at Malachi and Jenna. Did he even want to know what else happened?

Alan laughed nervously. "Good. You're still here. I found out what Lauren said. I had it out with her. It's a wonder the desk nurse didn't throw us off the floor. Anyway, Lauren got the message. So why don't you and Mal get something to eat and . . . "

Jenna pulled away from Malachi's embrace and confronted her big brother. Her tear-stained face was a mask of fury. "You can't reason with Lauren. You never could." With that, she walked away. She went through the entrance just as Julian was entering. Jenna greeted her father wearing the same thunderous look on her face. However, she didn't stop as she usually would. She just kept on walking, rubbing her throbbing temples.

Julian spotted Alan and Malachi. In seconds, he was at their side. "What's the matter with her?"

24

Jenna paced the parking lot like a restless tiger. When she calmed down, she walked over to a far corner and put on her headset. In seconds, she had Rosa on the phone. Jenna skipped the formality of saying hello.

"I need you to do something for me."

"What happened?" Rosa asked. She should've been aggravated by the call, but curiosity got the better of her. She almost didn't recognize Jenna's voice. It practically dripped with venom. Moreover, Jenna promised to let her rest. Now here was this sudden urgency.

"I can't go into it now," Jenna replied. "Just . . . just forget about the order of the plan." She lowered her voice. "Take care of Lauren." Jenna gritted her teeth. "And this time I want in."

Rosa had to process this sudden change in Jenna's attitude. Talk about an about face. This morning she was feeling guilty about her mother's coma and the neighbors anguish. Now she wants to take out her sister. "Come over to my house and we'll talk."

"I can't. Malachi's with me." Jenna searched the parking lot. No sign of him yet. No doubt, he was inside talking to her father and Alan about her meltdown. "I don't want anyone questioning me about going to Hudson. Alan was already grilling me today." She gave Rosa a recap about what happened after she returned home. "And to make matters worse, our little binge made the morning news."

Rosa laughed. "I heard. What's his deal?"

"Wish I knew." Jenna saw Malachi coming come through the exit. "I gotta go."

"Tell him to drop you off at the meadow," Rosa said. "Go to the farmhouse and meet me in the back."

"Right."

Malachi pulled up to the side of the rode by the meadow and put the car in park. He looked over at Jenna. She was more relaxed. Thank goodness. He smiled. No doubt, it was because of the venue.

She really loves this place.

It was good to see her react to Lauren's brusqueness instead of retreating into another world. Even so, her behavior was unsettling. "Alan picking you up?"

"No. I'm walking back. I can work off some more steam."

Malachi watched a chipmunk dash out of the bush. "I should've realized how angry you are about the past."

"Like, I told the detective, I don't let things bother me."

"Jenna, stop." Malachi was losing his patience. "Just stop." He sighed. "You were so heated up back there I could've grilled a hamburger on your head. Lauren was out of line. And Diane was acting like a—" He checked himself. "She was her usual charming self. Anyway, I don't care about them. I care about you. I'm worried."

"About what?"

"What I saw today. I saw the same thing at your wedding."

"Saw what?" Jenna asked.

"Rage. God knows how long you've been holding it in. I'm afraid when it finally comes out it's going to boil over onto anyone or anything in its path."

"What am I a volcano?"

"I'm concerned about what all that anger might be doing to you," Malachi said, ignoring her caustic wit. "Or what it might do to someone else if you don't take care of it."

Jenna crossed her arms.

"I'll let you in on something," Malachi said. "Lauren is insecure. Putting down others is the only way she feels good about herself."

Jenna uncrossed her arms. She turned to him with a bemused look on her face. "Lauren? My sister?"

Malachi nodded.

"The wealthy, famous, drop-dead gorgeous prosecutor?" Jenna asked.

"The one and only. And the same is true for Diane *and* your mother. Trust me." Malachi smiled ruefully. "I know a little something about low self-esteem and trying to compensate for it."

"All these years they said that I was the one with a problem."

"What problem?" Malachi asked.

Jenna played with her hair. "I'm a freak of nature."

He held her hand. "That's their opinion. It doesn't make it right."

"If I got my feelings hurt and I cried," Jenna began, "Mom said I made every little thing bother me. I was 'gonna have problems' cause 'I couldn't handle pressure.'"

"She was messing with your head. I used to do the same thing to people, as you already know. Still, that's a lousy thing to say to a kid.

"I know your relationship with God is shaky," Malachi began, "but believe me He sees everything. No one gets away with anything. I'm speaking on authority."

Jenna let go of Malachi's hand. She really didn't want to talk about God right now. He created her mother and her sisters. And for what purpose? She wondered if she was slowly becoming an atheist like Rosa.

Malachi beat a tune on his lap with his hand. What he was about to say could cause Jenna to end their relationship. He recalled Proverbs 27:6, 'Faithful are the wounds of a friend.' He took a deep breath. "I think you should see a professional."

Jenna's expression went from aloofness to incredulity. "You want me to see a shrink?"

Malachi swallowed. *I think I hear a harpsichord.* "The purpose is to work out your issues."

"I ain't got no issues."

Great. She's gone ethnic. "You have to channel your anger in a healthy way," Malachi said.

"I do. Through . . . art." She couldn't believe he wanted her to see a professional. She felt betrayed.

"True, but don't you think drawing someone getting swallowed alive by a snake is cause for concern?"

"It's art."

"That symbolizes an underlying problem," Malachi said.

"There's nothing wrong with me."

"I'm not saying there is," Malachi said. "I'm saying that you need to address that anger. For your own sake. Before it's too late."

He hesitated. "Psychotherapy worked for me."

Jenna's eyes widened.

"I didn't tell you everything about my past," Malachi said. "I couldn't. It's not something I like to talk about." He hesitated. "I had . . . problems. It started after I lost my job. I began thinking about some of my former colleagues. What happened to them? Did they lose their homes because of me? Maybe someone took his own life. That's when I began seeing them."

Jenna frowned. "You saw your former coworkers? That must've been so awkward for you."

"No, hon. I was having . . . hallucinations."

"Oh, Malachi." No wonder he resisted talking about his past on Wall Street. It was more than just about his being a conniving big shot executive. It took a lot for Malachi to reveal this part of his life to her.

"They were in my bedroom, the aisles of the grocery store, the subway platform. And the illusions were giving me these accusatory looks." He shuddered. "But it was the nights that were the hardest."

"Why?"

"In the stillness of the night I had no distractions. I was alone with my thoughts and my memories. That's where the conscience pricks you the most. And the visions, Jenna, the visions." Malachi looked down at his leather oxfords. "I thought I was going mad. That's why I wouldn't tell anyone what was happening to me." He sighed. "After so many weeks of sleep deprivation, I would just start to cry. No reason. I could be having a bowl of corn flakes or watching a sitcom and suddenly cry."

Jenna groaned. It was painful to know that he had lost control. That was a horrible feeling.

"My parents would ask me what's wrong and I wouldn't tell them. I'd just sit there and bawl. My brother and sister tried to find out." He took a deep breath. "I was incoherent. I had to swallow my pride and tell Brendan."

Jenna drew an imaginary design on the glove compartment with her pointer finger. "What did he say?"

"That I seek professional help."

"Oh."

"And like you, I refused," Malachi said. "It was bad enough I had to tell my parents I was seeing people who weren't there never mind seeing some psychotherapist and I was clearly cracking up."

They sat in silence listening to the sounds of the children coming from the meadow. Then Jenna said, "Brendan's a good friend."

"He's the best."

In a quiet voice, Jenna said, "Mom thought that Rosa and I should've been committed. She used to laugh about it."

Malachi looked dismayed. He didn't like jokes about putting people in mental facilities or suffering mental breakdowns. He came too close to that. He agreed that Jenna's friend was disturbed, but for her mother to make light of it was unconscionable. Especially where her own daughter was concerned, then again knowing Bella's history, it shouldn't have been a surprise.

"So that's why you don't want to go for counseling," Malachi said. "You're worried about what your mother and sisters are going to think. Your mom's condition notwithstanding. Well, it's not about them."

"Did psychotherapy work?" Jenna asked. He was so strong. A man of faith. It was hard to believe that he experienced something as frightening as hallucinations. Rosa would blow her top if she knew what Malachi was suggesting.

Malachi nodded. "But it took a little while for me to get to a place of normalcy. God forgave me. I hadn't forgiven myself. I'm still working on that though while I live with what I did to my former co-workers."

"I think the important thing is that you're no longer a slime ball."

"Thanks. I think." Malachi began stroking her cheek. "You're the only one besides Brendan and my folks who know about . . . my trip around the bend."

"I won't tell anyone."

He knew she wouldn't. That's why he finally decided to tell her. Keeping this part of his life a secret from Jenna was like a great weight on his shoulder. As painful as it was to talk about, if it would help her, then it was worth the discomfort. "I have to get back." Malachi looked at the clock on the dashboard. He should've been back at his desk already preparing the lesson plan.

Jenna had to be going too. Rosa must've been at the farmhouse by now. Going by way of the meadow was going to take longer but it was necessary. Malachi mustn't know that she was going to Thornbush Lane. He would have endless questions. Eventually he was going to get curios.

"Thanks for coming, Mal. I'm glad you were there. Again." She didn't even want to think about having to face her family's drama without him. Even Alan was a pain although he tried to make up for it.

"I'll always be there for you, Jenna," Malachi said, interrupting her thoughts.

"And I'm sorry about being crabby."

"Forget it. Will you at least think about what I said?"

Jenna started twisting her hair around her finger. "Yes." *Rosa must never know about this conversation.* "I'm sorry I flipped out before."

"We all have our moments."

Jenna smiled. "You should know. You think about pouring sugar in people's gas tanks."

"I like it when you smile." Malachi leaned over and kissed her.

*

When Jenna arrived at the farmhouse, she headed straight for the back yard. Rosa was sitting in the grass by the back porch.

"It's about time," Rosa said.

"He kissed me." Jenna took a seat on the grass. "And it was . . . wow!"

"And I'd love to hear about it. Later."

"But we made such a connection."

She wasn't going to betray his trust by mentioning his mental breakdown to Rosa and she definitely couldn't tell her that he suggested that she get psychotherapy. Even though his intentions were well meant, Rosa would've flipped out.

"Now, what did the princesses do that caused me my afternoon of rest?" Rosa asked with undisguised impatience.

Jenna looked toward the red barn in the distance as she told her friend about what happened between her, Lauren and Malachi as well as Nelson and Larry's condescending attitudes.

"Lauren dissed you? In front of your man?" Rosa began cursing a blue streak.

"But it's okay," Jenna said. Malachi's sticking by me. I know that now." She talked about how supportive he was, omitting his suggestion about counseling. Like a true friend, she didn't mention his delusions.

"I'm glad you have his support," Rosa said. "I really am."

Jenna deserved some happiness. She was so messed up especially after Everett left. Of all the relationships, that one nearly sent Jenna over the edge. She was unhappy with herself, unhappy with life and just . . .

lonely. She hated her sisters, but most of all she hated her mother. If only she could've admitted it. It would've been her first step toward liberation.

And healing.

But Jenna made her promise not to interfere. She had to stand by and regretfully watch Jenna fill her lonely heart with cheeseburgers, pizza, ice cream, cookies. A beatific glow would come over her face, as her pain temporarily disappeared with each bite she took of some high calorie dish, but it came with a price. Jenna put on the pounds. When the pain returned and it did, there was always more fast food to ease it.

On top of that, her family couldn't even see that Jenna's weight gain was a cry for help. Not even Alan. Her vulnerabilities became fodder for Lauren and Diane, who made fun of her constantly. Rosa picked a blade of grass recalling how she had to restrain herself from strangling them and instead coaxed Jenna to redirect her depression into exercise, diet and expressing her anger through drawing. That was the only time she interfered.

The best thing to happen to her was Bella banging her head into the wall. It made her finally wise up.

Rosa patted Jenna on the back. "Girlfriend, it doesn't matter what Malachi says. You can't forget how they treated you. Lauren and Diane are picking up where your mommy left off. Think Jenna. They'll keep chipping away at you 'til there's nuthin' left. Now they got reinforcements. Nelson and Larry."

Jenna watched a cottontail rabbit hop behind a bush. She was so glad to have a chance at love. Love? Where did that come from? *Does Malachi love me?* They barely knew each other a month. Jenna smiled. There went that good feeling inside of her every time she thought of him instead of panic and pessimism.

"So what's it gonna be?" Rosa asked, interrupting her thoughts. "Are we going to go after Lauren or do you want to spend the rest of your life in a cold, empty bed?"

Jenna looked dismayed. She shook her head.

"Well that's what's gonna happen if you don't do something about Lauren. She'll make sure that you're never happy."

Jenna's nostrils flared. They were not going to take Malachi away from her. They were not going to take away her joy. "Let's do it."

Jenna felt honored that Malachi shared his past with her. *He trusts me. If he didn't, he'd never share something so personal.* Where Lauren was concerned, Malachi would've insisted that she, 'turn the other cheek.' Given his past, he would've been sensitive to the need for mercy. But Lauren didn't deserve it and neither did Diane. *They need to pay.*

Rosa wore a silky smile. "You still want in?"

"Definitely."

"Dear sweet Lauren." Rosa sighed. "Guess we'll have to go to Pound Ridge sooner than planned."

Jenna grinned. "Guess who booked the Lilac Room?" She went on to tell Rosa about Lauren and Nelson's accommodations at The Lorelei House. "You shoulda heard Larry whining about his girlie room."

Rosa guffawed. "Why didn't you tell me this before? I was right, wasn't I?"

"As always." Moving their mother out of the picture really did bring them all back to town. Soon Jenna's smile disappeared. "I want Lauren to suffer."

Rosa stared out at the woods. "She will."

Then, Rosa dug her hand deep into the soil and pulled up a clump of dirt. Worms were sticking out of it. She examined the hideous cluster. A mischievous grin appeared on her face. "What does Lauren fear the most?"

Jenna smiled. Then, she threw her head back and laughed.

25

Detective Chang greeted Reverend Brooks then sat down. Thankfully, the clergyman's office had air-conditioning. After arriving at the old steepled, white-frame church, he spent the better part of the morning interrogating church staff in other rooms with ceiling fans which did nothing more than circulate hot air. He wondered if they couldn't afford to install central air.

Chang laughed to himself. No media damage to their reputation there. Everyone from the organist down to the woman who served refreshments in the Fellowship Hall had nothing but praises for Bella Crandall. They now knew about her and Julian's frail marriage and were very accepting. The situation was unfortunate, but at least they were still married.

A Bible was open on the reverend's desk. Revelations 3:16 was highlighted. " . . . So because you are lukewarm—neither hot nor cold—I am about to spit you out of my mouth." He winced. Unknowingly, the cleric was reminding him of his ongoing lackadaisical relationship with God. His mother phoned last night with the same thing and then some.

"You should go back to Mass, Richard and you should try to find a nice girl."

Detective Chang looked up at a wooden cross hanging on the wall in the corner. If he didn't know better, he would've sworn that God and his mother were ganging up on him. He pulled out his notepad.

"I just got back from visiting Bella," Reverend Brooks said. "Mayor Urbanowski stopped by too."

Chang tried not to grimace.

"It was hard to see Bella lying there," Reverend Brooks said. "Just yesterday, she was so full of life. Now . . . " He shook his head. "And it's a shame the way the media's spreading gossip."

"Oh?"

"Something about Jenna getting drunk."

Detective Chang raised his eyebrows.

"Jenna and her sisters got into a fuss because of it." "I'm not condoning her actions, but the family's going through a terrible time right now. Sometimes tempers flare. Stress does funny things to us."

You got that right. Chang tapped his pen against his notepad. He wasn't too surprised to learn that Jenna was drinking allegedly. It fueled his suspicion that she was masking tension. He was amazed that Jenna would allow herself to get intoxicated in public. The reserved woman was so meticulous about appearing proper. Controlled. It was almost eerie. "Her mother's attack notwithstanding, is Jenna under stress?"

Reverend Brooks arranged a stack of papers on his desk. "It would've helped if she came back to church," Reverend Brooks said. "Her brother and his wife come almost every Sunday. Her father comes once or twice a month."

"When and why did Jenna stop going?" Chang asked glad that the reverend brought up the family's church attendance even though he didn't answer the question.

The middle-aged pastor leaned back in his swivel chair and sighed. "It happened before I became a minister. Back then, I was a deacon serving under Reverend Joseph Wilson, who's since retired. Anyway, shortly after Jenna's eighteenth birthday, she stopped coming."

"Just like that?"

The Reverend shifted. "Jenna always struck me as unhappy. She didn't look it, mind you. Just something about her spirit."

Chang contained his excitement. He looked up from his writing. "Did Jenna ever talk to you about her feelings?"

Reverend Brooks rearranged the stacks of papers. I mentioned it to Bella a few times. She kept assuring me that Jenna was fine. She's just a loner."

There was a pause.

"You didn't buy it did you, Reverend?"

"There was—talk about discontent between Bella and her children." He closed his eyes as if in prayer.

"You're not gossiping," Detective Chang said. He could see that the spiritual leader was feeling uncomfortable. "I'm trying to determine what happened to a beloved member of your congregation. All you're doing is helping me. I have to investigate every lead. No matter how ugly."

Reverend Brooks opened his eyes and sighed. "I don't know all the facts, Detective. I wasn't in the loop. As I said, I was a deacon. But what I do know is that Bella didn't take too kindly to the talk. The *source* of the rumor nearly lost his or her job."

Detective Chang looked at Reverend Brooks with consternation. Did Bella have that much influence over the church board?

Reverend Brooks' face turned red. They weren't making a good impression. "As for there being unhappiness among the Crandall's," he continued, "the children were always happy. Laughing, joking around."

"The issue is Jenna," Detective Chang said. "Was she as happy as her siblings?"

"Sure. I didn't mean to imply that she went around looking all mopey. I just meant there was something about her that suggested something was off. I'm sure that Julian and Bella did everything they could for their children."

"All right, all of a sudden Jenna stops coming to church," Chang said, taking a fresh tack. "Wasn't that unusual considering her mother was an elder?"

"Detective, sometimes young folks just want to go their own way."

"True."

"I tried bringing Jenna back to the fold. Getting her to tell me what was on her mind. But she wouldn't. It didn't mean she lost her walk with the Lord. I knew that as long as Jenna was with Bella, she was in good hands."

"You believed that knowing what you did about Bella's character?"

"I don't adhere to rumor mongering."

"With all due respect Reverend, you knew that Bella had influence. So much so, that she had the power to have that person's job. And you heard talk about discontent within the family."

The cleric fell silent. Detective Chang watched the expression on the reverend's face as the reminder sank in. "You did have your doubts didn't you, Reverend? You never believed that line about Jenna being a loner, did you?"

"Bella's a good mother." Reverend Brooks sounded defensive.

Detective Chang resisted the urge to groan. What is it about this woman that mesmerizes people? "Did Bella strike you as a strict mother?"

"She was very gentle and loving with her children."

"Did you know that Jenna had to make tea for Bella?" Detective Chang asked.

The clergyman waved his hand in dismissal. "Is that such a bad thing? Have we become so jaded a society that doing kindness for a parent is an outrage?"

Again, Detective Chang decided to switch gears. "I understand Bella was coming here for a meeting last night."

Reverend Brooks nodded. "I was talking to her about it over the phone just yesterday."

Chang straightened. "What time?"

"Around one-ish."

Detective Chang scribbled down the information.

"Although," Reverend Brooks began, a frown forming on his ruddy countenance, "when she told me someone was at the door, I didn't hear the doorbell or anyone knocking."

"Did she mention seeing anyone at the door?"

"No."

Chang stared at a coffee mug on the reverend's desk. He was calm but inwardly excited. Bella didn't see anyone or hear the doorbell yet she knew someone was present. She probably did know her visitor and therefore had no need to feel threatened by his or her prescience. Someone who had a right to be on the premises.

Someone with a key . . .

That made Alan and Jenna persons of interest in his mind. *There were two place settings. Bella knew her visitor. Did a friendly discussion suddenly turn ugly?* "Can you remember anything else, Reverend?"

"At one point, I thought she wasn't listening. She seemed a bit distracted."

"Nervous?"

"No. Just unfocused."

` Chang stood up. "Well, thank you for your time, Reverend, Brooks."

"Anytime, Detective Chang. I'm going to pray that the Lord guides you in the investigation."

"Thanks. I appreciate that." *They are conspiring against me.*

"And I'm going to pray for whoever did this. That person needs help."

Detective Chang stood on the front steps outside of the church. His suit jacket draped over his shoulder, contemplating his next move. A movement caught his eye. A thin, medium height black man in his early sixties and wearing a cap was watering some larkspurs. His instincts kicked in.

*

Roscoe Addison chuckled as the detective sergeant approached. He saw Chang watching him and knew that the officer was going to come over eventually.

"Nice work," Chang said looking with admiration at the church's garden as after they introduced themselves to each other.

"Thanks."

Upon closer inspection, Detective Chang noticed that Addison was a Vietnam War Veteran. "My neighbor's son was in Cambodia. I wished I knew him before he went over there. His name was Hugh. His parents told me he was never the same when he came back. They said he used to be sweet, intelligent. Had lots of promise."

Roscoe nodded his expression serious. "Vietnam. Fort Riley, 1st Infantry, 1971-74."

"Ah. The Big Red One."

Roscoe smiled brightly impressed with the detective's knowledge of his infantry's nickname. "My sister got me into gardening. Wanted to give me something to concentrate on besides blood and guts." Roscoe began trimming shrubs. "You know what I love about planting, Detective? Knowing that something beautiful's gonna bloom." Roscoe looked off into the distance. Then he said. "Something pretty. Instead of ugly." He resumed working in silence. "It's spiritual."

"And sometimes it's edible." Chang smiled and pointed to the vegetable garden in the distance.

Roscoe chuckled. "The church runs a soup kitchen."

"Speaking of gardening," Detective Chang began, "I saw Bella Crandall's. "Charming. Like something out of a fairytale. Did she get her inspiration from you?"

Roscoe paused. He stared pointedly at Detective Chang before going back to his task.

"I take it you and the victim are not on friendly terms."

"But I wouldn't try to kill her either. Bella Crandall ain't worth spending my time in jail."

Detective Chang nodded. "I need to ask you some questions." He pulled out his notepad and pen then draped his suit jacket along a nearby bench. "You a member here?"

"Twenty-five years."

"Then you know the Crandall's."

Roscoe smiled sardonically. "Yup."

"Did Bella have any disputes with anyone?"

The Vietnam Veteran laughed with derision. "You mean recently?"

Chang gave him a puzzled look. "She's not well-loved after all?"

With his thumb, Roscoe pointed to the church. "I don't have to be a fly on the wall to know that everybody's singing Bella's praises to you. If I were you, Detective Chang, I'd think about the number two as in two faces. The first time I saw it happen was on Communion Sunday."

"Saw what happen?" Detective Chang already knew that the veteran was referring to the first Sunday of the month when his church's denomination celebrated Holy Communion.

"It was my first year here. "Jenna could've been six, seven-years-old. I saw Bella grab a fistful of that child's hair. Some of it even came out."

Chang raised his eyebrows.

Roscoe nodded. Saw it while I was trimming the rose bush outside the classroom where they hold Sunday school. Her son was there too. What's his name? Alan. Yeah. He coulda been about . . . fourteen. The boy was upset. He said something to Bella. Whatever it was, she didn't like it. Boxed Alan right in the ears."

"What was that all about?" Chang asked.

"Don't know. What I do know is that if she knew I saw her, she would've been different. Huh. The way she struts around town like she's some big shot. I knew all about her by the time I got here." Roscoe grabbed his water bottle again and took another drink. "Reverend

Wilson, he was our senior minister back then, didn't waste time telling me about her majesty."

"Was she having an off day?" Detective Chang knew the question was silly but he asked anyway. He was still processing this data. He already suspected that Bella was tough and demanding behind closed doors, but not a child abuser.

"Bella Crandall had a lot of off days," Roscoe said. "Another time I was getting the soil ready for the spring planting and I overheard her tell Jenna she was ugly. You've seen her. There ain't nuthin' ugly about her."

Chang agreed. "What about Lauren and Diane?" "Huh. They're every bit like their mother. While Bella was giving their brother and sister hell, Lauren just stood there and Diane was laughin' like a hyena. Now the congregation's all excited because they're famous."

"Wait a minute. Lauren and Diane were there?"

"Yup."

Chang made a note. The girls would've been minors and wouldn't been able to do much, but the least they could've done was care. On the other hand, if they found Jenna having her hair yanked out amusing what did he expect? "Did Bella ever hit Lauren or Diane?" He knew the answer, but he asked anyway.

Roscoe snorted. "She adores those two." He walked over to the hibiscus.

Detective Chang followed. Two. There goes that number again. "What about Julian?"

"What about him?"

"He's their father. He must've had some say in his children's upbringing."

Roscoe turned away from the hibiscus and looked Chang straight in the eye. "Bella was in charge. Even now. She's got the whole church board sewn up. She's the life of the party and generous to a fault. Likewise, Lauren and Diane. Those three sign checks with lots of zeroes. Somethin' wasn't right up there on Haven Road. Now the '*chickens come home to roost.*'"

"Roscoe, did you ever tell anyone about what you saw?"

"Yeah. Nearly lost my job."

Detective Sergeant Richard Chang stormed back to his unmarked car. He cursed as he opened the door. He tossed his suit jacket on the passenger side then slid behind the wheel. Lauren, Alan, Diane and Jenna had each taken him for a ride. They were all part of a stormy and dismal past. They all had something to hide. Evidently, Alan and Jenna thought that he might've found a motive for attempted murder. Lauren and Diane on some level have to feel some kind of shame for their past. Detective Chang snorted. Crandall-Door had the gall to threaten his career and his credibility while she had this skeleton in the closet. Bella, Lauren and Diane's generosity was definitely for show.

Or was it guilt?

Detective Chang frowned. What occurred between Bella, Alan and Jenna was a long time ago. Why want payback now? Assuming they did. Unless the abuse never really stopped . . .

He sighed then leaned his head on the headrest. Was Bella continuously abusing Jenna? Bree, the college intern, when questioned said that she did relieve Jenna at the phone for lunch, a witness had spotted Jenna in the park and Alan was at his business meeting. When Alan went away to college. Jenna would've been around eleven. Why did he leave her alone, knowing what their mother was like? Importantly, why didn't he or Jenna tell someone?

If he followed Roscoe's implication, Alan and Jenna were co-conspirators. Detective Chang sighed again. He just couldn't get that look Alan gave his younger sister out of his mind.

Then, there was Julian. The mechanic came across as pleasant and reasonable. He too was out of the loop. He could be harboring a smoldering rage behind that façade. He was the head of the family, yet he walked out and left his wife and children. Bella must have been some formidable force for him to leave his family. Then again, look at the way she treated her own son and daughter. Why?

Chang massaged the back of his neck. This case was becoming less about a fiend running loose in Gordonville and more about an enemy within. He hated to play with the public's emotions. For now, it was paramount that the community continues to believe that a stranger was responsible.

He started the car. "I think I'm gonna pay my man Alan a visit."

Shortly after he pulled away from the church, Detective Chang saw an entourage heading toward him. He sighed. Mayor Urbanowksi. Soon, Hizzoner's limo pulled up alongside him. Now he was obligated to stop. Chang pasted on a smile as he and the mayor stepped out of their respective vehicles.

"Detective," the mayor greeted as security stood beside his limousine.

"Mr. Mayor."

"I was just on my way to your office," Urbanowski said. "I just came from visiting Bella Crandall."

Chang was still wearing his pasted-on smile.

A small crowd started to gather at the sight of the city official and the detective sergeant. Seeing this, Urbanowski puffed out his chest.

"What're you doing about the current situation, Detective Chang?" The mayor's voice was a tad high. "The citizens of Gordonville need reassurance."

"My team and I are working on it as we speak." Detective Chang's smile faltered. The nerve of this glory hog humiliating him in public.

If you'd get out my way, I could get some more work done. The mayor was delaying his interview with Alan Crandall and time was of the essence. Who knew if he was getting rid of evidence this very moment? Moreover, there was no way he was going to tell the mayor what he just learned about the Crandall's.

"I'll be staying on top of things," the mayor said. He acknowledged the crowd with a nod then turned his attention back to Detective

Chang. "I want the citizens to know that I intend to take back this town from this criminal."

Chang hoped he wasn't going to hurl from the mayor's grandstanding.

"Good Day, citizens, Detective."

Urbanowski stepped back into his limousine. Soon he and his entourage drove away, leaving Detective Chang free to go about his work.

Elise was in the kitchen preparing dinner. She was surprised Alan decided to return to the office; his reason being that work would help keep his mind off his mother. It made sense and yet, she sensed there was something else going on. She opened up the spice rack and took out a bottle of rosemary. She rubbed it over the chicken she was preparing for tonight's dinner. For the second time in a matter of days, she saw her youngest sister-in-law display uncharacteristic anger. Alan and Jenna never showed such tension toward each other before. Elise paused. Usually, Alan always confided in her. If something was wrong, he could tell her. Hadn't she always been his confidante?

The doorbell rang. It was probably another neighbor coming over to offer sympathy. When Elise went to the door, Detective Chang was standing on the step.

26

R.B. Consulting, P.C. was located on the fifth floor of a flatiron edifice on Main Street. Alan sat in his office staring at the walls, the plans for a new children's wing for the Gordonville Library spread across his desk. Beside it was a bottle of antacid. As he expected, his associates were surprised when he suddenly showed up for work that afternoon. Barely twenty-four hours ago, someone put his mother in a coma. He should be at home awaiting news of her prognosis, comforting his family, getting over his initial shock. But he needed to focus on something else. Work would help him to relax. Fortunately, they accepted that excuse. No doubt, they were discussing him at the water cooler.

Alan sighed as he spooned out some of the antacid. He was alone in his speculations about Rosa. Diane blew him off. So did Lauren once he got a chance to talk to her. What should he do? His stomach had been churning since Elise called to warn him that Detective Chang was on his way. He assured her that he had no idea what the detective wanted, which was true. He wished he could be forthright about Rosa but how could he when his own father didn't know about her? He rubbed his hand over his face. Elise was going to want answers later.

"Oh, Mom," Alan said aloud. "What happened yesterday?"

He turned his swivel chair around and looked out the window at the mountains. He watched the residents on Main Street going about their business laughing and smiling others wearing a complacent look. Beneath the surface, however, lay apprehension. He knew it. He recognized it. He lived it all his life. Gordonville believed that some twisted person was running around their village and they were right. What they didn't know was that the monster wasn't after them.

Detective Chang sat in a guest chair across from Alan, notepad in hand. Immediately, the architect began explaining to him why he returned to work, not that he asked. His wife already told him when he came to the house. Chang noted the bottle of antacid sitting on top of the desk. Either Alan ate something that didn't agree with him or he was extremely nervous. Could it have something to do with him and his sisters playing him for a fool? Chang was still steaming from his encounter with the mayor and from discovering Lauren, Alan and Diane's lies; nevertheless, he kept his anger in check.

The detective's calmness didn't fool Alan. He knew annoyed when he saw it. He didn't live with his mother for eighteen years without sensing it. He just wondered what he was dealing with.

"How were things between you and your mother?"

Alan blinked. "Fine."

"Ever argue with her?"

"I was a nerd so I didn't give my mom much trouble."

"Did you ever argue with your mother," Detective Chang asked again.

"Sometimes . . . I guess. What's this about?"

"Are you familiar with the old adage, *'walls have ears?'*"

"Sure."

Without mentioning Roscoe's name, Detective Chang repeated what the groundskeeper witnessed. He never took his eyes off Alan who, reminded him of a scared rabbit.

Someone saw. Alan looked toward the door. "Please lower your voice." He couldn't risk any of his associates overhearing. Importantly, they mustn't find out about his and Jenna's abuse. It was bad enough that someone saw what happened at the church. Well, whoever it was didn't see everything or this interrogation would be taking an entirely different turn . . .

"Fine," Chang said. Alan was still determined to maintain the family's pristine image. He lowered his voice, which wasn't that loud to begin with. "You and Jenna neglected to mention you and your mother's past likewise Lauren and Diane. How about it?"

He didn't have a comeback. He wasn't prepared for this. Alan looked into the detective sergeant's unsmiling eyes. "What does that have to do with this case?"

"Try vengeance."

"I would never do anything to hurt my mother."

"How old were you and Jenna when your father moved out?"

Alan glanced at the door again. "Twelve." His parents' de facto separation was now public knowledge but the details weren't.

"That would've made Jenna, what, five?

"Yes," Alan said.

"And Lauren?" No need to ask about Diane since she's Alan's twin.

"Fourteen." Alan sounded abrupt. "Is any of this relevant?"

"Your father leaving must've left you feeling angry and confused," Chang said, deliberately disregarding Alan's query and indignant tone. "Especially during your teen years. "Must've been awkward being the only male in a house full of females. The mean, domineering kind."

Alan pretended to study the library plan on his desk.

"Your mother must've been one tough cookie for your dad to jump ship.

Alan found the plans fascinating.

"I'm curious," Chang continued. "What did your father have to say about you and Jenna's treatment?" Based on Roscoe's hint about

Bella being in charge, he suspected that Julian was in the dark about the abuse.

Alan's thoughts went back in time. He was twelve years old again standing in his undershirt and briefs, legs covered in welts. Mom was beating Jenna. He came to his baby sister's defense and paid the price.

Bella grabbed his arm, her long nails digging into his skin.

"You stay out of my business, boy."

"I'm gonna tell, Dad."

"If you tell him or anyone else you'll be eating your tonsils."

"I'm waiting."

Detective Chang's voice brought Alan back to the present and the officer's furious visage. Alan sighed. He couldn't answer the query. He just couldn't.

"Crandall—"

"He didn't know." On edge, Alan's voice raised a notch.

I can't believe this is happening.

This wasn't the way it was supposed to happen. *He had played it out in his mind so many different times, so many different ways. He planned to have Lauren and Diane with him.*

Chang was unaffected by the retort. He waited patiently for Alan's reply. The architect owed him some answers.

"We weren't supposed to tell."

"Why?"

Alan rapped his fingers around the antacid bottle. "Because Mom said not to. And you didn't cross her. Ever."

"What about now? You're an adult."

"Why are we talking about this?" Alan asked.

"Because today I find out your mother was mistreating you and Jenna. You both had a chance to bring it up but you didn't. I wonder why."

"So Mom had her moments."

"Is that what you call them? Moments?" Detective Chang frowned. Alan sustained a fear of his mother after all these years even though she could no longer harm him. "Is that how Jenna dealt with the cruelty too? Calling them moments?" *Did his eyes just flicker?*

"Why do I get the feeling that you and Jenna may know what went down?

Alan shook his head vehemently. "No. We don't know anything. We were as shocked as everyone else." He wanted to shrink under Chang's skeptical expression.

"How about Lauren and Diane?"

"Of course they don't know who did it. That's what we want you to find out."

Chang gave him a skeptical look. There was something phony about his statement. There was something phony about him. He was trying too hard. "How come Jenna didn't leave home?"

"She and Mom worked things out."

"Jenna tell you that?"

"No."

"Then how do you know?"

"She and Mom were getting along great."

Chang gritted his teeth. "Every time you saw the two of them together you mean?"

"Yes."

"You have no idea what was going on or might have been going on between your mother and sisters over the years, did you?"

"I've looked out for my little sister her entire life," Alan said defensively. He was loaded with guilt, regretting not paying more attention to Jenna and to what was going on within his own household.

To not digging beneath the surface.

He took another teaspoon of antacid. He really believed that Mom and Jenna had a ceasefire. Rosa went away; Jenna finished high school, went on to college. Things seemed fine until the wedding and Diane's engagement. *I should've known better.*

"I know you looked out for her," Detective Chang said interrupting his thoughts.

"Jenna's a very caring person," Alan added.

"Is that why she was serving her tea?"

"Yes."

"Regardless of your mother's earlier treatment?"

"Yes."

"I'm supposed to believe Jenna made peace with Bella. Just like that."

"Yes."

Detective Chang glanced at the antacid bottle. "Without counseling I presume."

Alan breathed an audible sigh. "Yes."

"Have you and Jenna reconciled with Lauren and Diane?"

"We're sociable."

Chang started drawing a geometric figure in his notepad. "Does Jenna have any friends?" Despite what Officers Davidson and Vega said about Jenna's solitude, he wanted to see what else he could glean. If Jenna didn't have a friend, then she had an associate.

"My sister keeps to herself."

Chang put away his notepad. He stood up and leaned over Alan's desk. The architect shrank, becoming a frightened little boy again. He looked away.

"You and your sisters withheld evidence. I suppose your father's a part of the sport play-games-with-the detective?"

"No."

"Why should I believe you? You lied to me once?"

"Jenna doesn't have any friends and Dad didn't know what Mom was doing. It's like I said we weren't allowed to tell." Alan held his stomach. Chang towering over him was disconcerting.

"I don't give a rat's ass about The Crandall mystique," Chang said. "Now's the time for you to come clean. Because if I find out you're holding back, the-you-know-what's gonna hit the fan."

Alan nodded.

"Now, did Jenna have any friends?"

"No."

The detective looked at him for a moment. Alan didn't blink. He maintained eye contact. He could not allow himself to look away. Unknown to Chang he was pinching himself. Hard.

"Okay." Detective Chang left the room.

Alan slumped in his chair. *I just lied to a cop.*

Chang stopped at Delsey's for a quick bite. Over coffee and a complimentary vanilla cupcake, he decided to pay a visit to Julian.

27

Gordonville Mechanics was located just outside of town. Julian escorted the detective into his cluttered office. On the wall hung a football calendar. In the corner was a water cooler.

"I'll try not to take up too much of your time," Detective Chang said as he took a seat on a metal folding chair.

"It's no trouble at all, Detective."

"I see you decided to go back to work too." Chang mentioned Alan's return to the office. He noticed a candy jar on the mechanic's desk filled with caramel, assorted fruit-filled . . . peppermint and ginger candies.

"Activity helps." Julian said.

It also gets you away from your wife. Julian must've spent countless hours at Bella's side. "According to your son, Jenna keeps to herself."

"She was always a quiet girl." Julian smiled. "I think she only came alive when she was painting or drawing."

"Her work is remarkable," Detective Chang said. "I'm surprised she didn't make a career of it."

"She plans to." Julian told the detective all about Jenna's plan to enroll in art school. "She brought it up the same day Diane announced her engagement. It caused a stir." Chang pulled out his notepad. Julian went on to talk about Bella, Lauren and Diane's reactions. "I was furious

276

with Bella." Julian realized how that might've sounded to the detective. Quickly, he added, "Not enough to try to kill her."

Chang wore a contemplative expression. Bella Crandall had a serious mean streak. It wasn't enough she ill-treated Jenna, but she had to stifle her talent too? Could interfering with Jenna's artistic ambitions have been the final straw? *Could this have been a hit gone wrong?* Jenna didn't have the body strength to pull the attack. Someone was conspiring with her. That made Alan a suspect. He had reason to keep his troubled history with his mother a secret. "Mr. Crandall, how come you didn't know about Jenna's goal to become an artist?"

"Call me Julian. And in answer to your question, Detective, Bella was in charge of everything." His tone carried undisguised contempt. "That included raising our children."

Chang tapped his notepad with his pen. He recalled Roscoe's critique about Bella being in control.

"Once in a while she'd *allow* me to put in my two cents. Believe me, I tried my best, but Bella . . . She wore me down until one day I had no will left to fight."

Detective Chang watched as Julian picked up a stack of work orders and mulled over them. He continued watching the victim's husband while at the same time listening to the buzz of conversation and laughter coming from the workers in the garage. "So you left."

The patriarch's subliminal need to confide could prove invaluable. In addition, Bella's threat to his manhood could also hold a clue. He fought back the guilt of using Julian. Instinct told him that this man had been through a lot.

He was about to go through more.

Julian pushed aside the work orders. "I can just see the headlines now. Disgruntled husband loses cool. Pummels wife."

Was that a roundabout confession? "Would you say your wife dominated Jenna?"

Julian hesitated. He recalled witnessing Bella's unreasonable behavior toward Jenna. "I'm sure she has our daughter's best interest at heart."

Making excuses. *Like father like son. And like the Reverend Brooks.*

"Why are you asking about Jenna?" Julian stiffened. "She's not a suspect is she?"

"I'm sorry to break this to you," Detective Chang began, not answering Julian's query, "but your wife has been physically and verbally abusing Jenna when she was a child."

Disillusionment came over Julian's face.

"Alan was a victim too," Detective Chang went on, "but from what it appears Jenna bore the brunt of it."

Julian shook his head. "No. It can't be."

"Lauren and Diane were willing participants." Detective Chang repeated what Roscoe Addison said, careful not to reveal the identity of the Vietnam War veteran and groundskeeper.

"My daughters?" He shook his head. "That would mean they were tormenting their own brother and sister when they were just kids themselves."

Julian looked up mindlessly at the sports calendar. July was in black large font, a picture of a baseball player underneath it. Lauren and Diane did behave unkindly towards Jenna the last time they were together and Bella was indifferent about it. But what about Alan?

How could this have been going on and he not tell me?

"Any idea why your wife would want to maltreat your son and youngest daughter?"

"No." Julian could barely get the word out.

Chang looked skeptical. "You're sure?"

"Detective, why would I think that my wife and daughters would terrify Jenna and Alan?"

"You didn't answer my question."

The two men looked at each other for a beat. Then, Julian said, "No, I don't know why Bella would hurt Jenna and Alan. Or why Lauren and Diane would participate. They're their own flesh and blood." Julian swore. "I can't believe this. Bella. All these years. And Lauren and Diane. You think maybe Alan and Jenna were misbehaving?"

Chang studied Julian. "I think you know better than that."

"Why didn't Alan and Jenna tell me?"

"Why didn't they tell *me*?" Chang asked.

"Are you suggesting my son and my daughter had something to do with what happened?" Julian asked.

"I'm not suggesting anything," Detective Chang said. "But I do find it strange that Alan and Jenna kept silent when they had an opportunity to talk. That's a sign they had something to hide. And," he continued before Julian could retort, "while I'm on the subject of guilt, Lauren and Diane were putting on quite a show for the cameras."

Julian shifted in his chair. Their behavior was unprofessional.

"It was too big a show."

"I don't know what to tell you, Detective, except maybe Alan and Jenna were scared."

"Of who?"

"I don't know."

"I think they're protecting someone."

Julian's face registered surprise. "That's ridiculous."

"Then why keep silent?" Detective Chang asked.

"I have no idea."

Chang looked at the peppermints and ginger hard candies on Julian's desk. "Have either Alan or Jenna been to a psychiatrist?" He doubted it by he asked anyway.

Julian stood up feeling miffed that Chang would ask that. "My children know they could talk to me about anything."

"Answer the question, please."

Julian sighed. "I don't know. I don't think so. I even told Jenna that if anything was ever on her mind she could always talk to me. She wasn't all that happy my wife and Diane dragged her house-hunting."

"Really?" Detective Chang looked thoughtful. "Was there something troubling her?"

"Maybe. She wasn't too happy about being there that afternoon. Said she had to cancel plans."

So she was unhappy. Maybe Angry?

"My kids don't need therapy," Julian said.

"Alan's still terrified of his own mother. There's damage to his machismo. I'm also willing to bet that Jenna's still a frightened little girl in the body of a woman." He also suspected that the patriarch knew more than he was letting on. "There something you want to add, Julian?"

"No. What more can I add to this rotten news you're giving me?" The mechanic slammed his fist on the desk then paced the room. Why didn't Jenna just leave? Alan did. He went away to college."

"Where?"

"Cornell." Julian couldn't help smiling proudly. "Full scholarship."

"Commendable. And Jenna?"

"Gordonville State."

Chang nodded.

Julian grimaced. The detective's body language said it all. Jenna attended a local college while Alan left home to attend Cornell. Even if the Ivy League college was only two hours away, he was still testing his independence. Julian wore a stubborn expression. "So Jenna's a late bloomer. But if my son was that troubled he wouldn't have gone away to college or have gotten married."

"Interesting how the mind works," Detective Chang said. "Nevertheless, there seems to be some kind of perceived power your wife has over them. That's why Alan's still trapped." Chang pointed to his forehead. "In here." He took his pen and poked one of the peppermints in the dish. "Why do you have those?"

"Is that a problem?"

"I think you're a straightforward guy who doesn't go for bull," Detective Chang said.

"Got that right."

"Then answer the question. "Now, why do you keep peppermints and ginger candies? I think it's more than just a coincidence."

"They're for Alan aren't they?" Detective Chang asked.

"So what if they are?" Julian sighed. "He's got stomach problems."

"I'm not a trained professional, but I think your son's condition is psychosomatic."

Julian balled his hands into fists. He had permitted Bella to drive him away when he should've stayed and fought to maintain his position as leader in the family, but instead, he let her wave that one mistake he made over his head . . .

She said she'd let it go. She promised. So all this time she was breaking her pledge. Chang didn't need to know the details. Besides, it had nothing to do with the case. He wished that Bella would come out of her coma. He wanted some answers.

"It's inconceivable that Jenna could go through life without having at least one friend." Detective Chang hadn't ruled out the possibility of a stranger having committed the crime. "So far, I've been told that she doesn't have any friends. She must know someone other than Prof. Chase."

"Only Bella would know about that," Julian said bitterly. "Wait a minute who told you Jenna didn't have any friends? At least, she used to have one."

Chang flipped the page of his notebook.

"Her name was Rosa." Julian walked over to the water cooler and poured a cup of water for himself and Detective Chang. "It was weird. Just the mention of her name caused the whole family to get edgy. Except for Elise and me that is. We were in the dark."

"Explain."

Julian handed the cup of water to Detective Chang as he told him about everything that occurred at the impromptu engagement celebration. "Lauren and Diane kept baiting Jenna about Rosa. Finally, Jenna blew her top. It was so unlike her. But they had it coming."

Detective Chang contemplated Jenna's temper as he drank the cool water. She was showing irritability lately. "What's Rosa's last name?"

Julian thought for a moment. "Garrison.

Detective Chang frowned. *I can't believe Alan kept this from me. He's more afraid of his mother than he is of me. And she's in a coma.*

"I hope what I said shows you that Jenna can stand up for herself. Even though she did back down eventually, she still stood up to her mother. Jenna even left with Malachi that same afternoon."

"What do you mean?"

Julian explained about Bella's disapproval about their children leaving in the middle of a family gathering. "It practically became a showdown between her and Jenna. I found out something else too. If it hadn't been for me, Malachi would never have gotten the chance to set foot in the house."

"He's your daughter's boyfriend and he's never been to the house?"

"*Inside* the house, Detective. Bella wouldn't allow him in." Julian explained about the parking. "My wife's a trip. Now you understand why I gave her space?"

"Did it ever occur to you that something may be mentally or emotionally wrong with Bella?"

"No." What's with this detective and the psychology trip? Julian began refilling his cup with more water. *Amelia.* It never occurred to him that Bella was suffering repercussions all this time. She was always so strong. And vocal.

If she had a problem, she would've said something. She said they'd work things out. Julian took a big gulp of water. He didn't know his world anymore.

Detective Chang stared intently at a chip in the wood on Julian's desk. Prof. Chase never mentioned Bella's hostility toward him. No doubt, for the same reason Alan and Jenna didn't tell him about her hostility toward them. *He was afraid of becoming a suspect too.*

"Malachi was nice about it though," Julian said interrupting the detective's thoughts. "Jenna found a remarkable guy." Julian sighed. "I didn't want to her to have to go through the pain of another breakup again."

"They broke up before?"

Julian returned to his desk. "Some other guy. Alan told me." He stacked and restacked a pile of papers. "Needless to say Bella didn't tell me. And they dated for almost a year I think. I guess Jenna was in too much pain to talk about it."

Pain. "What was the ex-boyfriend's name?"

"Everett Long." He looked at Chang with incredulity. "You don't think . . . ?"

"And what about the argument at the hospital?"

Julian told him what he learned from Malachi and Alan.

"Tell me what you know about this Rosa Garrison."

"Not much. My wife said she was an old childhood friend."

"Really?" Detective Chang drained his cup then crushed it.

28

"I didn't expect to get dragged into this," Everett said after Detective Chang and Officer Vega arrived and sat down in the home office of his Tudor-style mansion. Everett tore a sheet of paper from a legal pad and crumpled it in his tan-colored hands. "I did not harm Bella. From the day I broke up with Jenna, I cut all ties with the Crandall's. That was almost two years ago. Am I gonna need a lawyer?"

"Relax, Mr. Long," Officer Vega said using the soothing tone she reserved for reassuring nervous witnesses. "You're not in any trouble." She could see why Jenna fell for him. At six foot one with unblemished skin and gorgeous light brown eyes, Everett looked as if he could've been a model or an actor instead of a financial analyst.

"How long did you and Jenna date?"

"Nine months."

"What caused you to breakup?" Officer Vega asked.

She ignored that feeling she got after she said the word breakup. The question unearthed memories of her split with her fiancé. The Philmont, New York native was grateful for the transfer to the Gordonville P.D. from the Hudson Police Department where she had worked for six years. The change in units and the decision to move to a new town gave her a new focus and a chance to stop thinking about her cancelled wedding and the humiliation that went with it, a chance to stop cursing herself for missing the signs that her fiancé had met someone else.

It'll be a long time before I fall for another man again.

"I'll give you three reasons," Everett began snapping Nanci out of her reverie. "Bella, Lauren and Diane." Flustered, she glanced at Chang who fortunately was deep in thought to notice she had been staring into space.

Unknown to Officer Vega, her sergeant was too busy steeling himself against the sound of her voice. He decided to bring her along because she might be able to get through to Jenna's ex-boyfriend in a way that he couldn't. So far, he was right. She had calmed him down and Everett was talking. *It was not an excuse to be around her. He* adjusted his tie. "What did Jenna's mother and sisters have to do with it?"

"Jenna and I didn't have what one would consider normal dates. She always had to be home before four o'clock." Everett laughed shortly. "Now I know why."

"So Jenna never told you about her mother's tea," Chang said.

"No. And she always had an excuse for why she had to be home no later than three-thirty. Chores for Bella, favors for Lauren or Diane." Detective Chang and Officer Vega exchanged glances. "We could be in the middle of a date and Jenna's mother or one of her sisters could suddenly need something and BAM! She stops dead in her tracks and takes care of it."

Everett leaned back in his swivel chair. "I wouldn't forget the time I got us tickets to a jazz concert in Rhinebeck. Weeks in advance. The day of the concert, Jenna calls me to say she can't go. Diane's throwing a dinner party and the family has to be there. She needs her family's support."

Detective Chang looked at Everett with incredulity. "You're kidding."

"I wish. Naturally, I went ballistic, which only made things worse. Jenna was in tears when she called. See, she and her mother got into a fight over Diane's dinner party conflicting with our plans. Not to mention Jenna feeling mega guilty."

"Over not wanting to attend Diane's dinner party?" Officer Vega was mystified. "You had concert tickets."

Everett laughed without mirth. "Bella could make Jenna feel responsible for a tsunami. It occurred to me some time after we broke up that Diane probably knew about the concert and helped set the whole thing up. She, Lauren and Bella set up a lot of things. Why do you think our relationship crashed?"

"Why?" Officer Vega asked.

"Spite." Everett picked up an eraser and began playing with it. "Bella, Lauren and Diane didn't like me."

Officer Vega's eyes widened. How could the victim and her elder daughters have found fault with this handsome, successful man?

Everett shrugged responding to her unspoken question. "I guess I didn't meet their standards whatever those are."

Chang tapped his pen against his notepad. *Or maybe their antagonism had nothing to do with you.* "Did you ever get around the four o'clock tea situation?"

"We went out *after* four."

"Tell us about your relationship with Bella," Chang commanded.

"Nightmarish." They could see the discomfort on the financial analyst's face. "She gave me the silent treatment every time I came over. I thought she'd warm up to me once she realized my intentions towards Jenna were honorable." He sighed. "Not that woman. She was rough."

"You were actually invited inside the house?" Detective Chang asked.

"Yes. Surprisingly. Not that I was enjoying myself. The atmosphere felt like the inside of a meat locker."

Chang twiddled his pen. *Bella must've changed her modus operandi when Malachi came around.* "Where did you park?"

"In front of the house." Now Everett looked at the detective sergeant strangely. "Why?"

Chang brushed aside Everett's question. "Tell us about Jenna's sisters."

"There was this one time Jenna invited me over for dinner. She was cooking my favorite. Baked ziti."

Officer Vega smothered a smile. Everett Long looked like a man more accustomed to filet mignon.

"It was supposed to be just the two of us," Everett went on. Bella was going to some church function so Jenna and I would have the house to ourselves. We were going to eat in the kitchen then later watch a video. When I got there, Bella gave me her usual chilly greeting. I didn't care. She was leaving. Jenna and I were counting the minutes.

"Then lo and behold the church function's cancelled." Everett chuckled dryly. "Instead of finding something else to do and giving Jenna and me our alone time, Bella makes herself comfortable."

"Awkward," Officer Vega murmured.

"It got even more interesting. Lauren miraculously showed up." Detective Chang and Officer Vega exchanged glances. "Yeah. That was my reaction too. And Jenna's. Lauren was living in Wallkill. She couldn't be just passing by. But *Bella* was expecting her. I saw a look pass between her and Lauren. Like they were sharing a private joke."

Chang grunted. *Runs in the family.*

Everett stood up and began pacing the room. "Needless to say, there never was a church anything. Next thing we knew Bella and Lauren invited themselves to *our* dinner. We ended up eating in the dining room instead of the kitchen. Why? Because, Lauren, the prima donna, wanted it that way."

Chang laughed to himself. The adjective fit the attorney to a tee.

"Lauren was on a mission to make me feel uncomfortable. While I was taking up the gravy boat, I spilled a drop on the tablecloth. Lauren. Flipped. Out. It wasn't even her tablecloth. It wasn't even her table."

"What did Jenna say?"

"Nothing. She just shut down. Like when the lights go dark in a house. Funny though. I could tell she didn't like it. Everett slammed his hand on the desk. The officers stared. "Sorry. It's just reliving it." He took a moment to collect himself. "She never reacted to anything. That was my problem with Jenna. And it wasn't the first time she let them ride roughshod over her."

"Why did Jenna allow it?" Officer Vega asked.

"Wish I knew. Bella, Lauren and Diane had this . . . power over her. Especially Bella. It was uncanny but understandable." Everett looked rueful. "They almost had me under their spell. You wanna lash out at them but you can't." He glanced sheepishly at Officer Vega. "It was . . . emasculating."

Chang wiggled the pen in his hand. On the afternoon of Bella's attack, Lauren and Diane insulted Jenna publicly and she didn't retaliate. She didn't even make a negative gesture.

"I could still see the smirk on Bella's face while her first born was ripping my face off," Everett said. "Sitting like a queen at the head of the table presiding over her throne. She was like that at the barbecue."

"What barbecue?"

Everett laughed sardonically. "To this day I'm still kicking myself for going. But I went for Jenna's sake." He sighed. "Lauren was having some housewarming. She bought a townhouse in Bronxville. Jenna had to go."

Chang was in deep thought. Jenna *had* to go to Diane's dinner party and she *had* to go house hunting. Too many obligations.

"Going to Lauren's really bummed her out," Everett said.

Detective Chang wore a slight frown. "Oh?"

"Unless you're deemed worthy by Lauren, she'll never make you feel welcome. That's why it came as a surprise when Jenna said that Lauren was inviting me. Of course, I didn't want to go. The woman was insulting me every time she had a chance. But for Jenna's sake, I went."

"Not only was I treated like crap, but I got roped into killing a bunch of spiders and their eggs." Detective Chang made a face while Officer Vega flinched. "Lauren didn't want me there as her guest. She just wanted a houseboy. Even Alan resented it."

Detective Chang looked up, startled. "He was there?"

"The whole family was there," Everett said. "Including Larry and Nelson." He rolled his eyes. "Nelson was too good to catch spiders on his own girlfriend's property. And Larry's got too much of a fathead. It's a wonder he can wear turtlenecks."

Detective Chang began clicking his pen. "Tell me about Alan."

"He's an okay guy. He's successful in his field, but he doesn't let you know it. You can sit down with him and have a beer. Julian's like that. I wish Jenna had a fraction of his guts."

"What do you mean?"

"Alan got into Lauren's face about using me to kill spiders. And would you believe she complained to her *mother?*" Chang raised his eyebrows. "I couldn't believe it. She almost sounded like a little girl. Thing is she didn't know she had an audience until she turned around and saw me. Lauren had this look in her eyes like I caught her with no clothes on. The look was there for a few seconds. Then it disappeared."

"Then what happened?" Detective Chang asked.

"She avoided me for the rest of the party, but Bella got crazy mad at Alan. She lost that public relations façade she always wears. She had this scary look on her face. My man Alan backed down like he saw a rabid dog."

"And what was Jenna's reaction to all this?" Chang asked, knowing what the answer would be but decided to ask anyway.

"Like the gravy boat she didn't have the backbone to stand up to Lauren. And she sure wasn't going to stand up to her mother. Everett sat down at his desk again. "When we got back home, I begged Jenna to stand up for her rights. I even offered to take her away from all that madness, but she refused. That's when I knew I had to get out of the relationship. Fast. That last visit with her family was the turning point for me. Her father had the sense enough to leave that house."

"Did you know that Julian Crandall split from his wife when Jenna was a small child?" Detective Chang asked.

"No, I didn't. He should've taken her with him." Everett walked over to the window and looked out at the hawthorn tree in his front yard. "Jenna and I got into a huge fight about her mother and sisters. "See, before I met her, I was this self-assured, healthy guy. I ran the personal financial planning division at my firm. My employees respected me. I got along with my neighbors." Everett turned and faced Detective Chang and Officer Vega. "After I met the Crandall's, my confidence started going south along with my emotional health. Look, I cared a lot about Jenna. I really did. The last thing I wanted to do was cause her heartache, but if I didn't get away, I'd become like her. A wuss.

"As sharp as Jenna was, something was missing. Now I think I know what it was, her essence. Bella, Lauren and Diane were consuming her." Everett sighed. "You see, Bella had this eerie ability to get into your head and play with it like a lump of clay. The woman could smell fear like an animal. Lauren was just like her." Everett made a face. "She is a lawyer, you know. As for Diane," he waved his hand in dismissal, "she's just a follower. Point is they love messing with peoples' heads. So imagine what they must've been doing to Jenna?"

Chang stared into space. So far, Bella, Lauren and Diane managed to traumatize three men. "I've heard only wonderful things about Bella. She and her elder daughters are so generous."

Everett snorted. "The public doesn't know them."

But someone out there does. Detective Chang closed his notepad. Placing it in the inside pocket of his suit jacket, he said, "Thank you for your time."

All three shook hands.

"By the way," Detective Chang began, "did Jenna ever mention a friend named Rosa Garrison?"

"No."

"Jenna's been lying," Detective Chang said as he and Officer Vega drove back to headquarters. "Now there's a surprise." Lying seemed to be inherent with the Crandall's. "And she's not just lying to me but to herself. No one could put up with that nonsense without feeling some anger."

"I agree," Officer Vega said. "That family isn't healthy. I thought my family was bad." They drove in silence. Then she said, "Shutting down is a defense mechanism. Like us cops and our gallows humor. You're feeling powerless or you don't want anyone to know how you really feel. I did that a lot when I was fifteen."

"But Jenna's not fifteen anymore." Chang, who was at the wheel, made a left turn on Main Street. "When she was a kid, she never once told her mother or her sisters how she felt."

"Her family wasn't exactly open to dialogue."

"Maybe so. But now she's an adult who they're continuing to exploit."

"She's allowing it," Officer Vega said.

Chang drove in silence then said, "It's a psychological cage. Why is Alan so afraid of his mother that he's willing to lie to the cops?"

Officer Vega didn't have an answer to that. Instead, she said, "What I don't get is why Bella, Lauren and Diane disliked Everett. They're so status conscious. He's the complete package. He's good-looking. *Ay. El hombre es tan guapo.* And he has lots of money."

"Yeah." He didn't mind her acknowledging his wealth. But he could've done without Nanci saying Everett was handsome. Chang stopped at a red light. He tried to take her compliments about Everett Long at face value. He was sure Nanci was being objective. Still, he was annoyed. "I don't think they were against him personally. I think it was more about sticking it to Jenna."

"But why?" Officer Vega asked. "Suppose she and Everett got serious which my intuition tells me would've happened. That man would've had a ring on Jenna's fingers by the end of the year. She would've been out of her mother's house and out of her hair."

"Ahh. You're assuming Bella wanted her out of the house."

"What're you saying?"

"That Bella wanted Jenna under her control. Everett Long threatened the natural order of things. This leads me to believe that he may not have been the only guy Mrs. Crandall and her elder daughters played head games with."

"There's Malachi."

"No. I mean before Everett and Malachi."

"That house is an asylum," Officer Vega said.

"Jenna's outraged," Detective Chang said. "I just know it. And that fury has to be going somewhere."

Officer Vega loosened her ponytail holder. Detective Chang inhaled sharply as he watched her hair falling down her shoulders, grateful that she didn't loosen it while they were still in traffic. He was wondering what it would feel like to run his fingers through her hair.

"Are you going to question Lauren and Diane further?" Officer Vega asked.

"I should, but I won't." Chang grimaced. Diane was one experience. Lauren was another. He'd have to get loaded before he decided to interrogate them again. Lauren was cunning and knew her way around the law for obvious reasons. "I wouldn't get anywhere with those drama queens. I will get to her though. Somehow, she fits into this picture. No, Alan's the common denominator. He's apprehensive. He's the one to shake." Detective Chang continued gazing at Officer Vega.

She turned toward him and smiled. He smiled back. Suddenly, a car honked. Then several. Chang looked up at the traffic light. It had turned green. Flustered, he put his foot on the gas.

29

Alan sat behind his desk in his office, staring into his coffee mug, which was much better than staring into the angry eyes of Detective Sergeant Richard Chang who was standing before him. It was all he could do to appear calm. Why was he back and angry? Emotionally exhausted and taut as a rope, Alan thought he would find solace at the office.

Earlier Lauren called. After having words with Dad, she talked endlessly making it difficult for Alan to get a word in edgewise as she proclaimed her innocence, denying that she, their mother and Diane did anything to him and Jenna and using very colorful language.

How could she lie to herself? Then again, what else does this family do?

Then, Diane phoned. Alan rolled his eyes and let the machine take it. He couldn't deal with his twin right now, not after Lauren's diatribe. He could only pray that she didn't blow out his voicemail with one of her tirades.

To his surprise, his father called. That was one call Alan had to take.

Had Mom taken a turn for the worst?

He didn't want their relationship to end this way. In spite of their past, if there was any room for reconciliation before she passed away, he was all for it. The call from his father wasn't what he thought it was, however.

"Detective Chang stopped by the shop today. Why didn't you tell me? Why did I have to find out about this from a cop?"

His father started ranting about what the detective told him. The angry words didn't affect him. The pain in his father's voice did.

"Dad, did you mentioning anything to Elise?"

"No, son, I didn't." Julian paused. *"She doesn't know about this does she?"*

"Not yet."

"Well, at least I'm not the only one who's been in the dark. We're gonna talk about this later."

Alan sighed. He should've known that Chang would tell their father about the abuse. Growing up, he used to imagine telling his father about everything. Afterward he would take him and Jenna away to live with him in his bungalow on Harbor Street, where there was love and safety. Just thinking about his father's house made him feel secure even now during this nerve-racking moment. He wondered how Jenna would feel if she knew that the secret was out. Would she tell Rosa? Naturally. Jenna told her everything.

"Care to tell me about Rosa?" Chang asked, bringing Alan out of his reverie and back to the present.

Alan reached for his coffee mug then took a few sips. His hands were shaking. Droplets of coffee landed on the desk, staining the plans for the library. He put the mug back down, picked up a napkin and gently dry patted the blueprints.

"And," Detective Chang continued as he plunked down into a chair, "if you can give me a good reason why you withheld that piece of information, I *may* not drag you out of here in handcuffs."

Now the genie was out of the bottle. Dad neglected to mention that he told the detective about Rosa. Alan cleared his throat. "I didn't think it was important."

Chang pinned Alan to the chair with a furious gaze. "Did I or did I not ask you if Jenna had any friends?"

Alan took another sip of coffee. He could use the standard story. She was just an old friend that Jenna used to have which was true. But Chang probably knew that already since he had spoken *to Dad*. He twitched his foot, considering whether or not to lawyer up, but that would only make Chang suspicious, angrier.

And make me a person of interest.

Chang whipped out his notepad. "Now where can I find this Rosa?"

Alan stared into his coffee mug. "She's gone. Jenna and Rosa stopped talking around the end of their junior year of high school."

After taking down some notes Chang asked, "How did they meet?"

"Grade school."

The detective lowered his pen and notepad. "What made them suddenly stop speaking?"

Alan began fiddling with his paisley tie.

"I don't have all day, Crandall. What's the story besides them being old friends?"

Alan tapped his foot. *So much for using that theory.* "I guess Jenna decided it was best to part company."

"What do you take me for an idiot? Girls who've been buddies since grade school don't suddenly stop speaking in the latter part of high school without a reason. So, what's going on, Crandall? What's your family hiding?"

Alarmed Alan looked towards his office door which although closed wasn't soundproof. It was embarrassing enough that he returned to his place of work.

Alan looked back at Detective Chang. "What makes you think we're hiding something?"

Chang gave Alan the you-gotta-be-kidding-look.

Alan sighed. "Rosa used to get my sister into all kinds of trouble.

"Like getting plastered?"

Alan shifted in his swivel chair. "Oh. You heard about that. Jenna was having trouble dealing with Mom's condition that's all."

"You know what I think, Crandall? I think that Rosa's still in your sister's life. He didn't know that for sure. It was all instinct. He just wanted to get Alan's reaction by springing on this theory.

"I wouldn't know." Alan didn't blink. Deep down, he was anxious. He couldn't admit to anything without talking to Lauren and Diane first. Once they knew that the authorities suspected that Rosa was around, they'd have to listen to him. "She was Jenna's friend. I didn't hang out with her."

"She makes you nervous."

"Who?"

"Don't play with me, Crandall. I know that this Rosa Garrison makes you, Bella, Lauren and Diane extremely nervous. Now why is that?"

"What does she have to do with anything?" Alan asked testily.

"You tell me. I think you know more than you're saying."

"What do you want from me?"

"The truth."

Alan chuckled dryly. "I was living my life. Minding my own business. Suddenly I'm the whipping boy."

"No pun intended?"

"Don't even joke about that."

"I'm glad to see you man up." Chang looked quizzically at Alan. "Okay. Let's put Rosa out of the picture. You stopped by your mother's, things got out of hand and you lost control."

Alan stood up. "You know I wasn't there. And I wouldn't do such a thing."

"Then you sent someone else to do it." *Did he just blink?*

"Don't be ridiculous."

"Well someone out there is *very* unhappy with your mommy."

Alan picked up a memo pad and pencil then started to draw.

Chang watched Alan work, aware of the irony that both he and Jenna had taken up drawing. The sketch turned out to be a belt. Considering he and Jenna's past, it made sense.

Is Alan Crandall carrying some residual resentment? Is he responsible for what happened?

"I'm waiting," Detective Chang said.

Flustered, Alan blurted, "I don't know. She's never been this violent."

Alan could barely look into the angry sergeant detective's eyes. He wanted to kick himself. Hard. He let his emotions take over. Now his tongue slipped.

"What do you mean, 'She's never been this violent?'"

Alan needed some antacid and fast.

Jenna wiggled her toes in her red ankle socks. She sat the computer in the family room surfing the internet for art schools in New York City. She finally had the place to herself. Alan was at the office and Elise went grocery shopping. She could've gone with her. Elise invited her. Accompanying her would've been the polite thing to do. Elise might've needed help with making purchases, but a part of her kept insisting, *'You're free. Do what you want.'* Besides, she wanted the afternoon to be with her thoughts and to do some research. Fortunately, her sister-in-law presumed that she still needed time to grieve.

Taking a sip of raspberry iced tea, she imagined herself sitting in a classroom in rapt attention while a professor lectured on medieval art. Then, she was picturing herself visiting one of several New York City museums then having lunch at a sidewalk café.

In the middle of her daydream, Rosa called. "I'm at work so I gotta make this quick. We need to discuss Plan B. Or should I call it Plan L—for Lauren." Rosa laughed at her own corny joke.

Jenna winced. "How about this evening?"

"That's what I had in mind," Rosa said.

When they finished arranging a time, Jenna hung up. She got up off the couch, took a sheet of paper from the printer and sat back down again. She began to draw a picture of Malachi.

Elise was in the kitchen unloading groceries when Alan returned home. He gave her a kiss then began helping her. He didn't dare mention Detective Chang's return visit to the office. That would've invited all sorts of questions. It was enough that he had to come up with excuses for why the detective was there in the first place. Alan put away jars of mayonnaise, pickles and balsamic vinegar while playing over the interrogation in his mind. He decided to stick to the old standby: Rosa Garrison was Jenna's childhood friend and a hell-raiser but she was never violent. He played down the fact that she was a potential killer by neglecting to mention the food poisoning and arson incidents. He stuck to the story with such conviction until Chang finally backed off.

He knew he was adding fuel to the fire with more lying. It was only a matter of time before Chang found out, but he needed to buy himself some time. Their fabricated life was starting to unravel like a piece of moth-eaten cloth. When questioned, Alan played down the part about Jenna exploding in the living room.

Did Dad have to mention that?

Alan sighed as he picked up a bottle of barbecue sauce and began wiping it off with a dishcloth. His father had no idea the trouble he had created.

Elise glanced at Alan from time to time. "Are you okay?"

"Besides someone wanting to kill my mother, just dandy."

"You know what I mean." Elise started sulking.

Slowly, Alan began to put away the eggs, once again glad to have something to do. He chastised himself for snapping at her. He had to control his emotions better. He was still feeling rattled over Detective Chang's visit. "I'm sorry. I'm just jumpy."

"You know you can always talk to me. We always talk remember?"

"I know."

"Something we used to do," Elise said.

Guilt blasted through him, making him feel worse than he already did. She was right. They always talked. Spending moments in the university cafeteria or somewhere outside on campus just talking is what drew them together as a friends before becoming a couple. He should've told her about Rosa ages ago, but he couldn't. It was his default mechanism. Mom trained them never to discuss her, and Mom's threats, regardless of the passage of time or her distance, didn't make her any less threatening. "How's Jenna?"

"She's fine." Elise's tone was dry. Alan's sudden change in topic was so obvious. Evidently, he didn't want to confide in her. What else was new? "We watched some TV, talked about her going back to art school. She's adjusting. In fact, she seems happier."

Alan tried not to squeeze the loaf of rye bread he had just taken up. "Where is she now?"

"Right here."

Alan nearly dropped the bread as he and Elise turned around to see Jenna standing at the threshold.

"Am I interrupting something?" Jenna asked.

"No," Elise replied. "You can help us unload."

As Jenna entered the kitchen, Alan looked down at her stocking feet.

Jenna noticed. "Does it bother you that I'm not wearing slippers?"

Alan stared at her with a blank look on his face. He didn't even hear Jenna approach. *Was that how Rosa did it?* That's probably how she was able to overpower Mom. Sneak attack.

"Don't you remember how Mom hated it when we walked around in our socks?" Jenna turned to Elise. "She hated dirty socks so we always had to wear our slippers in the house."

"Oh yeah." Alan smiled nervously. "How could I forget?"

That evening in the kitchen, Alan leaned back in the chair. "Elise, dinner was great."

"Glad you enjoyed it."

"It was delicious," Jenna said. "The tenderloin was a work of art. That is, until Alan carved it."

Her brother made a face.

Elise laughed. It was nice to see them getting along and to feel some joviality in the atmosphere for a change. Despite feeling anger and confusion toward Alan, it was nice to see him looking relaxed for a change. For a moment, she watched Jenna and Alan teasing each other. It was curious how he bonded with Jenna instead of with his twin sister. Diane bonded with Lauren. *Was it because Lauren was female?*

Elise picked up her napkin and covered her mouth to hide an impish grin. The evil twin theory crossed her mind. She soon sobered. Jenna was female. Why didn't she form an attachment with her sisters? Sure, Lauren and Diane may be older and there may have been some long-standing grudges, but they were all adults now. Shouldn't the three of them have outgrown their childhood differences?

Elise remembered what Alan had asked her on the night of the attack. *"What if a person got so fed up that he just snapped?"* An eerie feeling came over her. No. Alan couldn't have done it. He did have a strained relationship with Bella, but he never showed any violence towards her. Were the signs there all along and she just hadn't noticed? But Alan has been testy and nervous lately. Was that because of guilt?

It couldn't be. It just couldn't be. Elise listened to Alan and Jenna's happy chatter, refusing to give in to this dark line of thinking.

Alan cut another slice of tenderloin then dipped it into some mustard sauce. He felt as if he were living out one of his fantasies. Besides daydreaming about their father rescuing him and Jenna, he rewrote the family history. Their parents were a loving couple who doted on their children and he, Lauren, Diane and Jenna got along like normal human beings. Alan played with his fork. If his parents had gotten along, Rosa would never have been born.

"I bought sugar cookies from Delsey's today," Elise said cutting into his thoughts. Alan was fond of them.

"I'm going to pass," Jenna said. "I want to go for a drive."

"Where?" Alan asked.

Jenna's smile was critical. "Nowhere special." In truth, she and Rosa had planned to meet at the farmhouse not that it was any of his business.

Alan heard the screeching sound as the serene background music of his fantasy world came to a halt. Jenna was going to meet with Rosa. He just knew it.

Elise looked at the guarded expression on Alan's face and at the annoyance on Jenna's. She crumpled her napkin. The period of peace was over. "Just be careful, Jen."

"I will."

From the kitchen window, Alan watched Jenna get into her Honda and drive away.

"She's a grown woman," Elise said. "You're her big brother. She doesn't need you picking up where her mother left off."

Alan spun around, a furious expression on his face. "I am nothing like that woman."

Elise stared, dumbfounded. She didn't know her husband anymore. The smart, shy easy-going man had turned into an edgy, irritable individual practically overnight. "I never said you were like Bella," Elise said when she found her voice again. "What is your problem, Alan?"

"I've been interrogated enough for one day, Elise."

"Is this about Detective Chang?"

Alan continued putting away the groceries.

"What happened?" Elise asked.

To himself, Alan counted to ten then said, "I just didn't like his coming to the office that's all."

"He's just doing his job," Elise said fighting back the suspicion that she fought hard not to give into a while ago. "What did he want?"

You finally got around to asking. Alan turned back to the window and stared out at the front lawn. "He had questions about my past I didn't care to go into." He hoped that that would satisfy her. "How about some coffee to go with those cookies?"

His sudden shift in topics didn't surprise Elise. Alan could change subjects at the drop of a hat. He turned around as Elise opened the kitchen cupboard and began taking out a bag of hazelnut coffee. Soon she was pouring the beans into the coffee maker. The aroma of hazelnut coffee filled the kitchen.

"I'm sorry I snapped at you," Alan said. He always seemed to be sorry lately.

"How have things been between you and your mother?"

Alan moistened his lips. Elise didn't say *That's okay* or *Apology accepted.* Instead, she asked an odd question. "Everything's the same as usual. Prickly. Why?"

Frowning, he walked over to Elise. For a moment, husband and wife stared at each other. The anxiety in her eyes was devastating. And that's when it dawned on him.

She thinks I did it.

"Oh, sweetie, no." Alan took Elise into his arms and held her. "I didn't do it. You've got to believe me."

Elise choked back tears. "I want to believe you. Yes. I believe you. I do."

Alan smiled tenderly. "Sounds like our wedding day."

Elise giggled through her tears.

Alan kissed the top of her head. "I'm so sorry." His wife thought he attacked his mother.

What a mess.

"It's perfect," Jenna said after Rosa told her the details of Plan B. "I love it."

"I knew you would," Rosa said.

They were sitting down in the parlor room of the farmhouse where Jenna kept her art supplies, paintings, sketches and works in progress. Jenna smiled as if she were attending a banquet and all her favorite foods were on the table before her. How good it felt to be part of the plan, to know what was going on for a change.

"Too bad I won't be able to see Lauren's face," Jenna said.

"You'll see the footage on the news," Rosa said. "She'll be all drama for the cameras. Next case. You gotta go back to work."

Jenna stopped smiling. "FYI, I plan to look for a job in an art gallery or a museum. I'm also putting together a new portfolio and checking out art programs in Manhattan."

"That's wonderful," Rosa said. "You have to go back to work."

"If I go back to Wheat Prentiss & Associates, how am I supposed to look for a job?"

"You need an alibi, girlfriend. So tomorrow morning, you're gonna call the office and tell them that you need to get your mind off things. Like Alan's been doing."

Elise told Jenna about Alan's reason for returning to work while she and Jenna were alone. She told Rosa about it.

Jenna stood up and kicked an old paint tube across the floor. She loved getting up in the morning knowing that she didn't have to go to the office, to a job decided for her by her mother, a job that she absolutely despised.

"It's only for one day," Rosa said.

Jenna was aware of Rosa staring at her, waiting for her to calm down. Returning to work was just a means of establishing an alibi. And it was just for one day. Afterward, she could return home, play the shocked and devastated sister, then get on with her life.

Finally, Jenna relaxed.

"Get it out of your system yet?" Rosa asked, undisturbed by her friend's hissy fit.

"Yeah."

"Good. Now, all we need is a room. Here's how you're gonna do it."

Elise was pouring another cup of coffee for Alan and herself when the doorbell rang.

"I'll get it," Alan said. He grabbed a sugar cookie on his way out the kitchen.

Walking down the hall, he couldn't help wondering about Jenna's whereabouts. What was she getting herself into now?

The doorbell rang again.

When Alan opened the door and saw his father standing there, he almost wished that it were Detective Chang with more questions. Julian looked as if he could've taken the house apart brick by brick. Elise came up behind him. She took one look at her father-in-law and grabbed hold of Alan's arm.

"Good evening, Elise," Julian greeted her, aware of his daughter-in-law standing there, although his infuriated gaze never left his son. "We need to talk. Now."

Alan sat at the table looking as badly as he felt. Thanks to an irate Julian, Elise now knew about the abuse he and Jenna suffered. Elise knew that he, his mother and sisters had a turbulent past, but she didn't know just how tumultuous it was. He deliberately didn't tell her about how vicious his mother really was or about how mean Lauren and Diane were. Instead, he skirted the truth. He told her enough to understand how he related to his mother and sisters. Wherever possible he whitewashed. He knew why he didn't tell her about Rosa. It was complicated, but he wasn't sure why he didn't tell Elise about the abuse. He just knew he didn't like to talk about it.

Alan held his breath, hoping against hope that his father would not mention Rosa's name. No doubt, it came up during Detective Chang's visit to his father's shop. If Dad mentioned Rosa in front of Elise, he'd have even more problems. Neither the physical abuse nor Rosa's vengeful spirit was not how he wanted Dad to find out about that part of his and Jenna's childhood. He didn't want Elise to find out this way either.

Alan summoned the courage to look over at Elise. She was looking right at him, her expression livid. He blew out an anxious breath.

When Jenna returned home and heard her father's voice, her face brightened. She entered the kitchen and ran into her father's outstretched arms. After what Detective Chang told him, Julian held her as if she were a lost treasure.

Afterward, Jenna stood back. She searched her father's face. She saw the love in his eyes and something else. Jenna turned toward her brother and sister-in-law. Their features showed distress and shock mixed with anger, respectively. Only then was Jenna aware of the tension in the kitchen. Her heart skipped a beat. *Did Mom pass away?* She was the one loose thread. Just thinking about her waking up from her coma and telling everyone about who attacked her made her jittery, but if she were dead, there'd be no need to worry . . .

"What's going on?" Jenna asked finally. As much as she wanted it to happen, she couldn't bring herself to ask the real question aloud.

"Julian, why don't you and Jenna go out in the yard and talk?" Elise suggested.

Father and daughter sat beside each other in the gazebo. Jenna looked out toward the horizon. It was sundown. The sky reminded her of a giant canvas covered in azure, peach, pink and lavender oil paints.

It's like God's here with me.

Jenna frowned. *Where did that come from?*

She never felt His presence before; at least she didn't remember feeling it. She was almost tempted to ask God how to handle this latest event. Daddy finally found out what Mom had been doing to her and Alan. He even knew about Lauren and Diane's part in it. He also wants to know why neither of them told him about it. No doubt, Elise was inside grilling Alan for answers. Jenna smothered a grin. It was going to be a long, cold night for Alan, but for now, this was her moment to tell her side, to tell him all about those years with Mom, Lauren and Diane. The funny thing was that she didn't want to talk about it.

Maybe now that Rosa was handling things it didn't matter anymore.

Not having a deep, philosophical answer ready Jenna said, "I was little. And I was scared."

Julian twisted his cap. "Your brother said the same thing."

"Mom threatened us." Jenna explained the rules about not telling anyone about what she said or did.

Julian could just imagine the horror that his children went through all those years. He couldn't find fault with them for keeping silent. If Bella could drive him, a grownup, out of his own home, what would she have done to two vulnerable children?

He thought about that sweet, tiny bundle he held in his arms thirty-two years ago. *Could that innocent child have been the reason that drove Bella to such rage?*

It would make sense.

But we reconciled. We were gonna make a fresh start. And why would she attack Alan?

If she awakened from her coma, he had questions. Julian sighed. He and Bella had also been carrying a secret. After he got his answers, *if* she gave him his answers, he would make a full confession to his children. No. Maybe he should confess to his children whether he got answers from Bella or not. Perhaps silence did more harm than good . . .

"Daddy?" Jenna was staring at her father who seemed to have zoned out. "Are you okay?"

Julian hugged his youngest child before the setting sun. "Yes, Jenna. I am."

30

"I have a bone to pick with you, Professor," Chang said as soon as he entered the lecture hall on the following day and took a front row seat. Detective Chang wore an icy expression as he watched who was at the blackboard copying down phraseologies from the notes he held in his hand. He should've summoned the professor down to the station, but he decided to accommodate him and come to the university instead. For some unknown reason he liked the guy. He wasn't sure why, considering the professor lied to him.

Chang was in a foul mood. Breakfast was a cup of coffee and half a blueberry muffin that he purchased at a gas station on the way to another press conference. To add insult to injury, it was a lousy cup of coffee. The aroma of hamburgers, French fries, hot dogs and other foods coming from the cafeteria was maddening and tempting.

Bella was in a coma for four days now. Lauren was claiming that the Gordonville Police Department was mishandling the job, giving Mayor Urbanowski that much more power to use against him. Chang loosened his collar. What if public opinion turned against him? He was not in a good place right now. Plus, he was hungry. "You left out the part about Bella having a beef with you."

I am in big trouble. The slightest sign of apprehension was risky. He didn't want Detective Chang leading him out of the university in handcuffs. *Talk about sinking your career.* He had to play it cool. "Good Morning, Detective," Malachi greeted in a voice that defied his nervousness. He turned back to the blackboard and continued to write down the points he was going to cover in his lecture in less than an hour.

Malachi could feel the detective's eyes boring into the back of his skull, but he wasn't going to look in Chang's before he collected his bearings. His old nature was just below the surface, tempting him to say, *"You didn't ask me."* That wouldn't be wise. He was already in trouble for omitting information.

Just a few more seconds. Finally, Malachi put down the chalk. He stepped away from the blackboard, pulled up a chair and sat down by Detective Chang. He sighed, then began telling him about everything that took place between him and Bella, including Lauren and Diane's antics.

Chang grunted. So far the information Malachi was giving him meshed with what Everett told him and Officer Vega. Bella, Lauren and Diane exhibited a pattern of behavior to isolate Jenna. The question was, why. Malachi's explanation for keeping his chilly relationship with Bella hidden from him was as he expected. The professor was afraid of becoming a suspect.

"As nasty as she was to me," Malachi continued, "I didn't try to get rid of her."

"You could've hired someone."

"How much does a hit man go for these days?"

Chang frowned, not in the mood for jokes.

"Sorry," Malachi said. He stood up, picked up his notes and returned to the blackboard.

"Did Jenna ever talk about her childhood?"

Malachi had resumed writing down sociological phraseologies. He wondered what he should say without actually lying.

Chang could tell that Malachi was stalling. "I was starting to forgive you, Professor. You don't want to slip out of my good graces."

Malachi paused then sighed. *Forgive me, Jenna.*

He began telling the detective what he knew about the abuse. He also talked about Jenna's love of art and Bella's discouraging her from pursuing it. Of course, he left out the part about the Enchanted Forest. He had to. He made a promise to Jenna that he wouldn't tell anyone about it. Besides, her childhood fantasies had nothing to do with this.

Regret flowed through his body like a rivulet. It didn't matter that he didn't have a choice. Discussing Jenna's past made him feel as if he were betraying her. Malachi paused. He didn't mention Rosa. She was part of Jenna's childhood. A big part.

Okay, God, You gave me a chance to avoid getting into deep you-know-what after lying to a cop. I think I did it again. But I just don't see the point in mentioning Rosa.

"Jenna never told anyone about her past," Chang said cutting into his prayer. Not even her previous boyfriend. "She must really trust you."

"Really?" Malachi grinned with pride temporarily forgetting his anxiety.

"Still, you had the chance to expose Bella, Lauren and Diane the other night."

Malachi put down the chalk. He wiped his hands together. "Not without consulting Jenna first. She spoke to me in confidence. That's what makes this conversation so hard. Funny, I think on some level she loves her mother and sisters in spite of what they did. And still does. I think she's more hurt that she never earned their respect."

Detective Chang nodded. He could see that. Still . . . "What're you not telling me?"

"Excuse me?"

"Cops instinct, Prof. As a teacher, you know when a student's trying to pull a fast one. Now I'm asking. What're you hiding from me . . . again?"

Malachi paused then said, "It's nothing important."

"I'll decide what's—" Was *it possible?* "Did Jenna mention a Rosa Garrison to you?"

Malachi looked as if he'd seen a ghost.

Chang flipped a page over in his notepad. "All right, Professor, start lecturing."

Malachi couldn't feel his legs as he walked over to the nearest chair then sat down. *How did Chang find out about her?* He took a deep breath then started talking.

Chang had that maniacal angry look on his face as Malachi told him what he knew about Rosa. So far, it wasn't anything that he hadn't already heard: former friend, bad influence. He was practically tuning out the professor until he began hearing tales of food tampering . . . and *arson? Rosa Garrison was psychotic.*

Detective Chang's face began contorting. "Why didn't Bella lodge a complaint against this girl? And how come her name never came up during the initial interrogation? It's obvious Rosa's hatred was directed at Bella, Lauren and Diane."

"Since Bella was abusing Alan and Jenna, going after Rosa would mean calling attention to herself," Malachi said. "There was no way Rosa was going down without taking Bella down."

Chang regarded Malachi with renewed respect. "I like your thinking, Prof."

"Anyway, Rosa's out of Jenna's life," Malachi said.

Chang stood up and walked about the room. "Is she?"

"Yes. Jenna told me."

"If you really believed that, you wouldn't have gone to such lengths to keep it from me."

"They haven't been friends since childhood."

"Oh yeah? What if I told you that her brother said that their friendship ended by the eleventh grade?"

Malachi frowned. The late teens wasn't exactly childhood. She lied again. *Like not telling me about the four o'clock tea.*

Chang grew deep in thought. Then he said, "You know, Rosa's beginning to sound to me like an angry relative. Like a cousin or a sister."

Malachi laughed nervously. "Jenna would've told me. Especially about another sister."

Chang grunted. "Because she and her family have been so forthcoming."

Malachi smiled ruefully. The Crandall's had been leaving out key information left and right. Like Rosa. Did she matter?

"Something more you want to tell me?" Detective Chang asked.

"Not really." Malachi hesitated. "You're gonna think I'm off my gourd."

"I'll keep an open mind."

He had nothing to lose anyway. Malachi stood up and stretched. Then, he told Detective Chang about the nightmare. The investigator listened patiently and without judgment.

When Malachi finished telling his story, Detective Chang said, "Then, a few days later, Bella Crandall's attacked."

Malachi nodded. "I've been weirded out ever since."

"Three skeletons? Obviously, Bella was the first. Evidently, two more attacks are to follow."

The men looked at each other knowingly. *Lauren and Diane.*

"But it was just a dream," Malachi said.

"So, what're you trying to say?" Detective Chang asked. "You're psychic?"

Malachi laughed. "Hardly. But I think God was trying to tell me something."

"Ah the dream technique," Detective Chang said. "Like with Jacob and Joseph."

It was Malachi's turn to look at him with respect. "What? I remember a thing or two from Catholic school. "So, what do you think God was trying to tell you?"

"I haven't the foggiest."

"Maybe you do and you don't want to face it."

"Come again?"

"In your nightmare, the woman in the Loki mask is Rosa. You suspect her."

Malachi did not like where this conversation was going. He checked his watch. Twenty-minutes to class. Enough time for questioning. Malachi swore. Why couldn't a student walk in with a profound question?

Like that would ever happen.

None of his students ever came early to Sociology 101. The dean probably warned them not to come into the lecture hall. By now, everyone knew Detective Sergeant Chang was questioning him. Jenna and her family's pictures have been in the paper. They've already seen him with her and must've connected him to Gordonville's most celebrated family and the crime of the decade.

I wonder if my students are gonna want my autograph? What's the matter with me? Is this gonna effect my job?

Not that it mattered. He was going to stick by Jenna no matter what.

Malachi looked down and noticed that one of his shoelaces was untied. He bent down to tie it.

"Professor . . . "

"I'm tying my shoe." *And stalling for something to say.*

"Rosa is a person of interest," Detective Chang said. "Possibly a relative. And I don't think your Jenna's all that innocent. And neither do you."

Malachi straightened. He couldn't hide his indignation. "Maybe I'm a little suspicious. Of Rosa. And she's no longer around."

"So you said."

"Jenna came running to me the day her mother was attacked remember?" Malachi said, defensiveness in his voice.

"So far, your girlfriend and her brother were abused by their mother, their relationship with their siblings is anything but healthy, Jenna had an amoral friend and Bella doesn't like you."

"That's pretty much it. But I think Bella's dislike of me has more to do with control over Jenna than anything personal."

Chang nodded. "Perceptive, Professor."

"Thank you."

"You're sharp."

Embarrassed, Malachi looked at the floor then smiled.

"And you know something's off," Detective Chang said. Malachi's smile faltered. "Jenna. Didn't. Do it. And neither did Alan."

"No. He doesn't have the stomach for it."

"Then why are you—?"

"Because something stinks," Detective Chang replied. "People are feeding me half-truths or bits and pieces of information and I don't. like. it." He paused then said, "There might be something to this Garrison angle. A strange woman in a Loki mask. The Norse god of tricks." Chang harrumphed. "There's certainly been a lot of that goin' around."

Malachi looked away.

Detective Chang examined the phraseologies that Malachi wrote on the blackboard. *Loose or rigid boundaries. Difficulty forming intimate relationships. Extreme loyalty even when undeserved.* Jenna certainly was loyal. She tended to her mother's needs and her sisters even at the expense of her personal relationships.

"Did you ever tell Jenna about your dream?" Detective Chang asked.

"I couldn't tell her I dreamed about her best friend killing off half her family. I don't even like thinking about it much less talking about it."

Chang walked over to the window and stared out the window at the nineteenth century edifices dotting the campus. *I think it's time I had a talk with Jenna.*

31

Jenna took a down message for a senior account executive then put it inside his message box. Yesterday she did what Rosa instructed and phoned the office. She smiled to herself. When she came in that morning, everybody greeted her warmly, even the major players of the firm, most of whom were borderline obnoxious. It was almost worth being back there.

Jenna checked the clock on her computer. 12:55 P.M. She was going to need a five-minute head start. She picked up her travel bag then signaled to an attractive, chubby brunette. Bree, the college intern, came over.

"Would you mind taking over the phones now?" Jenna asked.

"Sure," Bree said.

*

First stop, the Olympia Mall. Jenna always felt pride every time she stepped through its doors. Unlike the other patrons, she could say, *my big brother designed this.* She tried not to think about how disappointed and revolted Alan would feel if he knew that she was using his creation to exact revenge.

She rode the escalator down to the lower level where a ladies room was located. That one was cleaner and had less traffic.

As soon as she entered it, she grinned. Empty. Still, she entered a stall. Like Rosa always said take precaution. Jenna hung the travel bag on the hook behind the stall door then quickly changed into a pair of skinny jeans, scoop neck tank top, flip-styled wig, a black and gold head scarf, cotton gloves and a pair of butterfly sunglasses.

Jenna stepped out of the stall then checked herself in the mirror. Wig and scarf was straight. Sunglasses sat properly.

She smiled at herself with approval.

Ten minutes later, Jenna walked into The Lorelei House. Cream and lavender colored wallpaper covered the walls of its massive entryway. A wide sweeping staircase led to the upper floors. The aroma of fresh-baked cinnamon rolls from the inn's dining room filled the air. Her stomach started to growl. She couldn't have lunch until after she secured a room. She had to focus.

Jenna rubbed her temple. Hunger and nervousness was stressing her out. *I have to do this job right.* Trying not to think about her empty stomach, Jenna walked over to the front parlor where the registration desk was located.

An auburn haired girl in her late teens stood behind it. She greeted Jenna with a warm smile. "Welcome to The Lorelei House. My name's Moira. How can I help you?"

"Good Afternoon!" Jenna greeted with a southern accent. "Y'all have any rooms available?"

"I believe we do." Moira began to type on the computer.

Jenna tried to keep a straight face. They had vacancies. Rosa Googled it.

"Is it for you?" Moira asked.

"Yes, it is." Jenna was about to tell a story about traveling across the country, but since Moira didn't ask why bother wasting a good lie.

"Here we are," Moira said. "The Poppy Room. It's perfect. It's gotta queen-sized bed, TV, sitting area, private bath and a beautiful view of the garden."

"That sounds nice," Jenna said.

"There's a minimum two night stay and our rooms come with a full breakfast and check-in is from 3:00 P.M. to 7:00 P.M."

"Okay." Moira handed Jenna the registration form.

Jenna smiled graciously. *You owe me money, Rosa.* She filled out the information using the name Doreen Bennett, as Rosa had planned. Jenna wanted a different first name like, Cassidy Rae or Jo Lynn, but Rosa shot it down. She said it was overkill.

"We accept all major credit cards," Moira said after *Doreen* handed the form.

"How's cash?" Yesterday, she went to the bank and made a withdrawal to cover expenses for the plan.

"We take that too."

While Moira was assembling the paperwork, Jenna looked around the parlor room with admiration. "This place is so charming. Is the Poppy Room on this floor?"

"It's on the second floor."

"I was wondering," Jenna began. "I've heard so much about the Lilac Room and . . . "

Moira shook her head and smiled. "Sorry. It's not available. But if it's any consolation, you're on the floor below it."

Jenna's lips twitched. Thanks to the perky teen's naiveté, she now knew the location of Lauren's room. It was the one problem they had in implementing Plan B; hence the ruse to get into the Lilac Room. Plan B was going to be that much easier.

"Oh." Moira hesitated. "We're obligated to tell our guests we don't leave the front door open after nine o'clock."

"You lock your doors at night?" Jenna put her hand over her heart. "Isn't Gordonville a safe community?"

"You didn't hear about the attack on Bella Crandall?" Jenna pretended to look puzzled.

"She's the mother of Lauren, Alan and Diane Crandall." Moira went on to tell 'Ms. Bennett' all about the assault and about the renowned family of whom Gordonville was so proud.

Jenna slapped her forehead. "Oh right. I remember reading about that. What a shame."

"Yeah. Everybody's a little jumpy. Otherwise, Gordonville's safe. You should stop by the Olympia Mall during your stay. Alan Crandall built it."

Jenna grinned. "I'll do that." She grew serious. "Come to think of it, didn't the Crandall's have another child? I think a daughter." She couldn't help noticing that Moira didn't mention *her*. It was all she could do to remain unruffled while Moira kept going on and on about her mother, Lauren and Diane.

Moira shrugged. "Maybe. I guess. I don't know."

Jenna kept smiling even pain and fury was rising with her. *Breathe.*

"Anyway," Moira continued, "ever since the attack, "Lorelei, she's the owner, wanted to take precautions even though it happened in broad daylight." Moira glanced around then lowered her voice. "You're not supposed to know this, but Lauren Crandall-Door, her husband and her sister is staying here."

Jenna gasped. "Nelson Door the producer and Diane Crandall the supermodel?"

"Uh huh. Lawrence Belmar is here too. Lauren and Nelson rented the Lilac Room.

Jenna pretended to look starry-eyed. She knew Larry had booked the Tulip Room. He was still lamenting about the name's non-masculinity. Her future brother-in-law's only consolation was that the room had a connecting door to Diane's suite.

"If you happen to run into any of them," Moira continued, "don't ask them for their autographs."

"Aww!" Jenna feigned disappointment.

"Yeah," Moira said. "They're really uptight." Jenna adjusted her butterfly sunglasses. *You don't know the half of it.*

"They've been under so much stress," Moira said. "Reporters have been camped out here for days. We even had to take the phone out of Ms. Crandall-Door's room. A reporter got a hold of her number."

"It's a shame how people try to take advantage of others," Jenna said. *Wish I could take credit for that.*

"It's funny," Moira began. "Before the attack, nothing ever happened in this town."

"Is that right?"

In the Lorelei House's sunflower garden, Jenna phoned Rosa. Still disguised as Doreen, she told her that Phase 1 of Plan B was complete. "And guess what? I found out where Lauren and Nelson's room is."

Rosa gasped.

Jenna smiled proudly. Quickly, she told her about the location of the Lilac Room.

"This is great."

Jenna expressed her concern about the inn's closed-door policy. She expected them to be able to sneak in together after hours. "How are we supposed to get inside with the stuff without anyone seeing?"

"Leave that to me," Rosa said. "Just find out when Lauren and her posse will be away from their rooms."

"All right."

After Jenna hung up, she checked her watch. Twenty-two minutes left of her lunch break. There was still time for her to change and pick up some lunch.

When Jenna returned to the office, she stopped short. Detective Chang was sitting in the reception area. She hadn't seen or spoken to him since that fateful afternoon. This can't be good.

This wasn't part of the plan. Jenna forced herself to smile. "Good Afternoon, Detective."

"Nice to see you again, Jenna." Chang stood up. He noticed her travel bag as well as the sack from Delsey's. Although it was subtle, he didn't miss her stunned reaction at seeing him. "No brown bagging it today I see."

"I had errands." Jenna looked toward her desk where Bree was still minding the phones. The college intern was also looking dreamily at the detective sergeant. "Is there a break in the case?" Jenna asked trying to not to giggle.

"As a matter of fact, some information came my way that I'd like to discuss."

Jenna tried not to appear reluctant. All she wanted to do was eat for the remaining six minutes she had left of her lunch hour. She didn't want to have to think about what to have to say. Especially since she and Rosa hadn't gone over anything.

"Or we could do this later at the station," Detective Chang said sensing her hesitation.

"No, here's fine." There's no way she was going to the station after work. Phase Two of Plan B was already set for tonight. They couldn't afford any delays. She held up the Delsey's bag. "Mind if I eat while you ask questions?"

"Not at all." He took up some newspapers.

Again, Jenna glanced towards her desk. "Bree, could you man the phones a little longer while I speak with Detective Chang?"

"No, I don't mind." Bree had that high-school-girl-meets-star-quarterback look in her eyes.

"On behalf of the Gordonville Police Department," Detective Chang began, "we appreciate your cooperation,"

Bree giggled.

Jenna and Detective Chang sat in one of the available conference rooms. He set the newspapers down on the table then took out his notepad wondering if he should've brought Nanci along. The line of questioning was going to get rough. There was no telling how Jenna was going to react. She might need placating. He soon dismissed the idea, however. He needed to observe Jenna with little distraction. He was looking for just the slightest sign of uneasiness, which might be a challenge since he had reason to believe that Jenna had long mastered the art of hiding her emotions.

"How's your mother?" Detective Chang asked.

Jenna looked rueful. "No change." She broke off a piece of Kaiser Roll and dipped it into a takeout container filled with thick pea soup.

Detective Chang's mouth watered. Delsey's made yummy soup. "I'll cut to the chase. Tell me about your friend Rosa Garrison."

Jenna smiled enigmatically, then looked down into the Styrofoam container of soup. She stared at the peas, carrots, onions and pieces of ham floating at the top.

"And spare me the old friend spiel," Detective Chang said. "Your father and brother already covered that."

Jenna spooned a mouthful of pea soup. It would've been nice if Alan had informed her of this development. He did seem edgy this morning. She thought it was about him and Elise arguing about him not telling her about how evil Mom was and that their father didn't know.

Don't panic. Think.

That's what Rosa would've advised. Jenna looked up at Detective Chang and smiled. "I'm surprised that Rosa's name came up at all."

He admired her poise. "Where is she now?" Detective Chang asked.

"We haven't spoken since forever."

"Be that as it may I have reason to believe she may be in town."

Jenna raised her eyebrows. "You're serious?"

"I understand you two were best friends since grade," school. "To suddenly end it at what? Seventeen, eighteen years old must've been devastating."

Jenna picked up a salt packet, opened it, then sprinkled a dash of it into her soup.

"Wouldn't you have wanted to spend your senior year of high school with your best friend? That's one of the most important years of your life."

Jenna shrugged.

Chang used his most encouraging tone. "Tell me about Rosa."

"What does she have to do with the attack on my mother?"

Beneath her calm exterior, Chang detected a slight unease in Jenna's eyes. "I have to cover all bases."

"We grew apart," Jenna said. "And anyway, she moved. And we lost touch."

Alan didn't mention that the Garrison's moved. Could it be that he didn't know? Or was this just one more thing he was hiding? "According to your brother, she was a bad influence."

"Rosa was a good friend. She had my back."

Chang picked up a leftover syllabus from a meeting on travel media off the table and began flipping through it. "You needed protection?"

Stay calm. "You remember the schoolyard bully, Jenna said."

"Sure. I think that's why I became a cop." Detective Chang paused. "But Bullies aren't just in the schoolyard."

Jenna shifted.

Chang pushed the syllabus aside. Clearly, Jenna wasn't comfortable about this conversation. And things were about to get worse. "I know what happened to you and Alan."

Jenna stirred her soup. "Yes, he told me."

"I wish I was told about it," Chang continued. "It must've gotten on your nerves watching your mother and sisters put on that goody-goody act all these years." He shook his head for dramatic effect. "Lauren prosecuting criminal after criminal when you knew she was a first-class jerk. And let's not forget Diane. Flying all over the globe, gracing the front cover of fashion magazines, appearing on TV. We both know she's a mean, egotistical ditz."

"Don't talk that way about my sisters."

Chang looked at her quizzically. "You like your sisters?"

"I *love* my sisters." Jenna held the Kaiser roll so hard she squashed it. "I'm happy about their successes. And if you think, I live in the past, I don't. Alan and I don't even talk about it. It's forgotten."

"Is it? One doesn't just forget about abuse. Especially what your mother and sisters put you and your brother through. You know about Alan's nervous stomach?"

"Yes."

"What about you?" Detective Chang asked.

"I don't have a nervous stomach. In fact, I have no allergies."

"Fantastic. But something's gotta be bugging you."

"I'm fine."

Chang spread out the newspapers he had brought with him. One showed a photo of Jenna looking outraged in the lobby of Gordonville General Hospital. Another one showed her wearing a demented grin as she was coming out of a convenience store carrying a six-pack. Jenna looked down at the pictures, shrugged, then calmly picked at the Kaiser roll.

"I think Rosa's responsible for what happened to your mother," Detective Chang said, using the same tactic on Jenna that he used on Alan.

Jenna laughed.

To his trained ear, the sound carried a hint of high anxiety.

"Why would she do that?" Jenna asked.

"To settle a score. Rosa knew the truth about your family. You said yourself, she had your back."

"When we were kids."

Chang wanted to point out to her that Rosa knew about the real, Bella, Lauren and Diane and therefore would've been furious, but he couldn't, not without outing Malachi. He was the only who told him about Rosa's antics.

Jenna took a deep breath. "In order for Rosa to put Mom in a coma, I'd still have to be in touch with her, *which I'm not*. The whole thing would be like . . . hiring a hit man. I'd have to hate my mother to do something like that."

"Do you?"

"Do I what?"

"Hate your mother."

"NO." Jenna placed her hand over her mouth. She didn't mean to raise her voice. She hoped that no one heard.

Chang was calm, not disturbed by her outburst. Jenna was giving him exactly what he hoped for: signs of discomfort. "You don't hate her? Not even a little?"

"Of course not."

"And you don't hate your sisters."

"No."

"When you threw the jar of Vaseline across the room it was because of Diane."

"No. Why are you accusing me?"

Chang turned to a page he folded in the Gordonville Gazette then read, "' . . . Jenna Crandall, while in the arms of an unidentified man, later identified as Dr. Malachi Chase, Professor of Sociology at Gordonville State University, tearfully cried out, "I hate Lauren," after what witnesses say was a spat between her and her sister Assistant D.A., Lauren Crandall-Door.'" He tossed the paper on the table. "Witnesses also said your boyfriend and brother tried to calm you down because Diane and Larry were getting under your skin."

Jenna spooned some more soup. "It was nothing. People love gossip. And I didn't mean what I said about Lauren. Sisters say things all the time they don't mean. And for the record, I love my mother."

"Even though she tortured you and Alan? With Lauren and Diane's help. Lauren who you don't hate."

Jenna clutched her napkin. "I told you I'm not angry."

Chang leaned back in the swivel chair. "Why?"

"Because anger is wrong."

Chang recalled the term *extreme loyalty* that Malachi wrote on the blackboard. Jenna was nauseatingly loyal. Why? What did she owe her sisters? Her mother especially? Yes, she gave birth to her, but isn't more than that? What about love? Nurturing? Compassion. Brothers and sisters have their differences, but where was the so-called togetherness that Lauren and Diane claimed they had for all of their family?

"Jenna," Detective Chang began, "anger is a part of being human. Everyone gets angry at one time or another."

"It's one of the seven deadly sins."

Wow. It hadn't occurred to him that Christian doctrine would still matter to her even after she'd left the church.

This could be significant.

"Mom always said I was bad whenever I got angry." She twirled a finger around a strand of hair. "Just the sight of a teardrop would make her crazy with rage."

Chang could scarcely breathe. Could Jenna, unable to express her anger, use someone else as a conduit to release it, such as, Rosa? "It's a question of not allowing anger to get you into trouble. Psalm 4:4, says 'Be angry, and do not sin . . . '"

Jenna widened her eyes. "You're Christian?"

"Well, you don't have to look so surprised. And the answer is yes. Although I'm not a terrific one."

Jenna's laughter sounded edgy. "I seem to be running into you people lately."

"You people as in . . . "

"Christians."

"Is that a bad thing?"

"No. Malachi's a Christian."

"Something about Christians make you uncomfortable?" "I grew up in the church."

"That you no longer attend," Detective Chang said.

Jenna toyed with her spoon. *You've certainly been digging.*

"Come on. We both know that your mother and sisters were poor representatives of the Gospel. They turned you off from anything to do with Christianity."

"Could we move this along?" Jenna asked. "I have to get back to work."

Detective Chang wore a half-smile. "Were the Garrisons members of your church?"

"They were Roman Catholic."

"Me too. Were they practicing Catholics?" He saw a tiny flicker of annoyance in her eyes.

"No," Jenna said. "And Rosa did not hurt my mother."

Detective Chang held his hand like a steeple as Malachi's dream came to mind. "Suppose your friend hated Bella enough to want to kill her?"

"After sixteen years?"

"Yeah. To vindicate you."

Jenna made a frustrated sound. "The abuse is over, Detective Chang."

"So you all live together in peace and harmony?"

"Rosa's no longer a part of my life."

"You didn't answer my question."

Jenna blew a frustrated sigh.

"You didn't feel like a servant in your own home, Jenna?"

"No, I didn't."

"All right," Detective Chang said. "It's my duty to investigate leads. For some reason your friend's name keeps surfacing."

"Well, somebody's pulling your leg. And anyway, I don't know where she is."

Chang closed his notepad. Jenna was lying. It was just a matter of proving it. "If you remember anything, anything at all let me know."

"I will."

*

Jenna waited for Detective Chang to step into the elevator before rushing into the ladies room. To her dismay, Dina, an account executive was standing in front of the mirror reapplying her makeup.

The dark-haired beauty noted Jenna's unease. "Everything okay? I heard a detective was here to see you." Dina paused. "It, got a little loud in the conference room."

"It was nothing. The situation just has me edgy that's all." Not wanting to answer any more questions, Jenna went over to the sink and splashed some cold water on her face.

Dina looked at her with sympathy. "We're here for you, Jen."

"Thanks." Jenna pulled a paper towel from the dispenser and began drying her face. She watched as Dina reached into her handbag, take out a hairbrush then begin to brush her hair. Jenna tapped her feet on the tile floor. She had to speak to Rosa right away then get back to reception. She'd been away from her desk long enough. She would've enjoyed her lunch in peace had it not been for Detective Chang.

Dina, you're gorgeous. The whole office knows it. Trust me. Now hurry up and go.

Jenna opened her pocketbook, took out a plum-colored lipstick and began applying it. She needed a reason to stay in the lounge without arousing Dina's suspicion.

At last, Dina said, "See you inside."

Jenna smiled and waved, inwardly shrieking for joy. As soon as Diane left, Jenna grabbed her cell phone from her pocketbook. In a moment, she had Rosa on the phone.

Before Jenna could explain why she was calling, Rosa said in a cold voice, "This isn't a good time."

Jenna blinked, completely taken aback by the reception.

"I'm at work," Rosa continued. "My boss doesn't like me taking personal calls right now."

Jenna's face fell. She didn't mean any harm. Didn't Rosa know that what she had to say must be important or she wouldn't have called? She felt a lump in her throat.

"I'm sorry," Jenna said, feeling hurt and embarrassed at the reception she was getting from Rosa. "Something happened." Jenna swallowed. "D-Detective Chang was here."

"Why?" Rosa's tone was intimidating.

Petrified almost to the point of speechlessness, Jenna talked about Chang's visit. "I didn't know he was coming." She began sobbing.

"Relax." Rosa sighed. "I'm not mad at you."

"Did I do all right?" Jenna asked her voice child-like.

"Yeah, you did." Rosa paused. "Doesn't sound like the detective has any real evidence. Chang's just fishing. Find out when the Doors will be out the gate at The Lorelei House and report back to me."

The pun brought a smile to Jenna's face. "When do you want me to call back?" She was still gun-shy even though her mood was lifting.

"Anytime. I'll set my phone on vibrate. Sorry I snapped at you. I'm under pressure at the studio."

Jenna sniffled. "It's okay." She was just glad to get this burden off her shoulders.

32

When Lauren saw Alan's number on her BlackBerry, she went into panic mode. Sitting on the king-size bed in the master suite of the Lilac Room, she pushed aside the legal briefs she was working on then answered the call. "What happened? Is Mom . . . ?"

"Relax. Her condition's the same. But we have another problem. Chang knows about Rosa."

"You had better be joking."

"You hear me laughing?" Alan asked.

"First, you give Dad and Detective Chang that sob story about abuse," Lauren said. "Now this."

"Stop lying. You, Mom and Diane were all in on it. And FYI, Chang found out about the abuse from someone else."

"Who?"

"I don't know. But he was the one who told Dad about Mom's *tender loving care.* Alan told her about the detective's visit to their father at his mechanic shop. "During the conversation Dad told Chang about Rosa."

"Dad?"

"Yeah, he must've remembered Rosa's name coming up last time we were all together. Maybe if you and Diane weren't so busy acting like hyenas that day, Rosa's name wouldn't have come up in the first place."

"Spare me the lecture, okay.

"Dad wanted to know why Jenna and I kept quiet all these years," Alan said.

"What did you tell him?"

"That we were too scared to tell him what Mom and you guys," he added dryly, "were doing." Alan went on to tell her about their father's fury over not knowing about the abuse all these years.

"Did you tell Dad about Rosa?"

Alan let out a frustrated sigh. She cared nothing about the mess that she, Mom and Diane created. It was all about damage control. Classic Lauren. "Don't you think if I did, they would've carried him out on a stretcher? Finding out about the abuse from a third party had him so worked up that Rosa's name never came up; which doesn't mean he won't get around to asking about her. I just thought I'd give you a heads up." Dad's questions brought back painful memories for him and Jenna. They "compared notes" later that evening after talking to their father separately.

For years, he and Jenna stayed silent about it. When the beatings first started, however, they used to talk about it among themselves. They would comfort each other; sometimes tearfully or just sit beside each other in quiet contemplation. Other times, he and Jenna would spend an afternoon of fun to channel their pain. Alan took a breath. "Lauren, I think it's time we did the right thing."

"Meaning?"

"I think you know."

"Forget it."

"You people created this monster," Alan said. "Not me. Chang's been on my case. I've been doing my best to hold him off, but he keeps finding out stuff. And I got an earful from Elise last night because I didn't tell her that my own father didn't know what Mom did. Imagine how she's gonna feel when she finds out we're actually related to Rosa. Don't ask me how I managed to keep that from her so far."

Lauren made a sound of disgust. "My sister-in-law is in La-La Land if she thinks she has to know everything. Even I don't tell Nelson everything."

Alan let the comment about Elise slide. "Rosa's here. She's dangerous and she's got to be stopped."

Lauren stiffened. "Rosa did not attack Mom. She wouldn't do that. Jenna would've stopped her."

"Would you grow up," Alan said. "Jenna's turned against you."

"She'd have to have the strength of Atlas to knock out Mom," Lauren said.

"Rage can give a person amazing strength," Alan said. "Especially when it's been stored up for years."

"You're exaggerating, Alan." She felt her nerves growing tense. She didn't need to hear this right now.

"Who else would do these things, Lauren?"

The attractive prosecutor got up and went over to the window. She looked out at the inn's formal garden. The Black Eyed Susans were blowing in the mid-July breeze. *Was it possible? Did Jenna pit Rosa against Mom like a Doberman pinscher?* Jenna was always docile. Most of the time anyway. Lauren ran her fingers through her long copper hair. "I don't want to talk about this."

"Well you're gonna," Alan said. "For years, this 800-pound gorilla has been sitting in the room. Now I warned you all, that this was going to backfire, but would you listen to me? We all have our breaking points. Jenna reached hers a long time ago." His voice began to crack. "I knew from the moment Larry called and told me how they found Mom. A person could only take but so much."

"Shut up, Alan. Just shut up."

"It's only a matter of time before Jenna and Rosa come after you *and* Diane," Alan went on, ignoring his sister's outburst.

Lauren watched two preschoolers playing in the garden outside her window. "I've got work to do before I leave for the hospital."

She turned away from the window, put him on speaker and picked up the files that she put aside when he first called. In the back of her mind, she was thinking it was pointless to try concentrating on cases when she was feeling distress. Alan was disturbing her. She almost wished she hadn't picked up the phone.

"Don't you think as the eldest and as a *prosecutor*, we should do the right thing?" Alan asked.

"You're insane. Think of our reputations."

"You should've thought of that before."

"Don't be a fool," Lauren said. "We'll be ruined."

"No. You people will be. I, on the other hand, will be acutely embarrassed and possibly divorced." Alan moistened his lips. "Jenna's fate is in the cards." Victim or no victim she was going to be in an awful lot of trouble.

"Alan, don't do anything stupid."

"I'm sick and tired of holding down the fort. I tried to tell you about Rosa the day she put Mom in the hospital. Now, the next time I see Detective Chang, I'm telling him everything about the other little sister."

Lauren switched off her BlackBerry then began massaging her forehead. She'd have to make the decisions. What if Mom never recovers? She couldn't think about that now. Family secrets were about to be revealed. *I've got to stop it.*

Lauren swore at Alan as she began slipping her feet into a pair of thong sandals. She quickly left her bedroom suite and headed down the hall to Diane's room.

She repeated to Diane everything that Alan had told her while they were having lunch on the terrace of the inn's dining room. "I still don't believe it. He's just exaggerating."

"Remember when Rosa beat up that girl?" Diane asked.

Lauren poured dressing on her Waldorf salad. "Jenna did that."

"Oh. Right." Diane gazed intently at her elder sister. Lauren was wearing an uncharacteristic look of worry. "You *do* believe Alan." Diane lowered her voice. She picked off pieces of her sandwich bread and made tiny balls out of them.

Lauren didn't answer. Instead, she ate a forkful of salad.

"Why is this happening now?" Diane asked.

Lauren shrugged.

Diane's voice dropped even lower. "Maybe Alan's right." "We should tell Detective Chang."

Lauren nearly choked on her salad. "I think you're both as loopy as Jenna. Do you realize what would happen?"

"So what do you suggest?"

"That you fix your face." It had anxiety written all over it. Appearances still mattered regardless of their mother's condition. Lauren felt indecisiveness returning. "I have to think." Tears stung her eyes, but she blinked them back. She couldn't crack. Not now. Lauren reached into her handbag, pulled out a tissue and dabbed at her eyes.

Diane took a bite of her turkey sandwich. She could hardly get it down. Their mother's life was uncertain and Lauren, who was always so strong, was showing weakness. It was natural, but abnormal for her. Perhaps, they were in over their heads.

"I think we let this go on too long," Diane said. "It's gotten out of hand."

"Now you sound like Alan."

"If Mom dies," Diane continued, ignoring Lauren's sarcasm, "Rosa would be guilty of murder. Don't you see? We have to tell Chang about . . . our other little sister." She took a breath.

In a glacial tone Lauren said, "That's never going to happen. I am going to do to Rosa what Mom should've done a long time ago: put her away."

"How?"

"I'll trick Jenna into coming to my house. I'll tell her to bring Rosa. 'We want to let bygones be bygones.' The authorities will be waiting for her. That wench won't be able to do a thing."

"Lauren, that's crazy."

"We'll subdue her if we have to."

"Rosa's a psycho. She'd kill you for sure." Diane shuddered at the thought. This plan was all kinds of nuts. "I thought Mom's goal was to keep Rosa's existence a secret."

"It is," Lauren said.

"And how is this crazy plan supposed to accomplish that. Once Rosa's in custody, the cat's out of the bag."

"I have friends in high places, little sister. I can make information disappear." Lauren jabbed at a slice of red delicious apple with her salad fork. She bit into the sweet, crunchy fruit. For the first time since she spoke to Alan, she was enjoying her lunch. Her confidence had returned. She was feeling like herself again; in control. She could see that Diane wasn't buying the plan. She loved Diane dearly, but her hypersensitivity could be irksome sometimes.

Lauren sighed. "Would you stop worrying?"

"I can't help it. Suppose the guys find out about Rosa?"

A brief look of worry flashed into Lauren's eyes then quickly disappeared. "I can't worry about that right now. Everything's going to be okay and Nelson and Larry will be with us."

"But we can't ask them to stick around 24/7," Diane said. "They might start asking questions. Besides, Larry has to get back to work. He told me this morning."

"Nelson too," Lauren said. "For now we'll stick around the guys as much as possible and when they're not around, we'll make sure that we're always in public. Rosa won't do anything in front of witnesses. It's not her modus operandi. And we'll also keep our room doors locked."

"Now that's sure to make Larry and Nelson suspicious," Diane said. "Guests at The Lorelei don't lock their room doors. And anyway they lock the front door as of nine o'clock. Anything more is overkill."

"We tell the guys that we're scared. With this maniac running around. They'll understand."

Diane took another sip of tea. Even though Lauren was showing a little vulnerability, the guys would never believe that she could be scared. At least not of people. "Everything's gonna be fine," Lauren said as if reading her sister's mind.

"How can you be so sure?"

"Trust me," Lauren said

Diane gasped. "Suppose she attacks Mom again?"

"Too many witnesses. Rosa's crazy. Not stupid."

"I can't even look at Jenna now," Diane said.

"Well, you have to. Otherwise, you'll make her suspicious *and* Detective Chang. We can't have that. If he comes sniffing around, remember to stay calm."

Diane started to giggle.

Lauren resisted the urge to slap her. "Don't blow this. Get a grip."

After taking a message from an advertising client, Jenna called The Lorelei House. Recognizing Moira's lively voice, she introduced herself—as herself.

"This is sooo weird. "I just spoke with someone today who was asking about another sister. And here you are."

"Well isn't that a coinkydink," Jenna said at the same time wondering if Moira was taking uppers or just drank a lot of coffee.

"I had no idea there was another sister," Moira said. "It's so nice to speak with you."

Before Jenna had the chance to ask about her sisters' whereabouts, Moira, with her usual chattiness, went on to say how sorry she was about what her family was going through.

"Why, Thank You. You're so sweet." Finally getting a word in edgewise, Jenna asked, "Is Lauren or Diane around? Their cell phones are off." Actually, they had changed their cell numbers and didn't bother to tell her. Their inconsiderateness worked to her advantage.

"You just missed them," Moira said. "I think they went to the hospital to visit your mom."

"Oh. Well, may I speak with Nelson or Larry?" Jenna spoke in a calm voice masking her inner excitement.

"They left with them."

"Oh nuts!" Jenna had to keep the smile out of her voice as she faked regret. She was feeling eager. Not only was the room vacant, giving her and Rosa time to carry out Phase 2 of Plan B. Importantly, Lauren and Co. weren't around to question her or Rosa's presence. "I wanted to know if they needed anything from Delsey's. We keep eating at the hospital's cafeteria. You know what that's like."

Moira chuckled. "Yeah I've eaten hospital food."

"I'll try them later, thanks bye." Jenna hung up before Moira could start talking about her misadventures with hospital cuisine.

Jenna pulled out her cell phone to call Rosa when line 2 lit up. Jenna muttered a mild expletive. "Wheat Prentiss & Associates."

"Hi there."

Malachi's deep, warm voice thrilled her. It was great to hear his voice. Last night and a part of this morning, he had to take over classes for a colleague who was absent. He was worth the interruption.

"When I called the house, Elise said you went back to work," Malachi said.

Jenna detected mild surprise in his voice. She explained her need to want something to do. She turned her face and winced. She was lying to someone who she cared deeply for. Still, she'd been lying to him about Rosa all along.

"I called to see how you were feeling," Malachi went on, "and to give you a lift to the hospital. I figured we could catch up on some alone time."

Jenna's smile faded. She and Rosa had to set things up in Lauren's suite. What to do, what to do. Tension began rising within her like the mercury in a thermometer on a summer day. She had to tell Malachi yes or he'd wonder what was wrong. She looked at the clock on her computer. 4:45 P.M. "I do want to see you. How's seven-thirty?"

"That doesn't give you much time with your mother. Why so late?"

"It's been a hectic day." *And that's no lie.*

"I just want to go home freshen up and take a nap."

"All right. Seven-thirty it is."

After Malachi hung up, Jenna picked up her cell and called Rosa. Quickly, she informed her that Lauren, Nelson, Diane and Larry were en route to the hospital. "They're probably already there. But we have a problem." Jenna could hear Rosa groaning over the phone. With a sharp intake of breath she added, "Malachi's picking me up."

"What?"

Jenna explained the situation. "I had to say yes. Otherwise, he would've wondered what was wrong."

"Your man's becoming a pain in the butt."

"He doesn't mean to be. I love being with him," Jenna said.

Rosa sighed. "This means we're gonna be on a tight shift. We'll have to work faster."

After five o'clock, Jenna poured out of the office building along with the other workers. She approached her Honda in the parking lot.

Officer William Tedesco, sitting in an unmarked car, watched Jenna pull out. He followed at a discreet distance.

33

The officer drove for approximately five minutes before he realized Jenna was heading toward Thornbush Lane. "She couldn't be going down that street," Officer Tedesco asked himself aloud. He didn't buy into the haunted street rumor, but like everyone else, he avoided it. Soon, he had his answer. Jenna did indeed make the turn down the isolated road. He'd have to follow. Officer Tedesco was under orders by Detective Sergeant Chang to tail Jenna and he took his assignments seriously. He made a face. He was aware that some of his fellow officers thought he took his assignments a little bit too seriously, to the point of taking unnecessary risks. He chuckled. What would they think if they saw him heading toward Thornbush Lane? He had no choice. He had orders.

This was going to be difficult. With no other vehicles on the road, tailing Jenna without arousing her suspicion would require him to don the cloak of invisibility. "Maybe she's taking this road on the way to someplace else?"

Periodically, Jenna glanced at her rearview mirror. She noticed the car following her from back in town. Grateful that she had put on her

Bluetooth headset before pulling off, with her right hand she picked up her cell and pressed Rosa's number.

"I was just about to call you," Rosa said by way of a greeting. "I'm at the farmhouse so—"

"I'm being followed," Jenna said.

Rosa cursed. "Is it that detective?"

Jenna's voice was trembling. "I don't know."

"It's gotta be a cop," Rosa said.

"What am I gonna do?" Jenna asked.

"Relax," Rosa snapped. Her friend was getting hysterical. She couldn't let that happen.

Jenna did become quiet. A reprimand conjured up feelings of inadequacy even if it done to her best friend. Rosa could sense right away that she had struck a nerve. She didn't mean to hurt Jenna's feelings again. Jenna losing her cool could ruin everything. Whoever was following her was another loose thread, much worse that Bella possible waking up. She was going to have to handle this person fast.

In a soothing tone, Rosa said, "I want you to calm down." Already Jenna began to breathe easily. Knowing that Rosa was there was reassuring. She would take care of this situation.

"Don't let whoever it is know that you're on to them. I'll be at the door to let you in. I'll take care of Gordonville's Finest."

Jenna stiffened. She knew that tone. It meant trouble. Gulping she asked, "What do you mean by that?"

"Just do as I say," Rosa said.

"He's a cop!" Tormenting her mother and sisters was one thing. Messing with the law was an entirely different matter. "Rosa, I don't think you should—"

The phone went dead.

Soon, Jenna arrived at the farmhouse. She didn't see Rosa's car. She wondered where she parked it. She couldn't think about it now; already she had a pain developing in her left temple. The approach of that cop was making her anxious. Jenna parked, flew out the car, then jogged up the dilapidated steps. She paused to rub her temple. How did things get out of hand?

Rosa flung opened the door. Jenna, in pain, stepped inside and closed the door.

Officer Tedesco pulled up. He got out of the car hand over his holster. He looked around him. Why did Jenna come here and where did she disappear to so quickly? He looked at the dilapidated structure. There's no way she could be in there.

Officer Tedesco went to the back.

From inside the parlor room, they watched through the slats in the window. Jenna gasped. "I remember him."

"Lower your voice," Rosa commanded.

"Sorry."

They watched as Officer Tedesco looked warily at the farmhouse. Rosa grimaced. The cop heard Jenna's voice. She was hoping that he wouldn't get nosy and come over to investigate. Fortunately, he didn't. Afterward, Jenna whispered that she first saw the officer when the police came to question them.

"Good," Rosa said. "You can use it as an icebreaker when you go to distract him."

"*Me?*"

"Yeah. You're on, girlfriend."

Jenna looked as if she was about to have a conniption. "You're the one who wanted in on this."

Jenna let out a ragged breath. It was fun playing Doreen Bennett, but she had to force it when Detective Chang suddenly showed up at the office. Pretending to feel cool, making believe that his suppositions about Rosa were inane took its toll. She had enough of law enforcement for one day and she still didn't know what Rosa was planning to do to the officer.

"You can do this," Rosa said. "You pulled it off at the Lorelei House."

Jenna held her hand to her temple. "What do you want me to do?"

Tedesco frowned as he looked toward the dilapidated back porch. Wooden slats covered the door and windows. There was no way in there from out here and evidently, Jenna was in the house—with someone.

*

"I don't know about this," Jenna said after Rosa finished telling her about the impromptu plan.

"We have no choice. We have to get to the inn and we're on borrowed time. We're already falling behind schedule. Now hurry up."

Jenna hesitated before she finally left the parlor room and came out of the farmhouse.

Officer Tedesco was heading towards the front of the house when he heard a twig snap. Turning, he drew his gun.

Alarmed, Jenna threw up her hands.

Officer Tedesco lowered his gun. "What're you doing here?"

Jenna was shaking from her near-death experience. How close she came to being at the other end of a bullet. She swore at Rosa. *I didn't sign up for this.* "I——I came here to relax." Jenna gulped then tried to muster up as much charm as she could. "Peaceful here isn't it?"

Officer Tedesco stared at her intently.

"I know. You think I'm strange. How could I love this out-of-the-way place? But I just do." Jenna began playing with the bun in her hair while reading his nameplate. "Officer Tedesco. I remember you. You and Officer Davidson brought water for Detective Chang and me."

"Yeah." The small talk wasn't easing his wariness. He continued to stare at Jenna guardedly. This was a weird place for her to relax. Thornbush Road and this whole property were starting to give him the creeps. Moreover, something wasn't right. "I thought I heard voices."

An edgy look appeared in Jenna's eyes. She looked at the farmhouse then back at Officer Tedesco who became even more wary. "What's wrong?"

Jenna started playing with the bun in her hair.

"There someone in there?" Officer Tedesco asked.

Jenna lowered her gaze. She saw a thick, medium-sized branch on the ground. She picked it up and stared at it as if fascinated by its shape.

"Put that down and answer the question."

Jenna dropped the branch. "You have to leave. Now."

Officer Tedesco looked at her warily. "Why?"

Jenna was quiet as she played with her hair.

"Is someone threatening you?"

"Shh! She'll hear you."

"Who? Rosa?" *I did hear voices coming from the house.* Rosa Garrison was a person of interest." The sergeant had brought them all to speed about Jenna's old friend. "Ms. Crandall, were you in that house with Rosa?"

Jenna continued playing with her hair.

"Ms. Crandall, is Rosa in there?"

"No." Jenna rubbed her temple. Knowing what possibly awaited him made her head feel as if it were about to explode.

"You're a bad liar. Stay here while I take a look around."

Jenna idly picked up the branch that she had dropped and began twirling it like a baton. Did she stall the officer long enough? She hoped Rosa was ready. She drew in her breath then followed the officer.

Tedesco looked doubtfully at the dilapidated stairs before he climbed up the front steps of the old farmhouse. Sarge was gonna ream him. He didn't tell him to go to the house or in the house. He didn't tell him to approach the suspect. Just tail her. Now he was about to advance on Rosa Garrison. Jenna didn't exactly say it was Rosa, but she implied it. He could also see that Jenna was scared. And a little weird. What if it was Rosa? He shrugged. He could handle her. Unlike Bella Crandall, he was prepared.

He put his hand on the door handle then turned. His eyebrows shot up. It opened so easily. *They oughta seal this place. It's a wonder it hasn't become a drug den. It may be creepy but it was the perfect location.*

Officer Tedesco was about to enter the house when he heard a creak. He turned around. To his annoyance, Jenna was standing at the bottom of the steps. Jenna was looking uncertain and a little embarrassed. She had forgotten about that first step. It squeaks.

He eyed the tree branch in her hand. "I thought I told you to stay back."

"I don't want to be alone. And I thought I heard a noise."

"Get back in your car and go home."

"What're you going to do?" Jenna asked.

"Go home," Officer Tedesco said. "I'm handling this."

Jenna made an about face. Dropping the tree branch, she began walking towards her car. She had to figure a way around this pickle. Rosa was waiting for her. And him. She turned around. Officer Tedesco was watching her. She had to keep going.

Cursing, Jenna kept walking. When she reached her car, she got in then checked her rearview mirror. Officer Tedesco was still watching. She stuck her tongue out at him. Then, she started the car and began driving away.

Officer Tedesco entered the house.

Immediately, Jenna stopped the car. She got out then jogged back to the house. She picked up the tree branch and stealthily climbed up the steps. She started rubbing her temple again. Officer Tedesco was making her tense. She resented him for even being there. Why did he have to follow her? She couldn't dwell on that now. Rosa was waiting. Stealthily, Jenna entered the house.

Gun hand over his holster, Tedesco stepped through the door. A ray of light shone through a window revealing a well-polished parquet floor in the center hall. He frowned.

Why was the floor so clean?

Unlike the officer, Rosa and Jenna knew the farmhouse's layout and hiding place. In the shadows they waited.

Officer Tedesco took out his flashlight. The beam revealed the wainscoting and the banister leading to the second floor shining from the waxing it had received. Someone's been staying here.

He continued down the hallway.

Rosa smiled at the unsuspecting officer. The tree branch that Jenna held had now became a weapon in Rosa's hand.

She brought it down on the officer's head.

When Jenna and Rosa pulled up in front of The Lorelei House, storm clouds started gathering. Good thing they finished at the farmhouse. It looked like it was going to pour any minute. After Rosa was finished with Officer Tedesco, Jenna helped her load the materials they were going to need into the car, then got dressed in her Doreen Bennett costume before they left for the inn.

Jenna wiped away tears.

"Oh, would you stop?" Rosa was growing irritated. Jenna had been sniffling since they left the farmhouse considering she wasn't the one who KO'd the cop.

"Suppose he doesn't make it?"

"Then our problems are solved."

"Don't say that. That's cruel."

"You wanna get hauled off to jail? You're lucky that officer was too high-handed to call for backup. Now dry your face. You got the sunglasses, but I don't need you going in there with tear-stained cheeks."

Jenna pulled out her compact from her handbag and applied it to her face. Then she blew her nose and sniffled.

"Hurry up." Rosa said. "And get into character. Time's wasting."

Jenna yawned. They still had a long evening ahead of them.

All smiles, Doreen Bennett reentered The Lorelei House. This time, the owner, Lorelei Kelly, was at the reception desk. She was in her mid forties, with ash blonde hair and perfect makeup. Also behind the desk was Dave, a college senior studying hotel management, who was assisting for the evening.

"Where's Moira?" Jenna asked after they made introductions.

Lorelei smiled. "Moira made an impression on you didn't she?"

"She's unforgettable."

"Moira had an evening class," Lorelei replied. "She's an art major at Gordonville State. She's quite good. In fact, she did the mural on the second and third floors. One of her oil paintings is hanging in the living room. Here's your key."

It was old-fashioned with a red ribbon tied on the end of it in keeping with the inn's antiquity. It looked similar to the key to her mother's bedroom, the person who ruined her life. Jenna hesitated.

"Something wrong?"

"No." She had to guard her emotions. She nearly gave herself away. She took the key from Lorelei then changed the subject. "So, Moira's an art major."

"A sophomore."

Jenna put on her best imitation smile. The chatty teenager failed to mention her talent. She talked about everything else. Jenna turned to leave.

"Enjoy your stay," Lorelei said.

Jenna gripped her room key. "Thank you."

As she climbed the stairs to the second floor, Jenna stopped smiling. Thoughts of where her talent could've led her raced through her mind like stock cars on a racetrack. Her artwork could've been hanging in this very inn or perhaps in a library. Maybe in a New York City art gallery. An office suite.

As soon as she reached the second floor, Jenna recognized Moira's talent right away. It was amazing. The mural was a garden scene. The college sophomore used the trompe l'oeil method, giving it a three-dimensional effect. Jenna continued walking down the carpeted hall. Deceiving Moira didn't bother her anymore.

It took her a few minutes to find the Poppy Room, which was located down the hall and around the corner, giving it a secluded feel. Rosa would approve of the spot.

As soon as she entered the room, she understood why they named it the poppy room. The wall covering had poppies, likewise, the bed linen. As on the main floor foyer, it too had a mouth-watering aroma. She put her travel bag down on the antique double bed. When she turned toward the dresser, Jenna cried out in delight. On display was a colorful array of miniature teddy bear candles. They filled the room with the scent of strawberries and cream, whipped pumpkin pie, fruitcake and coconut. She walked over to the dresser and picked up a candle, a tiny light brown bear. There was a sign next to them that read:

For decorative purposes only.
Please do not light.

Jenna sniffed the candle then smiled. Whipped pumpkin pie. She held the tiny brown bear in the palm of her gloved hand. It would've made a wonderful character in the Enchanted Forest. It would've been a boy and he definitely would've been a friend. Again, she breathed in the room's sweet fragrance. She could've stood there longer savoring the room's fragrance and charming atmosphere, but she couldn't. She had to go back for Rosa.

"Lorelei's at the front desk," Jenna said as soon as she returned to the car. "She can't see you or this bag." She was referring to the large shopping bag on the backseat, which contained a large cardboard box.

With her gloved hand, Rosa pointed to a busload of conventioneers that had just pulled in for the evening while Jenna was inside. They watched as the driver opened the bus door. Shortly, travelers were alighting from the bus and heading for the inn. Others were waiting for their luggage in the cargo area.

Looking smug Rosa asked, "Shall we?"

Quickly, Jenna got the bag out of the car and together they blended in with the conventioneers and entered the building.

"Isn't it charming?" Jenna later asked when they were safely inside the Poppy Room.

"It brings tears to my eyes."

Jenna made a face. Rosa could be so sarcastic sometimes. "I'm glad I brought my sketchpad. I want to draw this room."

"We don't have time for that." Rosa was glad that Lorelei and an assistant was too busy checking people into the bed and breakfast to notice them going by. "You have to get back to Alan's. Malachi's picking you up remember? And we already lost time because of Officer Nosy."

Jenna didn't need the reminder. She was just starting to feel relaxed now that they had gotten past Lorelei Kelly. Rosa had given the officer a good blow. Her breathing became ragged.

He must be dead by now.

"Stop daydreaming," Rosa said. She sat down on the bed and began removing her pumps. "Well, don't just stand there. Take off your shoes."

"Oh. Right." On the way to Lorelei House, Rosa did explain the importance of not leaving evidence around. As Jenna removed her loafers, she watched as Rosa getting rid of any traces of footprints off the floor and area rug as well as outside their room.

"Doesn't the place smell heavenly?" Jenna asked.

Rosa grunted.

"And the teddy bear candles are adorable."

Grunt.

"I sniffed one," Jenna said.

Rosa's hand froze in mid-air. "You *what*?"

"I wore gloves."

"What part of take no chances do you not understand? Ever hear of nose prints?" Rosa had to compose herself before she opened her mouth again. If she didn't, it would not have been pretty. She was already removing prints and fibers. She could just imagine the crime lab combing through this room and finding Jenna's DNA. "Now which one of these hokey candles did you touch?"

Embarrassed, Jenna walked over to the dresser. Retrieving the candle she touched earlier, she handed it to Rosa who stuffed it into her pocket.

With lightening speed, Rosa finished removing all clues. "Now pick up the bag and let's go."

Sulking, Jenna did what Rosa said.

Rosa sighed. Jenna was going to need some major reassurance. "Sorry I snapped at you. I'm just tense. We're on borrowed time and every second counts. I can't be stopping to fix mistakes."

Jenna didn't nod or say a word. She just stood there. Silent.

Rosa looked up at the ceiling as if in supplication. Jenna needed more than just words. She gave Jenna a hug.

Like a pacified child, Jenna smiled.

"Just remember why we're here," Rosa said.

A wicked smiled spread across Jenna's face. Together, they left the room. Rosa led the way. Jenna held the shopping bag.

When they reached the stairs leading up to the third floor, they heard a man humming a tune. Quickly, they rushed back around the corner outside their room. Rosa waited a second before peering around the wall. One of the guests, a man, was approaching the stairs heading down to the main floor. At that moment, there was a hissing sound. The man paused then frowned. He turned in the direction of the sound. Rosa ducked. She turned toward an anxious-looking Jenna who was standing directly behind her. Rosa signaled to her to be quiet then silently counted to five before sneaking a look around the corner again. She watched as the man shrugged then started walking down the stairs. It wasn't until after his footsteps faded away before deciding it was safe for them to come out of hiding. Rosa and Jenna stepped from around the corner, then proceeded up the stairs.

"If we run into anyone," Rosa began in a low voice, "do *not* look guilty. Remember you're Doreen Bennett. A guest and I'm your friend Shamira. Act as if we belong."

Jenna nodded. "Right."

They reached the third floor. Thankfully, it was deserted. Rosa was grateful. Despite what she told Jenna earlier about acting confident, the near run in with the guest made her feel a tad uncomfortable, not to mention the clash with Officer Tedesco. That was one disruption too many.

Rosa and Jenna continued walking down the hall, studying the name on each door. The Orchid Room, The Azalea, The Lavender. "What is it with these people and flowers?" Rosa muttered.

At last, they located The Lilac Room. With her gloved hand, Rosa turned the knob . . . then blinked.

Locked.

She frowned in puzzlement. Rosa turned towards Jenna who looked equally as stunned.

"*What's* going on?" Rosa sounded forbidding.

"I don't know why it's locked." Jenna could feel her mouth going dry. Rosa always planned things out carefully, down to the finest detail. For that reason, she hated surprises. Unless they worked in her favor. "I didn't say anything. I swear."

Rosa scowled. "Be quiet." Jenna's high, squeaky voice might as well have been a gong ringing in the quiet hall. All they needed now was for a guest to stick his or her head out of a room and see them standing outside of Lauren and Nelson's suite.

'"Maybe they just locked the door by coincidence," Jenna said.

Rosa continued to stare at the door. This was no coincidence. The princess was onto something. Why else would she lock her room? Following her own advice, Rosa took a few deep cleansing breaths. She had to. She was about to lose it. She didn't need this. Time was of the essence.

Needing something to do while Rosa decompressed, Jenna examined the lines in her fingers. After a moment, she looked up and noticed that Rosa was smiling at her. "What?"

"Gimme a hairpin."

Jenna removed one from the bun in her hair then handed it to her. Right away, Rosa began picking the lock. Within five minutes, she got the door opened.

Jenna gasped from the moment they entered The Lilac Room. Its old world décor mixed with a lilac theme and wide sweeping views of the Hudson River was breathtaking. She gazed at the hand-carved fireplace, mahogany moldings and ornate furnishings.

Unimpressed, Rosa tapped her watch.

"Yeah, I know," Jenna said. "We have to hurry." She griped to herself about the luxury that always seemed to be at Lauren's disposal. "I guess the bedroom's back here."

They located the master suite. Jenna also admired its décor, especially a pair of champagne-colored Queen Anne wing chairs. Rosa took the shopping bag from Jenna and placed it on the bed. Together they pulled the box from out of the bag.

Rosa opened the box and grinned.

Outside, thunder boomed. Then, the heavens burst.

34

The rain slowed to a drizzle by the time Malachi pulled into the hospital parking lot. He put the car in park then turned to the front passenger seat. He smiled tenderly. Jenna looked even prettier when she was sleeping. Malachi tapped her shoulder. "Jenna." When she didn't respond, Malachi reached over and kissed her. "Wake up, sleepyhead."

Slowly, Jenna opened her eyes.

"We're here," Malachi said.

Jenna looked around in confusion. She remembered getting into Malachi's car. She remembered talking to him about work. The rest was all a blur. Through the car window, she looked at the neon lights of Gordonville

General Hospital. Gradually, it all came back. After she and Rosa arranged the little surprise for Lauren in her bedroom suite, they left The Lorelei House and went their separate ways. Back at Alan and Elise's, she just had time for a quick shower. Evidently, she ended up getting her catnap in Malachi's car. They were supposed to spend the time talking.

Jenna fingered the zipper of her pocketbook as she thought about the locked door to the Lilac Room. As a guest, she would've known about Lorelei Kelly's nine p.m. door policy. Then why lock the door.

Rosa was convinced Lauren knew something. *Maybe she did.* Should they be worried? Maybe it didn't matter now.

Jenna yawned then stretched. The exhaustion was worth it. If only she could see the expression on Lauren's face when she saw what was waiting for her. And Nelson. Rosa referred to him as collateral damage. She gave Malachi a lazy smile then yawned again.

"You weren't kidding when you said your day was hectic," Malachi said. "We were talking and next thing I knew I was talking to myself." He chuckled. "Now I know how Brendan feels when my mind wanders and I leave him talking to myself." He kissed her on the lips. Jenna responded. Neither of them cared if a roving reporter spotted them.

"Sorry I wasn't much company," Jenna said in between kisses.

"Not. A. Problem," Malachi said.

Dr. Gennaro, The neurologist, was conferring with the family when Jenna and Malachi arrived and joined them. Jenna wore a slight frown. Where were Nelson and Larry? Seeing her sisters without their mates by their side was like seeing them shopping in a discount department store. Never gonna happen.

Nelson and Larry couldn't have gone back to The Lorelei House. That would ruin everything. She and Rosa set the trap specifically for Lauren.

"Your mother's circulation is intact," Dr. Gennaro said interrupting her train of thought. "But we have to guard against infection. On the plus side, we're moving her out of intensive care tomorrow." He excused himself to make other rounds.

"That's great news," Julian said.

"Where're Nelson and Larry?" Jenna asked. "Didn't they come with you?"

"They went to the cafeteria," Diane replied. "Is that okay with you?"

Jenna smiled with puzzlement . . . *The hell?*

Lauren adjusted the strap of her handbag. She wanted to slap Diane for being an ass. Didn't she tell her not to make Jenna suspicious?

"Why wouldn't I be okay with it?" Jenna asked. She took in her sisters' chic appearance, a silk leopard print top, wide-legged pants and black boots. Lauren who was in a sleeveless top, slim leather pants and thong sandals. She tried not to feel plain in her jeans and T-shirt.

"Hi, Malachi," Diane greeted. "It's nice to see you again. How're you doing?"

Malachi blinked. *Is she talking to me?*

"I'm fine," Malachi replied. He felt as if he stepped into a bizarro world. "Thanks for asking." He and Jenna exchanged glances. Then he asked, "And you?"

"Just great."

No, you're not. Jenna frowned. Diane was acting strangely even for her. Why was she being so nice all of a sudden? *You're scared.* Diane and Lauren were pretty tight. It was odd that Lauren and Nelson locked their suite. Jenna's eyes narrowed. *This dope knows something.* "What's going on?"

Alan looked curiously at his twin. He was wondering the same thing. Elise was curious too, but she didn't comment.

"Nothing." Diane's voice came out squeaky.

Lauren started wiggling her nose. She hoped that Diane would remember their secret signal to each other and take the hint to stop talking.

Just then, Nelson and Larry returned from the cafeteria with two trays of coffee and tea. Exuding a cool confidence, they looked as if they stepped right out of a page from a fashion magazine in their sport shirts and medium-wash jeans. Lauren was grateful for their entrance as they began handing out beverages. If they ever needed a distraction . . .

Suddenly, Diane said, "I was just trying to be nice."

"Why?" Jenna asked now looking at her elder sister warily.

Lauren pretended to cough. She could've choked Diane. She was going to blow their cover. She had the chance to bow out of an awkward situation when the guys showed up.

"Because we're sisters," Diane answered.

Jenna turned to Alan who looked equally as puzzled. "Are you afraid of something?" She couldn't get that locked door out of her mind.

"Who?" Diane asked. Me? No. Of what?"

Lauren fake-coughed again. For someone who worked before cameras, Diane knew nothing about playing it cool. *Was she listening to anything I said at lunch?*

Jenna gave her a peculiar look. Tired of her, Jenna took Malachi by the hand. "We're going in to see Mom now. Okay?"

"Yes."

Jenna gave her one more curious look before she and Malachi disappeared into the ICU.

Julian had been observing Diane's obvious apprehension and Lauren's subtle guardedness. "Girls, I wanna talk to you. You too, Alan."

The siblings looked at each other. What did Dad want?

Once they were out of earshot, Julian addressed Diane. "What was that?"

"What was what, Daddy?"

"Look, that dumb act is not gonna work with me." The shocking revelations of the past few days enlightened him to the importance of being aware of what was in front of him. And their behavior was off.

Diane's mouth fell open.

Lauren started massaging the tension that was growing in the back of her neck. He wouldn't have called this impromptu meeting if it hadn't been for Diane. Now she had to figure out how to stop Dad from asking any further questions. Managing Rosa was supposed to be the most difficult task outside of awaiting news of her mother's recovery.

Lauren flipped her hair then looked at Nelson, who was standing beside Larry and Elise, staring at their little group. Of course, they were curious. She put on a reassuring smile and wondered what to tell Nelson later when they were alone. He was going to have questions for sure about this family gathering that didn't include him, Larry and Elise. *I'll have to distract him tonight.*

"There's something going on," Julian said, breaking into Lauren's thoughts. "And I wanna know what it is."

Alan shoved his hands into his pockets. An ironic twist of fate. He begged his sisters to deal with this situation. Now it's become complex.

"I had to find out from a cop about abuse in my own home," Julian said in a low tone. The bitterness in his voice was evident. He looked at Diane. "Now, you're being polite to the same sister you practically despise."

Diane managed to find her voice. "Daddy, I don't despise Jenna."

"Don't you dare deny it. Now, what's the story?"

Diane looked into her father's angry face. A few times, she tried to reply; however, no sound came out of her mouth. Usually she had a speech prepared or a canned phrase or two. That's how she dealt with the public. But this was Daddy. And he was in a bad mood. He's been snappy lately. She felt a lump in her throat. She blinked back tears.

Julian crossed his arms. He was in no mood for one of Diane's poor little orphan scenes.

"Diane's trying to make up with Jenna," Lauren said. Furious with her sister, she had to step in and fix this train wreck.

Julian looked skeptical. "And how about you?"

"Oh, I don't have any problems with Jenna." Lauren flipped her hair. "It was so long ago. Memories get distorted."

"Reconciliation my Aunt Minnie. Diane is terrified and I want to know why."

"She's scared of whoever did this to Mom," Lauren replied.

"Your sister can't answer for herself?"

Silence followed.

"How about you, Alan?" Julian asked. "What's your take on this?"

Alan was staring at a gum wrapper on the floor. Here was another chance. He could tell his father about Jenna's companion although this wasn't how he planned it. He needed to know. He should know.

Alan could sense Lauren and Diane staring at him, waiting for him to reveal the one thing that neither Dad nor Detective Chang knew.

In the ongoing silence, Julian sensed their shame. Their panic. It was in the very atmosphere. Then, realization came over him as if they had each taken turns pouring a bucket of cold water down his back. "No. You think Jenna did it. My baby." Julian sank into a nearby chair. "Does Detective Chang think so too?"

Alan continued staring at the gum wrapper. Diane twisted her engagement ring. Lauren stood by, her expression unemotional.

"What the hell's going on over there?" Larry asked as he, Nelson and Elise were looking on in wonderment. Julian appeared to be talking angrily in low tones to his children. Their curiosity soon turned to concern when Julian began to look extremely dismayed.

Nelson was feeling especially miffed that he was left out of the meeting. After all, he was Lauren's husband and Julian's son-in-law. "I'm going over." He began moving forward, Larry too.

Elise decided to follow too. She was especially concerned. She couldn't shake the feeling that something else was going on. She'd been feeling that way ever since she found out that Alan had been less than honest about his past. Diane's more than unusual goofiness and this spontaneous family made it even more apparent that something was amiss. Elise looked at how rattled her father-in-law appeared. Julian was a good man. She hated to see him like that.

Seeing her husband, Larry and sister-in-law approaching, Lauren held up her hand. Inwardly, she was horror-struck. No. This conversation was not for their ears. "It's okay. We got this."

Alan looked at the three of them and shook his head. *Stay where you are.* For once, he and Lauren were in accord. He didn't know in what direction this complicated conversation was going to go, but just in case, he didn't want the others involved either.

Nelson, Larry and Elise stopped in their tracks. They looked at each other. What was going on that they couldn't listen too?

Alan sighed. Once again, he was going to have to deal with Elise's relentless questions in addition to her ire. That was the lesser of two evils.

He looked over at his father. The elder man looked so broken. Alan went over and sat beside his father. The last time he saw his father like this, he was he was ten years old. His parents had another one of their vicious arguments. It would've been just another day at home except that whatever his mother said had shattered his father, reducing the man to tears. As a small boy, he couldn't articulate his feelings upon seeing his father that way.

Alan put his arm around Julian's shoulder. "No, Dad, the detective doesn't think Jenna did it." He didn't know if that was true, but he had to tell him something. He had to make him feel better. That far surpassed the story behind the story.

At least for now.

Chang was sitting in his office staring up at the ceiling.

Officer Davidson entered. "I got Jenna's yearbook." He placed it on the desk. Chang sent him up to Gordonville High School to retrieve a copy.

"Hope admin wasn't too upset about going into the archives," Chang said never taking his eyes off the ceiling.

"Didn't have to. Nanci told me to get it off Jenna's bookshelf. She noticed it when we were there."

Chang grunted.

"How's the view?" Officer Davidson asked.

"They're protecting them."

"Who?" Davidson pulled up a chair.

"Jenna and Rosa." Chang stopped looking at the ceiling and turned his attention to Davidson. "The groundskeeper insisted something wasn't right at the Crandall house, which was obvious. But I believe that whoever or whatever was going on up there got out of control."

"And that would be?"

"What if Rosa weren't a friend?"

Officer Davidson paused then said, "Let me guess: You think she's the crazy relative who lives in the attic."

"Bingo. Emphasis on the crazy. She doesn't sound like somebody who's wrapped too tight."

Davidson grinned. The detective sergeant clued him in about Rosa's spitefulness when she was a child. "That's why I said it."

"So far, they've been hiding child abuse and an unhappy marriage. That brings me back to Rosa. No one wanted to talk about her. Why? Why has Julian been kept out of the loop?"

"It is strange," Davidson said. "But if she is a relative wouldn't Julian know about her?"

"You would think." Detective Chang paused. It was incredible that so much could be happening in his home and he not be aware of it. He frowned. Was it possible that he knew more than he let on?

"Unless *he's* hiding something."

"Like what?"

Chang opened the yearbook. "Do I even want to know? Rosa sounds like the personification of a Voodoo doll." He started turning pages then suddenly stopped. He looked puzzled. "She never told her parents."

"What?"

"Why didn't Rosa tell her parents what was happening to her best friend?" Detective Chang picked up a pen and started tapping it on the desk. "If she did, the Garrison's would've done something about it. Spoken to a teacher. Told the authorities."

"That's true," Davidson said.

Chang resumed turning the pages in the yearbook until he found Jenna's picture. She wore a dark velvet gown along with a strand of pearls and matching earrings. She had on light make up. Her hair was in French braids and she wore the sweetest smile. The officers looked at one another, marveling at the way in which the pretty seventeen-year-old had masked her inner pain.

Detective Chang started searching for Rosa's picture. Soon, he and Officer Davidson were frowning.

"Didn't Rosa graduate with her class?" Davidson asked.

Chang rubbed his hand across his face. Jenna mentioned something about her friend moving. "We assumed she was still part of the graduating class.

"Or maybe she doesn't like pictures," Officer Davidson suggested.

The detective sighed then stood up. "They say 'A picture is worth a thousand words.' I'm going back to Haven Road and recanvas the crime scene. And do me a favor. Tell Tedesco I wanna see him." Chang checked his watch. 7:15 P.M. "I asked him to tail Jenna. He should've been back already."

By 7:45, Chang was back in the Crandall residence. The reason for why Bella felt such hostility towards her own son and daughter and for why Rosa put Bella, Lauren and Diane on edge had to be here. It was something they overlooked. The crazy relative theory was starting to sound more credible. He decided to start in the basement where he recalled seeing some of Jenna's artwork the first time he and his team had arrived at the scene. They had lain the canvasses aside while they searched the premises. Tonight, he wanted to study those pictures.

Detective Chang approached the closet under the stairs where several paintings were located. Putting on a pair of latex gloves, he opened the door and pulled out the canvasses. Jenna's talent was unquestionable. He paused to look at a painting of a barn. It looked . . . Finding nothing particularly revealing in the other artwork, he went upstairs to Jenna's bedroom.

Chang especially took note of the art posters, figurines and book collection. He combed through the volumes in search of anything that he might've missed the first time. He walked over to the dormer window. Jenna's antique fairy tale book tweaked his interest. He picked up

the tome, sat down began leafing through its colorful pictures. *So, Jenna has a whimsical side.* He returned it to its place then started scanning the room again.

Leaning against the wall in a corner was another portfolio. He strode over, pulled up a chair, and began looking through it: nature scenes, still lifes, portraits. All bore Jenna's spectacular detail. Then, he suddenly stopped at another picture of a farmhouse. It was similar to the one he found in the basement. Where had he seen it? He thought for a moment. He snapped his fingers. *The old farmhouse* on *Thornbush Lane.*

Drawn in pastel, Jenna drew the property in its original beauty, a milky white frame structure with double porches and ebony-colored shutters. Odd. Most of Gordonville avoided this area like the plague. But Jenna had been spending quite a bit of time there. Why?

I gotta talk to Tedesco to find out what he learned.

Detective Chang continued looking through the portfolio. To his surprise, there were an assortment of farmhouse pictures and the surrounding outbuildings done in watercolor, crayon and charcoal.

Afterward, he walked over to the night table. He pulled open the drawer. He found a small and medium-sized sketchpad. He took the medium-sized pad first, sat on the edge of the bed and began looking through it. It contained numerous drawings of the meadow.

"So, she likes this place too." Could Thornbush Lane and the meadow have a connection to this case? He cursed. The further he went into the investigation, the more he uncovered. He rubbed his tired eyes.

Next, he examined the small drawing pad. A moment later he cried out, "Whoa!"

He was staring at the anaconda drawing.

"You're sure you're okay?" Nelson asked. He was looking at Lauren with concern. He was over his feelings of anger and inferiority over them leaving him out of the family discussion, a conversation that he noticed was emotionally charged. Lauren did explain that her father was having difficulties dealing with stress and was embarrassed and loathed having to reveal his weakness in front of his son-in-law, Larry and Elise.

The couple had just returned from the hospital and were about to enter their suite after saying goodnight to Diane and Larry, who since entered their respective rooms. Lauren was also grateful that they arrived before Lorelei locked the door for the night. They didn't have to disturb the innkeeper who may have retired for the night.

"Yes, Nelson, I'm fine." Lauren made herself extra sweet and patient. It was the second time he had asked the question. It wouldn't do to get annoyed and risk having Nelson become suspicious. It would be foolish to blow it. She smiled feeling relieved and confident. Nelson bought her explanation for the "Crandall Family Caucus." Importantly, Dad was pacified. He accepted Alan's assertion that Jenna wasn't a suspect. Alan was so glib about it too. He had the perfect opportunity to spill the beans, but he didn't.

Lauren smirked. *He's no different from the rest of us.*

"And how about Julian?" Nelson had never seen his father-in-law look so shaken. It must be awful to feel powerless when someone who you care about gets hurt and you can't do anything to stop it. "Will he be okay staying by himself?"

"Of course. Dad's stronger than he realizes. Besides, he can always call us if he feels down."

"Jenna's weird," Nelson said interrupting his wife's thoughts.

Lauren blinked. Nelson's comment seemed to come from out of the blue. He never commented about her baby sister before, not even when they were dating.

"No offense," Nelson added quickly. "Just something about her."

"None taken. I gave up trying to figure out Jenna long time ago." A cool look crossed Lauren's face. "Weird or not, she's the apple of Dad's eye."

"Well that's to be expected."

"Does Jenna even have any friends?" Nelson asked.

Yes, she does. But you don't need to know about them.

Suddenly, Lauren kissed him. Delightfully surprised, Nelson kissed her back.

"I wish you didn't have to go back to work," Lauren said in between kisses.

Nelson deepened the kiss. Ever since Bella's attack, the interrogations, the trips to the hospital, they'd both been under a lot of stress. It was a relief to have some romantic time with his wife. "I'd stay longer if I could," Nelson said after finally stopping for air. "But the film's been on hold long enough. I'll be back as soon as I can." He began planting kisses along Lauren's neck. Nelson chuckled. "We better get inside."

Lauren snuggled against him. She was happy and proud at the same time. She was enjoying her husband's company and she was proud at how he simply accepted what she said. Her ruse was working.

With one hand around her waist, Nelson used the other to insert the Victorian key into the door. He turned the handle. "That's funny."

"What?"

"Door's locked."

"You locked it instead of opening it." Lauren's voice sounded accusatory to hide her anxiety. The door should've opened as soon as Nelson turned the key in the lock.

"What do you mean I locked it," Nelson began. "That would mean that the door was open. You said you locked it didn't you?"

Lauren swallowed then said, "Yes." Diane was even standing there when she did it. Lauren looked down the hall. Diane was already in her room; likewise, Larry, who had no reason to lock his door. What would she have done if she saw Diane? Question her about the door? Not without arousing Nelson's suspicion.

Nelson tried the key again. This time the door opened with ease. It proved that the door was inadvertently locked in the first place.

Lauren drew in her breath. *The door was open in the first place.*

When they entered, their suite the living area was in total darkness. "That's funny," Nelson said again. "Didn't you leave the lamp on?" He ran his hand along the wall and felt for the light switch.

Lauren ran her fingers through her hair. She did leave the lamp on. She distinctly remembered. *Right before we left for the hospital, I locked the door.* Lauren blanched.

"You all right?" Nelson saw the panicked look on her face. "You look like you've seen a ghost."

Rosa was here. Somehow, she got in. She may still be here. "We have to leave. Now."

Nelson frowned. "Lauren, what's going on?"

"She's here."

"Who?"

Lauren closed her eyes, wishing she could take back the pronoun. It was only a matter of time before Nelson put two and two together and figured out that she knew more than she was letting on. She couldn't think about that now, however. Now was a matter of life and death. There was no telling what Rosa might do. Alan's warning about her seeking vengeance on her and Diane began to haunt her.

"You're all playing with fire. And someday you're gonna burn."

Lauren began to tremble. Her eyes became suspiciously moist.

Nelson stared at his wife like a frightened child. Lauren was scared. A raw, intense dread. She was never afraid. Who was this *she*? *Why didn't she tell the authorities about this she?* A sickening feeling came over him. Was this the person responsible for attacking Bella? Why would Lauren suddenly start talking about this person all of a sudden? Especially if she truly was a suspect?

He doubted that anyone was in the suite, despite Lauren's unprecedented fear. Nevertheless, Nelson began searching for a weapon. In a corner of the living area, he spotted his long-handled shoehorn. Its decorative metal handle could do some serious damage. Striking a female was against his principles, but if this mystery woman were responsible for putting his mother-in-law in a coma and could put so much fear into his wife—a woman who wasn't afraid of anyone or anything except for worms and snakes, the he was gonna do whatever it takes to protect her.

Nelson signaled to Lauren to be quiet. Wearing a dogged expression, he headed for the master bedroom.

Lauren gasped. One good strike with the shoehorn and Rosa was as good as dead. She never liked her. She never acknowledged her kinship. None of them did. Except for Alan and Dad who didn't know of her existence. At the

end of the day, however, Rosa was family. She choked back tears.

Nelson started moving towards the master bedroom.

Lauren widened her eyes. What if Rosa had a gun? She envisioned her lying in wait. The gun going off. Nelson lying on the floor . . . "No!"

Nelson spun around, furious. So much for the element of surprise. Then again, the intruder must've heard them enter the suite anyway.

"Let's just go," Lauren said. "You don't have to play hero."

"Sweetheart, I'm just going to check it out. Anyway, I doubt anybody's here."

"I'm going with you."

"The hell you are." His duty was to protect in spite of how bewildered and hurt he was feeling.

"Then, let's leave. Now. Please."

Nelson stared at her in disbelief. *Who's this person that has you terrified?* The desperation in her voice, the apprehension. He'd seen Lauren in action in the courtroom many times, like the first time he met her when he was researching a character for a screenplay. He watched how she related to people who got in her way outside of the courtroom. To Lauren, they were appetizers.

"All right," Nelson said. He had to get her out of there before she freaked out. "But I'm calling the police."

Lauren gasped. They couldn't involve the police—yet. Alan was right after all. Except that instead of telling Dad the truth about the other child, they now had to speak to the authorities. Now, it was too late to go to Detective Chang. She looked around every corner of the elegant room as if expecting to see Rosa appear. Lauren shivered. Her mind carried the bloody picture of her mother's wounds. What would Rosa do to her? For the first time in her life, she knew what defeat felt *like*. It's too late.

Or was it? They could just walk out of the suite right now. She'd find Alan and Diane and together they'd go to the police. She would explain everything to Nelson later. "We'll call the police," Lauren said. "But not now."

"Dear, you've been panicking since we came in here." Nelson paused then said, "You haven't told me who this *she* is you're so afraid of?"

"Have you forgotten that I work with criminals every day?" Lauren's tone was brash. Nelson was heading into dangerous territory. All she wanted to do was make an about face.

Nelson looked wounded then confounded. She never spoke to him like that before. "I'm your husband. "I'm supposed to protect you."

"I don't need your protection."

Nelson turned away, even more grieved and baffled. What was happening here? What was happening to his wife?

Lauren choked back tears. She saw Nelson's shoulders shudder. He was trying to control his emotions. She never meant to hurt him, but it was for his own good. She knew whom she was dealing with. Nelson didn't. She hated herself for disrupting his peace. For wounding him. With all her might, she ignored the guilt and the pain she was feeling. She never needed her mother more than she did right now. Not because she was sentimental. She needed her to be well again. She needed her to take care of family business again.

When Nelson turned around, Lauren saw the pain on his face. She took a deep breath.

"Is there something you'd like to tell me?" He asked after he managed to find his voice.

Lauren sniffled. "Do you think now's the time for us to discuss this?" She had to get them out of here and somehow keep Nelson away from the truth until she had a chance to talk to Detective Chang. "Maybe I'm wrong. There's no one here. I'm just tired and stressed."

Nelson stared at Lauren cagily. She's hiding something. "Fine. We won't call the police. But we're gonna talk about this later. I resent it that you'd think so little of me that you'd just throw that at me when just a moment ago you were beside yourself." He frowned. "That discussion your father was having with you guys. It was more than what you said, wasn't it?"

Lauren sighed. She didn't have the strength or the time to challenge him. "Yes."

"So you lied to me."

"Yes."

Nelson looked at her in disbelief. "So Julian's not feeling weak?"

"No."

Nelson shook his head. She'd never lied to him before. What else had she been lying about? He couldn't think about this now. "I'm going in the room."

"I'm going with you," Lauren said. She held out her hand. Nelson stared at it briefly before taking her hand in his.

When they arrived outside of their bedroom door, they found it shut. Lauren and Nelson looked at each other. Lauren stiffened. She hadn't left it that way and neither of them was in the habit of closing the door before they left for the day. The cleaning staff hadn't either.

Nelson looked grim. Forgetting about their argument and his injured pride, he pushed Lauren behind him. Nelson put his hand on the doorknob then turned.

In her mind's eye, she saw Alan and Jenna cowering as their mother came at them while she and Diane laughed uncontrollably. She put her hands to her mouth. Jenna really did order the attack on their mother.

She is getting revenge. Lauren shook her head. She couldn't think about this right now.

The door opened with ease. The alleged intruder closed it but didn't shut it. Gingerly, he pushed open the door. Like the living area, the bedroom was in total darkness.

"There's no use hiding," Nelson said. "Security's on the way."

Nelson gripped his makeshift weapon as he listened for the sound of the intruder's breathing or any other movement. To Lauren it felt as if hours were going by instead of just seconds.

Nelson relaxed his grip on the shoehorn. "There's no one here."

Lauren breathed a sigh of relief. Then, together they entered the bedroom. Nelson turned on the light switch. As soon as the lights came on, the shoehorn fell from his hand. Their voices stuck in their throats.

Garter snakes!

Myriads of them were lying on the bed, coiled up. One raised its head and protruded its tongue as if taunting them. Another one was slinking on top of the Queen Anne chair.

Nelson recovered first. *Lauren.* He turned to look at her. Her body was almost stiff from sheer terror. "It's alright, sweetheart. We're gonna get you out of here." Nelson wrapped his arms around her.

Almost catatonic, she allowed him to escort her out of the room. They were almost at the door when Lauren gasped. She became rigid in his arms. Something brushed against her thong-sandaled feet. Her heart went into arrhythmia.

"What is it, honey?"

Lauren couldn't speak. Her spirit didn't want to accept what her mind already knew. She dared to look down. A garter snake was slithering across her feet. She could feel its scales rubbing against her skin. At that moment, Lauren found her voice. She let out a blood-curdling scream.

Nelson kicked at the snake but missed. He forgot about it, however, when Lauren clutched her chest. Her eyes went blank then rolled up into her head. Then, she passed out. "Lauren!" He caught her before she fell to the floor. He didn't care about the garter snakes all around him as he bent over Lauren's unconscious form. Anxiety numbed his insides as he searched for a pulse.

35

Lauren and Nelson's cries sent Larry and Diane flying from their rooms. Guests were flinging open their doors, either coyly holding them ajar, or cowering behind their entrances. Lorelei, who was still working in her first floor office, took the stairs two at a time.

"The screams were coming from in there," an elderly female said, pointing toward the Lilac Room just as Lorelei, Diane and Larry arrived on the third floor. Without pausing, they ran toward the suite.

When they arrived, Diane said, "We need a key." Bafflement and irritation came over Lorelei and Larry's faces, respectively.

"You mean Lauren really locked the door?" Larry asked. "Nelson permitted this?" Both men heard the women talking about it, but he personally thought it was overkill. "That was asinine." Lives could be at stake and they were going to waste precious time unlocking the door. He was about to ask Lorelei for a spare set of keys when the innkeeper turned the knob. The door opened.

"They didn't lock it," Larry said.

Anxiety filled Diane. Lauren was supposed to lock the door.

Lorelei entered first, followed by Larry and Diane. Not seeing the couple in the living area, Diane, Larry and Lorelei ran into the bedroom then stopped short at the horrific sight: A tearful Nelson sat surrounded by snakes cradling Lauren's unconscious form. Larry stared in horror as Diane and Lorelei cried out. Simultaneous gasps came from a few guests who wandered in and gazed upon the hideous scene.

"Is she . . . ?" Diane didn't have the courage to finish the question.

Nelson choked up. "There's a pulse. Oh thank you, Jesus!"

Lorelei pulled out her cell phone and dialed 9-1-1.

Detective Chang examined the picture of the hand sticking out of the anaconda's mouth. It didn't fit in with Jenna's other drawings. Was this a random sketch or was she experimenting with a different genre?

Did Jenna have someone in mind when she drew this?

A moment later, he got his answer. Inside of the draw of her night table, in the other sketchpad was the illustration of the woman hanging from a tree. She bore an incredible likeness to Bella Crandall. Chang looked from the hand in the anaconda picture to the sketch of Bella's effigy then back again. They weren't the same person. Whomever the snake was devouring was light-skinned. And female. The hand was too delicate to be a male. Whose hand was it? Lauren's? Diane's?

He turned his attention back to the chilling sketch of the tree. Sections of the paper contained streaks as if water had dripped on it. Was Jenna crying when she drew this? She wasn't just sad, however.

She was furious.

On a hunch, Detective Chang put down the sketchpad, walked over to her bedroom closet, then opened it. He began rummaging. He turned up some clothes, several pairs of shoes, ping-pong paddles and an old pair of roller skates. Then, he backed out of the closet to get a better view of the items on the top shelf. Instincts aroused, he pulled over a chair and climbed on top of it. After a few more minutes of searching, he found a large sketchbook. From the date scribbled in the bottom right-hand corner it was from Jenna's high school days. He took it down and got comfortable on the chair.

Detective Chang studied a sketch of Jenna and Alan with padlocks drawn where their mouths should've been. The next sketch was Jenna inside of a cage. Beside it was a small table with a ring of antique jailer keys, just out of her reach. He looked at the backdrop then frowned. He looked around the room then back at the picture again.

It's the same room.

A teen-aged girl saw herself as a prisoner. She saw herself and her big brother as having no voice.

Detective Chang turned to the next picture then drew in his breath. A drawing, done in artist crayons, was of a familiar looking forest at night. In it, Bella was pinned against a tree, her body impaled by a spear. Also drawn into the picture, was a young black woman standing by and watching with a self-satisfied grin. A triumphant cry escaped from Detective Chang's lips. This had to be Rosa. By the looks of her, she could've been another sister. There was a resemblance. Now the crazy relative theory was really looking more realistic.

So what happened to Rosa? Did she live here once? *And Julian never knew? How was that possible?*

Something happened. Something bad. "Bella, what did you do?" Detective Chang looked back at the drawing. Jenna was also in it. She was standing next to her friend. She too was looking at Bella on the tree, but Rosa was smug; Jenna was hesitant as if unsure about the events happening before her in the scene.

That's when it hit him. The familiarity of the forest. It's the path leading to the farmhouse.

It's Thornbush Lane.

Detective Chang turned the page . . .

Then did the sign of the cross.

In a pastel drawing, The Grim Reaper, wearing his sickening grin raised his scythe over Bella, Lauren and Diane, their faces drawn in bizarre expressions of terror. Again, Jenna drew herself and Rosa in the picture; and once more, Rosa looked satisfied, while Jenna looked miserable. It was just a painting; nevertheless, as in literature, it revealed a lot about the human spirit.

Chang put down the sketchbook and began pacing the room. Behind the genial and sometimes controlled façade, Jenna was a ticking time bomb.

She set up her mother. And that Garrison woman is involved. She may have looked unwilling in those drawings as Rosa was eager, but Jenna was still behind it. He stopped pacing.

Alan had to know Jenna was furious with their mother and sisters. Detective Chang stared in bewilderment. Except for Elise and maybe Julian, they all must've known about how Jenna was feeling. There's no way they couldn't have known.

"What the hell were they thinking? That's it. I've had it with their lies. I'm rounding up every one of those Crandall's and this time . . . "

His cell phone rang. "Chang . . . *What?!*"

Jenna finished braiding her hair and was in bed reading another paperback. She heard the telephone ringing in Alan and Elise's bedroom. She had plugged out the jack in her room since Rosa rarely called on the landline. She tuned out the buzz of conversation and lost herself in a whirlwind romance with a larger-than-life hero. It was a tiring evening. She was glad to be home again. Jenna smiled. She was looking forward to tomorrow. She was turning the page when she heard the sound of running footsteps outside of her room.

Elise burst into the room. "Lauren's had a heart attack. We have to go to the Lorelei House."

The paperback slipped from Jenna's hand.

Pandemonium awaited Detective Chang outside The Lorelei House. The antique bed and breakfast inn was cordoned off and teeming with police, reporters and animal control. The morbidly curious some holding lantern flashlights, huddled together in the night, as the bulletin of the prosecutor's heart attack and the cause of it hit the airwaves.

The detective took a lungful of air. Déjà vu. The scene looked just like Haven Road did nearly a week ago. After what he just saw in Jenna's room, this latest incident was no coincidence. Rosa was definitely carrying out these deeds.

With Jenna's say-so.

Detective Chang marched past the crowd. Immediately, reporters started firing questions.

"Will a special investigator be called in?"

"Is there any truth to the rumor that someone who's been indicted may have a vendetta against the Crandall's?"

"Do you have a suspect in mind?"

"No comment," Detective Chang replied after each query.

The last question provoked him. The media had no idea how close they were to the truth. He wasn't about to leak what he found to the press, not without upsetting police brass for not informing them first. Importantly, it would've thrown his case. He was about to crack it. He could feel it. There were trade-offs. Mayor Urbanowski's head was gonna explode when he found out the ugly truth about his beloved Crandall's.

That's worth seeing.

Detective Chang was nearing the entrance to the inn when his instincts began to kick into overdrive. Something was off about this case. He just couldn't put his finger on it.

But I'm gonna find out what it is. The same way I found those paintings.

In the entry hall, Officer Vega was questioning Lorelei Kelly. "All the guests have been instructed to remain in their rooms," Officer Vega said after Detective Chang introduced himself to the visibly shaken innkeeper and to Dave who was also present. The college senior was white as a sheet.

"Levi and Davidson are questioning them as we speak," Officer Vega added.

Chang nodded. The sound of crying coming from the front parlor room drew his attention. A college-aged girl was sitting in a rocking chair. Her shoulders were slumped.

Detective Chang looked questioningly at the officer and the innkeeper.

"That's Moira Connolly," Lorelei said. "She works here part time."

Officer Vega gave Chang a significant look. "She feels responsible."

Chang raised his eyebrows. *What did Jenna do that affected this kid?* "I'll wanna talk to her." He looked back at Moira's forlorn figure. "Nanci finish up with Ms. Kelly then try to comfort the kid."

"I will."

"I'll make her some herbal tea," Lorelei offered. "I know I could use some."

With that, Detective Chang flew up the stairs. He overheard snippets of Lorelei wailing about what that person had done to her beautiful suite. "It's tainted now. No one's going to want it."

Chang laughed to himself. *Jenna and her sadistic friend may have done you a favor.* Tourists will come from miles just to sleep in the now nefarious room. He took the stairs two at a time up to the third floor. He couldn't help admiring the artwork.

Ironic.

"I heard him with the snakes," the male guest who heard the hissing sound earlier when Rosa and Jenna were hiding said to Officer Levi.

"How do you know the perp was a he?"

"Only a man would have the nerve to handle snakes."

Chang arrived in time to overhear the comment. *Guess again.*

"I would've seen him too if I'd investigated that sound," the guest went on.

And if you had, there might've been a chalk line of your body in this hall. Chang nodded to Officer Levi as he continued down the hall towards the Lilac Room.

"They cleared out the snakes," Officer Davidson said as soon as Detective Chang arrived at the scene.

Chang nodded. He didn't mind snakes. Just not up close.

"The paramedics are tending to Lauren and the crime lab is dusting for fingerprints," Davidson went on. "Oh and you'll love this. Our snake charmer picked the lock."

Chang grunted. "Wanna bet they don't find any prints other than the vic's, her husband's and housekeeping?"

"How could this happen?" Diane wailed. "We locked our doors."

The officers looked in the direction of the grieving model who was sobbing outside the lavish suite. A bewildered-looking Larry was standing by her side with his arms around her. Nearby, Nelson sat in a chair, staring into space.

Chang fought back the urge not to lash out at Diane. Perhaps this latest incident wouldn't have occurred if she and her family hadn't been withholding vital information. There's no way that she, her siblings and even her mother didn't know that there were serious family issues. Whatever it is involved Jenna and one very angry relative. "Davidson, your aunt stays here when she's in town. Does she usually lock her room?"

"Nope." His aunt, a native of Emerson, New Jersey enjoyed Gordonville's close-knit community spirit and always felt reasonably safe. "The only ones who might lock their doors," Davidson went on, "are the paranoid. Or people from the city. No offense. And anyway, Ms. Kelly did make a change in policy." He told the detective sergeant about the front door.

"Ms. Crandall, as guests of the inn you and Counselor Crandall-Door must've known about the front-door policy." "Yet, you locked your room doors. Why?"

Diane gulped then sniffled. "We needed extra security."

"The inn's front door being closed wasn't enough for you?"

Diane sniffled again. She took a tissue from her purse, dabbed at her eyes and blew her nose. Chang turned to Nelson who was staring out at nothing.

"Mr. Door," Chang began, "can I get you anything?" Nelson sat staring into space. He was afraid to move. Afraid to breathe. If only he could turn the clock black. He should've known something was wrong. Lauren wasn't afraid of anyone. *If only I'd turned on the bedroom light first.* If only they hadn't entered the suite. Period. He started choking back tears.

Detective Chang had an officer get some coffee for Nelson before turning his attention back to Diane. His gaze was anything but sympathetic. "Let's cut to the chase, shall we? You and your sister knew you were in danger. Didn't you?"

Nelson snapped to attention. Something began to nag him. Something in the back of his mind.

"There's a potential murderer running around," Diane replied in a snippy voice. Feeling helpless made her resort to cheekiness. Mom was lying comatose. Lauren may not make it. *Who am I going to go to now?* "We were taking precautions." She pulled away from Larry then began rubbing her hands up and down her arms as if she were cold.

Chang marveled. Even now, Diane refused to come clean. She was determined to live in denial even though whatever Bella Crandall started had gotten out of hand. *What secret is worth all that?*

The officer came back with a cup of coffee for Nelson then handed it to him. Nelson took it. Distracted, he thanked the officer. That nagging feeling persisted. What was it that he was trying to remember?

"What are you getting at, Detective?" Larry asked. He didn't want anyone upsetting her; he didn't care who it was. While he agreed that locking the door was a bit much, he didn't like Chang's tone. For the second time, his fiancée had to see a loved one lying close to death.

"The culprit knew exactly which room to go to, that's what I'm getting at."

Diane held her breath. This was getting too close to home. How long will it be before Detective Chang starts asking questions about Rosa? And in front of Larry and Nelson? She wasn't prepared to answer them. Not now.

She felt a lump in her throat. Lauren promised her that everything would be okay.

Then, Nelson remembered. "Lauren said, 'She's here.'" His voice shook when he said it.

Chang pulled out his notepad. "So who's this *she*?" Diane stiffened. She had to remind herself to breathe. Was she really going through this without Mom and Lauren? *There's Alan.* Diane looked towards the wide sweeping staircase. She wouldn't have mind seeing her twin brother arrive. They were never close like most twins, but she could use him now. He'd know what to do.

"Lauren didn't say," Nelson replied breaking into her thoughts.

Diane relaxed. Nelson knew nothing. She had some time.

"But I had the feeling that she knew who this person was. Lauren was freaked out." Nelson started crying. "She was acting so strange. First, she wanted to call the police. Then she changed her mind."

"Really?" This was proof that Lauren knew that Jenna was angry. The angry pictures Jenna created were still vivid in his mind.

"I've never seen my Lauren like that. We started arguing." Nelson began crying again. "I couldn't understand her attitude. She was so snippy. Why would she be act like that if she thought someone was a threat?"

Chang tapped his chin with his pen. "I know this is hard, but try to tell me what happened."

Nelson retold the terrifying tale. Diane nibbled on her bottom lip. It was unlike Lauren to be scared. Outside of Mom, she was the one who held everything together. On the other hand, she did seem tense at lunch.

Nelson sniffled then said, "I told her we were going to talk about this later. Now . . . I don't know."

Chang looked at Diane with disdain. "Six days ago, I asked you if anyone had a conflict with your mother. Now I'm going to ask you again. Is there someone who would want to hurt your mother?"

"No."

The detective sergeant gave the supermodel a sarcastic look. *You have got to be kidding me.* The drawing of Bella impaled to the tree was still in his head. "Is there anyone who would want to hurt your mother or your sister?"

Diane grabbed hold of Larry and buried her face in his chest. "I don't know."

"Does anyone want to hurt you?"

"No." Her reply came out sounding muffled.

Chang's temper was rising. "Are. You. Sure?"

"She says she doesn't know," Larry said.

The detective glowered. Any respect he held for the fashion maven was beginning to vanish. Can't he see what Nelson was technically saying? Lauren knows the guilty party. Rosa Garrison. It had to be her. He thought about the woman's self-satisfactory grin in Jenna's gruesome artwork. The woman fed on torture. Even this latest scheme was sick and personal.

Rosa's style.

Would Larry be able to handle the truth about his soon-to-be-family when it finally came out? Bella was abusive, Lauren and Diane were cruel and deceptive; Jenna had twisted fantasies and a friend who was willing to carryout them out; a friend, who, he now believed, was one seriously pissed-off relative. Perhaps Rosa is a cousin or a stepchild who they kept ignoring over the years. Perhaps that was that the secret? They're ashamed of Rosa's existence. *Perhaps the details behind her birth would tarnish the Crandall image.*

Besides, the abuse of Jenna why else would she want to retaliate? Chang tapped his pen against his notepad. "Solving this case is as much about you and your family's welfare as it is about the citizen's of Gordonville. They're peace of mind is my obligation."

Larry was about to challenge him when the paramedics came out of the Lilac Room with Lauren. She lay on a gurney, an oxygen mask on her face and wires attached to her.

Nelson stood. He looked at his wife and started moaning. Lauren looked almost lifeless.

Diane looked at her sister and gasped.

Detective Chang blew out a ragged breath. *The second skeleton.*

In spite of his dislike for her, as a law enforcer and a Christian, he could not condone this violence. It had to stop.

Nelson followed the paramedics. Diane rushed behind him, followed by Larry.

Detective Chang wasn't finished with the interrogation, but considering the circumstances, Detective Chang let them go. He'd catch up with them later.

In a low voice, Davidson asked, "All right, what's the dirt?"

Chang signaled to the officer to follow him into The Lilac Room.

After greeting the forensic technicians, Detective Chang and Officer Davidson headed for the master bedroom. The room was indeed clear of garter snakes; nevertheless, Chang started looking around. Animal control may have missed one. Then, he told Davidson about his discovery at the Crandall house.

The officer whistled. "Now what?"

Chang was about to respond when Officer Vega said, "I have an update." She stepped into room. Admiring the décor, she said, "!Qué bonita! How pretty."

"I agree," Detective Chang said.

Davidson coughed.

"Some guests were spending the evening in Rhinebeck or Hudson and came back to this chaos," Officer Vega continued. "They know nothing. Others were in the dining room or in their rooms watching TV when they heard the screams. And everybody's alibis check out. Except for one."

Detective Chang and Officer Davidson looked at her then at each other.

"That person's disappeared," Officer Vega said. "Oh and Moira has a *very* interesting story."

"Step back," an officer was commanding spectators who were getting a little too close just as Jenna, Malachi, Alan, Elise and Julian arrived outside The Lorelei House. They identified themselves to the officer whose name was Jackson.

"Sorry I can't let you in. I'll let Detective Chang, know you're here."

"But we're family," Julian said. "I'm Lauren's father."

"I understand, sir, but it's a crime scene. The paramedics are in there with her."

Just then, the paramedics came out of the inn with Lauren on the stretcher. A hush came over the Crandall's, Malachi, the crowd, officers and firefighters as they caught a glimpse of her ashen features by the glow of the inn's lamplight.

Jenna looked down at her eldest sister. She shook her head. Lauren was supposed to be frightened to death.

Not literally.

When she called Rosa to tell her about what happened, she laughed hysterically. Jenna bristled. She should've known she'd find Lauren's heart failure hysterical. Jenna hung up and called Malachi. Naturally, he was shocked and outraged. Talking to him was soothing even though she had a hand in it. Malachi was compassionate. Understanding. That's what she needed now.

"What's happening?" Elise asked.

Her sister-in-law's impassioned query tweaked Jenna's conscience. She started playing with the ends of her tan satin headscarf, which was hanging loose over her brown T-shirt. It had the symbol of a red dragon. It was one of the blouses she bought when Elise took her shopping. *Lauren was only supposed to freak just like she did at her wedding after she saw the earthworm.* It didn't make sense. She should feel ecstatic. Not guilty. Lauren made her life miserable. Jenna reminded herself about everything she endured throughout the years because of Lauren.

The paramedics put Lauren into the waiting ambulance. A distraught Nelson climbed into after her.

Sensing Jenna's tension, Malachi put his arm her. He felt sorry for Lauren. There was no love lost between him and her, but she didn't deserve this. No one did. Yet there was something strangely familiar about this scenario . . .

Alan spotted Nelson, Diane and Larry coming out of the inn. He jogged over to them. The others followed.

"What did the paramedics say?" Alan asked.

"She's stabilized." Larry looked bewildered. Seeing Bella on the floor was enough. "They're taking her to emergency.

The paramedics closed the ambulance door. After a few minutes, they drove away.

"Come on, Di," Larry said.

As they were heading towards Larry's Lexus, Diane saw Jenna. "What are you doing here?"

Cameras flashed. A tabloid reporter turned to the cameras and began reporting live what was happening. Diane ignored the curious looks from the crowd. She disregarded the irritated looks from her family and Larry. Malachi was irritated and curious. What happened to her desire to be courteous to Jenna?

"Why shouldn't I be here?" Jenna asked. "Lauren's my sister."

"Yeah, Di, take it easy," Larry said as reporters went wild.

"Stay away from us!" Diane cried. Seeing what happened to her big sister and being afraid to face the future devastated her, causing her to become reckless.

Jenna gripped Malachi's arm. Did Diane know what she and Rosa had done? But she couldn't have. Could she? She had to stay calm. That's what Rosa would advise.

Alan's breathing became rapid. What was wrong with Diane? She knows upsetting Jenna was the last thing she should do. She need not get an attitude. Didn't he warn them? Teeth clenched, he said to his twin, "Shut. Up."

Jenna looked around. Media persons, curiosity seekers, guests, police and firefighters all had their eyes on her and Diane. Humiliated, she choked back tears. "Why are you acting like this?"

Diane glowered, unmoved by her little sister's pain. All she could see was the person responsible for the potential deaths of their mother and big sister. She had the nerve to act innocent.

"Why are you antagonizing Jenna?" Malachi asked. Only a few hours ago, she was anxious to please her.

"That's what I'd like to know," Alan said.

Davidson, followed by another police officer, approached. "There a problem?"

Loathing the negative attention they were receiving, Larry took charge. "No, officer. We're good."

The other officers looked skeptical.

"Really," Larry said. "No more drama."

After the officers left, Diane said, "Larry, you don't understand—"

"We're going to the hospital," Larry interrupted. "Lauren needs you and so does your mother."

"I agree," Alan muttered. It was best to get Diane out of here. He gave his twin sister a nasty look. Hopefully, she didn't incite more problems . . .

As Larry was leading Diane away, Malachi was wondering what was it about this scenario that seemed vaguely familiar.

"What was all that commotion outside?" Detective Chang asked as Davidson reentered the Poppy Room where he, Officer Vega, Lorelei and Moira were present. They were asking the innkeeper and Moira further questions. Lorelei said that she went to check on her other guests after what happened to Lauren and after calling the ambulance. When she discovered that Ms. Bennett hadn't slept in her bed, she immediately became suspicious. The bed hadn't been touched. Forensics came up with no fingerprints after they examined The Poppy Room. "Diane was making like a diva and having a fit," Officer Davidson said.

Chang frowned. "Oh?"

"Yeah. When, the rest of the Crandall clan showed up, Diane was ready to get into a catfight with Jenna." Davidson explained what happened. "Alan wasn't happy either. He looked liked he wanted to strangle Diane."

"We have enough villains," Chang said wryly. "Besides, Alan wouldn't attack her. Too many witnesses." This also proved that Diane as well as Alan know something about Jenna's true feelings or at least suspect them. He tried not to think about how much of his time they wasted. Detective Chang continued to examine the antique room. "No luggage. Ms. Doreen never intended to stay here."

Moira's eyes were red from crying. "It's all my fault."

Lorelei hugged her. "No one's blaming you."

"But she asked about The Lilac Room," Moira said. Detective Chang became alert. "She did?"

"That's not unusual," Lorelei said. "It's one of our most desired rooms."

"What else happened, Moira?" Detective Chang asked.

The college sophomore looked down at her sneakers. "I told her Lauren was staying there."

A stern look came over Lorelei's face.

Moira hung her head down. "And I told her where it was located. Sort of." She recounted the conversation.

Lorelei groaned. "Moira, she tricked you into revealing where the room was situated. You made that creep's job easier."

"She seemed nice." Moira looked up. Her voice trembled. "I didn't think it mattered."

"That's right you didn't think."

"Doreen Bennett was going to find that room whether anyone helped her or not," Detective Chang said, his voice rising slightly. He refused to allow Lorelei to jump all over the teenager. Perhaps Moira was garrulous, but she was young. From what Lorelei was telling them earlier about her encounter with Doreen, the suspect charmed her also. Didn't Lorelei say that Moira painted some of the rooms? How come it didn't occur to the innkeeper that wearing sunglasses indoors was odd?

Detective Chang hoped that this unpleasant incident and Ms. Kelly's behavior would not rob Moira of her friendliness or her desire to be kind to others.

"But why was she going after Lauren?" Lorelei asked.

Chang didn't answer. The detective sergeant grew pensive. What was the connection between Doreen and Lauren?

Lorelei glanced at the dresser. "One of my candles is missing."

Everyone turned toward the dresser.

"Do you think Doreen took it?" Moira asked shyly.

"Why would she take that?" Lorelei asked.

Chang rubbed his tired eyes. This case was getting weirder and weirder. He turned to Moira and smiled reassuringly. "You're a very talented young lady."

Moira sniffled. "Thank you."

"As an artist you must possess an ability to recall objects and faces."

Moira nodded and smiled. "Yes."

"We need your help. Can you give me a description of Doreen Bennett?"

Still visibly shaken and red-faced from embarrassment, Moira nodded. Detective Chang addressed Officers Davidson and Vega. "You two question the guests again and see who remembers anyone fitting her description."

*

By 1:00 AM, Detective Chang and Officers Davidson and Levi parked outside The Lorelei House in Chang's patrol car. He ordered Officer Vega to go home for the night. The news crews, police, fire department personnel had left. So did the crowd.

Chang looked at the bed and breakfast. The only lights on were coming from the parlor room windows and the porch light illuminating the wooden sign. Something was still bothering him. "Besides the bag from Delsey's, Jenna had a traveling bag with her." He snapped his fingers. "Jenna booked the room—as Doreen Bennett. She helped set the trap. No wonder she didn't have time to eat during her lunch hour. 'She had errands to run'. I bet."

"How and when did Rosa gain entry into the inn?" Officer Levi asked. "Only four guests maybe remember seeing Doreen Bennett." He made air quotes with his fingers. "But none of them remember seeing her or anyone else entering the building holding a container of snakes."

"Give her some credit," Officer Davidson said. "She didn't go in there advertising the parcel."

"Jenna/Doreen is sneaky," Detective Chang said in a frustrated voice.

"The best witness we have is the guy who heard the snakes."

"I didn't say I worked out the entire equation," Chang said. And we're keeping under wraps this Doreen Bennett—Jenna Crandall angle." Garrulous by nature, Moira told him about Jenna's phone call. "I'm glad Moira didn't make the connection that Jenna's call was a ruse. Let's hope it stays that way."

Detective Chang yawned again. Thank goodness, Hizzoner was out of town on an emergency call. The last thing he needed was for him to get in the way of his investigation. His grandstanding was going to be worse now that Lauren was a victim. By now, he must've heard the news and was already at the town border.

"So who're we dealing with, Sarge?" Officer Levi asked. "A coupla Houdini's?"

"Evidently. I want Alan and Diane down at headquarters. I'm arresting them for obstruction of justice. Once I start asking them what they know about Thornbush Lane, the meadow and their sister's unusual artwork, I'm willing to bet either one or both is gonna crack like an egg."

"Or lawyer up," Levi said.

"Why" Davidson asked. "They haven't done it up to now. Oh. In all the uproar I almost forgot about," Davidson began. "We never heard back from Tedesco."

Chang frowned. "That's not like him."

"You know how Bill is," Officer Levi said. "He probably made a project out of it.

"He was supposed to tail Jenna then report back to me," Detective Chang said. "I don't like this. "She's beyond furious and her pal Rosa's not playing with a full deck. Snakes in someone's bedroom." He groaned.

"You don't think he met up with Rosa do you?" Levi asked.

The sound of the crickets filled the silence. What could've happened to their fellow officer?

"No," Detective Chang said, breaking the silence. "He didn't. He wouldn't approach a suspect without backup." In a resolute tone he added, "Those were not my orders."

"I'm sure he's fine," Davidson said wanting to ease the tension. "And we'll find him and then you can ream him for going against procedures for not reporting to you."

The detective sergeant managed to smile a little.

"In the meantime," Officer Levi began, "we can give a description of Rosa from the artwork you found to our sketch artist then put out an APB."

"No," Chang said.

"No?" Officers and Davidson responded in unison.

"My instincts tell me to hold off on that," Chang said. He sighed. If his officer did have an encounter with Rosa, he didn't know what shape he might be in, if he was injured or even alive. He didn't want his thoughts to go there. He couldn't. *Bill had to be alive.* Therefore, he didn't want to tick her off. "I wanna look into Tedesco's whereabouts."

In the dark, silent, musty parlor of the farmhouse, Officer William Tedesco laid bound and gagged.

36

Larry, Julian, Alan, Elise and Diane gathered around Nelson in the cardiac unit of Gordonville Hospital. Larry placed his hand on Nelson's shoulder. The film producer buried his face in his hands. His grief was so deep, he couldn't talk.

Jenna and Malachi sat beside each other in a corner. Jenna rested her head on his shoulder. Malachi whispered reassuring words to her. Mortified by Diane's public display and worried about what might happen to Lauren, Jenna was quiet on the way to the hospital.

Malachi watched Diane comforting her sister's husband. In a just a few short hours, she went from being oddly nervous around Jenna and having a strange need to placate her to suddenly lashing out. *There's something wrong with her.* Even if she suspected Jenna of *The Great Snake Caper,* she didn't have to do it on national television. Malachi kissed the top of Jenna's head. *Why was Diane angry? No. Why was she so suddenly afraid of Jenna?*

Because she thinks Jenna has something to do with what happened.

No way. Rosa was the one who hated them and she's gone. Ancient history. But Jenna had a reason to hate them too. And Alan. *What is happening here?*

386

Dr. Marie Bradhurst, the cardiologist assigned to Lauren's case, walked through the swinging double-doors. "Mr. Door?" As she approached Nelson, fatigue showed on her copper-toned face.

Nelson raised his head. He looked . . . haunted. He stood up. His legs were wobbly legs. Larry and Julian helped steady him.

Jenna and Malachi came over. Each wondered what the doctor was going to say.

"Your wife's going to be fine," Dr. Bradhurst said.

If it weren't for Larry and Julian, Nelson would've dropped to the floor from relief, while at the same time, a collective sigh of relief escaped from the family.

Jenna hugged Malachi. *Lauren wasn't going to die.*

"There was no damage to the heart," Dr. Bradhurst continued. "We're prepping her for a cardiac catheterization. Lauren's extremely lucky."

"M-May I see her?" Nelson asked.

"All right. But only for a minute. She mustn't get excited. She needs her rest. I'll let you know when it's okay to see your wife."

"Thank you, Doctor Bradhurst." Nelson gushed laughing and crying at the same time.

After the doctor left, Alan tapped Diane on the shoulder. "Let's get something to eat."

"I'm not hungry."

"Yes, you are."

Diane searched her brother's face. He wanted to talk. No doubt about something she didn't want to hear about right now. She can't take the stress. Diane sighed then went with Alan to the hospital cafeteria.

Tact was never one of your strong points," Alan said when they stepped off the elevator and headed toward the cafeteria. "Like Mom and Lauren. And you lack judgment."

"Just get to the point. I don't have the strength to deal with you now."

"Fine. Jenna's no fool. Neither is Detective Sergeant Chang." Alan stopped walking and faced her. "We have to tell him the truth."

"But Lauren said not to."

"You're kidding, right? Her credibility is shot. She almost died. Mom's still in a coma. It's over, Diane."

"Lauren had a plan." Diane told him about the plan to lure Jenna to Lauren and Nelson's house.

Alan looked at his twin sister as if she suddenly grew three heads. "Jenna in captivity? That idea was stupid, deadly and did I say stupid?"

"It might've worked."

"You can't even say that with a straight face." Alan lowered his voice. "She would've summoned Rosa faster than you could take a picture?" He saw visions of blood in his head. "I only hope Detective Chang has me in custody before Elise finds out the rest of the story. She's gonna barbecue me."

"Custody? Will I get arrested too?"

"Yes."

Diane looked horrified. "But why?"

"Withholding evidence." Alan watched the expression on his twin sister's face change from dismay to comprehension to finally sadness. "Welcome to reality. This is what life with Mom and Lauren has led us to. And they can't help us now. I only hope that when this whole thing blows over, it doesn't send Dad over the edge. Lauren's lucky if she doesn't get disbarred."

Diane started choking back tears. "Do you think it'll come to that?"

"Let's hope not. And don't forget the truth has to come out."

Diane gasped. "How's Larry going to feel? Suppose he wants back his ring?"

Alan wanted to wring her neck. She should be thinking about all the chaos and pain she Mom and Lauren had caused, instead of her own problems but, when Alan looked into his sister's eyes, he saw genuine fright. He couldn't help feel a little bit sorry for her. "If Larry's love for you is strong, he'll cut you some slack."

"I'm scared, Alan."

"You should be. To you people, Jenna and Rosa was all a sport. You can't go around treating people like crap all the time and think you're gonna get away with it." Alan resumed walking towards the cafeteria.

Diane followed.

"I really thought Rosa was gone for good," Alan said. "I knew something wasn't right."

Diane started pouting.

"Now what?"

"Rosa was never really gone."

Alan stopped dead in his tracks. "Say what?"

"Mom caught them talking a month before the wedding."

The look Alan gave Diane could've frozen water. "When exactly did Mom share this information with you?" Diane told him about the conversation that took place between her, Lauren and Bella at the wedding reception.

Alan began to laugh like a mad scientist drawing the attention of nearby visitors and hospital staff.

"People are looking," Diane whispered.

"I couldn't care less if reporters took my pictures and plastered them in newspapers all over the Eastern Seaboard. You all stood there in Mom's kitchen and denied to my face that Rosa was back. The three of you. And at the wedding." He rubbed the nape of his neck. "Mom even threw me out of the house just to call her bluff. What the hell was she thinking? That she could control Rosa? Now? She might as well have smacked herself over the head."

"We didn't know Rosa was so angry." Diane sounded like a small child.

"You mean you didn't want to know. She isn't Jenna's rebellious little playmate anymore. She's a pissed off insane woman."

"So what do you want me to do?"

"You're coming with me to see Detective Chang."

"We can't. Lauren said not to."

"Seriously? She's not running this show anymore. Come on, we'll get something to eat."

When they reached the entrance, Diane stopped. She looked at Alan with terror-filled eyes. "Rosa's coming for me next."

Nelson sat by Lauren's bed in the ICU. He listened to the heart monitor beeping. It was a beautiful sound. His bride was alive. He hated to think that a quarrel nearly became their last words to each other. Then, Lauren's eyelids began to flutter. Nelson smiled and laughed a little. In a voice barely above a whisper, he said, "Baby."

Lauren opened her eyes.

Nelson thought it was the most beautiful sight he'd ever seen next to the first day he met her and when he saw her walking down the aisle on their wedding day. Lauren looked into Nelson's eyes. He took her limp hand in his and whispered, "Hi, sweetheart."

She looked around at her surroundings: the IV bag, the monitor. Gradually her memory returned. Her eyes filled with tears.

"It's okay," Nelson said softly. He gently stroked her cheek. "You're safe. The doctor says you're gonna be fine."

Nelson pulled out a tissue from out of the box on the side table then gently he dried her tears.

Lauren wanted to tell him, "No, things weren't going to be okay." But she didn't have the strength. She couldn't even shake her head no. She was too weak.

How am I going to tell him?

She was going to have to tell the truth. Knowing what was about to happen filled her with dread. How was Nelson going to feel about her and her family after the truth about Rosa's relationship to them and the role she herself had played?

Lauren started getting upset. The monitor began beeping rapidly. Anxious, Nelson took Lauren's hand in his. "Baby, please, you have to relax. The family's here. They all love you and they're here to support you."

Not all of you. Lauren struggled to speak; however only guttural sounds kept coming out of her throat.

"Shh," Nelson said. He moved a stray hair away from her forehead. Again, Lauren tried to speak, but with no success. Lauren closed her eyes. She was tired, frustrated and anxious.

"Honey, please, you have to take it easy," Nelson said. "The doctor doesn't want you getting excited. Soon, the nurse is gonna come back and make me leave."

Lauren's eyes flew open. *No. Not before I make you understand. She's gonna kill Diane. She's gonna try to kill Mom and me. And none of you will be able to stop her.*

Her anxiety upon awakening stirred up Nelson's memories of her fear just before the grim discovery in their master bedroom. Evidently, Lauren wanted to tell him something. Desperately.

"I have an idea," Nelson said.

Alan and Diane were coming back from the cafeteria just as Nelson was returning from visiting Lauren. They placed the beverages and pastries on a nearby table. Julian, Elise and Larry helped themselves to coffee, assorted muffins, bagels and tea. Diane offered Nelson a blueberry muffin.

"Just coffee, thanks," Nelson said.

"How's Lauren?" Julian asked.

Nelson smiled weakly. "Fine. She's anxious to get out of bed. You know your sister." He lowered his voice. "I want to talk to you and Alan."

When, Alan, Diane and Nelson moved out of earshot, Nelson said, "Lauren wanted me to give this to you two." He reached into the front pocket of his shirt and pulled out a small slip of paper and showed it to them. In scrawled lettering, Alan and Diane read:

Beware Rosa tell twins

Diane gasped, drawing the attention of Jenna, Elise, Malachi and Julian.

Jenna, who was standing by the nurses' station with Malachi and sipping honey lemon tea, watched the three of them intently. Diane conversing with Nelson made sense. But with Alan? What is he showing them that would make Diane react like that? *Something's up.*

"Everything okay?" Malachi asked. He noticed Jenna staring warily at her siblings and Nelson.

Jenna turned toward Malachi and smiled. "Yeah, it is." She took another sip of tea. *Or maybe not.*

*

Alan looked up and saw that Jenna was watching them. Raising his voice a tad, he said, "Diane, modern art isn't *that* bad."

Nelson gave him a peculiar look. The statement was out of left field. "What's going on?"

Alan muttered that he didn't want to make the others suspicious. "They're already looking this way."

"So?" Nelson asked.

"Nothing. What's on your mind?" He had to divert his brother-in-law as best he could. Anything to delay explaining Jenna and the family nemesis with Nelson. *Of all times for Lauren to let the cat out of the bag.*

"You talk," Nelson said. "Who's this Rosa and why is my wife so anxious for you to be aware of her? Is she the one who left those snakes in our suite?" Nelson began to rehash Lauren's behavior before the incident. He was growing angrier by the second, even with Lauren, now that he knew the name of the person who had spooked her. If she, Alan and Diane suspected this person, why didn't they tell Detective Chang from the beginning? Maybe tonight's near-fatality wouldn't have occurred and Bella wouldn't be in intensive care. "Detective Chang said the person responsible for attacking Bella was someone you knew, Diane. I want some answers."

Alan reached into his pocket, took out a piece of ginger candy, then popped it into his mouth. The candy was a great substitute for the antacid. So Lauren had a meltdown and Detective Chang came close to the truth. Something tipped him off. It would've been nice if Diane informed him this. He would've made a suggestion.

"Hello? Someone going to give me an answer?" Nelson took another sip of coffee. Who was this Rosa anyway? And why was he just hearing about her now? Lauren was afraid of her and evidently so was his in-laws. *Just who was this person?*

Slyly, Alan stepped on Diane's loafer. Divulging anything to Nelson was a no-no. He would go off half-cocked. Alan didn't even want to think about the media circus that would ensue. No. They were much better off talking to Chang. The detective was gonna hit the roof, but he would know how to handle the situation.

Diane picked up on her brother's message. She cleared her throat. "Rosa was just a childhood nightmare."

Alan rubbed his eyes. That was ridiculous. What happened to the "old friend" story they've been using all these years? It was gonna have to do now that she put it out there.

Nelson looked from Diane to Alan. "Lauren wanted me to warn you about a nightmare? Who do you take me for an idiot? A fantasy didn't break into our room and booby trap it with garter snakes."

Diane looked over at the rest of the family. Julian, Elise and Malachi were giving them questioning looks, no doubt because of Nelson's body language, but the worst stare of all was Jenna's. It was . . . piercing. "Tone it down." Diane gestured to Alan to look across the room.

Her twin smiled and waved at Jenna, keeping up appearances. Fortunately, the ginger candy soothed his nervous stomach. Their sister's intent stare was disturbing.

Jenna waved back. She turned to Malachi. "Be right back. Ladies room."

She walked down the hall. Nelson seemed upset. Jenna started rubbing her temple. There was no way that those three were discussing art. Diane wouldn't know the difference between a Renoir and a child's finger paint project. If Rosa were here, she'd say, "*I smell a rat.*" Why did Nelson pull the twins? Jenna continued walking down the hall. She looked back. Malachi wasn't watching. Good. She approached the door marked LADIES LOUNGE . . . then walked past it.

Nelson was baffled. He expected more of a reaction to Lauren's note from Alan and Diane. Where was their sense of urgency and cooperation? "I'm still waiting for a satisfactory answer."

"What more do you want us to tell you?" Alan asked. He spoke up before Diane could respond. He didn't trust his sister not after that crazy line she gave about Rosa being a nightmare. He was afraid of what else might come out of her mouth.

"Your sister nearly died. She gave me a note with a cryptic message to give to you and you have nothing to tell me except that it's a nightmare." Alan and Diane shrugged as if they were performing a mirror exercise in an acting class.

"All right, then." Nelson pushed the note back into his pocket. "I'll see what the police have to say about it."

"So, you're talking about art," Jenna said.

Alan, Diane and Nelson jumped. All three looked at her in wonderment. Alan especially marveled at the way in which Jenna was moving around like a cat. How much of the conversation did she hear? He prayed that she didn't hear any of it—for their sakes.

"That's a favorite topic of mine," Jenna said.

"It is?" Nelson asked, recovering from shock. Jenna's sudden appearance was unnerving. Was she sneaking up on them? Now he felt more annoyed by her presence. Jenna was a strange one.

Jenna smiled innocently. It was fun watching Diane squirm and Nelson frightened. Alan was looking guilty though. Whatever they were talking about wasn't for her ears. This can't be good. *What did they know?* She began to tremble. She crossed her arms so her mounting anxiety wouldn't show. *All right. I'll play along.*

Broadening her smile, Jenna went on to talk about her artwork.

Alan, who believed that Jenna was eating up the ruse, corroborated. He was relieved and rambled a bit.

"I didn't know you were so creative," Nelson said. He was genuinely surprised yet unimpressed. "Lauren never mentioned it."

Jenna played with her hair. *Of course not.*

"Uh, sorry about before, Jenna," Diane said. "No hard feelings?"

"I guess."

Jenna looked perplexed. She didn't see that coming. "And I promise not to give you a hard time anymore."

Nelson, who was about to take another sip of coffee froze. What was going on in this family?

Alan winced. *Too much, Diane.* Nelson must be more suspicious than he already was.

Jenna looked searchingly at Diane and saw fear. Was it because she didn't have Mom and Lauren with her. "I'll forget about what happened." She turned to Nelson. "I'm just glad Lauren's going to be okay."

"Me too." On a hunch Nelson asked, "You know anyone named Rosa?"

Alan grabbed hold of a nearby chair to steady himself. Diane held her breath.

Jenna didn't bat an eye. It was important that she remain calm. "What about Rosa?"

Nelson told her about Lauren's note.

Jenna chuckled, shielding her apprehension. So that's what this meeting of the minds was about. "She's an old friend of mine."

Alan closed his eyes for a moment as if he were in great pain. Why couldn't Diane have said that?

Now we look like morons masquerading as idiots.

"So Rosa's not one of Lauren's nightmares." The statement was like a question.

Jenna covered her mouth to prevent herself from doubling over from laughter. "She's as real as I am."

Diane sat down in a nearby seat. Alan feigned interest in some doctors who were conversing on the other side of the room. Jenna had just shot an arrow through Diane's reason for why Lauren sent them that warning.

Furious, Nelson told Jenna about the nightmare angle. Her laughter ceased. Jenna looked at the twins with dismay. "Why would you tell him that?"

Caught off guard, Alan and Diane stared at her with dumb expressions on their faces.

"Okay," Nelson began, "What was she warning them about?"

Jenna shrugged. "I don't know. Rosa and I were childhood friends. Lauren and Diane didn't get along with her. Kid stuff. Anyway, Rosa's not even around here anymore. We're not even friends."

Nelson frowned at Alan and Diane. "Then why would they make up a story like that?"

"I wouldn't give it another thought, Nel." Jenna started rubbing her temple.

Nelson scowled. One of his pet peeves was when people abbreviated his name. She knew that. Jenna kept rubbing her temple. That would make anyone become suddenly repugnant. "Headache?"

"Just stress. It's been a rough night. See you guys later." As he watched Jenna walking away, Nelson wasn't sure about what annoyed him more, her misuse of his name or that ridiculous yarn Alan and Diane told him.

Malachi's headlights pierced the early morning darkness. The road was quiet save for the occasional passing car or delivery truck. Three hours to sunrise. Malachi yawned then lowered the window so that some of the cool morning air could wake him up. Silently, he thanked God that he didn't have a faculty meeting scheduled for later or didn't have to give a lecture.

Malachi stole a glance at Jenna who was sitting in the front passenger seat. She was twisting the tissue she was holding in her hand. Turning his attention back to the road, Malachi reached out and patted her on her leg. He couldn't get that anaconda drawing out of his mind. Whoever put those snakes in the room had to be the same person who attacked Bella. He was getting that bad feeling again.

He didn't want to believe that Jenna would do something twisted like booby trap her sister and brother-in-law's room, and anyway, one person couldn't do all that. *But two people could.*

Malachi tried not to think about that. It put a whole new spin on Diane's outburst at the inn. She implied that Jenna had something to do with what happened. Where did that even come from all of a sudden? Even it was true, why would Diane be foolish enough to accuse her in public?

Malachi turned down Donnelly Drive. Presently, he pulled into the driveway of Alan and Elise's Cape Cod. Alan, who left the hospital ahead of them, parked his in the driveway. He saw how Alan bolted out of the hospital shortly after he and Diane had that talk with Nelson. Malachi frowned. Jenna just planted herself right into the middle of their conversation. After Diane's histrionics, he was surprised to see Jenna anywhere near her.

"Wanna talk?" Malachi asked.

She couldn't tell him about the note and Nelson's inquiries. Malachi would wonder why Rosa's name came up. Keeping the continuing friendship a secret, was hard enough. Why did Lauren have to write that note? She had to speak with Rosa. Things were getting too hot. Besides, she had a change of plans.

"No thanks, Mal," Jenna said in response to his query. "I'm tired." She opened the door and stepped out.

Malachi did the same. He came around the car. "Jenna." She stopped. He took her into his arms and held her. He had so many questions but he didn't press her for answers. He stroked her back. *What are you not telling me?*

After saying goodnight to Malachi, Jenna went inside. It was quiet. Not the foreboding quiet that was pervasive at her home, but rather, from the silence of sleeping occupants.

Jenna did a fist pump. Alan left the light on at the stairwell. Mom wouldn't have done that. He was a great brother even if he was annoying sometimes. She too noticed how quickly he left the cardiac unit, Elise desperately trying to keep up with him. He must've broken the speed limit to get home so quickly. Why? To avoid further questions by Nelson? Elise wasn't going to give him any less relief. She was a terrific sister-in-law, but once she sensed an anomaly, Elise didn't stop pursuing an answer until she found it, sort of like a bloodhound sniffing for wild boar. That must've been an interesting ride home.

Jenna began climbing the stairs to her room. *I wonder what Alan told her?*

When she entered her room, she quickly changed into loungewear then climbed into bed. She glanced at the clock. 3:00 AM. Predictable, the office was going to understand when she called up too distraught to come to work. That was one benefit to this plan. Jenna began playing with the satin cap covering her head. Her conscience was still chafing from Lauren's near-fatal encounter.

Alan heard the car pull up. That's because he was restless and counting the hours to when he and Diane would go to see Detective Chang. Now that Nelson was going to the police, they were on borrowed time. What made Diane decide to tell Nelson that Rosa was a nightmare? All these years, Rosa was an old friend as far as anyone else was concerned if it ever were to come up. Of all times, she decides to veer away from the script today. He should've known she'd goof. Diane was never good when she was nervous.

Alan sat up carefully. He didn't want to awaken Elise. He was so grateful she was finally asleep. He rubbed his hand over his face. Elise was on his case. Again.

"What did Nelson want? And since when does he talk to you and Diane?"

At first, he was going to tell her that they really were discussing art, but he had a feeling that that wasn't going to fly. So, he decided to tell her a little bit of the truth. Nelson was asking questions about Rosa. Naturally, Elise pounced:

"Why was he asking about her?"

He told her that Lauren was murmuring her name in and out of consciousness. What's one more lie?

"That's odd. But why was Nelson talking to you and Diane?"

"Because we know more about Rosa."

"Then shouldn't he have asked Jenna?"

"That's why she came over. Honey, you know Nelson and Jenna are not close."

Elise bought it. At least, she stopped asking questions. Alan made a promise before God that once he and Diane went to see Detective Chang, he would come clean to his wife. He reached for the roll of antacids on the nightstand, which was almost finished.

37

Malachi crawled into bed and groaned. He looked at his digital clock. 3:30 AM. By the time his afternoon class began, he should be well rested. And loaded with caffeine. He felt as if he could sleep for a hundred years. He was going to need a lot of caffeine in order to teach class. He began nodding off the moment his head hit the pillow. Seconds later, he opened his eyes. The attack on Bella was personal. The assailant didn't take anything. Malachi sat up. The dream. The woman in the mask. *And Jenna's drawing.* The hand sticking out of the snake's mouth was slender and light-skinned. *Like Lauren's.*

No wonder Jenna was uncomfortable about the anaconda drawing. *She never meant for me for to see it.* The feeling of déjà vu returned. Jenna said she was angry when she drew that anaconda picture. But was she angry enough to put snakes in her sister and brother-in-law's suite?

Malachi groaned. "Now, it all makes sense," he said aloud in the darkness. *Rosa.*

He turned on the lamp and sat up in bed. "She lied to me. Jenna's been talking to Rosa all along." That was the reason for Diane's theatrics. She knew. But what exactly did Diane know? And how about the rest of the family? Why didn't they say something? *What is happening here?*

Malachi went downstairs to the kitchen and poured himself a glass of milk. He couldn't sleep now. He had to think.

When Jenna opened her eyes the next morning, the bedroom was aglow with morning sunlight. The wrought iron clock on the night table read 9:45 A.M. Jenna sat up. She overslept. She was late in calling the office. She was going to tug at their heartstrings with another Oscar-winning performance. By now, they must've heard the "shocking news" to quote the media about what happened to A.D.A. Crandall-Door. *"Our hearts go out to Nelson Door and the family . . . "*

Jenna wore a half-smile. Everyone at work would assume that she was too overwrought to call in, never mind come into the office, but as a formality, she still had to make contact. Her smile grew wider. What would her colleagues think if she didn't call in feeling sad and distraught? *Image.*

Her half-smile soon disappeared; however. Was there a chance that Rosa would get into trouble? How did Lauren find the strength to write that message? Fear began to wrap her like a blanket, followed by guilt. Her sister deserved to be terrified, not have a near fatality. Revenge was supposed to feel good. Wasn't it? Malachi's words came back to her. *"God gives us free will . . . Some of us choose to do evil."*

She picked up her cell phone then pressed Rosa's number. "Can we talk?" Jenna asked when Rosa answered on the first ring. "I'm sorry to bother you," she added quickly. She didn't want Rosa flipping out on her again. "We need to talk" Jenna said. " . . . No, Lauren didn't die . . . If it wasn't important would I call?" In fairness, Rosa was probably still tired from all that activity last night. She would've been willing to bet that Rosa's attitude would've been more receptive, if she called with the news of her sister's demise. "I know you're working. I just said I was sorry . . . Of course, it'll be after work."

After they arranged a time and place, Jenna hung up. She sat on the edge of the bed. She pushed her feet into her pink open toe terry cloth slippers. "She's not going to like what I tell her."

The law offices of Mirsky, Mirsky & Walden occupied a large Greek Revival house on Green Street. Malachi entered the reception room of the swanky law firm, greeted the receptionist, then entered Brendan's office. The defense attorney, who was sitting behind an L-shaped desk, taking a call signaled to Malachi to have a seat. Brendan was expecting him.

Malachi picked up a stress relief toy, a yellow rubber ball with a smiley face. He squeezed it, watching it expand and contract.

Brendan frowned slightly. He knew something was on his friend's mind when he called his house earlier that morning asking if he could squeeze him in today. Whatever it was, it was heavy. He hadn't seen Malachi looked so stress since that down period he was having after he lost his job. As soon as Brendan ended the call, he asked, "What's the latest on Lauren?"

"She's doing alright." The question was another way of asking what's wrong. Malachi gave Brendan the rundown on Lauren's recovery.

"Good." Lauren wasn't on his list of favorite people, but he didn't wish her ill either. Brendan leaned back in his swivel chair and lazily scribbled on a legal pad.

Malachi continued to squeeze the stress-relief toy.

Brendan cleared his throat. Evidently, Malachi had something to say and needed help in getting it out. "You know, rumor has it that the incident is a family affair."

"I know," Malachi said in a quiet voice. "What else have you heard?"

Brendan mentioned the shouting match he saw on the news last night. "It kinda reminded me of reality TV."

"That's what I came to talk to you about," Malachi said. "Off the record."

Brendan nodded. "Shoot."

Malachi needed another moment to get his bearings. What he was about to say wasn't easy for him to admit to another person, even if he was his best friend. Finally, in an even lower voice, Malachi said, "I think Jenna's behind the attacks."

Brendan stopped scribbling, then put down the pencil.

"At least she's responsible for part of it," Malachi added.

"You mean she's an accessory."

Malachi nodded solemnly.

Brendan cursed. His uncle was gonna love this. He sat forward. "Talk to me."

Malachi went on to tell him everything about Jenna and Alan's past and about Jenna's friend Rosa. Regardless of his confusion and disappointment, Malachi didn't discuss Jenna's childhood game. A promise was a promise. He still cared about Jenna, but she had been lying to him.

Brendan mouthed the word, wow and widened his eyes as Malachi told him about the type of things that Rosa did as a teenager. He told him about his volatile relationship with Bella and his reluctance to share it with the police, Jenna's nervousness on their first day and why now that he knew about serving Bella and about the anaconda drawing that he realized in retrospect she never meant for him to see. Malachi even talked about the nightmare. "And I suspect that their family may know about Jenna's latent hatred."

"So," Brendan began in a teasing tone, "you tried to withhold information from the cops. "Back to your old tricks again?" He wasn't making fun of the situation. He just wanted Malachi to relax.

"FYI, I told Detective Chang what I thought he needed to know at the time, smart guy." Malachi picked up the stress relief toy again. He could hear the I-told-you-so's in his head. But Jenna wasn't the problem. At least not entirely. It was her mother and her sisters.

"Sounds to me as if Rosa Garrison is looking for restitution," Brendan said interrupting his thoughts.

"Restitution?" Malachi clutched the stress toy until it looked as if it would burst.

"Yeah." Brendan reached over the desk and took the toy away from him before he destroyed it.

"After all these years? Well, you did say you thought Jenna was holding back."

"I wasn't talking about murderous intentions towards her family." Brendan sighed. "Anyway, you wanted my advice." He cringed. "Although I wish I didn't know this stuff you were telling me."

Malachi looked rueful. He put Brendan in an awkward position should he ever have to testify. Hopefully that would never happen.

"Go to Detective Chang and tell him your suspicions. But you already knew that."

"I've told him things . . . after he found out I was holding out."

"Well, now you're gonna tell him your suspicions. Apparently, she and this Rosa person have some kind of vendetta going on. According to the formula, aka your dream, Diane's next." Brendan ripped off a page from the legal pad then started draw a triangle on a fresh page. "I know you're in love with Jenna, but maybe next time Rosa won't miss."

Malachi looked grim. If he stayed silent and something happened to Diane, he'd never forgive himself. "I don't get it. Why would Rosa risk life imprisonment or," he swallowed, "the death penalty, just to avenge Jenna for stuff that happened so long ago?" He got up and started pacing the room.

Brendan added an eye to the triangle. He didn't point out that Jenna was risking the same punishment. Malachi would figure it out himself eventually.

"Alan was abused too and he didn't go after Bella and Lauren," Malachi said.

"You sure about that?"

"Brendan, I assure you this is all this is Rosa's doing. Alan is not a sadistic guy."

"Neither was Jenna until you found out otherwise."

Malachi stopped. He gave Brendan a defensive look then sighed. His pal was right. Jenna had a vindictive side or she'd never maintain a friendship with a person of Rosa's caliber or acquiesce to her actions. Did Alan have any hidden brutal traits? "None of this makes any sense."

"It does if Rosa is more than just a friend."

Malachi gave Brendan a funny look. "Jenna likes men."

"No, fool. She could be a relative. Ergo, Rosa's need to take revenge."

"That's what Detective Chang said."

"Why didn't you say that before? If he's coming up with the same theory, there might be something to it."

Malachi shook his head. "Jenna would've told me."

"Like how she told you that she and Rosa were history when they were still hanging out."

Malachi started pacing again.

"Think," Brendan began, "why's Diane weirding out all of a sudden? If they know something that could crack the case, why not talk to the cops?" Brendan's face lit up. "Maybe Rosa is Lauren's daughter?" He smiled sadistically. What a thrill it would be to see his opponent knocked off her high horse.

"Your math's wrong, Counselor. She's the same age as Jenna who by the way is thirty-two."

"Then Lauren's lying about her age. Have you even met Rosa?"

"No and I don't want to." Malachi resumed pacing.

"Dude, you're wearing out my carpet." Brendan wore a slight frown. "What if Jenna doesn't know."

"What do you mean?"

"That Rosa's a relative and not just her best friend. She could be the proverbial crazy relative they've kept hidden in the attic all these years and she got loose."

"She was always loose."

"Well, something went wrong." Brendan came from around the desk and sat on the edge of it.

"What's the point of passing Rosa off as a friend?"

"Shame."

"Of what?"

"Her birth," Brendan replied. I happen to know that Bella's a stickler for image. If Rosa's illegitimate, that would've put Bella on edge." He chuckled sardonically. "I think she would prefer a crazy relative than an out-of-wedlock grandkid."

Malachi paused. It made sense, but he still wasn't sure about Rosa being her sister. He blew out a sigh. "I'll do what I have to do." Tears began gathering at his eyes.

Sometimes doing the right thing hurts," Brendan said. "A good friend told me that once."

Malachi nodded too overwhelmed to speak.

Brendan put his arm around Malachi's shoulder. "You know I'm here for you."

Detective Chang stood before Officer Tedesco's desk. He looked at the photos of his family and fiancée. "He goes missing the same day I send him to follow Jenna which happens to be the same day that Lauren and Nelson have an encounter with garter snakes. I don't believe in coincidences. He was supposed to follow Jenna nothing more." Detective Chang took a deep breath. "If Tedesco saw the suspect, he was supposed to call for back up."

"We don't know what happened," Officer Vega said.

"What else must I think, Nanci? He's not answering his calls. He's noticeably absent. It doesn't fit his pattern." Chang wanted to kick himself for sending him on that assignment in the first place. Tedesco, on the other hand, was available. He did have a tendency to take risks, but all he had to do was watch from a distant. "His family's going out of their minds." Chang rubbed his hand over his face. He had to stay positive.

"Maybe he has a lead," Officer Levi said as he and Officers Davidson and Jackson joined them. "You know Bill. He thinks he can handle one female. As soon as he gets a chance he'll call in."

"Two," Vega corrected. "Jenna's the lookout."

"But she's not the aggressor," Levi said.

Detective looked grim. He turned to Officers Vega and Levi then handed them a warrant. "Arrest Alan and Diane Crandall." He turned to Officer Jackson. "Put out an APB on Rosa Garrison."

"I'm on it."

Chang had changed his mind earlier that morning and showed one of the paintings to the police sketch artist. He turned to Officer Davidson. "You and I are going to Thornbush Lane."

A hush fell over the department. Police officers and other personnel ceased activity.

Chang looked around the department. Evidently, they were horrified at the orders he just issued. "Come on. What're you eight?" He turned back to Officer Davidson who was looking suspiciously pale. The detective sergeant shook his head. "Now based on the artwork I found, Thornbush is where we'll find Tedesco." He looked grim. "Or a clue to his whereabouts." Would they find him alive?

"There's the meadow," Officer Davidson suggested. He was hoping he could steer his superior away from a trip to the Thornbush Lane also known as the farmhouse. Yes, he was a cop and he did not want to go down there. The place wasn't a notorious drug den. There was no gang activity. He didn't want to go there because it looked and felt creepy. Even worse, he's going to want to enter that farmhouse. The young officer was aware of the irony.

"The meadow's not a bad idea," Detective Chang said. The site was the subject of quite a few of Jenna's pieces, "but unlike Thornbush Lane, there's no place for them to hide."

"But Sarge," an officer spoke up, "the structure is insecure."

Other officers agreed.

Chang silenced them with a look. "If that were true, the building would've fallen down ages ago. Bill is our brother. Are you going to let your fears of the boogeyman stand in your way? We're police officers. We have to uphold the law. Now grow up and let's move it."

Davidson and the other officers looked at each other shamefaced.

They were about to leave on their respective assignments when they stopped dead in their tracks.

Malachi just walked into police headquarters.

38

Alan parked across the street from the Lorelei House. He looked baffled. He was calling Diane for the past twenty minutes. No response. Before they left the hospital last night, he and Diane had quietly arranged for him to pick her up and together they would go see Detective Chang. She was supposed to wait for his call, then come downstairs. He wasn't going to go into the inn. That way Nelson or Larry wouldn't start asking questions. Her excuse for going out was that she needed to be alone for a while.

Alan crunched on what was left of a piece of ginger candy. He wasn't proud of himself. He had to lie to Elise yet again. He told her that he was going to the office. He got out of the car.

Alan stood in front of the French Normandy manor. He sought out the third floor windows. Diane and Larry's suites were located somewhere on that floor. He became uneasy. Did Rosa get to Diane somehow? He dashed into the bed and breakfast inn. All thoughts of nosy reporters watching his actions or running into Nelson or Larry fled from his mind as he was racing up the stairs. The only thing that mattered now was his sister's safety.

When Alan arrived at her suite, he knocked on the door. Five seconds went by. Ten. *She has to be okay.*

He tried the door. Locked. After a full twenty seconds, Alan gave up waiting. He was going to have to call the police. Lorelei Kelly was gonna just love having the cops show up at her establishment again. Alan pulled out his cell phone and was about to call 9-1-1 when he heard movement behind the door. *Someone's in there.* "Diane?"

He knocked again. Again no answer. But Diane was safe. He knew that now. She was simply ignoring his call. If Rosa were in the room, she would've opened the door and given him a big fat greeting. Rosa loved drama. Just like a Crandall.

Furious, Alan stormed down the hall. Soon, he was back outside again. Standing before the bougainvillea, he redialed his twin sister. This time, Diane picked up. In a quiet steel-like voice Alan asked, "What're you trying to pull? I thought you were hurt. Or worse." He couldn't bring himself to say the d-word. "What do you mean pulling a stunt like that? . . . Oh, you were in the shower." Alan spoke sarcastically. Her excuse was bogus although plausible. "What do you mean you're not ready? . . . Well how much time do you need?" He rolled his eyes. "You're stalling. I'm gonna tell you what I told Lauren. I'm not keeping up this game anymore. You people started it. I didn't. It's ruining my life and it's jeopardizing my marriage. It ends. Today. I'm going to Detective Chang with or without you." Alan hung up.

He looked up at the sky. The sunny day was suddenly turning gray and menacing. Alan got into his BMW.

Malachi too noticed the storm clouds gathering outside the window of Detective Chang's office where he was about to talk about his theory on Jenna and Rosa. Now that he was in front of the detective, he felt an unease that he hadn't felt since he was in psychotherapy for the first time. On the way to police headquarters, he was feeling confident; that was after a good cry and some prayer. He envied the people in the park across the way, reading, snacking, chatting with friends. For a moment,

Malachi wished he were one of them, uninvolved in this situation and clueless. Not even, the chimes coming from nearby St. Anthony of Padua was comforting.

Chang shuffled some papers around, giving the professor time to get himself together. It had to be something big to make him come down here. Instinct told him to hold off on Alan and Diane's arrest, which he still intended to do, but first, he wanted to hear what Malachi had to say.

"Looks like we're in for a downpour," Detective Chang said.

Malachi nodded.

Chang tossed a few knickknacks into a file drawer then watered the azaleas. After a few more minutes of keeping busy, he could no longer wait. A maniacal female and her partner in crime were roaming around his town. "What did you want to see me about, Prof?"

Malachi stared at a paper clip. "I—I think Rosa Garrison committed both crimes." He took a deep breath. "And that Jenna may have been her accomplice." He never took his eyes off the paper clip.

Detective Sergeant Chang didn't respond. Malachi could feel Chang watching him. He held his breath as he waited for the censure: *Why didn't you mention this before?*

Finally, Chang said, "I know."

Startled, Malachi looked up. "You do?"

Detective Chang picked up his notepad. Given what he knew about Jenna and how the professor felt about her, he couldn't condemn him when he decided to come clean. It took courage for him to reveal Jenna's guilt. "You didn't reach this conclusion overnight. What happened?"

Careful not to mention his visit to Brendan, Malachi discussed the anaconda drawing and its similarities to Lauren's booby-trapped room and the possibility of Rosa being a vengeful relative.

"I appreciate you telling me." Detective Chang sighed. "We too considered that Rosa might be a vengeful relation. That or an extremely loyal friend."

"I was wondering," Malachi began, "if Jenna doesn't know Rosa is really her sister or her cousin, "why are the Crandall's hiding it?"

"I don't think the father knows."

"How could he not know—?" Malachi stopped. Hadn't Julian been in the dark about the abuse?

"What if Bella were Rosa's mother?" Detective Chang asked.

"By another man," Malachi said. That would be a secret worth hiding. From the world as well as from Julian. "Why did Jenna hide her ongoing relationship with Rosa from me?"

Chang noted Malachi's disillusionment. He remembered the afternoon he first met the professor, a polite yet cool confident individual. Today, he wasn't hiding his emotions. He was nervous. He felt betrayed and he was grieving.

With a sympathetic tone, Chang said. "Whatever Jenna did or didn't tell you, they made her that way."

"You're talking about the abuse." Malachi groaned. "I could just kick myself. The signs were right in front of me. How could I not see it?"

"Love has a way of messing with our heads sometimes," Chang said. "And sometimes we don't want to see what's right in front of us."

Malachi felt the blood rushing to his head. He had been in denial. God even sent him a dream and he wouldn't use it.

Detective Chang was about to thank Malachi and send him home when he had a thought. "Did Jenna ever talk to you about the meadow?"

Malachi smiled weakly. "We had our first unofficial date there."

He went on to discuss her obvious fondness for the place. "She was like a little girl. So carefree." That's when the significance of the Enchanted Forest hit him. *She used her make-believe world to fight off her enemies.*

"Besides the anaconda drawing, what other artwork of Jenna's have you seen?" Detective Chang asked.

"There's the meadow, some nature scenes. One picture did seem off though. That farmhouse."

Chang straightened. "Thornbush Lane?"

"Yeah." Malachi explained about accidentally driving up the infamous road and seeing the farmhouse. "I was surprised to see it in her collection, given its reputation. Anyway, she made it pretty." Malachi described the pretty details she added to the now decrepit house.

With a decisive look, the detective sat up. "Follow me."

Chang opened the trunk of his car and took out one of Jenna's portfolios. He opened it out to one of the drawings. "I have to warn you. This is more graphic."

Malachi took the portfolio. It was the drawing of Bella impaled to a tree. He made a retching sound.

"You okay?" Detective Chang asked.

Malachi nodded.

"Good. I don't want you getting sick all over the evidence." Detective Chang removed the disturbing picture from Malachi. He was supposed to log it and the other artwork into evidence, but with the chaos at The Lorelei House and the disappearance of Officer William Tedesco, they remained in his possession. Detective Chang pointed to the woman beside Jenna in the picture. "She your mystery lady from your nightmare?"

"I can't tell. She was wearing a mask. But, she does have the same shape if that helps."

Putting the portfolio away, Detective Chang asked, "Think you can handle another one?"

"Yeah." Soon, Malachi was gazing in alarm at the grim reaper, about to harvest the souls of Bella, Lauren and Diane.

Chang watched as Malachi's Adam's apple began bobbing up and down rapidly. "This next one might be easier on ya, Prof." He showed Malachi the sketchbook with the picture of Bella hanging from a tree.

Malachi shook his head. "She told me she was angry when she drew that anaconda picture. She was having an off day. I even allowed myself to believe it. It was the tranquil pictures that were the irregularity."

"That's the crux of this case," Chang said. "Denial. And dangerous secrets. It was like pulling teeth just to get her brother to admit their abusive past."

Malachi nodded. Jenna was reluctant to open up to him as well and he's her boyfriend. He noticed some other sketchpads in the trunk. They looked old. "What about these?"

"Go ahead. I didn't get a chance to look at them yet. After I got the call about Lauren, I managed to scoop these up."

Malachi picked up a sketchpad. It contained child-like drawings done in crayon. With Chang looking over his shoulder, they studied a picture of a little girl, presumably Jenna. She was alone in a garden sitting in a chair. Big droplets were on her face, a child's version of tears. The next drawing was a happy picture of Jenna. She was playing in the meadow with another little girl.

"Rosa," Detective Chang said.

"And look." Malachi pointed to a drawing of a teenage boy standing by a tree looking on. "That has to be Alan. It's a pretty good likeness."

Chang grunted. Even then, he was present at Jenna and Rosa's gatherings. The architect wanted him to have the impression that he didn't associate with them at all. Even if he was babysitting, this picture showed how far back his association with Rosa Garrison went.

When Malachi turned to the next drawing, he and the detective gasped. Little Rosa was defending Alan from a huge, ugly woman, obviously Bella. In her hand was a knife. Little Jenna had drawn droplets of blood coming down from it with a red crayon. In the background stood the farmhouse.

For a moment, they were silent. Jenna's hatred was born in childhood. She had been using art to express her latent desires.

Detective Chang was the first to speak. "So she, Rosa and Alan were going to that farmhouse," Detective Chang said. "I'm not even surprised that she didn't mention her brother's presence."

"Well, Rosa's family used to live there," Malachi said, returning the sketchpad to the trunk. He'd seen enough of Little Jenna's artistry as well as the adult version. "That's probably why she painted the place to look so nice. She wanted to recapture the past. You know. The way it used to look."

Chang gave him a strange look.

"What?" Malachi asked.

"I've only lived in this town for five years now but I know for a fact that that farmhouse hasn't been occupied in years."

39

Malachi stood at the same spot long after Detective Chang jumped into his car and drove off. He almost looked as shocked as Malachi was at the crazy lie Jenna told him. Malachi kicked a stone and watched it land in a patch of grass. First, she hid her ongoing friendship with Rosa; but of all the lies, the one about her friend once having lived in the farmhouse on Thornbush Lane, was the wildest. Now, she and Rosa were in trouble with the police. He had to talk to Jenna. Fast.

He checked his watch. "Great." In five minutes, he had a lecture on social deviance. He grimaced at the irony. Because a class was considered canceled when an instructor was fifteen minutes late, he was going to be twenty minutes late. He could just see his students gleefully signing the attendance sheet then running out the door and straight for the student lounge, forcing him to make up the class later. Not an option. Malachi pulled out his cell phone. A colleague owed him some favors.

Jenna lumbered up Thornbush Lane. Ordinarily, the trek relaxed her. The seclusion made her feel sheltered from her troubles. Here, Bella, Lauren and Diane couldn't get to her. They never came here. No one did. Or seldom ever. Only this time, she was feeling edgy. She had something important to say to Rosa. She'd been hashing and rehashing it in her mind. The more she thought about her decision, the better she felt. More relaxed. On the other hand, Rosa was going to explode.

The forest was growing darker. She looked up at the sky. Overcast. She heard something earlier on the weather report about rain but, with her mind filled with anxiety over Lauren's note, her nearly dying and Rosa's pending fury, she wouldn't have remembered to take her umbrella. Too late to turn back now. Rosa might already be at the farmhouse. They had agreed to meet there rather than at Rosa's place. Thunder clapped, signaling the arrival of a deluge. Jenna began jogging up the road.

She reached the end of the path where the forest ended and the old weathered farmhouse stood. Thunder clapped again. Jenna raced for the house, but not before the rain began to fall.

Very soon, she was climbing up the rotting steps. Getting wet was the least of her problems. Nevertheless, Jenna was annoyed. She arrived at the front door. Stressed, she began to rub her throbbing temple. Jenna put her hand on the door.

Rosa opened it. "This better be good, Jenna."

At Delsey's, Detective Chang sat down at a table in the back. He had to get away from Malachi. He needed to think. He was still reeling from that freaky story Jenna told Malachi. He took a bite out of a glazed donut, not giving a hoot about the cliché. He had to review the case. What was it that kept eluding him? It was obvious now that Bella's attacker was Rosa or someone who she knew and very well. The perp had easy access. That same person walked right into The Lorelei House. Alan and Jenna seemed reluctant to talk about this Rosa, who, apparently, is a relative. In addition, Lauren, Alan and Diane hadn't volunteered that information which proved that Rosa is a relative. *And they don't want the world to know about her.*

Detective Chang took another bite of his donut. A wicked grin crossed his face. *Did Bella have an affair and Rosa was the result?* Public news like that would've made the status-conscious woman nuts. That would be something worth hiding to her. In addition, an illegitimate child who felt slighted by her own mother could feel loads of resentment. But where did the other Crandall children fit in? Evidently, they were hiding Rosa's existence as well. Why would the kids care about another sister? And why the hostility toward Alan and Jenna, and why would Lauren and Diane aide their mother?

Jenna had to know that Rosa wasn't just a friend but a sister. The resemblance was unmistakable. Detective Chang frowned. They look like each other, but neither Rosa nor Jenna looked like Lauren, Alan or Diane. He took another bite of his donut. Jenna looked a little like Bella and yet . . .

Nina Murray entered the café with her eight-year-old twin boys. Detective Chang smiled and waved at his neighbors. He couldn't help thinking about Nanci Vega and settling down.

While a server handed Nina a takeout menu, Chang watched as the twins began to mimic each other. One boy raised his right arm at the same time as the other. Then the other boy raised his left arm at the same time as the other. Roscoe the Groundskeeper's words came back to him. *"If I were you, Detective, I'd think about the number two."* Detective Chang gasped. No. He didn't want to believe it and yet it made sense. They allowed it to go on. "Those dumb . . . " He cursed. His jaw dropped. *Tedesco.*

He leaped out of the booth and fled the restaurant, leaving Nina, the twins, customers and staff looking on in shock and curiosity.

Jenna was twisting her hair around her finger as she stared at Rosa, who was leaning against the wall in the parlor room, livid. For the first time Jenna found herself on the receiving end of her best friend's wrath. She had just finished telling her that she no longer wanted to settle the score with her mother and sisters after which Rosa called her pathetic.

Indecisive. Weak. Still, In the face of Rosa's anger, she managed to find the courage to continue. "I don't feel like killing anymore."

"No one's dead yet, Einstein."

The glow from the lantern flashlight showed the fury in her eyes as well as Officer Tedesco who lay in a corner, wounded, disheveled and sweating from the heat and humidity. Jenna felt sorry for him. He wasn't even supposed to be in this mess. If only he hadn't followed her. If only he'd just gone away . . .

Officer Tedesco began moaning from pain and sheer terror. Sometime in the night when he came to and found himself left alone, he tried to escape. The pitch darkness didn't deter him. He was determined to find a way to navigate in the dark in spite of the pain ricocheting through his head, the queasiness in his stomach and the absence of his flashlight that Rosa had kindly confiscated.

He struggled in the ropes she used to tie him up. The disturbed woman did an expert job too. No matter how hard he tried, he couldn't loosen the restraints. The officer berated himself. *How could I have let myself walk into this ambush?* After struggling into the wee hours, he grew exhausted. He fell asleep. Rosa's voice woke him up. It had a hellish sound.

Jenna looked down at the injured officer and the terror in his eyes. "I know you're angry with me, but at least you could give him some water. It's a miracle he's still alive."

"Are we getting spiritual now?"

"Things are getting out of hand, Roe. We're not supposed to have a hostage."

"Lauren wasn't supposed to have heart failure either," Rosa said, "but it works out. We got even." Rosa chuckled. "Now she'll shut up for awhile."

"Really?" Jenna told her about Lauren's note and the conversation between Nelson, Alan and Diane at the hospital. "I guess you think that's funny too."

Tedesco whimpered as he watched Jenna and Rosa arguing.

"Girl, you oughta know by now your family don't scare me."

"But Nelson's not going to buy that crazy story the twins gave him. He's gonna go to Detective Chang with the note. I just know it." Jenna pointed to Officer Tedesco. "It's all over the news that he's missing."

Tedesco's eyes sparkled with hope. *They're looking for me.*

"You think your brother-in-law's a threat to me?" Rosa asked. "I can off him like a duck in a shooting gallery."

Officer Tedesco's eyes glistened with unshed tears. How long before she gets tired of him and offs him like she was planning to do to Nelson Door? Already his hope was beginning to fade as he watched the exchange.

"Did you see the news?" Jenna asked. "They're getting suspicious." She told Rosa about Diane's accusation outside of the Lorelei House.

Rosa rolled her eyes. "I know. I saw the footage of Miss Prissy."

"Now they're saying it's a family matter," Jenna said.

Rosa started laughing. The sound echoed throughout the house. Officer Tedesco felt like a fly trapped in a spider's web of madness.

"Family matter?" Rosa asked in a mocking tone. "Oh am I family now? All these years I was the family secret." She snorted. "You and Alan didn't even count."

"Never mind that," Jenna said. "Detective Chang's getting close to the truth about your involvement."

"I don't get you. You cried out to me for help and I took care of Bella like you asked me to."

Officer Tedesco moaned again. It was hard to believe that that woman could do that. If he came out of this alive, he had so much to tell the Sarge.

"Would you shut up?" Rosa yelled. The officer was a nuisance. Not only was she going to have to kill him eventually, but thanks to Jenna's change of heart, she was about to get cheated out of sticking it to Diane. Rosa turned back to Jenna. "Bella's out of your hair. But are you glad? No. You feel guilty. You're worried about the neighbors' *feelings.* Next thing I know, you make a 180-degree turn and ask me to take care of Lauren. You even wanted in on it. And even then you were this close to changing your mind because Malachi gave you one of his Christian pep talks."

Jenna scowled at the way Rosa said her boyfriend's name in that derisive tone. She was also wrong about the "Christian pep talk." Malachi shared a sensitive part of his life with her and she felt grateful to him for that regardless of the choices she made.

Rosa shouted, "What do you want, Jenna?"

"I don't know."

"Well you better figure it out," Rosa said in a warning tone.

Jenna held her temples.

After Malachi got a colleague to cover for him, he decided to do a little detective work on his own. *Why would Jenna lie about Rosa and her family living at the farmhouse?* He questioned himself repeatedly as he drove to Thornbush Lane. Returning there wasn't easy. He promised himself he would never drive down that place again, but he was doing this for Jenna. Murderous hatred towards her mother and sisters and a certain bond between her and Rosa showed in her artwork, making her a person of interest. If not, she would be soon. Malachi was determined to find out what was going on and what other secrets that property held.

Malachi started getting jumpy as he got closer to his destination. He turned on the car radio to an R&B station to help him relax. As he listened to the smooth sounds of the saxophone, Malachi concluded that Rosa was unstable. Her actions when she was a teenager and over the past few days was an indication. No sane person would behave this way. He dismissed the idea that Jenna was disturbed too, although something had to be wrong with her to go along with Rosa's schemes. Even with the adversity she and Alan endured over the years, they turned out okay. He was a successful architect and had a nice wife. Jenna was doing well for herself too, although she wasn't working in her dream job. She was bright, funny, talented.

And a big fat liar.

He blew out a frustrated sigh. If it hadn't been for that ridiculous story about where Rosa lived, he wouldn't be on his way to Thornbush Lane now, the last place on earth he wanted to be. Obviously, the farmhouse was she and Jenna's hangout. She painted so many pictures of the place. Malachi frowned. *Maybe she does like girls.* He shook his head *and* quickly dismissed the idea.

"Uh oh," Malachi said as thunder started to rumble. Gordonville was in for another bout of rain. No sooner had the thought occurred than raindrops began to fall, followed by a downpour. The windshield wipers were no match. Blinded by the heavy rain, Malachi pulled over to the side. He leaned back in the driver's seat and waited for a break in the weather.

Wearing a cap, aviator sunglasses and carrying a dripping umbrella, Nelson walked into the Gordonville Police Department. Nelson questioned his decision on coming. He felt as nervous as an actor did about to do his first audition. The movie producer looked around at the wanted posters, the trophy case containing pictures and awards of decorated officers. Nevertheless, something was wrong and it involved Lauren. Therefore, he had to make it his business. Nelson folded the dripping umbrella, braced himself, then approached the front desk.

Officer Levi looked up. He sized up the dapper man. He looked familiar. "Can I help you?"

Nelson stared nervously at two officers bringing in a scary looking suspect. Finally, he said, "I need to speak with Detective Sergeant Chang. It's urgent."

"He's not here at the moment," Officer Levi said. "Perhaps I can help."

"Thanks, but I'd prefer to speak with the sergeant."

"I see." Levi narrowed his eyes. "What did you your name was?"

"I didn't. I'm here about the Crandall case. I really need to speak with the detective."

Officer Levi straightened. "You got information?"

Nelson sighed. He wanted to do this in private. Unfortunately, this cop wasn't going to make things easy. He removed his glasses.

Officer Levi raised his eyes. No wonder this guy looked familiar.

The rain stopped. Malachi started the car. The sooner he got to that dreaded farmhouse, the faster he could get this whole thing over with and get his answer. When he reached the corner of Thornbush, he made a left turn. That's when he got the message: *Do not drive up here.*

His relationship with God was too strong for him to think it was a result of nerves or a bad stomach.

Malachi slowed the car. The "entry" to Thornbush Lane was unusually dark because of the overcast sky. He swallowed. He was looking down the path of his own living nightmare. This was worse than the hallucinations he used to suffer from. This was real. He murmured something unflattering about his Cousin Omar. Now wasn't the time to think about his tales of terror. He recited a verse from Joshua 1:9 . . . "'Be strong and of good courage; do not be afraid, nor be dismayed, for the Lord your God is with you where you go.'" Then he asked, "So what do I do?" *Walk.*

"Up this place?"

Yes.

"Are you kidding me?"

Thunder boomed.

It was inconceivable that God wanted him to go up this creepy street on foot. Especially when He knows, he hates ghoulish places and things. Malachi looked through the rear window. Not another car or human being in sight. He turned back around then spotted a tall twisted tree about two yards from where sat parked in his Toyota. It looked like something used in some pagan ritual.

Malachi shook his head. "No. No way am I walking up there." Since becoming a Christian, he tried harder to obey God; however, this was not one of those moments. Like now. He was still determined to find out what was going on up at that farmhouse—his way. He started the engine then something dropped on his car. A bird's "calling card." To his vexation, another one followed. Then another. This was no coincidence. He put the car in neutral. Malachi looked up. "Thanks." Evidently, the Lord wasn't happy with his defiance.

"Okay," Malachi began, "I'll do it Your way." Still, the birds were relentless. His car was getting pelted. "I get it. Message received." Malachi put the car in park. With a wry grin, he grabbed his hooded raincoat from the backseat. He realized now that when he decided to take the coat with him at the last minute before leaving the house that morning he wasn't just being overly cautious. God had given him that urge. Malachi stepped out of the car. He winced when his leather oxfords oozed into the muddy ground.

Sulking, Malachi started hiking up the road.

The darkness of the forest and the shapes of the trees fueled Malachi's imagination. Memories of the ghost stories told to him in childhood started coming back. Passing by a gnarled tree, he thought he saw a headless specter perched atop its branches. Soon, he passed by another tree then stopped. It was the same one on which Bella's body hanged from in Jenna's drawing. How many times did she stand on this spot to do that?

Lightening streaked across the sky, illuminating the forest, followed by thunderclaps. Rain began to fall again. Malachi threw on the hooded raincoat then quickened his steps.

A deer bounded out of the forest. Malachi cried out then watched it run across the road and into the depths of the forest on the other side. What was he getting himself into going down this horrible place? He just wanted to return to the car and keep on driving even after he hit the Lincoln Tunnel. And he couldn't care less if a flight of California condors pelted him. Malachi looked up nervously, suddenly remembering that the Father could read thoughts.

"There had better be a Heaven," he grumbled. He continued hiking.

Now the rain was falling lightly, nevertheless, Malachi wasn't feeling any better. His shoes were history and he felt wet and miserable even though he was wearing a raincoat. After occasionally talking to himself, singing and praying, he was finally out of the forest and away from his living nightmare. Before him was the old farmhouse. Malachi stood there looking at it. He hadn't seen the place since he drove past that first afternoon. The farmhouse was in its natural state. Weather-beaten, decrepit. Not freshly painted and trimmed as it was in Jenna's pictures. The seasoned Victorian residence was no longer just an abandoned house at the end of a spooky country lane. It represented something more.

"Okay, God," Malachi said. "I'm here. Now what?"

Go to the back.

Malachi looked around the vast, desolate property. He shivered. This can't be good. He walked towards the back of the house.

The rain finally stopped and a summer wind began to blow just as Malachi reached the back of the property. The leaves on the trees swayed in the breeze, as did the ones in the orchid. Malachi looked toward the farmhouse. He frowned. He thought he heard muffled voices coming from the farmhouse. Malachi moved closer to the direction of the voices. He examined the rotting steps leading up to the farmhouse's ramshackle back porch. The second floor windows had torn and dirty screens. The windows on the first floor had boards nailed across them, some with torn screens protruding through the planks.

" . . . what we're doing is wrong."

Malachi froze. *That's Jenna. She's talking to someone.*

"So, you wanna go back to being your family's vomit bag?"

Malachi's eyes widened. That voice. It was menacing. *Like the woman in my nightmare.* His heartbeat quickened. *Rosa.* He was in no hurry to meet her, yet he had a morbid fascination for the woman Jenna revered, and on who she was now risking her entire future.

He was feeling vulnerable standing out there in front of the boarded-up windows. Exposed. If Jenna saw him, it might not be so bad; however, she might be upset about him being there. She'd think he was spying on her, which in a sense he was. Importantly, his sudden appearance might startle her, thus giving him away, sending Rosa rushing outside. He shuddered at the thought. The results might not be so pretty. Rosa Garrison was not well. He needed to move away from the window.

Mindful not to step on any twigs, Malachi approached the steps, some of which had rotted. It was going to take some maneuvering to reach the top of the back porch without alerting Jenna and Rosa, not to mention injuring himself. He took a deep breath then put one foot up on a good step. No mishap. He breathed a sigh of relief. Malachi stretched his long leg over a rotted step then placed his leg on another good step. *Talk about taking big steps.*

He made it to another level. Then the next. Little by little, he concentrated on the task. Jenna and Rosa's continuing dispute was the perfect diversion. No one would be paying attention to the window . . . After careful maneuvering, Malachi made it to the top of the porch.

"I've been thinking," Jenna said. "There's another way." She paused. "I want to learn about God."

Malachi did a fist pump. He had a positive effect on Jenna after all. Then, he heard Rosa laugh. He shivered at the maniacal sound. Afterward, he crept on stealthily. The floorboards on the back porch were decaying. One false move and he'd crash through to the foundation underneath. *Ow.* He kept moving until gradually, he moved toward a window with a small opening between the slats.

"God was such a big help to you before," Rosa said sarcastically. She laughed shortly. "You're a glutton for punishment."

"It's going to be different this time," Jenna said.

"How? A chariot's gonna come down from the sky and whisk you away from all your misery?"

"I thought I felt God's presence." Jenna talked about the experience she had when she was watching the sunset with her father.

"Are you trying to say you want to be a Christian?"

"I don't know. Maybe."

"I don't believe what I'm hearing."

"Malachi will help me."

He couldn't help grinning. His feeling of pride soon diminished, however, when, he heard groaning coming from inside the farmhouse. Malachi frowned. *There's a third person in there?*

*

"I told you to shut up," Rosa shouted. What followed was the sickening sound of kicking against skin followed by more whimpering.

"Stop!" Jenna cried. "You'll hurt him."

Malachi's eyes widened. He remembered hearing something on the news about a missing cop. *Oh, Jenna. What did you do?* He had to see inside. He had to prove to himself that she wasn't crazy enough to let Rosa talk her into kidnapping a police officer, but in his heart of hearts, he knew that she had. But why? And what did they plan to do with him? Regardless of Jenna's culpability, Rosa was the mastermind. Jenna was not devious.

Rosa snorted. "I don't believe what I'm hearing."

"Calm down and listen."

The argument continued. In between Malachi heard more groaning and whimpering. To kidnap an officer required subterfuge and strength. The same strategies she must've used on Bella . . .

Strength was the operative word. His spirit lifted. Perhaps neither Jenna nor Rosa was responsible for attacking Bella or the officer. They're women. He wasn't sexist. He simply doubted that either Jenna or Rosa had the upper body strength although he'd never met the much-lauded best friend. This small ray of hope, however, begged the question. If they didn't hospitalize Bella and take a cop as hostage, then who did?

"I just don't want to hurt anyone anymore," Jenna said.

"After everything they've done to you?" Rosa asked.

"I just want to do what's right."

"How did doing what's right work for you the first time?"

Malachi heard footsteps inside the farmhouse. Were they Rosa's? Maybe she was leaving. She was pretty steamed. He gulped. Was she coming outside? He'd only have a moment to hide. Malachi looked around. The area was vast. He could run toward that red barn in the distance. Perhaps he could lose himself in the orchid . . .

" . . . Forget about the past," Jenna said with force. Rosa wasn't going to talk her out of this.

"It's Diane's turn," Rosa said. "She should pay."

"I want out," Jenna said.

Malachi's shoulders sagged with relief. Thanks to Jenna, the argument would continue buying him more time. He must've lost 20 pounds wondering where to hide. He peeked through the window with the open slat. The light from the lantern flashlight in the parlor enabled him to see inside the room. His mouth fell open. On the floor bound and gagged was the missing officer.

"You're just scared," Rosa said. "Lauren's note, Nelson goin' to the cops, *possibly*, got you all nervous again. It's gonna be okay."

Malachi tried to get a glimpse but the direction of Rosa's voice was coming from a corner of the room, outside of his line of vision. He could see the officer. He needed medical attention. A horrified look covered his face as he stared in horror at his captors.

Rosa softened her voice. "You have nothing to be afraid of or feel guilty about. 'Cause I know that's what's bugging you."

"No it's—"

"I know how you think, Jenna," Rosa interrupted. "I'll take care of you. Don't I always?"

"Yes." After chewing her out, Rosa was trying to win back her affection. Her attempt to preserve their friendship, however, only made her feel worse. "But my mind is made up."

Malachi could hear Jenna, but he couldn't see her. The boarded window obstructed his vision and in spite of the lantern light, there were still shadows in the room. His body was beginning to ache from trying to see inside. He had to be careful. At any moment, he could reveal his presence by stepping on a creaky floorboard.

"Then, you deserve whatever happens to you," Rosa said. Jenna was a lost cause.

Tearfully, Jenna said, "It'll be better this time. I know it will."

Jenna finally moved into Malachi's line of vision. "I just want you to know that you'll always have a special place in my heart."

There was a pause. When Rosa spoke, her voice took on a dangerously low tone. "You're sending me away again."

Jenna held her head down. She felt as if she was betraying her best friend. "I'm sorry, Rosa."

"You're pathetic."

Jenna flinched.

Malachi moved away from the window. He started gagging.

Rosa's voice was coming out of Jenna's mouth.

40

Malachi tried not to gag. All these weeks he'd been with her and he never noticed it. *She has two personalities.* How could Jenna's family not know? Or did they? But why keep it a secret? There had to be a reason. He felt chagrined and horrified as he watched Jenna arguing with someone who wasn't there. Of course, in her mind, Rosa was there and very much real.

I gotta tell Detective Chang. There's no telling what Jenna, alias Rosa, might do to that cop. It was God's mercy that he was still alive.

Carefully, Malachi started backing away. He reached the steps then began descending, mindful of their rotting condition. However, when he put his foot down on the third step, it creaked.

Malachi froze.

"What was that?" He overheard Rosa asked.

"Probably a deer," Jenna replied.

Despite his horror, Malachi was impressed at how Jenna could play two distinctly different characters. His admiration came to a sudden halt, however, when once again he heard footsteps. This time they were exiting the room. *Rosa's coming to investigate the sound.* Jenna wouldn't hurt him. But Rosa would. If she could knock out Bella and trap a police officer, there's no telling what she would do to him. *I'd better get the heck outta here while I still have my head attached to my body.*

He leaped off the back porch and landed hard on his right ankle. Trying not to think about the searing pain shooting up his right leg, he bolted for the orchard. There, he crouched behind a tree. He watched as Jenna came around to the back of the house. No, not Jenna. Rosa. He looked in wonderment. This entity walked with a swagger. Immediately, she began observing the steps and the ground where Malachi was. For a while, she stood there watching.

From his hiding place, Malachi felt his insides growing cold. *Oh, God, please tell me I didn't leave any footprints.* As if Satan himself had whispered into her ear, Rosa began to look toward the orchard. Malachi held his breath. *Please God. Please God. Please God.*

Malachi started to shiver. He couldn't see her face too clearly, but he could still sense the evil emerging from her. He recalled the times he had seen Jenna's visage change from sweet to evil. Now he knew why. He was afraid to move. Afraid to breathe. Oblivious to his throbbing ankle, he surveyed his surroundings. This part of the orchard abutted the forest, which led out to the main road. The two places that he dreaded so much were about to become his refuge . . .

Finally, Rosa went back inside. Malachi breathed a sigh of relief. He waited for a few seconds just to make sure that the coast was clear then raced for the forest. Like a gazelle, he dashed through the forest, putting aside his fear of things that go bump in the night. Soon, he was sprinting on the main road as if a lion was chasing him.

Detective Chang kept berating himself while driving up Thornbush Lane. Why didn't he figure it out before? The Murray Twins mirror image game finally made him realize the bizarre, ugly truth about Jenna Crandall and the big secret her family had been keeping all these years, although he suspected that her father and sister-in-law were in ignorance. How long had Jenna been this way? He had a feeling quite a while. Why hadn't they taken care of it? Lauren and Diane were so dramatic the day of their mother's attack. Alan kept taking special pains to keep all findings a secret, even going so far as to lie to him. Detective Chang grunted. He wished he'd been more vigilant when Tedesco didn't report to him right away. *I should've known.* He was a by-the-book type of officer. Only this time something went wrong. If anything happened to Bill, he'd never forgive himself or the Crandall's.

He made the turn onto Thornbush Lane. Detective Chang drove for about a tenth of a mile before he spotted the Toyota. He stopped the car. A vehicle on the side of an isolated road like Thornbush was an anomaly around here. Detective Chang stepped out of the car to observe the auto more closely. The car was filthy. It also looked familiar. Could it be Jenna's? No. She would've parked it in front of the farmhouse. Not here where'd she have to hike up the road. The detective frowned. *Jenna drives a Honda.*

He was about to run a check on the license plate when he saw a familiar figure came running towards him at mach speed. Detective Chang gritted his teeth.

Professor Chase. No wonder the Toyota looked familiar. This was his car. Evidently, he was coming from the farmhouse. Of all the . . . He had better have a good explanation.

Malachi was so beyond overjoyed to see Detective Sergeant Chang he didn't care how furious he was going to be once he found out that he was at the farmhouse. Chang would bring safety and order. He stopped running when he reached the spot where Chang was standing. He was gasping.

"What. Are. You. Doing. Here?" Chang asked in the staccato voice he reserved only for those who got on his last nerve. He was too furious to care about Malachi huffing.

Malachi couldn't reply even if he wanted to. He was too busy panting and grateful to God for his narrow escape from danger. Not even a pissed off cop could intimidate him after what he just saw.

"Tell me you're not coming from that farmhouse," Detective Chang said even though he knew that was the case.

Malachi was still panting.

Detective Chang finally took in Malachi's traumatic condition. "What happened to you?"

"J-J-J-Jenna . . . I-I-I—saw . . . " Malachi gulped. His degree in sociology, the courses he took in psychology, not even his experience with hallucinations had prepared him for what he saw at the farmhouse. "Rosa, she's—" He couldn't talk. Malachi shook his head then started sobbing.

Chang took Malachi by the shoulders. He needed the professor to get a hold of himself. "What did you see?"

Malachi groaned. He couldn't talk. His mind was reliving the bizarre sight. Poor Jenna. Yet unknowingly she caused damage and chaos.

Detective Chang released Malachi. He went to his car and grabbed an unopened bottle of water. He returned to Malachi, opened the bottle then handed it to him. The distraught professor began drinking thirstily. "Whoa! Take it easy there, Prof." He was mad, but he didn't want him choking to death either. Malachi slowed down. Chang watched Malachi drink then pause to catch his breath. *What happened up there?*

Malachi looked back down the road from the direction he ran. No sign of Jenna or her evil counterpart. He would know Rosa by her walk. He turned back to Detective Chang. Calm and thirst quenched, Malachi found his voice again. "We've got to get out of here. They'll be coming any minute. I mean she'll be coming. She can't see us. We gotta hide." Malachi started getting hysterical.

"You're talking about Rosa," Detective Chang said gently. He had the feeling that Malachi found out what the Crandall's were hiding about Jenna.

Malachi grabbed Detective Chang by the shoulders. "Jenna *is* Rosa." He started crying again.

"I know," Detective Chang said quietly. He still hadn't digested the information himself. He put his hand on Malachi's shoulder.

"And they . . . I mean . . . she . . . has the officer," Malachi said in between sobs.

"Tedesco's alive?" The detective felt a rush of relief.

"Yeah." Malachi sniffled. He never caught the officer's name on the news so he just assumed he was the same one they were talking about on the news. He wiped away his tears with the sleeve of his raincoat, unaware of the fact that it was already wet. "He needs a doctor."

Chang jumped on the phone.

"What're you gonna do?" Malachi asked.

"Calling for back up and an ambulance."

"You can't," Malachi said.

"Excuse you?"

Malachi knew he had interfered enough already, but desperation for Jenna's safety was starting to make him reckless. He looked down the road again. Still no sign of Jenna. He turned back to Detective Chang who didn't look too thrilled with him right now. "You cops are ill-equipped to handle someone like Jenna."

"Is there no end to your nerve, Professor?"

"You're gonna go into that farmhouse like gangbusters. You might hurt her. I know the way cops *and* civilians regard the mentally ill. They're mean, sarcastic. You look at Jenna and see a perp. I see someone who's broken. She doesn't need to get shot."

"Do I tell you how to run your classroom, Professor? You're lucky I don't charge you with interfering with an investigation. Suppose something happened to you while you were up there playing deputy? When Jenna's in her Rosa persona, there's no telling what she'll do."

"You have to go about it another way," Malachi said.

Detective Chang looked at him askance. "You realize Jenna's wanted for more than one attempted murder."

"But she's two distinct people," Malachi said. "You can't treat her like she's your normal every day perp." He glanced down the road again. All clear. But for how long. He turned back to Detective Chang. "We need a plan. Let's go someplace else and talk."

"Now you're out of your mind," Detective Chang said. "Let's get something straight," Chang began. "There is no *we*. This is official police business. Instead of appointing yourself deputy," he paused to look at Malachi's Toyota, "try washing your car. Why is there so much bird poopie on it after all that rain?"

Malachi hobbled over to the detective's car and leaned against it. Now that his initial fear was ebbing, he was starting to feel the pain in his ankle again. Malachi clenched his teeth. Later he would tell Chang about his little disagreement with the Almighty.

Grudgingly, Detective Chang had to admit the professor had a point. Jenna was mentally unstable. A trained professional should be present. He glanced down the road. They really should leave now. He didn't want to run the risk of having to explain to Jenna why they were there and in the state Malachi was in, he didn't trust how he might act if he saw her again so soon. If it were Rosa, he didn't want to confront her. Not yet anyway. Clearly, Jenna and Rosa "worked together." Like twins.

"Hand me your car keys," Detective Chang said.

"Don't ever call me again."

Jenna trudged up the road. The last words Rosa said to her before finally storming out the farmhouse played repeatedly in her mind. She began sobbing. They had their differences before but never like this. *Rosa's gone. This time for good.* For as long as she could remember it had always been the two of them. Together they defied the world. Now she was going to have to figure out how to exist without her best friend.

She walked like a zombie until she reached the end of the forested path. Jenna was too preoccupied to notice the two sets of tire tracks in the mud . . .

Malachi was sitting in Detective Chang's patrol car on the service road. Behind them sat Malachi's Toyota, which the detective had also parked on the service road since Malachi's ankle was sore. Malachi's anxiety was growing and his sadness was increasing. He never dreamed when he met Jenna on that lovely June afternoon it would lead to this.

He remembered how beautiful she looked in that champagne-colored ball gown . . .

Detective Chang nudged Malachi's elbow, bursting the bubble of his daydream and bringing him back to reality. Jenna was turning off Thornbush Lane. Malachi noted her stride. She wasn't strutting. This was indeed Jenna only she was walking with hunched shoulders.

"The argument didn't end well," Malachi said.

He wanted to race from the car, put his arm around her and make her smile. He wanted to make her well, but he couldn't move. He'd have to explain to her how he and Detective Chang just happened to be on the service road. And Chang would kill him. He was sore at him as it is.

Chang got on his car radio. "Officer down. Send a bus to 61 Thornbush Lane . . . " He made a face. "Yes, the farmhouse. "I'm on my way. And arrest Alan and Diane Crandall. What's that? Nelson Door?" Detective Chang grunted. "Tell him to make himself comfortable. He'll get to meet with me and his in-laws very shortly." He turned to Malachi. "Now I gotta figure out how to keep Jenna away from the farmhouse over the next 24 hours so she doesn't discover Tedesco's not there." He let out a long-suffering sigh. He could only imagine what Tedesco must have been experiencing. If Jenna freaked out Malachi and she's his girlfriend, then what was his officer's emotional state?

"That shouldn't be a problem," Malachi said. "Since she and her second self are at odds, Jenna won't be in a hurry to go back there. That'll buy us some time."

"You've been plural lately."

Malachi wore a tiny smile.

"I have to supervise the ambulance," Chang continued. "I don't want them compromising the crime scene." Once Jenna was at a distance and there was no risk of her being able to identify them, he started the car. Soon they were heading to the farmhouse. Maybe it was a good thing Malachi's car was "disguised." It was less easy for her to recognize. "We'll pick up your car later, Prof. In the meantime, you're going to the ER."

"I don't need a doctor." Malachi winced with pain even as he said it.

"You can ride in the ambulance with Tedesco," Detective Chang said. "After you get treated, you can join me when I meet with the Crandall's at headquarters. Moron."

Malachi smiled. He just made a new friend.

41

They gathered in the interrogation room with Detective Sergeant Richard Chang: Alan, Elise, Diane, Larry, Nelson, Malachi and Julian, who was looking shell-shocked after having just learned the truth about Jenna. Alan was slouching. Diane was staring at the wall, both considering the enormity of what they and their family was about to face. Elise was looking equally as thunderstruck as her father-in-law was. In a corner were a few of Jenna's hideous paintings. With his ankle wrapped in an Ace bandage and elevated on a chair, Malachi repeated his adventure at the farmhouse. Chang already heard it since Malachi explained what happened to him in detail, while they were on their way to the farmhouse to rescue Officer Tedesco. EMT administered first aid before taking the injured officer to the hospital.

An infuriated Chang regarded Alan and Diane with acute disdain. He pinned Alan to the chair with a sharp gaze. "Start. Talking."

"Don't say anything without your attorney," Larry said.

Alan shook his head. "No. No more hiding."

"You're making a mistake, man."

"Larry's right," Nelson said. "He has no right to question you."

The detective blew a sigh of frustration. "Alan, are you sure you want to waive your rights to counsel?" To himself, he was fantasizing

439

about doing something evil to Nelson and Larry. He was in no mood. Yes, Alan did have a right to legal counsel, but Bella, Lauren and Diane were clearly guilty on so many levels.

Alan nodded. "I'm sure. I'm tired."

"Do what you want," Nelson said, "but leave Diane out of it."

"She's up to her armpits in this," Detective Chang said.

"Di, you don't have to answer any questions," Larry said.

"You do realize that Alan and your fiancée are witnesses and that Alan is also a victim, which FYI puts him in a unique position. You can't put whipped cream on a stale pastry and think it's gonna taste better."

Diane began nibbling her bottom lip. "Alan and I were supposed to go to Detective Chang earlier today and tell him the truth. But I chickened out."

There was a pause.

"I'm waiting," Chang said.

Alan straightened in his chair. This was it. No more evasions. This was what he wanted wasn't it? *Just not the way I pictured it.* He took a deep breath then said, "It was a game."

"A game?"

"It started after Jenna turned five," Alan said. "Everything was fine up until then. But one day, Mom just started getting mean. She'd look for any reason to hit us. Especially Jenna." He repeated the accounts that Roscoe the Groundskeeper told Detective Chang. "Mom shook Jenna's head like a rattle. When I stood up for her Mom gave me such a hit in the ear I don't know how I didn't lose my hearing."

"What was that all about?" Detective Chang asked.

"It was Communion Sunday," Alan said. "Jenna was supposed to recite a Bible passage. During rehearsal, she kept flubbing it. I told Mom she should be easier on her. She was just a little kid. That's when I got the right one to the ear."

"Out of curiosity, which passage was it?" Chang asked.

"Proverbs 23: 13-14."

"Figures she'd pick that one," Malachi said. 'Do not withhold correction from a child. For if you beat him with a rod, he will not die. You shall beat him with a rod. And deliver his soul from hell.'"

Elise, who was sitting beside Alan, placed her hand on his shoulder. She was livid as well as dazed. Alan had been lying to her all this time about so many things, but right now, he needed support. She looked over at her father-in-law. What must Julian be going through?

"When Jenna stopped getting affection from Mom, she turned to Lauren and Diane," Alan said. "She just wanted a little bit of their time. Play a silly game. Read her a story. She loves stories. Give her a hug once in awhile. That's what I did. But they kept chasing her away. After awhile, Lauren and Diane discovered that they could use Jenna as a scapegoat. They knew Mom would blame her for anything in a heartbeat."

Diane glared at her brother in spite of her guilt. If only Mom weren't lying comatose and Lauren weren't recuperating from a heart attack, she wouldn't have to face this shame with Alan the Perfect.

"When exactly did Rosa come into the picture?" Detective Chang asked.

"One day, Jenna came home from school all excited," Alan began. "She made a new friend. I was happy for her. There weren't any children her age living on our street.

"Didn't your church have a youth group?" Chang asked as Officer Davidson entered and took a seat in a corner in the unusually crowded room.

"Yeah, but they were older," Alan replied. "And Mom saw to it that Jenna had limited contact with classmates outside of school. Anyway, every day Jenna kept going on and on about Rosa. She was happy in a way that I hadn't seen in a long time. She even stopped needing Lauren and Diane's affection." He gave his twin a nasty look. "I think that bothered them.

"Why?" Chang asked.

"They needed Jenna to need them so they could have an excuse to treat her like garbage or to use her. Alan paused then said, "Mom was curious about Rosa Garrison and wanted to meet her." Alan made a face. "I know she was gonna do everything she could to nip that friendship in the bud."

Julian moaned. The story was painful yet he had to know about the things that had been happening to his child right under his nose.

"One evening," Alan continued, "Mom went to a PTA meeting at Jenna's school. When she came back home, she had this weird look on her face. Turned out that there was no Rosa Garrison in the second grade class. In fact, there was no Rosa Garrison in the entire school. We were all shocked."

"We." Julian's voice was dripping with sarcasm. "I didn't even know about that PTA meeting much less about Jenna's make-believe friend. The first time I heard about her was Diane's engagement. No wonder you were all acting strange." He looked at Chang. "Bella was in a hurry for the whole topic to go away."

"That's another thing," Detective Chang began. "Why was your father kept in the dark?"

"I wanted to tell him," Alan said. "But Mom threatened to beat me. And Jenna. I had to take her seriously. I still have the scars to prove it. Detective, we couldn't tell anyone."

Diane stared at a juice stain on the floor. "Lauren and I weren't allowed to talk about Rosa either."

"She speaks," Detective Chang was sarcastic. "I was wondering what happened to your voice. The supermodel had been noticeably quiet, quite a change from her brazenness. "Did Bella tell Jenna's teacher what Jenna was doing?"

"No, she didn't," Diane answered.

"Your mother ever tell Jenna that she knew that Rosa wasn't real?"

Diane shook her head.

Alan spoke up. "Mom decided to let it play itself out. She was amused. So were Lauren and Diane. I didn't see any harm in Jenna having a pretend friend. Lots of little kids have pretend friends. I thought it was a solution to her loneliness.

"How old were you then?" Detective Chang asked.

Alan gestured to his sister. "We were twelve. Lauren was fourteen."

Julian groaned again. All this time.

"One day, Jenna *brought* Rosa home. See, all along she was just a friend in school. Now Jenna was at home pretending that Rosa was sitting in a chair, say, at dinnertime or standing next to her. Eventually, Jenna created a whole history around Rosa. She had parents and an address."

"The farmhouse," Malachi said. He shivered involuntarily. Witnessing Jenna's illness and his near possibly harmful encounter with Rosa was still fresh in his mind. It was going to be a long time before he'd be able to get that picture of Jenna arguing with herself out of his head.

Alan gave Malachi a knowing look. Someone who wasn't accustomed to seeing Jenna's split personality would be shocked. "It really was harmless in the beginning. Then things took a strange turn. Jenna was almost thirteen and Rosa was still her friend and aging along with her. Rosa even had a boyfriend and her own phone."

Nelson and Larry winced. Things were getting out of hand.

"I kept pointing out the weirdness of it to Mom," Alan said. "But she kept laughing it off. She continued to play along with it and she encourage Lauren and Diane to do the same. Hence, the game. It even became a habit to treat Jenna and Rosa as if they were two people."

The room went silent.

"Mom even made jokes about Jenna *and* Rosa needing to be committed."

Malachi winced. What would they have thought about him if they knew about his narrow escape from mental illness?

Diane glanced at Larry then looked quickly away. *He must feel ashamed of me.* She returned her gaze to the stain on the floor.

"Does Jenna understand that Rosa isn't real?" Detective Chang asked.

"She told me that Rosa was real," Nelson said. Angered, he reminded his brother-in-law about their conversation at the hospital after Lauren wrote that note. "Nightmare," Nelson added scornfully.

Alan winced at the memory. "To Jenna, Rosa is very real." He held his stomach. "She doesn't remember what Rosa does. Only that she did it and only her. I tried to steer Jenna's mind toward reality, but . . . " He sighed.

"It's called dissociative identity disorder," Malachi said. "Jenna created Rosa to protect herself against enemies. It's also common for an abused child to use fantasy, especially when growing up in a dysfunctional home." Like The Enchanted Forest, her other means of channeling her aggravation when she was a little girl.

Until she graduated to bigger things . . .

"Rosa's more than just an imaginary friend," Malachi went on. "She represents the friendships that Bella wouldn't allow her to have. She represents the sister she never had. Rosa also built up Jenna's self-esteem by giving her positive reinforcement, doing the things *Jenna* couldn't do but Rosa could."

"Like projecting anger she denied feeling," Detective Chang said.

"Exactly," Malachi said.

"Like Maura Wynn?" Diane sounded a tad acerbic. Shame was making her revert to bitterness.

Detective Chang groaned. "Tell me that's not another personality?"

Diane shook her head. "She was a classmate Jenna had in high school. Maura used to pick on her all the time. Jenna used to complain about her all the time. Instead of getting Rosa to handle it, she let her have it."

"Meaning?"

"She beat the crap out of her," Alan answered. "That's the one time Jenna ever took on somebody by herself."

Julian grunted angry and humiliated at yet another incident that he was not privy to but Bella, Lauren, Alan and Diane were.

"Never been this violent huh?" Chang asked sarcastically.

Alan shifted in his chair. "Mom was livid and nervous."

"Why?" Detective Chang asked.

"Because Jenna brought attention to herself," Diane said.

Chang nodded. "Of course. That would've meant trouble. By then, she'd been keeping Jenna mentally ill for nearly a decade. "So what happened?"

"She did a number on Maura. The principal suspended Jenna for a week.

"Didn't that put a blot on the Crandall name?" Malachi asked dryly.

"How come no one knew about this?" Detective Chang asked.

"Mom paid the Wynn's off to keep quiet."

Detective Chang raised his eyebrows. "That must've been some pay off."

"Oh, it was," Alan said.

"I don't get it," Nelson said. "Why deny she's pissed off? Jenna shoulda just done something."

"She would've if she was in an environment that allowed her to feel," Malachi said. "Allowed her to have a sense of purpose."

"She got older didn't she?"

"Conditioning a person is a strong effect," Malachi said.

"Brainwashing did this to her?"

Malachi was about to answer but changed his mind. Nelson's ignorance was already getting under his skin and the answer he was about to give him would've been inappropriate in present company.

"So all through high school, not one of Jenna's teachers had a clue that something was off?" Detective Chang asked.

Alan shook his head. "Rosa didn't appear around strangers. Only us."

"Everything seemed okay," Julian said. "So normal. Alan and Jenna were always smiling and laughing every time I came to the house."

Chang drummed his fingers on the table. No wonder Bella could fool her husband so easily. Just have the children display some sugariness and all's well. So many people bought into it as well. Jenna learned how to play pretend from the best. "Alan, you told me that Jenna and Rosa stopped speaking. What was that all about?"

"Jenna made this huge announcement that she was ending her friendship with Rosa," Alan replied. He looked rueful. "She'd been lying all these years."

Chang crossed his arms. "I wonder where she learned to do that?"

"Recently, Mom found out that Jenna and Rosa were still friends," Alan said ignoring the detective's sarcasm. "Neither she, nor my sisters wanted me to know. But I suspected it." He talked about Jenna's behavior at the wedding. "When I questioned Lauren and Diane, they denied it. The day when Diane announced her engagement, I brought up my suspicions about Rosa and that we should tell the proper authorities. Mom threw me out."

"What?" Elise exclaimed.

"I wanted Jenna to get help," Alan said deliberately ignoring his wife. "I was afraid of what Rosa might do now that she was older. The rest is history."

"I can't believe this," Elise began. "Jenna's so meek, so intelligent."

"She's all those things," Malachi said. "But she has a dark side. We all do. It's a question of which side we feed more. Jenna's been feeding her dark side a lot, subconsciously. She could never have separated herself from Rosa. Pardon the pun. She needed someone to look out for her. Someone on the inside." He winced. "Sorry. She needed someone who knew the family dynamics who would fight for her."

"But how did this happen to her?" Elise asked.

"Too many smacks in the head," Officer Davidson commented.

"That and abuse," Malachi replied. "Physical and mental. The isolation. No pals. No boyfriends. It finally pushed her over the edge.

"And Bella was so afraid of the truth coming out she didn't want her to socialize," Detective Chang said. He made eye contact with Diane. "So let me get this straight. Your mother thought she could continue to control the monster she created?"

"Yes."

"I'm adding stupidity to the charges."

Diane held her chin up. "Rosa wasn't dangerous just bratty."

Detective Chang banged his fist on the table. "This case could've been wrapped up from Jump Street and you're gonna cop an attitude?"

Malachi smothered a smile at the pun.

"Your sister set fire to the tool shed and tampered with food. Because of you yo-yo's, I nearly lost an officer and put out an APB on a figment of the imagination." Detective Chang looked from Alan to Diane. "You two are damn lucky that Lauren didn't die." He leaned forward. "And you better pray that your mother wakes up or you'll be lookin' at an even longer jail sentence than the one you're facing now. Same thing goes for Lauren." A speck of his saliva landed on Diane's cheek but she remained still too afraid to wipe it away.

"You must be joking," Larry said.

"You see me laughing?"

Nelson stood up. "Haven't they suffered enough, Detective? All right, in retrospect, they made poor choices. But they're already paying the consequences. The media must be having a field day with the twins' arrest."

"Mr. Door, I realize that your wife and mother-in-law's conditions are delicate. Nevertheless, Lauren is guilty of obstructing justice. As a prosecutor, she should've known better. When she was a kid, she was answerable to her mother. She should've cleaned up her act when she reached the age of maturity and especially when she knew she wanted to practice law. But instead, Lauren kept up this ridiculous, deadly charade. She brought this on herself. Likewise, Bella." Detective Chang looked at Larry. "The same thing goes for Diane."

"This is outrageous," Nelson said.

"No, this is the law."

"We didn't even know about those pictures," Diane wailed.

"You knew what you wanted to know," Detective Chang said. "You sat on your high-handed butts before, during and after the attacks."

"While you're planning to arrest my wife," Nelson began, "just what do you intend to do about Jenna and her . . . *other* half?"

"She'll be dealt with appropriately."

"How?" Nelson asked.

"I ask the questions, Door."

Elise addressed the twins. "You allowed Jenna to go near Bella. She could've murdered her at anytime. Alan, you stood there and watched me invite her into our home."

"We weren't in any danger." Alan sounded expasperated. Miserable, embarrassed and worried about Jenna, he didn't need Elise's nagging. The little boy within was still disappointed his fantasy didn't go as planned. "*Jenna* stayed with us. *Jenna* visited Mom. That part of her is incapable of harm. You and I weren't the enemies. Bella, Lauren and Diane are."

"It still doesn't make it right. You kept this information from me. It was bad enough when you didn't tell me that Bella was abusing you and Jenna and you didn't tell your father. This is even worse."

"Elise," Alan mumbled, "this isn't the time or the place."

"So we know that Jenna only sics her doppelganger on people she hates or feels threatened by," Detective Chang said bringing the conversation back to the topic at hand. "She's no fool. As Rosa, she never left a clue at any of the crime scenes."

Alan broke down. "I tried to make Jenna's life easier. When they were making her feel ugly, I tried to make her feel pretty. I told her she was beautiful way before her first boyfriend did."

Elise put aside her fury and once again reached out and put her hand on his shoulder.

"I bought her gifts," Alan went on. "Art supplies. Toys. I took her for walks. I made her smile. I did the best I could."

An uncomfortable silence followed.

Detective Chang coughed. The debilitating affect of Bella's dominance over Alan was evident. He could only imagine what it must've done to Julian. He stole a glance at the patriarch whose face was all sorrow. Yet, Chang felt annoyed with Julian for allowing these events to occur right in front of him. Or was obliviousness convenient? There were still some unanswered questions. If Bella was so volatile that she was too difficult for even Julian to live with, wasn't that an indication that there was a flaw in her character? Shouldn't he have thought it over carefully before allowing his wife to raise their children? Detective Chang sighed audibly. "Julian, when I came to your office, I suggested the possibility of Bella needing psychiatric help. Have you reconsidered? Her behavior illustrates an individual who's clearly disturbed."

Diane gasped. "Mom is not disturbed? Jenna is."

Silence.

"There's nothing wrong with Mom," Diane said.

"Yes there is," Julian said. "Her actions weren't normal any more than Jenna's." Wearing a contemplative look he added, "Something was troubling her."

Detective Chang looked skeptically at Julian. He wasn't sure if he liked his tone . . .

"The fact still remains Jenna's a psycho," Nelson said.

Malachi gave him a dirty look. "That was uncalled for and insensitive to Julian."

Nelson looked sheepish. "I'm sorry."

"Ms. Crandall," Detective Chang began, "you're close to your mother. Why was she so hard on your brother and younger sister?"

Alan turned his tear-stained face toward her. Diane stared back. She was twisting her engagement ring. For a moment, they stared at each other as if silently communicating the question, *You know?*

Julian was looking as if he wanted to disappear. There was no doubt as to what set off Bella's rage. He didn't want to believe it himself. What he thought they could keep hidden had grown into a toxic monster.

Chang noticed the expressions on the Crandall's faces. A feeling of inevitable destruction was in the air. His instincts were spinning out of control. Julian seemed to be wrestling over something and Alan and Diane, for the first time since he met them were finally behaving like twins as they continued to glance at each other uncertainly. "Now what?"

Silence.

"You mean there's more?" Chang broke into fluent Mandarin.

Malachi was trying hard not to laugh. He didn't have to know the language to know that the detective sergeant was wishing them a wonderful afternoon.

Julian stood up. "I'll take the bullet." He had no choice. So much damage had been done because of too many secrets.

Alan and Diane exchanged glances. What was Dad going to say?

"Kids, everyone," Julian began, "your mother and I have been carrying a secret. "Jenna is not Bella's daughter."

42

"*What?!*" Detective Chang cried.

Officer Davidson whistled.

"Her mother is Amelia Saunders," Julian said. "My former mistress."

Malachi was picking his jaw off the floor. Elise lost the power of speech. Larry muttered a few unrepeatable words in Jamaican patois. Nelson was catching flies. Chang threw his head back and looked up at the ceiling as if he were appealing to God. He straightened then asked, "And when did you intend on telling me this?"

Julian shrugged. "Maybe never. I didn't think it was important."

"Withholding information." A deranged sounding laugh came out of Detective Chang. "I'm gonna lose my badge, I'm gonna lose my badge. 'Cause I'm about to do something I'm gonna regret. I sat in your office what two, three days ago?"

Malachi pretended to cough. This was better than television.

Detective Chang took a deep breath. "So what's the story?"

Julian shifted his cap. "Amelia and I met at a coffee shop. At first, we would just talk. She was young, but mature for her age. Her mother's from Ghana and her father's from London. We didn't—I didn't expect anything to happen. It just did." He hesitated. "Bella and I were having problems in our marriage. I'm not making excuses for my behavior. It's just that Amelia gave me what I couldn't get from my wife. Love, respect.

"I kept Jenna's birth a secret at first. She might've remained one too had Amelia been able to bond with her. Yes, I know it's wrong. Anyway, Amelia couldn't handle Jenna. My girlfriend—"

"Mistress," Elise interjected.

"—Couldn't deal with the demands of motherhood," Julian finished aware of the shot coming from his daughter-in-law. "Even though I was there for her and the baby, it wasn't enough. Not even her parents' support was sufficient." Julian started playing with his cap. "Amelia was young."

"How young?" Elise asked.

"Still in college."

"Please tell me she wasn't a freshman."

"She was a junior, Elise. Give me some credit."

Nelson and Larry exchanged surreptitious glances. They were shocked and appalled but at the same time, they wanted to high-five him.

"Amelia wanted to pursue her education and her career," Julian said. "So, I had to bring the baby home."

"Your wife must've been thrilled," Officer Davidson murmured.

We got into a bitter fight. Needles to say she was enraged but mostly devastated. I didn't blame her. I betrayed her in the worst possible way. She barely spoke two words for weeks."

"Can you blame her?" Elise asked stunned at what she learned about the father-in-law she'd looked up to all these years.

"In the end, Bella and I managed to work things out. At least I thought we did."

"How was she with the baby?" Detective Chang asked.

"Kind and gentle, considering." Julian grew quiet, remembering how Bella used to be with Jenna. "We couldn't tell the children the truth. They were too young. The twins were seven and Lauren was nine.

So we told them we were adopting a baby girl. With the addition to the family we moved from our old place in Rhinebeck to Gordonville."

"I remember our old house," Alan said in a quiet voice. "I loved it."

Guilt showed in Julian's eyes. He remembered how much his son cried the day they moved, but he had to. With a fourth child they needed the space that Haven Road provided. Importantly, he and Bella could make a fresh start. "When Jenna got older, we wanted her to believe that she was part of the family so the word adoption was never to come up. There were no stepmother, stepsister or stepbrother."

"Bella and I talked about telling Lauren, Alan and Diane the truth someday. It came up from time to time about when and how we'd tell Jenna and the other children the truth and whether or not it was even necessary, but before Bella and I could come to any agreement, our marriage began falling apart. The issue never came up again.

"We were fighting about petty things in my opinion. It didn't occur to me that it was due to animosity towards Jenna. I thought it was just me." Julian sighed. "Well, now Alan and Diane know. And the rest of you. That leaves Lauren." He looked at his children. "I'm sorry. It probably sounds lame, but I truly am. I never meant for you to find out about Jenna like this. "When she comes out of the hospital feel free to tell Lauren. I just hope it doesn't overwhelm her. In spite of her hand in this she's been through enough as it is."

Alan and Diane looked uncomfortable.

Detective Chang noticed their reactions but remained quiet.

"In the meantime," Julian went on, "I made an effort to get Amelia involved in Jenna's life, but she wasn't having it. Not even to this day."

Malachi closed his eyes and sighed. First, Jenna's own mother rejected her. Then her stepmother.

Detective Chang thought about his own mother who still fussed over him and his sister. Not every woman is motherly. "This explains Bella's hostility towards Jenna and why she tried to stifle her talent. She's the other woman's child."

454 Debbie Boswell

"Something's not adding up," Officer Davidson said. "Why would Bella be nice to Jenna then after five years suddenly despise her? It doesn't make sense."

Chang tapped his pen on the table. "It does if the little girl starts looking more and more like the other woman." Detective Chang flipped through his notes. "So, let's rehash. Julian, you lied to your children about adopting a child who was, in fact, drum roll please, their very own sister. Meanwhile, your wife and children had been keeping abuse and mental disease a secret from you." "You people are some piece of work."

"We couldn't tell the kids the truth. That would've been inappropriate."

"Oh no," Detective Chang said, his voice dripping with sarcasm. "You wouldn't want to do anything inappropriate. Your family is accustomed to such things."

"Bella promised to love and raise Jenna as if she was her own daughter." Julian glanced at the hideous artwork in the corner of the room. "And that's why," his voice began to crack, "this whole thing is—" Julian lowered his head.

Alan and Diane were fidgeting. Chang's instincts were on fire. He gritted his teeth. "Whatever's on your chest I suggest you spill it."

"I already knew about Jenna," Diane said.

Fortunately, for Julian, a chair was nearby because he dropped right into it. "H-H-How did you know?"

"Mom told Lauren. Then Lauren told me."

"An I knew before Lauren did," Alan said. "I found out by accident, Dad."

"Tell me how, son."

"I was seven, but I didn't understand."

"Dear God. We were still living in Rhinebeck."

"I was playing under the kitchen window," Alan said. "I overheard you and Mom fighting. I climbed up on a milk crate to peek through the window. I saw you holding something in a pink blanket. I thought it was one of Diane's dolls. Then, I heard, How could you do this to me?

How could you bring her into this house? Then Mom started cursing. I didn't want to get caught so I got down and left. None of it made sense to me. In fact, I forgot about it until years later when Diane told me what she knew about Jenna.

"When did your mother tell Lauren?" Julian asked Diane in a strained voice.

When she opened her mouth, Diane sound like a little girl. "When she was starting high school."

Julian stood up again. Part of the reason for relocating was to make a clean slate. New neighbors. No one to question how a baby appeared so suddenly. As far as everyone else was concerned, Bella gave birth almost a year ago. When Julian spoke, his voice was stone cold. "Lauren was fourteen. And she told her twelve-year-old sister."

Diane began to cower.

That voice. Those eyes. Malachi braced himself. Julian looked beyond furious.

As if to confirm his thoughts, the elder Crandall slammed his fist on the table. "Bella had no right to tell Lauren without consulting me."

"Calm down," Detective Chang said.

Julian started pacing the room. "This is an example of how much respect Bella has for me. No matter what I did, she had no right to involve the children in grown up matters. Wait a second." He stopped pacing. He reminded Diane about how she and Lauren ridiculed Jenna about her looks, her job.

Her friendship with Rosa.

"They could only drop hints about it because Elise and I were the only jackasses in the room who didn't know," Julian said. "Now I know why Jenna went off. Bella was controlling my daughter like some kind of . . . Svengali. And you," he pointed to Diane, "were in on it. You were laughing." He looked at his daughter with repugnance.

Diane turned away. There was so much anger in her father's eyes.

"Were you, Bella and Lauren laughing at me too all these years?"

Diane cringed beside Larry. "No, Daddy."

His fury rose like lava from a volcano and before anybody knew what was happening Julian lunged at Diane. Nelson jumped out of the way, as his father-in-law grabbed Diane by the collar of her designer blouse, lifted her bodily off the chair and began slapping her. Diane screamed.

"You find that funny? You find that funny?" He asked her after each audible slap. "Feel what your baby sister felt. "Feel what your brother felt."

"Julian stop!" Elaine cried.

Officers Levi, Vega and Cooper, burst into the interrogation room just as Detective Chang, Officer Davidson, Alan and Larry were pulling Julian off Diane.

"Watch my ankle!" Malachi shouted.

When they were able to wrestle Julian away from a hysterical Diane, Larry swept her into his arms.

Julian glared at Diane while he struggled in Alan and the officers' grasp. "I shoulda done that to you and Lauren long time ago. Maybe you woulda turned out better. You destroyed my baby."

"Get him out of here," Detective Chang ordered.

"I'm okay, I'm okay," Julian insisted.

"You're a wreck," Detective Chang said. "I can't have this on my watch."

Julian went still. "I'm fine." Then, he began to cry.

Alan swallowed. He was reliving that moment from his childhood again when he saw his father in tears after his mother decimated him after another one of their fights.

Detective Chang, Officer Davidson and Alan let him go. Julian straightened his clothes then sat down again. Elise picked up his cap, which fell on the floor during the melee and handed it to him along with a tissue from her purse.

Nelson returned to his seat.

The detective signaled to Levi, Vega and Cooper to leave. "I can only imagine how you feel, Julian. But no matter what Bella promised you, in the end she couldn't look at Jenna without feeling resentment. That little girl was a living, breathing reminder of your betrayal."

Elise spoke up. "As a married woman, I can understand Bella's pain, but to take it out on two little kids . . . And why Alan? He was her own son."

"Think," Malachi said. He winced from the pain in his ankle as he adjusted his sitting position. "Julian committed adultery. Therefore, in Bella's mind, all men are scum. Alan was a little boy, who someday was going to grow and break some woman's heart like his father did."

Officer Davidson groaned. "Seriously? Then why didn't she get along with Elise since the male species is so bad."

Detective Chang rolled up his sleeves. "Don't you get it? It wasn't enough that she tried to rob Alan of his manhood. Elise made him happy. He didn't deserve that."

"Bella's always been so strong," Julian said. "So independent. I can't believe my wife was unstable."

"The ones who act the toughest are often the ones who need the most help," Malachi said.

"Why didn't Bella just get Jenna some psychiatric help?" Elise asked. "Why make it escalate?"

"For the same reason she kept her cut off from people," Detective Chang replied. "A doctor would've figured out what was going on."

"Bella's fury, cockeyed as it is, makes sense," Julian said. "But what about you, Diane? What were you and Lauren's excuse? Your mother forced you not to mention Rosa, but I didn't hear you say she made you torture Jenna."

"Mom didn't tell us to do what we did."

"Then why'd you do it?"

Diane stared at her father. Larry's eyes remained fixed on Julian, ready to shield her from him in case he suddenly decided to go on the attack.

"And when you're done you can tell me why you picked on Alan. Your twin brother."

Diane stared down at her father's work shoes.

"Or did you and Lauren just pick on them because you could?"

"What's the significance of the meadow?" Detective Chang asked. Diane deserved the dressing down, but he needed to move on with the interrogation. "I already know that Thornbush Lane was Rosa's address, if you will."

"She loved to play there when she was a little girl," Julian said, glad to know the answer to something that pertained to his youngest daughter.

"She also played there with Rosa," Alan said. "She didn't start hanging out at the farmhouse until high school. "She liked to do her artwork there too."

"Then what was all this talk about Hudson?" Malachi asked.

"Remember I said Jenna invented a life for Rosa? When she allegedly ended their friendship, she told us she that moved there."

"Oh, this just keeps getting better and better," Nelson said in a deadpan tone.

Detective Chang shook his head. "Amazing. Ms. Crandall, you all stood there and watched an abused and clearly disturbed little girl grow into an even more disturbed woman talking into a cell phone to an invisible entity. Tell me something, what was Mommy's grand master plan for when she departed from this world? For one of you geniuses to look after Jenna? Or did she think she was too important to die?"

Malachi had a flashback of Norma Beery praising Bella. "You may have a point. She's so magnanimous."

"What's the deal with all this charitable giving with you?" Detective Chang asked.

"We just like to do nice things," Diane said in a small voice.

Alan sneered. "Why don't you tell them about the charity you, Mom and Lauren donate to the most?"

Diane began to cry softly.

"Lay off her," Larry said. "Can't you see she's upset?"

"Tell them, Diane," Alan demanded.

"The National Institute for Mental Health," Diane said tearfully. "Happy now? Everybody knows you're the good boy now."

Alan glared. "Do not call me boy."

"All right," Larry began. "We've established the fact that Jenna got a raw deal, but she still did some crazy stuff."

Nelson stood up. "Larry's right. And she's not completely crazy. She meant to kill Bella. Then she returned to work like nothing happened. I can just see her at the reception desk with eyes like pinwheels." Nelson caught Malachi glaring at him. "Oh, come on, Chase. She let snakes loose in my suite. That psycho belongs in a rubber room."

"That's my daughter you're referring to," Julian said.

"Again, I'm sorry," Nelson said. "I meant no disrespect."

Malachi got up then hobbled over to Nelson. "That *psycho* was created by your wife and your sisters-in-law."

"Don't try to flip the script. Jenna even lied to you."

"To protect her friend. Her alter ego."

"She should be dealt with. And in case you didn't get it the first time, Jenna *is* Rosa."

"I was the one who saw my girlfriend come apart right before my eyes, you bozo."

"You still have feelings for her?"

"Yeah. And it's no more stranger than your feelings for that mean, nasty, callous, manipulative—"

"Watch it," Nelson interrupted. "That's my wife you're talking about."

Malachi grinned sardonically. "Ha! You knew I was taking about Lauren. Why is that?"

Nelson muttered under his breath. Julian didn't get defensive with Malachi when he took a verbal swipe at Lauren, his daughter. *And my wife.*

Chang held up his hands. "Gentlemen, Jenna's a victim who's also criminally insane. She needs help."

Nelson scowled. "She's beyond help."

"You don't know that," Malachi said.

"What's the plan, Sarge?" Davidson asked.

Chang pulled a handkerchief from his breast pocket and wiped his forehead. He had no clue. He only knew that the Crandall's were going to drive him crazy too.

43

Jenna was almost at Alan and Elise's house. She loved her brother dearly and Elise treated her just like a big sister, but right now, she just wanted to be alone to brood. There was no more Rosa. This time it was for real. She had to collect herself, put her game face on before she reached the house. Otherwise, they were going to bombard her with well-meaning, albeit intrusive questions. *What's the matter, Jenna? Wanna talk?*

No. She wouldn't want to talk. How could she tell them about her argument with Rosa? Having to admit that she'd been secretly keeping a friendship with her family's nemesis all this time would've led to an explanation that she didn't want to go into right now, not to mention how insane Alan would've gotten. Of course, Elise would've had a barrage of questions. Jenna moaned. It didn't help that Detective Chang had Rosa as a person of interest.

Later, Jenna stopped at a convenience store. She browsed the aisles, stopped to look through some paperbacks on a bookrack. Anything to delay going home.

"What is there to figure out?" Nelson asked. He was completely flabbergasted at the direction in which the conversation was taking.

Everybody except for Larry was making Jenna out to be a pathetic soul instead of dangerous individual. "Arrest Jenna. She's guilty."

"It's not that simple," Detective Chang said. "We're dealing with someone who has two personas. *Jenna* hasn't done anything. Rosa's the dominant character. "She's the one we need to apprehend. That's why I have to handle this delicately. As soon as the public gets wind of this, there'll be defense attorneys lined up and salivating to take this case, especially when your brother and sister-in-law's childhood comes out."

Nelson groaned. "Can we keep this out of the papers?"

Detective Chang stared at the film producer, wondering if he should charge Nelson for being an ass or just hurt him really badly and get himself indicted for police brutality. *But why should I lose my job and my pension for this joker?*

Officer Davidson, Elise and Julian, who had grown quiet since his outburst, were all looking at him in bewilderment. Detective Chang caught Malachi eyeing Davidson's gun then looking at Nelson and then looking at Davidson's gun again.

"Professor," Chang said in a warning tone.

"I wasn't gonna do it."

"What?" Nelson asked. He looked around the room. "We already have to deal with the disgrace of the twins' arrest. I can see it now, 'Alan and Diane Crandall, blah blah blah brother and sister-in-law to noted film producer Nelson Door, arrested for withholding information in connection to the suspicious attacks etcetera etcetera . . . 'right before they go into who was *really* behind the attacks."

"Your sympathy is overwhelming," Elise said sarcastically. He and Lauren were perfect for each other.

"Getting Jenna into custody is paramount," Detective Chang said. "Whatever happens after that, Mr. Door," Chang went on, "I have no control over."

Detective Chang looked at Diane. "It doesn't look good for you. But you already knew that."

Diane closed her eyes and prayed that when she opened them again she would wake up in her master suite in her upper West Side condo and find that this whole thing was a bad dream; but, when she opened her eyes, she was still in the interrogation room of the Gordonville Police Department.

"Jenna's no innocent bystander," Larry said.

"Weren't you listening to Alan?" Elise asked. "And what about what Malachi saw at the farmhouse?"

Nelson sighed. "We all heard it. It just proves my point. Jenna's been entertaining evil thoughts about her family causing her to manifest . . . that . . . that . . . entity. She needs to be put away."

"From what Malachi saw," Detective Chang began ignoring Nelson. "She's coming apart." He winced at his unintentional pun. "She's struggling to be good, but her rebellious side wants to punish everyone who's ever wounded her."

"Jenna must be wondering where we are by now," Elise said. "One of us is usually home by this time."

"That's true," Alan said.

Chang looked squarely at Alan. "Call her. No one's going home until we figure this out."

"Oh so now it's we?" Malachi said.

Detective Chang scowled in reply.

Alan brightened. "So Diane and I aren't going to jail?"

"I'm releasing you on your own recognizance."

Elise rubbed the bridge of her nose. They were going to have to answer these charges later, Lauren and Bella as well, assuming she lived.

Jenna was just a block away from her brother's house when her cell phone started ringing. That was Alan's ringtone. Now was not a good time. She let the call go to voicemail. The fight left her feeling strained. She didn't trust her voice. It might come out sounding worried. She had to prepare herself, get her game face on for when she got home. Alan had this ability to pierce through her with questions. That was okay when she was five, but she was thirty-two now and that approach was sometimes invasive.

Alan frowned. "She's not picking up. That's not like her." He had already called the house and there was no answer. He was thinking about what Malachi said about the quarrel at the farmhouse. "She's never had a major fight with Rosa before. She must really feel lost."

Nelson moaned. "Stop enabling her. This is how this whole mess got started. Jenna is arguing with herself. There is no Rosa."

Julian was struggling to keep his emotions in check. He couldn't lose his temper again as he did earlier with Diane, but it was hard. Nelson was acting like a jerk. He removed his mechanic's cap then started turning it around in his hands. "Alan, do you think she went to the meadow?"

"It's possible."

Malachi's breathing became shallow. Where was Jenna? Did anything happen to her? The old you-could-be-lying-in-a-ditch somewhere his parents used to use on him played in his mind. If anything happened, they would've known by now.

"Let's pray," Malachi suggested. He didn't plan on it. It just came up. He didn't know what to do or what to think. He needed encouragement from a greater Source.

And ideas.

"This is no time for a revival," Nelson said.

Malachi counted to ten. Nelson keeps acting like a butthead. "Praying can't hurt. It can only help.

Nelson snorted refusing to accept the fact that Jenna's condition wasn't her fault. The effect his words may have had on Julian didn't faze him. His anger at Jenna for nearly causing Lauren's death overshadowed his ability to feel compassion for his father-in-law.

"Are you forgetting," Nelson continued, "about separation of church and state? This is a government building in case you haven't noticed, *Dr. Chase.*"

Malachi's voice came out slow and quiet. "Separation of church and state means freedom to worship whatever way you choose. The founding fathers never meant for us to deny God although it is your choice to do so."

"Gonna preach a sermon now?"

"Yeah, I'll give you a sermon." Malachi held up his hands in worship. "Heal my foot, oh, Lord, so I could kick this guy's behind."

"Guys," Detective Chang began, "this isn't the time to—"

"Where was God when Jenna was causing all this chaos?" Nelson asked interrupting the detective. "She nearly killed her half-sister. Who knows what's going to happen to her stepmother?"

"SHUT UP!"

Malachi's loudness sent officers once again bounding into the interrogation room.

"It's all right," Chang said waving his hand in resignation. It was easier to let Malachi and Nelson get the testosterone out of their systems.

"How come you didn't ask God where He was when Bella, Lauren and Diane were tormenting Jenna and Alan?" Malachi asked.

The other officers left. Mesmerized by Malachi's diatribe, however, Officer Vega remained.

Detective Chang thought about his mother. She would've enjoyed this.

Malachi addressed the room. "Let's join hands."

Alan was the first to take Malachi's hand. Then, Elise took his. She didn't look at him, but Alan felt her love and support. The relief he was feeling at that moment was indescribable. Afterward, Julian took Elise's hand. Encouraged by her twin, Diane reached out her hand to her father. Julian looked at it then at her before finally taking her hand. Seeing that his fiancée was participating, Larry sighed then joined them. Officer Davidson looked at Detective Chang, shrugged then the two of them moved to join them around the table. At the same time, Officer Vega came over. She took Detective Chang's hand in hers. For a moment, they looked at each other. Malachi began to pray.

Nelson stood by watching in astonishment.

Malachi took a bite of his pepperoni pizza. He was grateful that Detective Chang ordered in. Pizza, drinks, and a garden salad for Diane. Guess she still had to watch her figure no matter what was happening. They were trying to devise a plan to catch Rosa. Tempers were still hot, but at least they weren't at each other's throats. Diane was adding some salt and pepper to her salad. Malachi began chewing slowly. The more he thought about it, the more it made sense; however, Larry wasn't going to like it.

"I got it," Malachi said. He took a drink of grape soda.

"I'm listening," Detective Chang said.

"We use Diane as bait."

Larry stood up nearly knocking over the drinks on the table. He questioned Malachi's sanity, before cursing him and his idea in Jamaican Patois. To which Malachi responded in Trinidadian Creole. He knew he was reverting to his old nature, but he was too angry to care. He realized that Larry wasn't going to be happy with this idea, but there was no reason to be rude.

Julian smiled for the first time that afternoon. He didn't know what Malachi said. He was just glad to see his future hoity-toity son-in-law put in his place.

Detective Chang held up his hand for silence. "Enough. Time was of the essence and there's been way too much fighting. "Larry, sit. Professor, speak in the King's English please."

"We tell Jenna that Diane ratted out Rosa to Detective Chang," Malachi said. "That'll put Jenna on edge. She'll go to the farmhouse and," he made air quotes with his index fingers, "tell Rosa. While Jenna's en route, she'll transform into her counterpart. Or maybe it'll happen while she's there. I don't know. All I know is that's how we catch her."

Chang gave Malachi a look. "Again with the *we*?"

"I still don't see it," Nelson said. "Why the elaborate ruse? Why not arrest Jenna and be done with it?"

Malachi picked off a pepperoni from his pizza and ate it while at the same time marveling at Sir Brags-a-Lot, his new nickname for Nelson. The man was a case study. How many times did they have to explain this? Malachi wiped his mouth with a napkin. "Rosa is the culprit." His tone was patronizing. "She's the character who committed the crime and who can answer the questions. Jenna won't remember doing any of it."

"How can you be sure Jenna will go to the farmhouse?" Larry asked. "And how do you know she won't go after Diane?"

"Because Jenna's not vindictive," Malachi replied. Rosa is. Besides, Diane's not involved in this. We're just using her name to lure Jenna and Rosa out, if you will." Malachi turned to Detective Chang. "Jenna will run, not walk, to the farmhouse. Of course, a professional will be on hand to deal with them . . . her."

Detective Chang gritted his teeth. He just loved the way Professor Chase was taking over.

"So far, Malachi's plan makes sense," Officer Davidson said.

"The hell it does!" Larry cried.

Malachi put his head on the table and prayed for strength.

"Look, I'm sorry if I'm not jumping with enthusiasm," Larry said. "But Jenna's story, unfortunate as it is, doesn't change anything. Diane is in danger as long as she's at large."

Chang leaned back in his chair. Annoying as he is, Larry had a right to be concerned for his fiancée's safety. He didn't want to add Diane to the list of casualties. Bella was still in a coma, Lauren was recovering from a near-fatal heart attack and Officer Tedesco was recovering from head injuries, dehydration and trauma. On the other hand, he wasn't going to use a civilian in a sting operation.

Chang glanced at a very subdued Julian. To find out about almost three decades of duplicity in one afternoon was beyond devastating. To have to reveal his indiscretion to his children only to find out that they knew about it all along was beyond reason. He couldn't tell the agonized man about the possibility of losing Jenna if a gun battle were to take place. Chang looked over at Malachi. Julian wasn't the only who was going to be a wreck . . . Then there was the fallout. They would take Jenna into custody. Gordonville and the rest of the world were going to know about everything. If Nelson thought the media was lapping up the news about Alan and Diane's arrest, wait until they find out about his wife's family secrets. A three-ring circus couldn't be more entertaining.

Chang exhaled slowly. "All right. We'll do it but with some modifications."

Larry put his hand on his forehead. Was there no one with an ounce of reason in this room?

Detective Chang looked from Alan to Elise. "Your place will be perfect. In fact, I'm gonna use you two to lead Jenna."

"Prof, I know it's your baby, but you have no part in this plan. I'm running this show. No. Playing. Deputy. Got it?"

Malachi wore a frozen smile. "Yes, Detective." Just like that, he lost control of his brainchild. He had visions of rescuing Jenna. Alan and Elise get to participate. *I would've gladly taken any role in the plan. My plan.*

"There's no way in hell I'm allowing you to use Diane as a decoy," Larry said.

Detective Chang raised his eyebrows.

"Suppose something goes wrong?" Larry asked.

"It won't," Chang said ignoring a renewed inner sense of discomfort rising within him. Belmar's pessimism was starting to get to him. He couldn't allow that. "For the umpteenth time, Diane won't be there. We're just using her name. Now let me do my job."

"I don't blame you, Lar," Nelson said. "Look at what Jenna's done. Or whatever she calls herself."

Malachi rolled his eyes. *You backed away when Julian was going after Diane.* "It's a good plan. Just hearing Diane's name will draw out the alter ego like a moth to a flame."

Larry glared. "You're all about anything that makes Diane and her family look like villains and your girlfriend look like the victim."

"That isn't what I meant and yes Jenna is a victim."

Nelson smirked. "Says the one with the nutty girlfriend."

"Who happens to be my daughter," Julian said his voice ragged. He glowered at Larry who was behaving equally as obnoxious towards Jenna.

"You just don't like her," Malachi said slowly and deliberately. He refused to let Nelson slide by easily.

Julian looked daggers at Nelson. The news shouldn't have come as a shock yet it did. Nelson's disrespect for Jenna had been obvious—if he'd bothered to look deep enough. Now some of the subtleties of the past made sense. The monosyllabic answers when she tried to make conversation. The refusal to make eye contact. Looking bored when Jenna was present.

Nelson looked at his father-in-law, who was looking back at him. His face was showing the obvious pain and betrayal he was feeling. Nelson wanted to tell him not to listen to Malachi that it was all a lie, but he couldn't.

Nelson turned to Malachi with an angry look. *You outed me.*

Malachi simply shrugged.

"I wouldn't have agreed to this if I didn't think it would work," Detective Chang said.

"Well, find another plan," Larry said.

Elise checked her watch. "It'll be sunset soon. We still haven't heard from Jenna and we have to visit Bella and Lauren at the hospital."

"Jenna can't go anywhere near Lauren or Bella."

Alan groaned. Tired of Nelson's cluelessness, he said, "For crying out—First, Lauren was living with Jenna way before you or Larry came into the picture. Two, Jenna's not going to be in a visiting mood and three, Rosa's not an idiot. If she wanted to bump off Lauren or Bella, she'd never do it in front of people."

In a beaten tone, Diane said, "I guess Malachi's plan is the only way."

Larry's eyes widened. "Julian, say something nuh mon?" Desperation caused him to revert to Jamaican patois. He couldn't believe Diane's father would encourage his daughter in this crazy scheme. Diane was acquiescing to this crazy scheme out of guilt.

Julian stretched his legs. He wasn't sure who to be angrier with, himself or Bella. Back then, Lauren and Diane were two little girls just following their mother and Bella was a poor, yet supreme role model.

She knew how to get their daughters to follow her. By the time Lauren and Diane were adults, they were as callous as their mother was. In addition, Bella was a fantastic actor. She tricked him into believing she was content with Jenna. She deceived him about Jenna and Alan's happiness. Were there clues staring him in the face and he just missed them or did he see what satisfied him? Did he not want to look beneath the surface? Like his wife and elder daughters, did he choose not to acknowledge that there was a problem?

Julian sighed. He couldn't blame Alan for not informing him. He was just a boy at the time. As a man, he felt trapped. He certainly couldn't fault Jenna. She was even younger than her stepbrother was and was even more vulnerable. Lord knows the two of them were living a nightmare."

He looked over at Diane. Even with a broken spirit she somehow, managed to pull off that chic magazine look. She wasn't nearly as broken as Jenna was. Her half-sister.

Julian sighed again. "Sorry to disappoint you, Larry, but I support it. I have faith in Detective Chang. He knows what he's doing."

Chang nodded in appreciation. "The basic pitch of Malachi's plan is good."

Malachi beamed. "Did you hear what he called it? *Malachi's Plan*."

"Well, bully for you," Larry said, furious that Julian wouldn't back him up. "You're really gonna make your daughter go through with this?"

Detective Chang swore. "For the first time in her life, Diane can do something right by Jenna. It may even be her last time."

The room became deadly silent.

The expression on Malachi's face was one of disbelief. Just moments ago, he was on a high, so proud of himself for coming up with a solution. His elation was gone, sending him crashing down to earth. Even with a professional on sight, it never occurred to him that Jenna's life might still be in danger.

Detective Chang swore. He wanted to kick himself. He never meant to reveal that. Like Julian and Malachi, he allowed his emotions to get the better of him. He knew better. "I'm sorry."

"You're sorry?" Larry's face had incredulity stamped across it. "You can't promise to protect Diane from Jenna."

Detective Chang pounded the desk. *Lord, give me the strength not to kill him.* "It's not about Diane. It's about Jenna whose worth just as much as her famous sister and anyone else's in this room. I don't know what my team and I may be facing." He glanced at Malachi. "Rosa is crazed and dangerous." Next, the detective turned to Julian. "I'm sorry. I really am."

Julian saw the sincerity in the lawman's eyes. He also felt his reproach. *This catastrophe wouldn't have happened if I had been a more attentive father.* The idea of losing Jenna . . . He didn't want to go there. "Detective . . . please."

Chang knew what the aggrieved husband and father was trying to say. *Save my daughters.*

Detective Chang looked at Julian and nodded.

Jenna was walking down Maple Street, a tree-lined block around the corner from her brother and sister-in-law's home on Donnelly Drive. Some of its residents were on their front porches, mowing their lawns, walking their dogs. Jenna waved to them as she walked by. To her surprise, some were giving her pitying looks. Others were smiling sadly or were avoiding having to look at her altogether.

Jenna frowned. What's going on?

When she arrived on Donnelly Drive, she stopped. A swarm of reporters standing in front of Alan and Elise's house. Jenna looked around. Just like on Maple Street, some of the neighbors were looking at her uneasily. Everyone seemed to know something except her. Immediately, Jenna became tense. She suddenly remembered the phone call. Did something happen to Daddy? Alan?

Malachi . . . ?

Her stomach started churning. She couldn't bear to lose them. Rosa taught her to remain calm and to think. Jenna took a deep cleansing breath, then continued walking towards the house.

A female reporter for the Gordonville Gazette spotted Jenna first the minute she arrived at the scene. "What do you have to say about your brother and sister's arrest?"

Stunned by the question, Jenna barely noticed the reporters beginning to flock around her.

They arrested Alan? Which sister did they arrest? It must've been Diane since Lauren was still in the hospital unless the authorities had a reason for handcuffing a cardiac victim. She tried not to smile. Despite the situation, she was getting excited picturing Lauren handcuffed to the hospital. The thrill soon left her, however, when the reporters began firing questions.

"What do you think your siblings knew about the attack on your mother and sister?"

"Were they involved?"

"What does the arrest of your brother and sister mean for your family?

"What are you talking about?" Jenna shouted above the din.

"You mean you don't know?" A male reporter for a cable network asked.

Jenna looked at him fiercely. "No. I don't know." The man's snarky voice stood out above the mayhem. She looked him over from head to toe. He reminded her of Nelson and Larry. He was good looking and he knew it.

That was irritating.

"Alan and Diane were arrested for obstructing justice," The dapper reporter said. He smirked. "Evidently, they knew something."

Jenna gasped. She was too shocked to concern herself with the obnoxious reporter. This must've been why Alan was calling. Of all the times for her not to have picked up. This was bad. Very bad. What was Detective Chang thinking? Now, her only concern was for Alan. He may have been annoying lately, but he was still her brother. They had a special bond. He had always been there for her even at his own risk. How was she supposed to get him out of this jam without incriminating

Rosa and herself? The thought of her glamorous sister sitting in a jail cell made her believe that maybe there really was justice in the world.

She felt the tension building up inside her as she stared at the ambitious reporters. Their voices talking all at once were cacophonous. What was she supposed to say? Jenna looked around at the newscasters and the camera crew. She could only imagine how foolish she must've looked on national television. Jenna turned back to the well-groomed reporter. He smirked as he waited for her to respond. For a moment, she envisioned doing to him what Rosa did to Officer Tedesco. Jenna put her hands to each side of her temples. *Don't go there. Think.*

That's when Jenna noticed the space between some reporters. She dashed through them past the throng and ran for the front door. She rang the bell frantically. Behind her cameras were flashing and reporters were still mercilessly firing questions. There was no answer. Of course, Elise was at police headquarters with Alan. Jenna started fishing for her keys in her handbag. Cameras continued flashing. It was taking forever for her to find her keys. Why did she bury them so far? Frustrated, she began to sob. She just wanted to get inside and away from the hungry media.

Finally, Jenna found the keys. She unlocked the door, rushed inside, slamming the door closed behind her. She stood panting in the foyer. She could hear the muffled voices of the reporters outside. Jenna hit the wall with her fist and started sobbing again. If Diane was incarcerated, that meant she and Rosa argued over nothing.

Officer Vega entered the interrogation room. "Sarge, you're gonna wanna see this. Them too."

On the television in the squad room was footage of Jenna surrounded by a flock of reporters.

"That's just great," Detective Chang said.

"It's a wonder she's not attacking the reporters," Larry said.

Detective Chang grunted. Larry had a point. The reporters were unknowingly provoking Jenna. That can't be good. The last thing he needed was for her to morph into Rosa on national television, blowing the cover off his case. It wasn't time for the whole world to know about Jenna and the Crandall's secrets before he closed the cases. "I better get them out of there before all hell breaks loose."

"I got Jenna on line 2," Officer Levi called out.

Chang instructed Alan, who he brought with him into his office, to take the call. He was going to put her on speaker. No doubt, Jenna was confused and upset after being hounded by reporters and hearing about Alan and Diane's arrest. Talking to her brother would calm her down. After the afternoon he's had, he was liable to be nervous. "Don't give any indication that you know that she's been hiding Rosa from you all these years. And more than ever, I want you to relax."

"Right." Alan cleared his throat. He was only talking to his sister. This should be a piece of cake. He took the phone from Detective Chang. "Hey, Jen." He couldn't believe how nervous he was feeling.

"Alan." Jenna breathed a sigh of relief. "Are you all right?"

"I'm okay."

"Wait a minute. How come they put me through to you? Why aren't you in holding cell?"

" . . . Uh, yeah . . . they're letting me to speak to you . . . Why?" Alan looked over at Chang.

The detective scribbled, 'a misunderstanding,' on a notepad. Jenna's quick-wittedness was something they needed to take into consideration. It was going to be much more acute when she became Rosa again.

"It was all just a misunderstanding," Alan said. His voice was raised an octave. "They're going to release us . . . yes, Diane too . . . " He cringed.

Likewise, Detective Chang. Detective Chang began tapping the pen on the desk. Jenna had a potty mouth. Already she may be transforming.

"Be nice, Jenna," Alan said. "She's our sister . . . Reporters are at the house?" Alan feigned shock as he kept up his end of the conversation. "I'll tell Detective Chang. He'll handle it."

After he dispatched officers to Donnelly Drive to clear the premises, Detective Chang asked the others to join them in his office briefly. "Remember any interaction with Jenna is to remain normal. She's astute. So behave as if you know nothing about her condition. Quarrel or no quarrel I don't want to take the chance of Jenna tipping off Rosa, if you will."

Recalling Diane's goofy behavior at the hospital the last time she was in Jenna's presence, Elise, Malachi and Alan hoped she was listening.

Afterward, Chang dismissed everyone except for Alan and Elise with whom he carefully went over the details of their roles in the plan in his office. In addition to their lines, they were to act as if it were any other morning.

"Now you're both clear on what you're gonna do?" Detective Chang asked.

"Yes," Alan replied.

Diane nodded.

The detective sergeant spent time with the couple going over what to say and what to do around Jenna. She may be family, but their feelings could get in the way. They had to act natural.

"And when are you going to say the lines we rehearsed?"

"Tomorrow when Jenna comes down for breakfast," Alan replied.

"And I will back anything Alan says, but without sounding fake," Elise said.

"And we'll call you the moment she leaves," Alan said. "If she leaves."

"Trust me," Detective Chang said. "She will."

44

Elise pulled up to the house. All was quiet, the reporters having been long gone, although the neighbors were probably peeping through their windows for any signs of activities at their home. They certainly got an eyeful today with that throng of reporters. The tongues that must've been wagging when the police handcuffed Alan and put him into the patrol car in front of their home. Elise started clenching and unclenching her hands. How could they ever show their faces around the neighborhood again? At the supermarket? *And Church?* Reverend Brooks was probably trying to get in touch with them.

She felt like someone else while she was driving to headquarters to find out the reason for her husband's arrest. This nightmare couldn't be happening to us, but when she saw Diane at headquarters in handcuffs, her jaw dropped. They arrested her illustrious sister-in-law at The Lorelei House. How humiliating. It couldn't have been much fun for the proprietor either.

She stared out the car windshield at the darkness. The nightmare was just beginning. Her in-law's scandal was about to come out. Today's arrest was just the tip of the iceberg. She couldn't begin to think about what this might mean to her job at Gordonville Elementary. Elise sighed. "I remember when we planted our herb garden."

Alan exhaled. *She's speaking.* He didn't know where the conversation was going. *The important thing is that she was saying something.* During the drive home, Elise had suddenly become silent. He was grateful for her support while he was at headquarters. He didn't know for how long he and Diane were going to be free. They were still guilty of obstruction. Even he had to admit that Lauren wouldn't have almost died had they just did the right thing.

He studied his wife's profile. She finally knew the truth. It felt as if someone had lifted a great weight from off his shoulder. Keeping the family's secrets had become too big a burden to carry; however, he didn't want Elsie to find out this way. Just like his father, she found out everything in a very horrible way. He didn't even know that his sisters knew about Jenna's parentage.

"We had brunch at Delsey's after church," Elise said, interrupting Alan's thoughts. "Afterward, we came back and planted basil and cilantro."

"Then you decided that the garden was sparse so you made me drive to the nursery and buy more herbs," Alan added.

Elise smiled, touched that he remembered. Then, recalling that she was still upset with him, she stopped smiling. "Life made so much sense back then. Even up until the moment the police showed up at our door, I thought I knew your family. I just knew something was off. Alan, you had so much opportunity to talk to me about this." She choked back tears. "This really hurts."

"I know and I'm sorry." He explained his reasons for not wanting to tell her before telling his father. "I wanted Mom, Lauren and Diane to do the right thing. Then it just came down to Lauren and Diane."

"Was it entirely up to them?"

Alan closed his eyes and leaned his head against the headrest.

"Look, I get it. You've been passive. But you're also analytical. And tough. And brave. You're a survivor. Otherwise, you couldn't have gotten through all this. Even Jenna has some of your qualities. Disassociative disorder notwithstanding." She sighed gain.

"Ready for tomorrow?" Elise asked wanting to move on.

"Yes and no."

"You'll be fine," Elise said.

Finally, they went inside. Before leaving the car, Alan and Elise reminded each other to act natural around Jenna; however, when they entered the kitchen, they stopped short. Their faces dropped. Jenna was making herself a cup of tea. The irony of watching her pouring hot water from a kettle into a mug was creepy.

Jenna looked at them askance. "Everything okay?" She saw when they pulled up and knew that they had been out in the car. She had been peering at them through the shutters and had concluded that Elise was lecturing poor Alan.

They had to pull themselves together. They were taking too long to respond. "Everything's fine," Alan said. He and Elise greeted her with big smiles and hoped that they were covering for their initial uneasiness.

Jenna put the kettle back on the stove. She blew into her mug then took a sip. The peppermint tea felt soothing going down. "So what happened?"

Elise adjusted her handbag strap. She could empathize with her husband. To look into the face of evil was daunting to say the least. Moreover, the way Jenna was staring at them was giving her the creeps. Her eyes held just the slightest tinge of leeriness. *Or maybe I'm just being paranoid because she knew about the real Jenna? More likely because Alan didn't answer right away. He was* rubbing his stomach. *Big mistake.* They had to think of something to say . . . fast.

Elise smiled evenly. "Detective Chang was upset with Alan and Diane for withholding information about the case." She hoped she sounded natural.

Jenna took another sip of peppermint tea. "What kind of information?"

"Secrets," Alan said after finding his voice again. Detective Chang prepped them for tomorrow morning's ruse. They didn't cover anything about answering direct questions from Jenna. Still, she asked a simple question. It shouldn't have freaked him out yet it did.

"What secrets?" Jenna asked.

"Mom's abuse, me not telling him about Rosa."

Jenna looked at Alan in disbelief. It sounded like a trumped up charge. A maneuver to make the detective sergeant look good. Jenna turned to open a jar of honey that was on the kitchen counter then added a teaspoon of it to her peppermint tea. *Why didn't he arrest me on the same charge?* She was about to ask when she suddenly grew apprehensive. Talking about Mom's abuse was no big deal, but talking about Rosa was. She still cared about Rosa even if they weren't speaking. She'd rather go to jail than Rosa. *I can't ask if Detective Chang mentioned Rosa. Not in front of Elise.*

"How are you doing, Jenna?" Elise asked. "Heard you had a tough time with some reporters."

Jenna stirred her tea then tasted it. Perfect. "I'm okay now." She took another sip. "Alan, would you mind if I don't go with you guys to the hospital?"

"No."

Elise groaned to herself. Alan responded a little too quickly. She hoped Jenna wouldn't get suspicious.

"You're not mad?" Jenna asked.

"Oh, no." Alan attempted to tone down his response. "After . . . everything I've been through today you're not visiting Mom or Lauren is the least of my problems." It was just as he predicted. Jenna wasn't in the mood to go to the hospital. Everyone involved would be more at ease. Neither he nor Elise would have to worry about Nelson and Larry saying something asinine in front of Jenna, thus putting her on the defense or worse making her suspicious.

Jenna looked at her brother askance. He was being awfully agreeable. "What's going on?"

"What do you mean?" Alan asked. He resisted the urge to hold his stomach and walked over to the refrigerator. He took out a bottle of ginger ale.

Jenna rolled her eyes. "Why are you being so accommodating?"

Understanding showed in Alan's eyes. He laughed with relief. "Jenna, tonight of all nights I'm not gonna argue with you about going to the hospital."

Jenna looked at her brother keenly. Okay. Maybe that's why he's not giving her the third degree.

The next morning Jenna lay in bed curled up in the fetal position. She stared through the window at the cloudy sky. *How am I going to face the day? I can't call Rosa.* Tears stung her eyes. She reached over for a tissue on the night table, dabbed at her eyes then turned over on her back. Staring up at the ceiling, she remembered what she said to Rosa in the orchard so long ago: *I have to learn to fight my own battles.* She sat up, threw the covers off, then got out of bed. Yes, there was the possibility of her mother waking up from her coma. Yes, there was the consequence of Nelson going to the cops with Lauren's note. She'd deal with it without Rosa. She can face a new day. She had Malachi now. Importantly, she was free, free to explore their new relationship and to enjoy it.

Elise poured blueberry pancake batter on the griddle while Alan was sitting at the kitchen table reading the sports pages and sipping ginger tea. Neither of them had an appetite but again they were keeping it real. "Poor Larry," Elise said as she stood before the stove watching the pancake batter bubbling. The fashion designer received an emergency call last night from an important client, forcing him to make a trip to Tribeca. He tried to get out of going to Manhattan by sending a representative, but the client only wanted him. Not wanting to lose business, Larry acquiesced. Reluctantly, he left the village this morning.

"He must be a basket case." Elise winced at her choice of words. "Sorry."

"Maybe it's best he's not in town," Alan said. "The diversion will do him some good."

In truth, Alan had been reading the same paragraph repeatedly and he still didn't understand what he was reading about last night's ballgame. He didn't want to tell Elise that he didn't feel relaxed or ready. This time, it wasn't about committing any sins of omissions. He needed to be calm for her and for himself. No matter how confident Malachi and Detective Chang spoke, they couldn't know how this whole thing was gonna go down. In the end, would Jenna and Diane be all right? Would they be injured or killed?

Alan tossed the newspaper aside. He stared at the pitcher of orange juice on the kitchen table as if it held a solution.

Suddenly, he and Elise became alert. Jenna was coming down the stairs. They looked at each other. This was no longer a rehearsal. Elise mouthed the words; *I love you*. Despite his anxiety, Alan felt as if he could face anything.

"Good Morning!" Alan greeted as soon as Jenna entered the kitchen, his voice defying trepidation. He tried not to cringe at the T-shirt she recently bought, a flaming skull. "Did you sleep well?"

"Yes." *Sort of.* Jenna poured herself a glass of orange juice. They didn't have to know about her inner turmoil. Even with Malachi in her life, she still felt empty inside without Rosa.

"I'm making blueberry pancakes," Elise said.

"Great." After she finished her orange juice Jenna asked, "Can I help with anything?"

"You can take out the butter and the maple syrup," Elise said.

Jenna opened the refrigerator and took out a tub of whipped butter.

"Detective Chang called," Alan said.

Jenna frowned in puzzlement. "I didn't hear the phone."

"You were still asleep." As Detective Chang said, Jenna was clever. As if, he didn't know.

"What did he want now?" Jenna asked sounding slightly annoyed. She went to the cupboard and took out a bottle of maple syrup. She brought it and the whipped butter over to the kitchen table but not before slamming the cupboard door shut.

Elise jumped. She stole a glance at Alan who furtively held his stomach. Jenna getting annoyed was not a good sign.

He cleared his throat. "He said you could go back home."

"It isn't a crime scene anymore?" Jenna asked.

"No," Alan answered.

"I can go back home. To my own room." She began whooping with joy, however, when she saw the expressions on her brother and sister-in-law's faces, she stopped. Alan smiled with uncertainty and Elise, who was standing by the stove preparing breakfast, seemed a little sad. Jenna felt a twinge of guilt. Elise was the one who jumped at the opportunity to have her stay at their home. "It's not that I didn't like staying here. You guys have been great. Thanks for letting me stay."

"You're welcome," Elise said. "We wouldn't have it any other way." She started removing blueberry pancakes from the griddle and placing them on plates. She wanted to gag. It was difficult pretending not to know that Jenna had a problem. It was difficult watching her act as if she were normal, but that's the way it's always been only she and Julian didn't know what was going on and of course, Jenna. *She doesn't know there's anything wrong with her.*

"The house'll be empty with Bella still in the hospital, Elise said. "Maybe you'll want to wait until she comes back."

"Yeah," Alan said. "You're welcome to stay." They couldn't look too anxious for her to leave. They had to show some a little enthusiasm for her to stay which was easy. He didn't want her to go. Yes, Jenna needed help, therefore apprehending Rosa was the best thing, but he was afraid of what was going to happen along the way.

"Thanks, but I don't mind being alone. Plus, I'm ready to go home.

Alan plastered on a smile for Jenna. "I'm glad you're happy."

Jenna really was eager to leave. Her zeal was unmistakable. When Detective Chang made telling Jenna that she could return home the initial part of the sting, he had disagreed with it. Why would she want to return to an unoccupied house? Nevertheless, Chang was right. Alan flinched. He should've known.

He knew that her alter ego had grown up, but almost forgot that Jenna had grown up too and like any adult, she desired respect, freedom and privacy, just as he was no longer a boy but a man who wanted recognition of his manhood.

Elise picked up the spatula and flipped over the blueberry pancakes.

The minute Jenna left the house Alan called Detective Chang. "She took the bait." He could barely eat the blueberry pancakes Elise prepared. The bravery he felt after his wife said she loved him had given way to fear. He didn't want anything to happen to Jenna or Diane regardless of her vanity. Before Jenna stepped through the door, he gave her a hug. Who cares if it wasn't something he'd ordinarily do? He just had to hold her.

After a brief conversation with Detective Chang, Alan hung up. He turned to Elise who had been standing beside him. "Well, this part is done."

She put her hand in his. "We will get through this."

Alan nodded, choking back tears.

Jenna stepped through the door of her childhood home. Whooping with glee, she began running through the house from room to room, upstairs and downstairs singing and dancing embracing the joy of freedom. Later, Jenna returned to kitchen. She looked around the room her mother adored so much. Jenna curled her lips. *I'm gonna make some changes.*

She opened the door to the backyard then stepped outside. The sun was braking through the clouds, promising a beautiful day after all. Jenna walked around the backyard. The rain-soaked grass was saturating her canvas shoes, but she didn't mind. She was too happy. She stopped to pick some baby's breath from a patch in the garden and placed them in her hair. Soon, she went back inside.

Again, Jenna looked around the kitchen. Suddenly she burst out laughing. "I get it now," she said to herself. "This is what it's all about.

Freedom. I have to call Rosa." She was going to yell, but she had to tell Rosa the good news. She had the house to herself now. More so, she understood what Rosa had been trying to do all along.

Jenna was about to pick up the telephone then stopped. She started twisting her hair. They did part on a bad terms. She took a deep breath. No. She had to do this. She picked up the phone. She began dialing. Then, the doorbell rang. Jenna scowled.

She continued scowling as she walked down the hall. Who could that be? She just got back home. Perhaps one of the neighbors saw her pull up to the house and decided to visit.

Before she opened the door, Jenna pasted on a smile. Then she opened the door . . . and blinked. Detective Chang was standing on the doorstep. Her smile faltered.

Chang smiled warmly. He pretended not to notice her discomfiture. Like Alan and Elise, he had a script to follow too. "Good Morning!"

Jenna reminded herself to smile.

45

"Make yourself at home," Jenna said as she reentered the kitchen, Detective Chang in tow.

"Thank you." Detective Chang took a seat at the kitchen table.

He played along maintaining an amiable expression. Jenna's hospitality wasn't fooling him. He saw the tiny glints in her eyes when she greeted him at the door. For that reason, he sat facing Jenna and kept her within eyesight as she was leading him down the hall to the kitchen. Jenna Crandall alias Rosa Garrison wasn't someone you turned your back on.

"So, glad to be back?" Detective Chang asked.

"Definitely." Jenna's cheeriness defied the annoyance building inside her. What did he want? She was enjoying her solitude. She paused then said, "So, you arrested Alan last night."

"And Diane."

"Yeah. Her."

Chang laughed to himself. Her so-called family loyalty was slipping. "You're probably wondering why I'm here."

"Kind of.

"I found out something about Rosa." The glints in Jenna's eyes returned. Detective Chang held up his hands for dramatic effect. "Just hear me out."

Jenna's smile was a little creepy. "Would you like some refreshments?"

"Okay . . . Thanks." What were the odds of Jenna trying to poison him? He doubted she had any toxins handy. Besides, she had no vendetta against him.

"We always have some kind of pastry in the house since Mom loves her teatime."

Detective Chang watched Jenna walk over to the cupboard, take down an unopened box of lemon cookies—store bought—and place it on top of the kitchen counter. Her cordiality sent a chill up his spine. It was weirdly incongruous. She possessed a whole other persona who lacked a conscience. Discovering Jenna's mental condition nearly traumatized Malachi. Tedesco's wounds and emotional distress was the result of having encountered this seemingly meek, delicate woman.

Chang watched her go to a cabinet filled with dinnerware. To his surprise, she took out a plate made of fine china. She returned to the table with it and the box of lemon cookies. She proceeded to set the table, opening the box of lemon cookies and pouring them out onto the plate. Next, she returned to the cabinet and took out a crystal drinking glass. Afterward, Jenna went over to the refrigerator and took out a can of ginger ale. She brought them over to the table.

"Thank you, Jenna. You didn't have to do all this."

"Mom stressed the importance of serving guests properly."

Chang opened the can of ginger ale, poured some into the glass, then took a drink. How ironic she'd bring up Bella's hospitality towards guests, considering how vindictive her stepmother treated Everett and now Malachi.

"What did you want to know about Rosa?" Jenna asked.

"First, Diane is staying over at your brother's."

Jenna looked at Detective Chang warily. "Why would she go there? They don't get along."

"Your brother just wants to be nice." He thought about how sharp Jenna can be. "Just like how you were considerate of your mother."

Jenna sniffed. "What about Larry? Diane would never leave him behind even with Nelson staying with him at the inn."

Calmly, Chang chewed on a lemon cookie. *Oops. Forgot about him.* "Larry's there too. Since the snake incident, they both checked out of The Lorelei House. They feel safer staying with your brother and sister-in-law." Larry would have a fit if he knew he just became a part of this ruse. It was a good thing he was out town.

"But the snakes weren't even in their suite," Jenna said.

"You have to understand. Diane and Larry are a bundle of nerves. This brings me to why I'm here. She told me Rosa's responsible for everything."

Dead silence.

Detective Chang drank ginger ale and pretended not to notice Jenna trying her darnedest not to blow a circuit.

Finally, Jenna asked, "When did she tell you that?" "When I stopped by Alan's." Was it his imagination or did Jenna's voice change pitch? He hoped he wouldn't have to use his gun . . . "I came looking for you, but Alan told me you'd already left."

Jenna helped herself to a lemon cookie. *Good thing I came home.* She couldn't handle occupying the same space as Diane and Larry. "If Rosa was guilty, why would Diane think she'd be dumb enough to return to the scene of the crime?"

"My thoughts exactly," Detective Chang said. "Yet Diane kept insisting it was Rosa. Imagine my surprise. Just when I was finally convinced your friend was someone from the past."

"But she is. I don't understand Diane at all. "I question her sanity."

Chang nearly spat out his ginger ale.

"First, she wouldn't give you information so you arrested her. Now she willingly shoots off her mouth."

"I heard how Diane practically pointed the finger at you outside the Lorelei House the night Lauren had that heart attack."

Jenna's eyes flashed angrily briefly. "My sister's hysterical. And I don't mean amusing."

"But even Lauren thinks Rosa's responsible." He examined the crystal glass then said, "Diane told me about the note. Neither you nor your brother bothered to mention it."

"Should we have?"

She is uptight. "You knew that I was interested in any new developments. You said you'd let me know."

Jenna nibbled on a piece of cookies. "Lauren and Diane are idiots. If I thought what Lauren said was significant I would've told you."

Jenna picked up another lemon cookie and began breaking it into pieces. "You can't take the ramblings of a sick person seriously, Detective. Does Alan know what Diane said?"

"Yes. And he's outraged. He denied everything she told me."

"Still, Rosa's name keeps coming up. So you see I gotta check out this new lead."

"What's there to check?" Jenna asked sounding testy.

"Beware of Rosa. Obviously she's dangerous."

Jenna began laughing sardonically. "Diane just arrived at Alan and Elise's and already she's making trouble."

Chang took a drink of ginger ale. Jenna's laugh sounded was a little disturbing. "I don't think Diane's trying to make trouble."

"I know that heifer."

Whoa. Chang cleared his throat. "When I was leaving, they were heading for the hospital."

Jenna stiffened. "Why didn't they call me? We always go together. Even if I say no, it's still nice to be asked."

"Maybe they wanted to give you some space. Alan and Elise said you were excited to be back here."

"And if that weren't enough," Jenna said, "she's ratting out my friend." It didn't matter if they were no longer friends. She had to protect her. What Diane did could mean trouble for both of them. "Anyway," Jenna went on, "it's not even true."

Chang wiped his mouth with the napkin then crumpled it. He felt a little guilty. Jenna was right. It wasn't true.

"I still can't believe they'd all go off to the hospital without me. It's not like Alan."

"Diane didn't go with them. She's still pretty shaken up. She and Lauren were close. But you already knew that."

"Yeah." Jenna stood up. She turned her back to Detective Chang. She had to think. What should she do? What should she say? *Okay. Breathe.*

While her back was turned, Detective Chang used the opportunity to plant a bug underneath the kitchen table. Everything was going according to plan. Jenna was falling apart bit by bit. Telling her that Diane ratted out Rosa did get her agitated. But she was more than restless. She was steamed. He almost felt sorry for her.

By the time Jenna turned around, Detective Chang repositioned himself. She faced him with a degree of self-control. "Like I told you the last time," Jenna began, "it's been a long time since I've spoken to her. I *may* be able to give you her last address. I'll see if I can find my old address book."

"Appreciate it."

Jenna smiled with relief. She bought herself some time.

Detective Chang let himself out. Jenna stood in the middle of the kitchen holding the receiver in her hand. Now she had no choice but to call Rosa. She had no time to fret over whether or not she'd yell at her. Jenna began rubbing her right temple. She needed Rosa's help. Soon a mechanical voice said, "If you'd like to make a call please hang up and dial again." A beeping sound followed. Because of her addled mind, she wasn't hearing it.

"What do you want?" Rosa asked in a venomous tone.

"Something's happened," Jenna said. "We've got trouble."

"No, *you've* got trouble. You don't need me anymore remember?"

"I never said that."

Parked outside the house but hidden from view, was a nondescript looking van. In it sat Detective Chang, Officer Davidson and Dr. Leslie Haddonfield, a forensic psychologist who Chang asked to assist with the case. The Harvard educated doctor jumped for the assignment. Wearing headphones, they listened in on Jenna and Rosa's "conversation". The beeping on the line was a distraction, however.

"Why don't you ask God to help you?"

"Please," Jenna said.

Rosa's response was an impatient sigh. "What happened now?"

"This is incredible," Officer Davidson said. "She really does sound like two people."

The dialogue was easier to follow now that the beeping sound to the phone changed to dead air. Detective Chang, Officer Davidson and Dr. Haddonfield continued listening as *Jenna* was telling *Rosa* about moving back to Haven Road and what Detective Chang had just told her about Diane moving in with Alan and Elise and about her accusing Rosa.

"Doesn't Rosa already know this?" Officer Davidson asked.

"No," Dr. Haddonfield replied. She pushed her shoulder-length chestnut hair behind her ear. "Rosa Garrison is separate from Jenna Crandall."

" . . . So I stalled Detective Chang," Jenna continued, "by telling him I'd look for your last address in an old address book. Did I do all right?"

"Yeah, you did well." Rosa paused then said, "So she fingered me."

"You gotta help me, Rosa. I don't know what to do." Jenna began sobbing. "There's gonna be trouble now. I just know it. I can feel it."

"All right. I'll help. Get a grip."

Jenna breathed a sigh of relief. Rosa didn't yell at her or decide to leave her in the lurch. "Oh, thank you. Do you want to meet at Hudson?"

"No. The farmhouse."

Detective Chang and Officer Davidson looked at each other knowingly. It was just as Malachi predicted.

"Wait a second," Rosa began. "Didn't you say Diane was staying at Alan's?"

"Uh huh." Jenna sniffled. "Detective Chang says she's 'shaken up'."

"Really? She's gonna know what shaken up really is when I get through with her."

"What do you mean?" Jenna asked.

"I'm goin' to Alan's."

Detective Chang and Officer Davidson stiffened, as did Dr. Haddonfield, who they brought up to date on the plan. That wasn't in the script. Levi, Vega and other officers were waiting for them at the farmhouse, expecting *Rosa and/or Jenna* to appear.

"Can I come?" Jenna asked.

"No!"

Rosa's loud response nearly caused the officers and the doctor to topple over in their seats. Detective Chang lowered the volume on the listening device.

"Stay home," Rosa commanded. "This is between Diane and me. Got it?" Jenna and Malachi almost cheated her out of getting revenge on Diane. Them and all that Christianity jazz. Here was her opportunity. She was not gonna get cheated again. Moreover, Diane dragged her into this when she fingered her to the cops. "I don't want you there."

"Yes, Rosa."

In the van, Detective Chang, Officer Davidson and Dr. Haddonfield heard a loud click.

Jenna took a deep breath. So what if she couldn't go. Rosa was going to take care of everything. They were going to be friends again. That's all that mattered. She smiled, but her grin wasn't lovely or pasted. It was perverse. Jenna turned on the radio and swayed to the cadence of R&B music.

"What is she's having a party?" Officer Davidson asked.

"With herself." Detective Chang frowned. Jenna was definitely happy about something.

Jenna stopped swaying. Didn't Diane know how much trouble she'd cause for her? Rosa was her best friend. "Why does Diane hate me so much?" Her tone of voice sounded plaintive.

"Well, she's not happy anymore, but she's definitely Jenna," Officer Davidson said. "So, now what?"

Before Detective Chang could respond, they overheard Jenna say, "Enough." There was something in the timbre of her voice that put Detective Chang, Officer Davidson and Dr. Haddonfield on the alert.

Jenna sniffled. She grabbed a napkin off the kitchen table, dried her eyes, then blew her nose. She began rubbing her temple. "Everything's going to be all right now."

She left the kitchen.

Upstairs in her bedroom Jenna went over to her closet and took out a leather satchel. She returned downstairs with it, went back into the kitchen then went over to the utensil drawer. There she pulled out a serrated knife. The expression on her face changed from docile to wild.

"This time, I'm gonna do it right," Rosa said.

46

Officer Davidson gulped. "Was that Rosa we just heard?"

"Yeah," Detective Chang replied. Rosa's voice even made him want to take cover. Her tone was beyond scary.

"What did she mean by, 'Do it right?'" Dr. Haddonfield adjusted her sleeves. Rosa's voice was disturbing and she worked with many unstable patients throughout her career as a forensic psychologist. And what was that riffling sound?"

Detective Chang was just as curious. There had been that lapse in time when Jenna had left the kitchen then returned. Who knows what she was doing?

Before Chang could reply, Officer Davidson cried, "Look."

They watched Jenna come out of the house. She stormed down the walkway then flung open the gate, nearly ripping it off its hinges. Her face was a mask of hatred. Detective Chang gawked. No wonder Malachi went to pieces that day. Jenna Crandall had transformed into a monster.

Rosa began walking speedily up the road.

Chang cursed. This plan was going awry. He got on the police radio. "Suspect is heading for Donnelly Drive. Repeat, suspect is heading for Donnelly Drive."

Officer Levi's voice came over the radio. "10-4." "She's like a human jetpack," Davidson said.

"I know a shortcut," Chang said. He put the van in drive. "And I have a new plan. We have to pick up Diane." Detective Chang groaned. He'd have to peel Larry Belmar off the wall if he knew what was happening. *Especially if he knew about the new plan . . .*

Malachi was peering through the eight-foot shrub that ran alongside Alan and Elise's front yard. Like the other officers on the premises, he too was on the lookout for Rosa Garrison. He saw when Detective Chang and a harried looking Diane arrived along with Officer Davidson and a woman he heard them address as doctor. She must be the forensic psychologist. He was lucky he could get that much out of Chang since he was out of the loop.

When he first arrived, Malachi was worried about Alan and Elise's neighbors seeing him sneak onto the property then deciding to call the cops considering the amazing job he'd done evading them at the farmhouse. He could only attribute that miracle to God. It was while he was over there that he overheard that Jenna wasn't coming. Rosa was going over to Alan's house to "shake up Diane." He had no time to feel awkward or guilty about his plan backfiring. He had to beat the cops to Donnelly Drive, which he did. Sitting in as comfortable a position as he could, the feeling of embarrassment and remorse for Diane's safety mixed with fear for Jenna's was washing over him.

He was so certain that Jenna and Rosa would want to strategize first. Larry was going to have his hide for this when he finds out.

If he finds out.

Who knew what was going on in Detective Chang's mind now? He must be furious with him for this unexpected change of events. Didn't he convince him that this plan was good even if Detective Chang did takeover *his plan*? Regardless, he couldn't afford to have Chang see him. He'd have him for lunch. He wasn't even supposed to be at the farmhouse never mind hiding out in these shrubs, which he prayed wasn't poison ivy.

All the same, he had to go against Detective Chang's orders and "play deputy." For him to just sit at home and wait to hear the outcome would never do and resentment towards Alan and Elise had nothing to do with it. It was the thought of losing Jenna. It kept him tossing and turning all night long. So what if they had a professional on hand? Yeah, he was the one who suggested it. But what if something went wrong? *Like bullets flying.*

Weren't things going wrong already? Besides, it wasn't just about Jenna having a dual nature. The evil within her wasn't going to release its grip that easily. It had been growing, developing, honing itself for twenty-five years. They were in for a fight.

While en route to Alan's house, he alerted Julian about what happened and promised to keep him posted. The elder Crandall, although deeply distressed was also grateful to Malachi for being at the farmhouse and now at Donnelly Drive. When Malachi asked him not to breathe a word to Nelson who was sure to tell Larry, he nearly blew his cover. He had to put his hand over his mouth to stop himself from whooping with joy.

Larry was out of town. What a relief.

Feeling cramped, Malachi shifted positions. He tried not to make the bushes shake, calling attention to himself. He also prayed that he wouldn't sneeze, burp—or any other sound. He was grateful that his ankle healed. Otherwise, this stakeout would be even more uncomfortable. Still, nothing would've kept him from helping Jenna.

"This is not happening, This is not happening," Diane said as she rocked back and forth on the living room couch in Alan and Elise's house while she and Detective Chang awaited Rosa's arrival.

Chang stunned the super model when he showed up at her suite to tell her about the change in developments. Uncharacteristically, Diane's face was void of makeup. She was dressed in one of Larry's old baseball jerseys and faded jeans. On her head, she wore an acrylic knitted cap. She had no time to change even if she wanted to. Chang had the van parked outside and they had to move fast. She wanted to call Larry, but Chang refused. Very loudly.

Diane choked back tears. She was going to have to go through this alone. No Larry. No Lauren. No Mom.

Alan.

She wanted. She needed him. "Can I call my brother?"

"No. I don't want to start a panic." Plus, Alan may let it slip to the others. "Now you remember what you're gonna say?"

"Yes."

Detective Chang came up with an impromptu script for her to follow. On the way to the house, Diane went over her lines. He was just as tense as she was; maybe even more if that were possible. The situation escalated into the very thing he wanted to avoid: having one civilian's life on the line.

"Now remember, when your sister, that is, Rosa arrives, you let her in, play your role as we discussed and I'll handle the rest," Detective Chang said. She was to show astonishment, then arrogance when Rosa first arrives. She wasn't supposed to be afraid. She doesn't expect Rosa to do her any harm. He was counting on her modeling as well as her acting skills. Diane had done two movies and a few commercials. She wasn't bad. Outside of work, she was questionable . . .

"I know you're scared," Detective Chang said, "but just try to relax."

Diane began nibbling her bottom lip. She had to be calm when she encountered Rosa. She shouldn't be afraid of Rosa, yet she was. She'd only lived with Jenna's double her entire life.

"She's the same Jenna/Rosa you, your mother and Lauren enjoyed making fun of all those years." He couldn't resist throwing that in. "I'm listening out for Davidson's signal. The second I get it, I'll be in there." He pointed to the study, which was adjacent to the living room. "When Rosa tries to make a move, we'll stop her."

"Who's we?" Diane asked, her voice quivering.

"My officers and I. We're spread all over the premises."

Diane rubbed her sweaty palms on her faded jeans. "Do I have to do this?"

"Yes. We went over this already." Detective Chang wished that he could find it within himself to care that she was afraid, but he couldn't. Like her mother and elder sister, Diane habitually played with Jenna's life as well the life of others like tokens on a game board. Still, he needed to put his feelings aside, do his job and importantly, keep her and Jenna alive. "We need Rosa. Otherwise, *Jenna* can claim all those years of abuse against you people." Which was probably going to happen anyway, but he left that part out. "Just try to pull yourself together."

"I want Larry." Diane sounded like his five-year-old niece.

"And I said no." Detective Chang sighed. "Wanna go over your lines again?"

Diane shook her ahead. She took ragged breaths then said, "I know what to do."

He patted her on the shoulder. "It'll all be over soon." Then he added, "It's gonna be okay." He added that to reassure himself as much as he said it to encourage her. Diane picked up a copy of *Architectural Digest* that was lying on top of the coffee table. Shakily, she began flipping through the pages of the design magazine. For the first time, she felt resentment towards Lauren. She insisted everything would be okay.

Why didn't they just confess like Alan said to?

If it hadn't been for the heart attack, she would've been here now waiting for Rosa instead of her. So what if she'd been acting a little scared lately. Lauren was still the tough one.

Diane saw a picture of an ad with a loving couple sitting cozily on the sofa in a family room. As she studied the magazine picture, she felt an awakening. Her whole life had been one big lie. She turned the page and saw another advertisement with a happy family. Angry tears fell down her cheeks at the same time bitterness began coursing through her veins. Mom should've just dealt with her anger then moved on. Dad was right. Mom had no right to drag us into this.

Diane put down the magazine. So what if Chang was going to be in the next room? And so what if the police were on the property? She could still be one of Rosa's victims. Things go wrong. *Mom couldn't control her. Lauren couldn't either.*

The muscles in Diane's stomach began clenching as her anger changed to fear. Suddenly, she doubled over.

Rushing over to her, Detective Chang asked, "Can I get you something? Some water?" He saw his case quickly going down the toilet. Of all times for Diane to have an emotional, relapse. Rosa would be here any minute.

"I'm fine." Diane raised herself up on the couch.

"You're sure?"

"Yes." She took one of those deep cleansing breaths she'd seen Jenna do many times when she thought no one was noticing. She tried visualizing herself in a happy place, like the photo shoot in Monte Carlo, the fun time she had in Cannes, but it didn't work. Her conscience started nagging her. Thinking about Monaco only brought back memories of how badly she treated Jenna that day when she announced her engagement to Larry. She was talking about her work and excursion in Monaco as if all were normal.

Detective Chang continued eying her with uncertainty. This had to work. This just had to work.

To Malachi, the waiting seemed endless. Carefully, he shifted again, ignoring the feeling of pins and needles in his leg. Just then, he heard some officers murmuring. He became alert. Malachi looked through the hedges. Officers stationed around the parameters assumed positions. Malachi spotted Davidson. The officer was pulling out his radio as he walked toward the house. Then he stopped right in front of the shrub, just inches away from where he was hiding. Malachi held his breath.

"Suspect approaching, Davidson said. "Repeat. Subject approaching."

"10-4," Detective Sergeant Chang said over the radio.

Malachi forgot about his fear of exposure. The ogress he nearly encountered at Thornbush Road was on her way. He just had to remember that she was also Jenna.

Detective Chang put away his radio then turned to Diane. "All right. She's here. Get ready."

Diane started to snivel.

"Don't lose it now," he added.

A figure cut through the yard.

Malachi stifled a gasp. The face was pure rage. Those beautiful eyes that first attracted him were now burning with hate. She was even angrier than the first day he encountered Rosa. She was angrier than the other times he'd seen Jenna display hints of the fury that was lying beneath the surface. Little did he know . . . Malachi considered everything that her stepmother and stepsisters had done to her, which drove her to this state of mind.

Malachi watched Rosa gun up the front walk and up the front door of Alan and Elise's house. *Lord, please guide the cops, protect Jenna and Diane.*

47

Rosa pounded on the door.

Diane yelped. Time to answer the door. Just the way she and Detective Chang rehearsed it. Trouble is she couldn't get her legs to move. She stood in the living room like a statue in The Louvre, the museum in Paris where she did a photo shoot.

Rosa pounded on the door again. Diane still hadn't moved. Detective Chang was growing antsy. Soon, one of his officers might try to radio him, wondering what the holdup is. The last thing he needed was for Rosa to hear the crackling of a radio and get suspicious. *I should arrest the Professor for suggesting this plan then arrest myself for listening to him.* Time was wasting.

Chang cursed then bounded out the study. He gently prodded her forward, but what he really wanted to do was shove her. "Get the door!"

Now the doorbell was ringing insistently. Finally, Diane took a step. Then another.

"Hurry!" Detective Chang whispered loudly.

Diane took a third step.

Detective Chang felt tension and anger skateboarding through his central nervous system. Diane Crandall, who was mouthing off to him just days ago, Diane Crandall who loved an audience was practically catatonic. He was about to reposition himself again in the study when suddenly, the doorbell stopped ringing. Chang's instincts went on overdrive.

Then, they heard a key turning in the lock. Diane and Detective Chang looked at each other. *Jenna* had a key. Chang wanted to kick himself. He had just seconds to remind Diane to do what they rehearsed and make a mad dash for the study before Rosa burst into the house and stepped over the threshold.

Terror gripped Diane. Rosa's face was a twisted visage. Chang warned her that Rosa, Jenna, her little sister, had become fury personified. She believed him. She put Mom in the ICU, Lauren in the cardiac unit and had the citizens of Gordonville looking over their shoulders.

"Remember me?"

Diane cried out. Rosa's voice was neither a child's make-believe playmate nor a rebellious teenager's companion. It was the voice of a lunatic. They'd never heard her voice, but it was never like this. What happened?

Chang felt the hairs rise on the back of his neck. The voice matched the face he'd seen coming out of the house on Haven Road: bloodcurdling.

Rosa swaggered over to Diane who immediately began to back away. She knew she was flubbing her "lines" from the moment she laid eyes on Rosa, but she was too scared to think. Too scared to show fake surprise and indifference. How was she supposed to tease her? She looked insane. Alan was so right.

"Been a long time," Rosa said interrupting Diane's thoughts. She cocked her head to one side. Why are you dressed like that?" Never in her life had she seen Jenna's sister look so unglamorous. She had to look her best just to put out the trash. "You look like a clod."

*

Chang laughed to himself. Diane did look unlike herself.

"I-I wasn't expecting company."

Rosa snorted. "You wear makeup and designer clothes to the grocery store just to buy a loaf of bread."

"I'm not feeling very well."

"Maybe it's guilt."

"I don't understand."

"Jenna told me what you said to that cop."

Diane gasped. She hadn't heard Jenna refer to herself in the third person in such a long time. Why did it seem so funny back then?

Rosa's eyes flashed. "What were you trying to do, bitch? Get me locked up?"

"No. I'm so sorry."

Rosa started laughing.

Diane cringed.

And so did Detective Chang. The laughter sounded demonic.

Rosa stopped laughing. She looked at Diane with loathing then began cursing at her.

*

Chang's jaw dropped. He hadn't heard language like that since he went undercover at an escort service providing prostitution.

Rosa stepped closer.

"What do you want?" Diane asked.

"If you have to ask then you're dumber than I thought."

Diane nibbled on her bottom lip. "Revenge?"

"Ding, ding, ding. And we have a winner."

"But why now?"

"'Revenge is a dish best served cold.'"

"Your mother crossed the line." Rosa smile. "So finally, I convinced Jenna that you people had to die."

Diane's mouth fell open.

Rosa practically danced. "She asked me to do it. Oh, come on. You have to see reason. "You know, Lauren's heart attack was a bonus. Too bad Nelson didn't join her. Arrogant jackass."

Diane nibbled on her bottom lip. *She really is crazy. I don't remember her being like this.*

Lauren played with the strap of her satchel. "So what was with the tantrum at the Lorelei House? Were you hoping a talent scout would be impressed with your drama and use you in his next picture?"

"I was stupid," Diane said. "I'm sorry."

"Honey, you've never been sorry about anything in your life. You told Jenna you wanted to make amends. You said it in front of the whole family. And Malachi. I know 'cause Jenna told me. Yet you kept screwin' her over. Why?"

Diane sniffled.

Chang clenched his teeth. *Come on, Diane. Remember what we rehearsed.* She had yet to push Rosa's buttons. When Diane should be baiting her sister, she gets cold feet.

"Why did you rat me out?"

Diane continued sniffling.

"You really think you can move me with those tears? Answer me."

"I don't know," Diane wailed. "Please, just go away and leave me alone." She didn't care about lines. She just wanted this monster who was once her baby stepsister to leave.

Rosa applauded. "You finally admit it. Unfortunately, I'm not going away yet. But I will. I promise."

Diane gulped. She started tremble.

Rosa examined the supermodel as if she were a specimen in a science lab. She wore a sickening smile. "I just love fear. "In fact, your mother had the same look that you do just before I bashed her head in."

Diane hiccupped. "I'll never hurt Jenna again. I swear."

"That's right you won't." Rosa pulled out the butcher knife from the leather satchel. "Cause you'll be dead." `Rosa tossed the satchel aside and lunged at Diane.

48

Rosa came at her again just as Detective Chang raced from the study. Davidson, Levi, Vega, Cooper and other officers stormed the house. Officer Davidson wrestled the knife away from Rosa but not before she head butted him causing him to collapse.

"Officer down!" Detective Chang yelled.

Dr. Haddonfield went over to help to Davidson. She had come in behind the officers and was standing by at a safe distance.

Shortly after, Davidson sat up. He was just temporarily dazed. He got up and Dr. Haddonfield scampered back to safety nearly colliding into Malachi, Larry, Julian and Alan who burst into the house. They and Dr. Haddonfield stood gaping at the sight of each other. The psychologist had no idea who these men were. Malachi, Larry and the Crandall's wore comical expressions. They didn't check with each other concerning his plans. Detective Chang, the other officers and even Rosa halted, distracted by the intrusion.

Malachi fought back the urge to laugh. The look on Detective Chang's face when he first saw them was priceless. He was also relieved to know that he wasn't the only one who was going to be in the doghouse. Still, he wondered how Julian, Alan and Larry managed to keep out of sight earlier.

Julian looked at Larry with eyes that were about to pop out of their sockets. "What're you doing here? I thought you were in Manhattan."

"That makes two of us," Detective Chang said. He couldn't believe that Julian, Malachi and Larry disobeyed his orders. Especially Malachi. He knew he didn't want him playing deputy again. "YOU SHOULDN'T BE HERE."

Malachi cringed. The man was apoplectic. *We're toast.*

Taking advantage of the situation, Rosa tried to make a rush for it, but Officer Cooper blocked her. She cried like the banshee then began punching, kicking and scratching. Officers were trying to maintain their hold on her. Knowing what she did to her stepmother and Officer Tedesco, it came as no surprise that she possessed Herculean strength.

Furious, Chang shouted, "I'll deal with you all later. Go home."

Rosa began to curse and swear at the officers. There were collective sharp intakes of breath from everyone except for Diane, Detective Chang and Malachi. They already heard the alter ego's malevolent voice.

Alan swallowed. *I don't remember her sounding so cold.*

Larry ran over to Diane who was cowering behind the sofa. He scooped her up in his arms and held her tightly.

Malachi and Julian watched in awe. It was hard to believe that Jenna possessed such brute force and knew such vulgar language.

Officer Levi doubled over in agony after Rosa kicked him in the groin. Detective Chang jumped in and took the injured officer's place. Shortly, he cursed. Rosa broke loose and headed straight for Diane who screamed at the top of her lungs. Larry blocked Rosa's path, not caring about his safety only Diane's.

"Get away from her, Belmar!" Detective Chang commanded wondering why the fashion maven was still there. He noticed the rest of Larry's crew. "You don't know who you're dealing with," Chang said. He couldn't concentrate on Malachi, Julian and Alan. He couldn't take his eyes off Rosa for a second.

Rosa looked at Larry with scorn. "Get outta my way, fool!"

"I'm not going to let you hurt her."

"Oh go sew a button."

Larry stared down the disturbed woman. He didn't see her as a victim of circumstances. He saw her as someone responsible for her own choices. Hiding her evil, psychotic intentions behind a creepy make-believe friend. "You stay away from her. *Jenna*."

Rage crossed Rosa's face. Larry smirked. Good. She needed to deal.

Malachi drew in his breath. *Bad move.* They may have been best buds, but even he knew that Rosa would not appreciate anyone calling her Jenna on purpose.

Chang swore. "Belmar, step back."

The words were barely out of his mouth when slowly and deliberately she said, "My name is Rosa."

Then, like a leopard, she pounced. Her fists were hitting him like bullets.

Diane shrieked.

Somehow, Larry managed to grab one of Rosa's arms and hold it even as officers moved forward to drag her off him. Exhausted, Rosa suddenly went limp.

Malachi, Alan and Julian breathed sighs of relief. It was over.

Malachi felt as if a great weight came off his shoulders. He wasn't even worried about the punishment that he, Julian and Larry faced from crashing the raid. Jenna and Diane had come out of the raid in one piece. That's all that mattered. He looked over at an exhausted Jenna. He knew that she was Rosa, but he preferred to think of her as Jenna.

Now you can finally get the help you need.

For Alan, a chapter in his life and in his family's life was finally ending and another one was beginning. The fallout. But that didn't matter. Everyone was fine. Sort of. Larry wasn't in such great shape, but he'd be all right.

Julian whipped out a handkerchief from his back pocket then began wiping the sweat off his forehead. His daughters were safe. That's the only thing that mattered.

Detective Chang remained cautious, however. Did Jenna/Rosa finally wear herself out? She was full of surprises. Perhaps Larry shouldn't stand so close . . . Finally, he said, "All right cuff 'er."

Officer Davidson was about to put handcuffs on Rosa when she shot up like a spring, taking him and everyone else by surprise. Before Larry could get out the way, she bucked his chin with her head like an angry cow. Blood spewed from his mouth. Disoriented, Rosa kicked Larry in the shin, shoved him aside and sprang for Diane.

Rosa grabbed her by the throat. "I'll kill you!"

While Dr. Haddonfield ran over to attend to Larry, Malachi, Alan and Julian moved forward to help Diane. "Stay back," Detective Chang commanded, furious and nervous, the situation was getting out of control and civilians were present at this raid. He cocked his gun at Rosa then cried, "Freeze!" He prayed that he'd never have to use it.

Rosa's face broke out into a derisive smile.

Sweat poured down Detective Chang's face. *She has no fear.* It was hard to believe that the crazed woman standing before him was the same relatively composed, decent lady he met just days ago, yet it made sense. Didn't he suspect that Jenna was struggling with something? Didn't he suspect that something was amiss? He tried not to think about her snapping off her sister's neck which is what she looked like she was about to do. Then he'd have to shoot her. Julian would lose two daughters right before his eyes. He didn't promise Julian that he'd keep them safe, but in spirit, he did.

"Step away from, Diane," Detective Chang said.

Her grip still on Diane, Rosa looked at the gun pointed at her then at him. "Even if I have to die, I'm taking Diane with me."

"You don't wanna do that," Detective Chang said. "Jenna needs you. What would she do without you?"

He hadn't prayed in years never mind attend mass. But if there ever were a time he needed to pray . . .

Lord, lives are at stake here. I can't do this alone. Please don't let Jenna and Diane pay for their parents' mistakes.

"She'll be fine," Rosa said.

Chang felt sick to his stomach. She had no concept that if she died, Jenna died as well. *I don't want to hit Diane.*

The detective's mind eased as he aimed for Rosa's foot. Just in case . . .

Malachi's heart was in his mouth. At any moment, Jenna could meet a bullet. He couldn't let that happen. Wasn't that the reason why he risked Detective Chang's wrath by following along on the stakeout?

Suddenly, Malachi cried out, "Rosa!"

Their eyes locked. Malachi went back to that June afternoon when he turned and saw a pair of beautiful chocolate-brown eyes staring back at him. An uncanny strength filled him. Unlike the time when he hid in terror from her in the orchard, he was ready to face Rosa. He understood his purpose for coming to Gordonville. Everything pointed to this moment. Slowly, Malachi approached her.

Bewildered, Detective Chang didn't know if he should feel angry or relieved for the interruption. Malachi actually got Rosa to face him. Maybe he would take her attention away from Diane.

Dr. Haddonfield pursed her lips. Who was this man? She accompanied Detective Sergeant Chang and his team to aid Jenna, not for this rank amateur to take over.

Rosa continued to stare fixedly at Malachi. Detective Chang, Davidson, Levi, Vega, Cooper and the other officers were ready to stop her at the slightest move. Malachi wondered which one of them was going to make a move.

Then, a ghost of a smile touched Rosa's lips. She finally had the pleasure of meeting him. Ordinarily, she hated interruptions. This was supposed to be her moment. But he was Jenna's man. She finally got to meet him even if it was under uneasy circumstances.

Malachi studied her grin. *I guess it's me.* "Don't kill Diane. She's not worth you going to jail."

Rosa lost the grin. "This doesn't concern you—Malachi."

"You know me?" He managed to keep his voice calm. Years of poor treatment had turned Jenna's voice as cold as a freezer.

"I saw you at the wedding."

"You did?" He had to process this. He hated to think that the woman he spoke to, laughed with and danced with at Lauren and Nelson's wedding was also Rosa Garrison and yet it was. Who was she but another side of Jenna?

"I told Jenna you were the one for her," Rosa said.

Malachi swallowed. Jenna was that broken that she had became two people in order to convince herself that it was safe to talk to a man.

"She wasn't gonna have anything to do with men anymore because of them." With that, Rosa yanked off Diane's knitted cap, revealing unkempt hair.

Diane began to moan. The exposure of her bad hair was like a punch in the gut. No one ever saw her with bad hair—not even Larry.

If Malachi was the vengeful type and if it weren't such a critical moment, he'd have taken her picture. The supermodel prided herself on always looking good.

"I must introduce you to my hairdresser," Rosa said. "Fernando." She deliberately rolled the r. Then, Rosa laughed derisively, freaking out everyone in the room except for Detective Chang and Diane. They already heard her satanic laughter.

Calmly, Malachi said, "Rosa, you have to stop."

"Why do you care? The chick don't even respect you. Neither did her crew."

"'Do not render evil for evil.'"

Rosa snorted. "Jenna told me about your faith. I'm not impressed. Now, I have a score to settle. It don't concern you."

"But it does. I'm Jenna's boyfriend. Diane is her sister. Hurting her would make Jenna unhappy. And what makes Jenna unhappy makes me unhappy."

"I knew her before you came along. I know what makes her happy." Rosa yanked Diane's hair. She cried out in pain. "She never loved Jenna. Or Alan. I know what really went down."

Why did he tell her he was Jenna's boyfriend? Rosa's been by her side all these years. Maybe she was okay with him in her life as long as he didn't get territorial.

Diane whimpered. Rosa's words cut to the core. They unleashed a flood of memories of all they had done: scorning Jenna's looks, deriding her feelings, sabotaging her relationships. She was paying for it now.

Please God. I don't want to die.

Malachi was no longer an insignificant professor. He was her prospective liberator.

"We all know what happened," Malachi said in a laid-back sort of tone. In reality, he was panicking. At any moment, Rosa also known as Jenna was going to kill her own sister, forcing Detective Chang to shoot her. He could feel everyone waiting anxiously for him to make the situation right.

Then it dawned on him. *"I knew her before you came along."* She was her friend. Somehow, he had to call forth Jenna. He suddenly remembered that Jenna said she liked to go for walks to relieve stress. *Rosa walked to Alan's house.* She didn't drive. That means Jenna was still in there somewhere. "Diane and I may not have been on good terms, "but I still value her life."

"You're pathetic."

Malachi swallowed. He had to remind himself that she didn't mean it, that even if this were Jenna she'd never say something so mean to him. Quickly recovering, he said, "I'd like to speak with Jenna."

"She's not here." Rosa gave him a threatening look.

He knew he was taking a chance. Upsetting Rosa was perilous, but if he got her rattled enough, he might be able to distract her from Diane.

"Jenna."

"I said she's not here." Rosa spoke like a wild woman. Malachi's outcry startled her, causing her hold on Diane to ease slightly. He prayed that no one else would say anything and call her attention to it.

Dr. Haddonfield's alabaster skin was growing red as she observed the interaction between Rosa and Malachi. Now she knew who this gatecrasher was. Not only did Detective Chang appear to forget about her, but also he was allowing the suspect's boyfriend to take control of the situation. This was supposed to be her landmark case. "This is highly irregular."

Detective Chang signaled her to be silent never once taking his concentration off Malachi. He could see that the professor was trying to establish contact with Jenna and he didn't want the psychologist to break the delicate balance. The professor's success was more important right now, than Dr. Haddonfield's ego, which, he realized, may be suffering but he could only handle one wounded ego at a time.

Again, Malachi called, "Jenna, I want to talk to you."

"Don't you have Bible study or something?" Rosa asked.

"Jenna, I know you're not a killer." If he kept saying her name, it might incite her to come out.

For a moment, Rosa's face went blank. Then her face began contorting. Enraged, Rosa began screaming. She came for vengeance and Malachi wasn't gonna ruin it for her. Rosa cursed him out like a fishwife.

Detective Chang winced. The language she used with the professor was even worse than what she used earlier with Diane.

With a complacent smile, Malachi asked, "Didn't Jenna tell you about my past? That used to be my second language."

His smugness only infuriated her more. Rosa's grip on Diane loosened a tad. "Don't make me hurt you, Malachi."

"How would Jenna feel about that?"

"What if I said I don't give a damn?"

Rosa was wearing a murderous expression. Malachi gulped. *She's gonna rip off something I really need.* "Of course you care. You know how much Jenna cares about me. That's why you won't hurt me." At least he hoped not.

"Get. Out."

Malachi stepped back. He didn't think it was possible for Rosa's voice to get any colder. It sounded like it could freeze over the Hudson River.

Now it was her turn to smile. She had the desired effect. Now he would leave.

Malachi noticed her glee and became upset with himself. Fear was paralyzing. He knew first hand. He used intimidation to cause his fellow coworkers to feel helpless. He created an environment of dread when attempting to crush a competitor. He knew how debilitating fear was when he had to face his conscience. Malachi felt some disgust for Jenna's evil side. He saw a little bit of his old self minus the propensity to injure his enemies.

Malachi pulled himself together then stepped forward again. "Come out, Jenna. I know you don't want to hurt Diane."

Rosa was glowering.

"You wanted to put a stop the schemes didn't you, Jenna?" Malachi asked. He kept using the name of the id and ignoring the fury of the ego.

"Stop it!" Rosa cried.

"I heard you tell Rosa."

"SHUT UP." Rosa closed her eyes and put her hands to her temple.

Diane used that moment to slip away. A bruised and bloodied Larry grabbed her then the two of them ran over to the safety of the foyer.

"No matter what Diane's done, Jenna," Malachi said containing his excitement, "she's still your sister. You can't allow Rosa to hurt her."

When Rosa opened her eyes again, Jenna was present. Malachi could tell from the gentle look in her eyes.

"Malachi? What are you doing here?" Jenna looked around her confusedly. She saw Detective Chang, Davidson and the other police officers. "What's going on?"

Before Malachi could answer, Rosa returned. Outraged, she screamed at the empty space next to her. "What're you doing here? I told you to stay home."

Malachi tried to stay centered. The shock of seeing her at the farmhouse returned to him. This is what Alan was talking about at the station. Sometimes, Rosa was the make-believe friend and like a typical little girl, Jenna would talk to her in the space beside her. Other times Jenna and Rosa were in the same body.

"Malachi called me," Jenna said. "Where is he?"

"Who cares? Do what I say and go home."

"Focus on me, Jenna," Malachi said.

She began twisting and thrashing as she literally struggled with herself.

Rosa turned toward Malachi with a baleful look. Soon, however, she gradually transformed into Jenna again. "What's going on?"

"Never mind," Malachi replied. "Do you trust me?"

"Of course." A slight frown appeared on Jenna's face. "I do."

A few seconds past as Malachi enjoyed the good feeling that passed over him as he imagined hearing that phrase under more pleasant circumstances. Finally, he asked, "Do you still want to learn about God?"

"Detective Chang," Dr. Haddonfield began, "where is he going with this?"

"Shh!" The detective didn't want the forensic psychologist disturbing Jenna's aura. Rosa disappeared hopefully this time for good and no one had to get hurt.

Dr. Haddonfield put her hand on her hip. "Are we here to capture a psychotic woman or to evangelize?" Regardless of the hypocrisy in Jenna's family and her personal struggles with Christianity, faith had no place in this matter. The doctor glared at Malachi.

Detective Chang silenced her with a look. *Ruin this and you'll spend the night in jail.*

Malachi turned to look at Dr. Haddonfield. Her grating voice cut through the silence, causing him to lose his concentration. Annoyed, he turned back to face Jenna and blinked. He was looking into the eyes of a deranged woman.

"Damn it!" Detective Chang exclaimed. Rosa had returned. He would've arrested the psychologist on the spot, but he was afraid of any sudden movements.

Rosa gave Malachi a look that could crush a cinder block. Again, Malachi stepped back. *Now I know how Alan feels when he's with his mother.*

"She doesn't need God," Rosa said.

"Jenna can speak for herself," Malachi said.

Rosa laughed raucously. "Says the guy who backs away in fear from a woman."

Detective Chang winced. Low blow.

"Scaredy cat. Scaredy cat."

Calling her bluff, Malachi not only stepped forward again, but a tad closer.

Rosa spat in his face.

He reached into his pocket and wiped off the spittle with a tissue. "Jenna wouldn't like this."

"She'll get over it."

"Because she's forgiving?"

"Get lost."

"Maybe Jenna is really the strong one," Malachi said. Rosa put both hands to each temple.

"It takes more strength to love people than to hate them," Malachi said.

"I could just—" A moment later that soft look in her eyes returned. Jenna was back.

"Hi, Jenna," Malachi said.

"Hi. I have to go. I'm not supposed to be here. Rosa's mad at me. I have to go."

"No. It's okay. Talk to me. What is that *you* want?"

Jenna frowned. No one outside of Rosa had ever asked her that before. "I don't understand."

"Is there something, Jenna that you've always wanted?" Malachi asked. Concluding that she created this entity only to be her best friend and defender was too simplistic. There had to be a deeper reason.

"Yes, there's something."

"Tell me."

"For Mom and my sisters to love me."

You could've heard a pin drop. Almost everyone in the room knew that Bella wasn't her mother and that Amelia Saunders, her real mother, had abandoned her. It added insult to injury that her stepsisters treated her poorly.

Malachi nodded, trying not to tear up. He didn't know if she would ever get that request granted, but she was going to get help on coping with their denial of their affection. Once again, the ego refused to have the id win. Rosa broke through Jenna's conscience and addressed her as if she were standing right beside her.

"Did you tell Malachi the plan?" Rosa asked.

"No," Jenna's timid voice responded.

"Then why's he here?"

Jenna cowered as she looked at the empty space. Rosa was angry with her again. She didn't mean to make her angry. "I don't know. He called me."

"He's ruining everything," Rosa said.

Julian looked on in horror. Distraught, he watched his daughter fighting with herself. *What did they do to my baby?*

"I don't care what Malachi says," Rosa continued. "Without me you're screwed."

"Not this time, Rosa," Malachi said. He turned to the empty space, which was now his beloved. "Look around you, Jenna. The police know everything."

"Who're you kidding?" Rosa asked. "They can't arrest Bella for child abuse. The statute of limitations is over."

"There's obstruction of justice," Detective Chang said speaking up for the first time since Malachi stepped up. He was profoundly impressed with Jenna's knowledge. Bella, Lauren and Diane truly underestimated her.

Rosa looked at Malachi with disgust. "I suppose you're gonna preach to her too."

"Don't be ropin' her in with all that religious crap. What kind of God would allow Bella, Lauren and Diane to do what they did?"

"No one gets away with anything," Malachi said remembering a similar conversation he had with Jenna.

"He rewarded them, preacher man. I saw it all." Rosa glowered at Diane. "She and Lauren, that grasshopper, paraded their wealth and power in Jenna's face. Bella Crandall was a faker who tortured this girl and Alan every chance she got and no one did anything." Rosa was at the brink of hysteria. "Everybody praised Ms. Crandall, the pious, generous woman and her two daughters." Rosa laughed shortly. "No one else existed. So where's the justice . . . Christian?"

Malachi needed a moment. What were the right words to say to the anger? "Je-Rosa, I don't know why God allowed those things. And I'm sorry that that Jenna got hurt. But there are things we're gonna go through in this life that don't make sense—"

"Blah, blah, blah."

"—But later we learn why it was necessary for us to go through it. And sometimes we never know why we get a raw deal. The important thing is that Jenna will never be bothered by Bella, Lauren and Diane again."

"What're you gonna do? Bore them to death?"

"I'll let the authorities and God handle them. I'm gonna look after Jenna. She can depend on me."

Rosa sneered. "How does she know that?"

Malachi took a breath. Jenna, who was not too far away from the surface, was really asking him, how do I know that? "Jenna has to trust me."

Trust me.

The warmth and the softness in the way in which he said it pierced through Rosa's icy facade. She held her temples before looking around again. Jenna's restful gaze now looked at Detective Chang and his team, Julian, Alan, Diane . . . and Larry. She gasped when she saw his body stained with blood; skin all black and blue. His clothes were torn bloody clothes. "Did Rosa do that?"

"Yes," Dr. Haddonfield, replied before Malachi could respond.

"Who are you?" Jenna asked.

"I am Dr. Haddonfield. I am here to help you." Malachi snarled. He hated the tone the doctor was using. She sounded like she was talking to some bozo. Regardless of her issues, Jenna was not a space cadet.

"Everybody's here for me?" Jenna asked.

"Yes," Malachi replied looking deliberately at Dr. Haddonfield. He resisted the urge call out, Nah nah.

Jenna spotted her brother. She looked over at him for confirmation.

Alan nodded. "It's over."

Julian stepped forward. Tearfully, he said. "They're never gonna hurt you again." He couldn't bear to speak their names. He didn't know how to tell her about her mother. Should he?

"I lied to you," Jenna said. "I was still seeing Rosa."

"I know."

"I'm sorry."

"I know."

"Are you mad at me?"

Malachi smiled. "No." Watching Jenna come apart was alarming, but hearing her ask if he were upset with her was heartrending. Malachi opened his arms. Right away, Jenna flew into his embrace. They stood holding each other.

"Rosa told me to stay home," Jenna said. "But I didn't listen. She's angry with me. See?" She pointed to the empty space. "She's frowning." Jenna buried her face into Malachi's shoulder.

"Yeah, I see." He didn't think it was possible for his heart to break any more than it already had.

"I hate it when she's angry," Jenna said. "She's scary when she's angry."

"I can't argue with that."

"I don't want to lose her," Jenna said. "She's my friend."

"It's gonna be okay. In fact, we'll all talk to Rosa for you." Malachi caught Dr. Haddonfield's glare and promptly ignored it.

Jenna began to sway. "I don't feel so good."

"All right. I got you."

Jenna sank to the floor where Malachi joined her.

"I'm so tired," Jenna said.

Malachi leaned her head on his shoulder. No wonder she was weary. Plotting and carrying out revenge had finally taken its toll.

"Does God still love me?" Jenna asked.

"Yes, He does."

Julian walked over and kneeled beside Jenna. "I'm gonna make this up to you. Somehow. I promise."

Jenna looked into her father's tear-stained face. She wasn't sure what he was feeling sorry about, nevertheless she was glad he was here.

"Me too," Alan said joining them on the floor.

"I'm sorry too." Diane spoke from the safety of the foyer.

For a moment, the sisters stared at each other across the room before Jenna turned away but not before her eyes took on a vacant look.

"What's going on?" Chang asked in a hushed tone. "It's like she's someplace else."

"She's withdrawing." Dr. Haddonfield sniffed. "That's typical for people with psychiatric disorders."

Malachi didn't comment. Let the good doctor have her say. Instead, he rocked Jenna and whispered, "How're the pixies?"

Jenna smiled and said, "They're happy."

In her hospital bed, Bella Crandall opened her eyes.

49

Detective Sergeant Chang drove down Thornbush Lane. Since he had some available time before his press conference with Mayor Urbanowski who was going to be majorly depressed over his pet, Lauren Crandall-Door, he decided to visit the farmhouse. He didn't know what he expected to find there. Nevertheless . . . He yawned. He felt tired and overwhelmed by what he had just witnessed at Alan and Elise's home. Feeling remorseful, Jenna confessed to her part in the crimes. That is, she confessed to Malachi, who was sitting next to him in the front passenger seat. The professor begged him to come along. He could hardly turn him down after the golden job he did. Admittedly, when the professor and the others burst through the door, he wanted to kill them himself.

It turned out that Malachi's updates weren't enough for Julian. He had to do something and thanks to Malachi, he knew just where to find his daughters. Putting aside his feelings for his future son-in-law, Julian decided to tell Larry what happened and that Malachi was acting as lookout. It didn't occur to him that the agitated designer would have the guts to show up at a raid.

Chang found himself thanking God repeatedly that Malachi was there, for without him, the result might've been catastrophic. Yes. Things could've been a lot worse. *Mom would've said this was providential.* Like Bella's miraculous recovery. She came out of her coma with no brain damage.

They all listened in astonishment as Jenna told them about leaving the key under the planter for Rosa to find, their ruse for gaining entrance into The Lorelei House and booby-trapping Lauren and Nelson's suite. Chang thought he was going to pass out when she described the way in which she and Rosa had lured Officer Tedesco into their trap.

Of course, Jenna had no memory of Rosa's actions they pieced together the rest. She only had a three-minute walk from her office back to her house on Haven Road. Likewise, she had a short walk from her office to The Lorelei House where at the mall she transformed herself into Doreen Bennett. They were relieved that this wasn't a third personality.

"Good job, Prof."

"Thanks."

Malachi smiled sheepishly then stared at the lonely road, which although eerie was a lot less intimidating on a bright sunny day. Ghosts and ghouls were far from his mind, however. Right now, he just wanted to get a look into Jenna's secret world. A visit to Thornbush Road was the perfect opportunity. He counted himself lucky. Chang could've easily arrested him, Julian, Alan and Larry. After all, they did interfere with the investigation. Importantly, Jenna and Diane were alive.

And Bella.

"I see the farm up ahead," Detective Chang said.

"The answer was here all the time," Chang said as they stood in front of the farmhouse.

He began surveying the long-abandoned estate. He could understand the residents' fear. The deserted road. The scary trees. No doubt, they looked creepier in the dark. The wide-open, untamed space possessed a quiet peaceful beauty. Here was where a teenage girl came to escape pain and agony, to create beautiful works of art, to find harmony.

Chang sighed. Here was where a teenage girl came to commune with her other half.

Malachi too looked around at the place that had once given him the creeps. Emotionally, he felt a little betrayed. Logically, he understood that she had a condition, but when she was *Jenna,* she never mentioned that Thornbush Lane was her retreat. She had the opportunity to do so on their first date. She told him about the meadow. Then again, what if she had told him? What would he have done? Ask to come along on her next visit? The street, never mind the property, scared the living daylights out of him. Besides, he might've risked having an encounter with Rosa who at the time he didn't know was Jenna.

Malachi and Detective Chang walked around to the back of the property. Malachi tried not to think about his first near-encounter with Rosa. Chang looked toward the big red barn. Jenna told them that beyond it was a brook where she and Rosa got the garter snakes.

"Come on, Prof." Together, they walked back to the front of the property. They climbed up the decrepit front steps. Chang handed Malachi a pair of latex gloves while he slipped on a pair of his own.

"Sure you wanna do this?"

Malachi nodded.

They entered the house.

The center hall was in semi-darkness. Detective Chang turned on his flashlight. The pristine condition of the floors, wainscoting and banister didn't surprise them. They knew that Jenna was lovingly maintaining parts of the farmhouse from Tedesco's statement and Jenna's confession.

Now Malachi wasn't fine. As they continued down the hall, he started getting the heebie-jeebies. *It's this house.* It was Jenna's hideaway, but it also carried the essence of her evil side. He almost expected Rosa to jump out at them. That wasn't going to happen, however. Jenna/Rosa was in custody, led away in handcuffs forty-five minutes ago from Alan and Elise's house, in front of neighbors and friends who thought they knew her.

By now, the Crandall's dark secret was out. "What're we looking for?" Malachi asked, trying to shake off his uneasiness.

"I'll know when I see it," Chang answered. Jenna as Rosa spent a good while here. She must've hid evidence that they hadn't thought to look for the first few times they came to the farmhouse having been preoccupied with Tedesco and apprehending Rosa.

They entered the parlor where Malachi first witnessed Jenna's one-woman show. Like the hallway, the woodwork was well polished. Chang shined his flashlight around. Evidence of Jenna was everywhere. An artist's box sat in a corner. In another corner were some finished paintings and an easel with a painting in progress stood in the center of the room.

"This place really was Jenna's second home," Malachi said his voice barely above a whisper.

Chang shined his flashlight on one of the paintings. Malachi gasped. It was a portrait of him and Jenna holding hands and gazing down at the valley from the top of the mountain at the rest stop where he had taken her that afternoon. He began choking up. "May I have this?"

Detective Chang sighed. Obviously, the painting had some significance for the professor, but this was a crime scene. "I'll see what I can do *after* we close the case."

Next, they entered the kitchen. Chang trained his flashlight over the hardwood floor. He stiffened.

"What's wrong?" Malachi asked.

"Something about this room." Detective Chang began searching the cabinets, which revealed cobwebs, dirt and grime. He coughed.

"She only cleaned the outside," Malachi said.

"Runs in the family." He winced. "Sorry." Chang turned to a cabinet underneath the sink. When he opened it, a spider crawled up its web. Detective Chang jumped back nearly losing his and Malachi's balance.

"Lauren's not the only one who's afraid of creepy crawlies," Detective Chang said.

Again, he trained his flashlight under the sink then flinched. The missing cup, saucer, plate, teaspoon and napkin from the first crime scene had become living quarters for spiders. Also among them was the missing candle from the Lorelei House.

Malachi let out a sigh. "Oh, Jenna."

"So, what's next, Sarge?" Officer Davidson asked.

"A competency hearing." Weary, the detective sergeant took a seat behind his desk. He just returned from the press conference. He rubbed his eyes then yawned. "When the jury finds out what the Crandall's put Jenna through and Alan, their toast. It's a public relations nightmare."

"Didn't Jenna work for a PR firm?" Officer Davidson asked.

Chang laughed dryly. "Ironic huh?"

"Will Jenna ever be normal, Sarge?"

Chang looked at the azaleas. After what he witnessed, he'll never doubt anything again. "Yeah. She's gonna be fine. Take over." Then, he stood up and headed for the door.

Outside, Detective Chang ran into Officer Vega.

"Hi, Sarge! That was some case."

"Yeah. It was nuts." He winced. "Pardon the pun."

She laughed. He thought he was going to melt. An uncomfortable silence ensued.

Chang loosened his collar. He was looking more like a moron instead of her boss.

What's wrong with me? I worked with her over the past few days. I'm a detective sergeant. An ex-NYPD officer for crying out loud. I should be able to make conversation with a fellow officer.

He cleared his throat. "Like I said at the press conference, I couldn't have done it without my team."

Officer Vega smiled shyly.

"Uh, look, I was heading over to Mass. Care to join me? That is if you don't have any files to clear up." Where did that come from? Chang swallowed. He didn't intend on asking her.

"No, I'd love to go."

Detective Chang ran his hand around his collar. "Maybe after we could talk. Say . . . over coffee?"

Officer Vega smiled. "I'd like that."

He reached out his hand. She took it. Together they walked down the street.

50

Julian sat before the television in Alan and Elise's family room, mesmerized. Almost all of the networks were carrying the story of how Bella masterminded a plot to drive her stepdaughter insane. They had a field day with the news of Julian's infidelity. They went on to talk about the real mother of Jenna Crandall, Amelia Saunders. He and Bella were staying with their son and daughter-in-law since Julian didn't want to stay by himself. They also helped with looking after Bella who was upstairs in the smaller guest bedroom that she and Julian were sharing, recuperating from her head wounds.

Julian was set to give her a piece of his mind after he learned about all the things Bella had done, but when Dr. Gennaro called with the news that Bella had awakened from her coma, he forgot about all his rage. His wife confronted Jenna's warped side one last time, a side she could no longer dominate. He wondered what Jenna said to her right before she struck that near-fatal blow. Besides, because of Bella's deep-seated resentment and desire for revenge, she now had to face censure. Her sufferings were only just beginning. He had no need to punish her.

Julian listened to the newscasters going on about their family's scandal. They were using the terms stepmother, stepsister, stepbrother or half sister or half brother interchangeably. The patriarch groaned inwardly. All these years he never had to think of Bella and Jenna as stepmother and stepdaughter. It was easy and more pleasant to pretend they were biologically connected. He never wanted Jenna to have to refer to Lauren, Alan and Diane as half siblings and vice versa; hence, the need to want to keep Jenna's parentage a secret in the first place.

Julian let out a long-suffering sigh. "How did they even get Amelia's name?" He asked Malachi, who was sitting across from him. The sociology professor had been spending as much of his free time with them as possible. In addition to his loyalty to Jenna, her family needed a friend. The past week was torture. Reporters chased them. The telephone rang constantly. Small wonder Diane and Larry went into seclusion likewise Nelson and Lauren, who was still recuperating.

Malachi took a drink of orange soda then said, "Detective Chang probably mentioned it." What choice did the man have?

Not surprisingly, life for Malachi had also changed. He became an instant celebrity. The press dubbed him, *The Hero of Donnelly Drive* for talking Jenna out of butchering Diane Crandall, who the world now knew was her *step*sister. TV news magazines offered him guest appearances. He even received a book deal, all of these he refused to take. The old Malachi would've jumped at the lucrative deals. How could I live with myself if I became rich at the Crandall's expense?

On the other hand, fame had its price. Malachi became the butt of many jokes. One talk show host said he was an idiot for not figuring out that his girlfriend had two personalities. Another one suggested he could have an affair with Rosa without cheating on Jenna.

Julian looked up at the ceiling and sighed. Only a month ago, the hot celebrity gossip was the Crandall-Door wedding followed by Diane and Larry's engagement; and before that Lauren and Diane's accomplishments in the courtroom and on the catwalk, respectively. Now everything changed forever. He continued staring at the scenes on the television, which now had footage of the paramedics carrying Bella out on a stretcher from their home, to paramedics carrying Lauren out of The Lorelei House.

Julian and Malachi went on to listen to local residents receive their fifteen minutes of fame. The man in Lakewood Park telling reporters about Jenna scaring herself and then talking to herself. The convenience store clerk selling her a six-pack the day after Jenna, in his words, "Tried to wipe out her mother. She kept actin' like someone else was there."

Former classmates came forward. Encouraged by the talk show circuit, they chatted about what it was like to attend school with Jenna. Maura Wynn, the student who she beat up back in high school was glad to talk to the press about Jenna.

"Wasn't she the one who Alan and Diane said use to pick on Jenna?" Julian asked.

"You're point?" Malachi snorted. "And where were all these people before?" For Jenna's sake, he prayed that they would never find her former boyfriends or that the men would otherwise keep their mouths shut.

Reverend Brooks refused to comment, likewise Roscoe Addison, whom Bella had wronged, remained silent on the matter. However, some other church members felt differently. They demanded that its ministry remove Bella Crandall from the church board and strip her of her status as church elder. Leading this request was Norma Beery who, before the cameras expressed her, *"shock and disappointment. She had no idea they had marital problems; however, she "always knew there was something not right about that Jenna . . . "*

Julian and Malachi exchanged glances.

"You have got to be kidding," Malachi said. He looked with disdain at Mrs. Crandall's former friend and devotee. He shook his head. "Nice to know who your friends are." He picked up the remote and began flipping channels.

Suddenly, Julian cried, "Hold it a second go back." When Malachi turned back to the previous station, Julian was staring intently at a black woman on the screen, a very attractive, older looking version of Jenna.

Malachi straightened. *Amelia Saunders.*

From her home in Greenport Jenna's birth mother spoke to reporters. Malachi widened his eyes. That's the town where the Olana mansion was located, the place where he and Jenna spent the day. How close they were to Amelia. Malachi turned up the volume.

"*. . . Never should've allowed him to take her home to that woman. Bella was the reason why Julian was so miserable.*" She went on to talk about her and Julian's relationship.

Malachi cringed. Unlike Julian, he had the benefit of hiding his past. He wet his lips. Would reporters find out about his near brush with insanity? *They'd have a picnic.*

Julian balled his hands into fists. "I can't believe she's airing our business."

When asked, Amelia talked about her current husband and children. She addressed the camera. "Wherever you are, Jenna, you've got a family who loves you and wants to meet you."

Julian started to yell at the television. "You never gave Jenna the chance to get to know you."

Malachi tried not to gag. Amelia's display of grandstanding was as bad as Lauren's was. Maybe worse. She helped to set this whole thing in motion.

"You refused to bond with your own child," Julian continued. "All these years you never even acknowledge our daughter." He picked up a throw pillow and tossed it at the television. "Now you want to walk into Jenna's life. Lord, why can't You cut her a break."

Malachi switched to cartoons before Julian picked up a heavy object and smashed his son and daughter-in-law's plasma TV. He thought about the difficulties that he experienced dealing with guilt and hallucinations. "You will get through this."

"I wanna believe that."

"What's all the commotion?" Alan asked as he and Elise entered carrying trays loaded with an assortment of sandwiches, tortilla chips, guacamole, soda and water.

Malachi filled them in. Elise said, "She just wants to ease her conscience." Thinking about Bella, Lauren and Diane, she added, "There's gonna be a lot of that." She put down the tray on the coffee table.

"I bet she's getting offers to make appearances."

Feeling guilty even though he didn't do anything, Malachi took a chip and dipped it into the guacamole.

"I can't believe Jenna's mother resurfaced," Alan said as he grabbed a ham and cheese sandwich. Guiltily, he was hoping he'd see a live clip or catch a still photo in the paper. He couldn't help wondering what the woman who captured his father's heart and caused him to break his marriage vows looked like. Opening a bottle of water, Alan asked, "Mal, did you know that Wheat Prentiss & Associates is suing us, that is they're suing Alan, his parents and his sisters, Jenna excluded?"

"Dare I ask the details?"

Elise sat down on the sofa next to her father-in-law. She sighed then said, "They," she gestured to Alan and Julian, "endangered the welfare of the firm's staff and clients due to their negligence to provide Jenna with the psychiatric help she obliviously needed. Now the staff of Wheat Prentiss & Associates is suffering from emotional stress and psychological damage after having learned that they had been working side by side with a deranged coworker."

Malachi crunched on tortilla chips. *Every nut job in the village will be coming out of the woodwork wanting compensation. Mrs. Crandall was so intent on hurting the other woman's child; she chose to blind herself to the chaos she was creating around her. She corrupted her daughters who evidently, resented Jenna because she was Amelia Saunders' child and was therefore their mommy's enemy. Mrs. Crandall turned Gordonville upside down, abused Jenna's potential boyfriends, and got the police involved. Alan and Julian share the blame because they allowed the situation to go on out of chronic fear and ignorance, respectively.*

Malachi took another drink of orange soda. "Well, I'm no lawyer," Malachi began, *but I wouldn't put any stock into their clients suffering since they had little contact with Jenna. She took their messages over the phone, greeted them in the reception area and served them coffee."* He made a rude noise. "As for the staff, *maybe* they experienced stress. But I doubt they're that damaged. Wheat Prentiss & Associates is just trying to milk this thing because they're looking at Lauren, Diane and

Alan's assets, not to mention Nelson's. Poor sap." Malachi laughed dryly. "Larry dodged a bullet by only being *engaged* to Diane."

"Don't give them any ideas," Julian said. "They want my neck too. Remember Bella was the mastermind and we're still married. Plus, I was careless for letting this happen." Julian groaned. "Who's not trying to get a piece of us is scorning us. We can't even go to the mailbox or the grocery store without the neighbors gawking at us. "Others look at us like we're scum."

"I'm lucky that the school's still keeping me on." Elise took a bite of a bologna sandwich. She hoped the cameras wouldn't follow her the first day of school. It was going to be hard enough working around the other teachers as they tried not to bring up the obvious with her. She could just imagine her new fourth and fifth grade class asking her about the crazy lady.

"Do you have an attorney?" Malachi asked.

"No," Alan replied. "We just got served this morning." He was barely over almost losing two-thirds of his family. Now he stood to lose part of his net worth. He cursed himself for allowing his mother and sisters to drag him into this.

"I'll talk to Brendan," Malachi said. "He can't represent you, but he'll know somebody who knows somebody. I'm sure Alan can get off easily. "He's been under duress for most of his life. And Julian, everybody's not against you."

Thankfulness showed in Julian, Alan and Elise's eyes.

Julian choked up. "Thanks, Malachi."

51

"Has the jury reached a verdict?"

"Yes we have your honor," the jury foreperson replied.

After two weeks of listening to testimonies from witnesses, the Crandall's forensic psychologists regarding Jenna's ability to stand trial and from Jenna herself who discussed her part, as well as her relationship with her family and Rosa, the civil court jury had their decision. All of Gordonville sat by their televisions and radios as well. Reporters were agog.

Sitting in the gallery, Malachi watched the bailiff hand the slip of paper with Jenna's fate written on it to the Honorable Vincent Graves, a large African-American with a reputation for being tough but fair.

Malachi leaned forward. Along with the family, reporters and spectators he waited to hear the outcome of Jenna's competency hearing. *She doesn't even belong here.* A 7:30 exam should've rendered her incapable of standing trial, but the court-appointed psychiatrist who examined her pronounced Jenna competent, contradicting Dr. Haddonfield's finding. *"A make-believe friend didn't make her insane. Just quirky."*

The psych was biased. *Where did he get his degree?* Evidently, the state wanted to convict her very badly. *If she hadn't kidnapped that cop . . .* Then again, Jenna must've answered the psychiatrist's questions with such poise and confidence, it left no doubt that Jenna knew what she was doing when she was doing it. After all, besides himself she fooled her now former employer and Detective Sergeant Chang.

Because of the contradiction, the court decided to hold a competency hearing. Would the jury render her incompetent to stand trial? In light of the evidence they surely had to see that Jenna's mind had cracked beneath the strain of constant mistreatment. If not, she'd have to stand trial for attempted murder and kidnapping.

The special prosecutor called in for the Crandall's, Parker Lynch, was a shark. The well-groomed middle-aged man, fought to convince the jury that a split personality did not impair Jenna's ability to reason. *"She's a calculated psychopath bent on retaliation."* Malachi smirked. Rumor had it that Lynch had a personal grudge against Lauren Crandall-Door . . .

Lynch emphasized Jenna's schemes, how masterful they were, *"Not an imbalanced woman as counsel for the defense is trying to convince you all, but the work of an evil genius."*

Malachi swallowed. Lynch almost had him convinced that Jenna was devious. He had all but reduced Rosa to an insignificant figment of Jenna's imagination instead of acknowledging the alter ego, as the shrewd entity that Jenna manifested because of cruelty and neglect. Recalling his moment on the stand made him want to smack the guy.

"You're a sociology professor at Gordonville State University?"

"Yes."

"And you picked up on Jenna's inability to get along with her mother and sisters?"

"Yes."

"When?"

"At the wedding. Jenna went from being friendly and conversational to getting quiet."

The D.A. struck an exaggerated befuddled pose. *"Yet you didn't notice Jenna had two personalities . . . Professor?"*

Malachi bit back a snappy retort. The question came up constantly in the media. Why hadn't he noticed? He asked himself the question repeatedly and it nagged him. Wasn't the nightmare a foreshadowing? Was he so smitten that he became blind?

Or didn't want to know.

Malachi shifted. "No, I didn't notice. She seemed okay."

"Oh. So she fooled you?"

"No. Jenna is a separate person from her alter ego."

Lynch smiled cunningly, turned toward the jury then back to Malachi. *"Did she or did she not hide the fact that,"* he stopped to make air quotes with his fingers, *"she was communicating with Rosa, Dr. Chase?"*

Malachi sighed. "Yes."

"And wasn't she cunning enough to leave no fingerprints? And clever enough to plan the sabotage of her stepsister's suite?"

"Well, yes, but . . ."

"That'll be all . . . Professor."

*

Malachi looked to the front of the courtroom where Jenna was sitting beside her attorney, Morgan Gupta. A colleague of Brendan's referred the forty-year-old British Indian to the case. The celebrated case intrigued the defense attorney that he agreed to do it pro bono. The publicity alone was payback.

Morgan listened to the proceedings with self-assurance. The prosecution's zeal to take down the Crandall's got in the way of commonsense. Between Parker Lynch and that bozo psychiatrist they hired, he had this case in the bag. Jenna didn't belong here and he intended to prove it.

Malachi was seeing Jenna for the first time since that traumatic morning. His arms ached to hold her. He heard she'd been having difficulty separating her identity from Rosa. Malachi served as a character witness. He stated under oath that under pressure from her stepmother and stepsisters, Jenna couldn't function as a healthy normal individual in her home environment. At times, she was withdrawn, afraid.

Dr. Haddonfield and Dr. Eli Dorfman were among the experts who examined Jenna and gave their points of view. They were concerned about the effects the proceedings might have on Jenna. Dr. Haddonfield had advised the court not to have Jenna in the courtroom with Bella, Lauren and Diane. The mere sight of them might trigger Rosa's appearance. She didn't even approve of having reporters there. Dr. Dorfman agreed.

But Gupta continued to wear an impassive expression, masking his confidence. He had no desire to tangle with Rosa. He met Jenna's alter ego when she was staying in a temporary psychiatric ward. It was an experience and quite horrifying. Although he had no doubt that he was in a strategic position, Rosa's appearance would help clinch his case.

He glanced over at his legal adversary. Parker Lynch was wasting his time. There was too much evidence showing the Crandall's tortured Jenna, leading up to her psychological damage, which they deliberately left untreated. Not to mention public opinion was against them.

Jenna played with her hair. Everyone seemed to think her friendship with Rosa was an illness. The doctor said things that didn't make sense. Figment? Entity? *Disassociated Identity Disorder?* Rosa was her friend. Rosa was real. Her friendship with Rosa wasn't bad. *And I'm not ill.*

Jenna whispered to Gupta during the procedure that they were lying. Firmly, but gently he ordered her to calm down. "They know what they're doing."

Alan reached for Elise's hand. They both listened with baited breath for the verdict. He too testified as a character witness. His was a unique position. He was guilty of obstruction of justice but was also a victim and a sympathetic witness. Alan wasn't happy about having to reveal painful childhood memories before the court . . .

"*Your mother hit you?*" Lynch asked.

"*Yes.*"

"*Often?*"

"*Only if I got between her and Jenna.*"

Lynch nodded. "*Why didn't you tell your father what was happening to you and Jenna?*"

"*I was scared.*"

"*But, Alan, you got older and larger. In fact, you had a growth spurt at fifteen making you taller than your mother. And you were still growing.*"

"*Your Honor, is there a question?*" Gupta asked.

"*You were too scared to do something about Jenna's situation even now.*"

Alan held his stomach and fought to keep from getting sick on the witness stand. He took a few deep breaths.

"*The beatings were . . . bad. Mom threatened to do worse to me if I told. Or if Jenna told. Even Lauren and Diane couldn't talk and they were her favorites. I may not have told anyone but I did defend Jenna.*"

"*Who wasn't always scared,*" Lynch said.

"*Is there a question?*" Gupta asked.

The prosecutor sighed then asked, "*Why did Jenna set the fire?*"

Alan glanced at the jury then at the reporters. "*Mom slapped her for not washing the dishes . . . in front of Rosa.*"

"*So Jenna was in both forms when your mother struck her?*"

"*Yes.*"

"Would you elaborate please for the court what happened?"

Alan paused then said, "*When Mom hit Jenna, she was embarrassed. But Rosa was pissed.*"

"*So Jenna had the ability to come in and out of that fear?*"

Bella, Lauren and Diane stared straight ahead. Beside them sat, Julian, Nelson and Larry. Crushed in spirit, Bella confessed to the court the blow she struck that pushed Jenna over the edge and set her on an orgy of revenge. She went on to talk about the resentment she harbored over her husband's infidelity and the birth of his illegitimate child. Reliving her moment on the stand, the matriarch tugged at the sides of her print wrap dress.

"How old was Jenna when Julian first brought her home?" Gupta asked.

"Three months," Bella replied.

"How did you relate to Baby Jenna?"

"I took care of her."

"Mrs. Crandall, did you love her, hate her?"

Bella paused. "I bonded with Jenna."

"I'm confused, what exactly did you feel for Baby Jenna?"

Bella smoothed her dress. "I felt nothing. At first. Then I began to bond with Jenna. She needed a mother. She was helpless. She needed nurturing.

"What changed?"

"I clothed her and fed her." There was a hint of defiance in Bella's voice. She regarded the young British Indian who was Jenna's defense. He was even more irritating than Dr. Chase was.

"You didn't answer my question," Gupta said. When did your feelings change?"

Bella glared and said, "After she started kindergarten."

"Why?"

Bella smoothed her dress again.

"Answer the question," Judge Graves said.

Silence.

"Is it because she started to look so much like her real mother, Amelia Saunders? The other woman?"

"Yes."

Lauren and Diane, accompanied by Nelson and Larry, stared straight ahead, stone-faced and mortified. Her green eyes had a haunted expression. Her career was uncertain. She couldn't fix it. Mom couldn't fix it either. During cross-examination, she kept shifting her gaze from the floor to the attorney for the defense, looks that she knew spelled doom for a witness.

"*Why did you go along with your mother's maltreatment of Jenna?*" Gupta asked.

"*We don't have the same mother.*"

"*But you have the same father?*"

"*Yes.*"

"*So you didn't consider Jenna your sibling too?*"

Lauren hesitated. "No."

"*Why?*"

"*I told you. Because Mom didn't.*"

"You and Alan have the same parents?"

"*Yes.*"

"*Yet you showed animosity toward him. Why?*"

Lauren took a moment to answer. "Because Mom did."

"*Did your mother say why?*"

"*She had issues.*"

"*With little boys?*"

Lauren sighed. "No. With men."

"*By the way, congratulations on your marriage, Ms. Crandall-Door. Uh, do you have issues with men too?*"

"*Obviously, not.*"

The courtroom erupted with laughter.

"*Order!*"

Lauren ran her fingers through her hair. "I was just a kid."

"*So after you turned eighteen you still continued to obey mommy.*"

"*Objection!*" Parker Lynch cried.

"*Sustained. Counsel will refrain from personalities.*"

"*Alan testified earlier that he warned you, your mother and Diane that she was ill yet you chose to ignore it, correct?*"

"*Yes.*"

Detective Chang clutched the rosary beads in his hands that his mother gave to him when he was a little boy. He found the religious article buried in the bottom of a drawer. He tensed when the prosecution called Officer Tedesco to the stand. He was a sympathetic figure. Just like Jenna, Chang felt torn in half. He was loyal to his officer. At the same time, Jenna may have done wrong, but she wasn't responsible and anything Officer William Tedesco said on the witness stand could prejudice the jury.

"Will the defendant please stand?"

Morgan Gupta stood. Jenna, however, remained seated. "Uh, Jenna," he began in a whisper, "you have to stand."

Still, Jenna wouldn't move. She had that faraway look. Tension filled the courtroom. Witnesses and reporters murmured.

Morgan cleared his throat. Again, he said, "Jenna, stand up."

Yet, she remained seated, locked into her own thoughts about life without her best friend. She began rubbing her temples.

Jenna blinked. She looked around her, suddenly recalling where she was.

Malachi gripped the back of the bench in front of them.

Murmuring in the courtroom went up an octave.

Malachi stiffened. This can't be good.

Beads of sweat dripped down Julian's forehead. Detective Chang said a quick prayer.

Judge Graves banged his gavel. "Order in the court!" He kept his eyes on Jenna. Was she going to have one of those "moments" in his courtroom? "Counsel, approach the bench."

Parker Lynch and Morgan Gupta were about to come forward when suddenly Jenna stood. She said, "I just realized something."

Gupta was about to stop Jenna from talking, but the Judge signaled to him to let her speak. Spectators began murmuring again.

Energized reporters jotted down what looked like the makings of a major development.

"Order!" Judge Graves exclaimed. "What is it that realized, Jenna?"

"Rosa's not coming to see me today."

Gupta could hardly maintain his poker face. Lynch's expression was unreadable. Neither counsel wanted to show his feelings of displeasure and contentment, respectively.

Spectators murmured louder. Reporters and sketch artists scribbled and sketched with fury.

"She hasn't come to see me in awhile," Jenna continued. "She always checks on me. It's because she's angry with me." Jenna toyed with her hair. "I went to Alan's house after she told me not to. Now Gupta could scarcely contain his glee. Rosa may not be speaking, but *Jenna* was showing the court that she did not have a full grip on reality despite the fact that she can function in a corporate setting and possessed an alter ego that exceptionally genius.

"The only reason I went," Jenna continued, "was because Malachi called me." Jenna turned to him with a smile. "Hi, Malachi."

All eyes turned to Malachi. Earlier he had testified to being there that day at the raid and encountering Rosa. Malachi smiled and waved back at Jenna. Acutely, embarrassed, he began loosening his shirt collar.

Jenna turned back to the judge. "She probably thinks I favor him over her, but I don't." She rubbed her temples again. "Rosa did talk to Mr. Gupta. I heard Dr. Haddonfield and Dr. Dorfman say so."

The buzz of conversation grew louder.

Again, Judge Graves banged the gavel. "Order or I'll clear the courtroom!" In a gentler voice, he said, "Go on, Jenna."

"I'm not a bad person, Your Honor. "I always wanted to be good."

"I understand," Judge Graves said.

"That's all I want to say," Jenna said.

The judge nodded. "It is the opinion of this court that Jenna Michaela Crandall is incompetent to stand trial."

Jenna frowned in puzzlement. Gupta placed his hand on her shoulder. Now wasn't the time for her to refute. She said her peace.

Bella, Lauren and Diane kept their heads down. "The Trio" could not even look at each other or at Jenna. There was a collective sigh of relief from Malachi, Julian, Alan, Elise, Reverend Brooks and Detective Chang. As the family's spiritual advisor, the Reverend Brooks was present. A reluctant character witness, the clergyman shared his observations about Jenna, Bella, the rumors about the family and her influence over the board.

Judge Graves thanked the jury for their service and dismissed them. After they left the courtroom, he said, "I've listened to the facts concerning this case. This court hereby sentences the defendant to an undisclosed mental health facility where she can receive the proper restorative treatment until she's well enough to stand trial."

Malachi sat with hand at his jaw. That could mean never.

Judge Graves cleared his throat. "I'm also assigning Julian, Bella, Alan and Diane Crandall to family counseling along with Lauren Crandall-Door."

The Trio looked up at the judge.

He glowered at Lauren. "And you, Counselor, had one of the most glowing records I've ever known." He shook his head. "You've disgraced the office of the Columbia County District Attorney, obstructed justice, and sullied your character by going along with your mother's plot to torment your own sister. You, an officer of the court."

Judge Graves looked at each Crandall, Julian and Alan included, with a stern expression. "In all my years on the bench, this is the most bizarre case I've ever presided over. What were you people thinking? Playing with the mind of a child? Disregarding the actions within your own household. A household ruled by fear? Case dismissed." Judge Graves banged the gavel and arose from the bench.

The bailiff cried, "All Rise!"

As Judge Graves was leaving the courtroom, the officers came to take Jenna away.

"Wait, I don't understand," Jenna said. "Why do I have to go?"

Gupta put a reassuring hand on her shoulder. Evidently, the judge's rendering went over her head. "It's just for awhile."

"But what about Malachi? My dad, Alan and Elise?"

"You'll see them again," Gupta said.

"Rosa too?"

Gupta hesitated then said, "Yes. Now go with the officers."

Jenna paused to look at Bella, Lauren and Diane who was the only who at that moment with the courage to look at her. Jenna finally turned away. She looked at Julian, Alan, Elise and Detective Chang and smiled at each of them. Last, she looked lovingly at Malachi. "I have to go, but I'll be back soon, okay?"

Malachi nodded and smiled. He mouthed the words, okay. It was all he could do not to cry.

Then with a sad smile on her face, she went peacefully with the officers.

Under his breath, Julian said, "My baby girl." He broke down.

Cameras flashed in Lauren, Nelson, Diane and Larry's faces as they fled from the courthouse. They didn't pause for questions. A despondent Julian, his arm around Bella, followed. The once haughty church elder now appeared older, fragile. Neither she nor Julian had anything to say.

"We're glad this is over," Alan said when he and Elise came out of the courtroom. For some unknown reason he was willing to face the media. "Now my wife and I just want to put this all behind us." That sounded lame. They had a lawsuit pending.

"What about your lawsuit with Wheat Prentiss & Associates?" A reporter asked.

Bingo!

"We can't discuss the case," Elise said.

Alan looked grateful, glad that she answered for him, glad that she was by his side.

"Now we just want to go home," Elise added.

Together they walked away hand in hand, ignoring the reporters' questions.

"Detective, can you give us an opinion on the verdict?" A reporter for the Gordonville Gazette asked when Chang appeared outside on the courthouse steps.

"It was fair."

"Will the state be pressing charges against the Crandall's?"

With any luck no. He had just about enough of the Crandall's. But that would've been wrong to say. A remark like that would prejudice the authorities. Already the Crandall's were unpopular. Lauren, Alan and Diane were guilty of obstructing justice. Chang was about to reply, but paused. Mayor Urbanowski appeared on the steps of the courthouse.

"We're glad this case has been resolved," the city official said. "But we're saddened to learn about the corruption within Gordonville's own prominent family . . . "

Detective Sergeant Richard Chang shook his head then sighed. Leave it to the mayor to steal the spotlight. You just couldn't be like the governor and express your sadness and disappointment in a written statement?

Malachi opted to linger in the halls. The sweet sad smile on Jenna's face as they were leading her out of the courtroom haunted him. *My Jenna.* Not wanting to face reporters, Malachi dodged into the men's room. He splashed cold water on his face, combed his hair. He couldn't stay in there forever. He left the bathroom. Slowly, he walked out the building.

Malachi stepped outside. The day was sunny and bright. It had no right to be so pretty when Jenna was going to be locked away somewhere unable to enjoy days like this. He should be grateful, nevertheless. She was getting help, Bella, Lauren and Diane were getting what they deserved at least so far, but he and Jenna were gonna be separated for a while. Even so, she'd still have to stand trial. A good lawyer would find her guilty but not responsible. That Morgan Gupta seemed good . . .

"What did you think about the trial?"

"What's your thought on the decision?"

"Has any of this affected your job?"

Malachi kept walking, choosing to ignore the reporters.

"What're you gonna do now that your girlfriend's been sent to a mental institution?"

Malachi stopped. He turned and gave the reporter, male blonde-haired male with chiseled features a long hard stared. Malachi didn't care for the reporter's critical tone. For a second, he wanted to go back to his old self and tell this donut a few choice words, but instead he counted to ten. The press had enough performance for one morning. Malachi looked the dapper man in the eye. "I'm gonna stick by her."

Stunned, the reporter asked, "Why?"

"That's what you do when you love someone."

Then, Malachi turned and walked away, leaving the reporter standing speechless.

52

Jenna stared out the window of her room at the spectacular display of red, gold, orange and yellow foliage atop the Talcott Mountains of Litchfield, Connecticut. A year had gone by since the court admitted her into the mental health facility. Six months had passed since she spoke to Rosa.

That is, she hadn't evoked her.

Through psychotherapy, she was learning the importance of relying on her inner strength.

"I still can't believe Rosa isn't real," Jenna said during one of her earlier sessions with Dr. Arlene Goldberg, the psychotherapist assigned to her case. She was still coming to grips that she had a problem, one that she didn't know she had, dissociative identity disorder or split personality.

She listened patiently. Arlene Goldberg made it a point to know Jenna's background thoroughly; family history, failed relationships, conflicts with Christianity. Coping with Rosa's nonexistence was especially hard. It was a rough start before Jenna finally started to open up. Initially, Jenna was suspicious. She dismissed the psychotherapist's attempts to reach out to her such as, asking Jenna to address her on a first name basis. Why did Dr. Goldberg want to know how she felt or what was on her mind? No one ever cared before except for Rosa who people said wasn't real, and Malachi who she missed terribly. Next to Rosa, she could tell him anything.

Nevertheless, Arlene met with Jenna every day no matter how often the troubled young woman told her to get lost. It was still an opportunity for dialogue. Gradually, Jenna began to open up.

"I feel like part of me is missing," Jenna said.

"That's natural," Arlene said. "But Rosa's not really gone. She's a part of you. All that time you were going to see her, you were really comforting yourself and giving yourself confidence."

"Great. Someone inside me yearns to wreak havoc."

Arlene smiled. "We're gonna work on that. And your sense of humor is going to help you through this. And life in general."

Jenna watched a formation of geese soaring over the white oaks in the garden outside as she recalled her earlier moments in psychotherapy.

"When I tried to talk about things that made me feel scared or angry, people said I was too sensitive."

"How did that make you feel?" Arlene asked.

"Worse than before I told them what was going on." Jenna started to play with her braids. "Sometimes I'd get yelled at or punished just for saying how I felt. I couldn't cry. I made that mistake before. It only made things worse."

"I'm sorry your stepmother treated you so shabbily."

Jenna stopped playing with her hair. "I couldn't understand why my moth—I mean Bella, was doing these terrible things to me." Her father told her the truth about her parentage. He thought she had a right to know. She was stunned, yet it made sense. Bella stopped connecting with her.

Didn't she flinch every time I called her Mom? Lauren and Diane stopped treating me like a sister.

Jenna's eyes took on a faraway look. "I remember when everything changed between us. Bella just cut me off like a machete to a red rose." She came home from kindergarten with a picture she drew of their family. "She looked at it then at me. She had the coldest look in her eyes. I was frightened and confused, but I thought the picture would make whatever was wrong with her better."

"And subconsciously, that was also the moment you set about trying to endear yourself to your stepmother."

Jenna nodded. "My drawing didn't make things better." She paused then said, "Bella wasn't the only one who was against tears. My teachers used to say that if I expected to make it in life I had to be tough."

Arlene wore a wry smile. Rosa Garrison was tough—to the point of being dangerous. These mentors almost created a murderer. Jenna cleared her throat. "They were misguided. Bella wasn't even honest with herself about her own pain and anger. She took it out on you. As for Lauren and Diane, well, with all their successes, they have such poor self-esteem. You and Alan's misery gave them strength. Why else would they spend their life making you miserable? Especially because someone else told them to?"

Jenna smiled. "Malachi said that."

"He's right. The point is you were a little girl whose feelings no one ever validated and when you grew up the same situation continued. You're not weak because you express yourself. That makes you stronger than those other people you mentioned and it'll help you get through this. More than likely, they were stuffing their feelings or projecting them onto someone else. Or something else.

"It's okay to feel. It makes you alive. You don't have to listen to Bella or your teachers. They're part of the past. And you're not there anymore. But speaking of past, Alan played a big role."

"He's great. But Alan's a guy. Know what I mean?"

Arlene nodded. "You wanted a female connection."

"A lot of my sex ed came from books and whatever Bella did the favor of teaching me. Lauren and Diane were useless." She rolled her eyes. "I think they were thrilled about what they could get away with because Bella and everyone else thought they were sweet." She paused then said, "Rosa and I spent hours reading trash novels and magazines. Yeah, I know. It was all me."

Arlene chuckled. "And there's what you learned in biology."

Jenna began clasping and unclasping her hands. "It wasn't easy making friends. I couldn't get too close to classmates, you know. I couldn't go to anyone's house and no one could come to mine." She felt a lump forming in her throat. "I don't want to talk about this anymore."

"I know it hurts," Arlene said, handing Jenna a tissue. "But you have to own your feelings. Otherwise, you end up stuffing them. Then the wounds fester.

"So what if they do?"

"That's how Rosa was born."

Jenna continued admiring the scenery. It was liberating not to be in that awful past anymore with hateful relatives and an unrewarding job. For the first time in a long time, she was learning to feel good about herself and about life. She was socializing, making friends and associates. There was a knock on her door. "Yes?"

Gretchen Traugott entered. The slim longhaired woman's family admitted her eight months ago with bipolar disorder. Jenna's eyes lit up at the sight of her new best friend. She and Jenna's conditions gave them a common bond, causing them to eventually form a special alliance. It didn't start out that way, however. During one her manic moments, Gretchen had an encounter with Rosa. Wired, she dared to challenge Rosa. Arlene told Jenna about it afterward since she had no recollection. Jenna smiled to herself. That run in would go down in the annals of the institute's history. "Hey, girlfriend."

Gretchen pulled up a chair then sat down. "My life sucks."

"Okay. Talk to me."

"I just finished watching this movie where this guy bends over backwards to win this girl's affection."

Jenna shook her head in mock disapproval. Gretchen was married, but her husband divorced her after her diagnosis. "I thought we agreed that you'd avoid those types of programs or at least take your meds before watching them."

Gretchen stuck her tongue at Jenna. "I want to be normal."

"You are normal. And so am I. People like us just have . . . challenges."

"At least you have a guy that loves you."

"At least your family didn't make you crazy. They tried to help you."

Gretchen crossed her arms. In a mocking voice she said, "I thought we agreed not to refer to ourselves as crazy."

Jenna laughed. "Right. We're not crazy—"

Gretchen ran over to stand by Jenna, put her arms around her and they said simultaneously, "We're special."

It was great having a best friend. A *real* one. "At the risk of sounding Pollyannaish, if I can meet someone as wonderful as Malachi, then you can too. In fact, you will."

"Thanks, Jenna. Play you a game of gin?"

"You got it." There was a knock on the door. "Come in."

Arlene entered. The middle-aged psychotherapist, greeted Jenna while at the same time wondering how her patient would react to what she was about to tell her. Jenna might be fine with it. After all, she'd been making unusual progress for someone who's gone through as much as she has and for so long. Jenna had come a long way since the first time she came to the facility. She was happier, a little more self-possessed, a contrast to a year ago when she was feeling lost, confused, scared. Other patients in her situation would've needed more time just to come out of their rooms.

"Or maybe later," Gretchen said. Evidently, Jenna's doctor had something to discuss."

"Sorry to break this up," Arlene said.

"No problem," Gretchen said after she greeted Arlene. "Later, Jen."

After Gretchen left, Jenna asked, "What's wrong?" Arlene's coolness didn't fool her. She saw the concern on her face beyond the friendly mask. "Did something happen to Malachi?"

"He's fine." Arlene forgot about Jenna's uncanny ability to see through people.

"Is it Daddy?

"You're family's fine. It's Diane and Larry."

Jenna looked wary. "What about them?"

"They're here."

"*What?*" Jenna sat on the bed. She hadn't seen them since the competency hearing. Besides Malachi, her only other visitors were Julian, Alan, and Elise and to her surprise Detective Chang. Arlene had advised against her receiving visits from Bella, Lauren and Diane until she had learned to cope with her anger without summoning Rosa. Her pain and anger were too raw. For Jenna not to see the women who had damaged her was easy. She had no desire to see them. Once Arlene had given them the green light, however, Jenna still refused to see her stepfamily no matter how many times they asked for permission to visit.

Arlene joined Jenna on the bed. She rolled up the sleeves of her crewneck sweater. Bella, Lauren or Diane always called before coming. Diane must've been desperate. "You don't have to see them. It's your call."

Jenna crossed her arms. She could still feel the hurt from Diane's cruelty. She got up and picked up her study Bible off her dresser. Malachi had given it to her as a gift during one of his visits. Periodically, they studied the scriptures together. Jenna rubbed her fingers across her name, which Malachi had engraved in gold foil lettering on the front. Deep in her memory was something about forgiveness. Jenna made a face. "I'll talk to them."

Arlene raised her eyebrows. "Are you sure? You don't look too enthusiastic."

"I'll do it."

"It's good that you're putting your anger aside and granting your sister and Larry a meeting. This is a step forward,"

Jenna shrugged. Her decision was more out of curiosity. What could they possibly want? That is, what did Diane want? Larry was just there for support.

Or to protect her from me.

"You can meet in the Victorian Room," Arlene said.

Jenna wore a frozen smile. She just took a step backward.

Jenna and Arlene stood at the threshold of the Victorian Room. It was unoccupied, except for her its sole occupants, Diane and Larry. Her sister was wearing a black long-sleeved twill dress, permed hair combed back, perfect makeup. Larry wore a camel hair crew neck sweater and trousers. Jenna could feel aggravation rising inside of her. *Still the perfect, well-dressed couple.* It figures they'd choose the loveseat.

Jenna looked around the Anglo-styled room. How she loathed it. Not even the large picture window that offered a magnificent view of the garden satisfied her. Used as a combination recreation and visitors room, the Victorian Room's décor reminded her of Bella's beloved living room with its claw-foot furnishings, elegant chairs and graceful tables. Jenna shuddered. If she had told Arlene the truth about how she really felt about the room, she would've found another venue for them to hold this impromptu family reunion—and found another topic for them to explore.

Finally, the half sisters made eye contact. Diane and Larry stood up.

"Ready?" Arlene asked.

Jenna nodded. Together, she and Arlene entered the room.

Larry kept his eyes on Jenna. He shifted nervously in the seat. He couldn't forget how she attacked him.

Diane had a nervous smile while she stood facing her youngest sister. She didn't think Jenna would agree to see her. Of course, she has no memory of that day, but she did. For months, she had nightmares. Diane swallowed. "Hi."

Jenna couldn't get her lips to move.

"I'll give you all some space," Arlene said. "I'll be right outside."

"You're leaving?" Larry asked, obviously nervous. He was more receptive about this reunion when he thought that Dr. Goldberg would be joining them.

"She wants to give us some privacy, Larry," Diane said.

After Arlene left, Diane said, "Let's sit." Jenna took a seat in a spoon back chair opposite Diane and Larry. "You look good."

Jenna, who was dressed in a gray T-shirt, pair of camouflage pants and no makeup searched her half sister's face for any signs of deceit. *She seems genuine.* "Thank you." She turned to Larry. "What's up?"

Larry inclined his head in greeting, unsure of what to say to his future half-sister-in-law.

"You two married yet?" Jenna asked. Of course they weren't. Dad, Alan or Malachi would've told her. She was just trying to make conversation.

"We postponed it. For now. The public might think Larry and I are having a good time while you're in recovery and Lauren's career is in a shambles." Diane winced. "And mine."

Jenna leaned back. Alan told her Diane's career took a nosedive. Public opinion turned against her and she lost several endorsements. In addition, Lauren's license was suspended. She was awaiting reinstatement pending further investigation. The ethics board was upset with her for the role she played in the inquiry of her mother's attack, which subsequently led to her and Diane's near demise.

Larry took Diane's hand. "We can't make a move without somebody saying something."

Jenna admired him for standing by her stepsister. A lesser man would've bailed. *Now I'll have to respect him.* "It's not so fun to be wrongfully accused is it?"

"No," Diane replied.

Jenna gave her a sly look. "Like stealing a sweater for instance."

Diane nibbled on her bottom lip.

Larry looked curious and a bit guarded. He didn't know what Jenna was talking about as long as she wasn't about to have another *moment.*

"You could just ignore the public. You're good at ignoring people's feelings. Or you could get married on a desert island."

Larry braced himself. Diane began to chuckle nervously. Was Jenna just being funny or was this another display of her dark side? Dr. Goldberg said that Rosa was no more. Larry took hold of Diane's hand.

"I'm kidding," Jenna said. "Relax." She winked at Larry. "Don't worry. I'm not gonna put another beat down on you. Malachi told me what happened at Alan's."

Larry frowned. His cuts and bruises weren't nearly as painful as the damage to his manly pride. "I'm sure you two enjoy talking about that."

"Trust me, Larry; talking about you is not how Malachi and I choose to spend our time." Jenna crossed her legs. "So, how's Bella?" Not that she cared. She was just making conversation. She already knew that her stepmother stopped attending The Gordonville Community Church. It wasn't because Reverend Brooks didn't welcome her. Things just got uncomfortable. Alan and Elise told her how some of the congregants made Bella's life difficult; frosty stares, being ousted from the church board. That had to hurt.

"Mom's recuperating nicely," Diane replied. "In fact, she works part-time at the thrift shop downtown. Daddy's taking really good care of her."

Jenna nodded. She had to give their father credit. He made a mistake and his wife inflamed it. Nevertheless, he showed such love and devotion to her. Church wasn't easy for Julian either. He told her about having to endure some cold looks and a few stiff greetings. He went from having the congregation's respect for stoically maintaining his marriage, to being a poor husband and a failure as a father. Jenna uncrossed her legs. "How come Bella and Lauren didn't come with you guys?"

Diane looked down at her manicured nails. "They keep a low profile . . . and they didn't think you'd want to see them."

"I'm here with you aren't I?"

"And I appreciate it," Diane said. "I really do. But I took a chance."

Diane clasped her hands. "We all deal with things differently. None of us has been the same since the truth came out."

Jenna sat up. "Thank you by the way for watching me decline into madness and not telling me."

"Our lives have been difficult since . . . " Diane couldn't finish the sentence. They'd been paying the price for their betrayal.

Jenna gave her half sister a long, hard look. "I'm in a mental institution."

"We're sorry about everything," Diane wailed.

Jenna snorted.

"You did try to kill them," Larry said.

"Hush!" Diane warned.

Jenna looked at Larry. He stiffened. He should've kept his mouth shut. The words just flew out. Jenna could strike at any moment. He didn't even want to be here. He only came because of Diane. She desperately wanted to see her sister. He was against it, but his fiancée was coming with or without him and he certainly wasn't letting her come here alone. Larry cleared his throat. "At least meet your sister half way."

"Half being the operative word." Jenna turned to Diane. "You want something."

"Yes. To make amends."

Jenna laughed without humor. "Where have I heard that before?"

"It's true."

"She means it," Larry said.

"It would give your career a boost wouldn't it?" Jenna asked, ignoring Larry. She stood up. "What a great photo op that would make." Jenna looked toward the large picture window with its view of the garden and the mountains. "Where are the photographer's hiding?"

"There aren't any," Diane said.

"Well, next time bring them. Bella and Lauren too. Then you can move on with your lives while I'm stuck here." Suddenly memories of Bella's heartless words returned.

"God's going to strike you with a bolt of lightning." "You're the devil's child."

"You're ugly."

Jenna could hear the lash of the leather belt against her skin. She began rubbing her arms as she began to feel the pain. Then she heard Lauren and Diane's mocking laughter in her head. Jenna put her hands over her ears then doubled over.

Diane and Larry stared open-mouthed.

"Jenna?" Diane swallowed. "Do you want us to call someone?"

Larry jumped up. "Look nuh." Mounting nerves caused him to begin speaking in Jamaican Patois.

Diane could only make out a few words, but she thought he said something about Litchfield and not getting something or other beat out of him again.

Jenna raised herself up. "I'm okay, I'm okay." She took a few deep breaths then straightened out her T-shirt.

Diane nibbled on her bottom lip. *She's angry. She has every right to be.* "You're right, Jenna." Diane sighed. "My career's not what it used to be. My publicist suggested reconciliation, but even I know that's no guarantee. The public is fickle and unpredictable. Jenna, I've had a lot to think about over the last year. Apart from getting my career back on track, I really do want us to start over."

Jenna put a hand to her cheek where Bella used to slap her repeatedly. On rainy days, she swore she could feel the sting. She wouldn't have to feel this kind of pain, if it hadn't been for Diane. Jenna looked around the ornamental room so reminiscent of her stepmother's taste. She wouldn't be here if it hadn't been for Diane.

For all of them.

Jenna could feel herself descending to the dark place. That place of rage. Jenna's eyes narrowed. "You're not sorry. I hope you all burn in hell."

She began screaming obscenities at Diane. Jenna didn't spare Bella or Lauren from her fury either.

"Come on, Di," Larry sang in a funny singsong voice.

She didn't need any more convincing. She couldn't reach her sister. Diane and Larry raced for the exit just as Arlene along with two orderlies dashed into the room. The orderlies grabbed Jenna, who cried, "You'll never be sorry, Diane. None of you," as they carried her out of the room.

Jenna, who had awakened from a drug-induced sleep two hours ago, sat staring at Arlene who was sitting across from her. They were back in the psychotherapist's office. Jenna couldn't look at Arlene at first. It took almost ten minutes just for Jenna to say hello. After six months of learning to live without Rosa, she had returned. She heard the whispers. The things she said to Diane. The way she had behaved. This was a step backwards. *How could this have happened?*

Arlene handed Jenna a cup of orange tea before pouring some for herself. Jenna studied the cup, which was really a raspberry colored mug. She smiled her appreciation then took a few sips. She told Arlene about her favorite shades and colors.

"Why didn't you tell me how you felt about the Victorian Room?" Arlene asked. She realized now that it had been too soon after all for Jenna to meet with Diane. The information about its resemblance to Bella's living room and the association of all things British was information she wished she had. Although she knew a lot about Jenna's background, there was still so much that only the patient could tell her.

"It never came up." Jenna took a few more sips of orange tea. The citrus flavor was soothing and delicious. The aromatic scent was calming. "Just seeing my stepsister in—that room. Mom—I mean Bella loved fancy China. She used to sip it in the dining room, but mostly in the kitchen. It was English." Jenna went on to explain how she felt about the area and the flood of memories that came with it. "I couldn't stop them if I tried."

"Remember what we said about not suppressing feelings?"

"I have to own them."

"Then you're gonna have to be honest with yourself and me if you want to heal. For example, admitting that you don't like Bella."

Jenna lowered your eyes. She recalled how Detective Chang wanted her to do the same thing when he came to interrogate her at work.

"You don't need Rosa anymore to express your true feelings. You can speak for yourself."

Jenna took another sip of orange tea. She set down the cup. "I can't believe that Rosa came back."

"She didn't. That was you."

Jenna was glad she had set down the cup or she would've surely dropped it. "It was?"

"You were so angry you to use the vernacular, flipped out. It was that incident all over again with your high school nemesis Maura. So you see, you can admit your feelings."

"I'm sorry."

Progress. Jenna was reacting to her childhood past where Bella treated her as the bad little girl. Arlene took another sip. "There's no blame here, Jenna. Look, for years you've been going through traumatic experiences."

"I didn't embarrass you?"

"You're still healing."

"I wish I could forget about the past and all the pain."

"As long as your brain is intact your memories will always be with you," Arlene said. "They're part of what make you who you are. And unlike a tape recorder, you can't erase your past. And you wouldn't want that because then you'd have an even bigger problem."

"Diane wanted us to start over. But I didn't want it."

"Give it time," Arlene said. "No one expects you to get over trauma so quickly. Importantly, we now know we have to work on your anger management and your fear of admitting your feelings. There'll be other times for you to meet with her again and maybe next time Bella and Lauren."

Jenna doubted that. Didn't Arlene hear the words she used on Diane and Larry? It would be a long time before Diane would try to visit.

Or call.

"Now, let's work on our anger management," Arlene said.

53

Jenna picked up a yellow ochre pastel chalk from her art supply box then began drawing the golden leaves on the maple tree in the distance. The addition enhanced the red, green and orange leaves in the picture. Afterward, she paused to assess her work. "So what do you think?"

"Nice." Malachi was sitting on the bench beside her. He had come to visit and the October day was too beautiful to stay inside and talk. Thanks to her progress, Jenna had earned what she affectionately referred to as garden privileges. "But I'd add a touch of burnt umber."

Jenna looked back at the sketch. She studied it for a moment. "You're right. I'll make an artist out of you yet." She reached into the box of assorted pastels and began adding burnt sienna. She was enjoying the peacefulness of the garden, the crisp fall day and Malachi. She looked forward to his visits.

"Speaking of artist," Malachi began, "I've got some great news." He cleared his throat for dramatic effect. "You're no longer an amateur artist. Your paintings are famous. Even the gory ones." His smile grew wider as Jenna's eyes lit up the way they did when she first spoke to him about art the first day they met. *When she was two people.* He tried not to think about that part. "Bella's been bragging about your talent."

Jenna held the pastel chalk in midair. "She has?" She could hardly forget how diligent Bella was about suppressing her talent while praising her daughters. Not even Alan got his mother's high regard and he designed a mall and now a new library wing.

Malachi nodded. "Even to the media. Your dream has come true. God has turned a horrible thing around. Your stepmother has become your unofficial publicist."

Her wondrous look suddenly became flat. She finished the drawing. She closed the sketchpad then put away the pastels. "Why's she doing this?"

"People change. I did."

"You're not Bella."

Malachi frowned in puzzlement. He thought Jenna would've been happy at least although he could understand her being perplexed about her stepmother's sudden kindness after all these years. "She made a mistake," Malachi said. "King David messed up. Moses. Peter and Paul. It wasn't until after the Resurrection they got their *Acts* together." He put on a silly grin.

Jenna winced. The Acts of the Apostles was one of their Bible lessons and she almost forgot how corny Malachi could be sometimes.

He gave her shoulder a squeeze. "We all have our skeletons."

"Okay now I'm gonna go full out Rosa on you." She caught the inside joke. He had finally told her about his prophetic nightmare about Loki and the skeletons sitting around the kitchen table.

"Sorry. Couldn't resist." He gave her a peck on the cheek. "Relax. Celebrate this milestone. Even Bella and I are starting to get along. Who'd a thunk it?"

Jenna looked incredulous. Then she crossed her arms.

Malachi sighed then put his arms around her. "I'm not trivializing what Bella, Lauren and Diane did. It was horrendous and uncalled-for. But even I have to admit that Larry was right. You need to meet Bella and your sisters in the middle."

"*Half* sisters." She would never think of Lauren and Diane as real sisters. Ever.

"Whatever. But so much has been working your way."

"And I'm glad," Jenna said. "And grateful." Recently, the courts found her guilty but not responsible. They tossed out the case against her regarding Officer Tedesco. Furthermore, due to the nature of the case and their part in it, Bella, Lauren or Diane was not pressing charges. "But I also know that they're the reason why I'm here. Public opinion is against Bella, Lauren and Diane. That's what my stepmother's goodwill gesture is about. She's trying to buy back the respect she once had in Gordonville. "Well I'm not interested." Jenna pulled away from Malachi.

He gave her a long, hard stare. "So now what do you want blood? You should be thanking God this whole thing didn't end up in irreparable disaster. You could've killed any of your victims and reached a point of no return, but you didn't."

"I DO THANK GOD!" Jenna twisted a strand of hair. She didn't mean to yell. Malachi was her heart. Her knight in shining armor. In a quieter tone she added, "I thank Him every day."

Malachi rubbed the back of his neck. "Why were you so upset with yourself after Diane and Larry left?" A week had passed since Diane and Larry's disastrous visit. When Jenna called to tell him about what happened, he already knew. Julian told him who got it from Diane and a shaken Larry. His mouth twitched. He could just picture Larry quaking in his shoes.

"You know why."

He did. He wanted her to see for herself. Malachi gestured to her to explain.

Frustrated, Jenna said, "I got angry and lost control. That wasn't supposed to happen. I thought I was cured."

"You are. But you have layers of hurt to work through. No one taught you how to handle emotions. At the risk of sounding hokey, to tame the beast within, you have to conquer it with love."

"Love." Jenna snorted. "I know where you're going with this, Malachi. Jesus. The Cross. Redemption. Well, I'm not Him."

Malachi counted to ten. He couldn't lose his cool. Mercy wasn't going to come easily to her. It's not as if she had any good examples. "Forgiveness is a process. God doesn't expect you to get over three decades of trauma in three easy lessons.", his thoughts returned to his former coworkers. Were they as embittered toward him as Jenna was to her stepfamily?

"I'll be gray by the time I get out of here," Jenna said.

"That's entirely up to you." He watched a squirrel scurry across the grass with a nut in its mouth. It stopped then began to nibble on it. "Do you want to end up like Bella?"

"Don't even kid about that."

"Well that's what bitterness will do to you. You have to ask God for the strength to deal with the past until it stops controlling you."

Jenna rubbed her hand over her face. The idea of forgiving *them* made her sick. Forgiving Bella, Lauren and Diane was gonna be harder than letting go of Rosa.

"Remember what I said about starting over? Here's your chance." Malachi swallowed. If he were to run into one of his former colleagues, would they forgive him for what he had done to them? "Everyone needs forgiveness at one time or another. Including you."

"I feel bad about what I did to Officer Tedesco, but not to the others. They had it coming."

"Twisted, but I'll give you that."

"They destroyed my life," Malachi.

"Your life's not over yet and yes, Bella, Lauren and Diane caused a lot of damage. But you've got a chance to start over. Not everyone gets that opportunity. Don't let fury ruin your opportunity to heal."

"Forgive them and Diane and everyone else in between. Pretend none of this ever happened. 'And we all lived happily ever after. The End.'"

Malachi sighed. "I didn't say that."

"You didn't have to."

"Jenna—"

"I don't know about this, Malachi."

"Then do it for your own peace of mind. Because this time you're gonna be the one who ends up destroying herself. For real this time."

54

Jenna returned to the Victorian Room. She looked around the room that disturbed her so much. It was January. Holiday decorations were still up as well as the Christmas tree and Menorah. Unlike the last time, she was here, patients reading or playing board games or visiting with friends and relatives filled the room.

She headed over to the telephone. She couldn't believe what she was about to do. Not even Arlene knew. That way if she changed her mind, it would be easy to back down. Jenna's heart was beating fast. Maybe it was good that the room was in use. It took three months to make this decision. Three months for her just to return to this room. Day after day, she argued with herself against why she shouldn't do this. She stared at the phone. It was modern. It didn't match the décor. Why? Bella would never have had a phone that didn't match the theme of a room. Finally, she picked up the receiver . . .

"Hi, Jenna!"

She put it back down then turned to see her friend Gretchen wearing the sunniest smiles and waving. The slim longhaired woman had been sitting at a card table in a corner, unnoticed. Jenna walked over. At first, she felt slightly annoyed yet relieved. Jenna glanced over at the phone on the other side. Maybe this delay was like a gift. She could still change her mind and walk out.

Or play cards with her new friend.

Jenna looked back at Gretchen who was playing solitaire. "Are you winning?"

Gretchen laughed and said, "Yeah." She searched Jenna's face. "You're *Jenna* today."

"Yes, I am."

"Good. I like you better than Rosa."

Jenna smiled. That was an ironic statement considering Gretchen's bipolar disorder made her subject to withdrawal, hallucinations and delusions of grandeur.

"I'll be leaving soon," Gretchen said.

"For good? No wonder you're grinning. That's fantastic!" Jenna felt a twinge of envy. It was great when someone was able to leave.

"We have to stay in touch," Gretchen said.

Jenna brightened. "Definitely." So this is what it was like to have a real BFF.

"And you have to draw me a picture."

"You got it."

Afterward Gretchen went back to playing solitaire and Jenna went back to the phone. Her hand hovered over it before finally picking it up. Halfway through dialing however, she changed her mind. She put the receiver back into its cradle. She looked out the window. The garden looked like a Christmas card with its snow-covered trees. In the distance, she could see the snowman that she and Gretchen made. Malachi's words came back to her. *"Forgiveness is a process."*

Encouraged by her friends pending release, Jenna picked up the phone again and dialed before she lost her nerve. Soon, the call was connecting. She was still tempted to hang up.

"Hello?"

Dad. Relief poured over her like a warm shower after a workout. "Hey, Daddy . . . No, everything's fine." *I hope.* "I just called to say hi— and to speak to Bella . . . Yes, really. I can hold." Jenna's mouth twitched.

Dad probably wanted to faint. Understandable. If anyone had told her that a day would come when she would want to speak with Bella, she would've laughed him or her to scorn. Jenna stared twisting her hair around her finger. Would Bella even want to talk when she found out that she was the one on the other end of the line? She remembered their talk that last morning they ate breakfast together. Bella was austere, unfeeling. She remembered making a last ditch effort to protect her stepmother from Rosa; that is, from herself. She could also remembered waiting at work for Rosa to call her, but everything else in between was blank. She couldn't even remember striking Bella . . .

"H-Hello?"

Jenna grabbed hold of the nearest chair to steady herself. It didn't matter that her old nemesis sounded hesitant or that she was far away. Her voice still had the power to produce fear. She listened to the buzz of conversation in the room, the sound of players shuffling cards. Silently, she gave thanks that there were others around. Jenna swallowed. "Hello, Bella."

"Jenna." The matriarch wasn't surprised she addressed her by her first name. She would never be Mom to her again. "Are you well?" Bella asked.

Jenna watched the other patients with their visitors. She watched Gretchen playing solitaire. "Yes. I am. Thanks. It gets better and better each day."

Silence.

"Heard about your job," Jenna said.

Bella wasn't sure where this was going. She didn't know what to think when Julian told her that she was on the phone asking for her. She tried to meet with her several times, but Jenna refused to see her not that she blamed her. A day didn't go by that she didn't think about what she did and what it amounted to: Lauren and Diane's plummeting careers and Alan's job termination. So much damage.

For nothing.

Bella chuckled uncertainly. "Yes. Today's my day off."

"I'm making friends now," Jenna said. "Real ones. I even have a best friend. Her name's Gretchen."

"That's wonderful." Bella swallowed. She remembered when she had friends. "Friends are important. Especially true ones." She remembered when Norma Beery was her best friend. "I'm glad for you, Jenna."

Jenna sat down. So far, this was easy. Still they were talking about everything else except the obvious . . .

"You'd love the recreational room. It has an English theme." She described the room's appointments.

Bella chuckled. "I love it already. Maybe . . . maybe I'll get to see it sometime."

Malachi returned with two cups of coffee. He handed Jenna hers then sat down at a coffee table in the community room. It wasn't as pretty as the Victorian was, but Jenna said that she had her share of it. He was just proud of her reaching out to her stepmother. Reconciliation with Lauren and Diane couldn't be far; however, he wouldn't bring it up. He'd let Jenna get there on her own. He took a sip of the brew. "They're renovating Thornbush Lane," Malachi said.

Jenna made a face. "I know. Daddy told me." Regardless of her history with the place, she'd always think of Thornbush Lane as her home away from home. The place where she found peace and quiet, escape from her private hell. The ambience of Thornbush Lane and its environs enabled her to create. The lonely road allowed her to hear herself think, to walk off steam, to fantasize about the things that she didn't have the courage.

She hated the idea of strangers inhabiting her place; perhaps turning it into some whoo whoo museum because of the property's history. One consolation was that Alan had an offer from the village to refurbish the farmhouse. He was available since R.B. Consulting fired him.

"It takes a tragedy before the city decides to fix up such a beautiful place," Malachi said.

Jenna laughed. "*You* thought Thornbush Lane was beautiful?"

He smiled sheepishly. "In its own way." He took a sip of coffee. The place still creeped him out.

Jenna drew an imaginary line on the table. She was grateful that the university still kept him employed in spite of the negative press Malachi was receiving. It must've been difficult for him to have people whispering about him or making jokes.

"No matter what progress I make, I'll always be known for being . . . you know . . . " She made the universal sign for crazy by putting her pointer finger to her head and making twirling motions.

Malachi grinned. "Isn't that true of all you artistes?"

"I don't want to make trouble for you."

She's giving me an out. Malachi took her hand in his. "Jenna, if I wanted out, don't you think I would've left long time ago?"

Jenna played with her hair.

"Stop worrying." In spite of her progress, she was going to need time to feel complete trust and emotional strength. Malachi reached over and kissed her. "I love you, Jenna. And on the day they release you, I'll be here. Helping you pack."

Jenna laughed. And this time, Malachi liked the sound of it. She didn't stop laughing until he kissed her into a blissful silence.

CPSIA information can be obtained at www.ICGtesting.com
Printed in the USA
LVOW12s1151180913

352969LV00001B/2/P